THE WALKING DEAD

BOOK TWELVE

a continuing story of survival horror.

created by Robert Kirkman

image comics presents

The Walking Dead
book twelve

ROBERT KIRKMAN
creator, writer

CHARLIE ADLARD
penciler, cover

STEFANO GAUDIANO
inker

CLIFF RATHBURN
gray tones

RUS WOOTON
letterer

SEAN MACKIEWICZ
editor

Original series covers by
CHARLIE ADLARD & DAVE STEWART

Robert Kirkman
chief executive officer

David Alpert
president

Sean Mackiewicz
editorial director

Shawn Kirkham
director of business development

Brian Huntington
online editorial director

June Alian
publicity director

Rachel Skidmore
director of media development

Michael Williamson
assistant editor

Dan Petersen
operations manager

Sarah Effinger
office manager

Nick Palmer
operations coordinator

Genevieve Jones
production coordinator

Andres Juarez
graphic designer

Stephen Murillo
administrative assistant

www.skybound.com

Robert Kirkman
chief operating officer

Erik Larsen
chief financial officer

Todd McFarlane
president

Marc Silvestri
chief executive officer

Jim Valentino
vice-president

Eric Stephenson
publisher

Corey Murphy
director of sales

Jeremy Sullivan
director of digital sales

Kat Salazar
director of pr & marketing

Emily Miller
director of operations

Branwyn Bigglestone
senior accounts manager

Sarah Mello
accounts manager

Drew Gill
art director

Jonathan Chan
production manager

Meredith Wallace
print manager

Randy Okamura
marketing production designer

David Brothers
branding manager

Ally Power
content manager

Addison Duke
production artist

Vincent Kukua
production artist

Sasha Head
production artist

Tricia Ramos
production artist

Emilio Bautista
sales assistant

Chloe Ramos-Peterson
administrative assistant

www.imagecomics.com

For international inquiries: foreign@skybound.com. For licensing inquiries: contact@skybound.com.

Chapter Twenty-Three: Whispers Into Screams

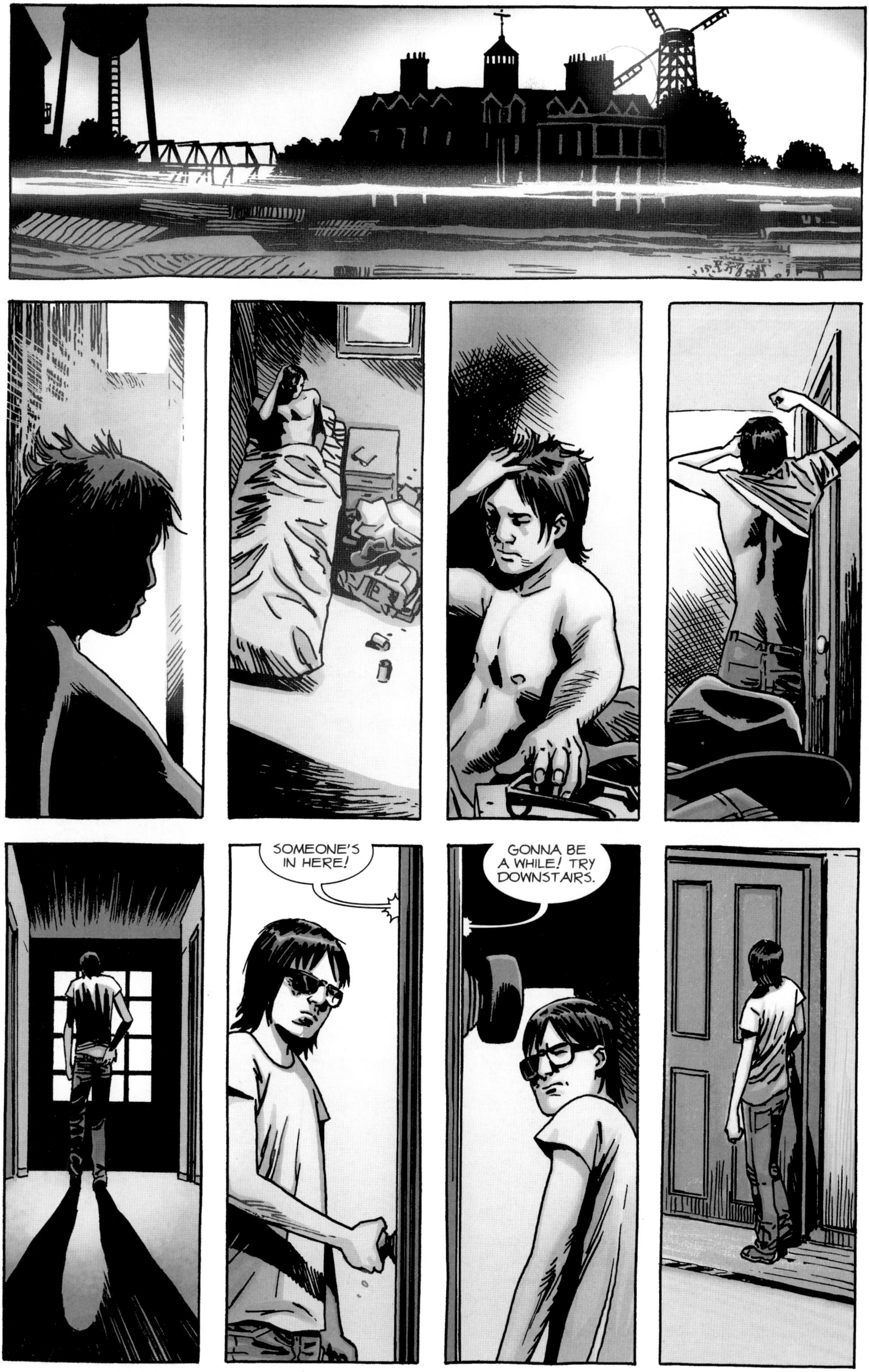
SOMEONE'S IN HERE!
GONNA BE A WHILE! TRY DOWNSTAIRS.

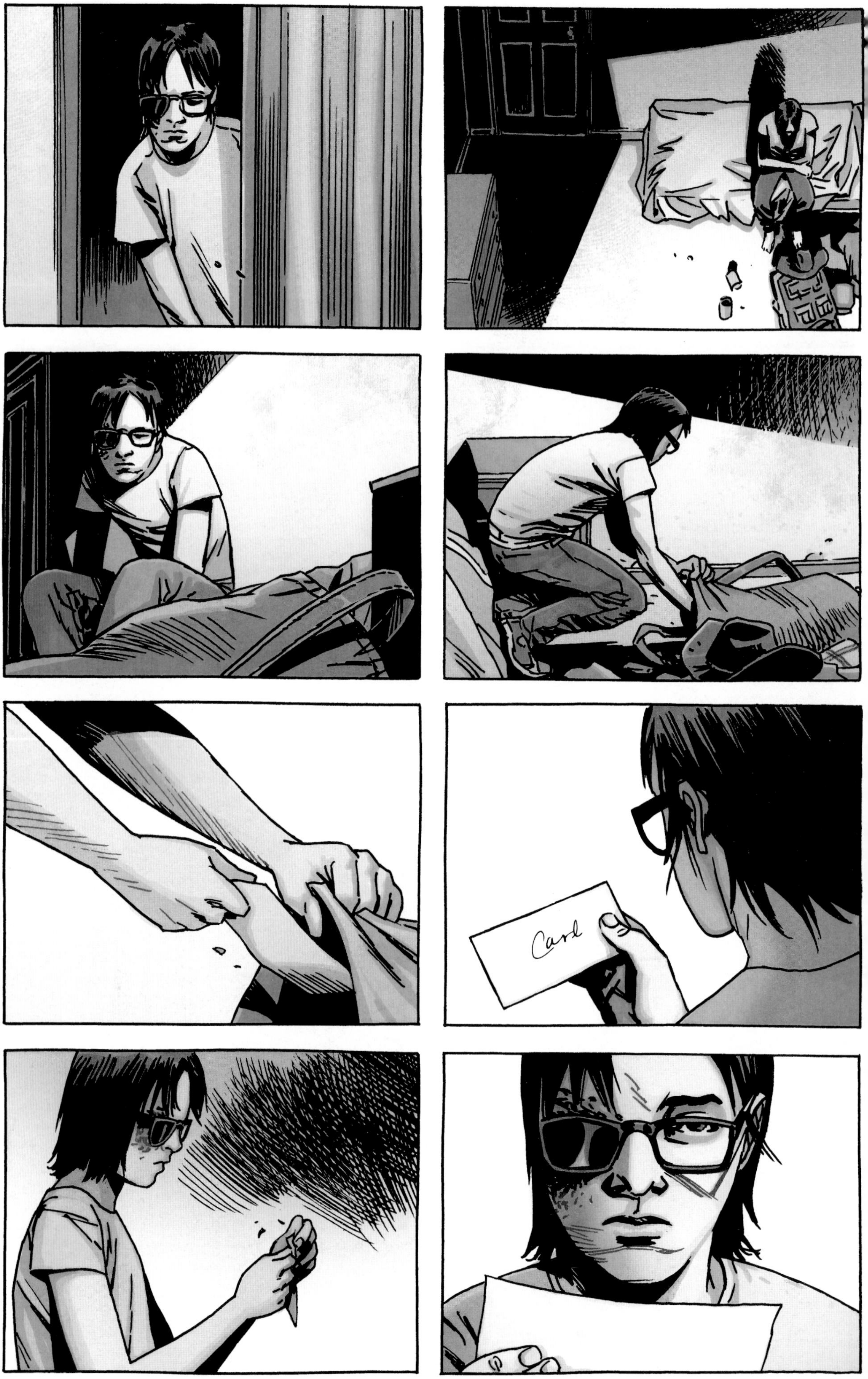
Carl

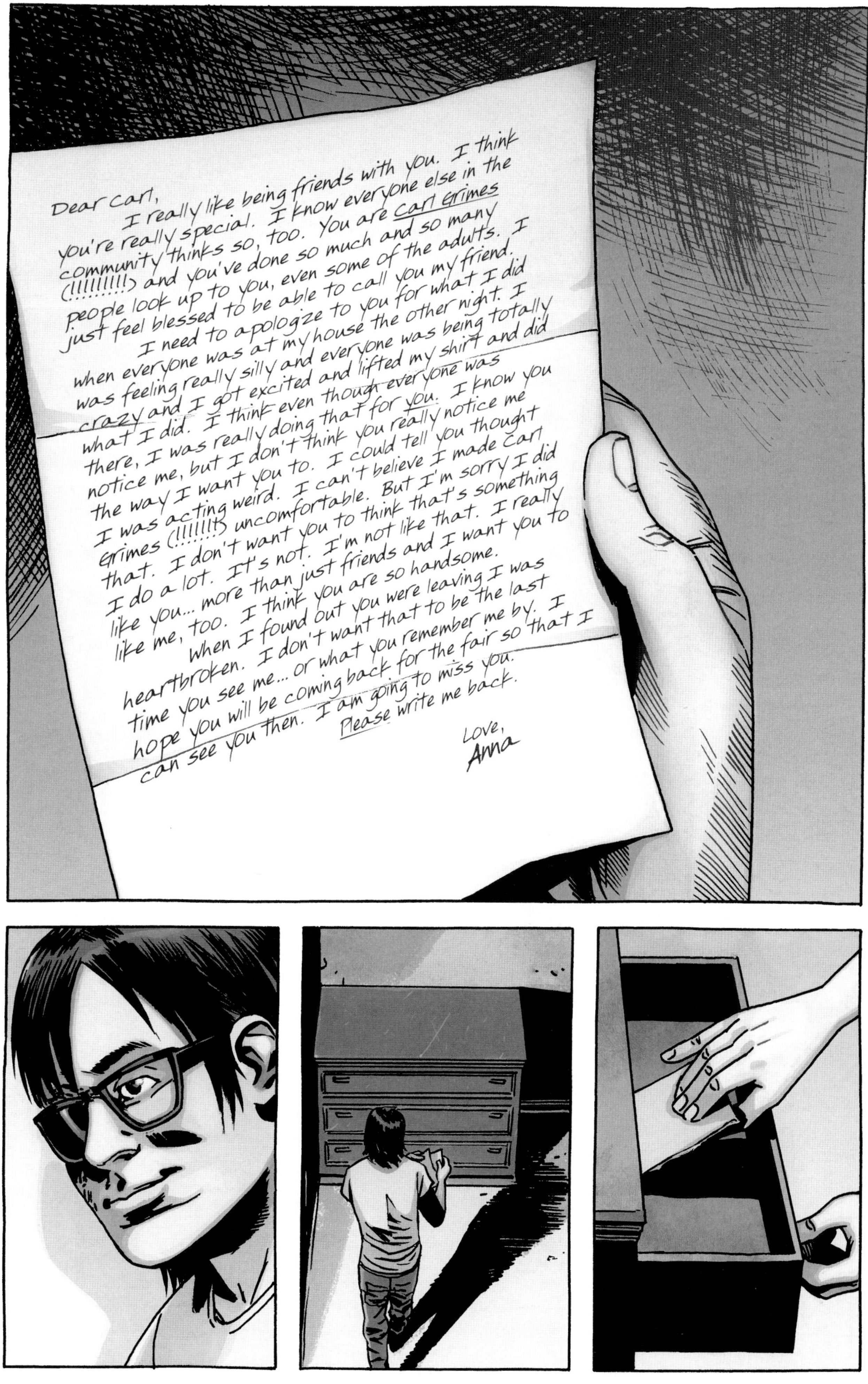
Dear Carl,
I really like being friends with you. I think you're really special. I know everyone else in the community thinks so, too. You are Carl Grimes (!!!!!!!!!) and you've done so much and so many people look up to you, even some of the adults. I just feel blessed to be able to call you my friend.
I need to apologze to you for what I did when everyone was at my house the other night. I was feeling really silly and everyone was being totally crazy and I got excited and lifted my shirt and did what I did. I think even though everyone was there, I was really doing that for you. I know you notice me, but I don't think you really notice me the way I want you to. I could tell you thought I was acting weird. I can't believe I made Carl Grimes (!!!!!!!!) uncomfortable. But I'm sorry I did that. I don't want you to think that's something I do a lot. It's not. I'm not like that. I really like you... more than just friends and I want you to like me, too. I think you are so handsome.
When I found out you were leaving I was heartbroken. I don't want that to be the last time you see me... or what you remember me by. I hope you will be coming back for the fair so that I can see you then. I am going to miss you. Please write me back.
Love,
Anna

HE WAS SHOT IN THE FACE? AND HE SURVIVED?!

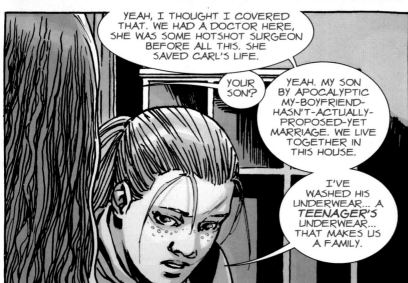

YEAH, I THOUGHT I COVERED THAT. WE HAD A DOCTOR HERE, SHE WAS SOME HOTSHOT SURGEON BEFORE ALL THIS. SHE SAVED CARL'S LIFE.

YOUR SON?

YEAH. MY SON BY APOCALYPTIC MY-BOYFRIEND-HASN'T-ACTUALLY-PROPOSED-YET MARRIAGE. WE LIVE TOGETHER IN THIS HOUSE.

I'VE WASHED HIS UNDERWEAR... A *TEENAGER'S* UNDERWEAR... THAT MAKES US A FAMILY.

THE GUY IN THE BASEMENT... THAT'S NEGAN, THEN? RICK ACTUALLY FOLLOWED THROUGH WITH THAT PLAN AFTER THE WAR?

YEAH. HE THOUGHT IT WOULD MAKE A STATEMENT... THE OLD WAYS ARE BACK... THAT KIND OF THING.

I DISAGREED... STILL DO, IF I'M HONEST. BUT I THINK IT WORKS. PEOPLE RECOGNIZE THERE'S A RULE OF LAW... AND PEOPLE LOOK UP TO RICK. THAT MOVE MORE THAN ANYTHING... THAT MADE HIM A LEADER.

I DON'T THINK HE REALLY ACCEPTED THAT ROLE UNTIL THEN.

WHAT HAPPENED TO THE REST OF THE SAVIORS?

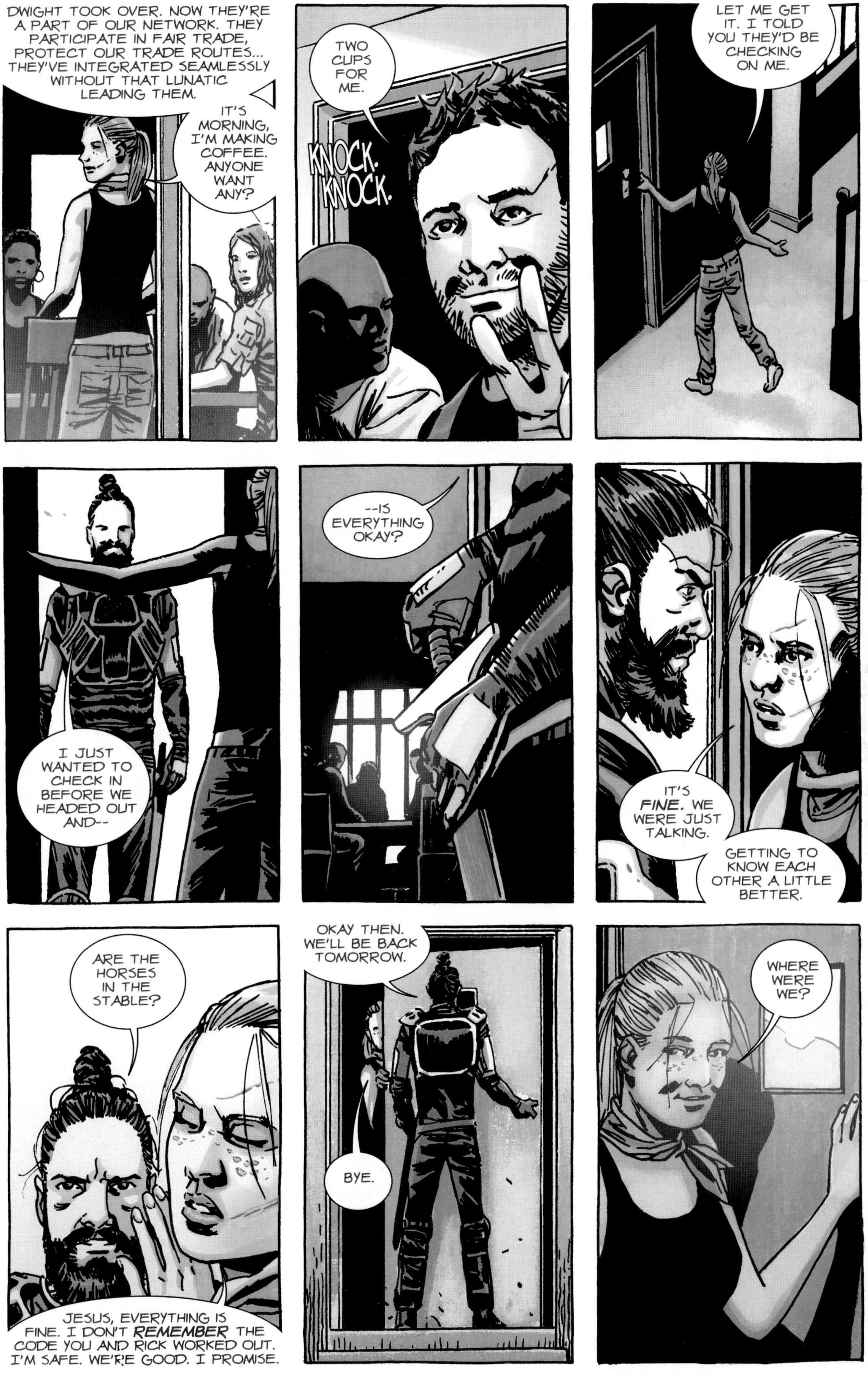
DWIGHT TOOK OVER. NOW THEY'RE A PART OF OUR NETWORK. THEY PARTICIPATE IN FAIR TRADE, PROTECT OUR TRADE ROUTES... THEY'VE INTEGRATED SEAMLESSLY WITHOUT THAT LUNATIC LEADING THEM.
IT'S MORNING, I'M MAKING COFFEE. ANYONE WANT ANY?
TWO CUPS FOR ME.
KNOCK. KNOCK.
LET ME GET IT. I TOLD YOU THEY'D BE CHECKING ON ME.
I JUST WANTED TO CHECK IN BEFORE WE HEADED OUT AND--
--IS EVERYTHING OKAY?
IT'S FINE. WE WERE JUST TALKING.
GETTING TO KNOW EACH OTHER A LITTLE BETTER.
ARE THE HORSES IN THE STABLE?
JESUS, EVERYTHING IS FINE. I DON'T REMEMBER THE CODE YOU AND RICK WORKED OUT. I'M SAFE. WE'RE GOOD. I PROMISE.
OKAY THEN. WE'LL BE BACK TOMORROW.
BYE.
WHERE WERE WE?

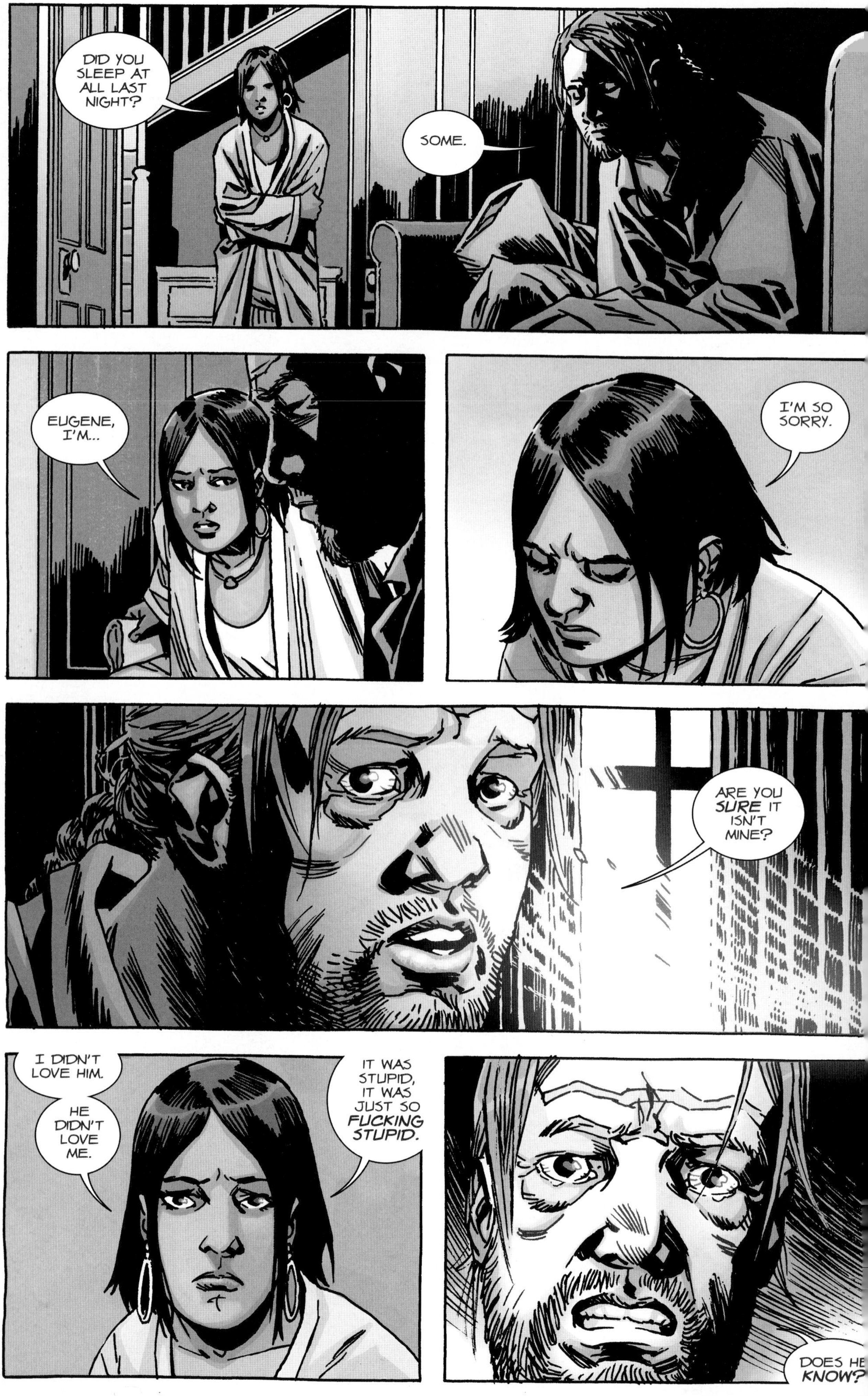
DID YOU SLEEP AT ALL LAST NIGHT?
SOME.
EUGENE, I'M...
I'M SO SORRY.
ARE YOU SURE IT ISN'T MINE?
I DIDN'T LOVE HIM.
HE DIDN'T LOVE ME.
IT WAS STUPID, IT WAS JUST SO FUCKING STUPID.
DOES HE KNOW?

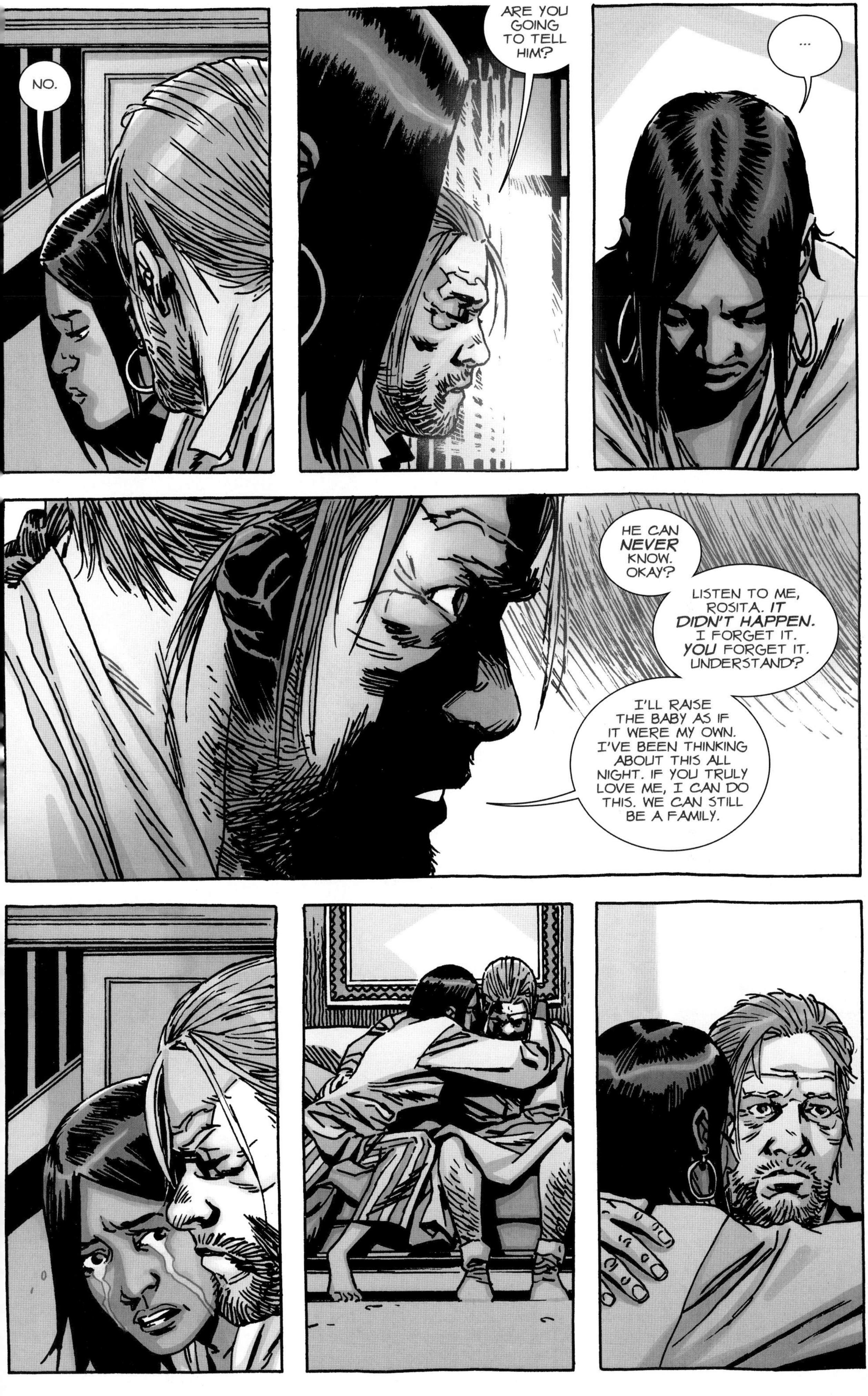
NO.
ARE YOU GOING TO TELL HIM?
...
HE CAN NEVER KNOW. OKAY?
LISTEN TO ME, ROSITA. IT DIDN'T HAPPEN. I FORGET IT. YOU FORGET IT. UNDERSTAND?
I'LL RAISE THE BABY AS IF IT WERE MY OWN. I'VE BEEN THINKING ABOUT THIS ALL NIGHT. IF YOU TRULY LOVE ME, I CAN DO THIS. WE CAN STILL BE A FAMILY.

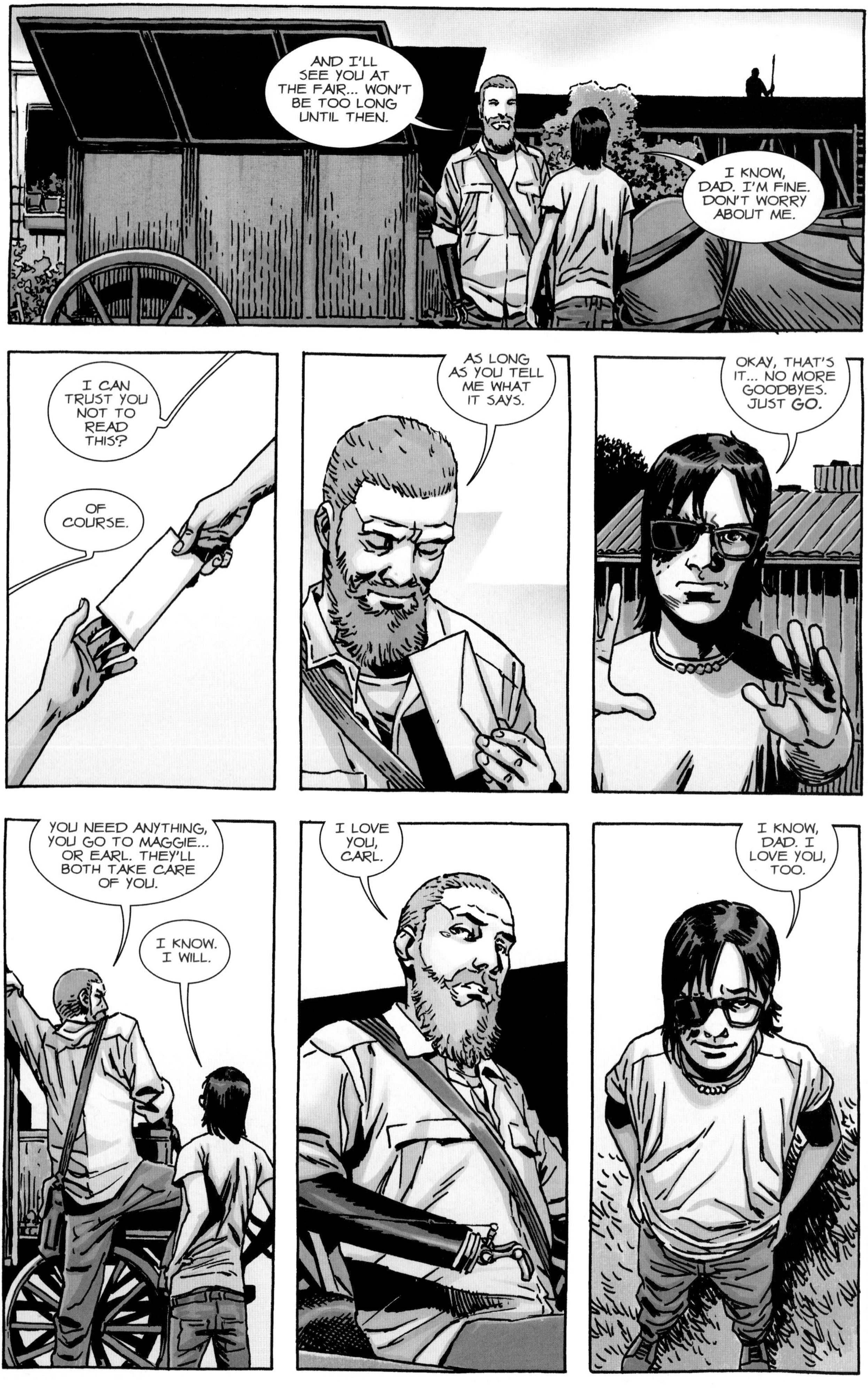
AND I'LL SEE YOU AT THE FAIR... WON'T BE TOO LONG UNTIL THEN.
I KNOW, DAD. I'M FINE. DON'T WORRY ABOUT ME.
I CAN TRUST YOU NOT TO READ THIS?
OF COURSE.
AS LONG AS YOU TELL ME WHAT IT SAYS.
OKAY, THAT'S IT... NO MORE GOODBYES. JUST GO.
YOU NEED ANYTHING, YOU GO TO MAGGIE... OR EARL. THEY'LL BOTH TAKE CARE OF YOU.
I KNOW. I WILL.
I LOVE YOU, CARL.
I KNOW, DAD. I LOVE YOU, TOO.

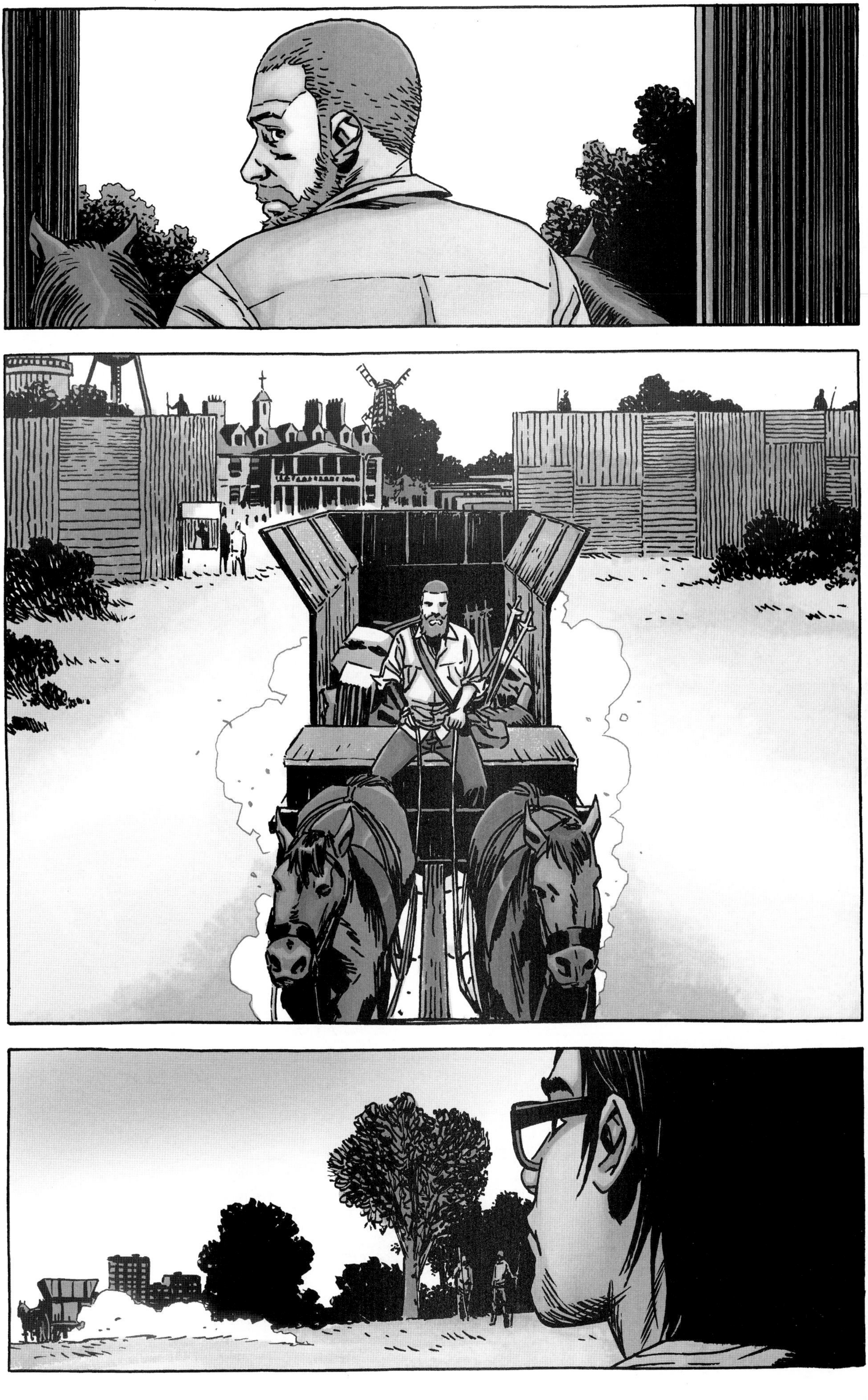

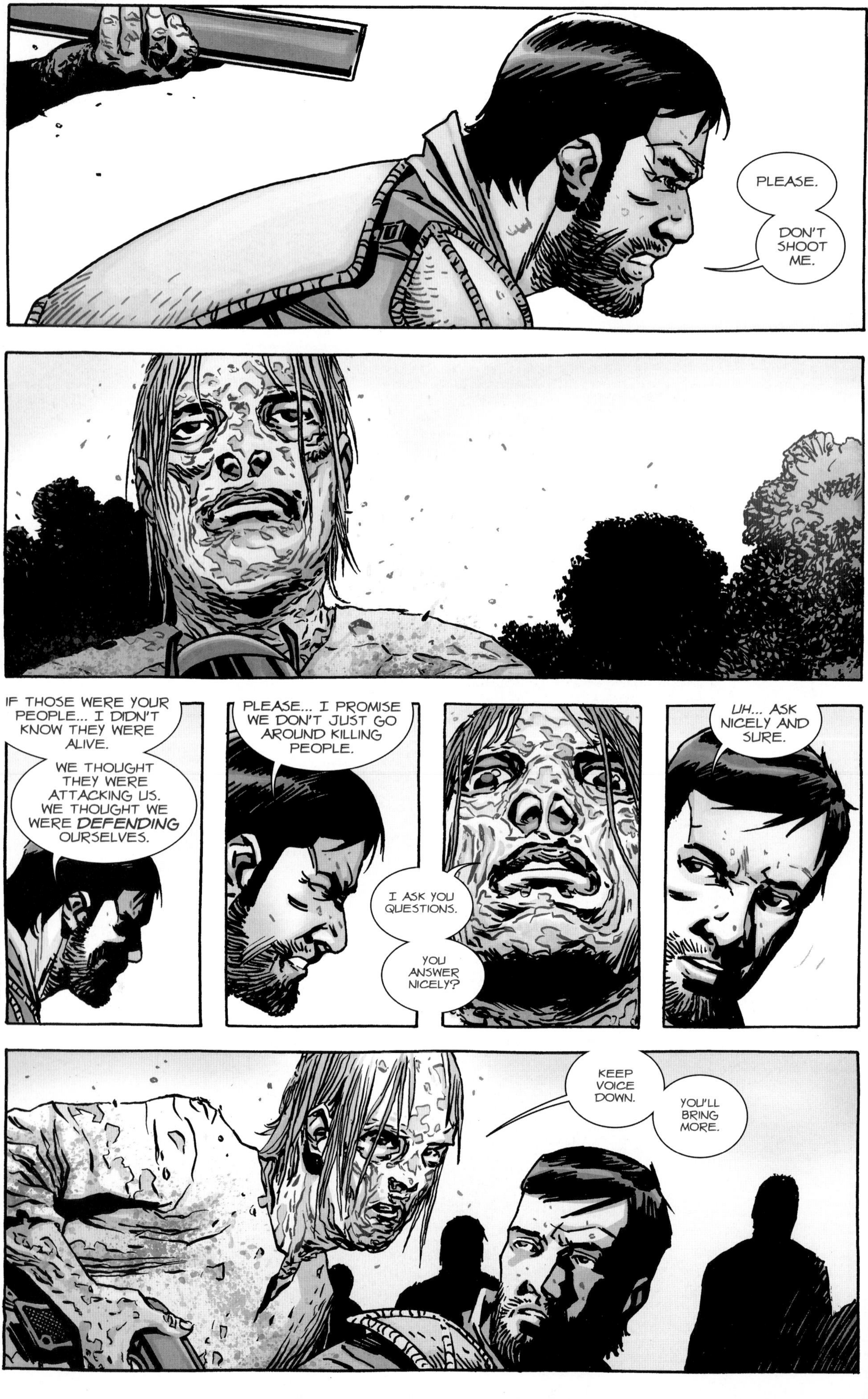
PLEASE.
DON'T SHOOT ME.
IF THOSE WERE YOUR PEOPLE... I DIDN'T KNOW THEY WERE ALIVE.
WE THOUGHT THEY WERE ATTACKING US. WE THOUGHT WE WERE *DEFENDING* OURSELVES.
PLEASE... I PROMISE WE DON'T JUST GO AROUND KILLING PEOPLE.
I ASK YOU QUESTIONS.
YOU ANSWER NICELY?
UH... ASK NICELY AND SURE.
KEEP VOICE DOWN.
YOU'LL BRING MORE.

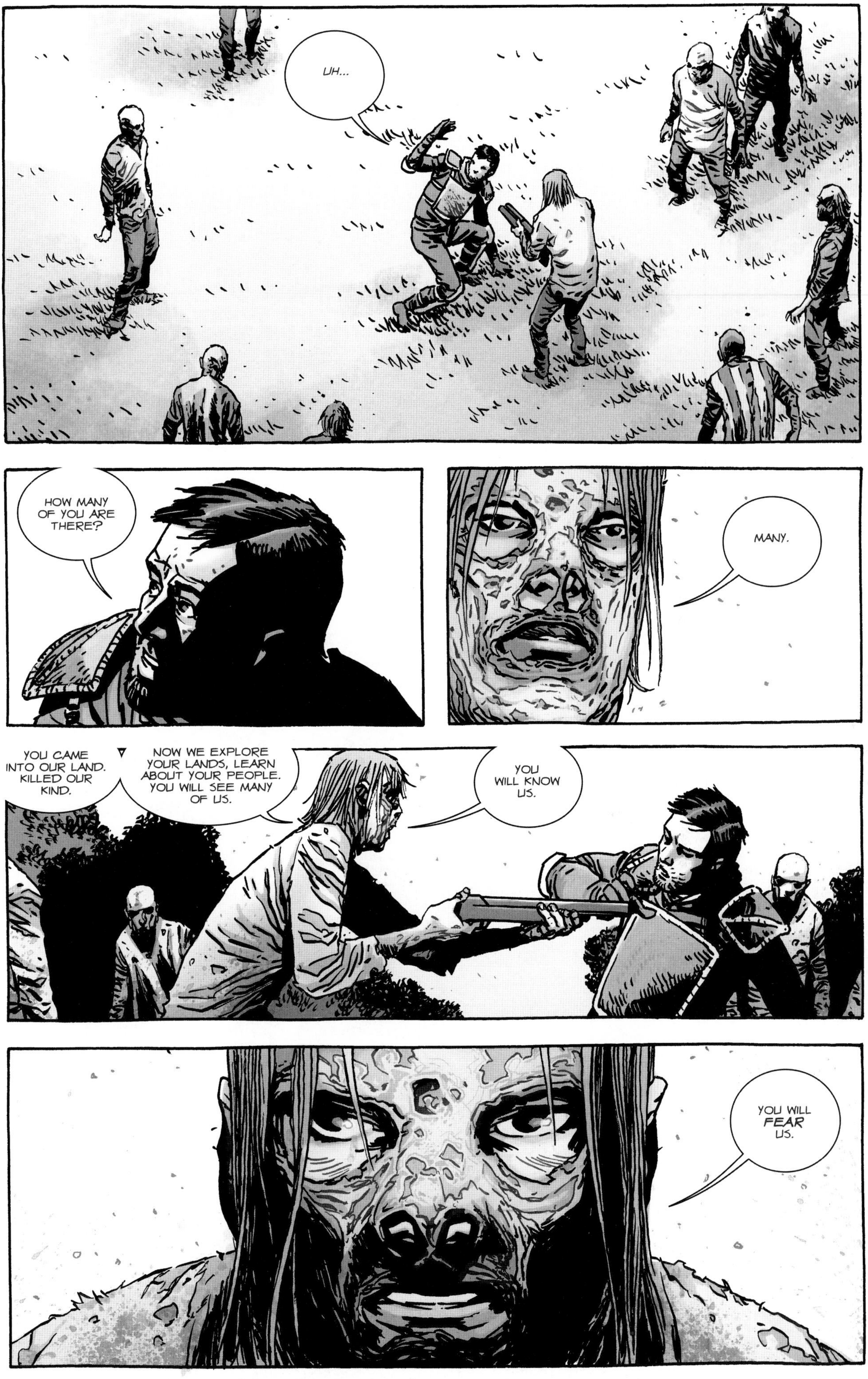
UH...
HOW MANY OF YOU ARE THERE?
MANY.
YOU CAME INTO OUR LAND. KILLED OUR KIND.
NOW WE EXPLORE YOUR LANDS, LEARN ABOUT YOUR PEOPLE. YOU WILL SEE MANY OF US.
YOU WILL KNOW US.
YOU WILL *FEAR* US.

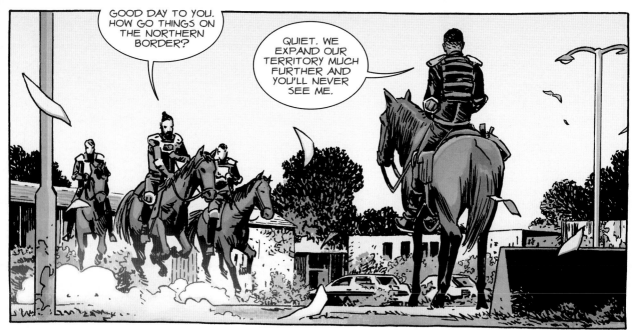

GOOD DAY TO YOU. HOW GO THINGS ON THE NORTHERN BORDER?

QUIET. WE EXPAND OUR TERRITORY MUCH FURTHER AND YOU'LL NEVER SEE ME.

I THINK RICK'S PLAN IS TO JUST SEE IF WE CAN MAINTAIN THIS FOR NOW, DARIUS. SO DON'T WORRY.

NO ACTION?

NOTHING UNUSUAL. PROBABLY ABOUT TWENTY ROAMERS IN THE LAST FEW DAYS. NO BIG GROUPS... I THINK ONE GROUP OF FIVE.

BEEN QUIET SINCE YOU GUYS STEERED THAT HERD THROUGH HERE.

NO NEWS IS GOOD NEWS.

HOW YOU GUYS ON SUPPLIES?

IF NATHANIEL WILL STOP EATING LIKE A GODDAMN PIG, OUR SHIT WOULD LAST US MUCH LONGER. WE'RE GOOD FOR NOW, BUT IT'S GOING FASTER THAN IT SHOULD.

YOU NEED TO TALK TO HIM AGAIN. FUCKER EATS LIKE IT'S HIS LAST MEAL.

I'LL HAVE ANOTHER TALK WITH HIM.

HE AT THE STATION?

NAH. HE'S STILL OUT.

HASN'T CHECKED IN.

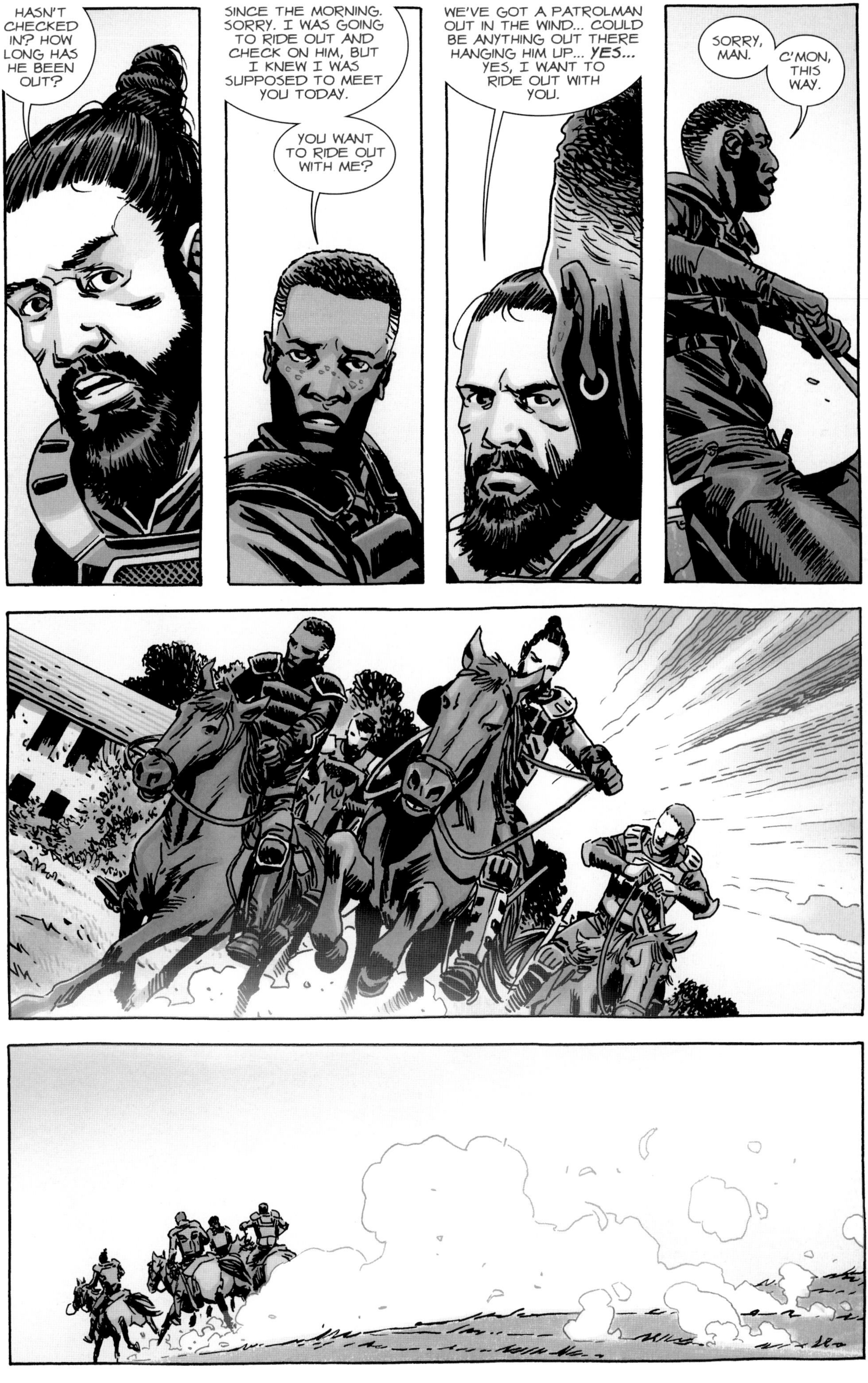
HASN'T CHECKED IN? HOW LONG HAS HE BEEN OUT?
SINCE THE MORNING. SORRY. I WAS GOING TO RIDE OUT AND CHECK ON HIM, BUT I KNEW I WAS SUPPOSED TO MEET YOU TODAY.
YOU WANT TO RIDE OUT WITH ME?
WE'VE GOT A PATROLMAN OUT IN THE WIND... COULD BE ANYTHING OUT THERE HANGING HIM UP... *YES...* YES, I WANT TO RIDE OUT WITH YOU.
SORRY, MAN.
C'MON, THIS WAY.

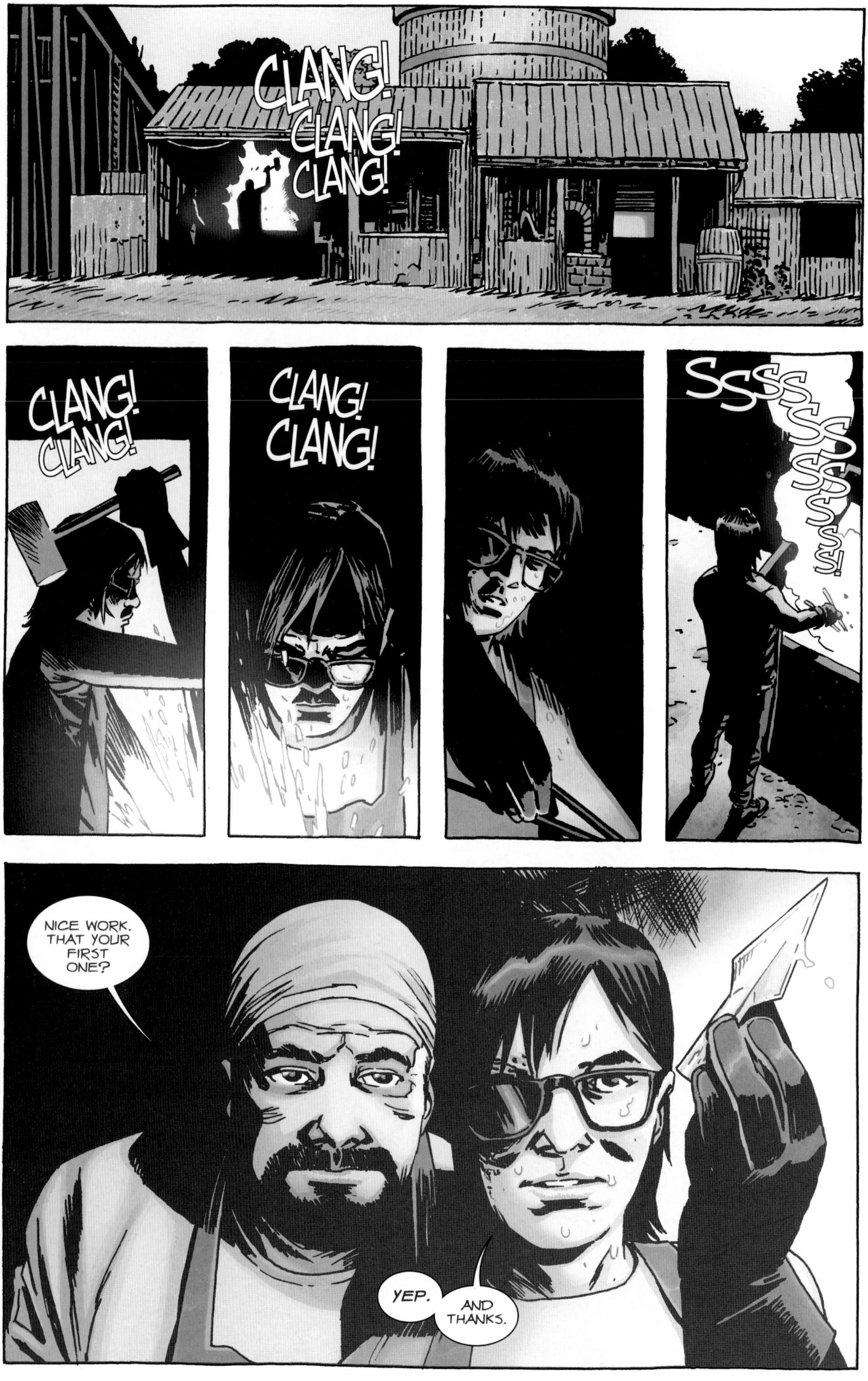
CLANG! CLANG! CLANG!
CLANG! CLANG!
CLANG! CLANG!
SSSSSSSSSSSSSSSS!
NICE WORK. THAT YOUR FIRST ONE?
YEP.
AND THANKS.

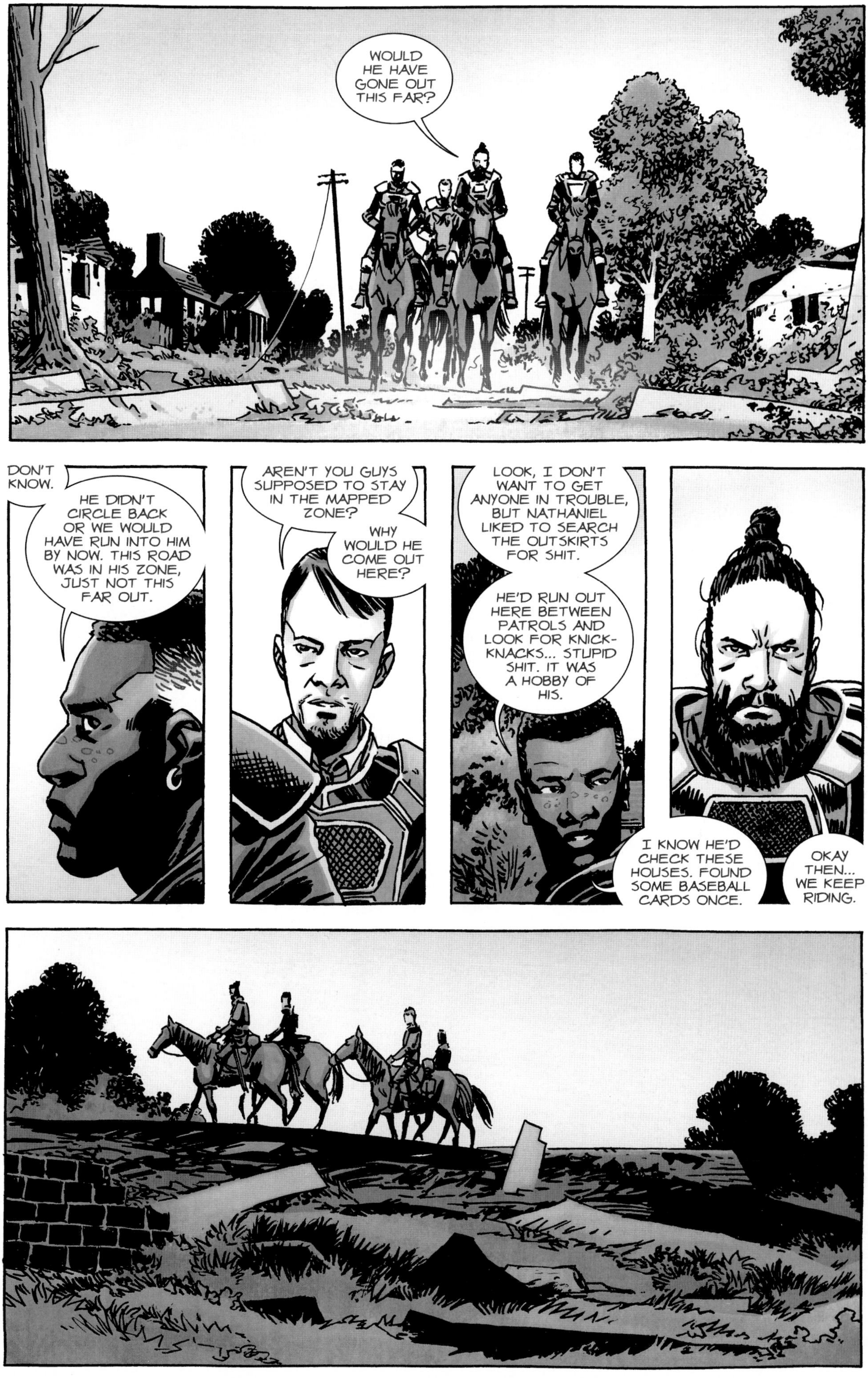
WOULD HE HAVE GONE OUT THIS FAR?
DON'T KNOW.
HE DIDN'T CIRCLE BACK OR WE WOULD HAVE RUN INTO HIM BY NOW. THIS ROAD WAS IN HIS ZONE, JUST NOT THIS FAR OUT.
AREN'T YOU GUYS SUPPOSED TO STAY IN THE MAPPED ZONE?
WHY WOULD HE COME OUT HERE?
LOOK, I DON'T WANT TO GET ANYONE IN TROUBLE, BUT NATHANIEL LIKED TO SEARCH THE OUTSKIRTS FOR SHIT.
HE'D RUN OUT HERE BETWEEN PATROLS AND LOOK FOR KNICK-KNACKS... STUPID SHIT. IT WAS A HOBBY OF HIS.
I KNOW HE'D CHECK THESE HOUSES. FOUND SOME BASEBALL CARDS ONCE.
OKAY THEN... WE KEEP RIDING.

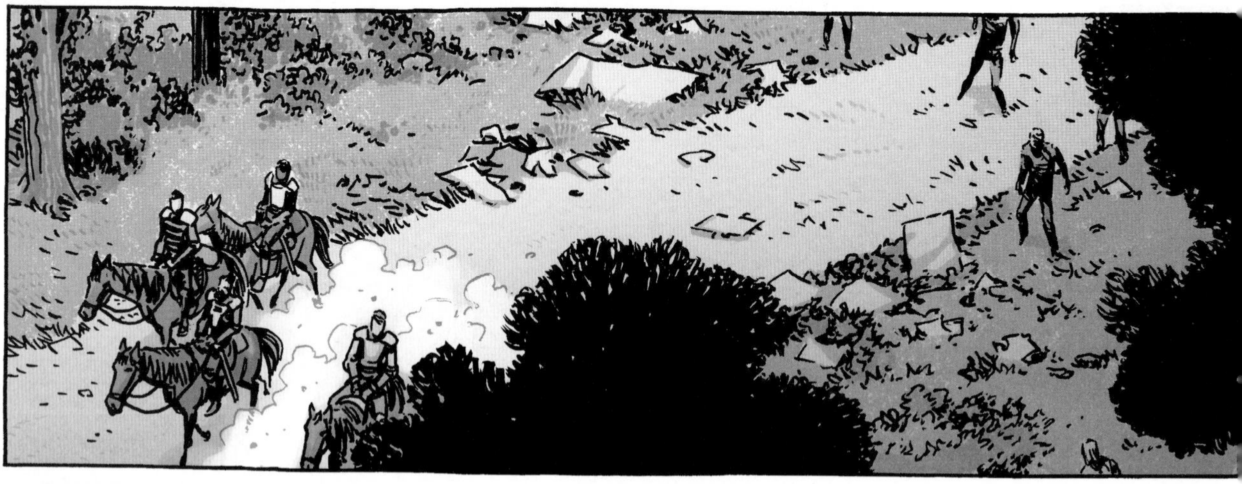

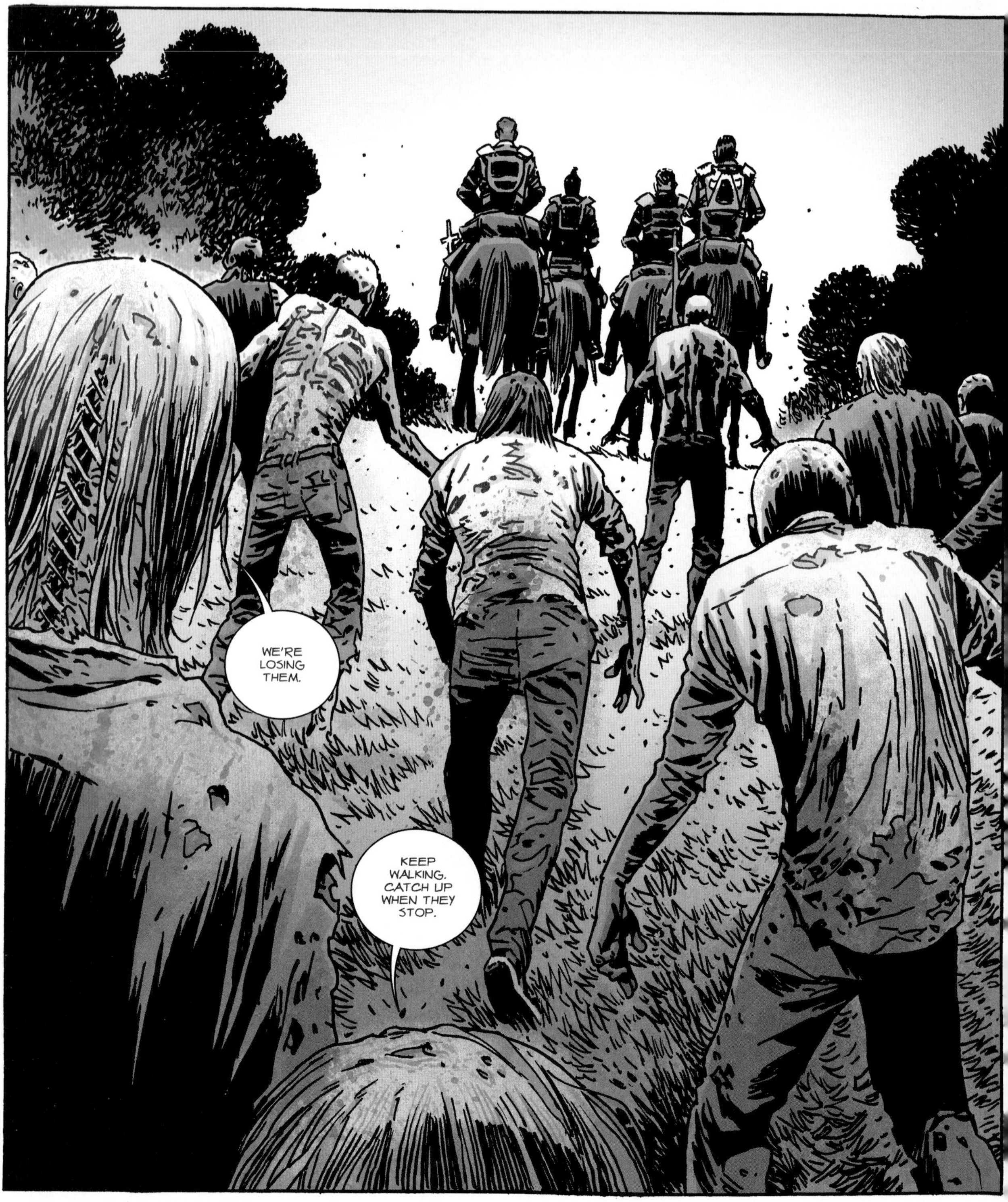
WE'RE LOSING THEM.
KEEP WALKING. CATCH UP WHEN THEY STOP.

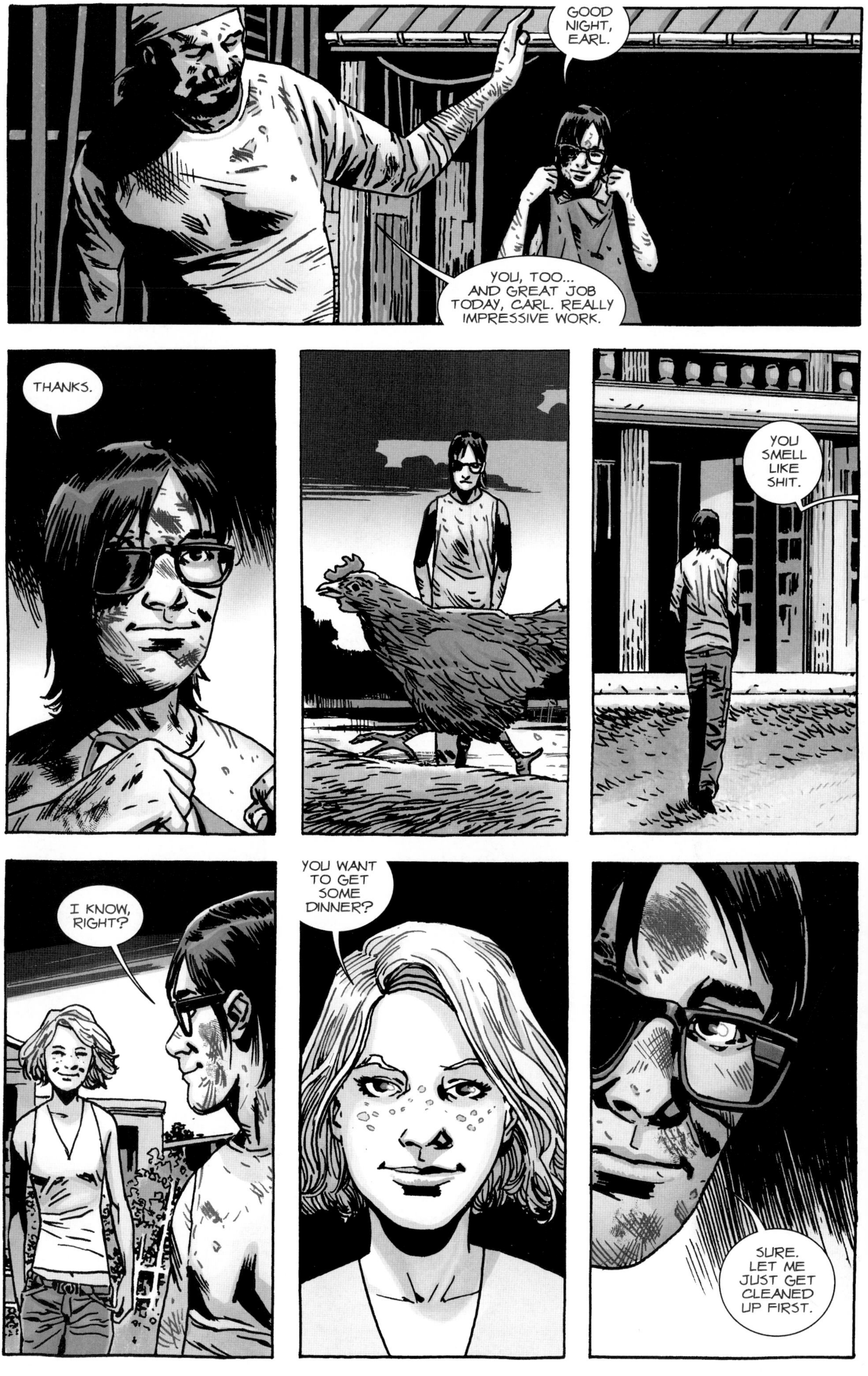
GOOD NIGHT, EARL.
YOU, TOO... AND GREAT JOB TODAY, CARL. REALLY IMPRESSIVE WORK.
THANKS.
YOU SMELL LIKE SHIT.
I KNOW, RIGHT?
YOU WANT TO GET SOME DINNER?
SURE. LET ME JUST GET CLEANED UP FIRST.

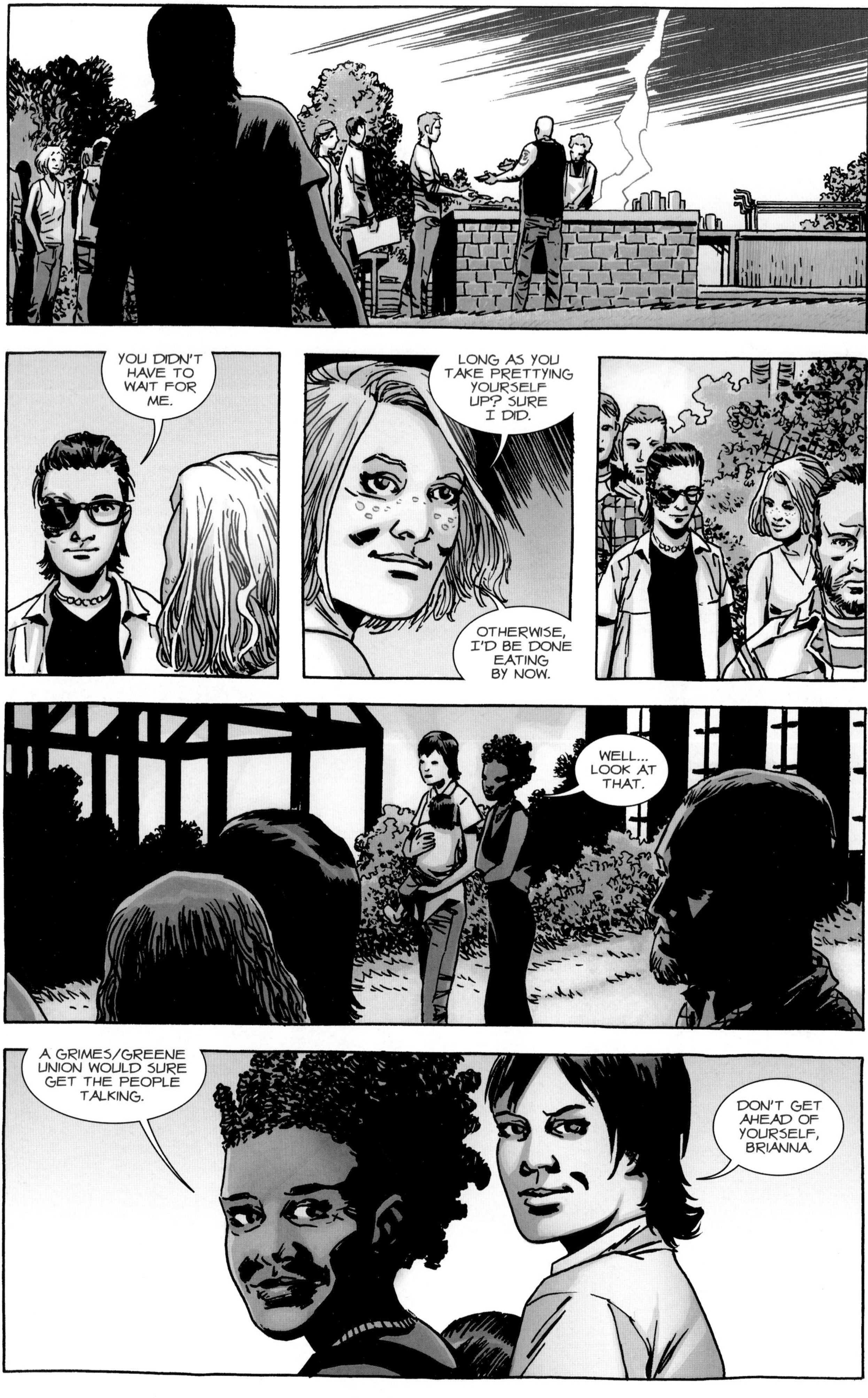
YOU DIDN'T HAVE TO WAIT FOR ME.
LONG AS YOU TAKE PRETTYING YOURSELF UP? SURE I DID.
OTHERWISE, I'D BE DONE EATING BY NOW.
WELL... LOOK AT THAT.
A GRIMES/GREENE UNION WOULD SURE GET THE PEOPLE TALKING.
DON'T GET AHEAD OF YOURSELF, BRIANNA.

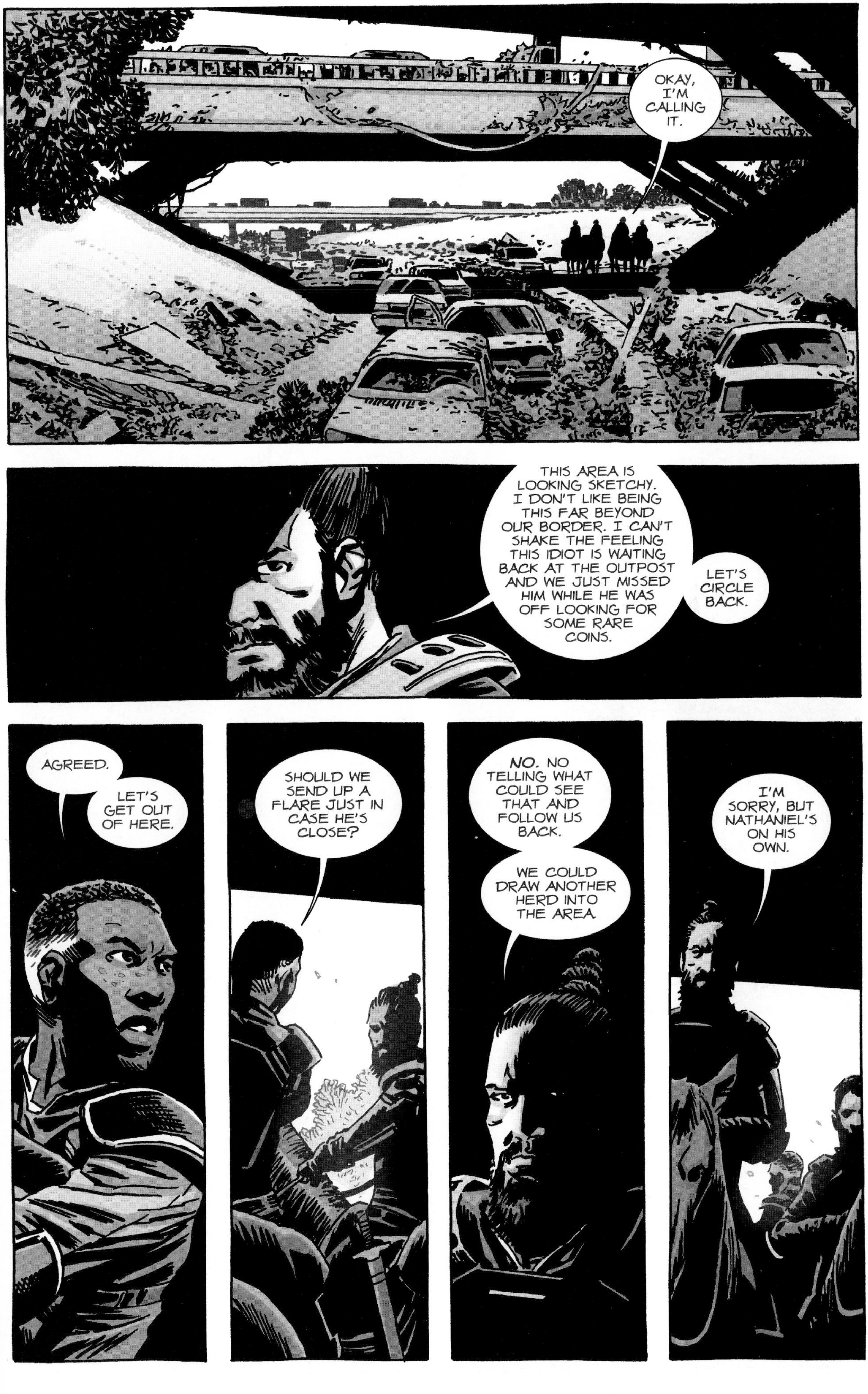
OKAY, I'M CALLING IT.
THIS AREA IS LOOKING SKETCHY. I DON'T LIKE BEING THIS FAR BEYOND OUR BORDER. I CAN'T SHAKE THE FEELING THIS IDIOT IS WAITING BACK AT THE OUTPOST AND WE JUST MISSED HIM WHILE HE WAS OFF LOOKING FOR SOME RARE COINS.
LET'S CIRCLE BACK.
AGREED.
LET'S GET OUT OF HERE.
SHOULD WE SEND UP A FLARE JUST IN CASE HE'S CLOSE?
NO. NO TELLING WHAT COULD SEE THAT AND FOLLOW US BACK.
WE COULD DRAW ANOTHER HERD INTO THE AREA.
I'M SORRY, BUT NATHANIEL'S ON HIS OWN.

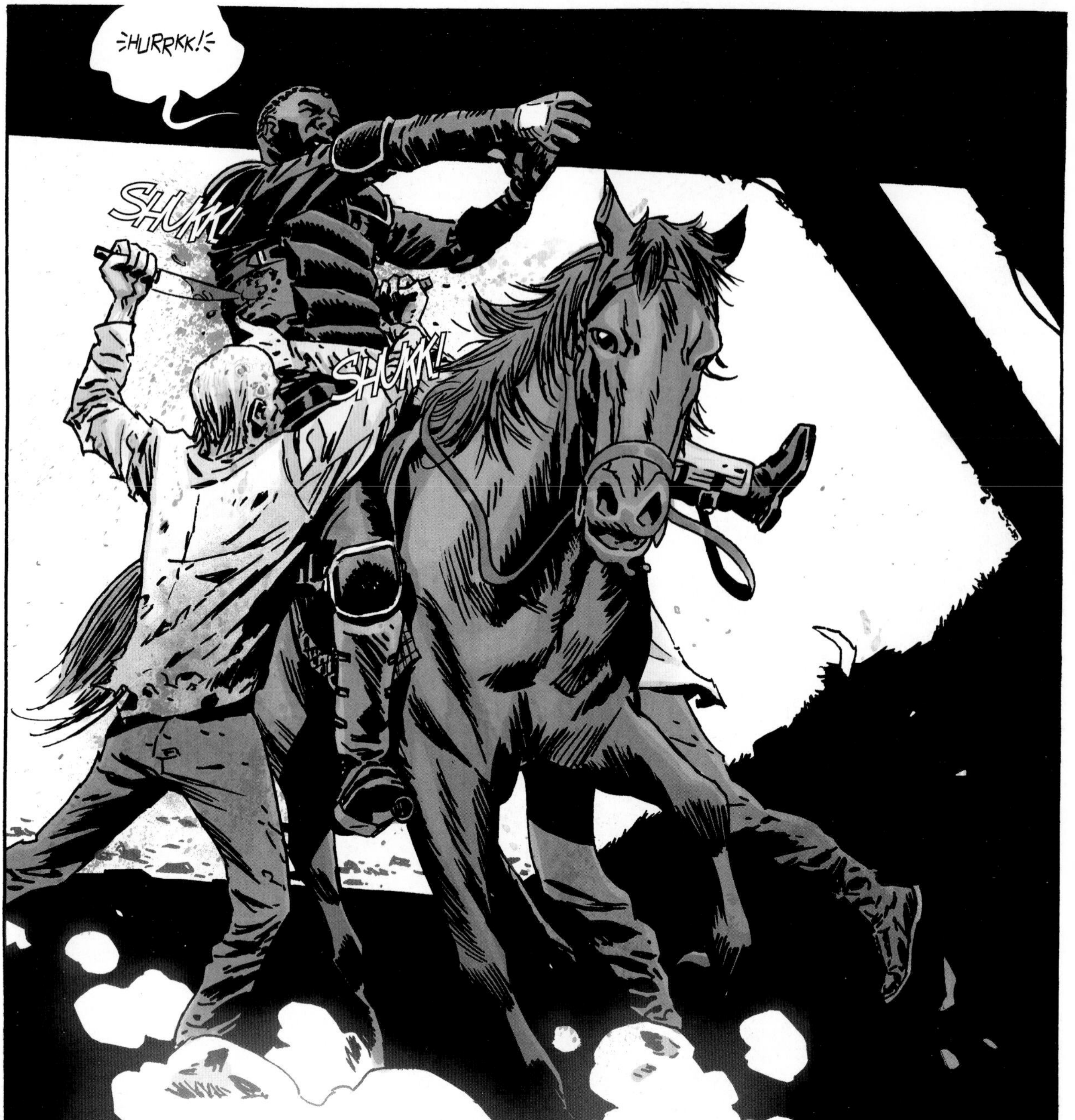
HURRKK!
SHUKK!
SHUKK!

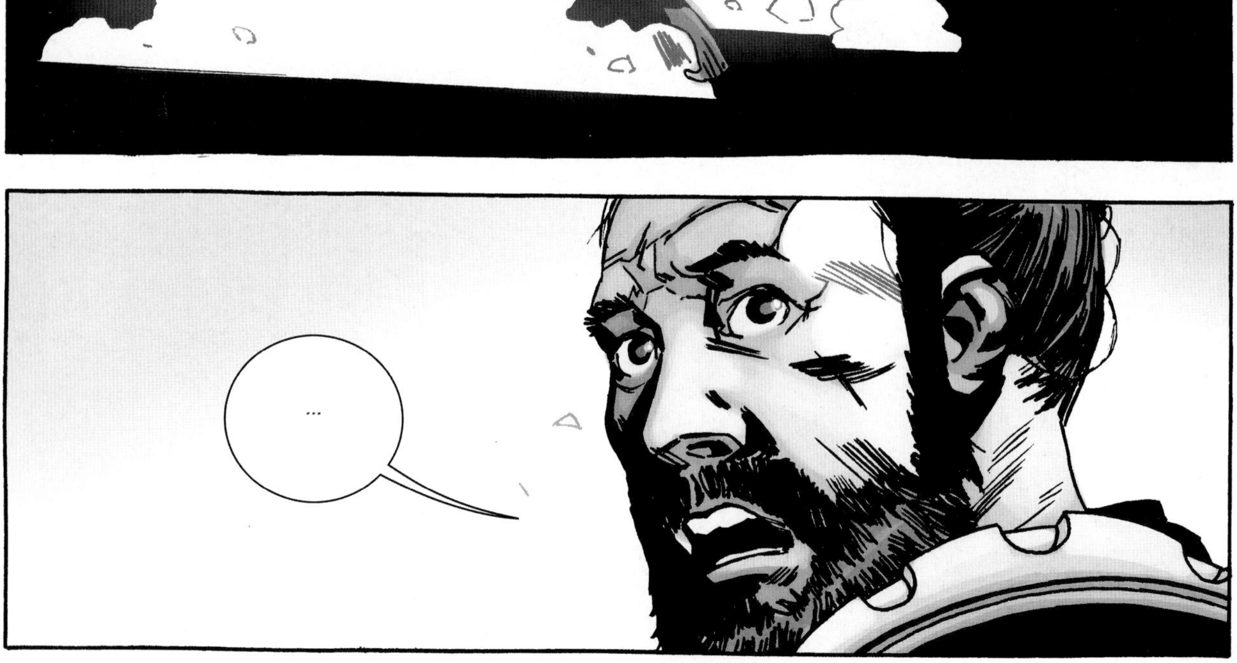
...

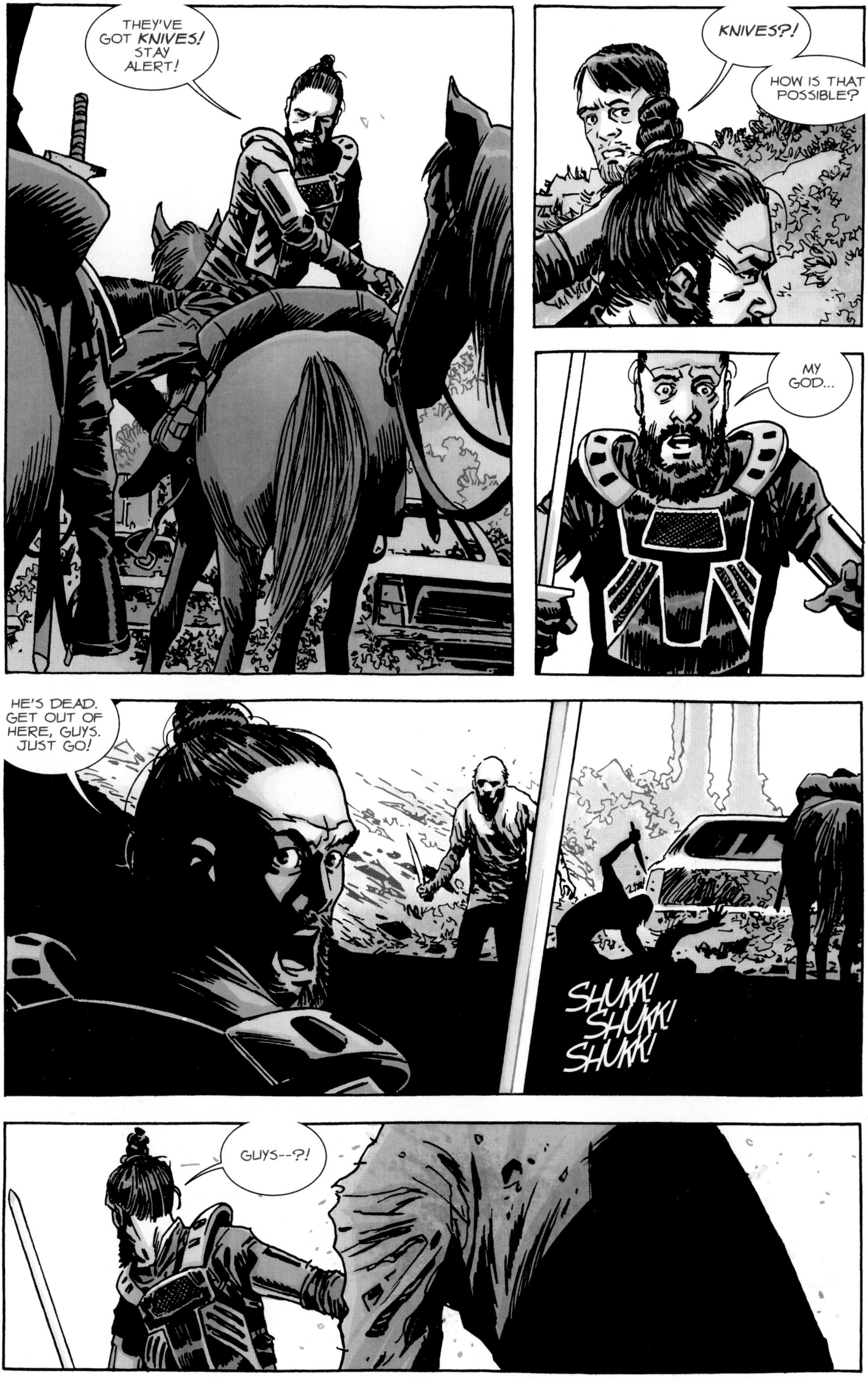
THEY'VE GOT KNIVES! STAY ALERT!
KNIVES?!
HOW IS THAT POSSIBLE?
MY GOD...
HE'S DEAD. GET OUT OF HERE, GUYS. JUST GO!
SHUKK! SHUKK! SHUKK!
GUYS--?!

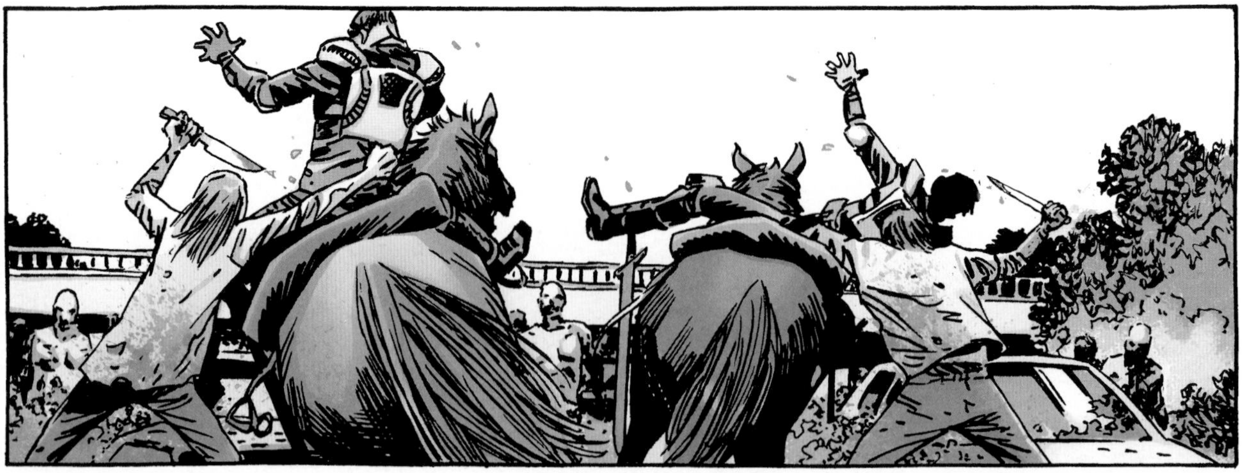

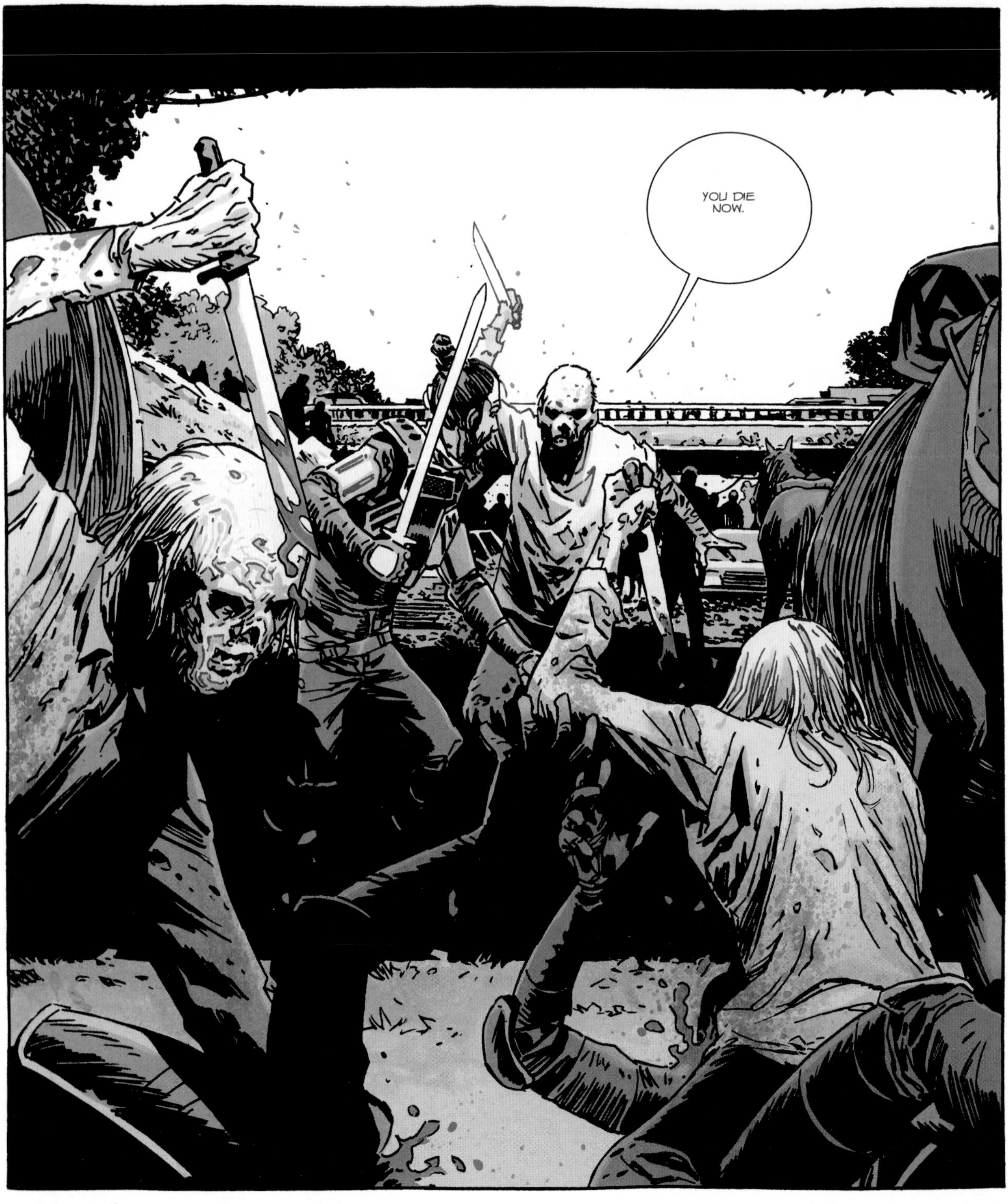
YOU DIE NOW.

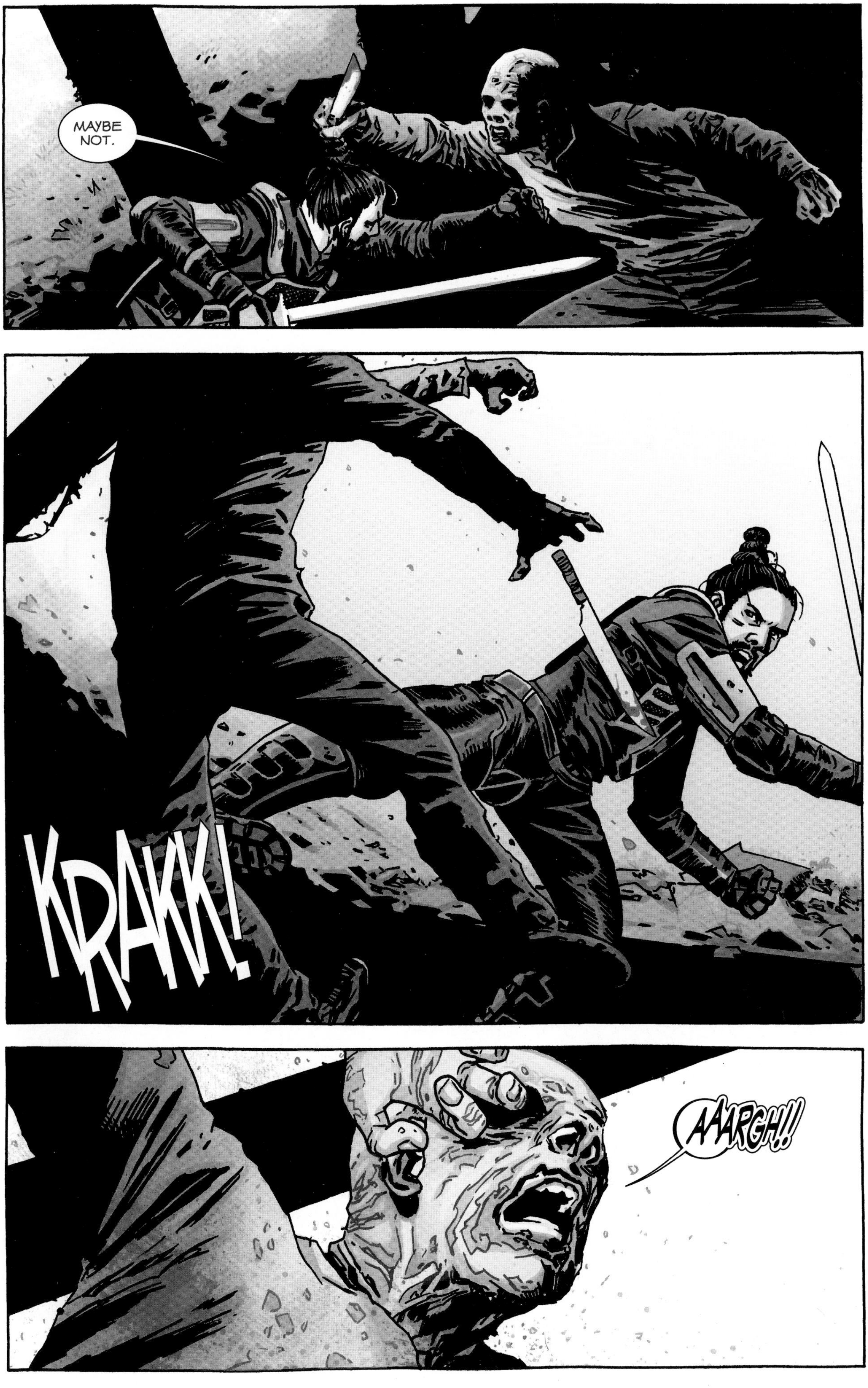
MAYBE NOT.
KRAKK!
AAARGH!!

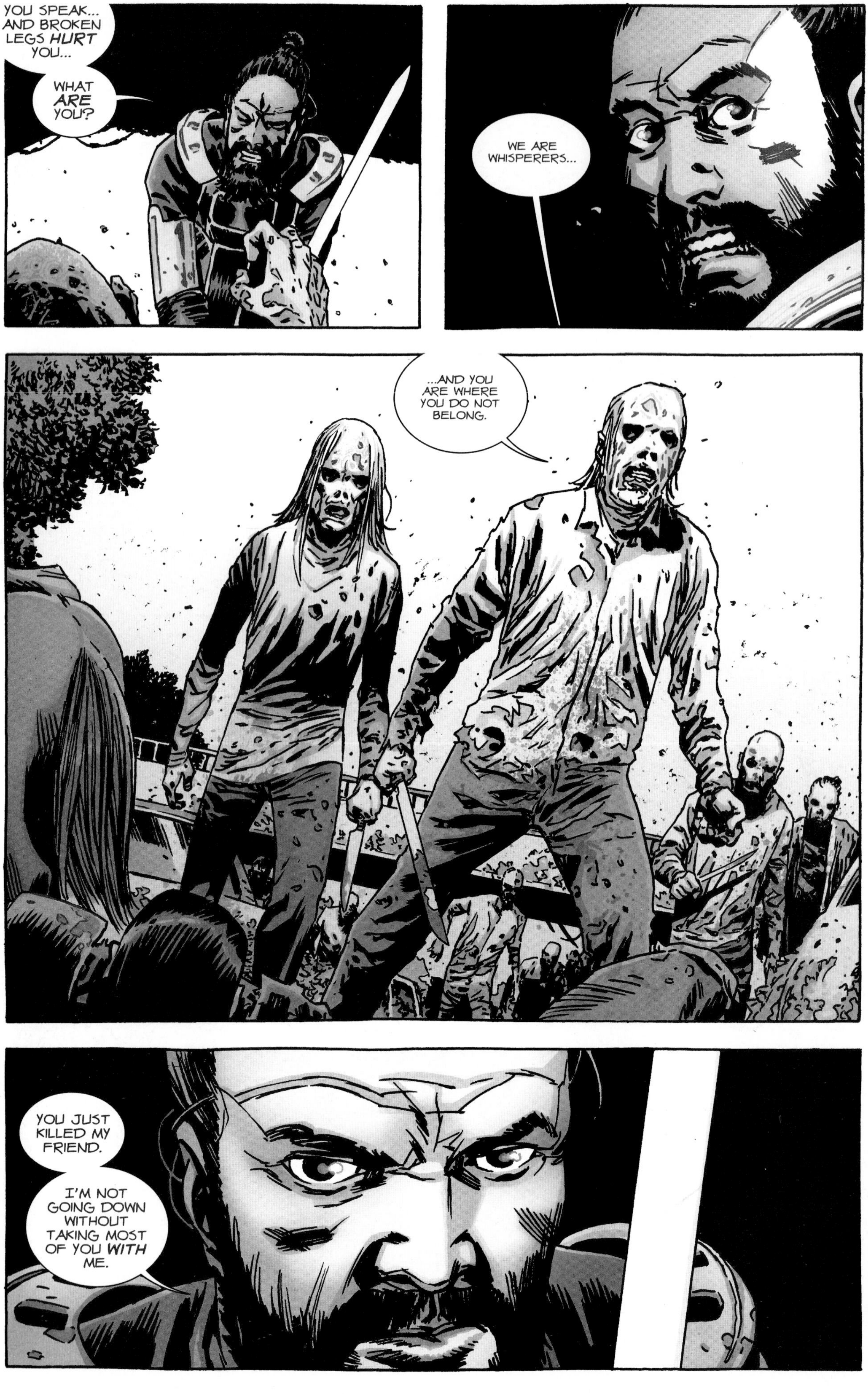
YOU SPEAK... AND BROKEN LEGS HURT YOU...
WHAT ARE YOU?
WE ARE WHISPERERS...
...AND YOU ARE WHERE YOU DO NOT BELONG.
YOU JUST KILLED MY FRIEND.
I'M NOT GOING DOWN WITHOUT TAKING MOST OF YOU WITH ME.

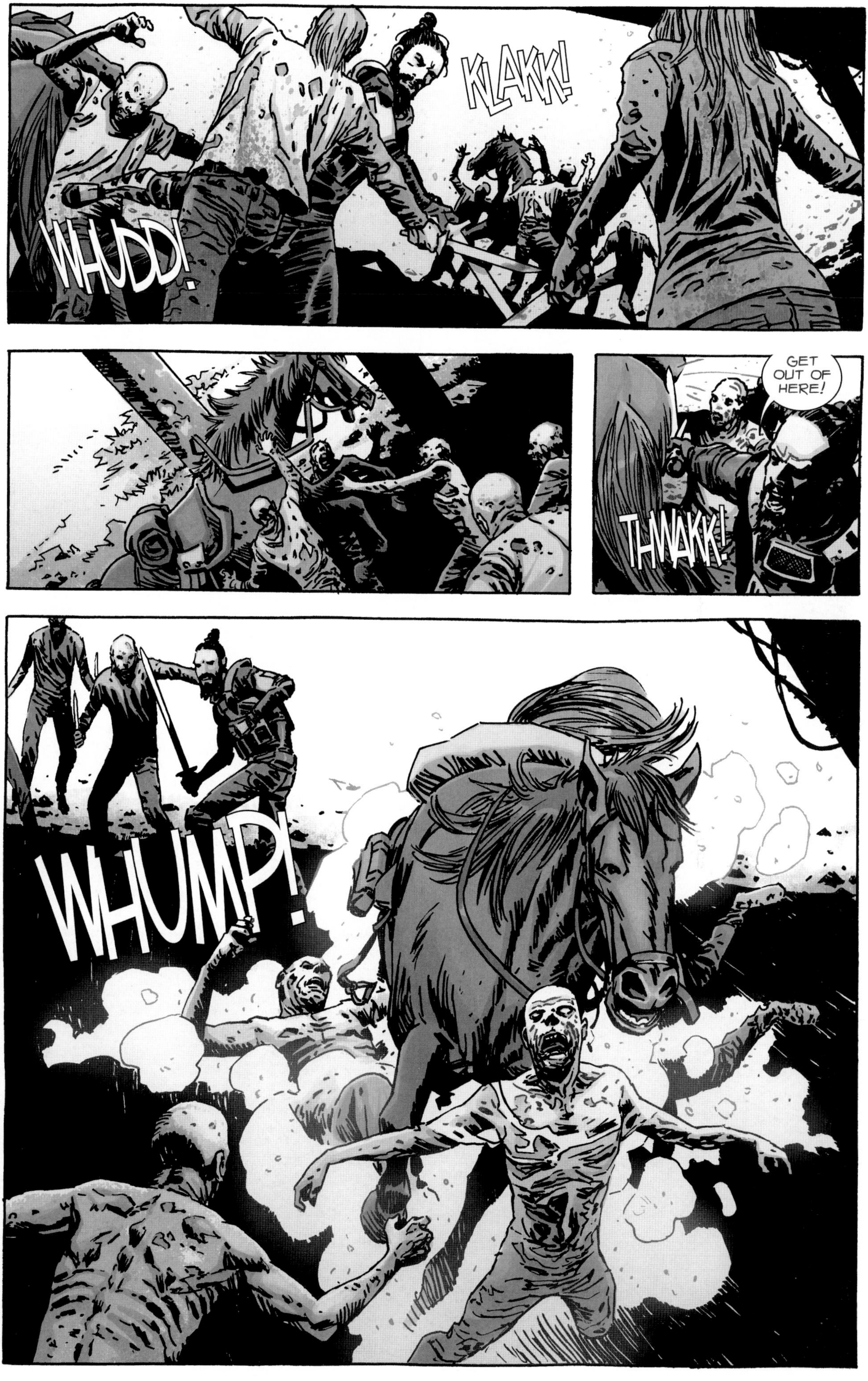
KLAKK!
WHUDD!
GET OUT OF HERE!
THWAKK!
WHUMP!

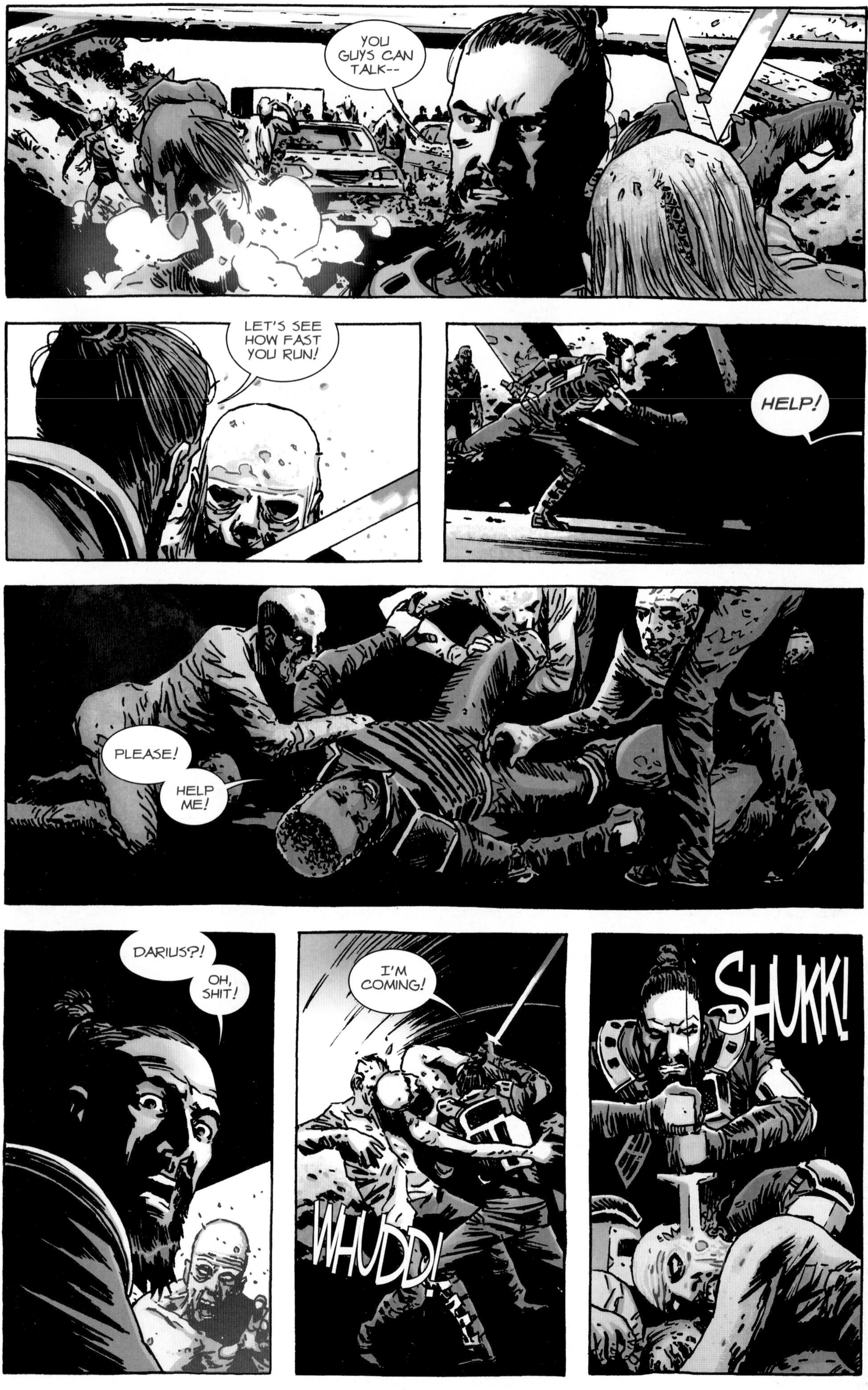
YOU GUYS CAN TALK--
LET'S SEE HOW FAST YOU RUN!
HELP!
PLEASE!
HELP ME!
DARIUS?!
OH, SHIT!
I'M COMING!
WHUDD!
SHUKK!

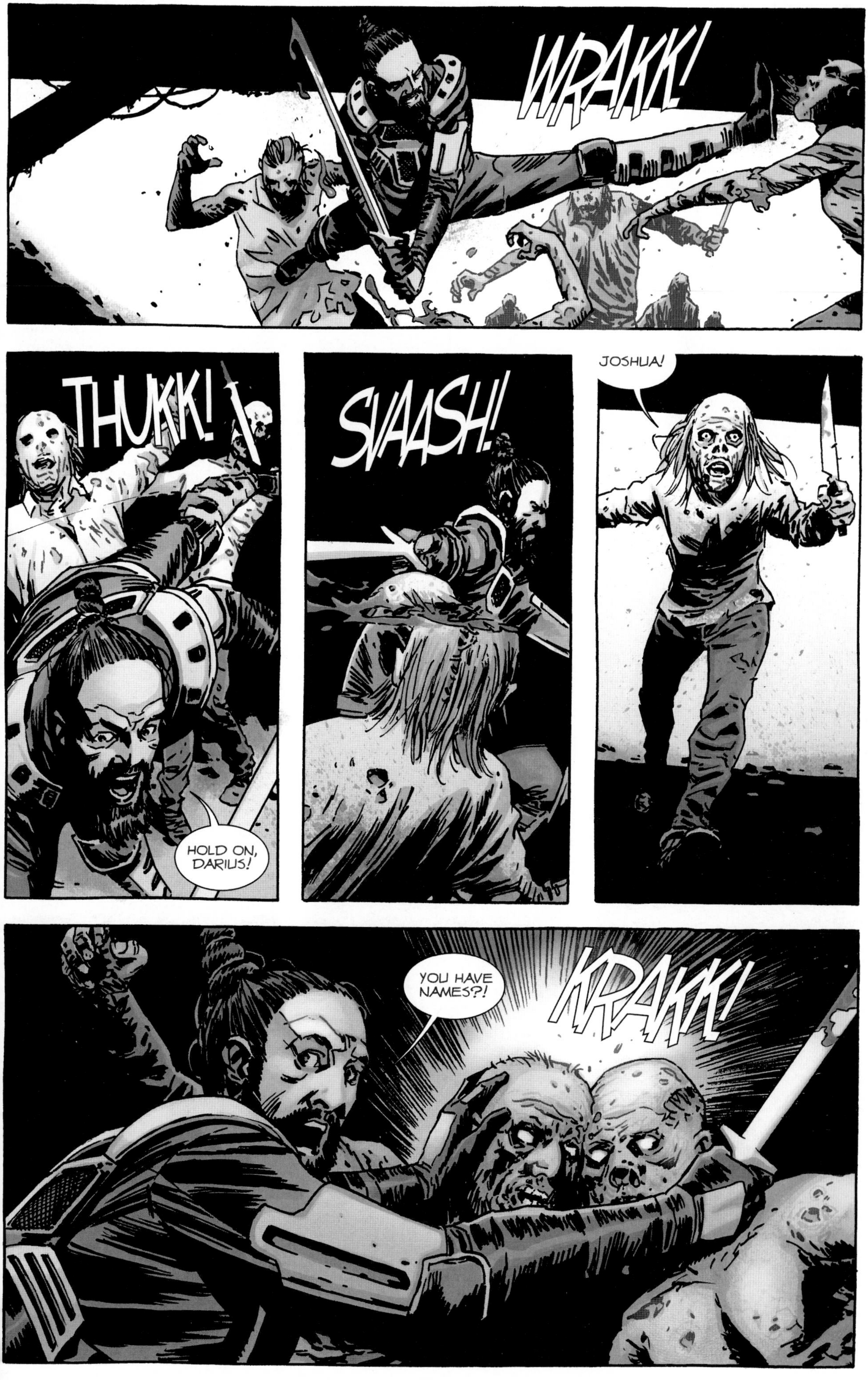
WRAKK!
THUKK!
HOLD ON, DARIUS!
SVAASH!
JOSHUA!
YOU HAVE NAMES?!
KRAKK!

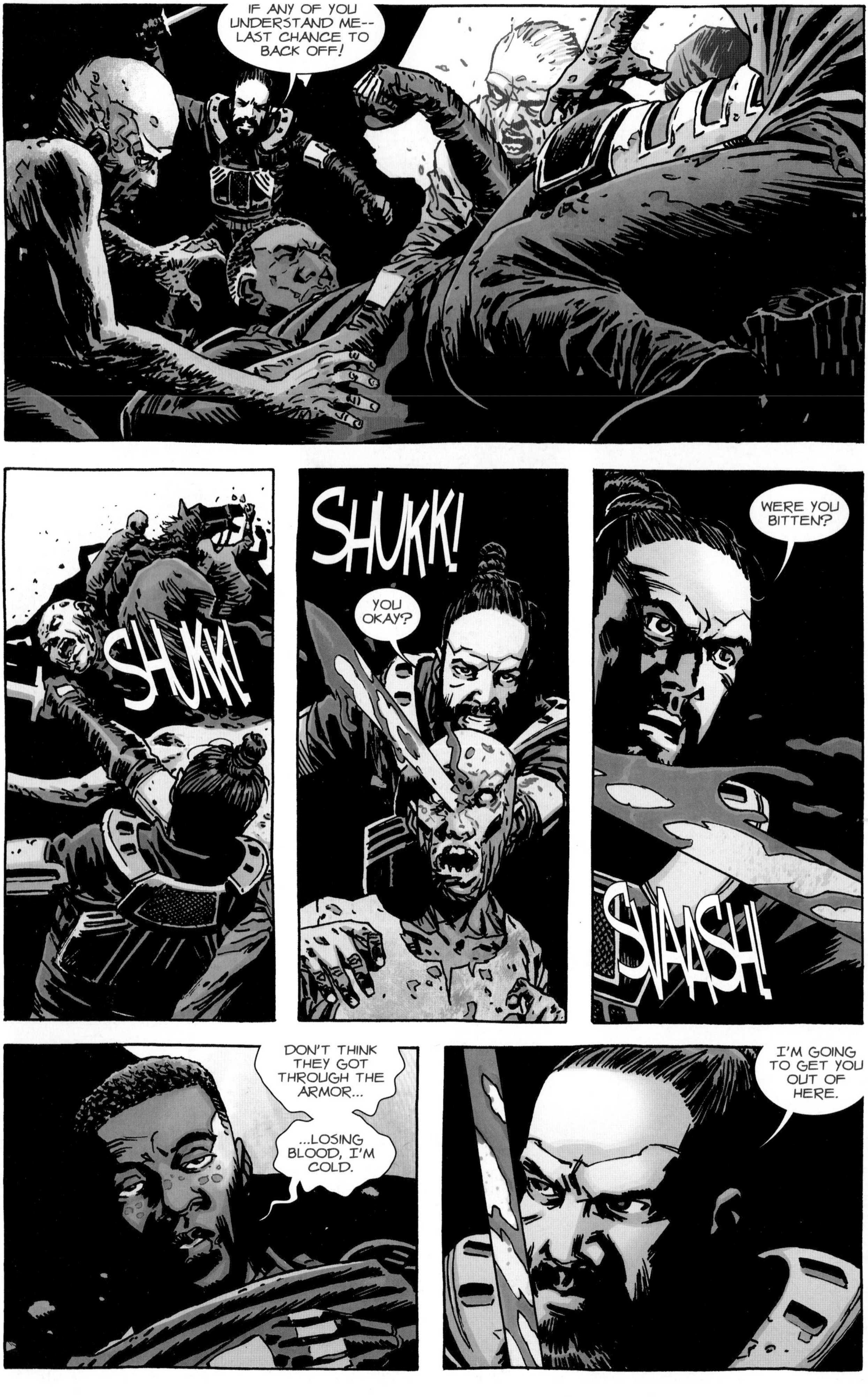
IF ANY OF YOU UNDERSTAND ME-- LAST CHANCE TO BACK OFF!
SHUKK!
SHUKK!
YOU OKAY?
WERE YOU BITTEN?
SNAASH!
DON'T THINK THEY GOT THROUGH THE ARMOR...
...LOSING BLOOD, I'M COLD.
I'M GOING TO GET YOU OUT OF HERE.

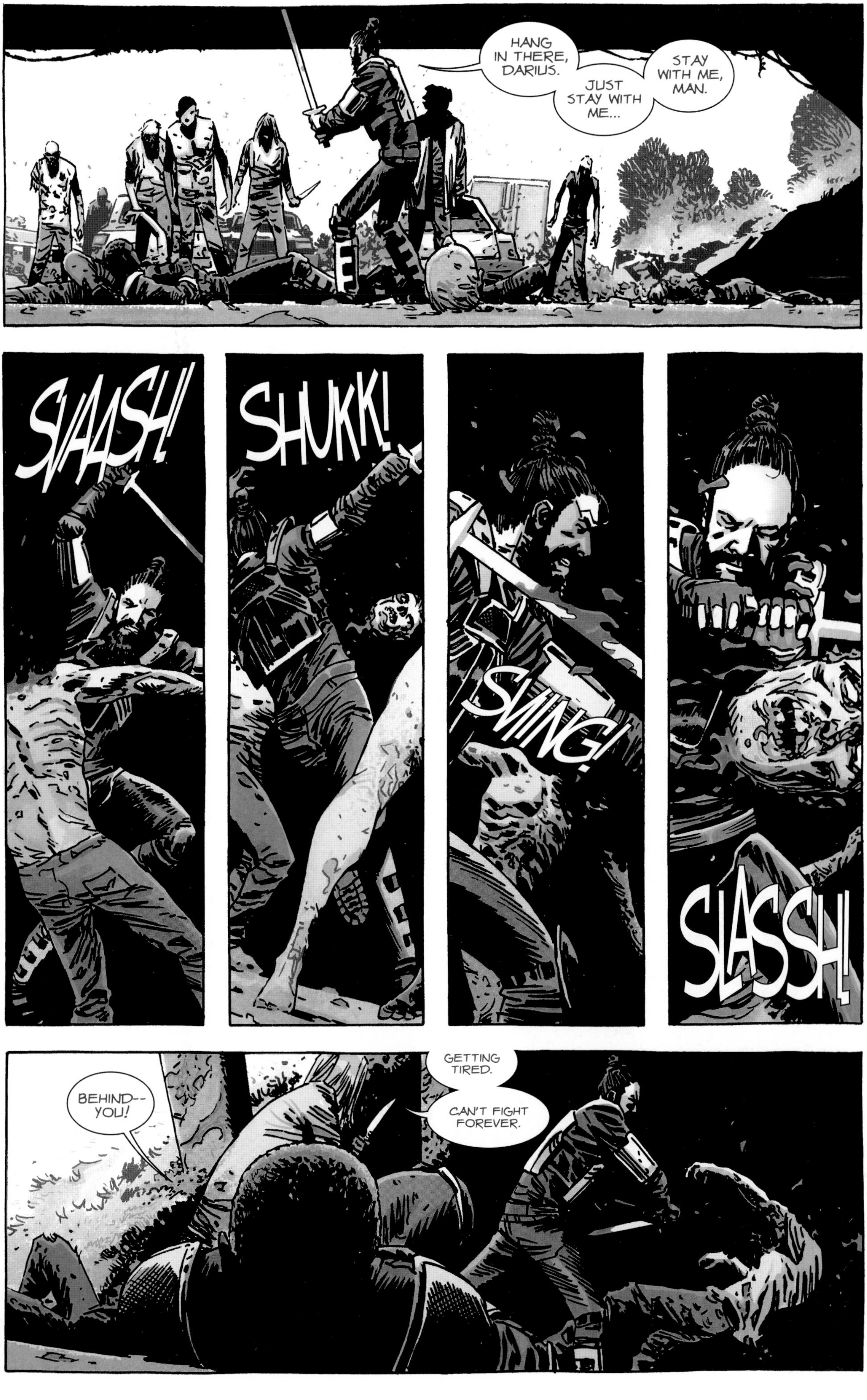

HANG IN THERE, DARIUS.
JUST STAY WITH ME...
STAY WITH ME, MAN.
SVAASH!
SHUKK!
SWING!
SLASSH!
BEHIND-- YOU!
GETTING TIRED.
CAN'T FIGHT FOREVER.

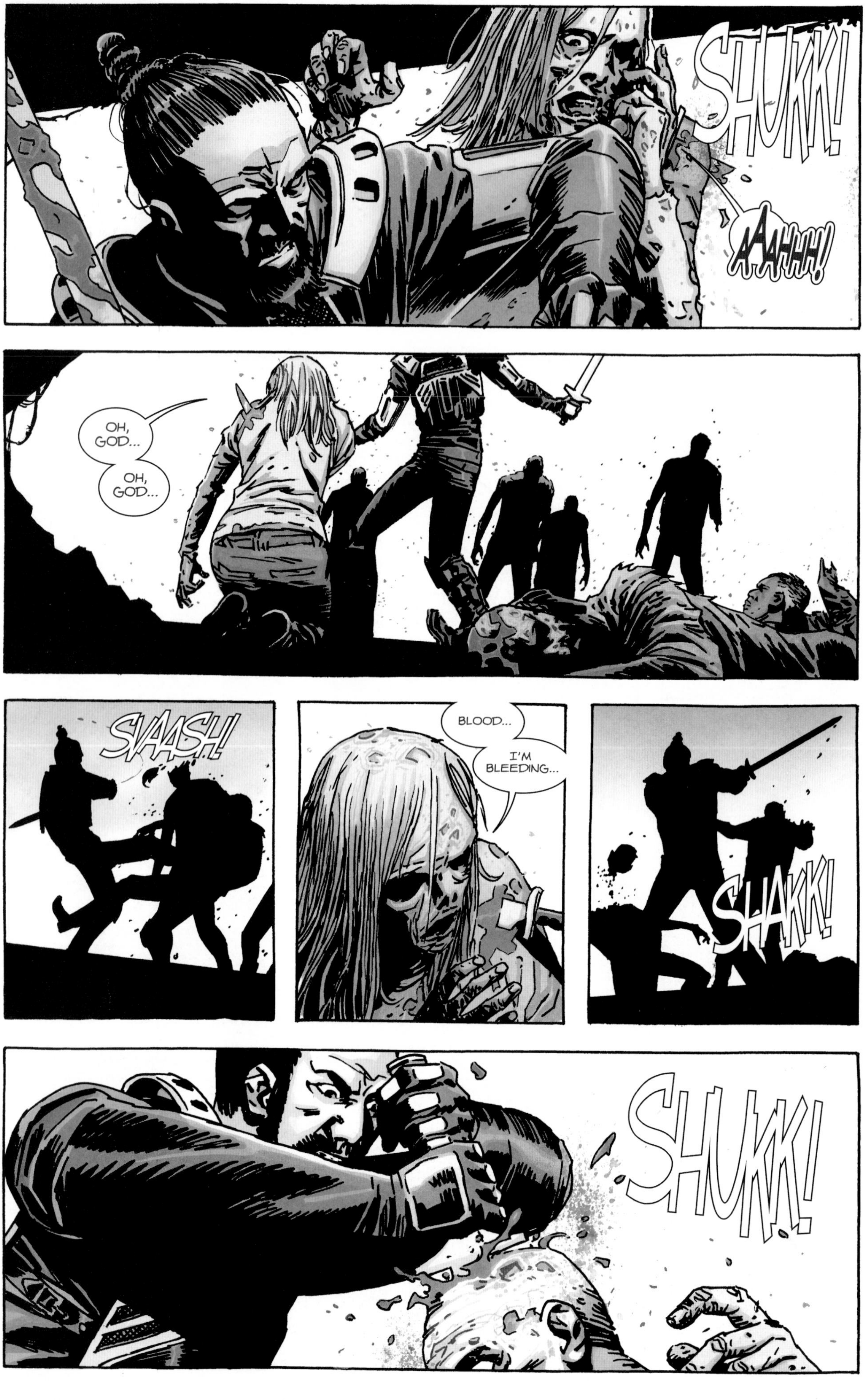
SHUKK!
AAAHHH!
OH, GOD...
OH, GOD...
SVAASH!
BLOOD...
I'M BLEEDING...
SHAKK!
SHUKK!

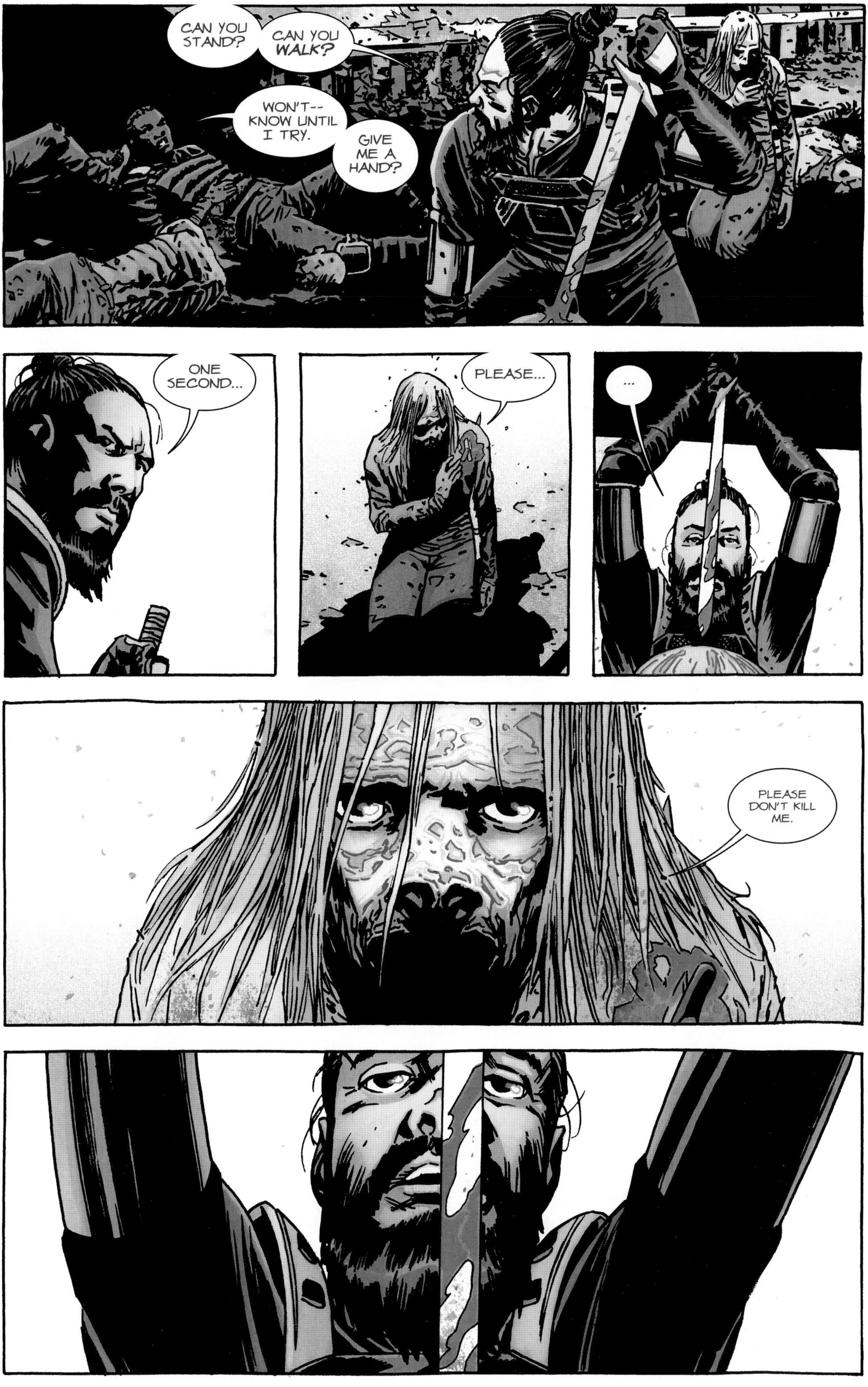
CAN YOU STAND?
CAN YOU WALK?
WON'T-- KNOW UNTIL I TRY.
GIVE ME A HAND?
ONE SECOND...
PLEASE...
...
PLEASE DON'T KILL ME.

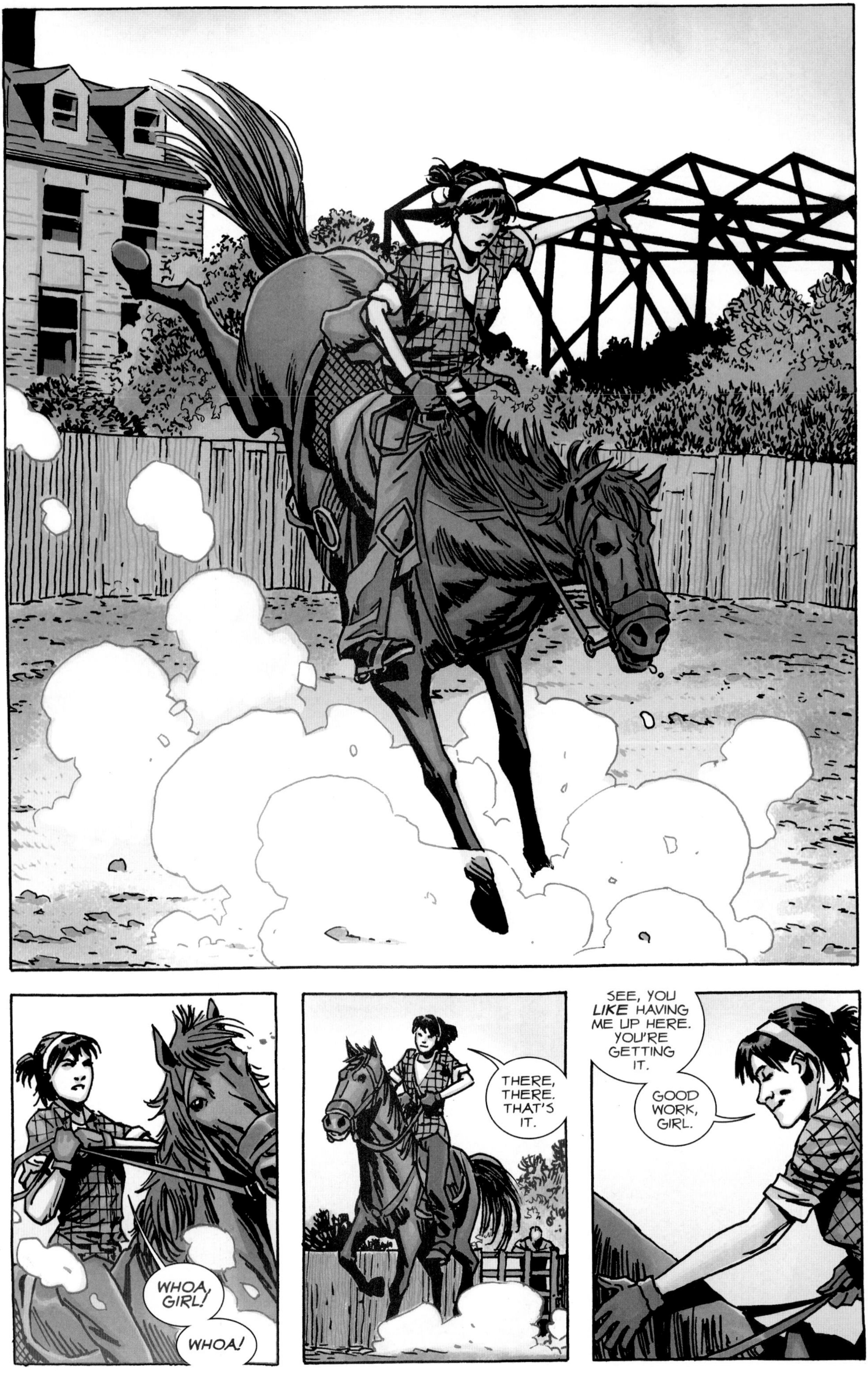
WHOA, GIRL!
WHOA!
THERE, THERE. THAT'S IT.
SEE, YOU LIKE HAVING ME UP HERE. YOU'RE GETTING IT.
GOOD WORK, GIRL.

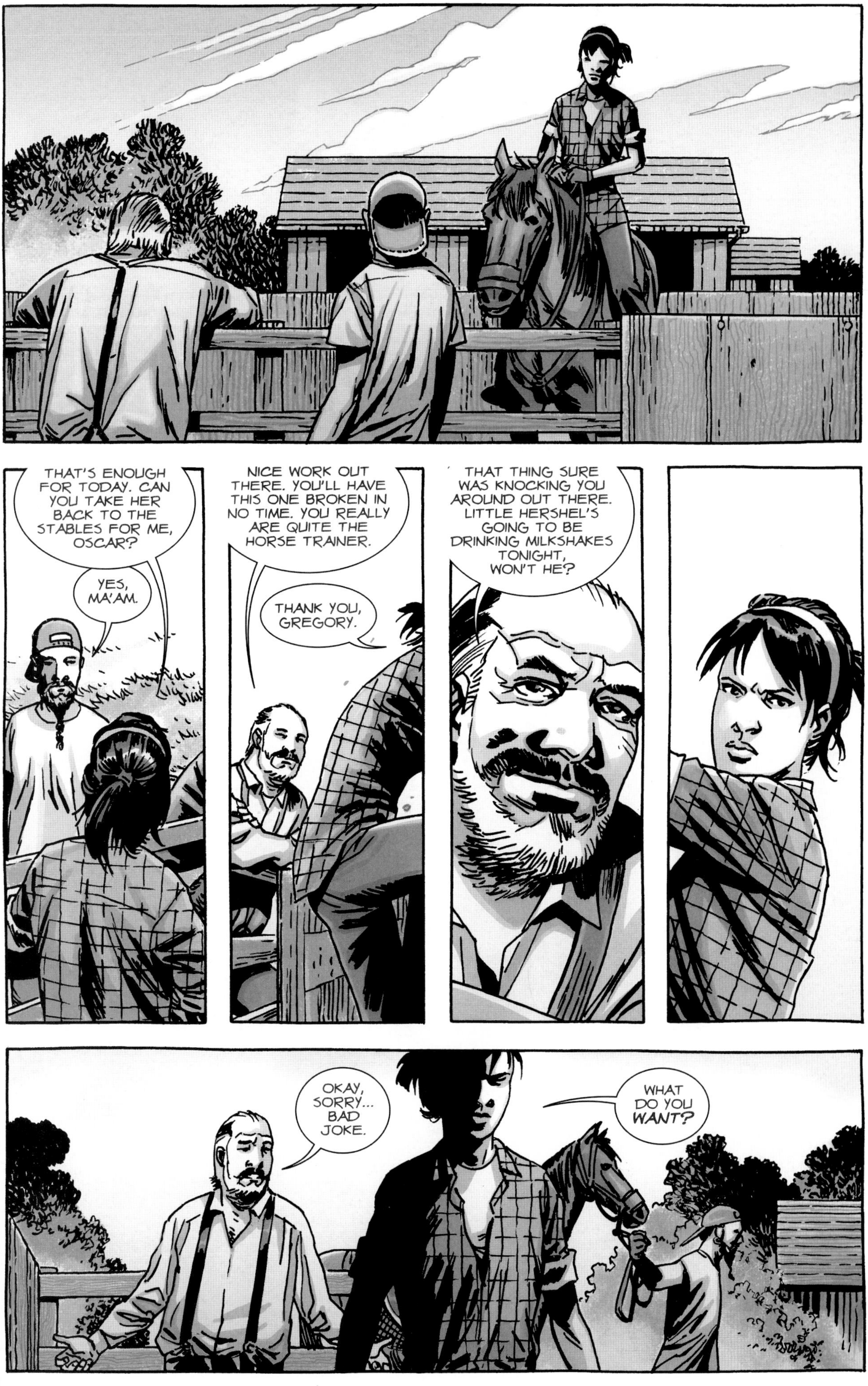
THAT'S ENOUGH FOR TODAY. CAN YOU TAKE HER BACK TO THE STABLES FOR ME, OSCAR?
YES, MA'AM.
NICE WORK OUT THERE. YOU'LL HAVE THIS ONE BROKEN IN NO TIME. YOU REALLY ARE QUITE THE HORSE TRAINER.
THANK YOU, GREGORY.
THAT THING SURE WAS KNOCKING YOU AROUND OUT THERE. LITTLE HERSHEL'S GOING TO BE DRINKING MILKSHAKES TONIGHT, WON'T HE?
OKAY, SORRY... BAD JOKE.
WHAT DO YOU *WANT?*

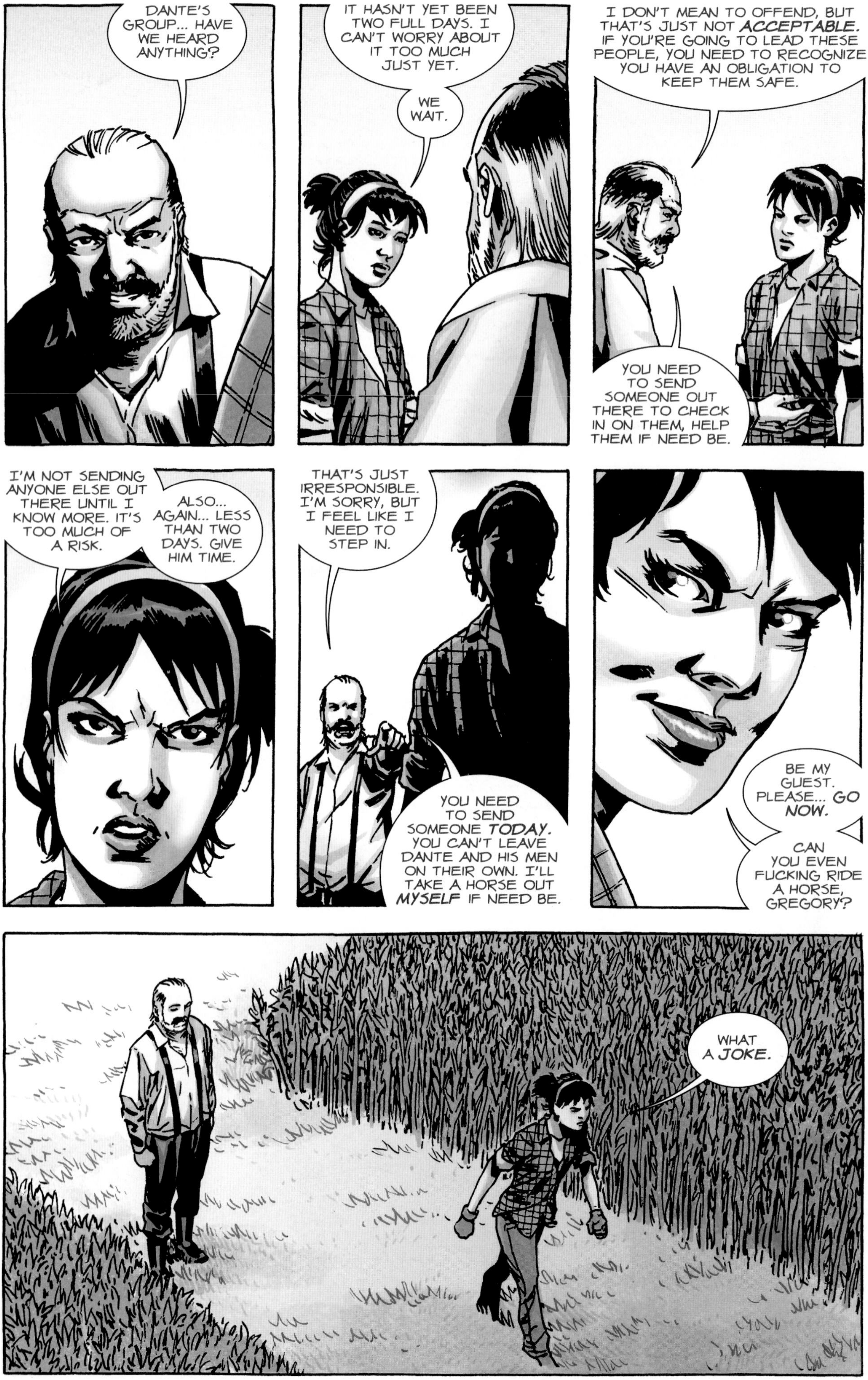
DANTE'S GROUP... HAVE WE HEARD ANYTHING?
IT HASN'T YET BEEN TWO FULL DAYS. I CAN'T WORRY ABOUT IT TOO MUCH JUST YET.
WE WAIT.
I DON'T MEAN TO OFFEND, BUT THAT'S JUST NOT ACCEPTABLE. IF YOU'RE GOING TO LEAD THESE PEOPLE, YOU NEED TO RECOGNIZE YOU HAVE AN OBLIGATION TO KEEP THEM SAFE.
YOU NEED TO SEND SOMEONE OUT THERE TO CHECK IN ON THEM, HELP THEM IF NEED BE.
I'M NOT SENDING ANYONE ELSE OUT THERE UNTIL I KNOW MORE. IT'S TOO MUCH OF A RISK.
ALSO... AGAIN... LESS THAN TWO DAYS. GIVE HIM TIME.
THAT'S JUST IRRESPONSIBLE. I'M SORRY, BUT I FEEL LIKE I NEED TO STEP IN.
YOU NEED TO SEND SOMEONE TODAY. YOU CAN'T LEAVE DANTE AND HIS MEN ON THEIR OWN. I'LL TAKE A HORSE OUT MYSELF IF NEED BE.
BE MY GUEST. PLEASE... GO NOW.
CAN YOU EVEN FUCKING RIDE A HORSE, GREGORY?
WHAT A JOKE.

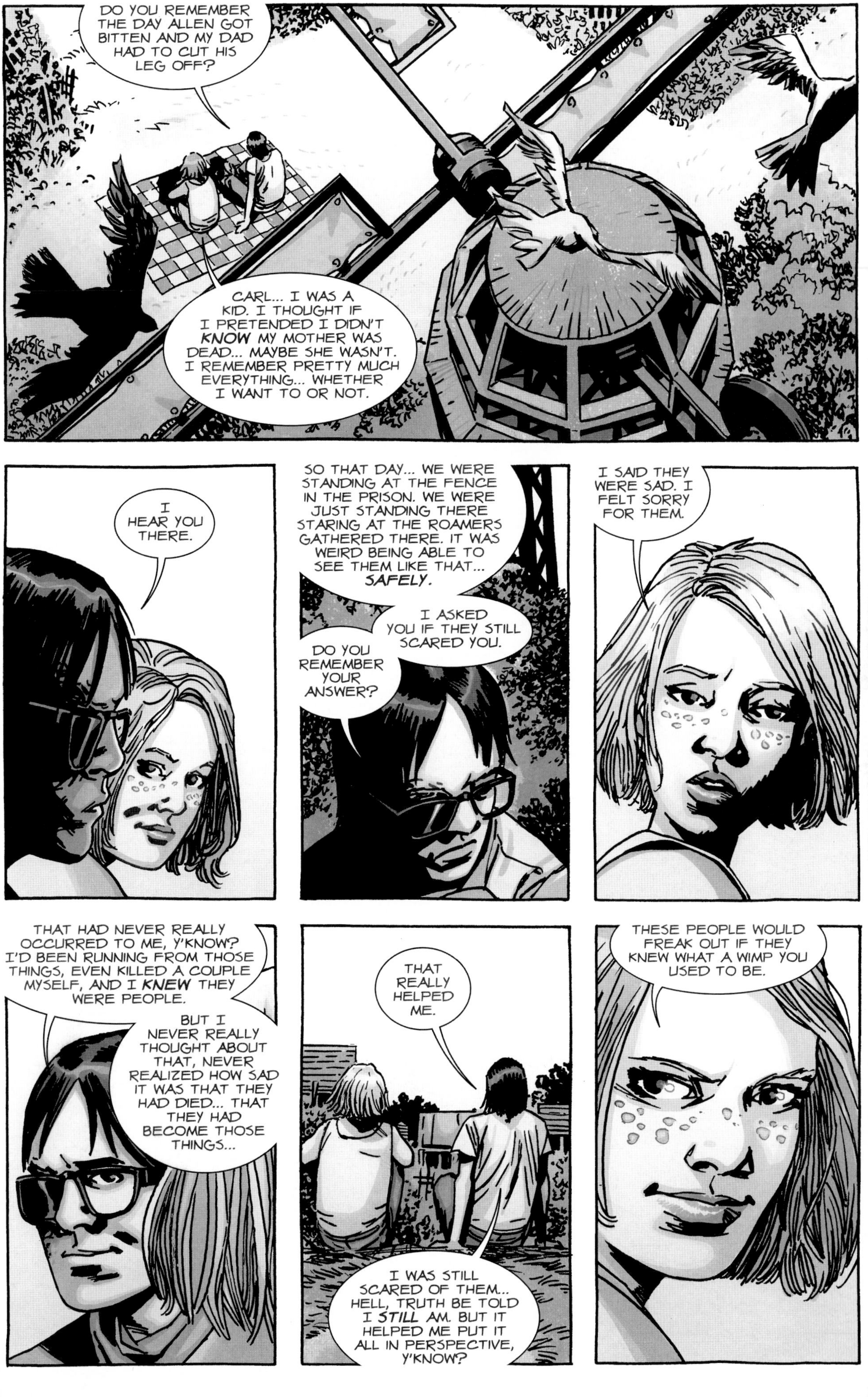
DO YOU REMEMBER THE DAY ALLEN GOT BITTEN AND MY DAD HAD TO CUT HIS LEG OFF?
CARL... I WAS A KID. I THOUGHT IF I PRETENDED I DIDN'T KNOW MY MOTHER WAS DEAD... MAYBE SHE WASN'T. I REMEMBER PRETTY MUCH EVERYTHING... WHETHER I WANT TO OR NOT.
I HEAR YOU THERE.
SO THAT DAY... WE WERE STANDING AT THE FENCE IN THE PRISON. WE WERE JUST STANDING THERE STARING AT THE ROAMERS GATHERED THERE. IT WAS WEIRD BEING ABLE TO SEE THEM LIKE THAT... SAFELY.
I ASKED YOU IF THEY STILL SCARED YOU.
DO YOU REMEMBER YOUR ANSWER?
I SAID THEY WERE SAD. I FELT SORRY FOR THEM.
THAT HAD NEVER REALLY OCCURRED TO ME, Y'KNOW? I'D BEEN RUNNING FROM THOSE THINGS, EVEN KILLED A COUPLE MYSELF, AND I KNEW THEY WERE PEOPLE.
BUT I NEVER REALLY THOUGHT ABOUT THAT, NEVER REALIZED HOW SAD IT WAS THAT THEY HAD DIED... THAT THEY HAD BECOME THOSE THINGS...
THAT REALLY HELPED ME.
I WAS STILL SCARED OF THEM... HELL, TRUTH BE TOLD I STILL AM. BUT IT HELPED ME PUT IT ALL IN PERSPECTIVE, Y'KNOW?
THESE PEOPLE WOULD FREAK OUT IF THEY KNEW WHAT A WIMP YOU USED TO BE.

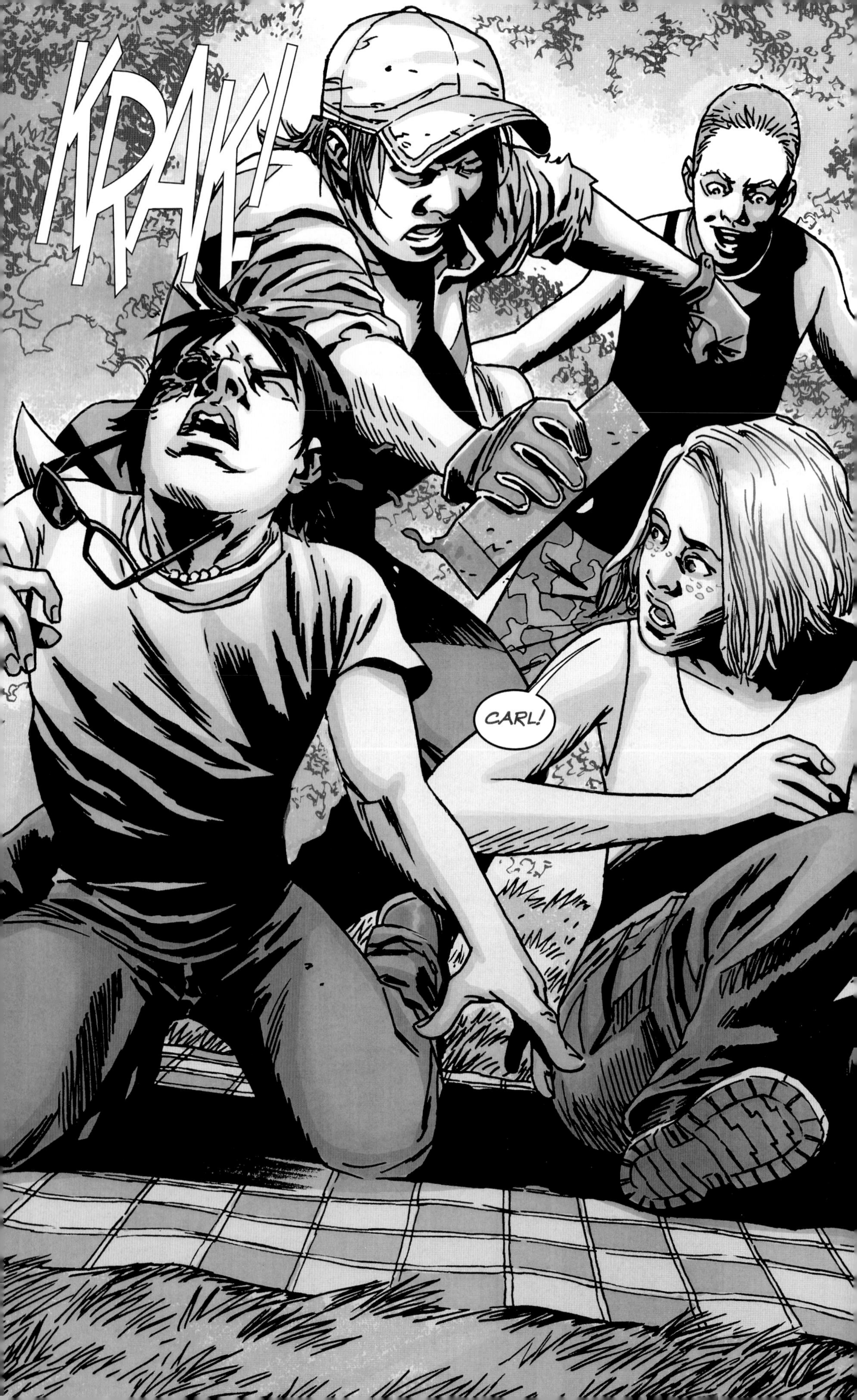
KRAK!
CARL!

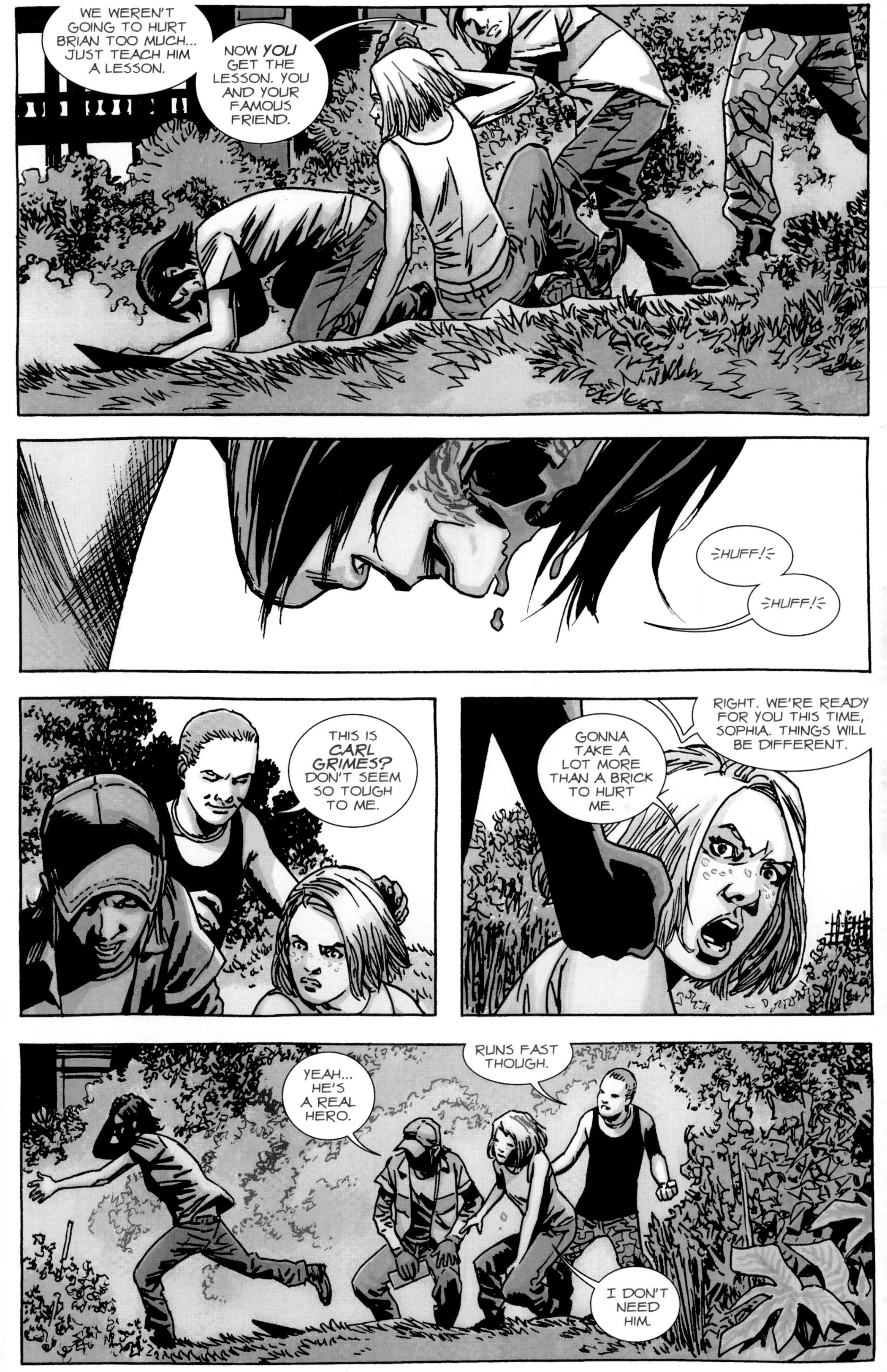
WE WEREN'T GOING TO HURT BRIAN TOO MUCH... JUST TEACH HIM A LESSON.
NOW YOU GET THE LESSON. YOU AND YOUR FAMOUS FRIEND.
HUFF!
HUFF!
THIS IS CARL GRIMES? DON'T SEEM SO TOUGH TO ME.
GONNA TAKE A LOT MORE THAN A BRICK TO HURT ME.
RIGHT. WE'RE READY FOR YOU THIS TIME, SOPHIA. THINGS WILL BE DIFFERENT.
YEAH... HE'S A REAL HERO.
RUNS FAST THOUGH.
I DON'T NEED HIM.

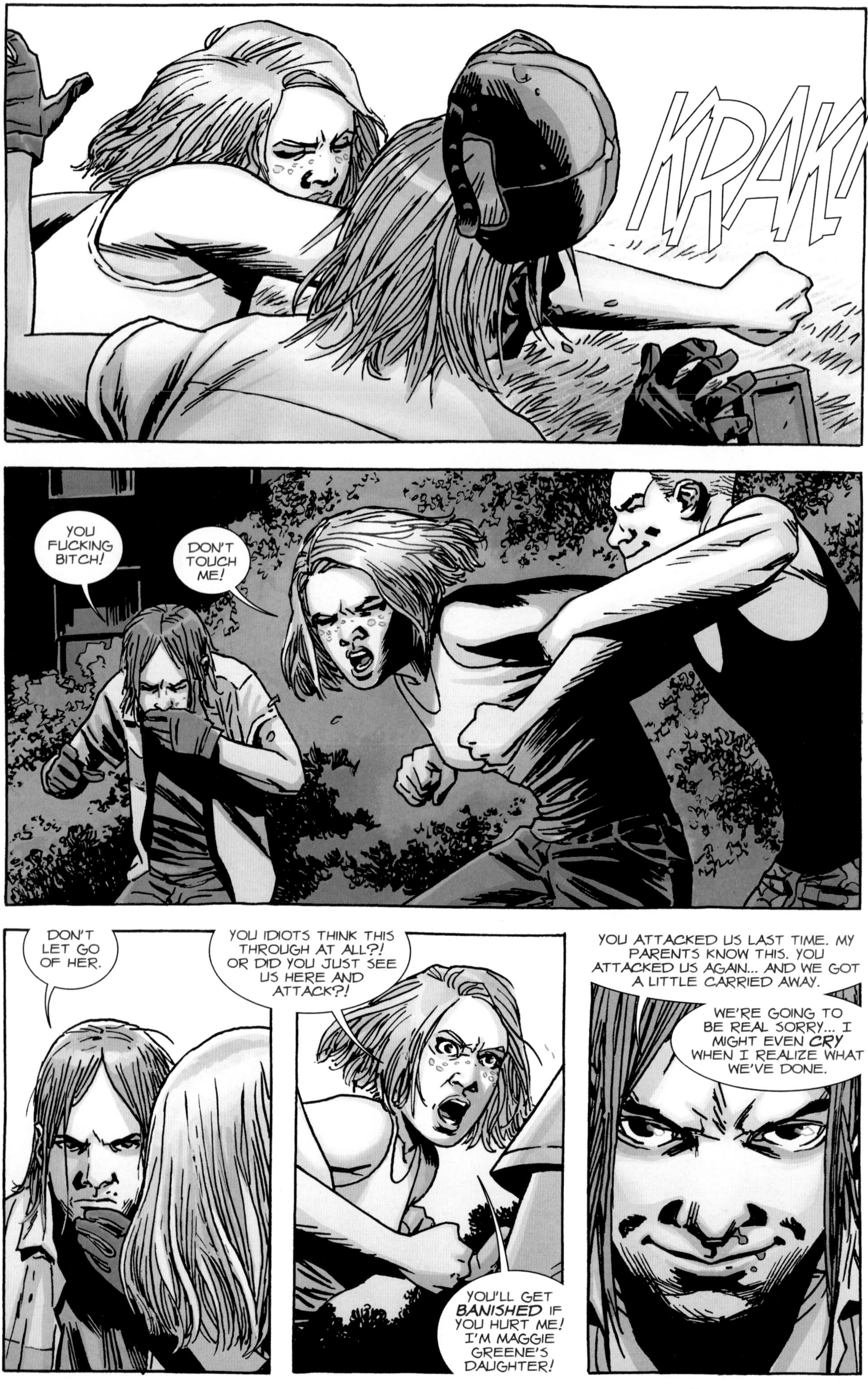
KRAK!
YOU FUCKING BITCH!
DON'T TOUCH ME!
DON'T LET GO OF HER.
YOU IDIOTS THINK THIS THROUGH AT ALL?! OR DID YOU JUST SEE US HERE AND ATTACK?!
YOU'LL GET BANISHED IF YOU HURT ME! I'M MAGGIE GREENE'S DAUGHTER!
YOU ATTACKED US LAST TIME. MY PARENTS KNOW THIS. YOU ATTACKED US AGAIN... AND WE GOT A LITTLE CARRIED AWAY.
WE'RE GOING TO BE REAL SORRY... I MIGHT EVEN CRY WHEN I REALIZE WHAT WE'VE DONE.

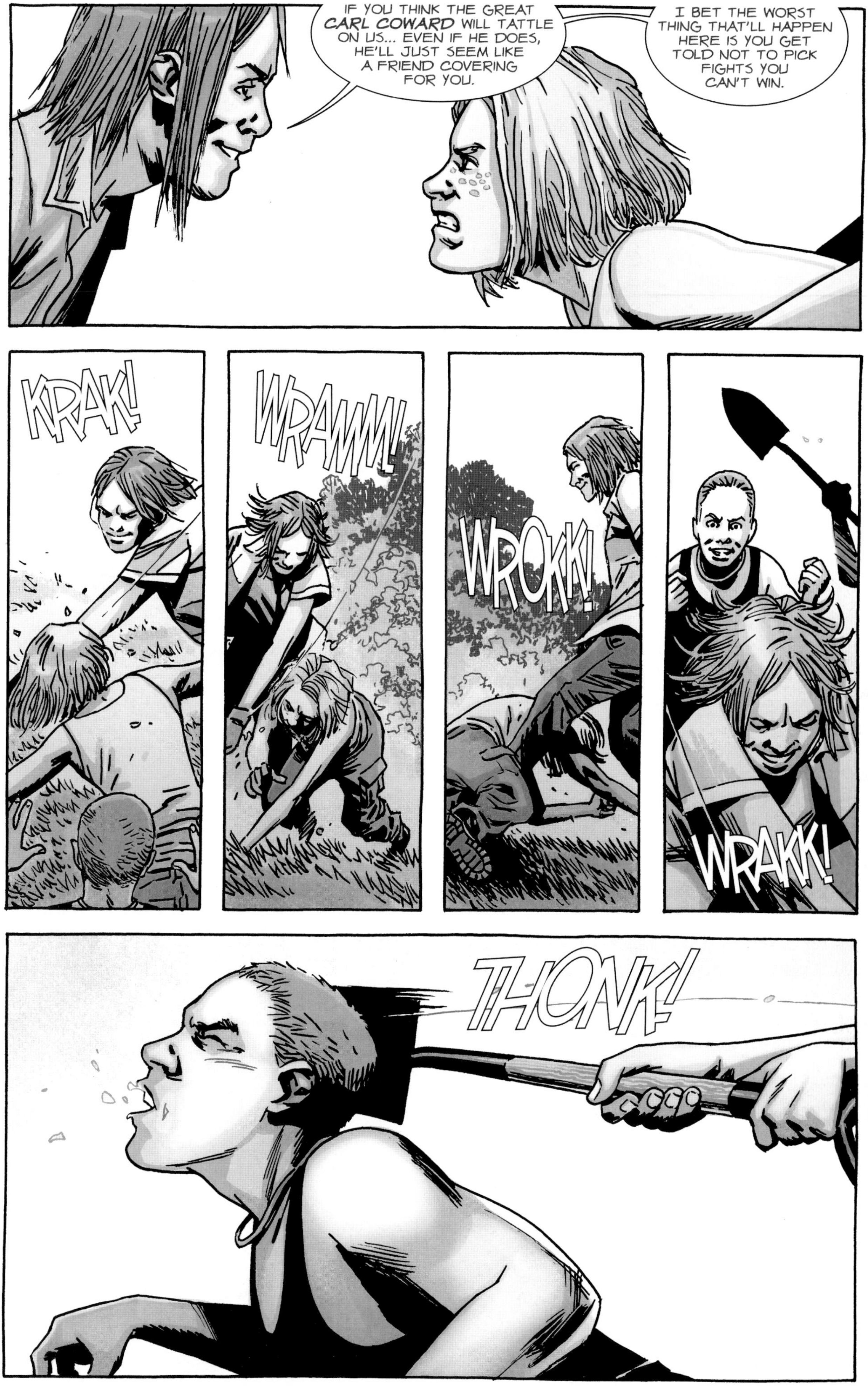
IF YOU THINK THE GREAT CARL COWARD WILL TATTLE ON US... EVEN IF HE DOES, HE'LL JUST SEEM LIKE A FRIEND COVERING FOR YOU.
I BET THE WORST THING THAT'LL HAPPEN HERE IS YOU GET TOLD NOT TO PICK FIGHTS YOU CAN'T WIN.
KRAK!
WRAMM!
WROKK!
WRAKK!
THONK!

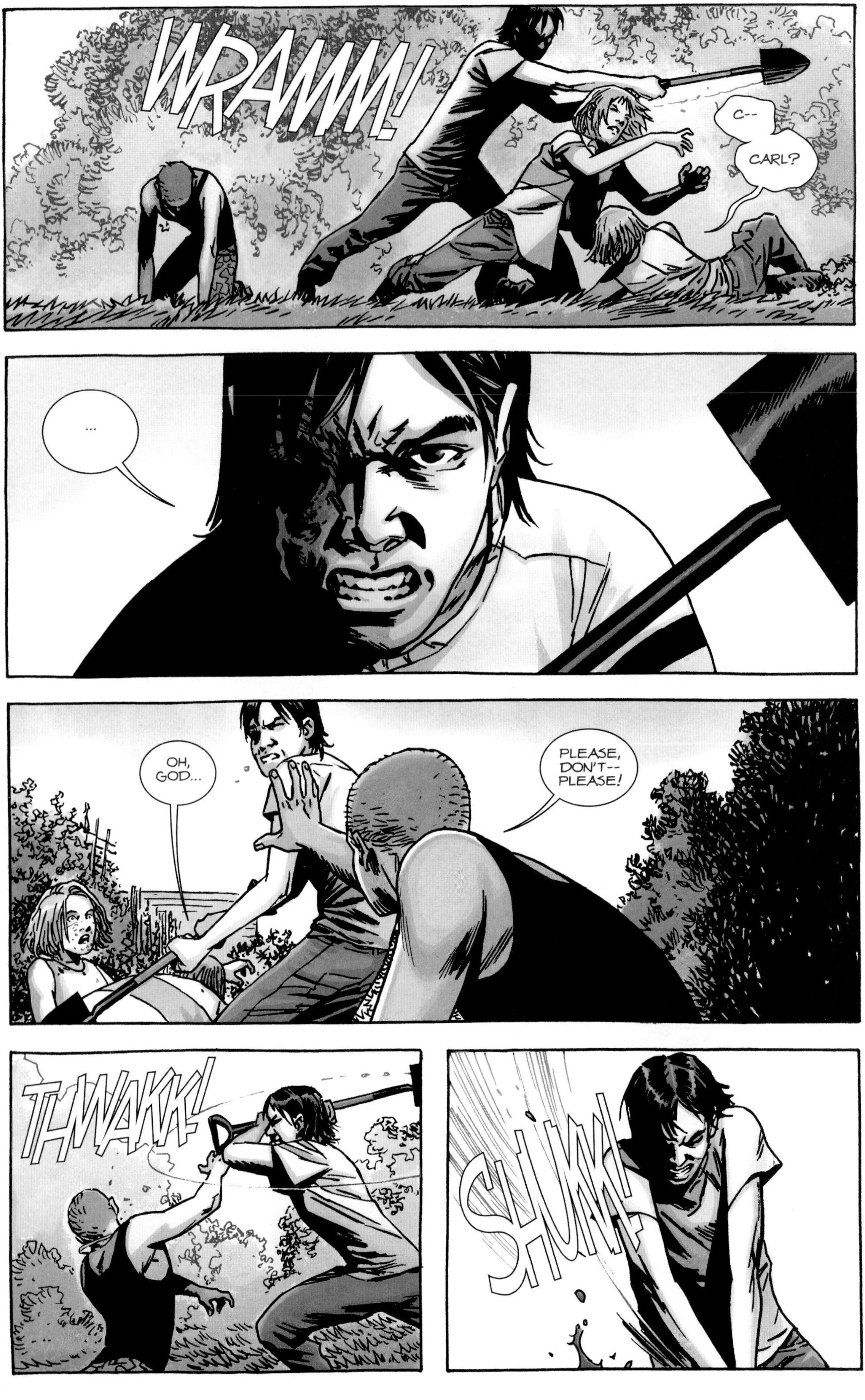
WRAMM!
C--
CARL?
...
OH, GOD...
PLEASE, DON'T-- PLEASE!
THWAKK!
SHUNK!

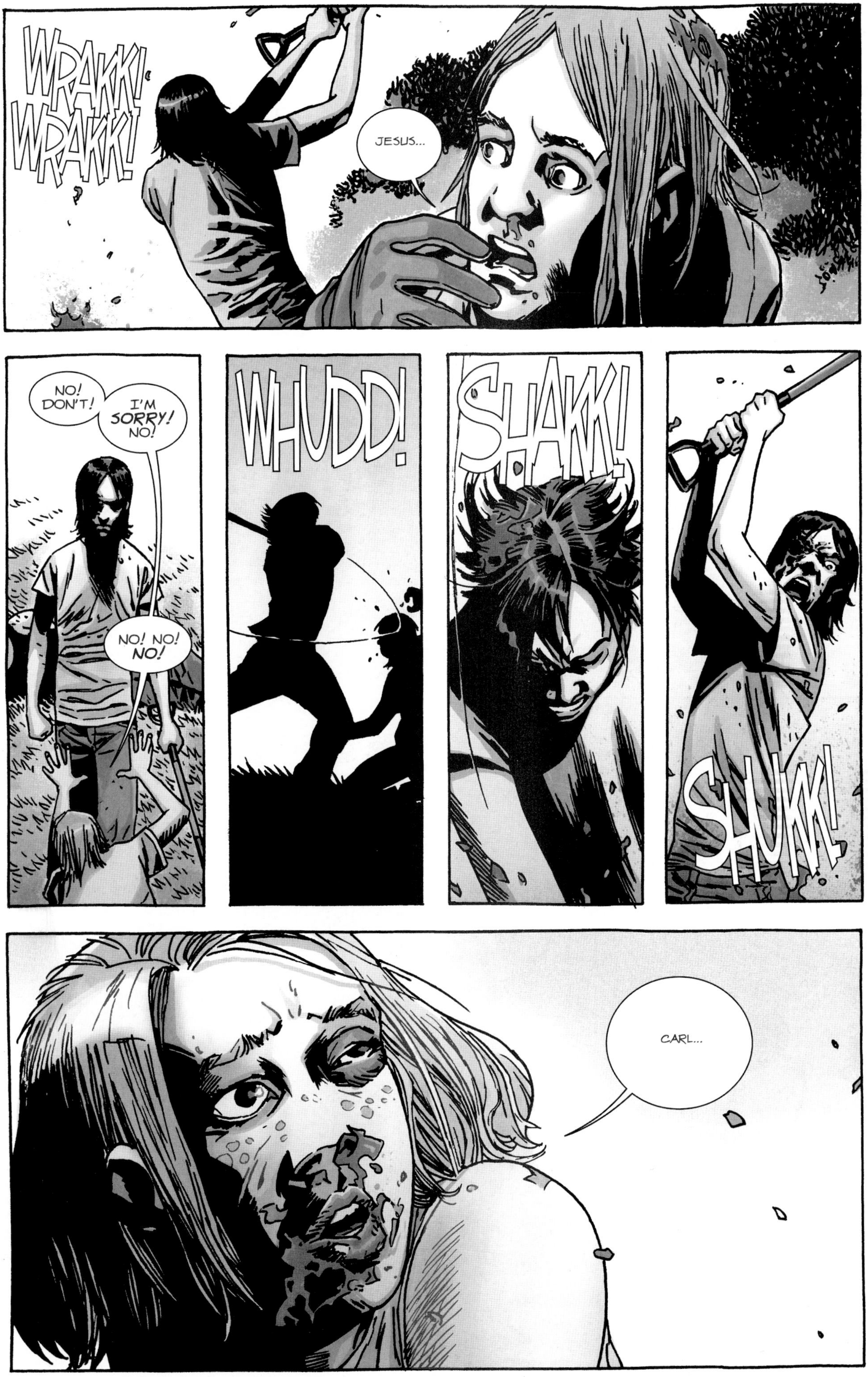
WRAKK! WRAKK!
JESUS...
NO! DON'T!
I'M SORRY! NO!
NO! NO! NO!
WHUDD!
SHAKK!
SHUKK!
CARL...

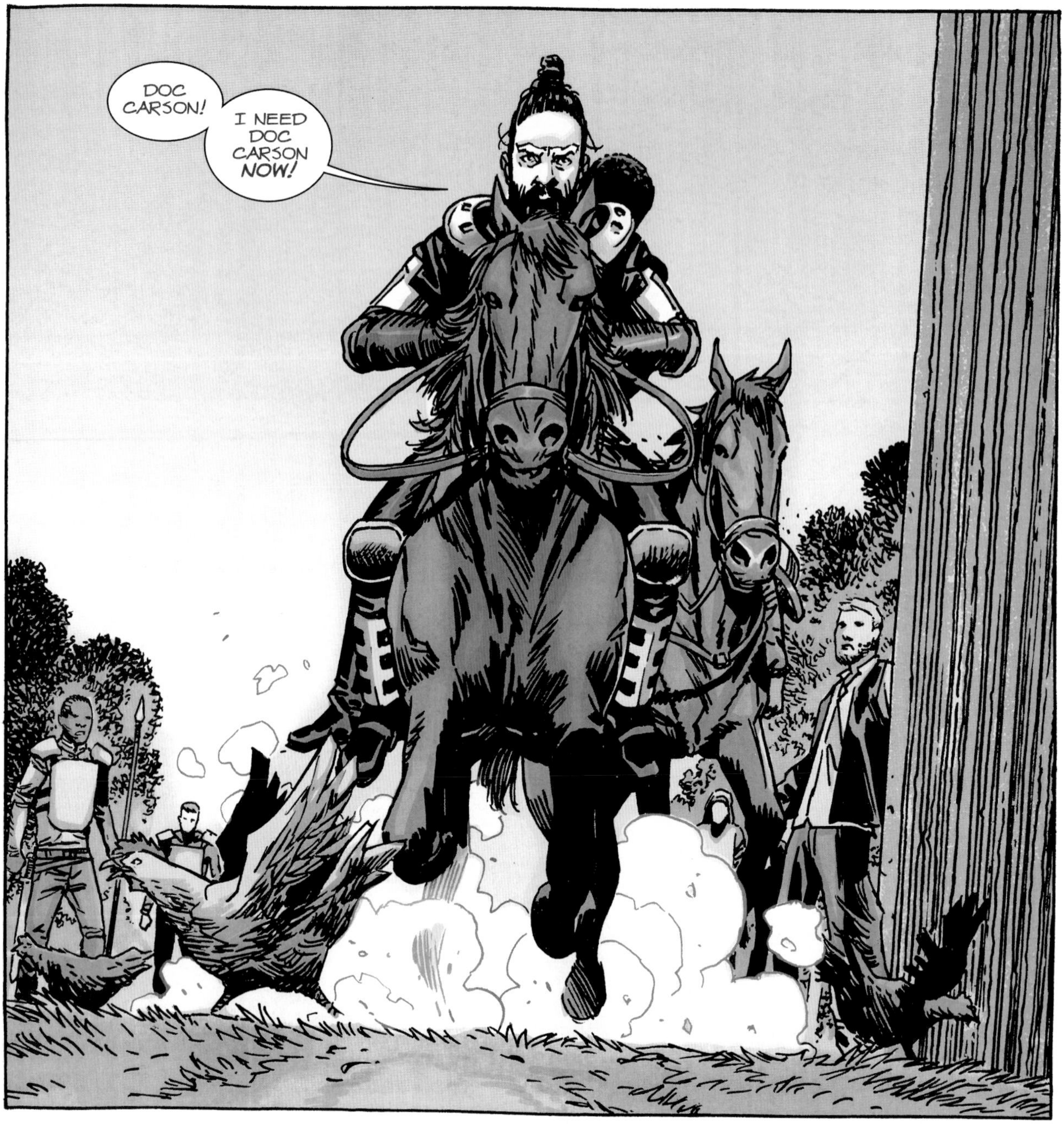
DOC CARSON!
I NEED DOC CARSON NOW!

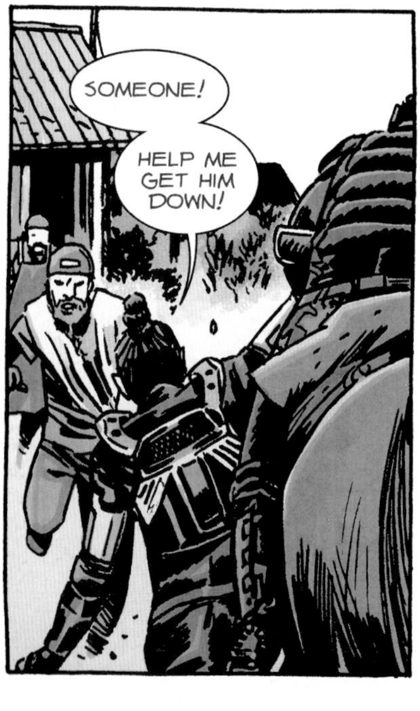
SOMEONE!
HELP ME GET HIM DOWN!

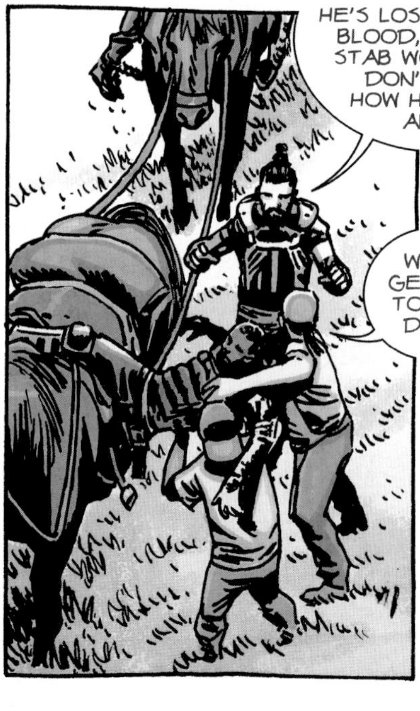
HE'S LOST A LOT OF BLOOD, MULTIPLE STAB WOUNDS... I DON'T KNOW HOW HE'S STILL ALIVE.
WE'LL GET HIM TO THE DOC!

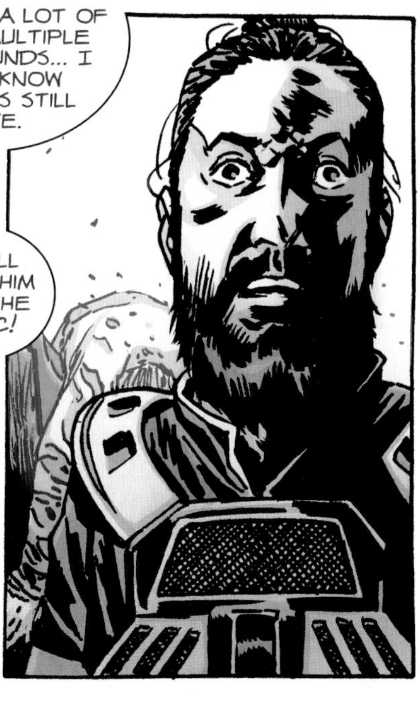

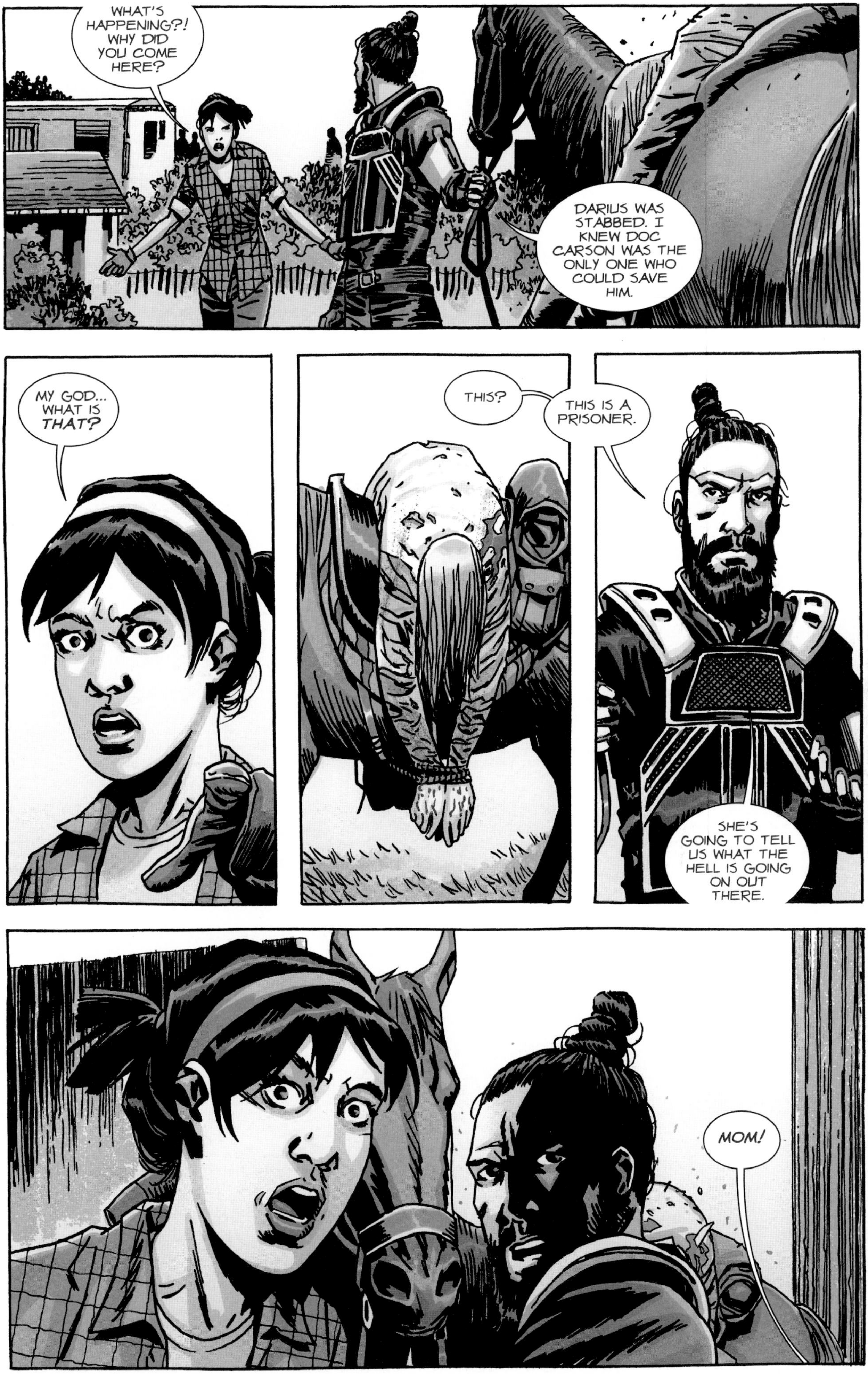
WHAT'S HAPPENING?! WHY DID YOU COME HERE?
DARIUS WAS STABBED. I KNEW DOC CARSON WAS THE ONLY ONE WHO COULD SAVE HIM.
MY GOD... WHAT IS *THAT?*
THIS?
THIS IS A PRISONER.
SHE'S GOING TO TELL US WHAT THE HELL IS GOING ON OUT THERE.
MOM!

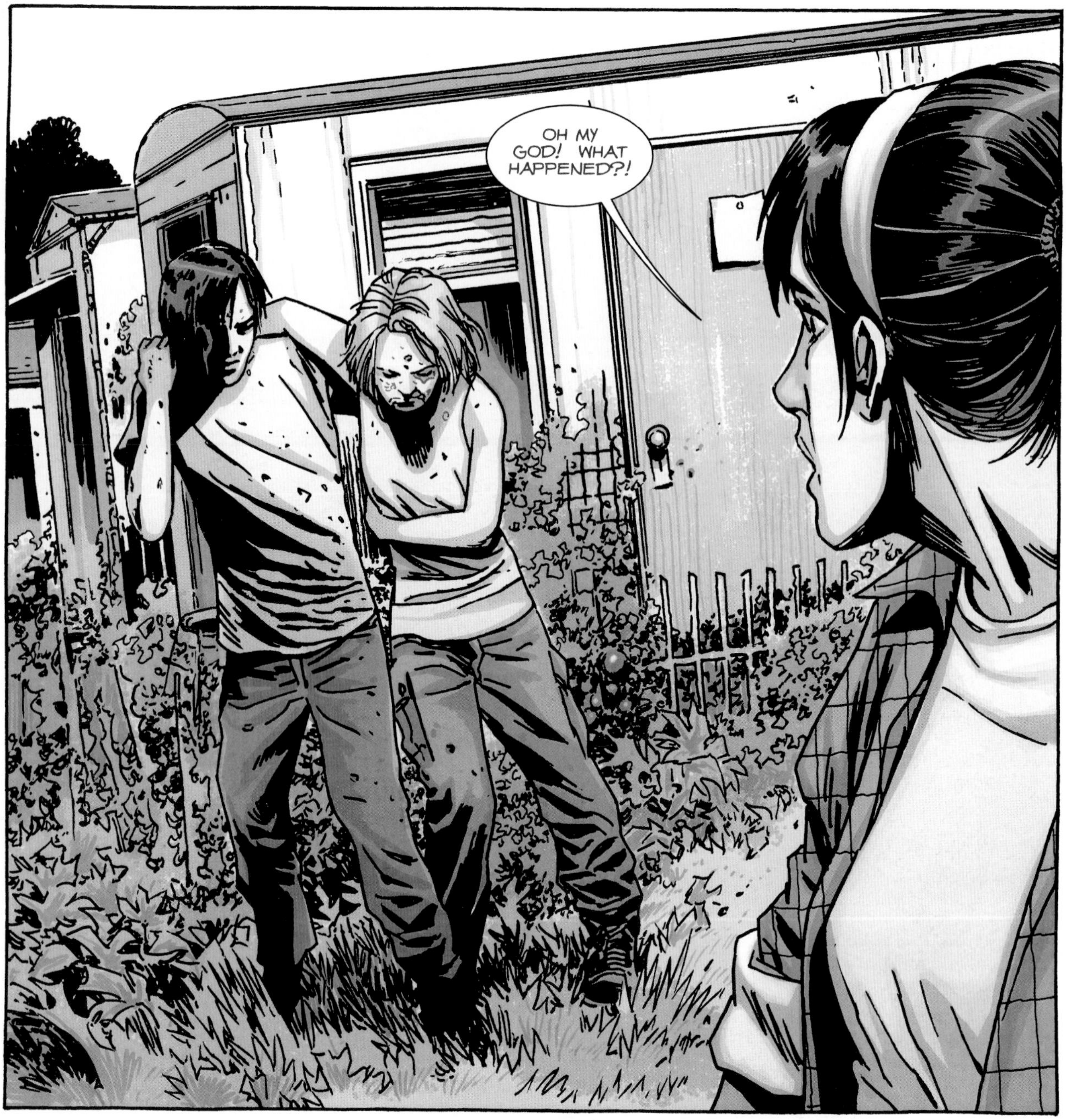
OH MY GOD! WHAT HAPPENED?!

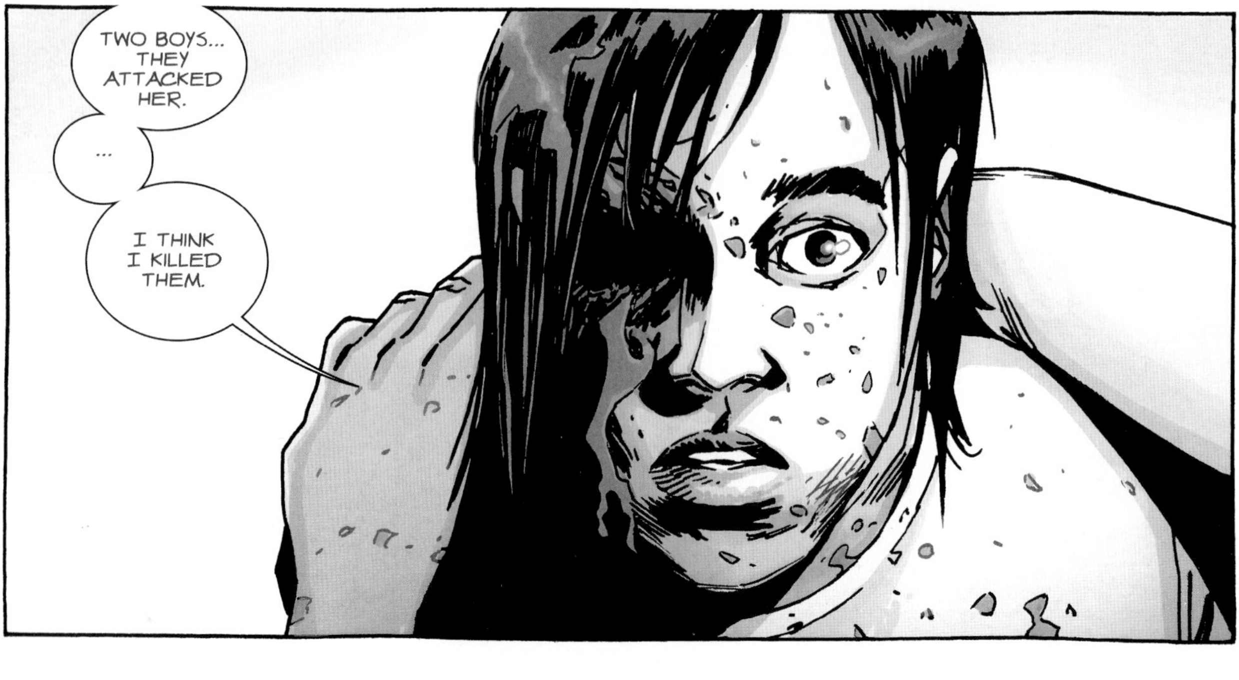
TWO BOYS... THEY ATTACKED HER.
...
I THINK I KILLED THEM.

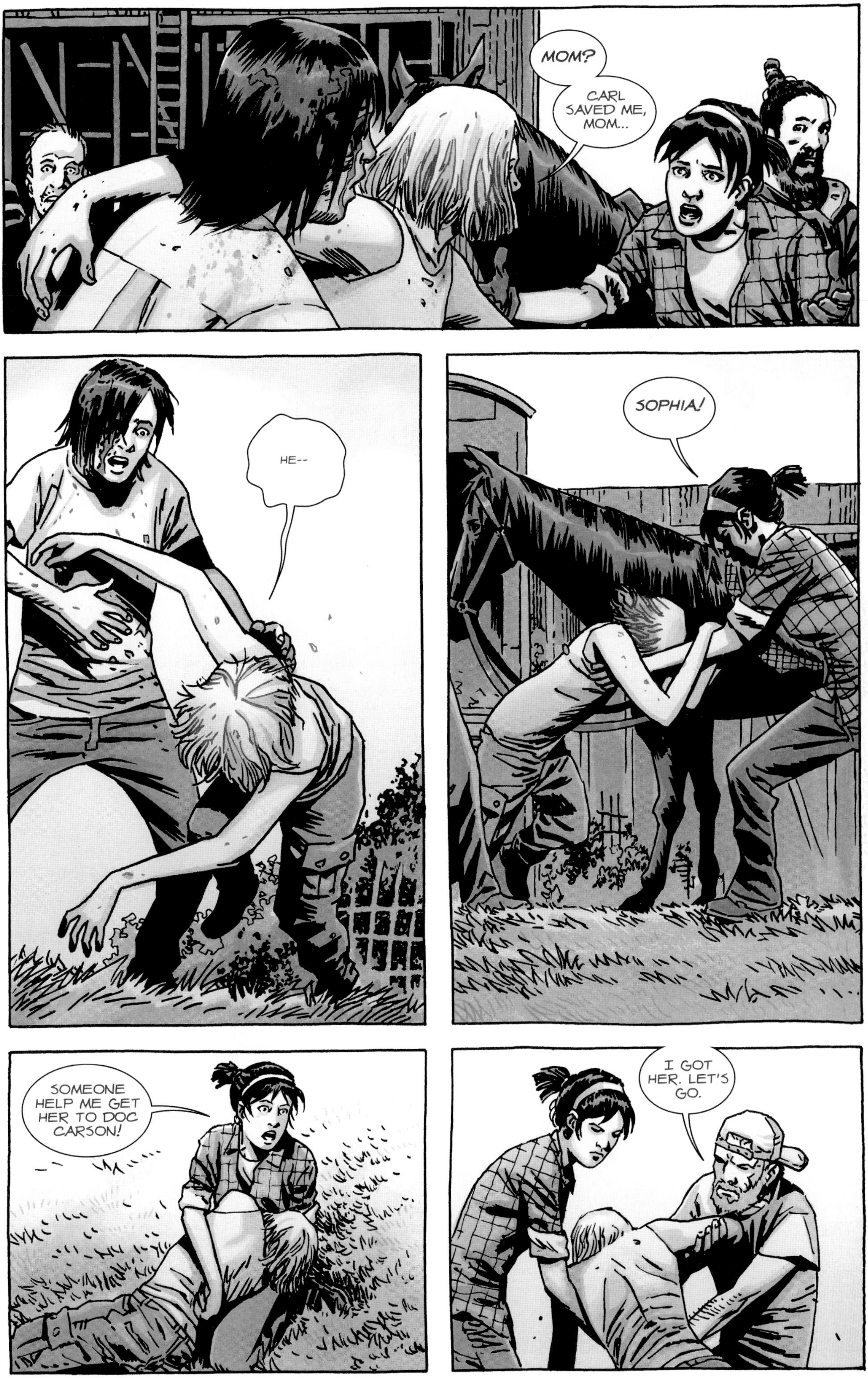
MOM?
CARL SAVED ME, MOM...
HE--
SOPHIA!
SOMEONE HELP ME GET HER TO DOC CARSON!
I GOT HER. LET'S GO.

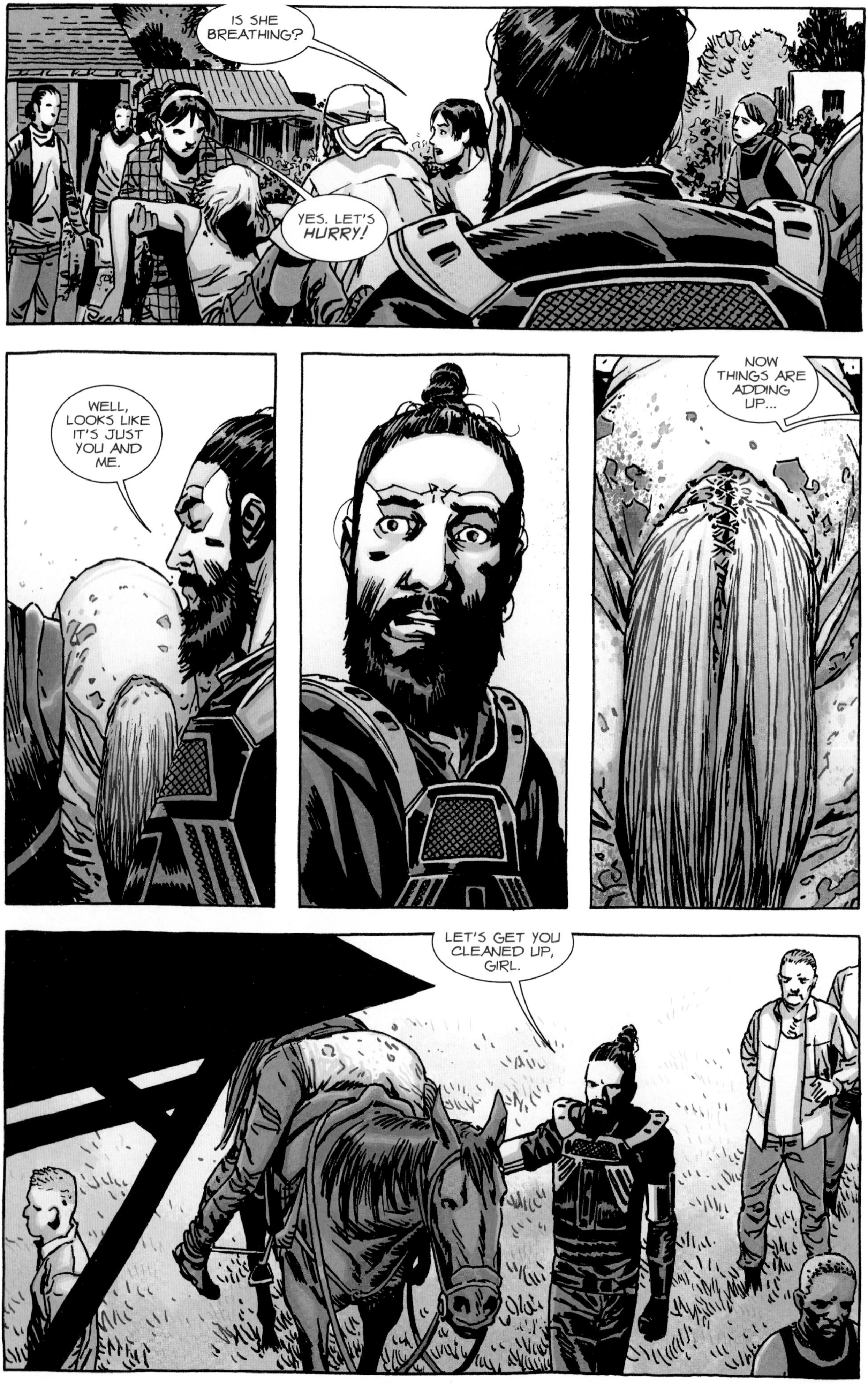
IS SHE BREATHING?
YES. LET'S HURRY!
WELL, LOOKS LIKE IT'S JUST YOU AND ME.
NOW THINGS ARE ADDING UP...
LET'S GET YOU CLEANED UP, GIRL.

WHAT DO YOU THINK, ALEX? IS SHE GOING TO BE OKAY?

SHE'S PRETTY BANGED UP... AND SHE'S PROBABLY GOT A CONCUSSION... BUT I THINK SHE'S GOING TO BE *FINE*.

DOC CARSON NEEDS TO FINISH UP WITH DARIUS... THEN HE'LL PATCH HER UP.

IT'S JUST A MATTER OF TIME.

TRY NOT TO WORRY, CARL. YOU HEARD ALEX. SHE'S GOING TO BE FINE.

I'M GLAD YOU WERE THERE FOR HER.

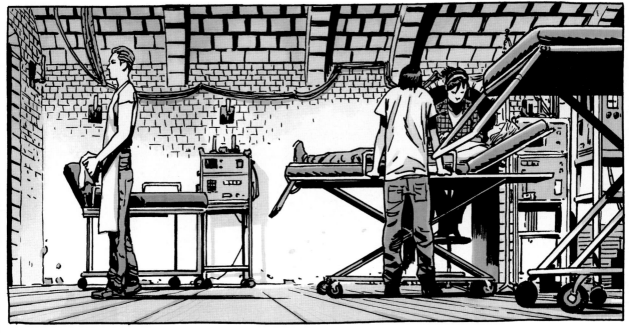

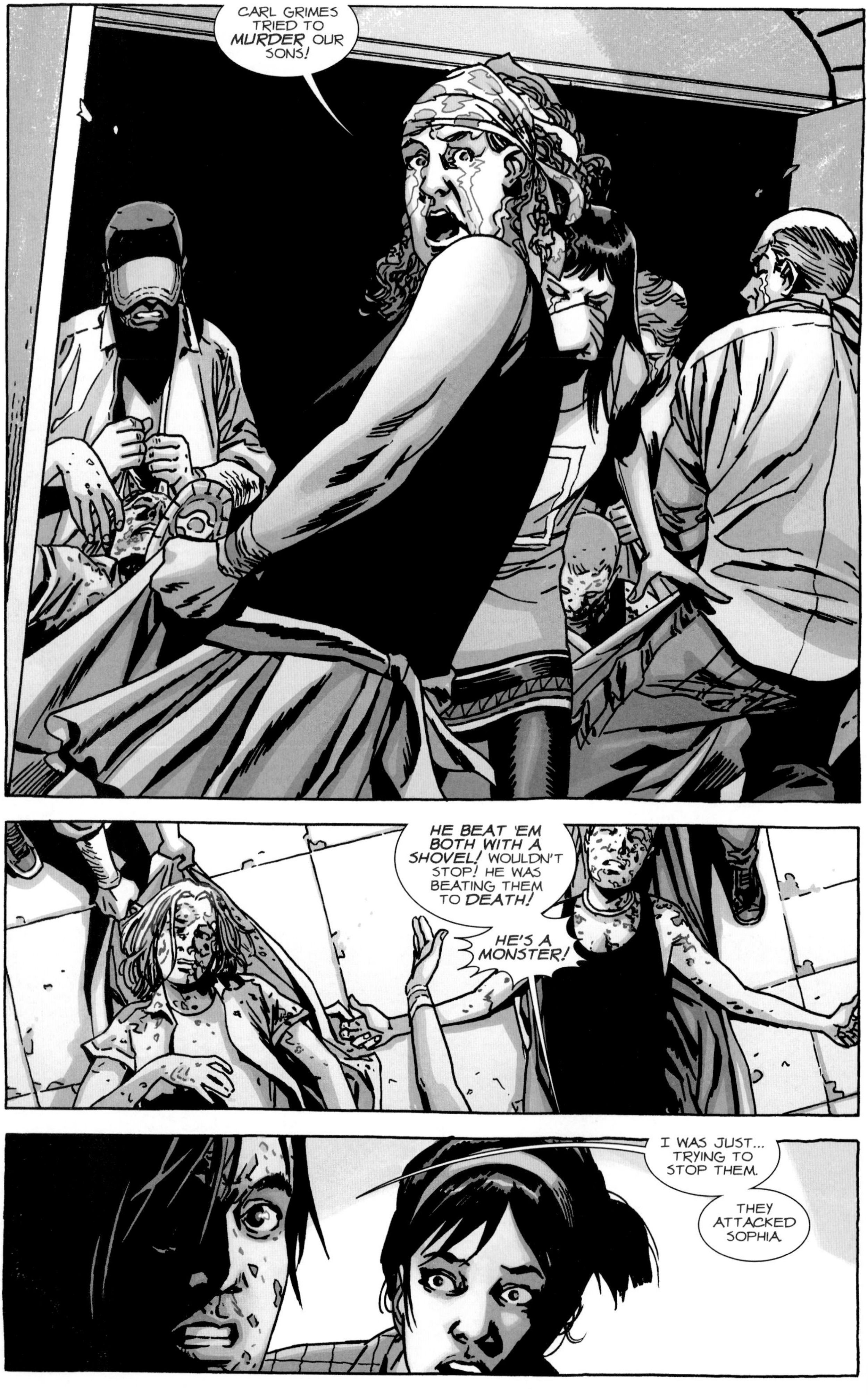
CARL GRIMES TRIED TO MURDER OUR SONS!
HE BEAT 'EM BOTH WITH A SHOVEL! WOULDN'T STOP! HE WAS BEATING THEM TO DEATH!
HE'S A MONSTER!
I WAS JUST... TRYING TO STOP THEM.
THEY ATTACKED SOPHIA.

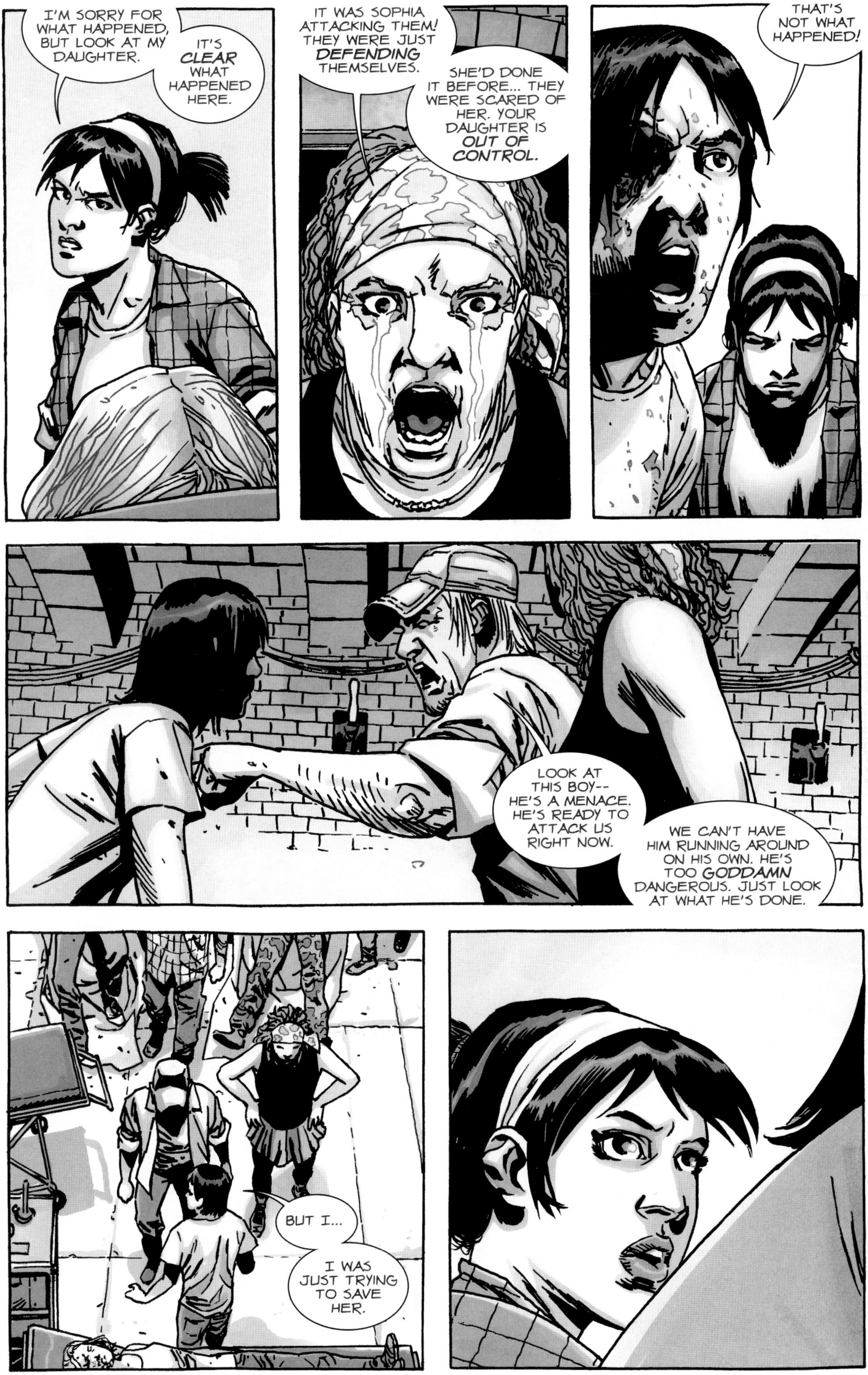
I'M SORRY FOR WHAT HAPPENED, BUT LOOK AT MY DAUGHTER.
IT'S CLEAR WHAT HAPPENED HERE.
IT WAS SOPHIA ATTACKING THEM! THEY WERE JUST DEFENDING THEMSELVES.
SHE'D DONE IT BEFORE... THEY WERE SCARED OF HER. YOUR DAUGHTER IS OUT OF CONTROL.
THAT'S NOT WHAT HAPPENED!
LOOK AT THIS BOY-- HE'S A MENACE. HE'S READY TO ATTACK US RIGHT NOW.
WE CAN'T HAVE HIM RUNNING AROUND ON HIS OWN. HE'S TOO GODDAMN DANGEROUS. JUST LOOK AT WHAT HE'S DONE.
BUT I...
I WAS JUST TRYING TO SAVE HER.

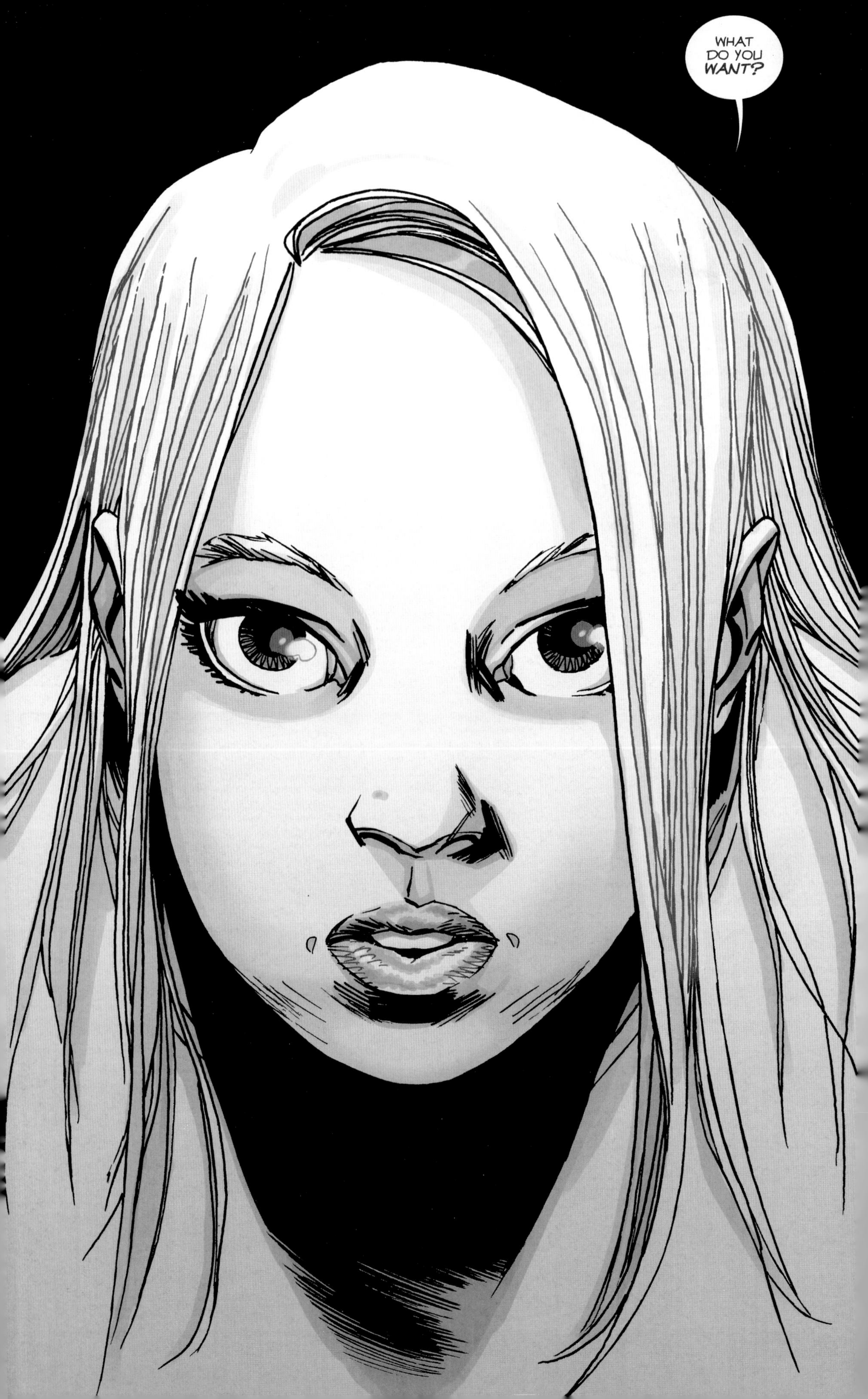
WHAT DO YOU WANT?

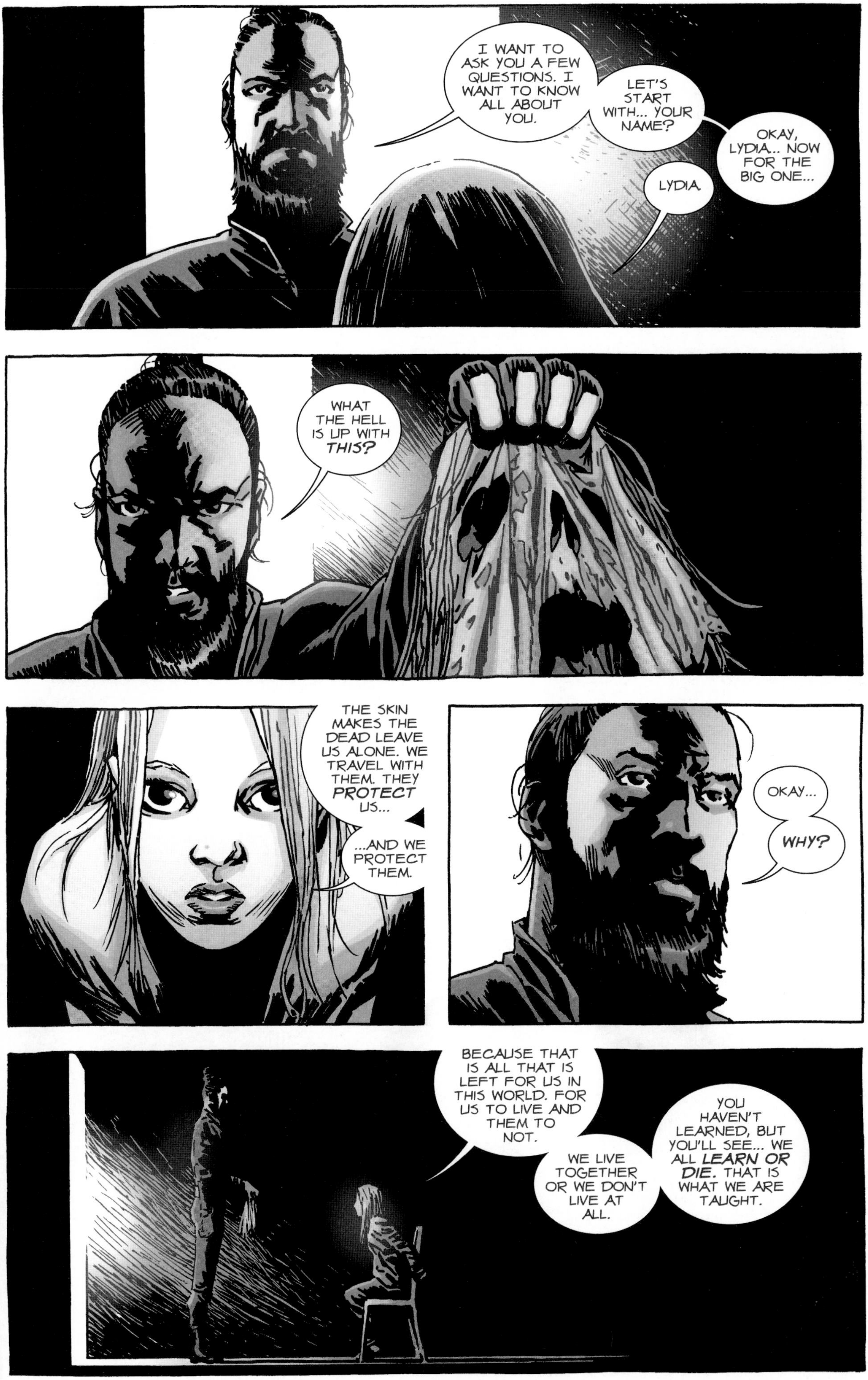
I WANT TO ASK YOU A FEW QUESTIONS. I WANT TO KNOW ALL ABOUT YOU.
LET'S START WITH... YOUR NAME?
LYDIA.
OKAY, LYDIA... NOW FOR THE BIG ONE...
WHAT THE HELL IS UP WITH *THIS?*
THE SKIN MAKES THE DEAD LEAVE US ALONE. WE TRAVEL WITH THEM. THEY *PROTECT* US...
...AND WE PROTECT THEM.
OKAY...
WHY?
BECAUSE THAT IS ALL THAT IS LEFT FOR US IN THIS WORLD. FOR US TO LIVE AND THEM TO NOT.
WE LIVE TOGETHER OR WE DON'T LIVE AT ALL.
YOU HAVEN'T LEARNED, BUT YOU'LL SEE... WE ALL ***LEARN OR DIE.*** THAT IS WHAT WE ARE TAUGHT.

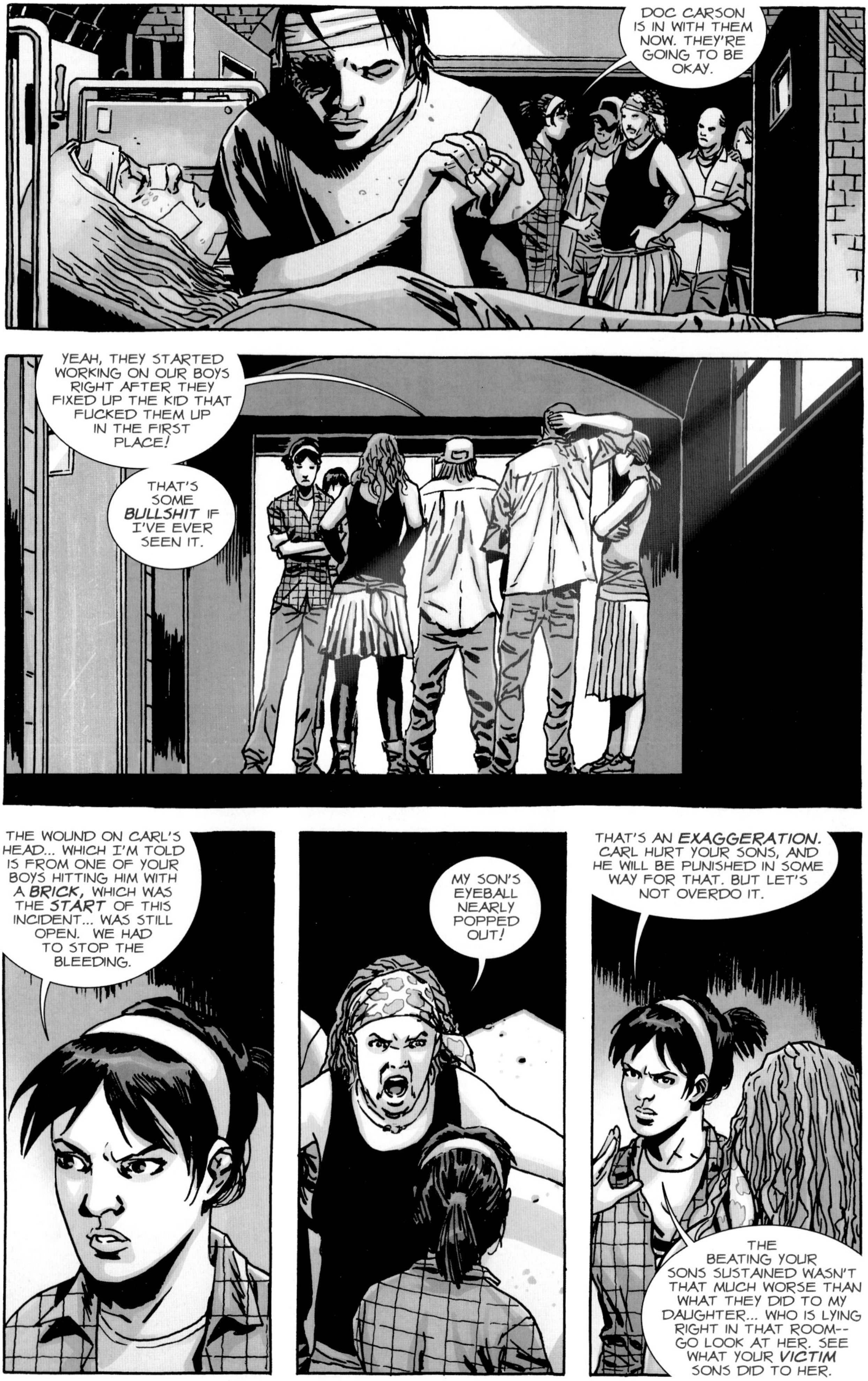
DOC CARSON IS IN WITH THEM NOW. THEY'RE GOING TO BE OKAY.
YEAH, THEY STARTED WORKING ON OUR BOYS RIGHT AFTER THEY FIXED UP THE KID THAT FUCKED THEM UP IN THE FIRST PLACE!
THAT'S SOME BULLSHIT IF I'VE EVER SEEN IT.
THE WOUND ON CARL'S HEAD... WHICH I'M TOLD IS FROM ONE OF YOUR BOYS HITTING HIM WITH A BRICK, WHICH WAS THE START OF THIS INCIDENT... WAS STILL OPEN. WE HAD TO STOP THE BLEEDING.
MY SON'S EYEBALL NEARLY POPPED OUT!
THAT'S AN EXAGGERATION. CARL HURT YOUR SONS, AND HE WILL BE PUNISHED IN SOME WAY FOR THAT. BUT LET'S NOT OVERDO IT.
THE BEATING YOUR SONS SUSTAINED WASN'T THAT MUCH WORSE THAN WHAT THEY DID TO MY DAUGHTER... WHO IS LYING RIGHT IN THAT ROOM-- GO LOOK AT HER. SEE WHAT YOUR VICTIM SONS DID TO HER.

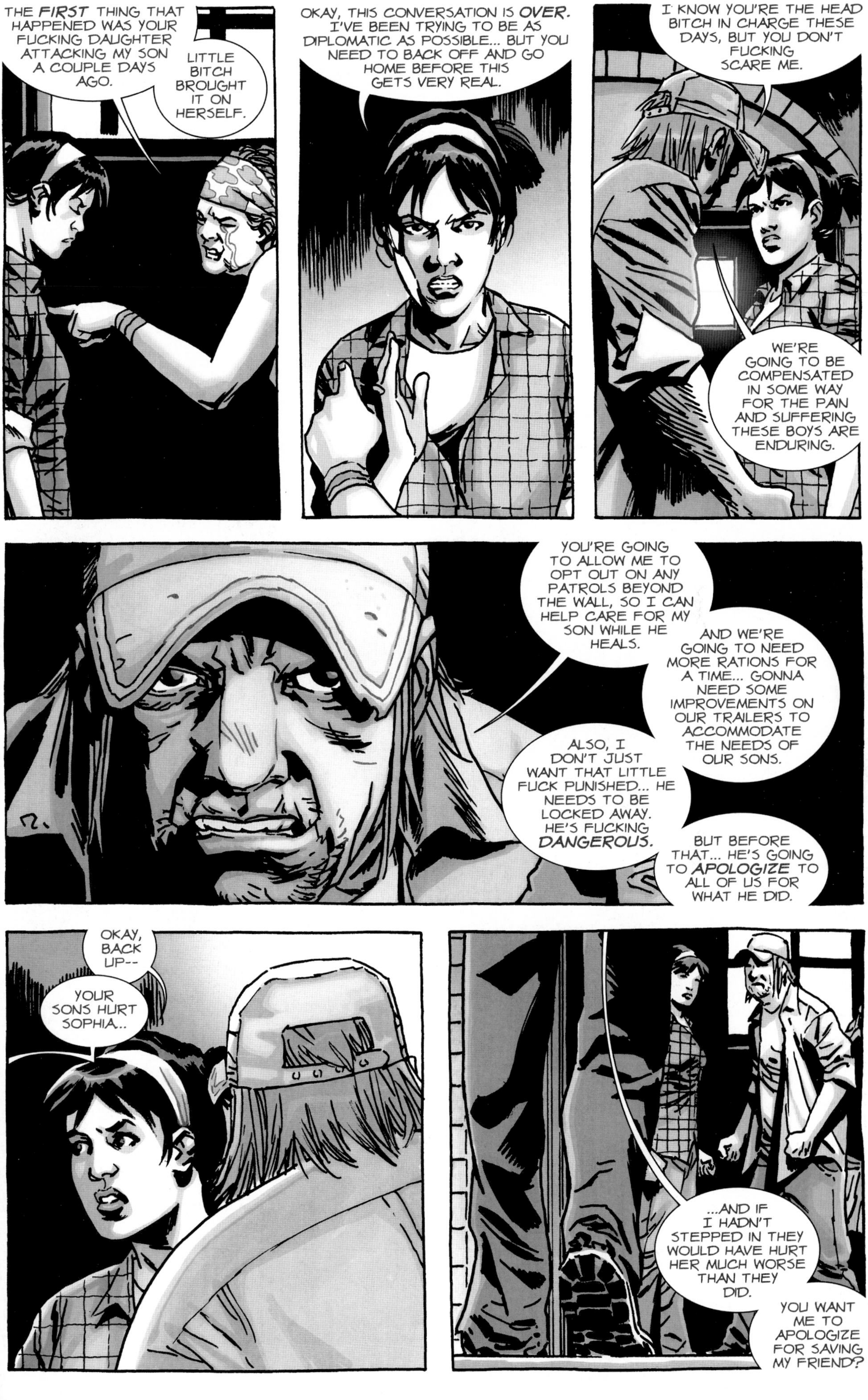
THE FIRST THING THAT HAPPENED WAS YOUR FUCKING DAUGHTER ATTACKING MY SON A COUPLE DAYS AGO.
LITTLE BITCH BROUGHT IT ON HERSELF.
OKAY, THIS CONVERSATION IS OVER. I'VE BEEN TRYING TO BE AS DIPLOMATIC AS POSSIBLE... BUT YOU NEED TO BACK OFF AND GO HOME BEFORE THIS GETS VERY REAL.
I KNOW YOU'RE THE HEAD BITCH IN CHARGE THESE DAYS, BUT YOU DON'T FUCKING SCARE ME.
WE'RE GOING TO BE COMPENSATED IN SOME WAY FOR THE PAIN AND SUFFERING THESE BOYS ARE ENDURING.
YOU'RE GOING TO ALLOW ME TO OPT OUT ON ANY PATROLS BEYOND THE WALL, SO I CAN HELP CARE FOR MY SON WHILE HE HEALS.
AND WE'RE GOING TO NEED MORE RATIONS FOR A TIME... GONNA NEED SOME IMPROVEMENTS ON OUR TRAILERS TO ACCOMMODATE THE NEEDS OF OUR SONS.
ALSO, I DON'T JUST WANT THAT LITTLE FUCK PUNISHED... HE NEEDS TO BE LOCKED AWAY. HE'S FUCKING DANGEROUS.
BUT BEFORE THAT... HE'S GOING TO APOLOGIZE TO ALL OF US FOR WHAT HE DID.
OKAY, BACK UP--
YOUR SONS HURT SOPHIA...
...AND IF I HADN'T STEPPED IN THEY WOULD HAVE HURT HER MUCH WORSE THAN THEY DID.
YOU WANT ME TO APOLOGIZE FOR SAVING MY FRIEND?

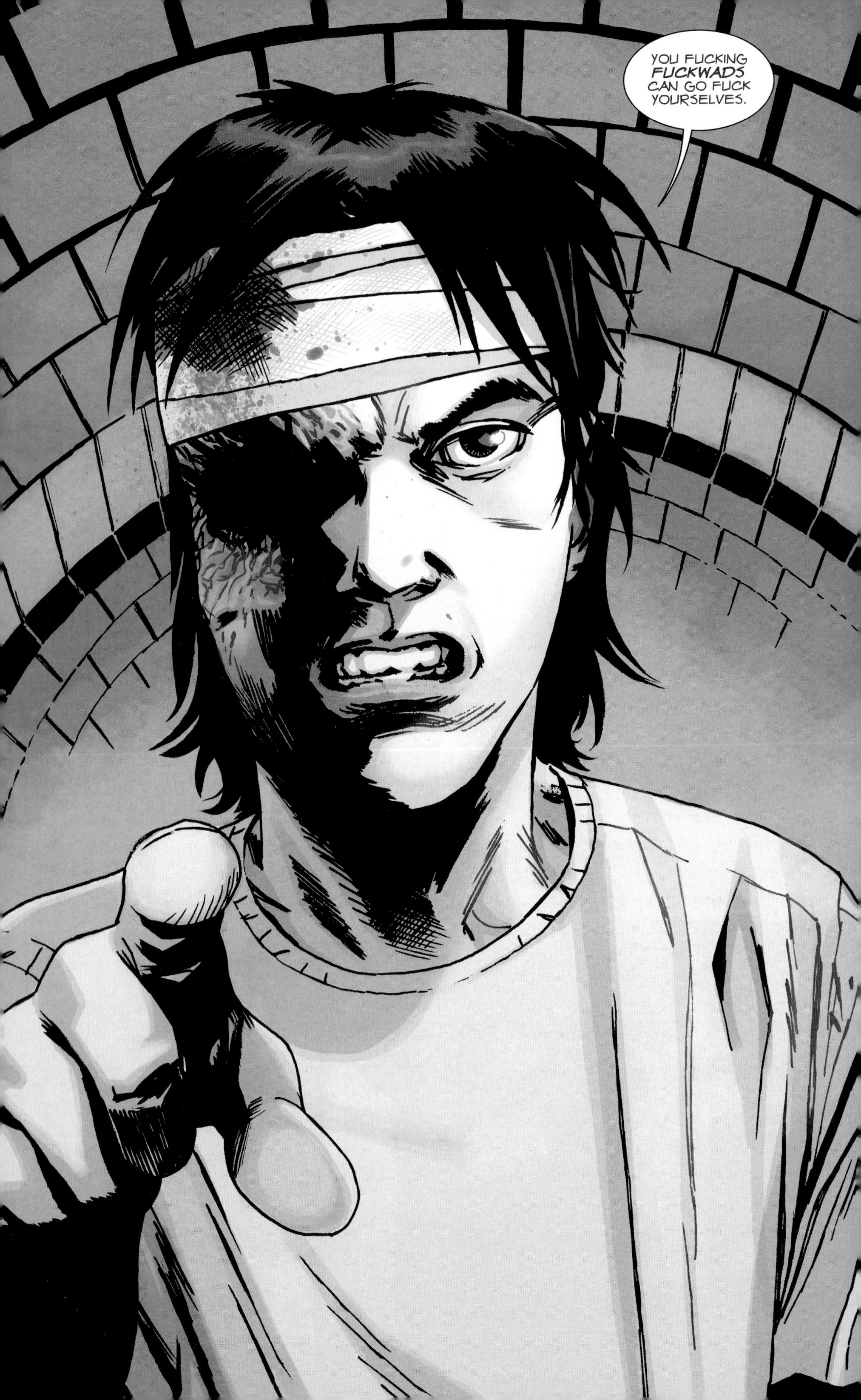
YOU FUCKING FUCKWADS CAN GO FUCK YOURSELVES.

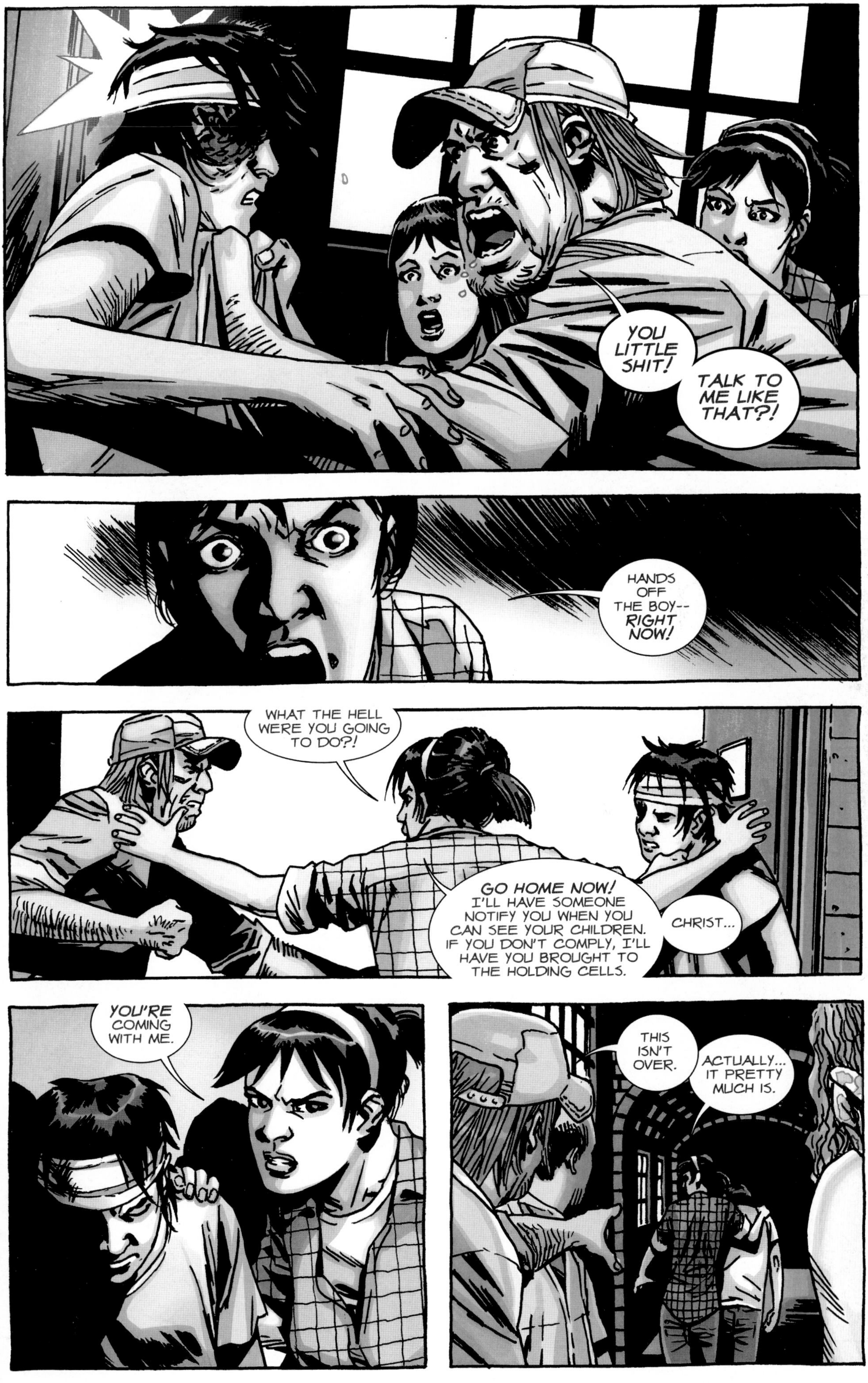
YOU LITTLE SHIT!
TALK TO ME LIKE THAT?!
HANDS OFF THE BOY-- RIGHT NOW!
WHAT THE HELL WERE YOU GOING TO DO?!
GO HOME NOW! I'LL HAVE SOMEONE NOTIFY YOU WHEN YOU CAN SEE YOUR CHILDREN. IF YOU DON'T COMPLY, I'LL HAVE YOU BROUGHT TO THE HOLDING CELLS.
CHRIST...
YOU'RE COMING WITH ME.
THIS ISN'T OVER.
ACTUALLY... IT PRETTY MUCH IS.

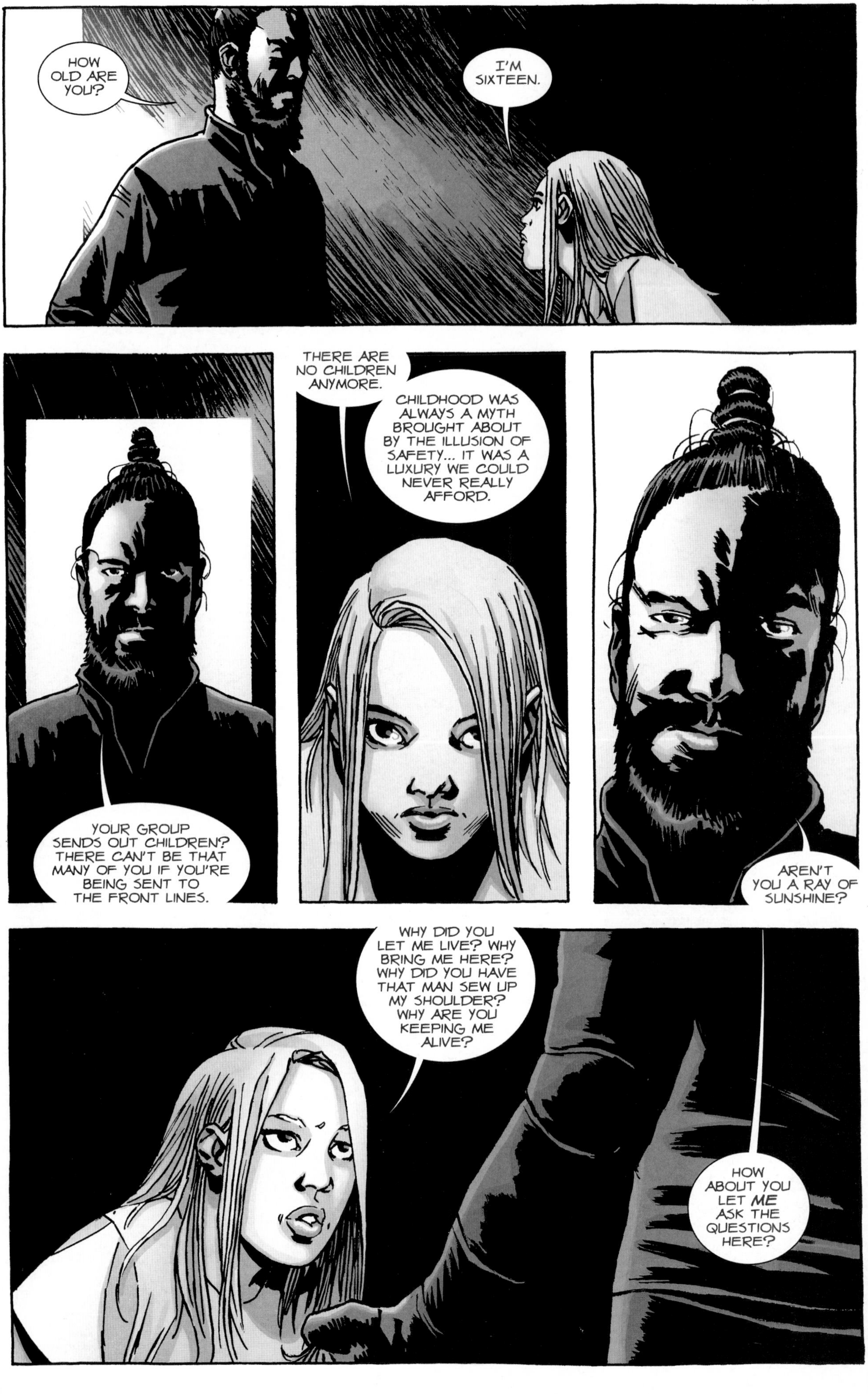
HOW OLD ARE YOU?
I'M SIXTEEN.
YOUR GROUP SENDS OUT CHILDREN? THERE CAN'T BE THAT MANY OF YOU IF YOU'RE BEING SENT TO THE FRONT LINES.
THERE ARE NO CHILDREN ANYMORE.
CHILDHOOD WAS ALWAYS A MYTH BROUGHT ABOUT BY THE ILLUSION OF SAFETY... IT WAS A LUXURY WE COULD NEVER REALLY AFFORD.
AREN'T YOU A RAY OF SUNSHINE?
WHY DID YOU LET ME LIVE? WHY BRING ME HERE? WHY DID YOU HAVE THAT MAN SEW UP MY SHOULDER? WHY ARE YOU KEEPING ME ALIVE?
HOW ABOUT YOU LET *ME* ASK THE QUESTIONS HERE?

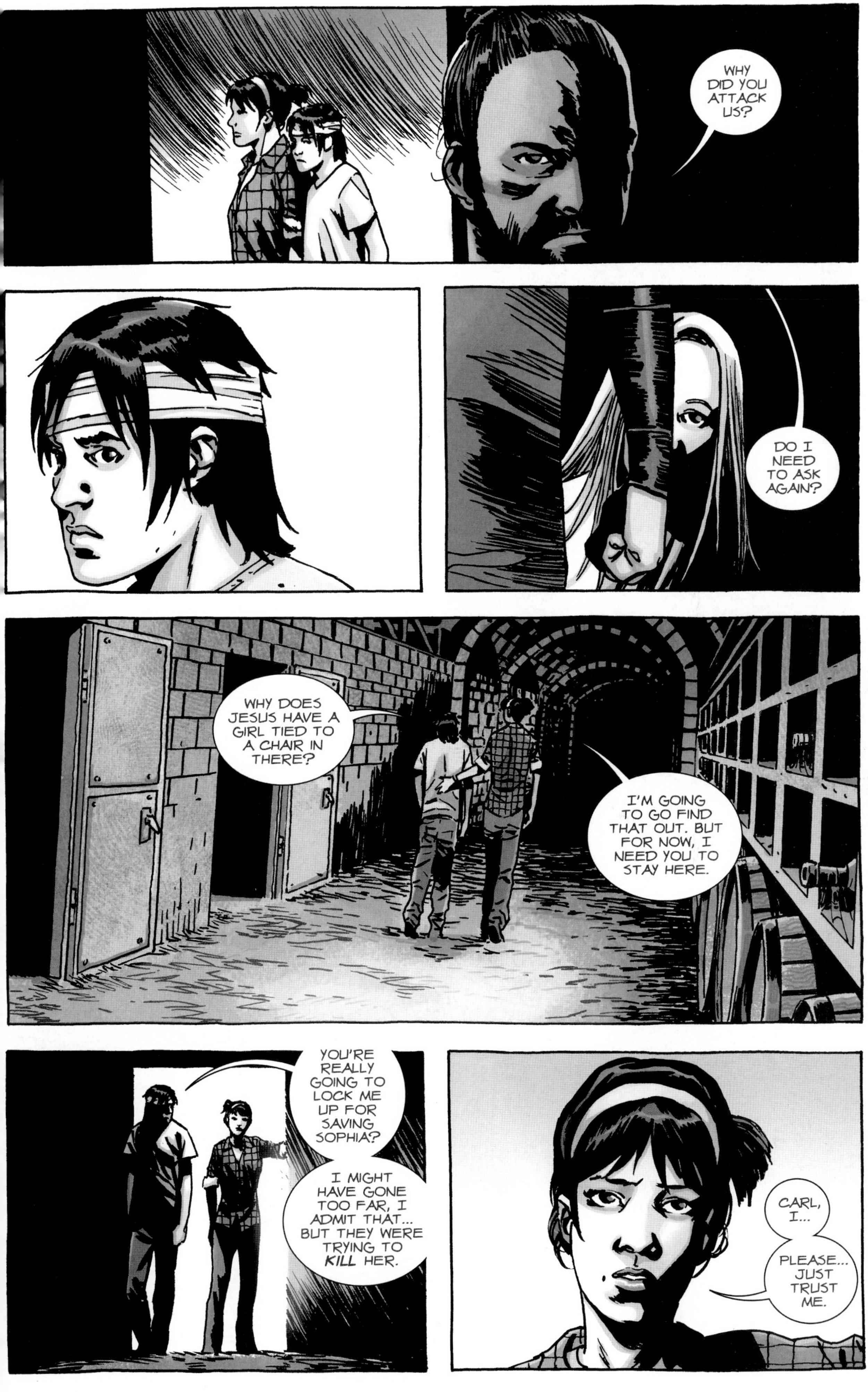
WHY DID YOU ATTACK US?
DO I NEED TO ASK AGAIN?
WHY DOES JESUS HAVE A GIRL TIED TO A CHAIR IN THERE?
I'M GOING TO GO FIND THAT OUT. BUT FOR NOW, I NEED YOU TO STAY HERE.
YOU'RE REALLY GOING TO LOCK ME UP FOR SAVING SOPHIA?
I MIGHT HAVE GONE TOO FAR, I ADMIT THAT... BUT THEY WERE TRYING TO KILL HER.
CARL, I...
PLEASE... JUST TRUST ME.

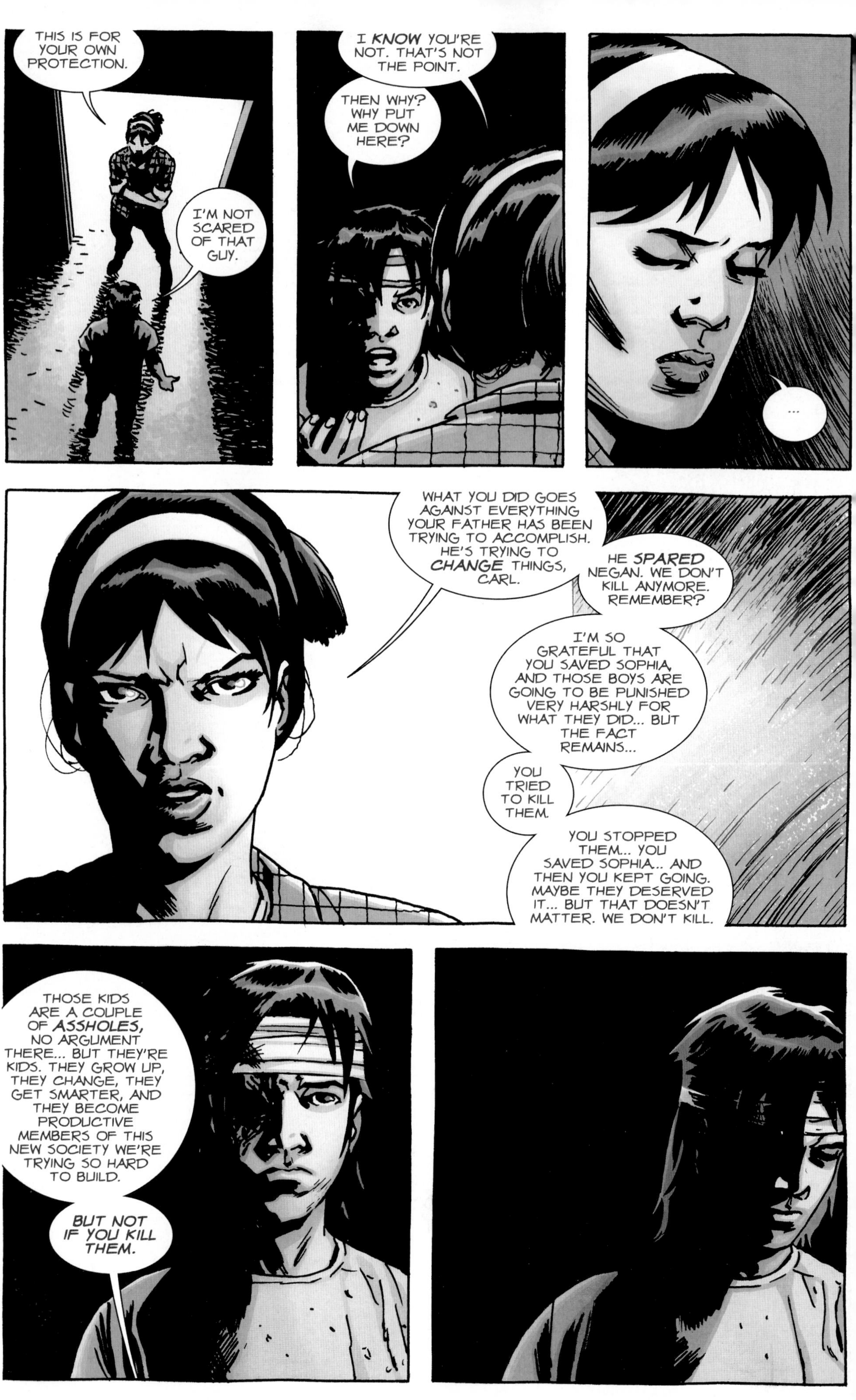
THIS IS FOR YOUR OWN PROTECTION.
I'M NOT SCARED OF THAT GUY.
I KNOW YOU'RE NOT. THAT'S NOT THE POINT.
THEN WHY? WHY PUT ME DOWN HERE?
...
WHAT YOU DID GOES AGAINST EVERYTHING YOUR FATHER HAS BEEN TRYING TO ACCOMPLISH. HE'S TRYING TO CHANGE THINGS, CARL.
HE SPARED NEGAN. WE DON'T KILL ANYMORE. REMEMBER?
I'M SO GRATEFUL THAT YOU SAVED SOPHIA, AND THOSE BOYS ARE GOING TO BE PUNISHED VERY HARSHLY FOR WHAT THEY DID... BUT THE FACT REMAINS...
YOU TRIED TO KILL THEM.
YOU STOPPED THEM... YOU SAVED SOPHIA... AND THEN YOU KEPT GOING. MAYBE THEY DESERVED IT... BUT THAT DOESN'T MATTER. WE DON'T KILL.
THOSE KIDS ARE A COUPLE OF ASSHOLES, NO ARGUMENT THERE... BUT THEY'RE KIDS. THEY GROW UP, THEY CHANGE, THEY GET SMARTER, AND THEY BECOME PRODUCTIVE MEMBERS OF THIS NEW SOCIETY WE'RE TRYING SO HARD TO BUILD.
BUT NOT IF YOU KILL THEM.

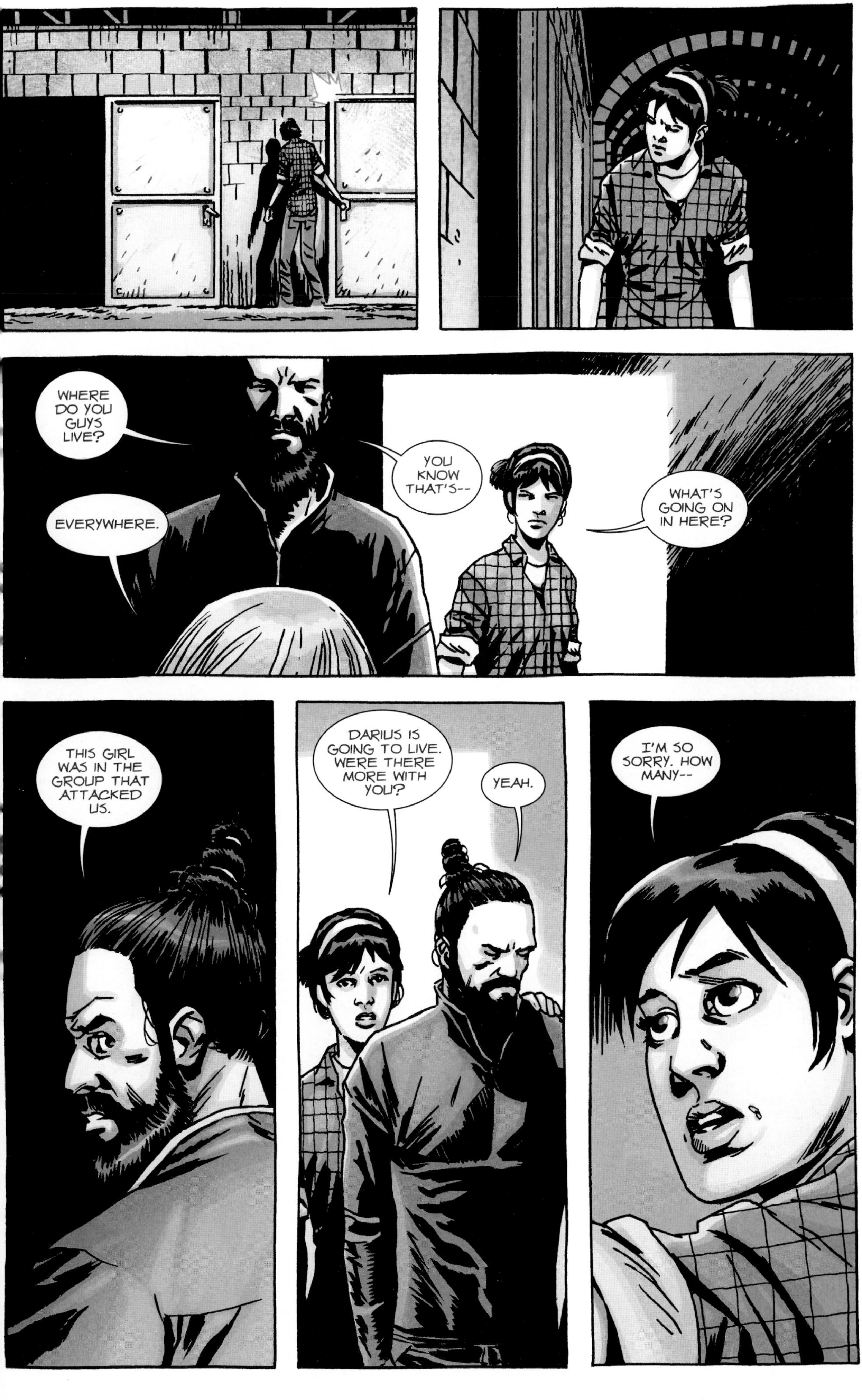
WHERE DO YOU GUYS LIVE?
EVERYWHERE.
YOU KNOW THAT'S--
WHAT'S GOING ON IN HERE?
THIS GIRL WAS IN THE GROUP THAT ATTACKED US.
DARIUS IS GOING TO LIVE. WERE THERE MORE WITH YOU?
YEAH.
I'M SO SORRY. HOW MANY--

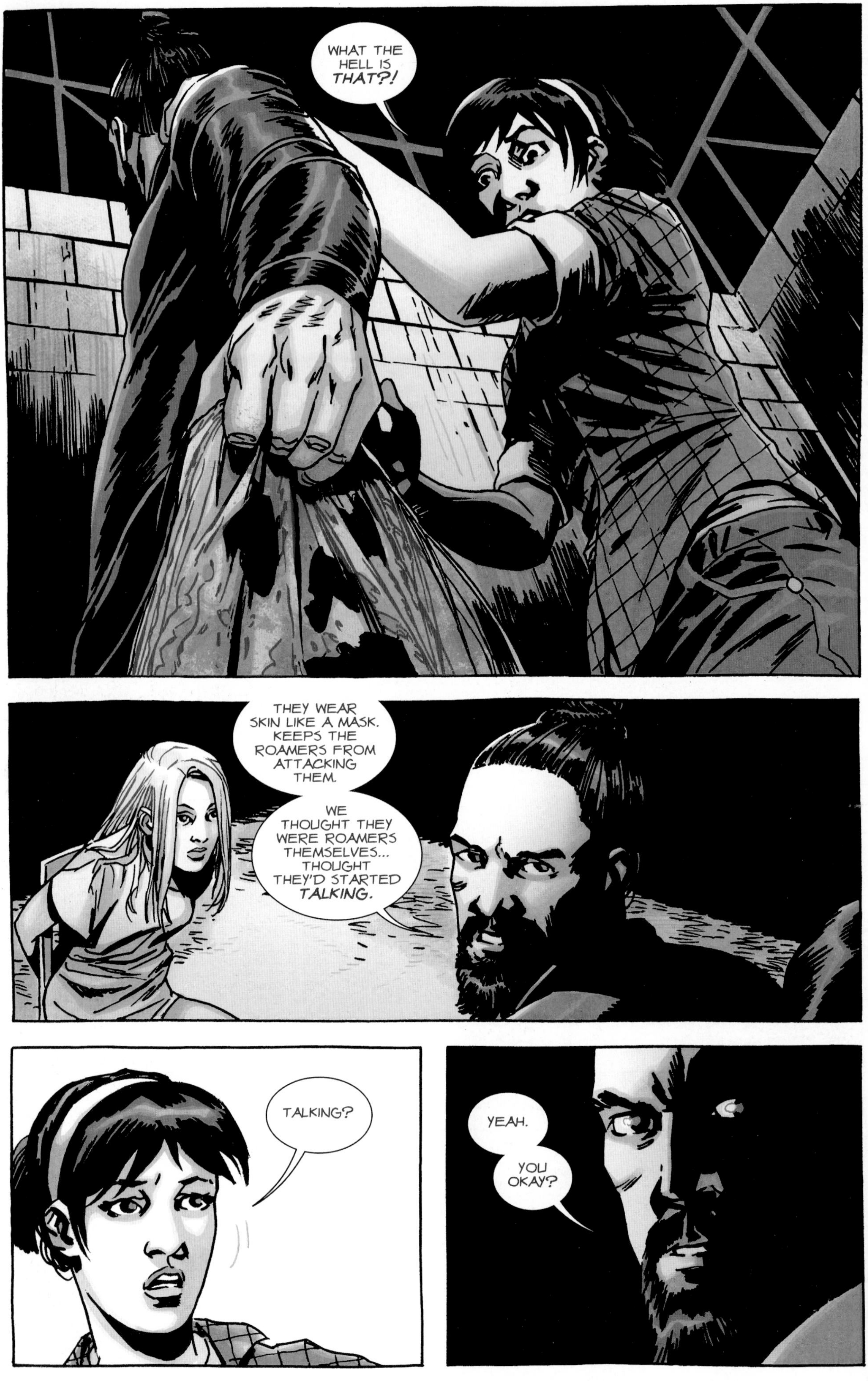
WHAT THE HELL IS THAT?!
THEY WEAR SKIN LIKE A MASK. KEEPS THE ROAMERS FROM ATTACKING THEM.
WE THOUGHT THEY WERE ROAMERS THEMSELVES... THOUGHT THEY'D STARTED TALKING.
TALKING?
YEAH.
YOU OKAY?

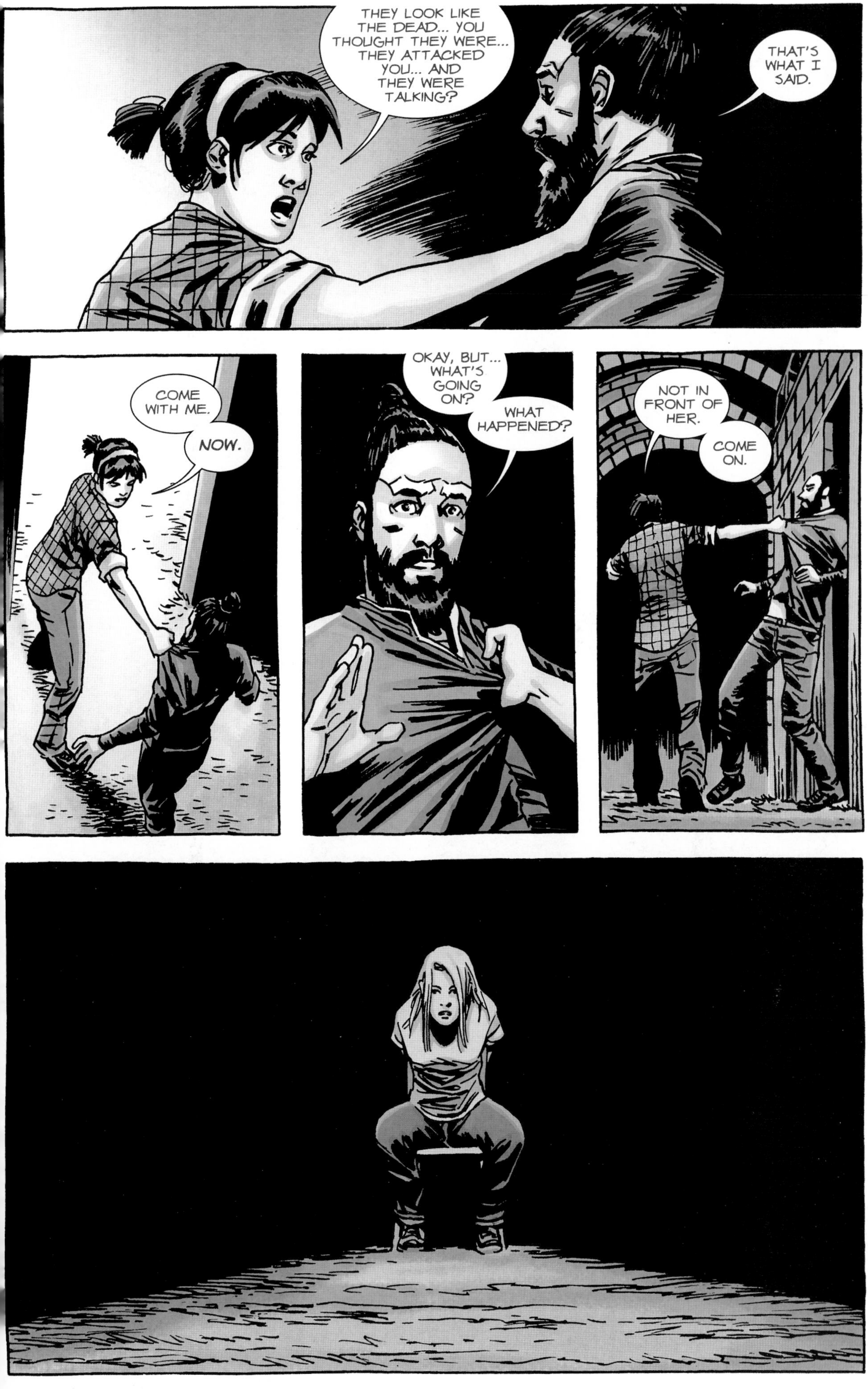
THEY LOOK LIKE THE DEAD... YOU THOUGHT THEY WERE... THEY ATTACKED YOU... AND THEY WERE TALKING?
THAT'S WHAT I SAID.
COME WITH ME.
NOW.
OKAY, BUT... WHAT'S GOING ON?
WHAT HAPPENED?
NOT IN FRONT OF HER.
COME ON.

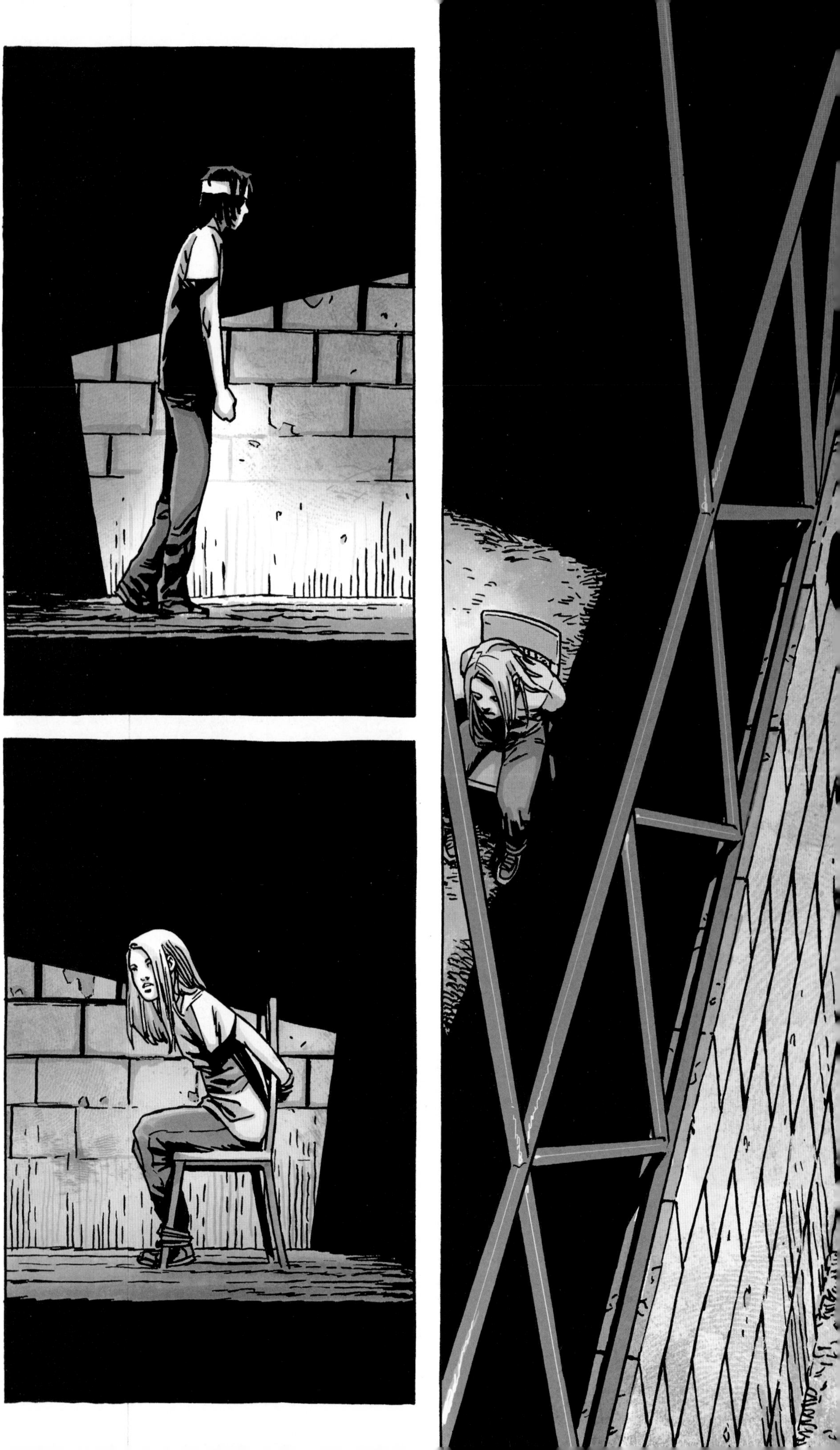

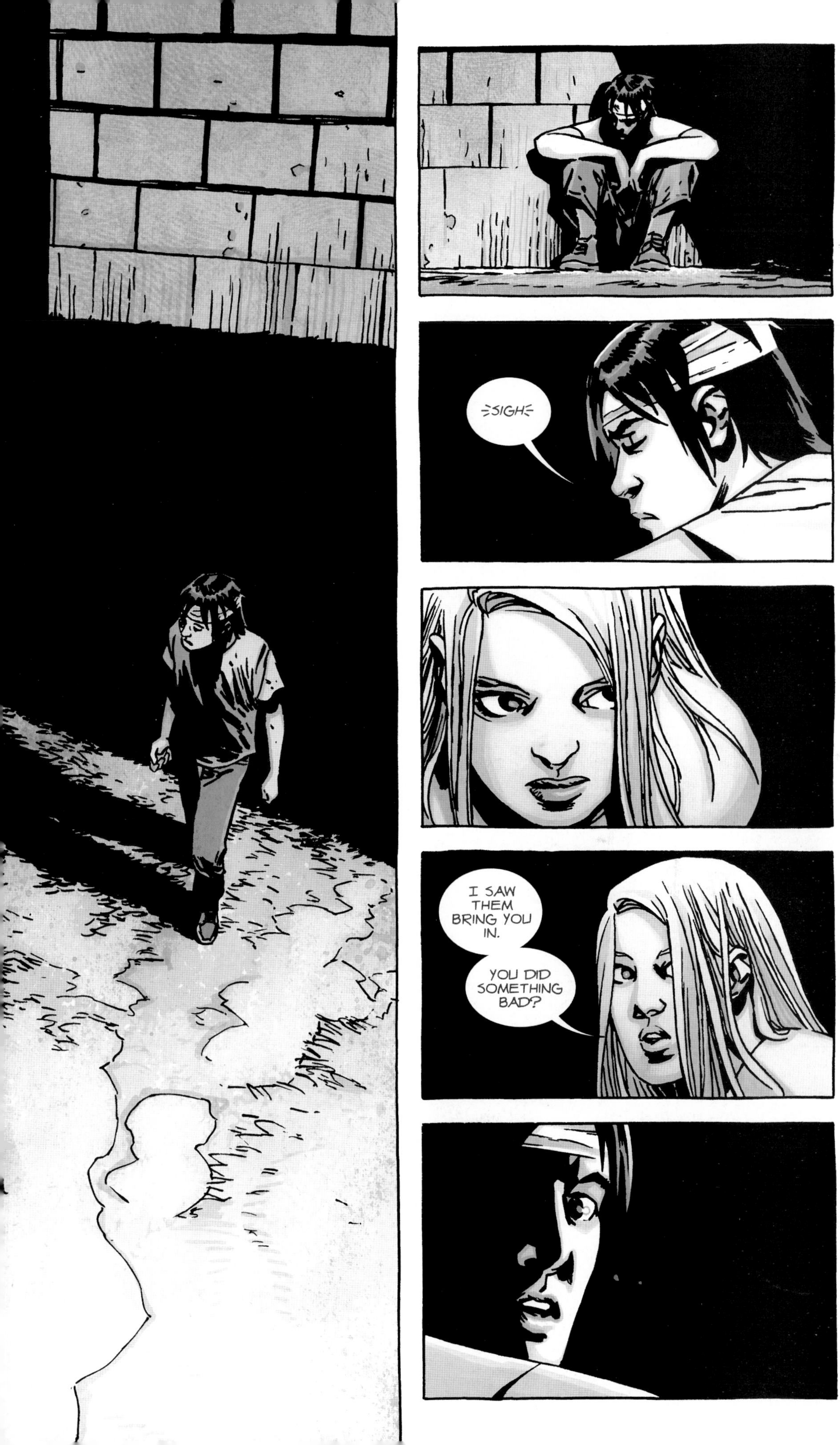
SIGH
I SAW THEM BRING YOU IN.
YOU DID SOMETHING BAD?

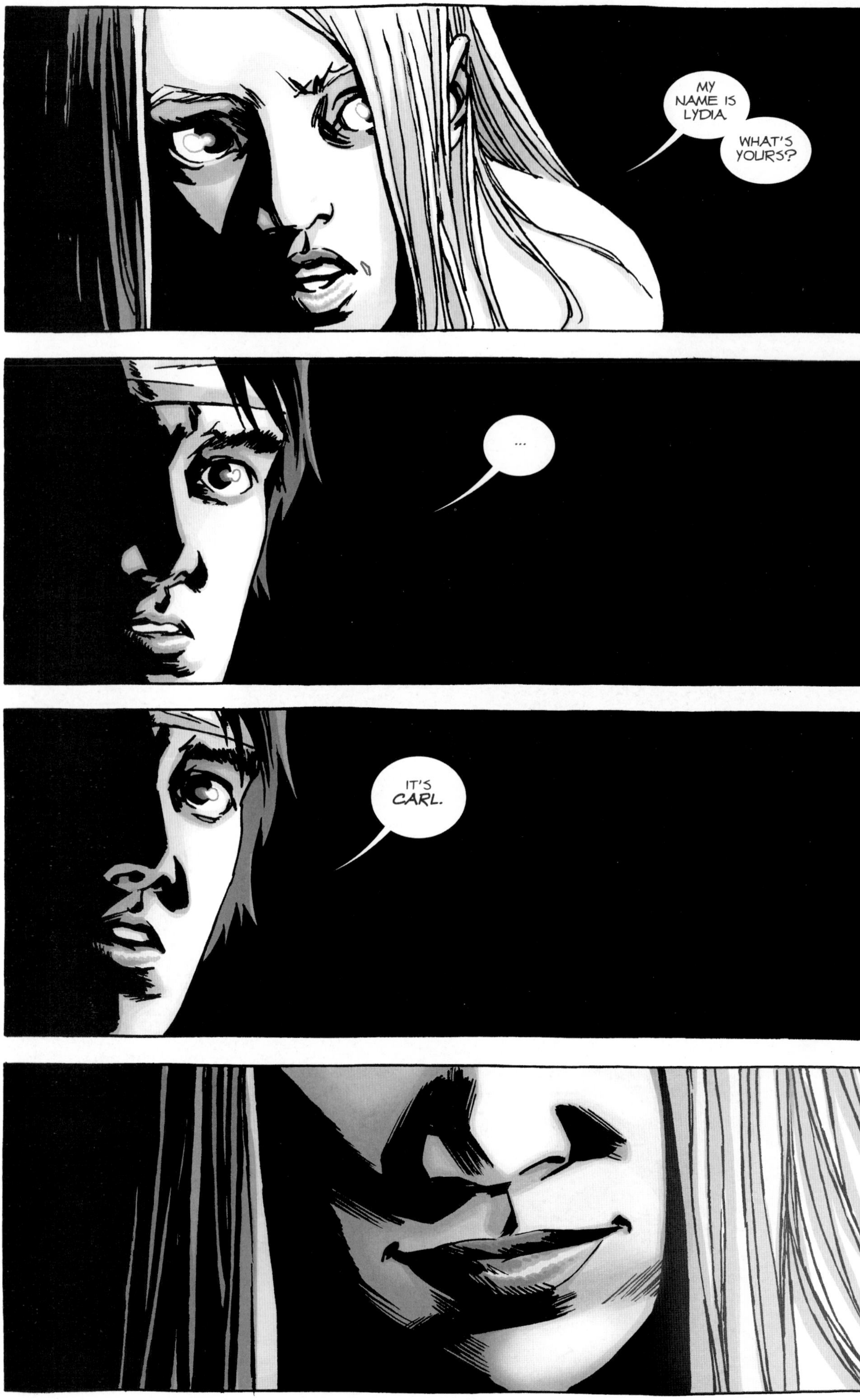
MY NAME IS LYDIA.
WHAT'S YOURS?
...
IT'S CARL.

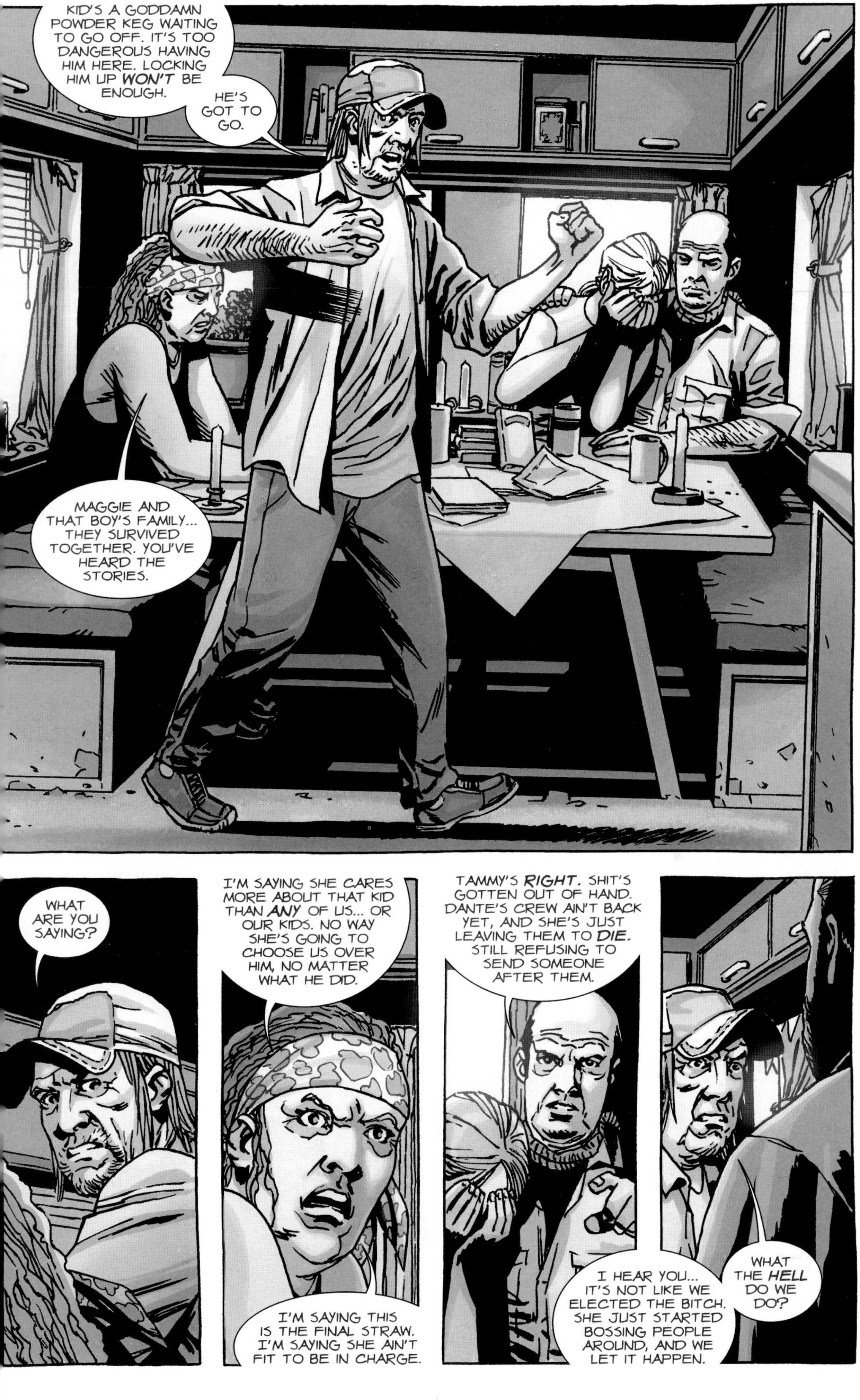
KID'S A GODDAMN POWDER KEG WAITING TO GO OFF. IT'S TOO DANGEROUS HAVING HIM HERE. LOCKING HIM UP WON'T BE ENOUGH.
HE'S GOT TO GO.
MAGGIE AND THAT BOY'S FAMILY... THEY SURVIVED TOGETHER. YOU'VE HEARD THE STORIES.
WHAT ARE YOU SAYING?
I'M SAYING SHE CARES MORE ABOUT THAT KID THAN ANY OF US... OR OUR KIDS. NO WAY SHE'S GOING TO CHOOSE US OVER HIM, NO MATTER WHAT HE DID.
I'M SAYING THIS IS THE FINAL STRAW. I'M SAYING SHE AIN'T FIT TO BE IN CHARGE.
TAMMY'S RIGHT. SHIT'S GOTTEN OUT OF HAND. DANTE'S CREW AIN'T BACK YET, AND SHE'S JUST LEAVING THEM TO DIE. STILL REFUSING TO SEND SOMEONE AFTER THEM.
I HEAR YOU... IT'S NOT LIKE WE ELECTED THE BITCH. SHE JUST STARTED BOSSING PEOPLE AROUND, AND WE LET IT HAPPEN.
WHAT THE HELL DO WE DO?

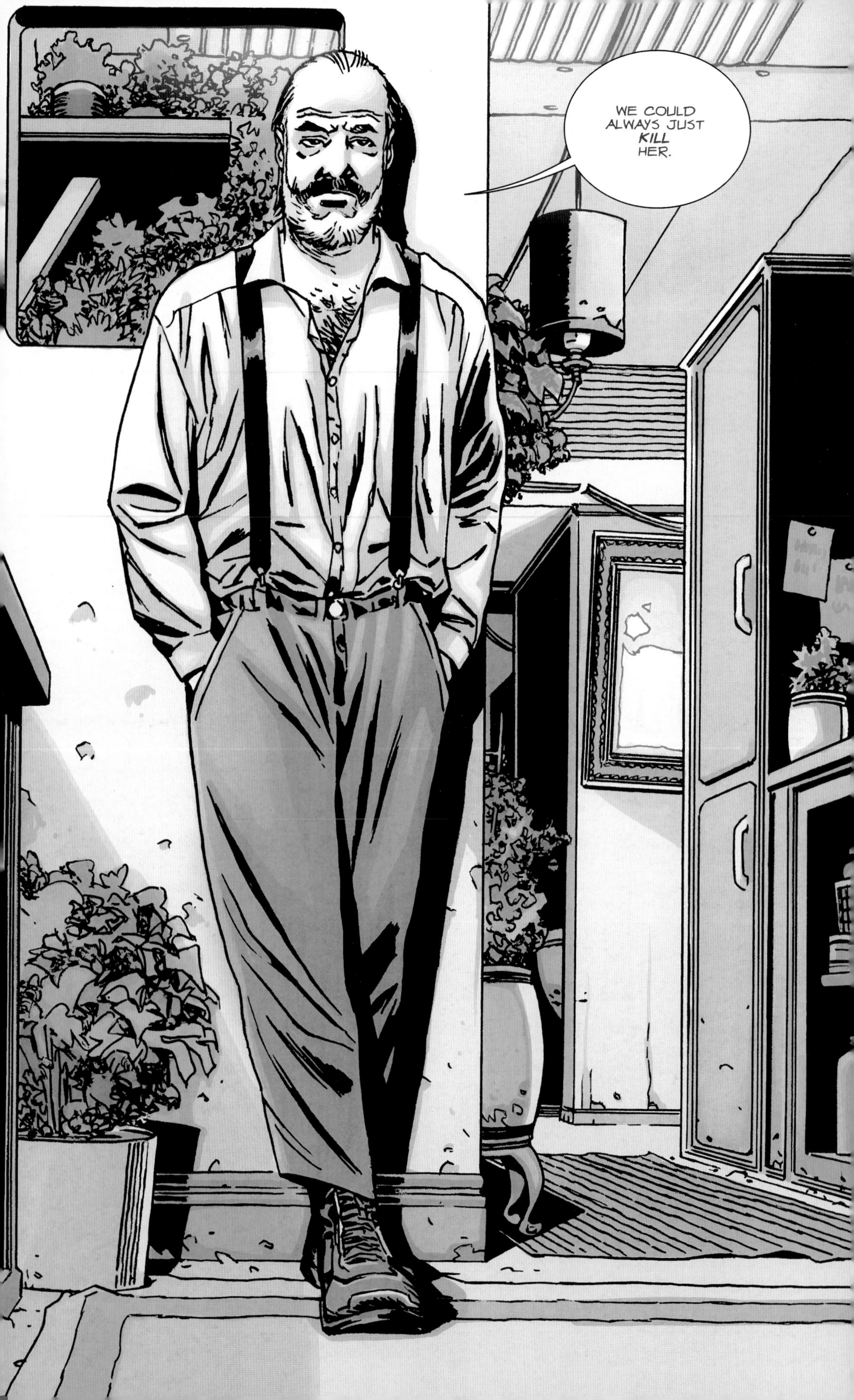
WE COULD ALWAYS JUST *KILL* HER.

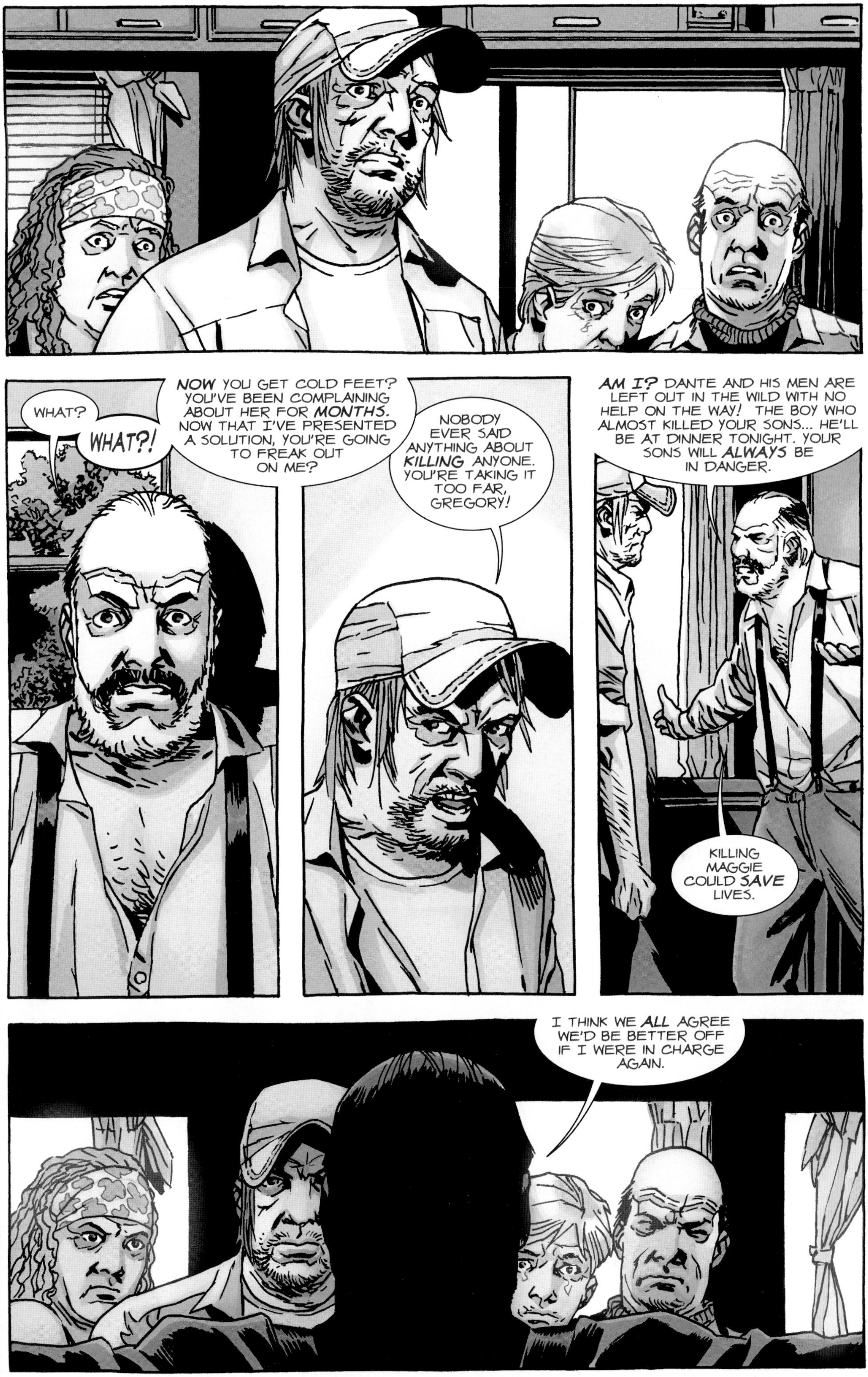
WHAT?
WHAT?!
NOW YOU GET COLD FEET? YOU'VE BEEN COMPLAINING ABOUT HER FOR MONTHS. NOW THAT I'VE PRESENTED A SOLUTION, YOU'RE GOING TO FREAK OUT ON ME?
NOBODY EVER SAID ANYTHING ABOUT KILLING ANYONE. YOU'RE TAKING IT TOO FAR, GREGORY!
AM I? DANTE AND HIS MEN ARE LEFT OUT IN THE WILD WITH NO HELP ON THE WAY! THE BOY WHO ALMOST KILLED YOUR SONS... HE'LL BE AT DINNER TONIGHT. YOUR SONS WILL ALWAYS BE IN DANGER.
KILLING MAGGIE COULD SAVE LIVES.
I THINK WE ALL AGREE WE'D BE BETTER OFF IF I WERE IN CHARGE AGAIN.

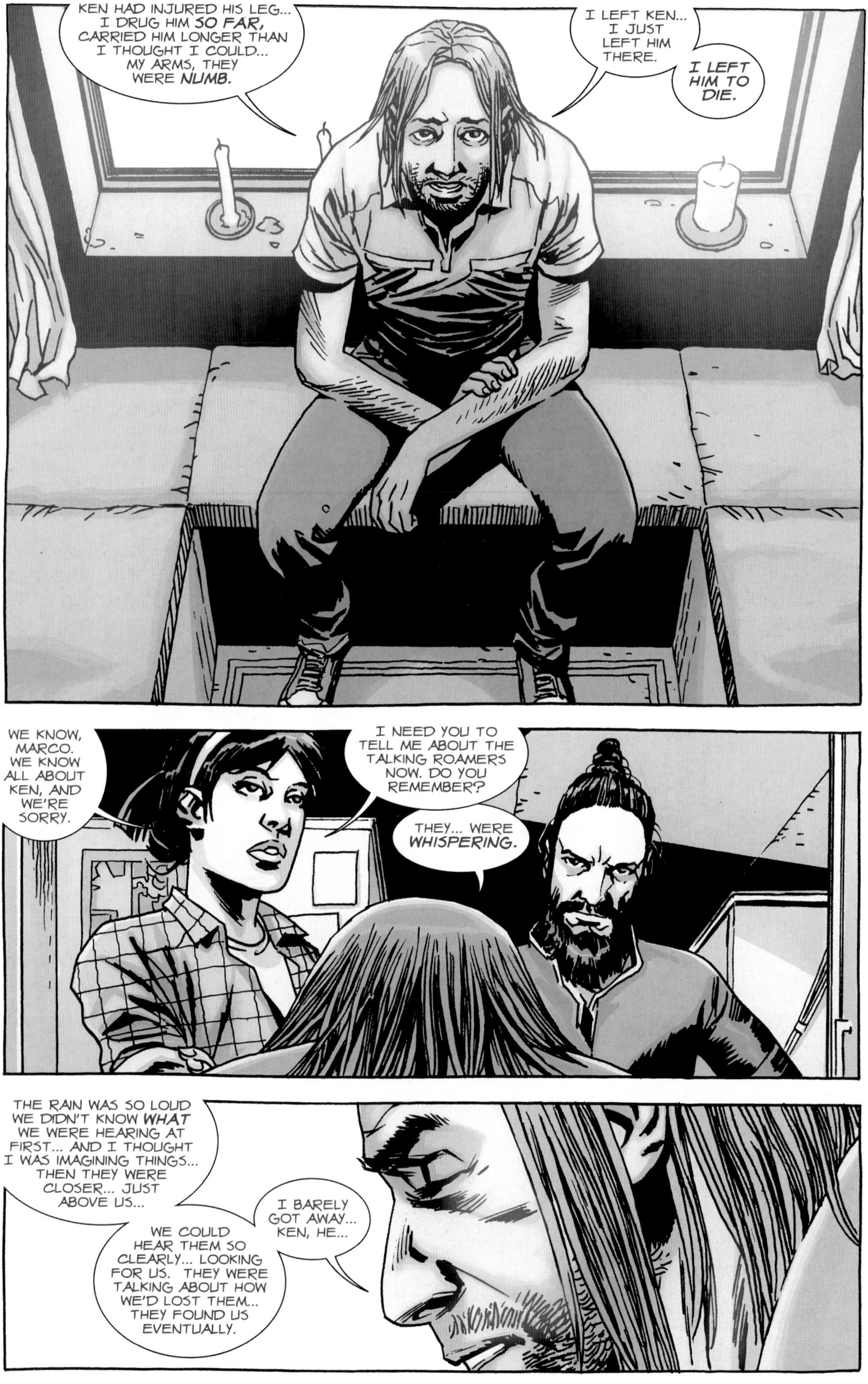
KEN HAD INJURED HIS LEG... I DRUG HIM SO FAR, CARRIED HIM LONGER THAN I THOUGHT I COULD... MY ARMS, THEY WERE NUMB.
I LEFT KEN... I JUST LEFT HIM THERE.
I LEFT HIM TO DIE.
WE KNOW, MARCO. WE KNOW ALL ABOUT KEN, AND WE'RE SORRY.
I NEED YOU TO TELL ME ABOUT THE TALKING ROAMERS NOW. DO YOU REMEMBER?
THEY... WERE WHISPERING.
THE RAIN WAS SO LOUD WE DIDN'T KNOW WHAT WE WERE HEARING AT FIRST... AND I THOUGHT I WAS IMAGINING THINGS... THEN THEY WERE CLOSER... JUST ABOVE US...
WE COULD HEAR THEM SO CLEARLY... LOOKING FOR US. THEY WERE TALKING ABOUT HOW WE'D LOST THEM... THEY FOUND US EVENTUALLY.
I BARELY GOT AWAY... KEN, HE...

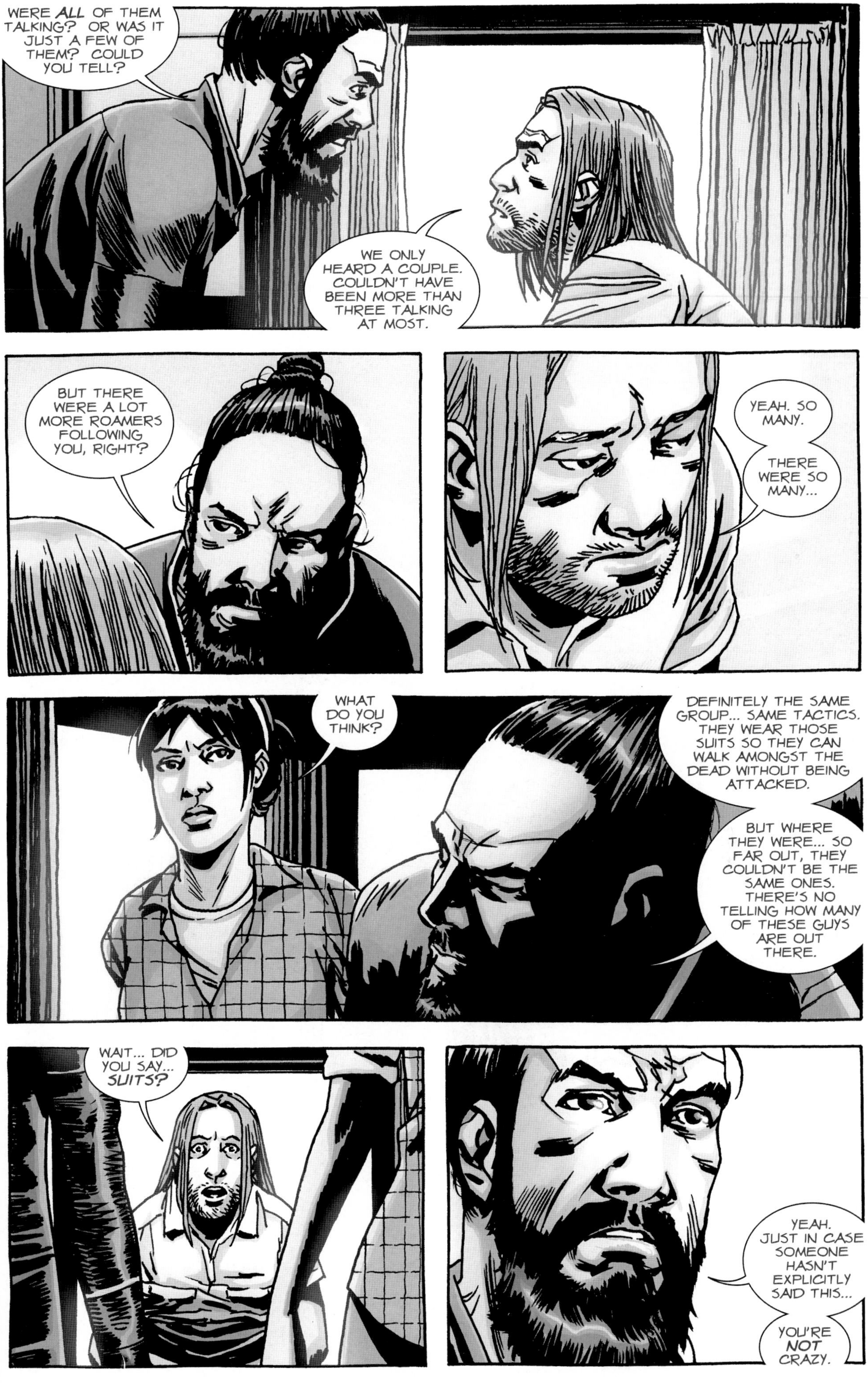
WERE *ALL* OF THEM TALKING? OR WAS IT JUST A FEW OF THEM? COULD YOU TELL?
WE ONLY HEARD A COUPLE. COULDN'T HAVE BEEN MORE THAN THREE TALKING AT MOST.
BUT THERE WERE A LOT MORE ROAMERS FOLLOWING YOU, RIGHT?
YEAH. SO MANY.
THERE WERE SO MANY...
WHAT DO YOU THINK?
DEFINITELY THE SAME GROUP... SAME TACTICS. THEY WEAR THOSE SUITS SO THEY CAN WALK AMONGST THE DEAD WITHOUT BEING ATTACKED.
BUT WHERE THEY WERE... SO FAR OUT, THEY COULDN'T BE THE SAME ONES. THERE'S NO TELLING HOW MANY OF THESE GUYS ARE OUT THERE.
WAIT... DID YOU SAY... *SUITS?*
YEAH. JUST IN CASE SOMEONE HASN'T EXPLICITLY SAID THIS...
YOU'RE *NOT* CRAZY.

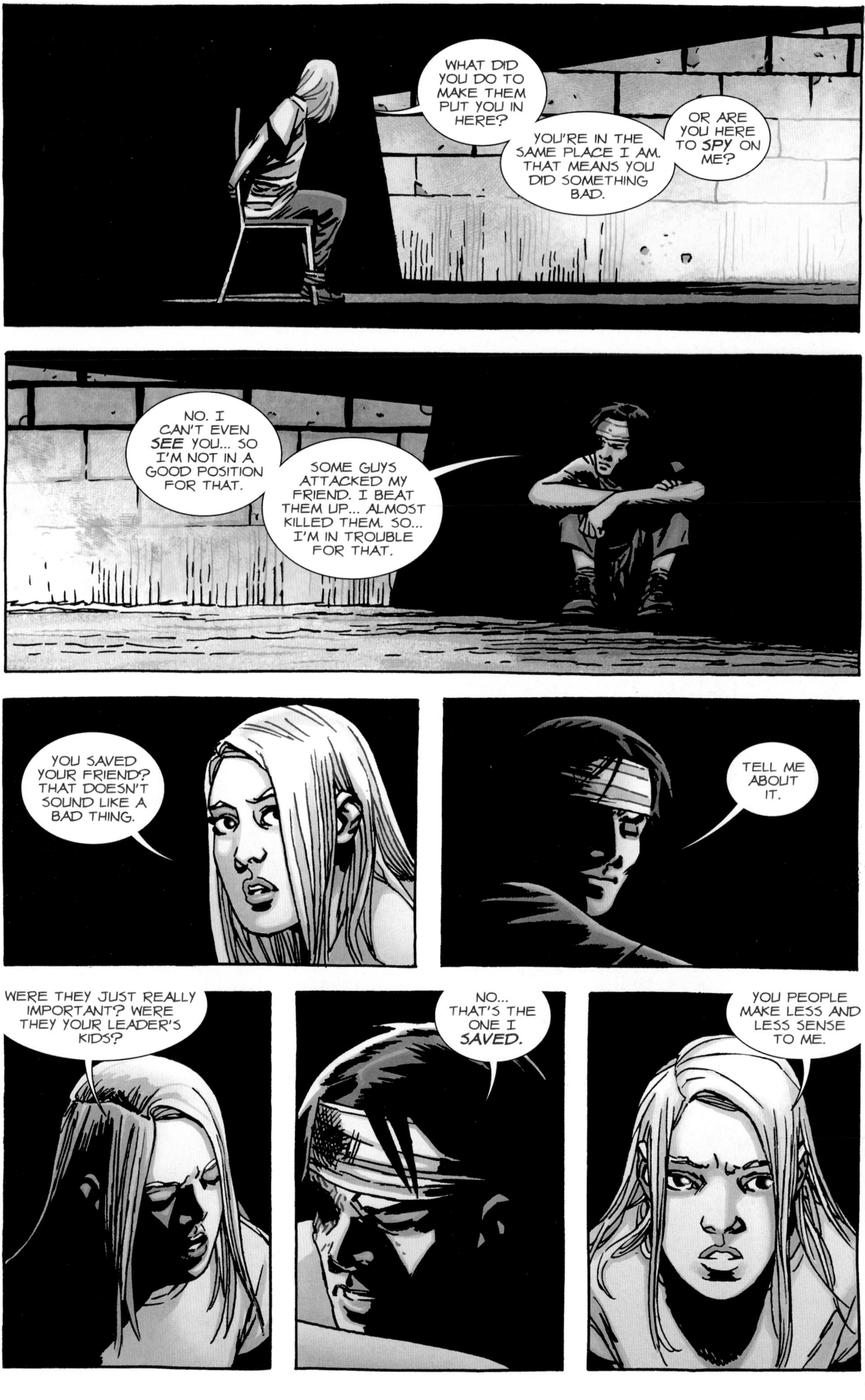
WHAT DID YOU DO TO MAKE THEM PUT YOU IN HERE?
YOU'RE IN THE SAME PLACE I AM. THAT MEANS YOU DID SOMETHING BAD.
OR ARE YOU HERE TO SPY ON ME?
NO. I CAN'T EVEN SEE YOU... SO I'M NOT IN A GOOD POSITION FOR THAT.
SOME GUYS ATTACKED MY FRIEND. I BEAT THEM UP... ALMOST KILLED THEM. SO... I'M IN TROUBLE FOR THAT.
YOU SAVED YOUR FRIEND? THAT DOESN'T SOUND LIKE A BAD THING.
TELL ME ABOUT IT.
WERE THEY JUST REALLY IMPORTANT? WERE THEY YOUR LEADER'S KIDS?
NO... THAT'S THE ONE I SAVED.
YOU PEOPLE MAKE LESS AND LESS SENSE TO ME.

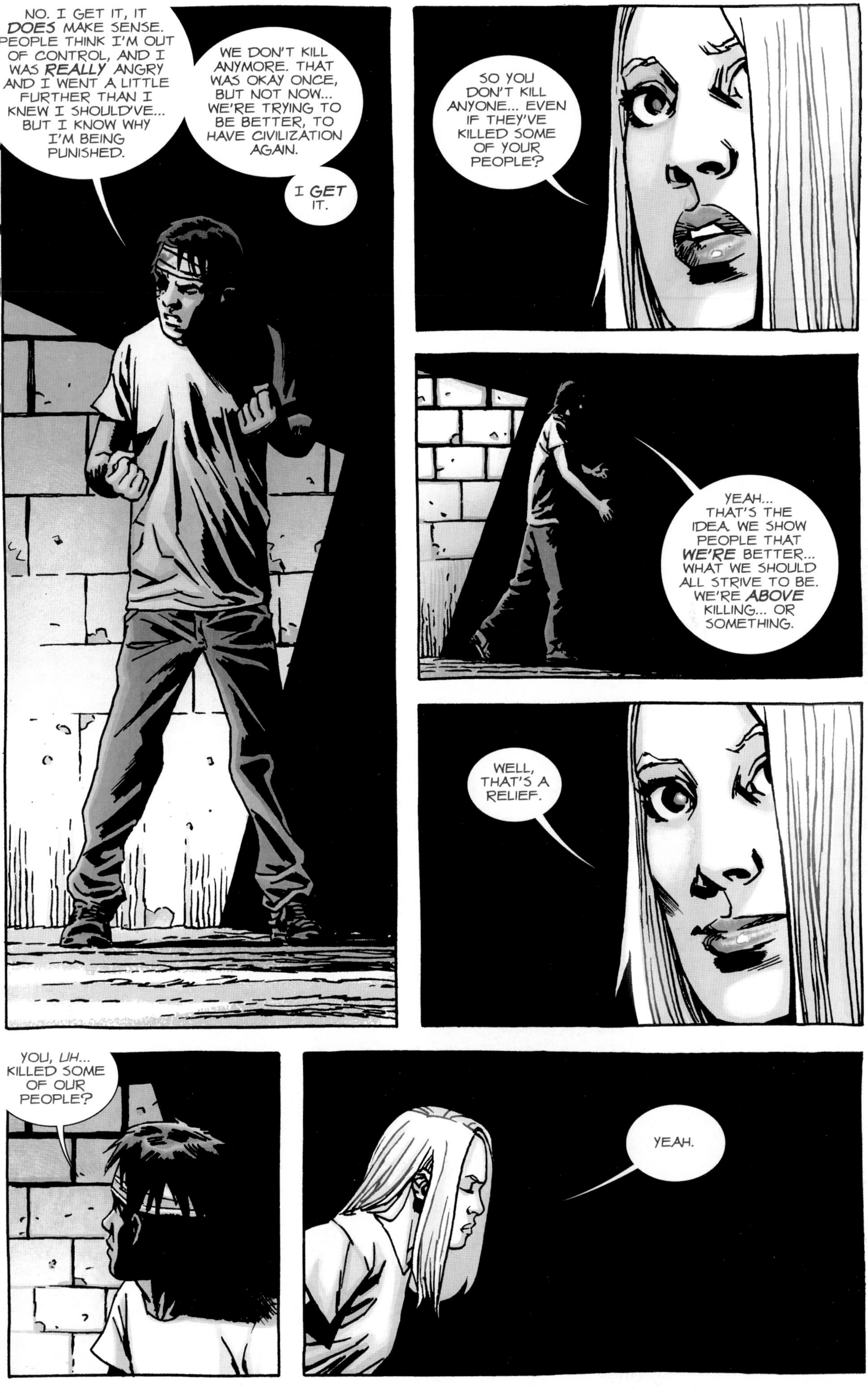
NO. I GET IT, IT DOES MAKE SENSE. PEOPLE THINK I'M OUT OF CONTROL, AND I WAS REALLY ANGRY AND I WENT A LITTLE FURTHER THAN I KNEW I SHOULD'VE... BUT I KNOW WHY I'M BEING PUNISHED.
WE DON'T KILL ANYMORE. THAT WAS OKAY ONCE, BUT NOT NOW... WE'RE TRYING TO BE BETTER, TO HAVE CIVILIZATION AGAIN.
I GET IT.
SO YOU DON'T KILL ANYONE... EVEN IF THEY'VE KILLED SOME OF YOUR PEOPLE?
YEAH... THAT'S THE IDEA. WE SHOW PEOPLE THAT WE'RE BETTER... WHAT WE SHOULD ALL STRIVE TO BE. WE'RE ABOVE KILLING... OR SOMETHING.
WELL, THAT'S A RELIEF.
YOU, UH... KILLED SOME OF OUR PEOPLE?
YEAH.

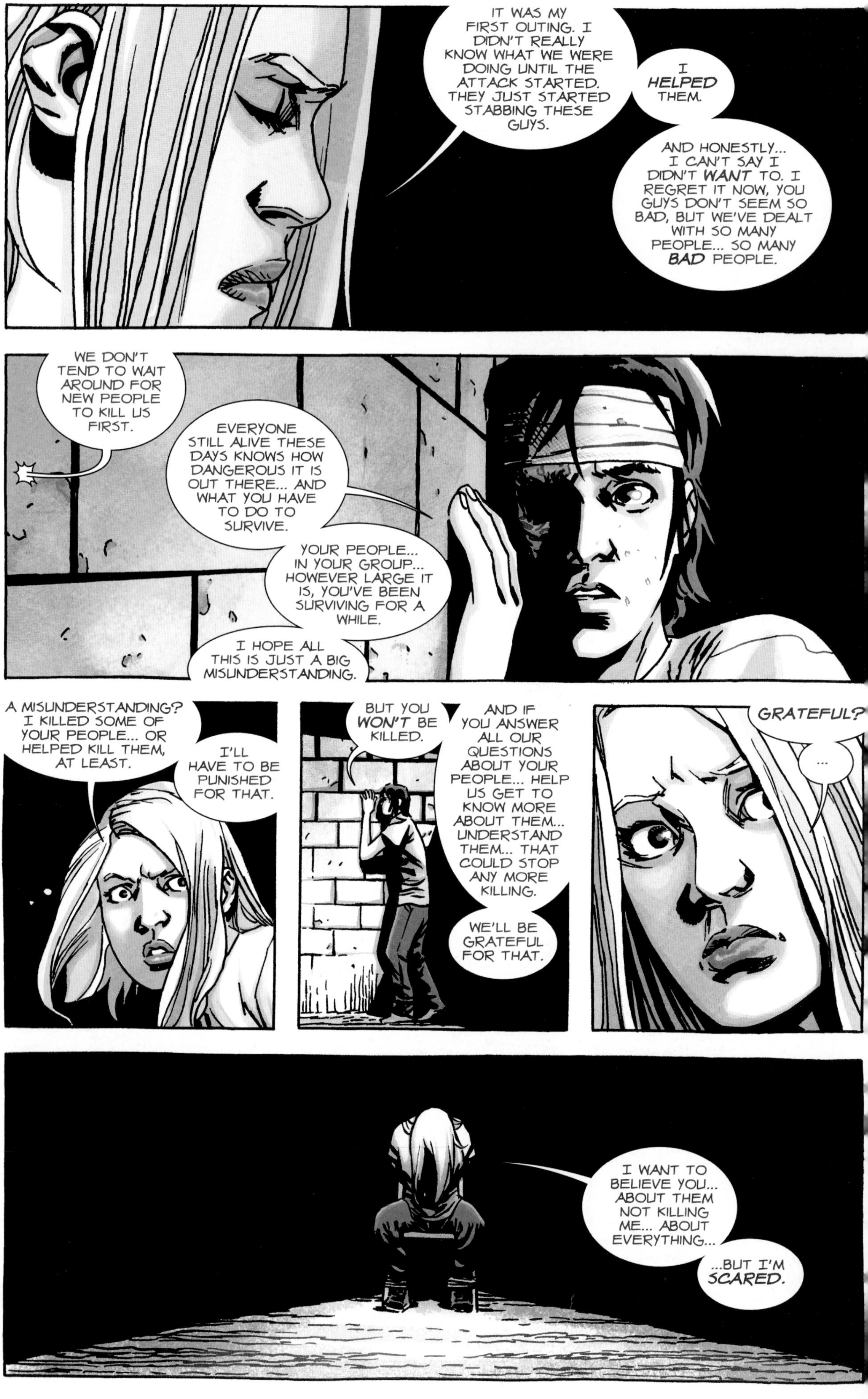
IT WAS MY FIRST OUTING. I DIDN'T REALLY KNOW WHAT WE WERE DOING UNTIL THE ATTACK STARTED. THEY JUST STARTED STABBING THESE GUYS.
I *HELPED* THEM.
AND HONESTLY... I CAN'T SAY I DIDN'T *WANT* TO. I REGRET IT NOW, YOU GUYS DON'T SEEM SO BAD, BUT WE'VE DEALT WITH SO MANY PEOPLE... SO MANY *BAD* PEOPLE.
WE DON'T TEND TO WAIT AROUND FOR NEW PEOPLE TO KILL US FIRST.
EVERYONE STILL ALIVE THESE DAYS KNOWS HOW DANGEROUS IT IS OUT THERE... AND WHAT YOU HAVE TO DO TO SURVIVE.
YOUR PEOPLE... IN YOUR GROUP... HOWEVER LARGE IT IS, YOU'VE BEEN SURVIVING FOR A WHILE.
I HOPE ALL THIS IS JUST A BIG MISUNDERSTANDING.
A MISUNDERSTANDING? I KILLED SOME OF YOUR PEOPLE... OR HELPED KILL THEM, AT LEAST.
I'LL HAVE TO BE PUNISHED FOR THAT.
BUT YOU *WON'T* BE KILLED.
AND IF YOU ANSWER ALL OUR QUESTIONS ABOUT YOUR PEOPLE... HELP US GET TO KNOW MORE ABOUT THEM... UNDERSTAND THEM... THAT COULD STOP ANY MORE KILLING.
WE'LL BE GRATEFUL FOR THAT.
GRATEFUL?
...
I WANT TO BELIEVE YOU... ABOUT THEM NOT KILLING ME... ABOUT EVERYTHING...
...BUT I'M *SCARED.*

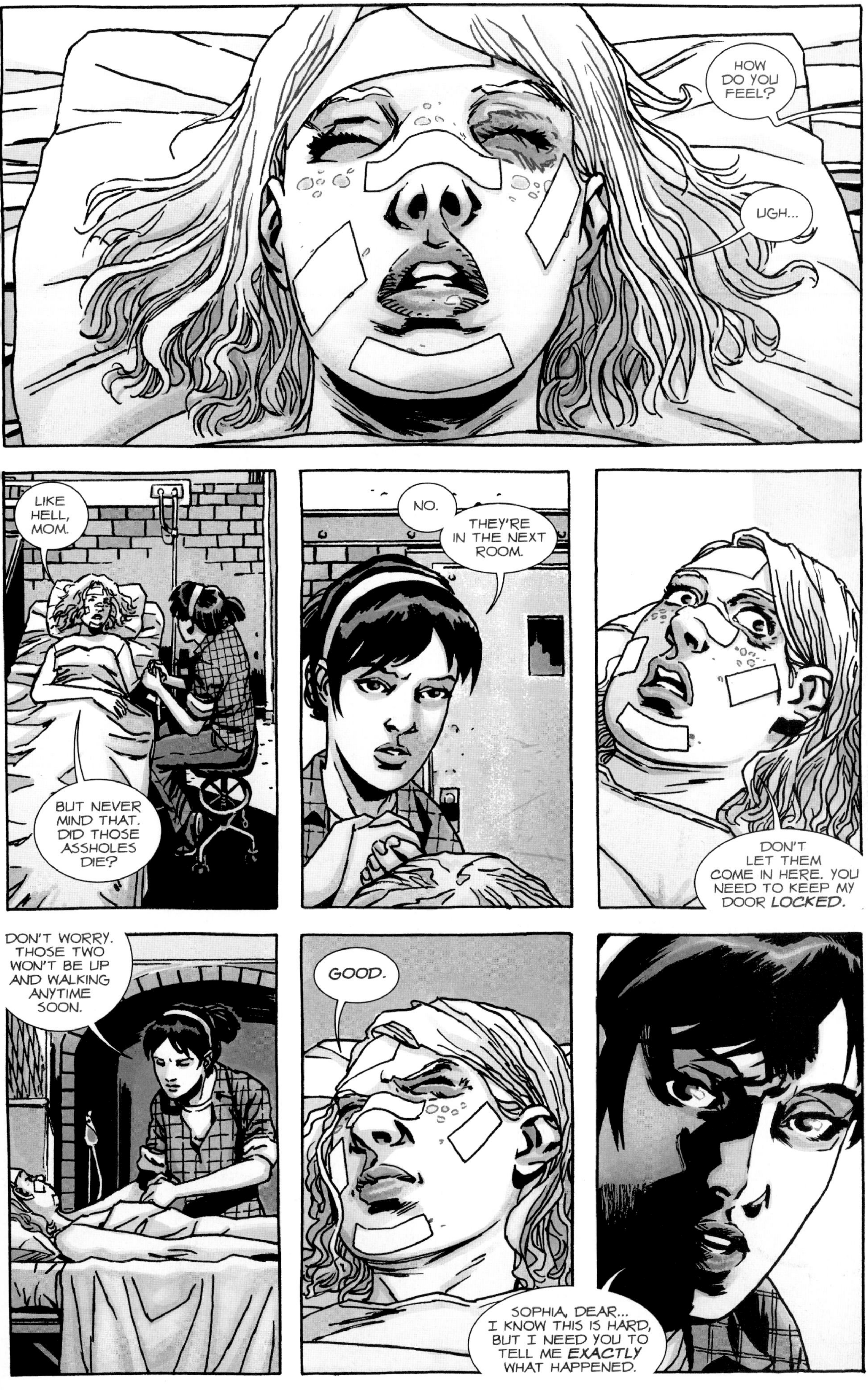

HOW DO YOU FEEL?
UGH...
LIKE HELL, MOM.
BUT NEVER MIND THAT. DID THOSE ASSHOLES DIE?
NO.
THEY'RE IN THE NEXT ROOM.
DON'T LET THEM COME IN HERE. YOU NEED TO KEEP MY DOOR *LOCKED.*
DON'T WORRY. THOSE TWO WON'T BE UP AND WALKING ANYTIME SOON.
GOOD.
SOPHIA, DEAR... I KNOW THIS IS HARD, BUT I NEED YOU TO TELL ME *EXACTLY* WHAT HAPPENED.

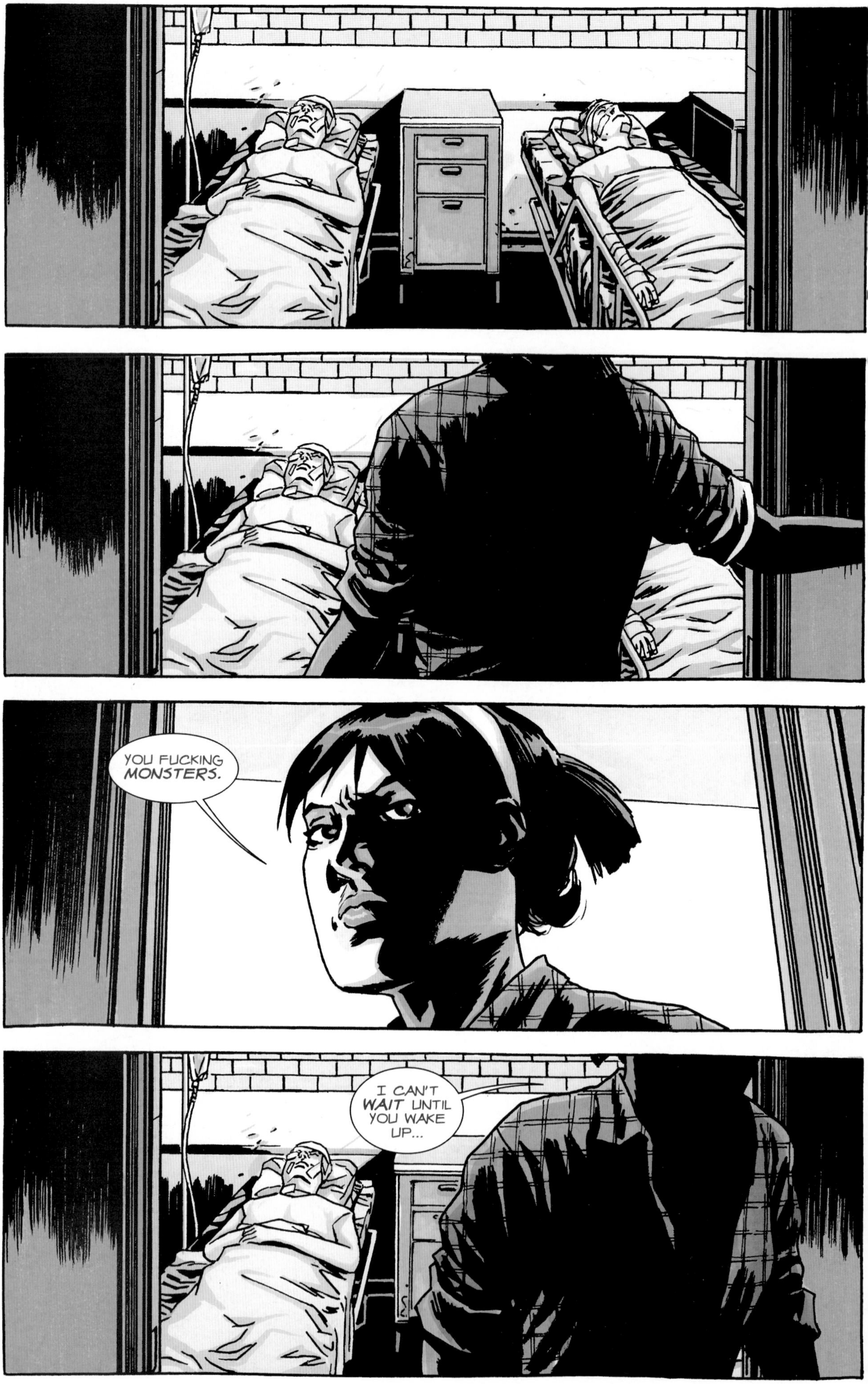
YOU FUCKING MONSTERS.
I CAN'T WAIT UNTIL YOU WAKE UP...

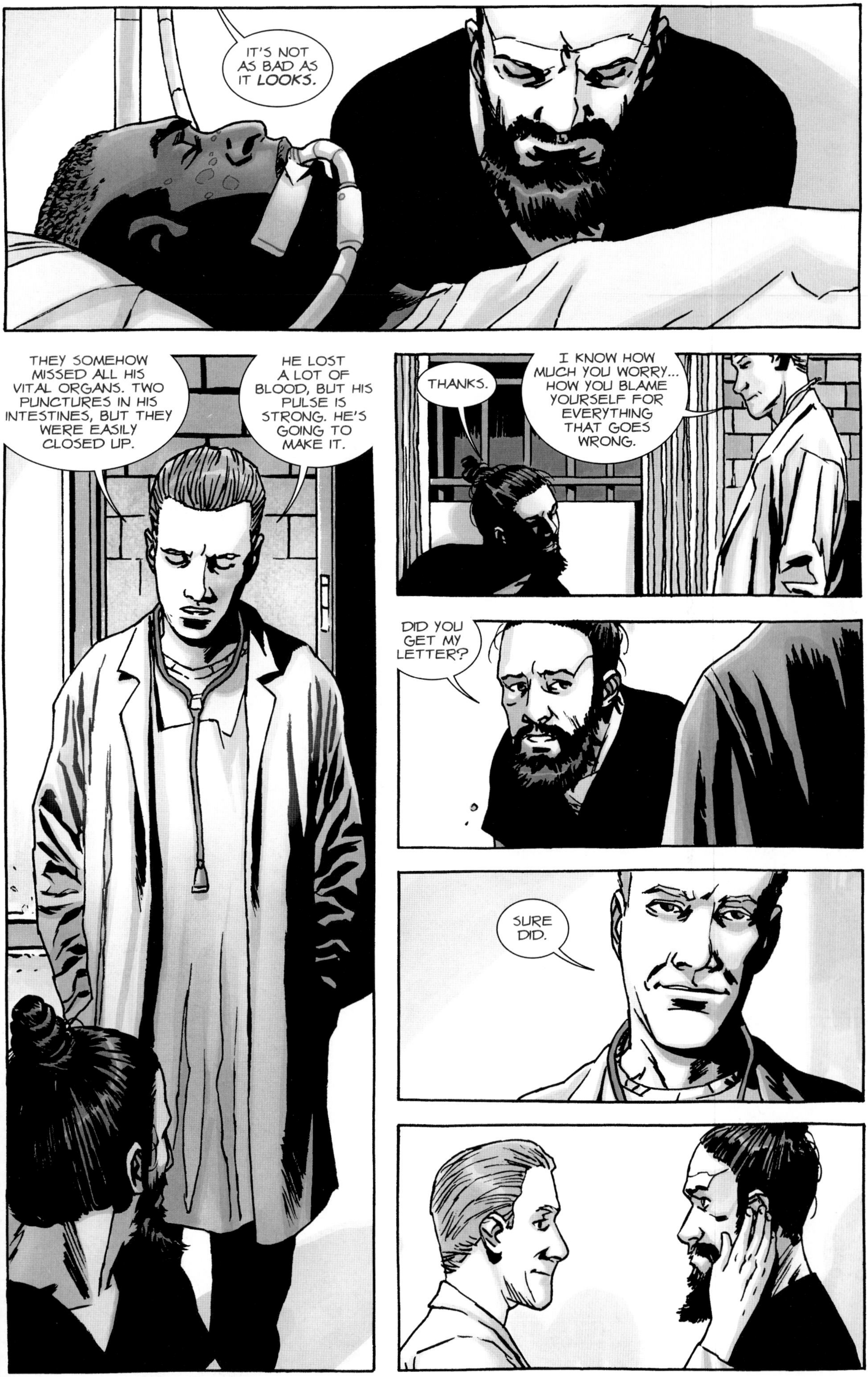
IT'S NOT AS BAD AS IT LOOKS.
THEY SOMEHOW MISSED ALL HIS VITAL ORGANS. TWO PUNCTURES IN HIS INTESTINES, BUT THEY WERE EASILY CLOSED UP.
HE LOST A LOT OF BLOOD, BUT HIS PULSE IS STRONG. HE'S GOING TO MAKE IT.
THANKS.
I KNOW HOW MUCH YOU WORRY... HOW YOU BLAME YOURSELF FOR EVERYTHING THAT GOES WRONG.
DID YOU GET MY LETTER?
SURE DID.

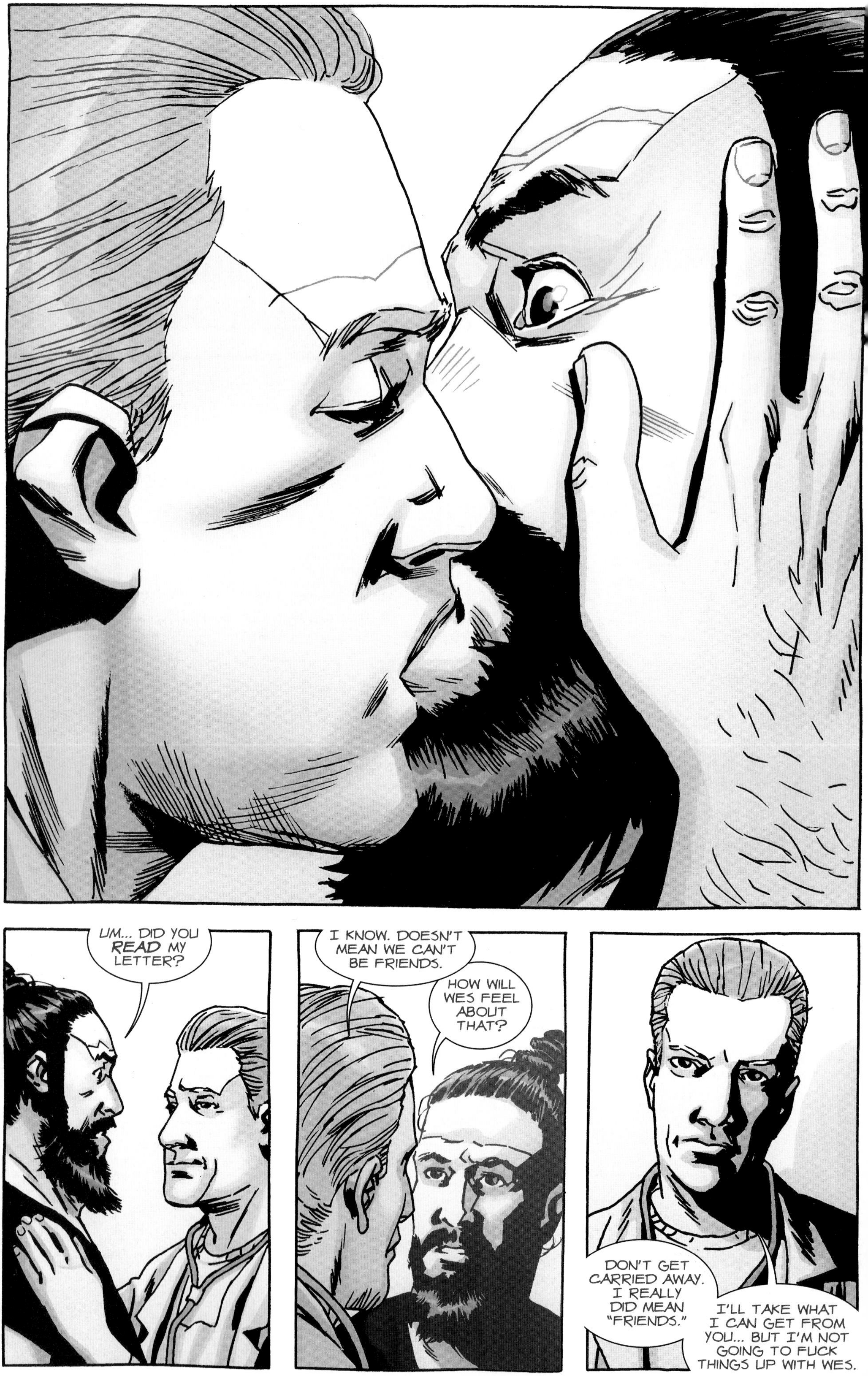
UM... DID YOU *READ* MY LETTER?
I KNOW. DOESN'T MEAN WE CAN'T BE FRIENDS.
HOW WILL WES FEEL ABOUT THAT?
DON'T GET CARRIED AWAY. I REALLY DID MEAN "FRIENDS."
I'LL TAKE WHAT I CAN GET FROM YOU... BUT I'M NOT GOING TO FUCK THINGS UP WITH WES.

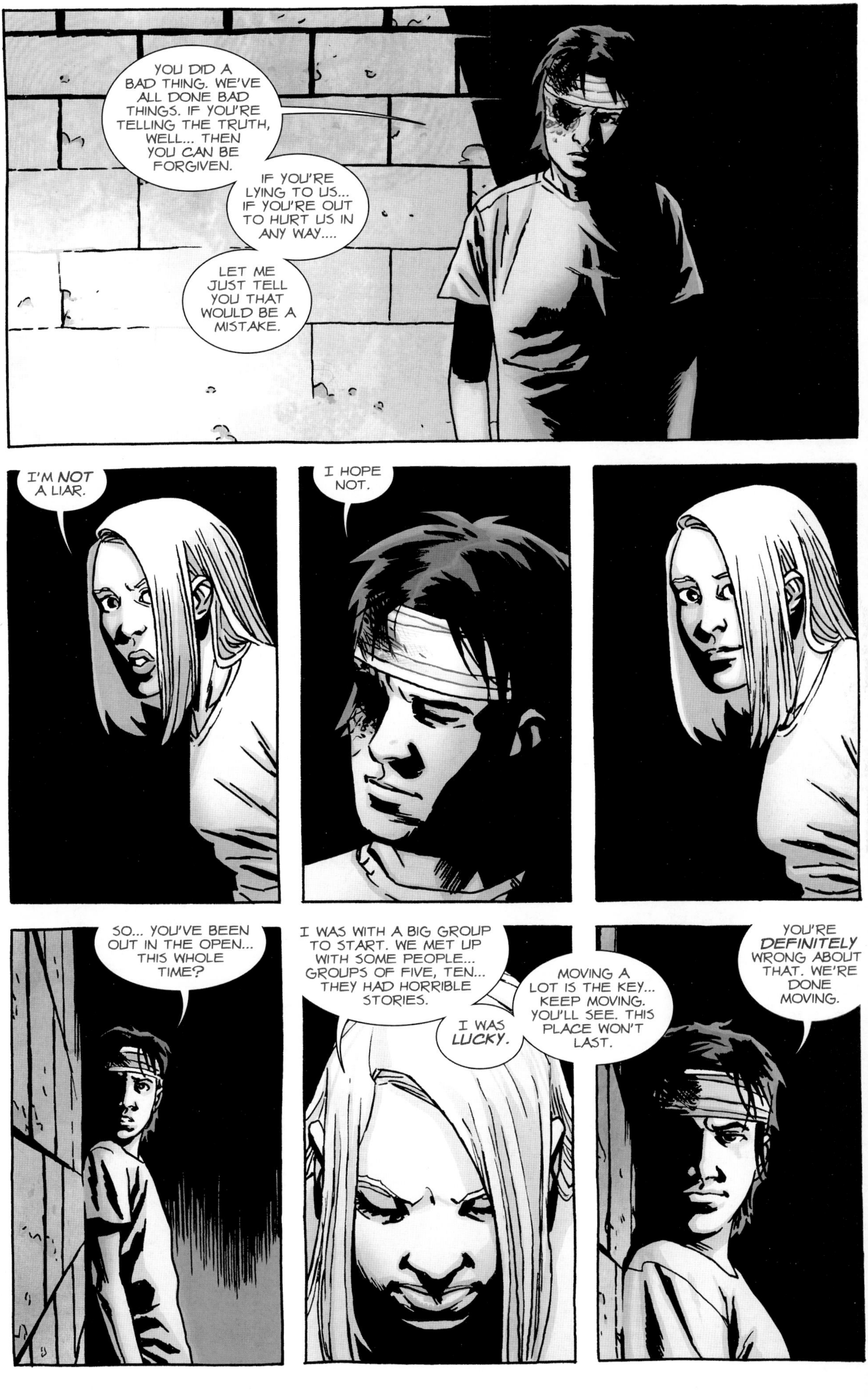
YOU DID A BAD THING. WE'VE ALL DONE BAD THINGS. IF YOU'RE TELLING THE TRUTH, WELL... THEN YOU CAN BE FORGIVEN.
IF YOU'RE LYING TO US... IF YOU'RE OUT TO HURT US IN ANY WAY....
LET ME JUST TELL YOU THAT WOULD BE A MISTAKE.
I'M *NOT* A LIAR.
I HOPE NOT.
SO... YOU'VE BEEN OUT IN THE OPEN... THIS WHOLE TIME?
I WAS WITH A BIG GROUP TO START. WE MET UP WITH SOME PEOPLE... GROUPS OF FIVE, TEN... THEY HAD HORRIBLE STORIES.
I WAS *LUCKY*.
MOVING A LOT IS THE KEY... KEEP MOVING. YOU'LL SEE. THIS PLACE WON'T LAST.
YOU'RE *DEFINITELY* WRONG ABOUT THAT. WE'RE DONE MOVING.

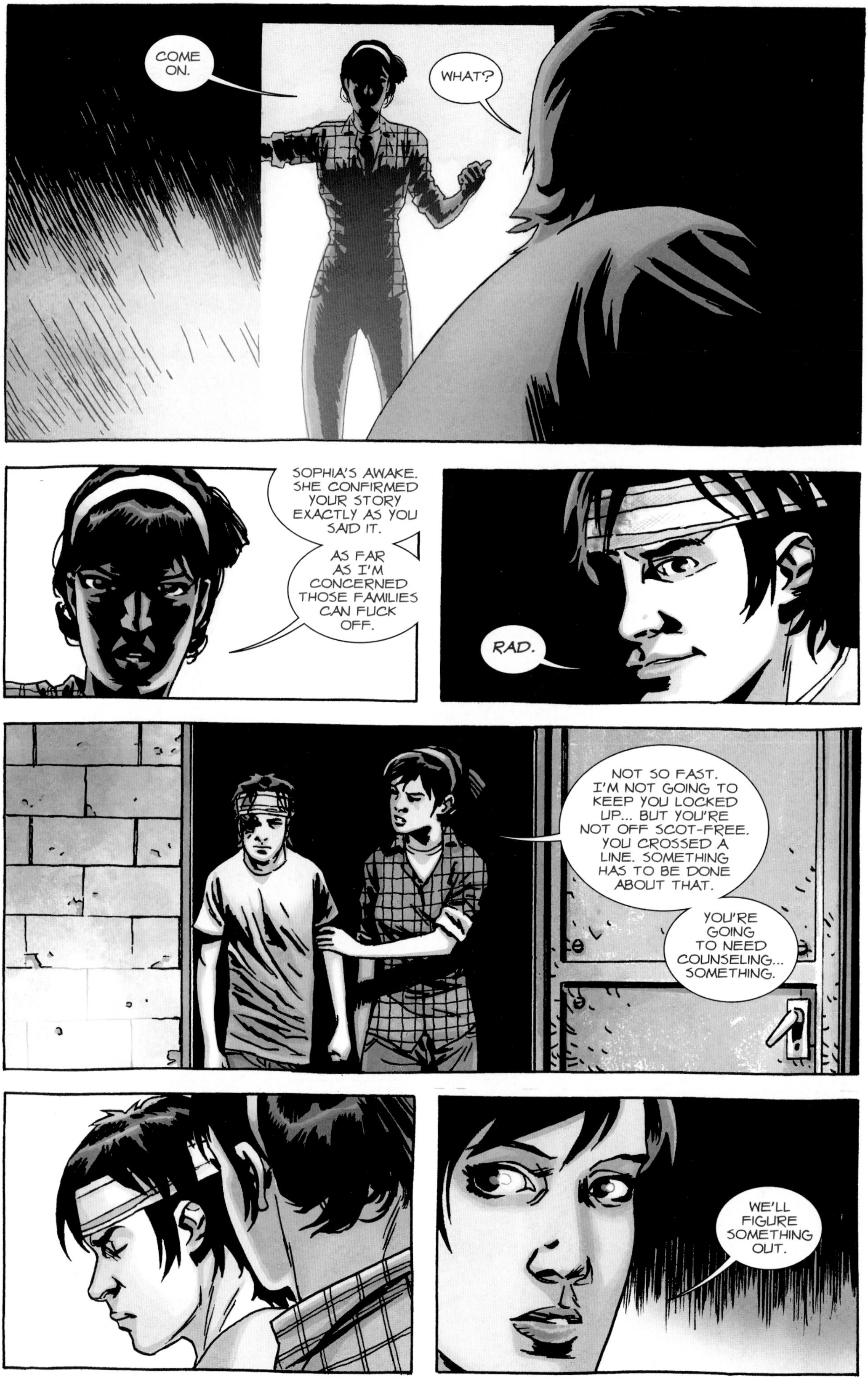
COME ON.
WHAT?
SOPHIA'S AWAKE. SHE CONFIRMED YOUR STORY EXACTLY AS YOU SAID IT.
AS FAR AS I'M CONCERNED THOSE FAMILIES CAN FUCK OFF.
RAD.
NOT SO FAST. I'M NOT GOING TO KEEP YOU LOCKED UP... BUT YOU'RE NOT OFF SCOT-FREE. YOU CROSSED A LINE. SOMETHING HAS TO BE DONE ABOUT THAT.
YOU'RE GOING TO NEED COUNSELING... SOMETHING.
WE'LL FIGURE SOMETHING OUT.

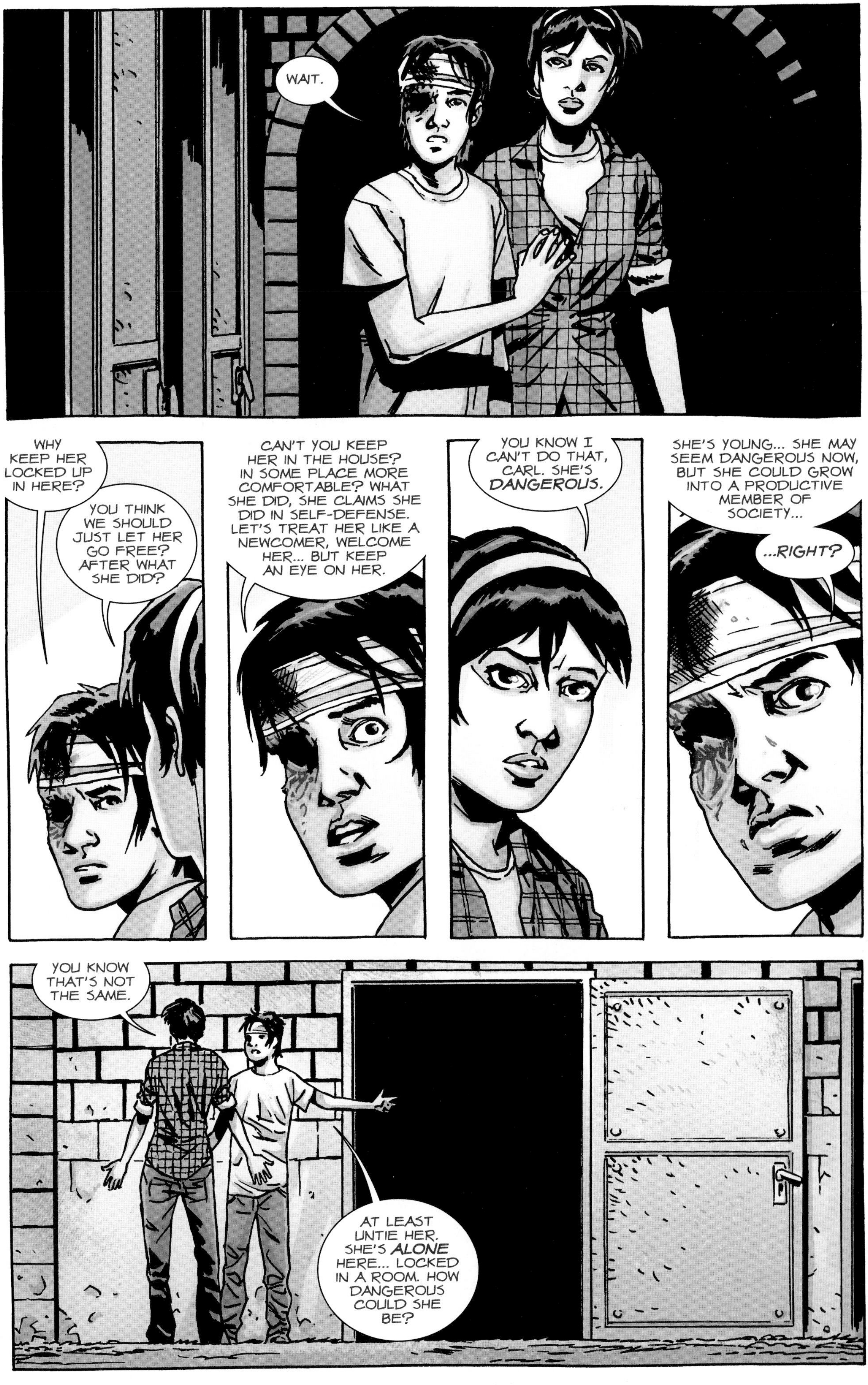
WAIT.
WHY KEEP HER LOCKED UP IN HERE?
YOU THINK WE SHOULD JUST LET HER GO FREE? AFTER WHAT SHE DID?
CAN'T YOU KEEP HER IN THE HOUSE? IN SOME PLACE MORE COMFORTABLE? WHAT SHE DID, SHE CLAIMS SHE DID IN SELF-DEFENSE. LET'S TREAT HER LIKE A NEWCOMER, WELCOME HER... BUT KEEP AN EYE ON HER.
YOU KNOW I CAN'T DO THAT, CARL. SHE'S DANGEROUS.
SHE'S YOUNG... SHE MAY SEEM DANGEROUS NOW, BUT SHE COULD GROW INTO A PRODUCTIVE MEMBER OF SOCIETY...
...RIGHT?
YOU KNOW THAT'S NOT THE SAME.
AT LEAST UNTIE HER. SHE'S ALONE HERE... LOCKED IN A ROOM. HOW DANGEROUS COULD SHE BE?

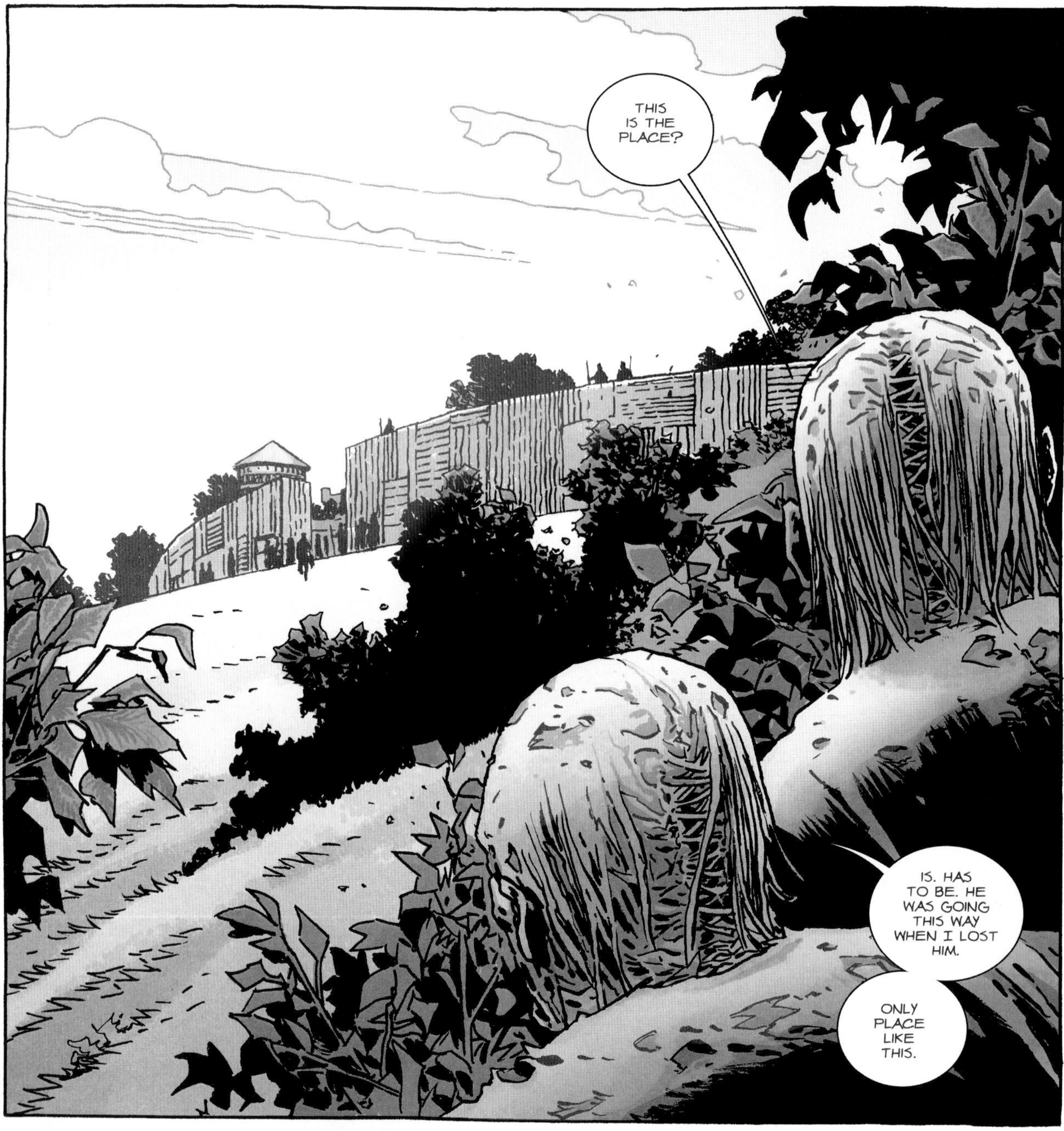
THIS IS THE PLACE?
IS. HAS TO BE. HE WAS GOING THIS WAY WHEN I LOST HIM.
ONLY PLACE LIKE THIS.

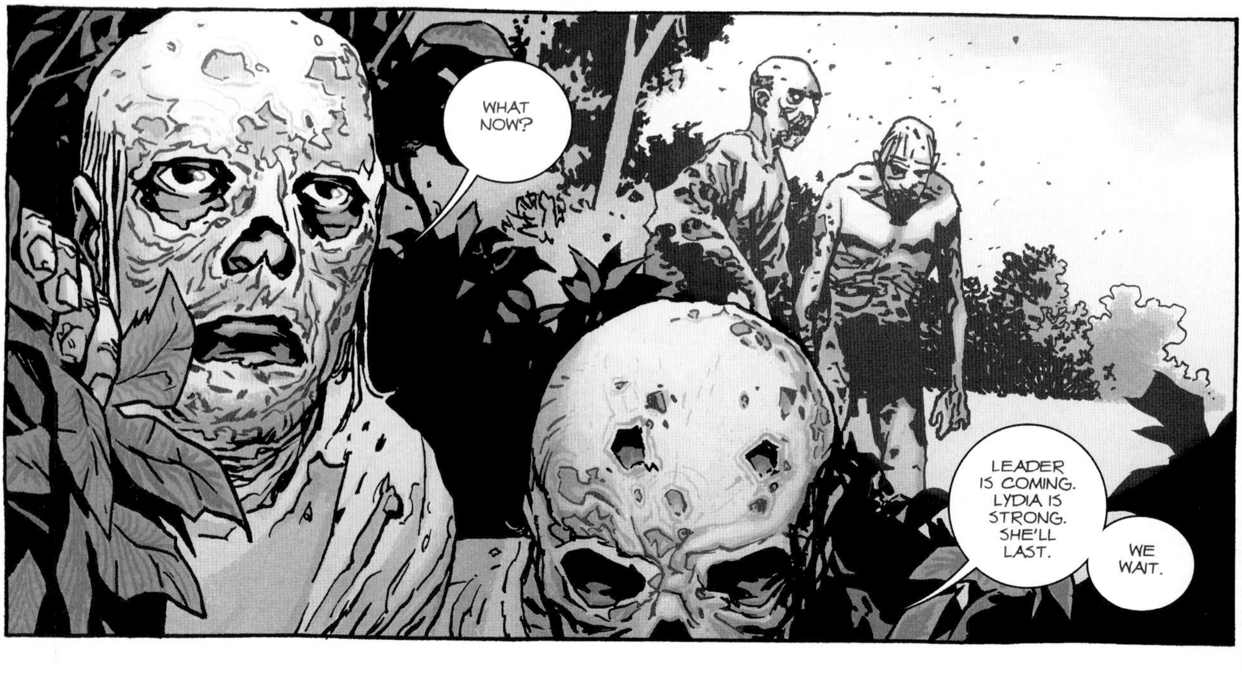
WHAT NOW?
LEADER IS COMING. LYDIA IS STRONG. SHE'LL LAST.
WE WAIT.

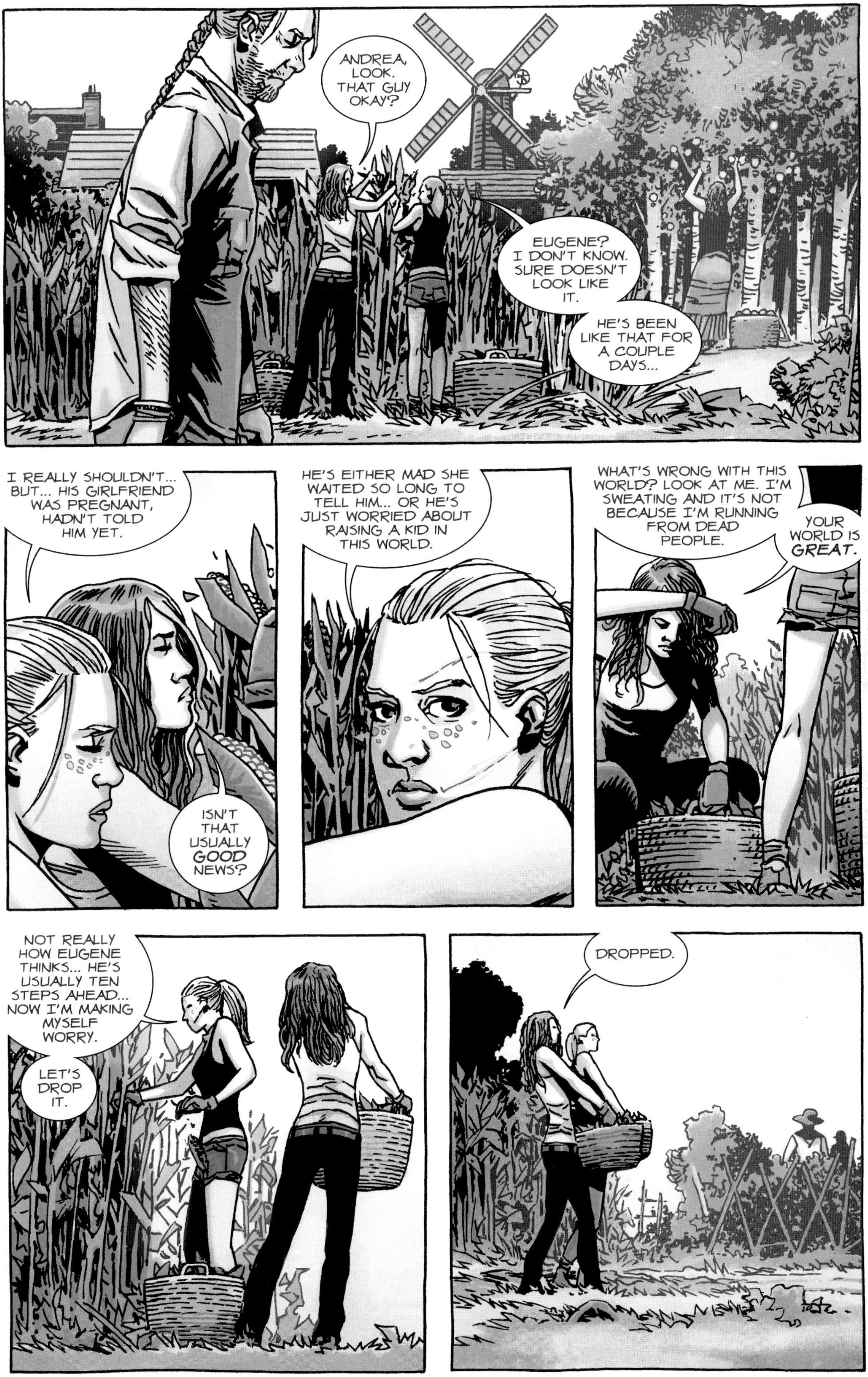
ANDREA, LOOK. THAT GUY OKAY?
EUGENE? I DON'T KNOW. SURE DOESN'T LOOK LIKE IT.
HE'S BEEN LIKE THAT FOR A COUPLE DAYS...
I REALLY SHOULDN'T... BUT... HIS GIRLFRIEND WAS PREGNANT, HADN'T TOLD HIM YET.
ISN'T THAT USUALLY GOOD NEWS?
HE'S EITHER MAD SHE WAITED SO LONG TO TELL HIM... OR HE'S JUST WORRIED ABOUT RAISING A KID IN THIS WORLD.
WHAT'S WRONG WITH THIS WORLD? LOOK AT ME. I'M SWEATING AND IT'S NOT BECAUSE I'M RUNNING FROM DEAD PEOPLE.
YOUR WORLD IS GREAT.
NOT REALLY HOW EUGENE THINKS... HE'S USUALLY TEN STEPS AHEAD... NOW I'M MAKING MYSELF WORRY.
LET'S DROP IT.
DROPPED.

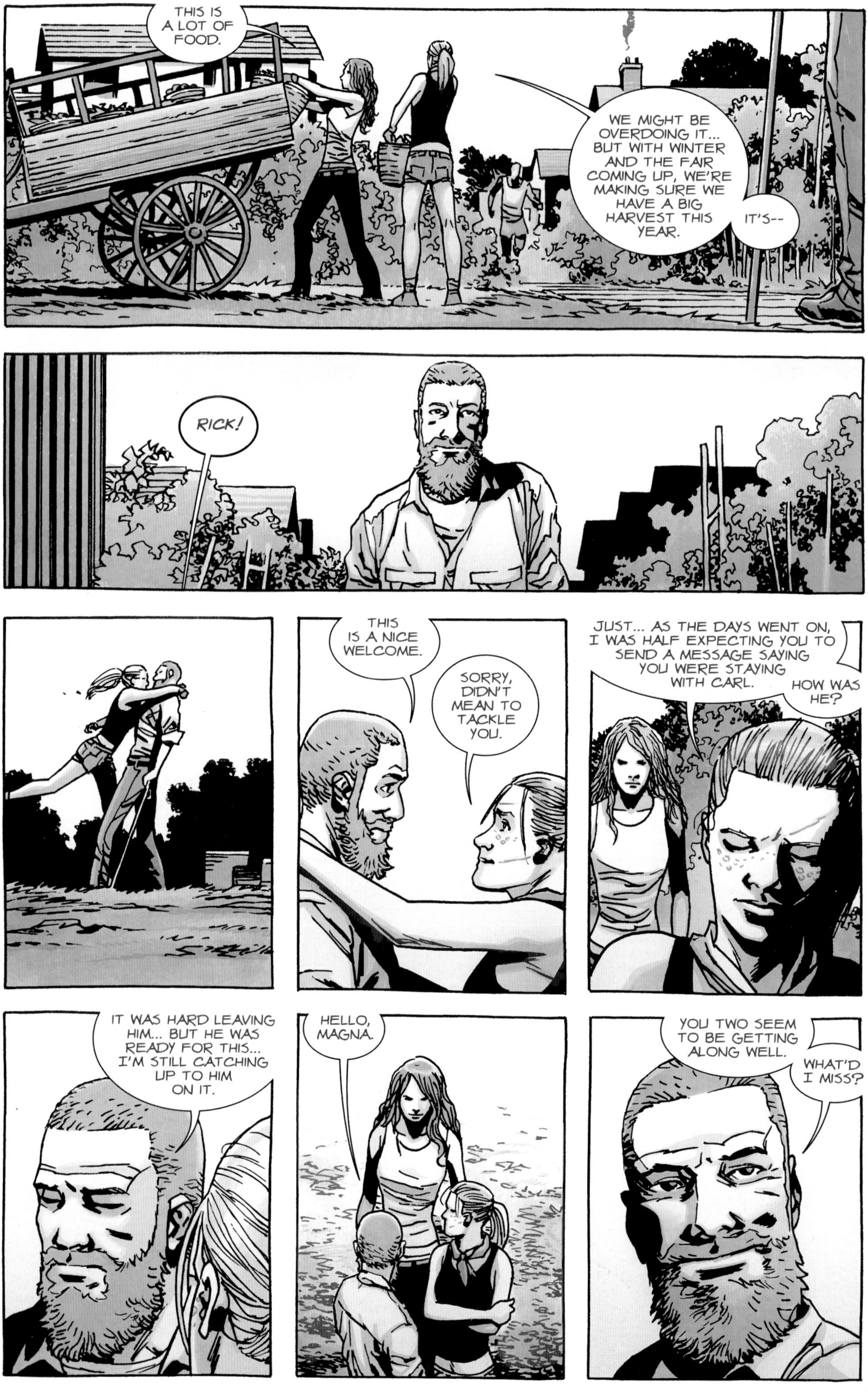

THIS IS A LOT OF FOOD.
WE MIGHT BE OVERDOING IT... BUT WITH WINTER AND THE FAIR COMING UP, WE'RE MAKING SURE WE HAVE A BIG HARVEST THIS YEAR.
IT'S--
RICK!
THIS IS A NICE WELCOME.
SORRY, DIDN'T MEAN TO TACKLE YOU.
JUST... AS THE DAYS WENT ON, I WAS HALF EXPECTING YOU TO SEND A MESSAGE SAYING YOU WERE STAYING WITH CARL.
HOW WAS HE?
IT WAS HARD LEAVING HIM... BUT HE WAS READY FOR THIS... I'M STILL CATCHING UP TO HIM ON IT.
HELLO, MAGNA.
YOU TWO SEEM TO BE GETTING ALONG WELL.
WHAT'D I MISS?

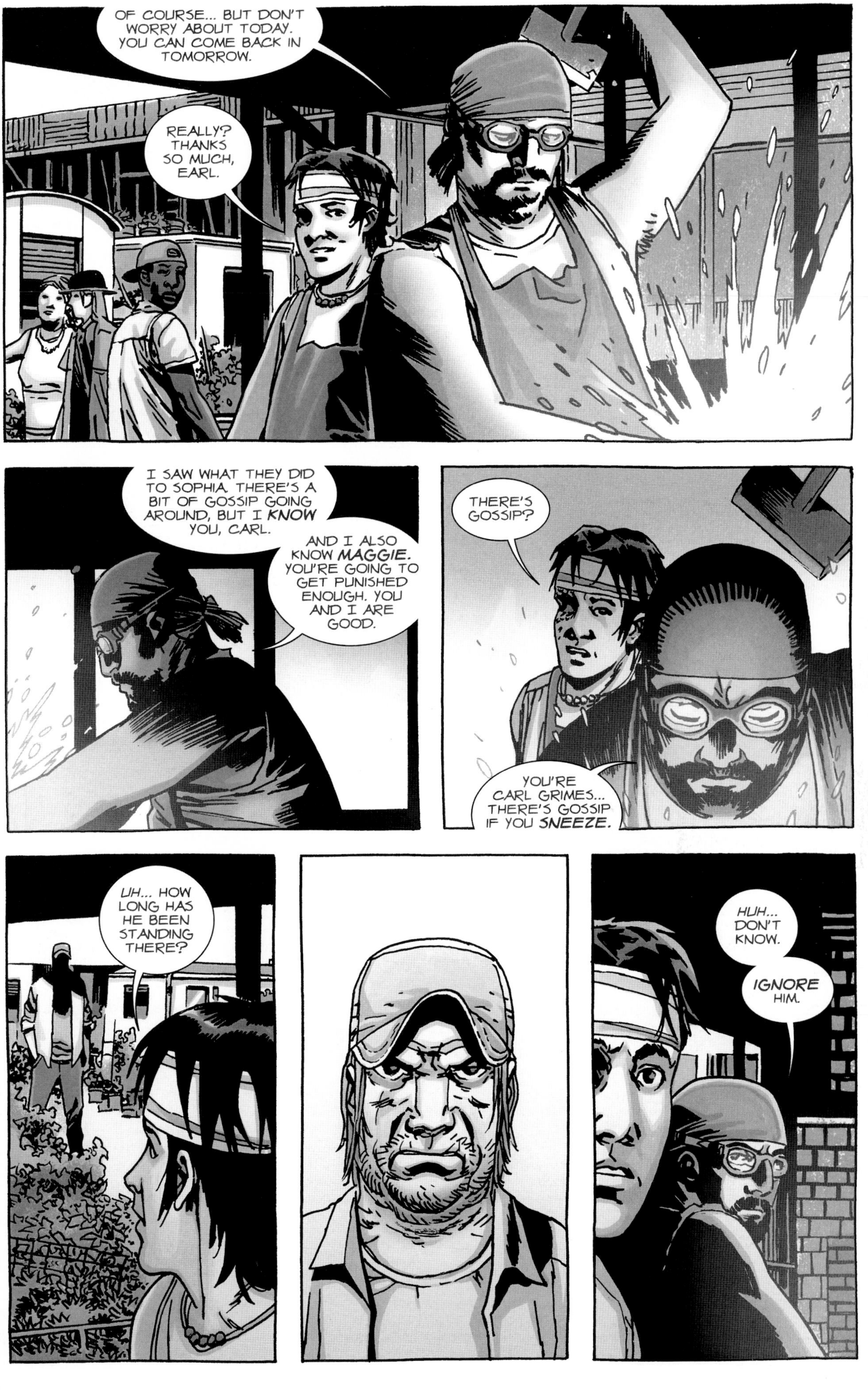
OF COURSE... BUT DON'T WORRY ABOUT TODAY. YOU CAN COME BACK IN TOMORROW.
REALLY? THANKS SO MUCH, EARL.
I SAW WHAT THEY DID TO SOPHIA. THERE'S A BIT OF GOSSIP GOING AROUND, BUT I KNOW YOU, CARL.
AND I ALSO KNOW MAGGIE. YOU'RE GOING TO GET PUNISHED ENOUGH. YOU AND I ARE GOOD.
THERE'S GOSSIP?
YOU'RE CARL GRIMES... THERE'S GOSSIP IF YOU SNEEZE.
UH... HOW LONG HAS HE BEEN STANDING THERE?
HUH... DON'T KNOW.
IGNORE HIM.

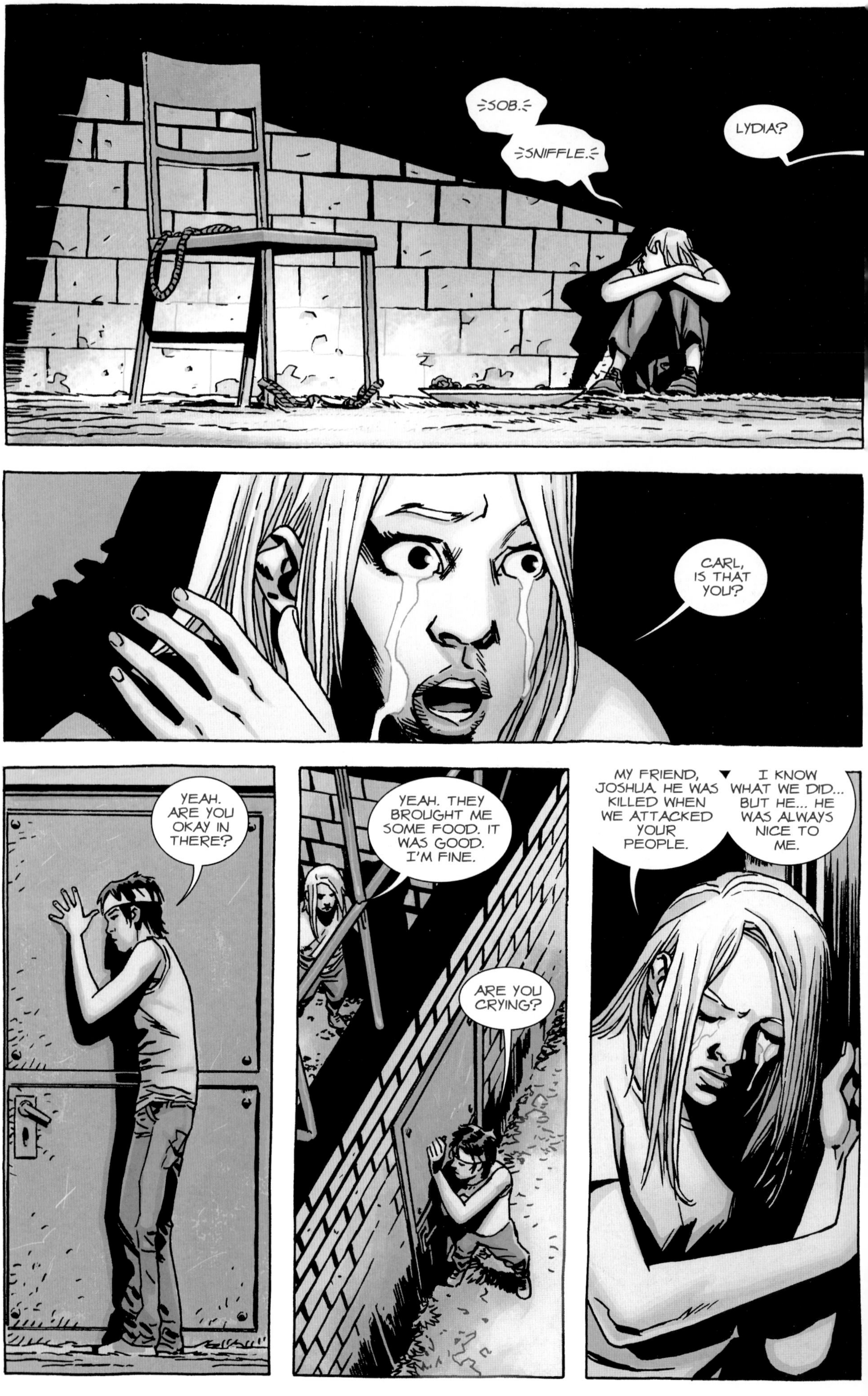
SOB.
SNIFFLE.
LYDIA?
CARL, IS THAT YOU?
YEAH. ARE YOU OKAY IN THERE?
YEAH. THEY BROUGHT ME SOME FOOD. IT WAS GOOD. I'M FINE.
ARE YOU CRYING?
MY FRIEND, JOSHUA. HE WAS KILLED WHEN WE ATTACKED YOUR PEOPLE.
I KNOW WHAT WE DID... BUT HE... HE WAS ALWAYS NICE TO ME.

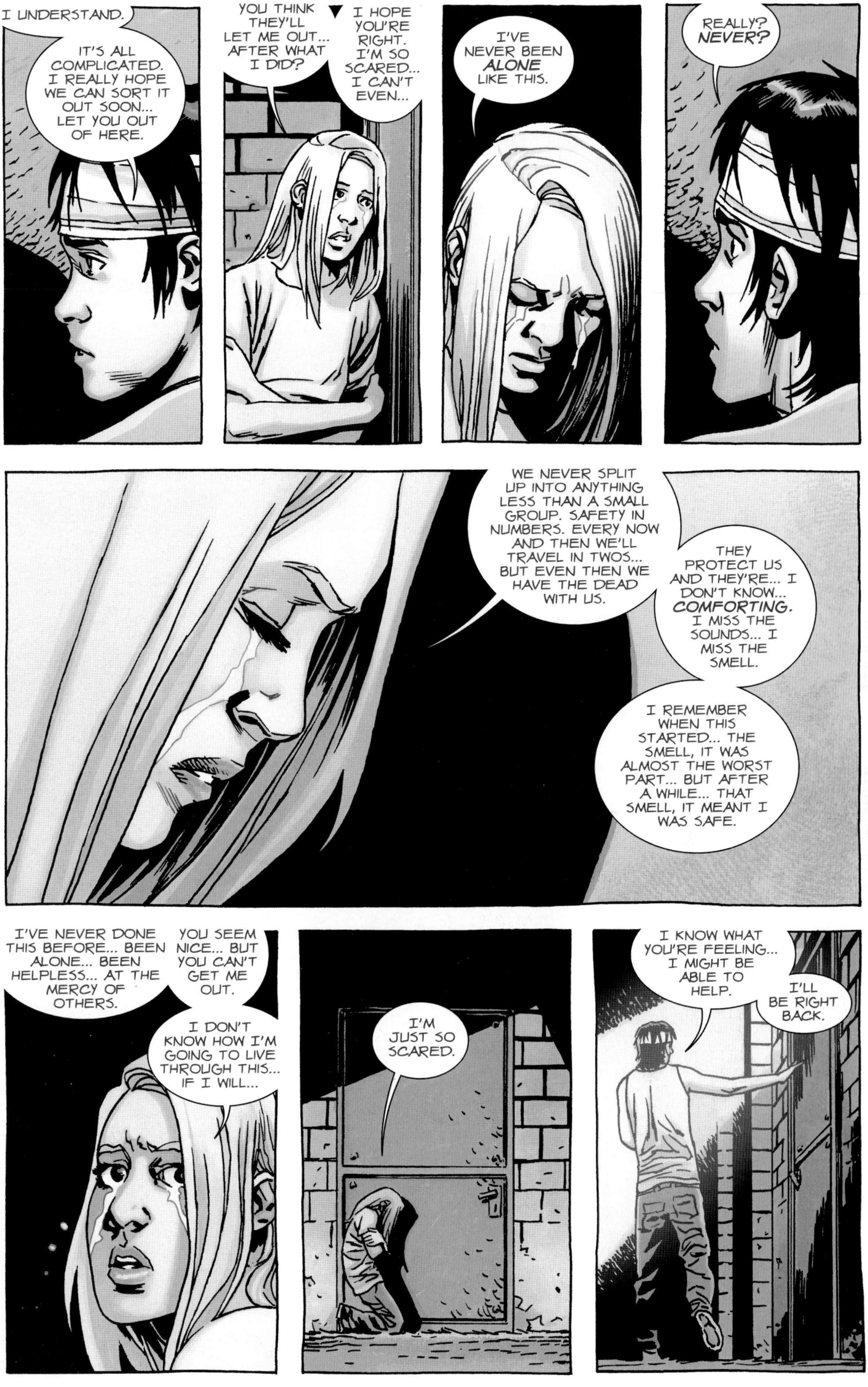
I UNDERSTAND.
IT'S ALL COMPLICATED. I REALLY HOPE WE CAN SORT IT OUT SOON... LET YOU OUT OF HERE.
YOU THINK THEY'LL LET ME OUT... AFTER WHAT I DID?
I HOPE YOU'RE RIGHT. I'M SO SCARED... I CAN'T EVEN...
I'VE NEVER BEEN ALONE LIKE THIS.
REALLY? NEVER?
WE NEVER SPLIT UP INTO ANYTHING LESS THAN A SMALL GROUP. SAFETY IN NUMBERS. EVERY NOW AND THEN WE'LL TRAVEL IN TWOS... BUT EVEN THEN WE HAVE THE DEAD WITH US.
THEY PROTECT US AND THEY'RE... I DON'T KNOW... COMFORTING. I MISS THE SOUNDS... I MISS THE SMELL.
I REMEMBER WHEN THIS STARTED... THE SMELL, IT WAS ALMOST THE WORST PART... BUT AFTER A WHILE... THAT SMELL, IT MEANT I WAS SAFE.
I'VE NEVER DONE THIS BEFORE... BEEN ALONE... BEEN HELPLESS... AT THE MERCY OF OTHERS.
YOU SEEM NICE... BUT YOU CAN'T GET ME OUT.
I DON'T KNOW HOW I'M GOING TO LIVE THROUGH THIS... IF I WILL...
I'M JUST SO SCARED.
I KNOW WHAT YOU'RE FEELING... I MIGHT BE ABLE TO HELP.
I'LL BE RIGHT BACK.

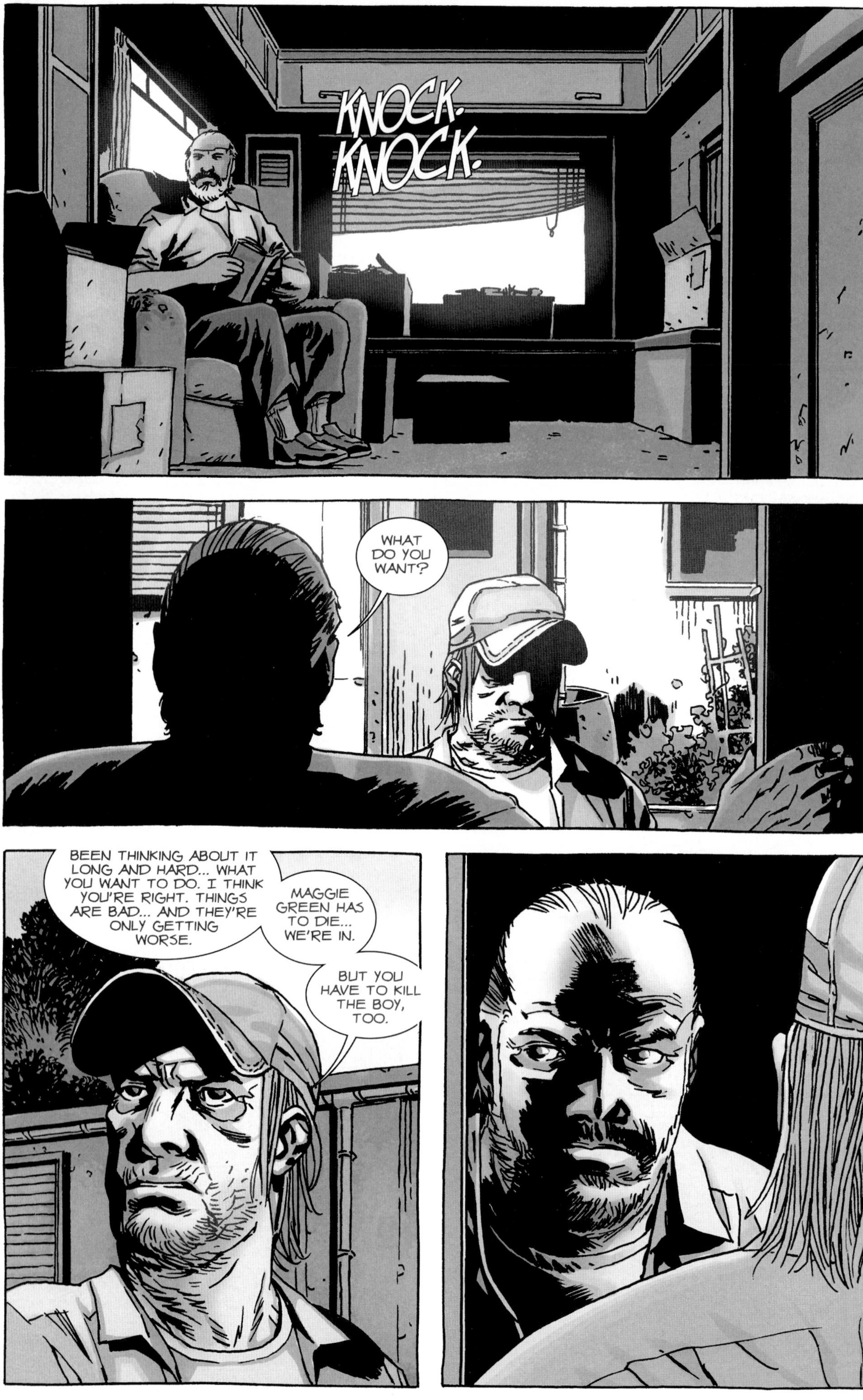
KNOCK. KNOCK.
WHAT DO YOU WANT?
BEEN THINKING ABOUT IT LONG AND HARD... WHAT YOU WANT TO DO. I THINK YOU'RE RIGHT. THINGS ARE BAD... AND THEY'RE ONLY GETTING WORSE.
MAGGIE GREEN HAS TO DIE... WE'RE IN.
BUT YOU HAVE TO KILL THE BOY, TOO.

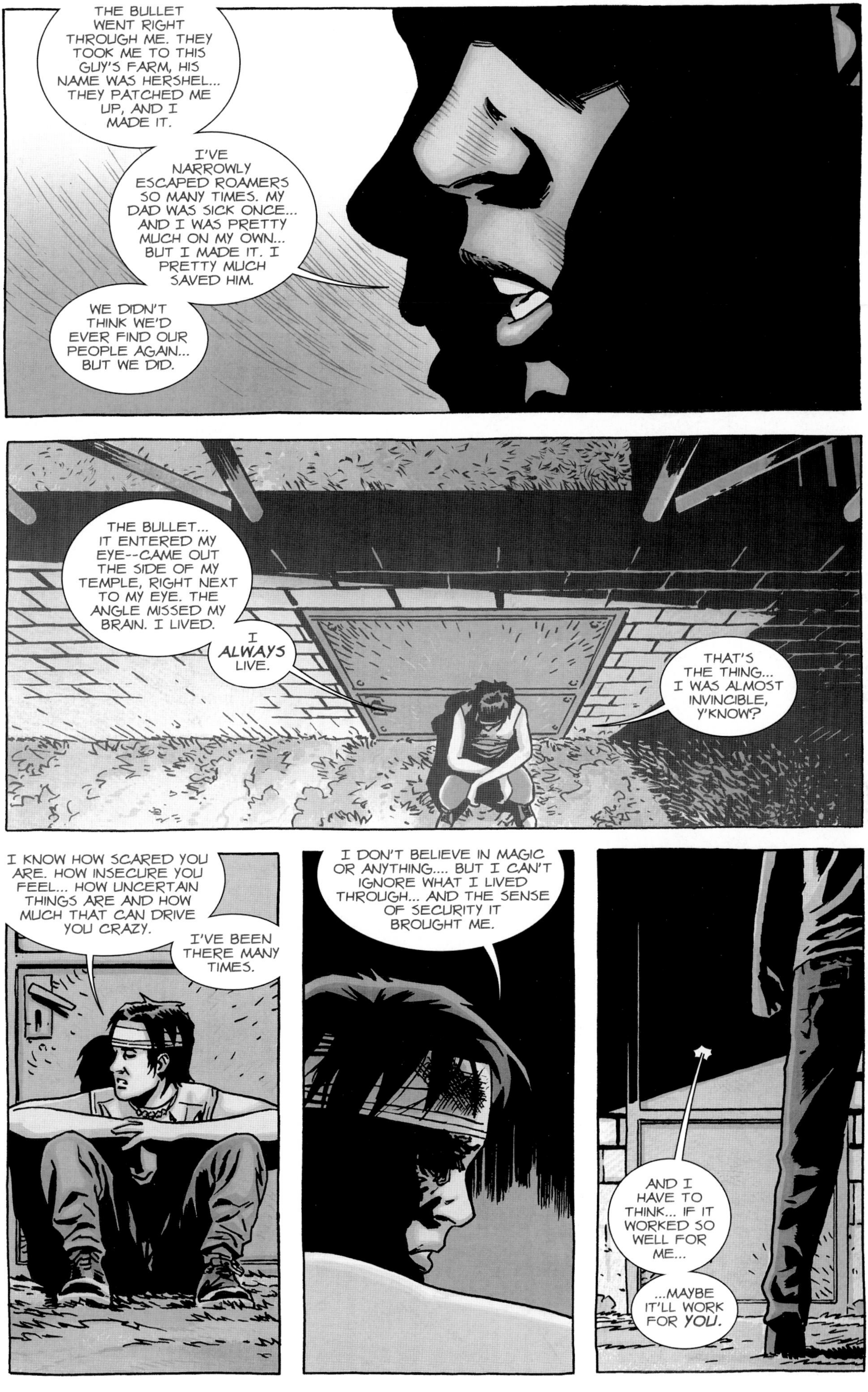
THE BULLET WENT RIGHT THROUGH ME. THEY TOOK ME TO THIS GUY'S FARM, HIS NAME WAS HERSHEL... THEY PATCHED ME UP, AND I MADE IT.
I'VE NARROWLY ESCAPED ROAMERS SO MANY TIMES. MY DAD WAS SICK ONCE... AND I WAS PRETTY MUCH ON MY OWN... BUT I MADE IT. I PRETTY MUCH SAVED HIM.
WE DIDN'T THINK WE'D EVER FIND OUR PEOPLE AGAIN... BUT WE DID.
THE BULLET... IT ENTERED MY EYE--CAME OUT THE SIDE OF MY TEMPLE, RIGHT NEXT TO MY EYE. THE ANGLE MISSED MY BRAIN. I LIVED.
I ALWAYS LIVE.
THAT'S THE THING... I WAS ALMOST INVINCIBLE, Y'KNOW?
I KNOW HOW SCARED YOU ARE. HOW INSECURE YOU FEEL... HOW UNCERTAIN THINGS ARE AND HOW MUCH THAT CAN DRIVE YOU CRAZY.
I'VE BEEN THERE MANY TIMES.
I DON'T BELIEVE IN MAGIC OR ANYTHING.... BUT I CAN'T IGNORE WHAT I LIVED THROUGH... AND THE SENSE OF SECURITY IT BROUGHT ME.
AND I HAVE TO THINK... IF IT WORKED SO WELL FOR ME...
...MAYBE IT'LL WORK FOR YOU.

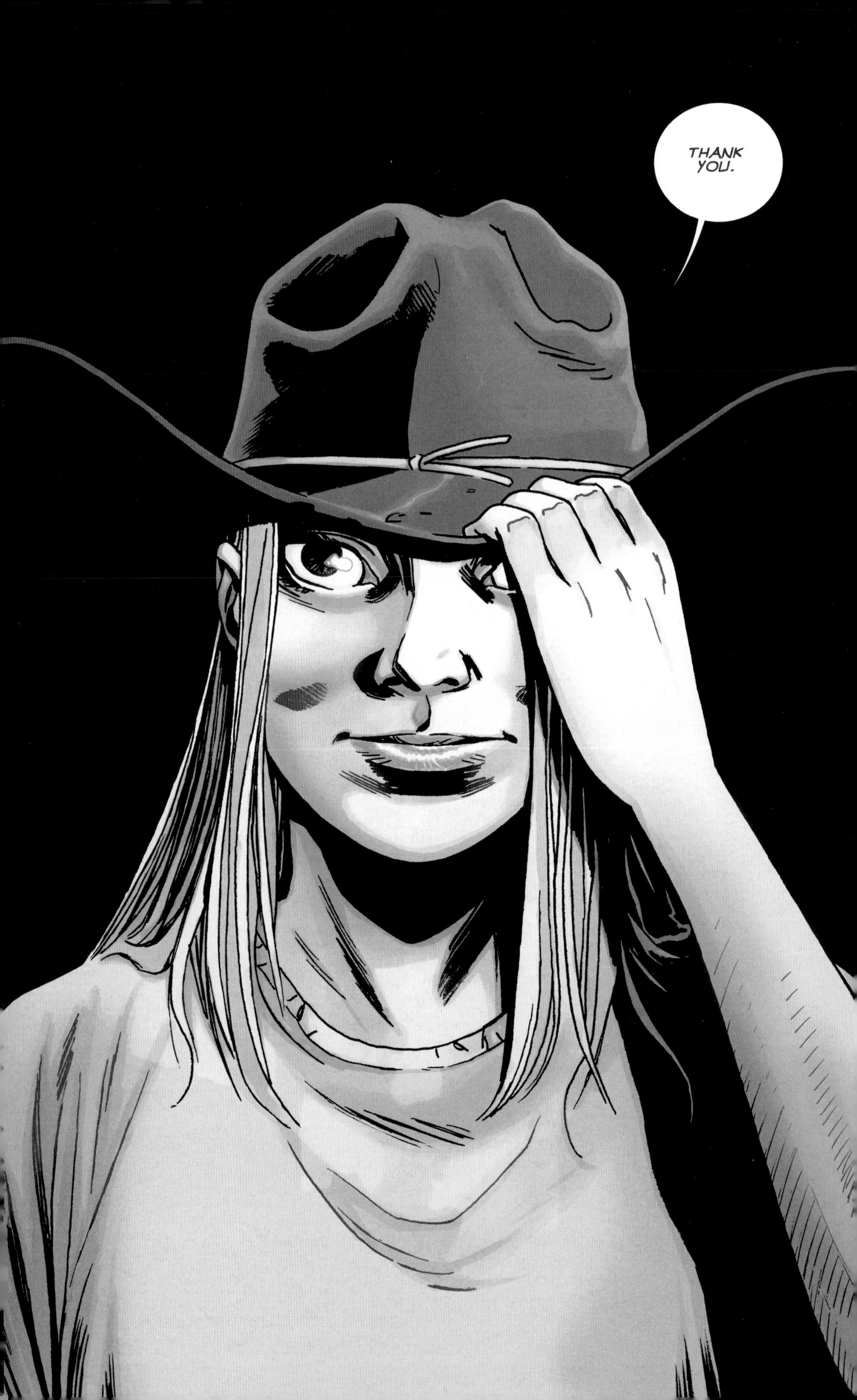
THANK YOU.

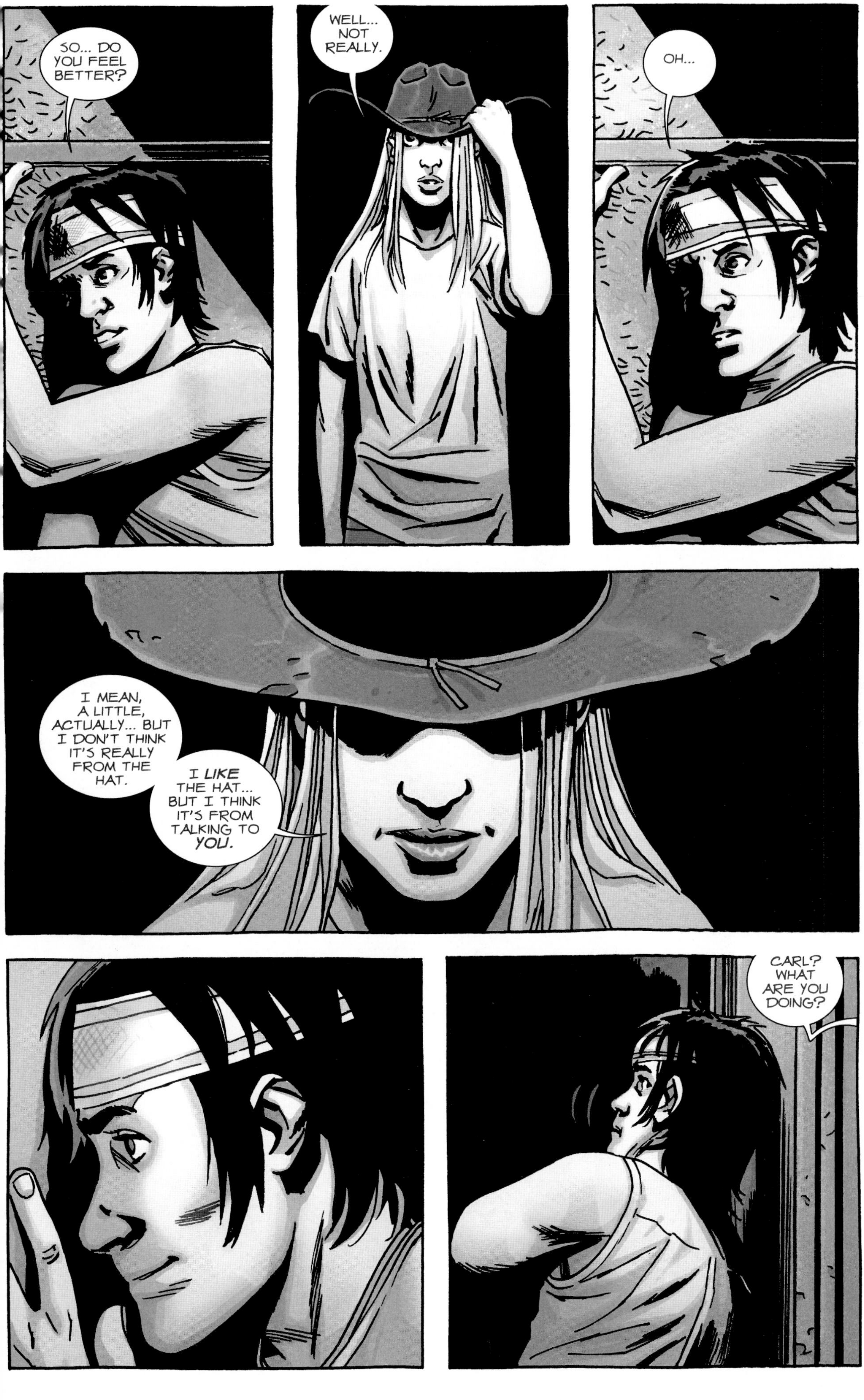
SO... DO YOU FEEL BETTER?
WELL... NOT REALLY.
OH...
I MEAN, A LITTLE, ACTUALLY... BUT I DON'T THINK IT'S REALLY FROM THE HAT.
I *LIKE* THE HAT... BUT I THINK IT'S FROM TALKING TO *YOU*.
CARL? WHAT ARE YOU DOING?

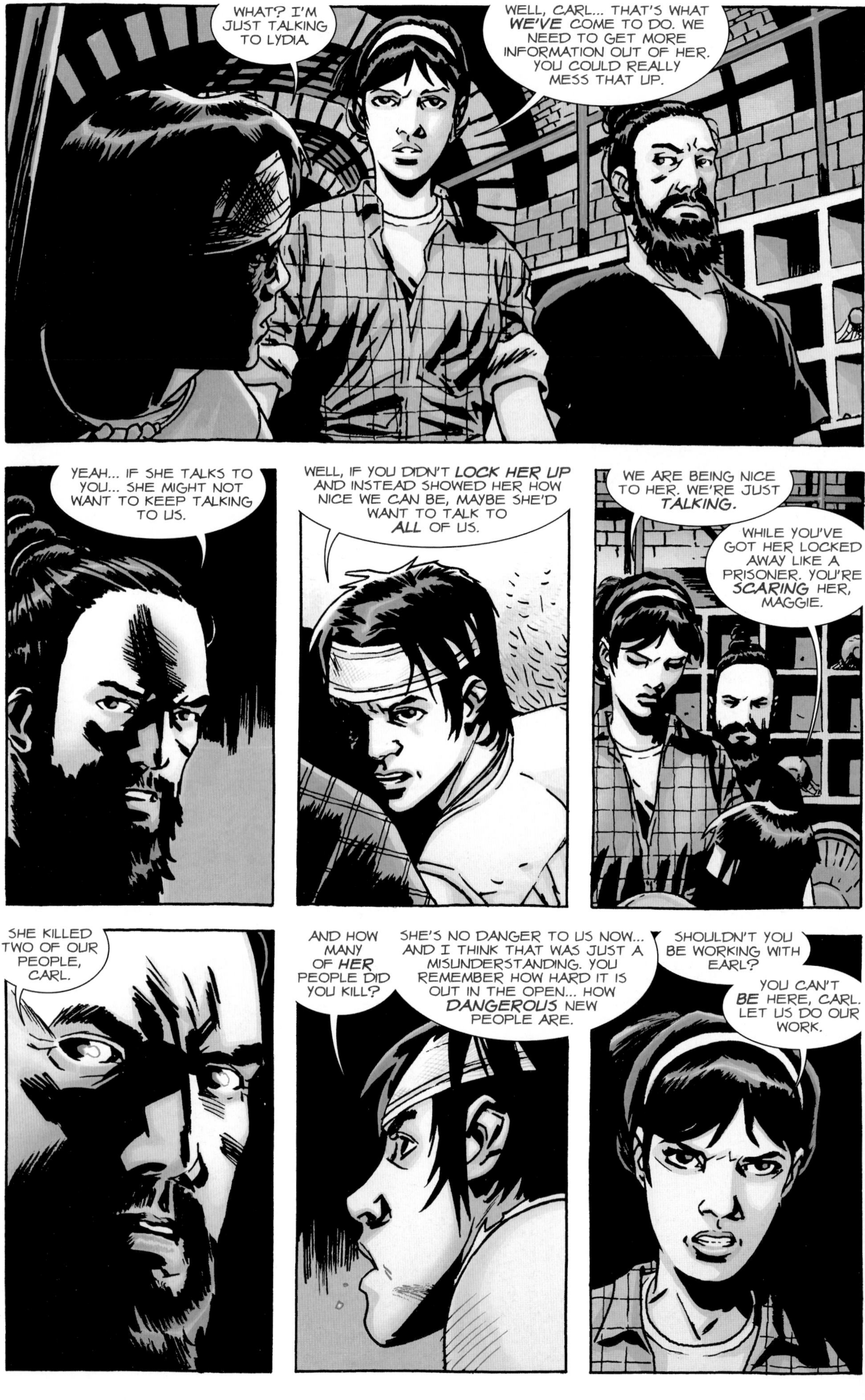
WHAT? I'M JUST TALKING TO LYDIA.
WELL, CARL... THAT'S WHAT *WE'VE* COME TO DO. WE NEED TO GET MORE INFORMATION OUT OF HER. YOU COULD REALLY MESS THAT UP.
YEAH... IF SHE TALKS TO YOU... SHE MIGHT NOT WANT TO KEEP TALKING TO US.
WELL, IF YOU DIDN'T *LOCK HER UP* AND INSTEAD SHOWED HER HOW NICE WE CAN BE, MAYBE SHE'D WANT TO TALK TO *ALL* OF US.
WE ARE BEING NICE TO HER. WE'RE JUST *TALKING.*
WHILE YOU'VE GOT HER LOCKED AWAY LIKE A PRISONER. YOU'RE *SCARING* HER, MAGGIE.
SHE KILLED TWO OF OUR PEOPLE, CARL.
AND HOW MANY OF *HER* PEOPLE DID YOU KILL?
SHE'S NO DANGER TO US NOW... AND I THINK THAT WAS JUST A MISUNDERSTANDING. YOU REMEMBER HOW HARD IT IS OUT IN THE OPEN... HOW *DANGEROUS* NEW PEOPLE ARE.
SHOULDN'T YOU BE WORKING WITH EARL?
YOU CAN'T *BE* HERE, CARL. LET US DO OUR WORK.

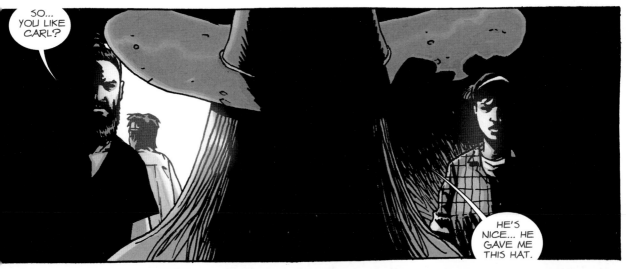

SO...
YOU LIKE
CARL?

HE'S
NICE... HE
GAVE ME
THIS HAT.

HE DID, DID HE?
THAT WAS REALLY
NICE OF HIM.

WHAT ARE
YOU GOING
TO ASK
ME?

WHO IS
THE LEADER OF
YOUR GROUP?

I DON'T
WANT TO
TALK TO YOU
ANYMORE.

WELL,
THAT'S
JUST--

MAGGIE?

WHAT
IS IT,
ALEX?

IT'S THE
BOYS... YOU
WANTED ME
TO MAKE SURE
YOU KNEW FIRST
WHEN THEY
WOKE UP.

WHERE IS SHE?!

WHERE IS THAT FUCKING BITCH?!

SHE'S RIGHT HERE.

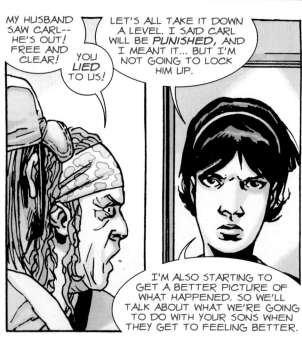

MY HUSBAND SAW CARL-- HE'S OUT! FREE AND CLEAR!

YOU LIED TO US!

LET'S ALL TAKE IT DOWN A LEVEL. I SAID CARL WILL BE PUNISHED, AND I MEANT IT... BUT I'M NOT GOING TO LOCK HIM UP.

I'M ALSO STARTING TO GET A BETTER PICTURE OF WHAT HAPPENED. SO WE'LL TALK ABOUT WHAT WE'RE GOING TO DO WITH YOUR SONS WHEN THEY GET TO FEELING BETTER.

WHAT THE HELL DOES THAT MEAN?

ARE YOU FUCKING JOKING? IS THAT A JOKE?! YOU CAN'T FUCKING BE SERIOUS!

I HONESTLY THINK IT'S TIME TO START DISCUSSING RELOCATION.

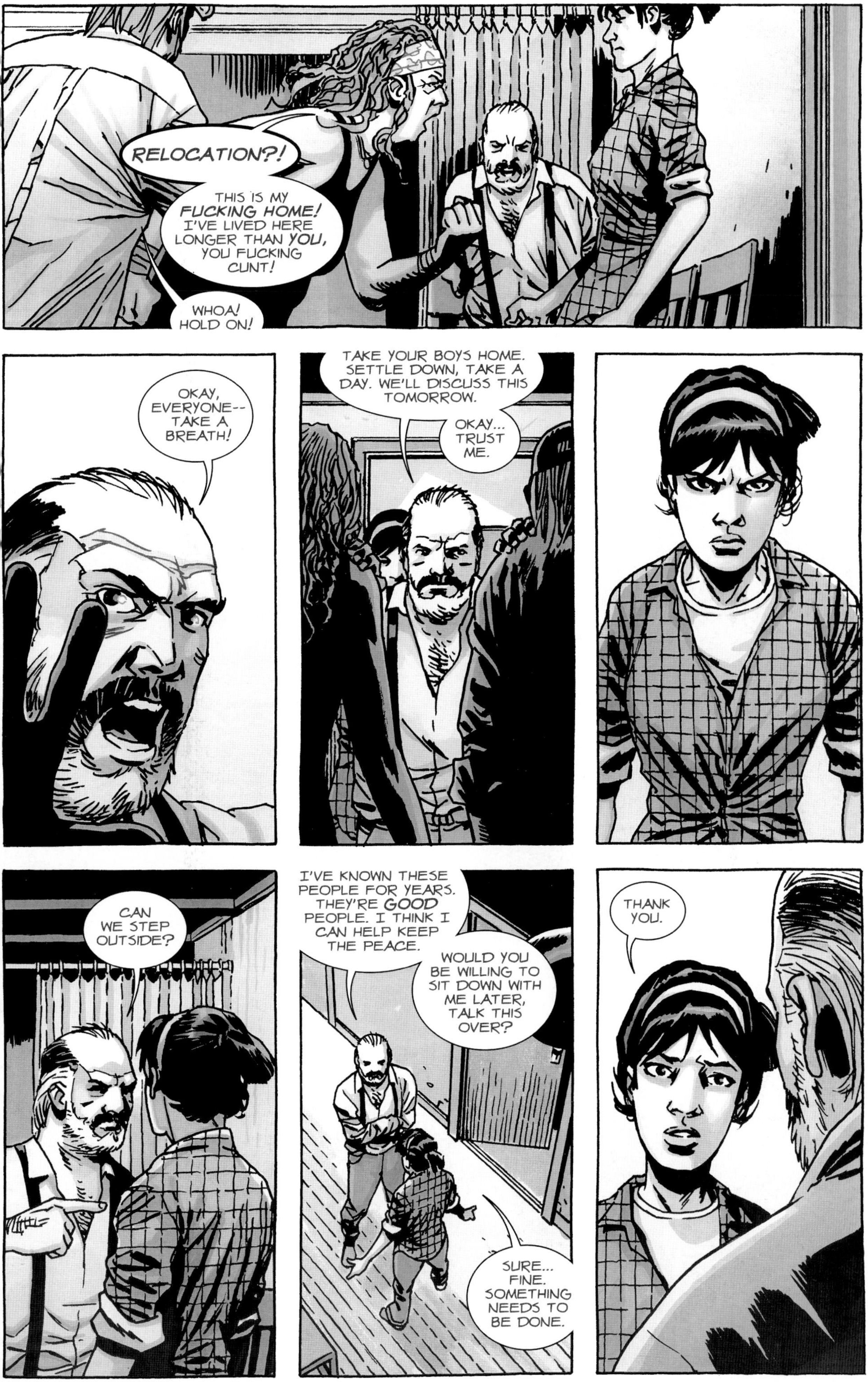
RELOCATION?!
THIS IS MY FUCKING HOME! I'VE LIVED HERE LONGER THAN YOU, YOU FUCKING CUNT!
WHOA! HOLD ON!
OKAY, EVERYONE-- TAKE A BREATH!
TAKE YOUR BOYS HOME. SETTLE DOWN, TAKE A DAY. WE'LL DISCUSS THIS TOMORROW.
OKAY... TRUST ME.
CAN WE STEP OUTSIDE?
I'VE KNOWN THESE PEOPLE FOR YEARS. THEY'RE GOOD PEOPLE. I THINK I CAN HELP KEEP THE PEACE.
WOULD YOU BE WILLING TO SIT DOWN WITH ME LATER, TALK THIS OVER?
SURE... FINE. SOMETHING NEEDS TO BE DONE.
THANK YOU.

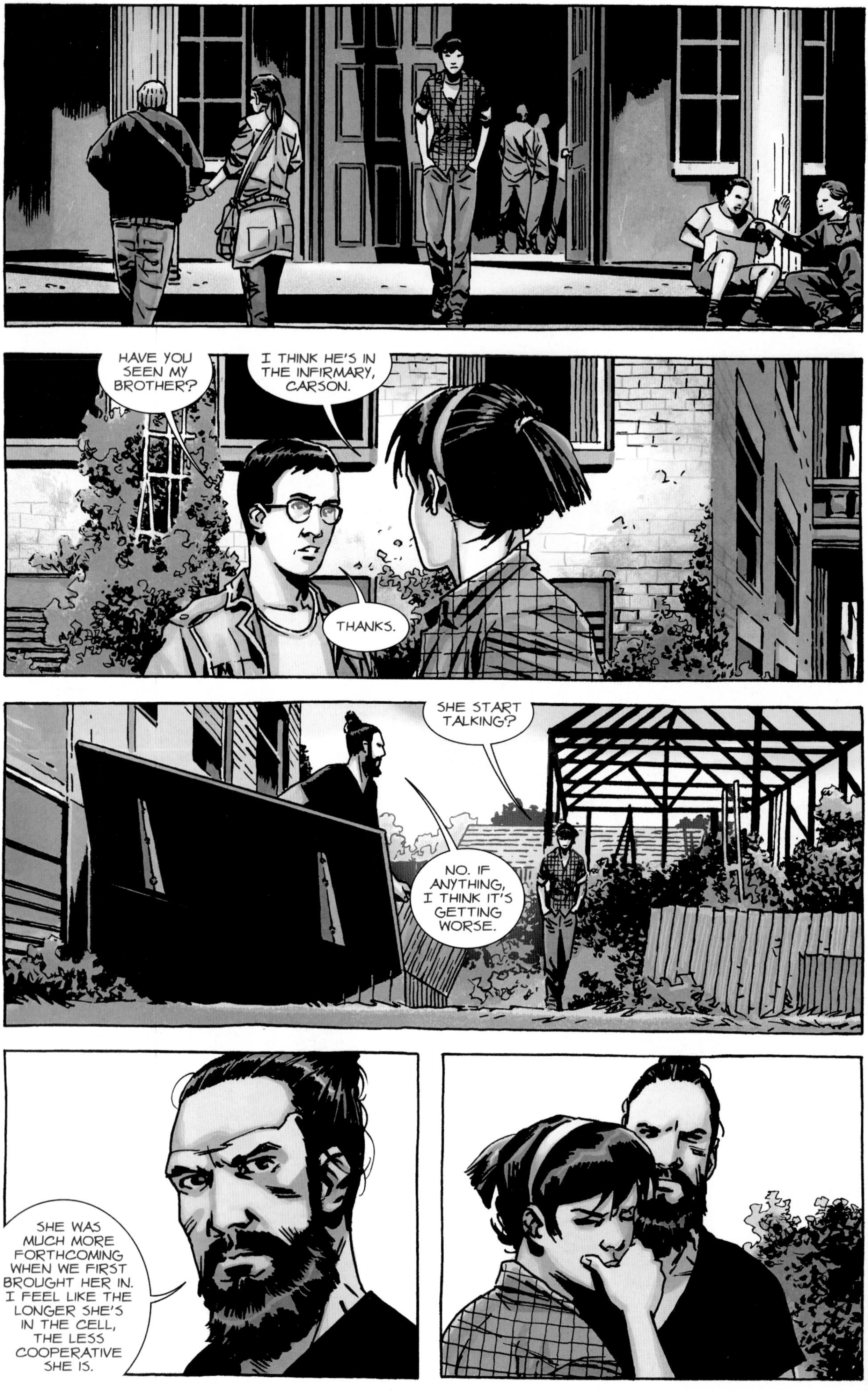
HAVE YOU SEEN MY BROTHER?
I THINK HE'S IN THE INFIRMARY, CARSON.
THANKS.
SHE START TALKING?
NO. IF ANYTHING, I THINK IT'S GETTING WORSE.
SHE WAS MUCH MORE FORTHCOMING WHEN WE FIRST BROUGHT HER IN. I FEEL LIKE THE LONGER SHE'S IN THE CELL, THE LESS COOPERATIVE SHE IS.

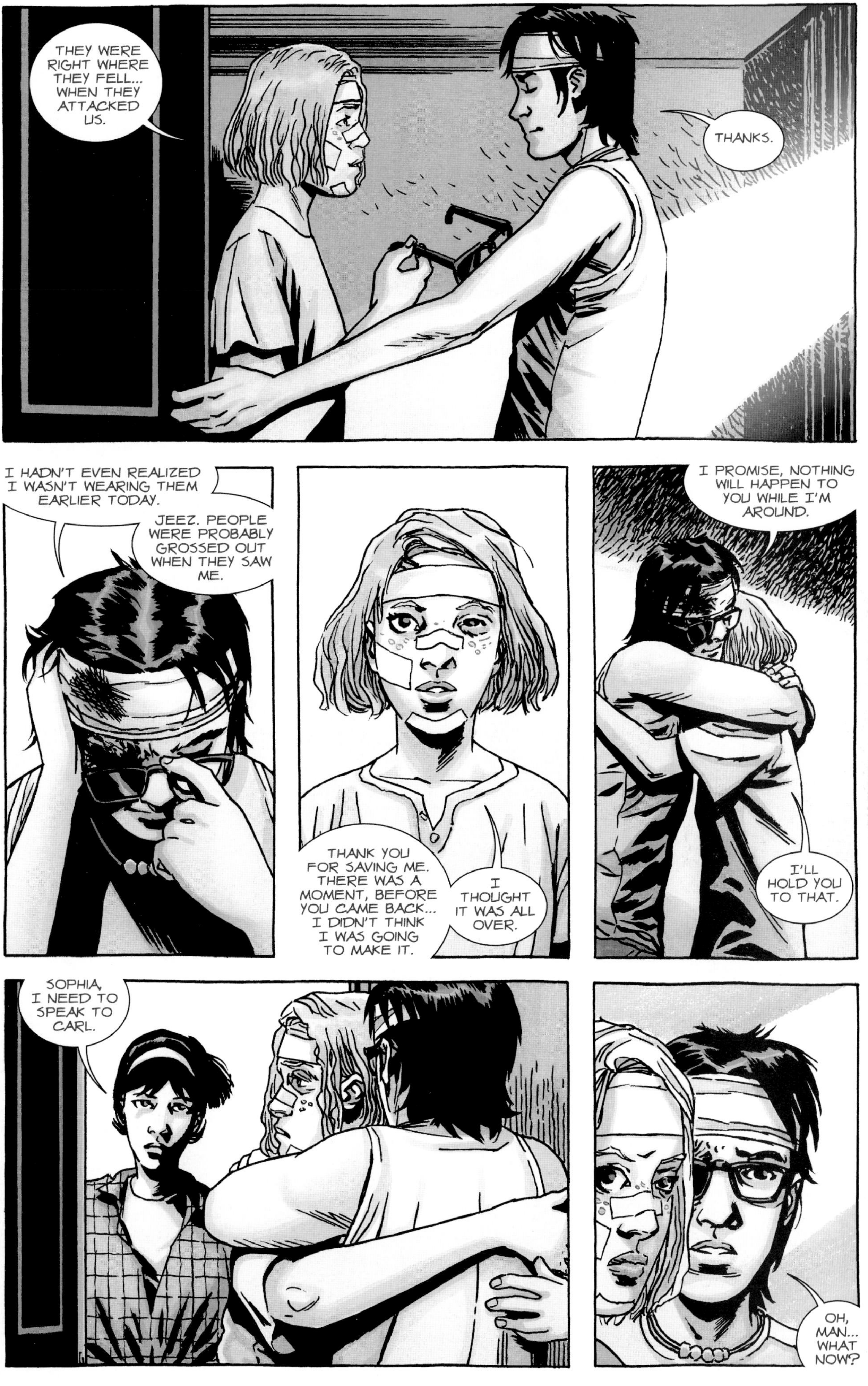
THEY WERE RIGHT WHERE THEY FELL... WHEN THEY ATTACKED US.
THANKS.
I HADN'T EVEN REALIZED I WASN'T WEARING THEM EARLIER TODAY.
JEEZ. PEOPLE WERE PROBABLY GROSSED OUT WHEN THEY SAW ME.
THANK YOU FOR SAVING ME. THERE WAS A MOMENT, BEFORE YOU CAME BACK... I DIDN'T THINK I WAS GOING TO MAKE IT.
I THOUGHT IT WAS ALL OVER.
I PROMISE, NOTHING WILL HAPPEN TO YOU WHILE I'M AROUND.
I'LL HOLD YOU TO THAT.
SOPHIA, I NEED TO SPEAK TO CARL.
OH, MAN... WHAT NOW?

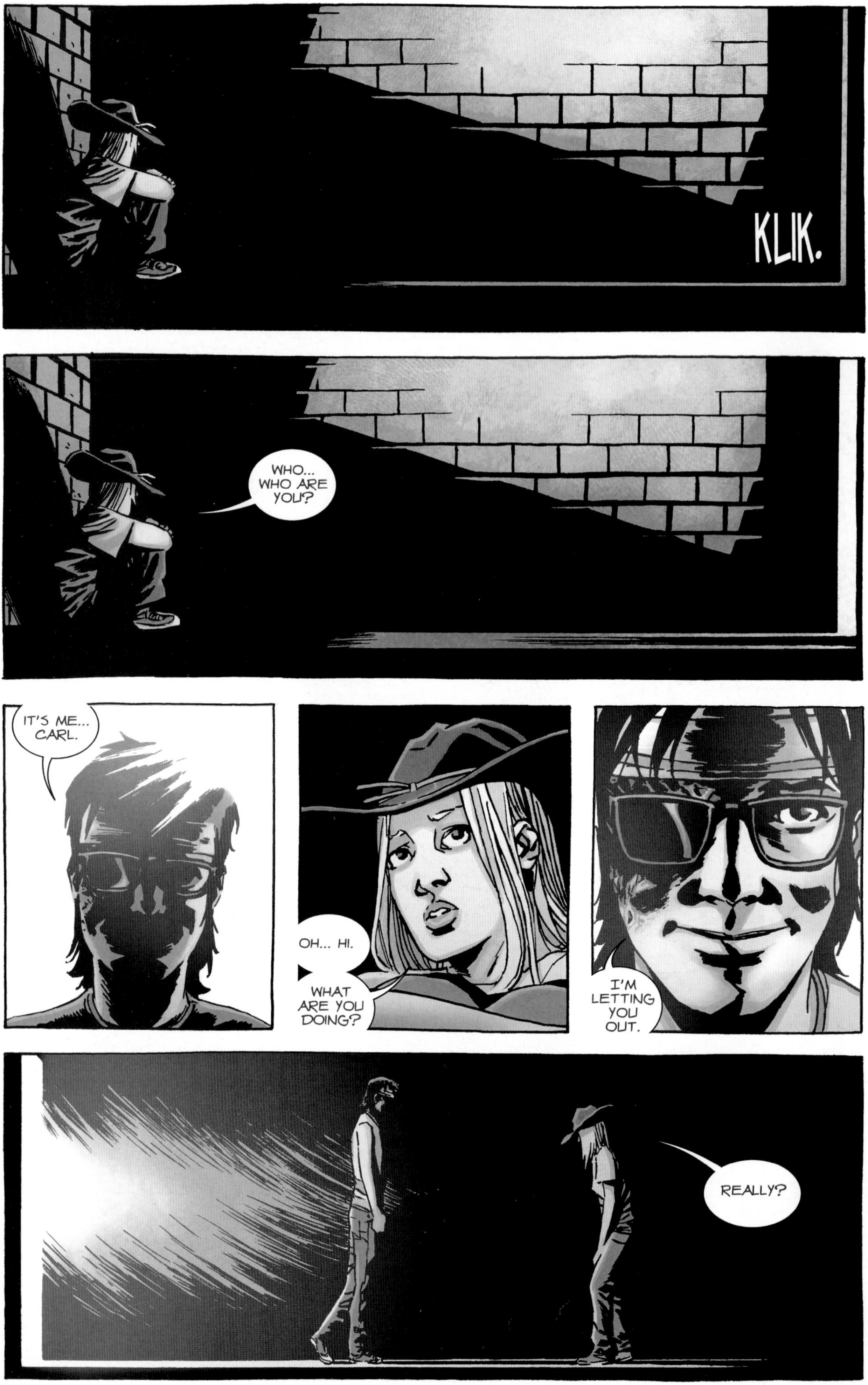
KLIK.
WHO... WHO ARE YOU?
IT'S ME... CARL.
OH... HI.
WHAT ARE YOU DOING?
I'M LETTING YOU OUT.
REALLY?

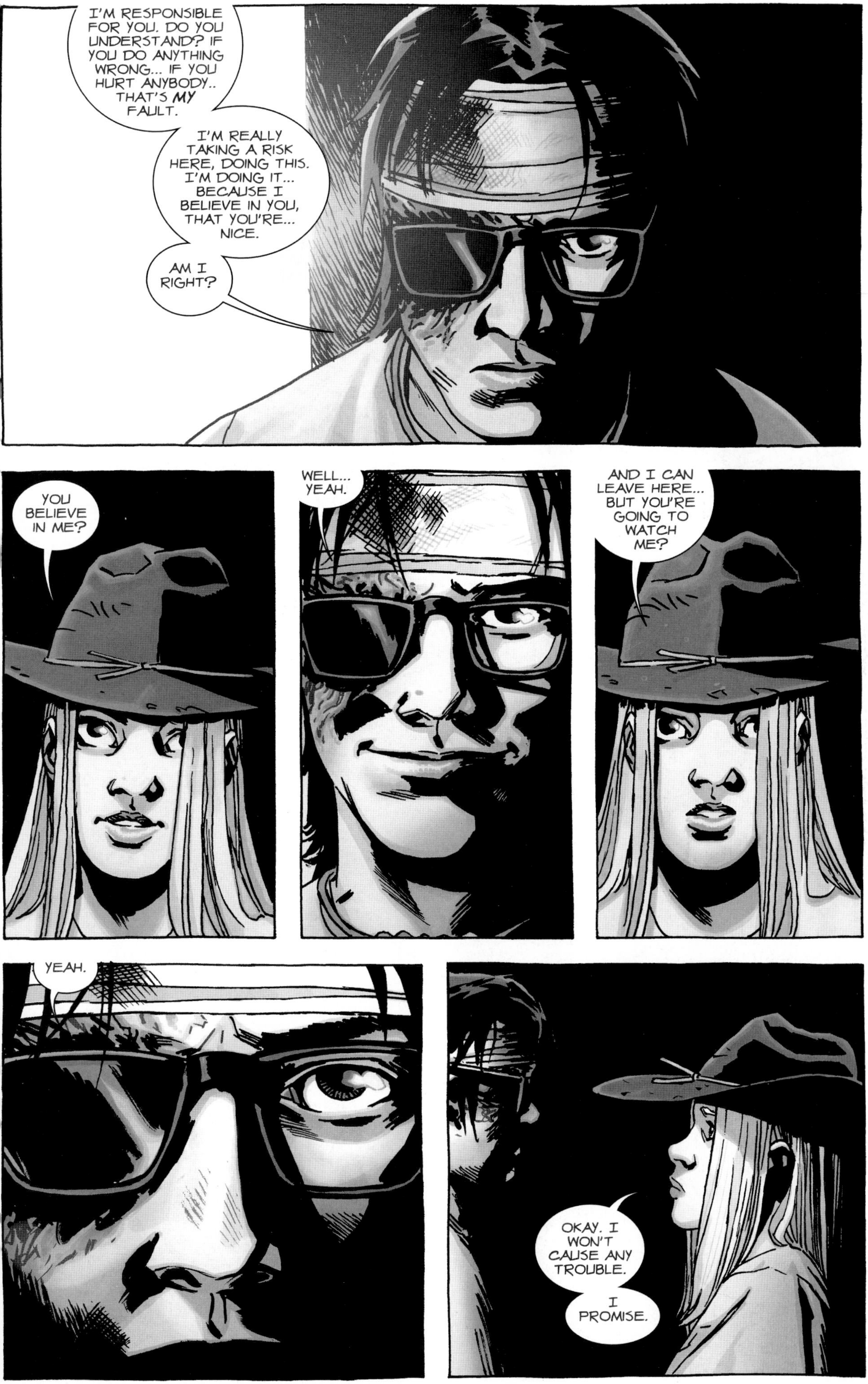
I'M RESPONSIBLE FOR YOU. DO YOU UNDERSTAND? IF YOU DO ANYTHING WRONG... IF YOU HURT ANYBODY.. THAT'S MY FAULT.
I'M REALLY TAKING A RISK HERE, DOING THIS. I'M DOING IT... BECAUSE I BELIEVE IN YOU, THAT YOU'RE... NICE.
AM I RIGHT?
YOU BELIEVE IN ME?
WELL... YEAH.
AND I CAN LEAVE HERE... BUT YOU'RE GOING TO WATCH ME?
YEAH.
OKAY. I WON'T CAUSE ANY TROUBLE.
I PROMISE.

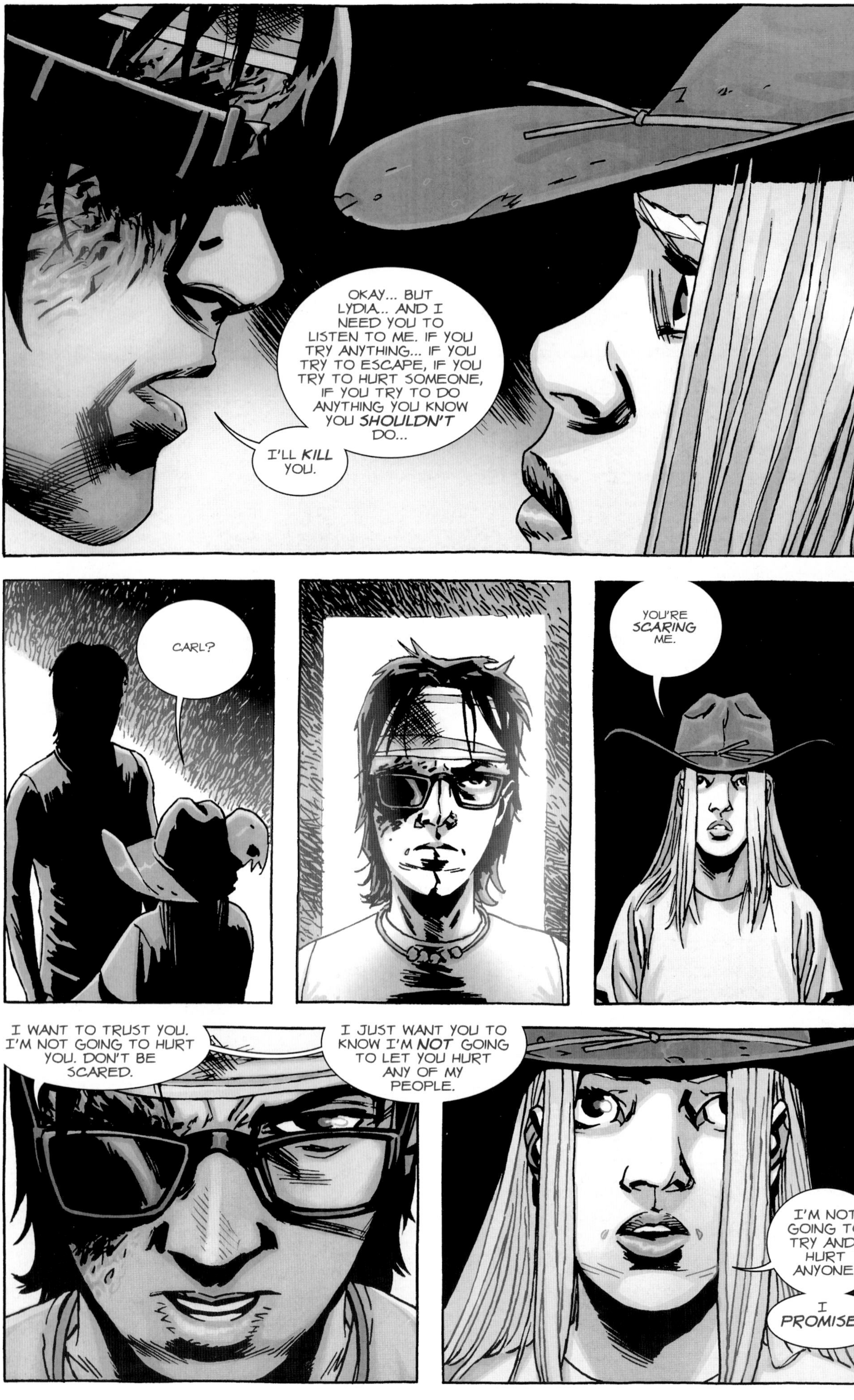
OKAY... BUT LYDIA.. AND I NEED YOU TO LISTEN TO ME. IF YOU TRY ANYTHING... IF YOU TRY TO ESCAPE, IF YOU TRY TO HURT SOMEONE, IF YOU TRY TO DO ANYTHING YOU KNOW YOU *SHOULDN'T* DO...
I'LL *KILL* YOU.
CARL?
YOU'RE *SCARING* ME.
I WANT TO TRUST YOU. I'M NOT GOING TO HURT YOU. DON'T BE SCARED.
I JUST WANT YOU TO KNOW I'M *NOT* GOING TO LET YOU HURT ANY OF MY PEOPLE.
I'M NOT GOING TO TRY AND HURT ANYONE.
I *PROMISE.*

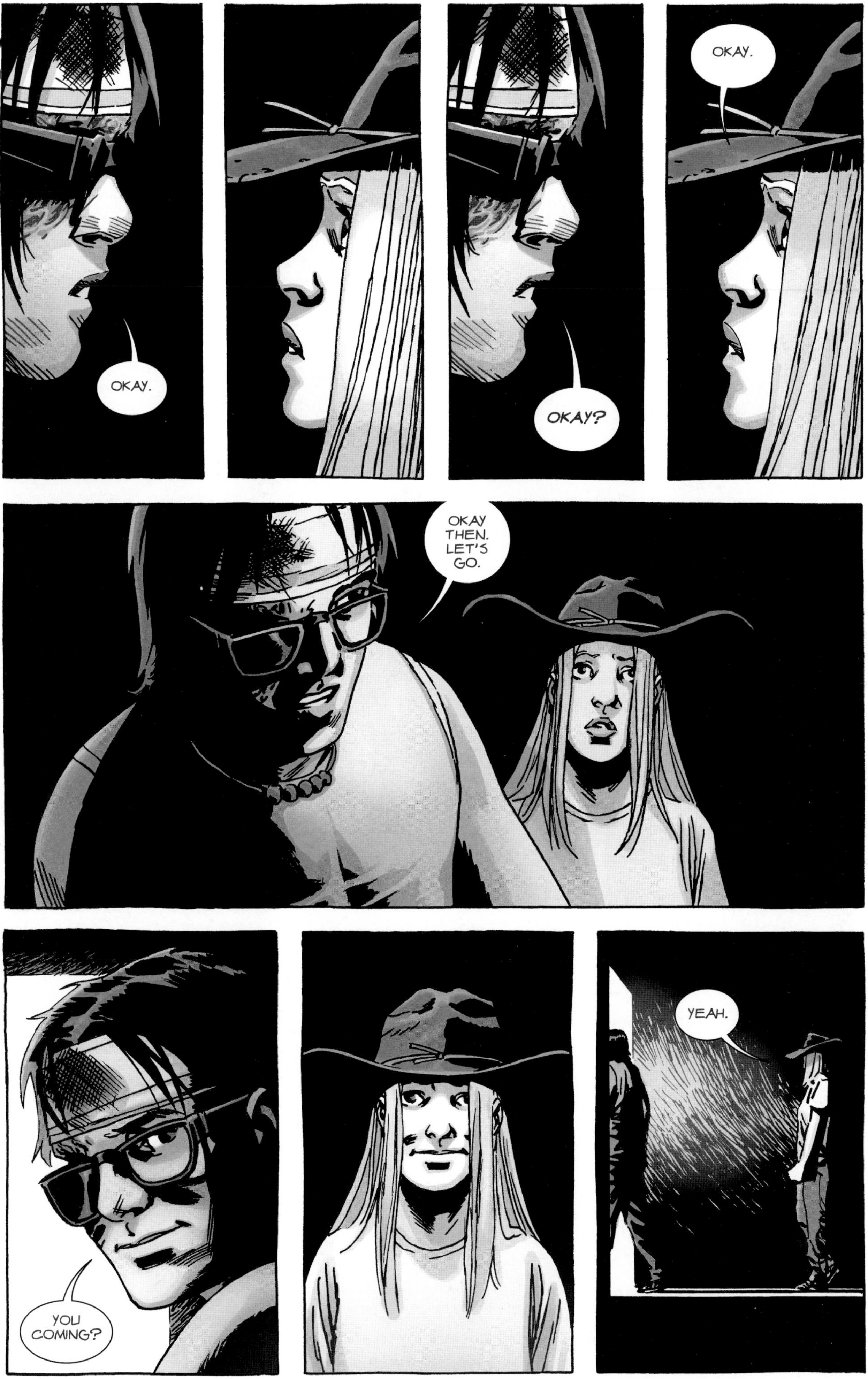
OKAY.
OKAY?
OKAY.
OKAY THEN. LET'S GO.
YOU COMING?
YEAH.

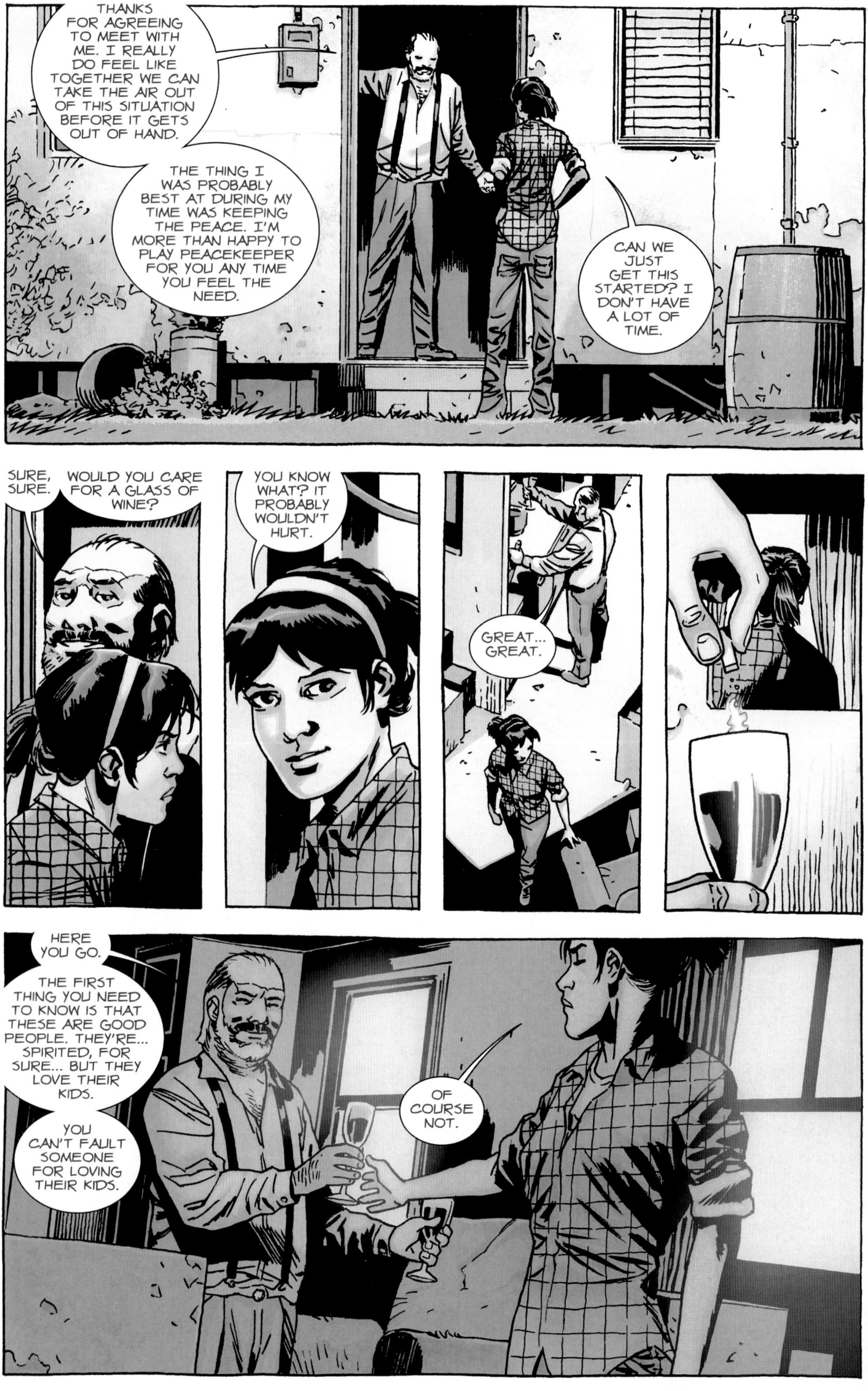
THANKS FOR AGREEING TO MEET WITH ME. I REALLY DO FEEL LIKE TOGETHER WE CAN TAKE THE AIR OUT OF THIS SITUATION BEFORE IT GETS OUT OF HAND.
THE THING I WAS PROBABLY BEST AT DURING MY TIME WAS KEEPING THE PEACE. I'M MORE THAN HAPPY TO PLAY PEACEKEEPER FOR YOU ANY TIME YOU FEEL THE NEED.
CAN WE JUST GET THIS STARTED? I DON'T HAVE A LOT OF TIME.
SURE, SURE.
WOULD YOU CARE FOR A GLASS OF WINE?
YOU KNOW WHAT? IT PROBABLY WOULDN'T HURT.
GREAT... GREAT.
HERE YOU GO.
THE FIRST THING YOU NEED TO KNOW IS THAT THESE ARE GOOD PEOPLE. THEY'RE... SPIRITED, FOR SURE... BUT THEY LOVE THEIR KIDS.
YOU CAN'T FAULT SOMEONE FOR LOVING THEIR KIDS.
OF COURSE NOT.

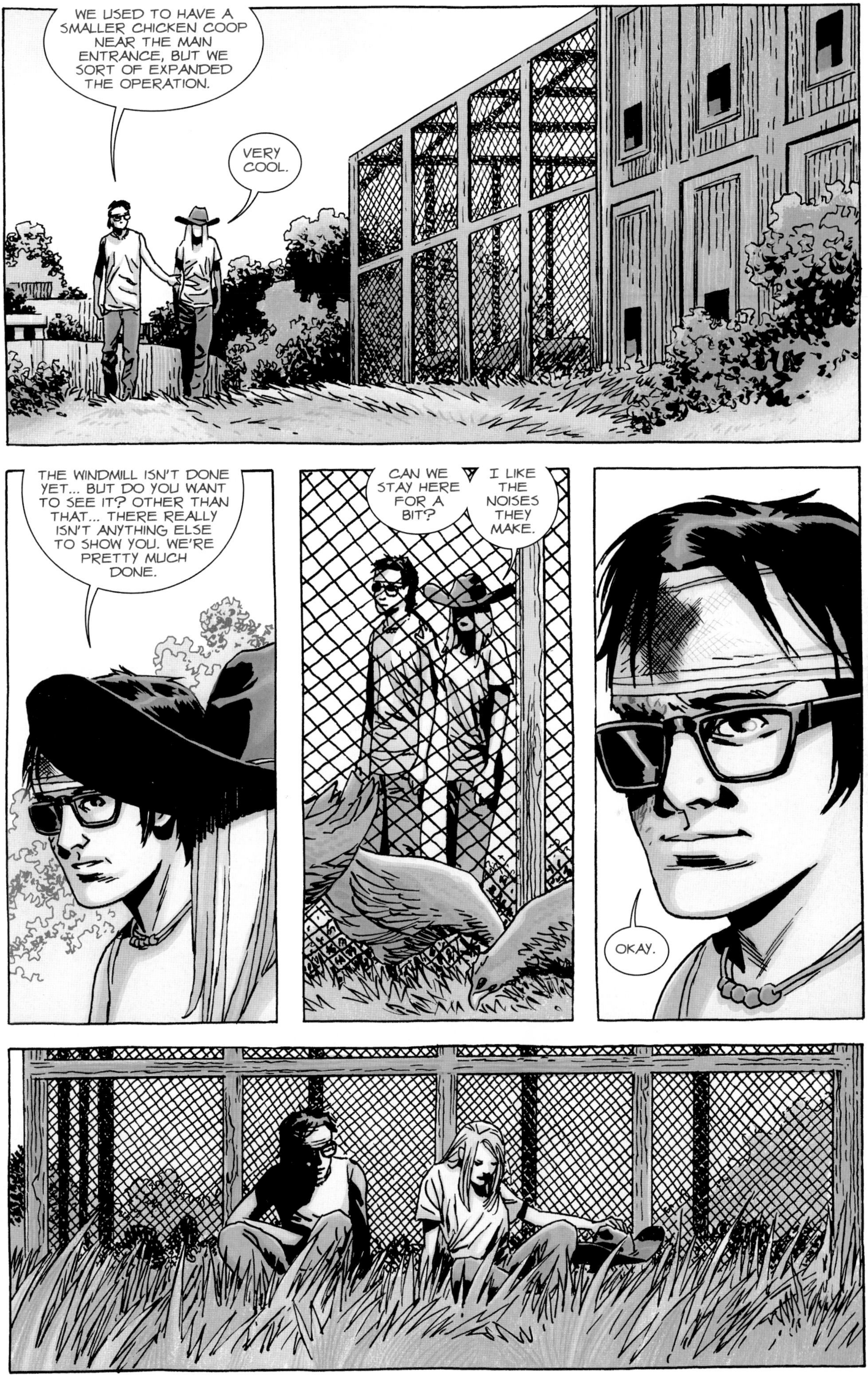
WE USED TO HAVE A SMALLER CHICKEN COOP NEAR THE MAIN ENTRANCE, BUT WE SORT OF EXPANDED THE OPERATION.
VERY COOL.
THE WINDMILL ISN'T DONE YET... BUT DO YOU WANT TO SEE IT? OTHER THAN THAT... THERE REALLY ISN'T ANYTHING ELSE TO SHOW YOU. WE'RE PRETTY MUCH DONE.
CAN WE STAY HERE FOR A BIT?
I LIKE THE NOISES THEY MAKE.
OKAY.

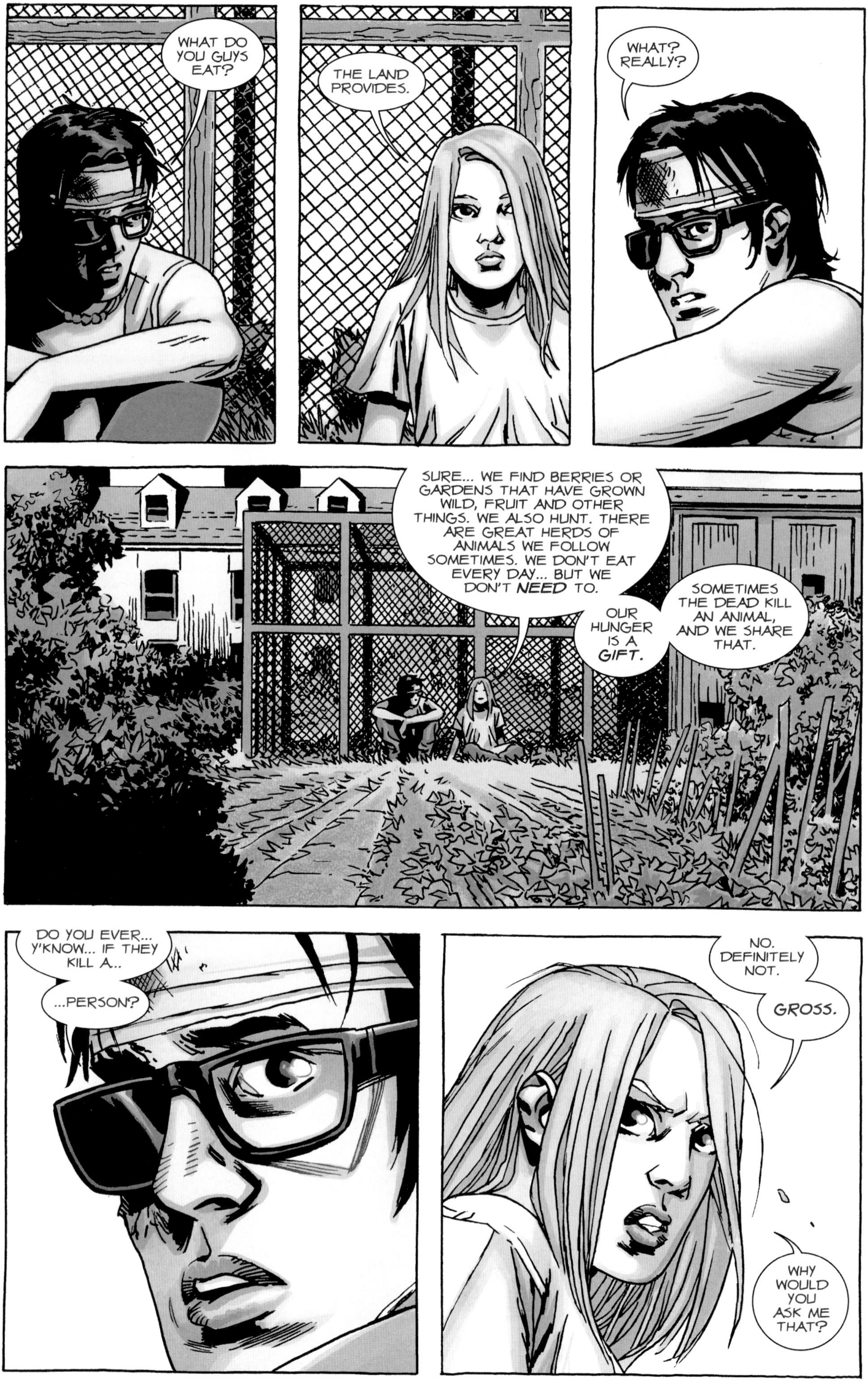

WHAT DO YOU GUYS EAT?
THE LAND PROVIDES.
WHAT? REALLY?
SURE... WE FIND BERRIES OR GARDENS THAT HAVE GROWN WILD, FRUIT AND OTHER THINGS. WE ALSO HUNT. THERE ARE GREAT HERDS OF ANIMALS WE FOLLOW SOMETIMES. WE DON'T EAT EVERY DAY... BUT WE DON'T NEED TO.
OUR HUNGER IS A GIFT.
SOMETIMES THE DEAD KILL AN ANIMAL, AND WE SHARE THAT.
DO YOU EVER... Y'KNOW... IF THEY KILL A...
...PERSON?
NO. DEFINITELY NOT.
GROSS.
WHY WOULD YOU ASK ME THAT?

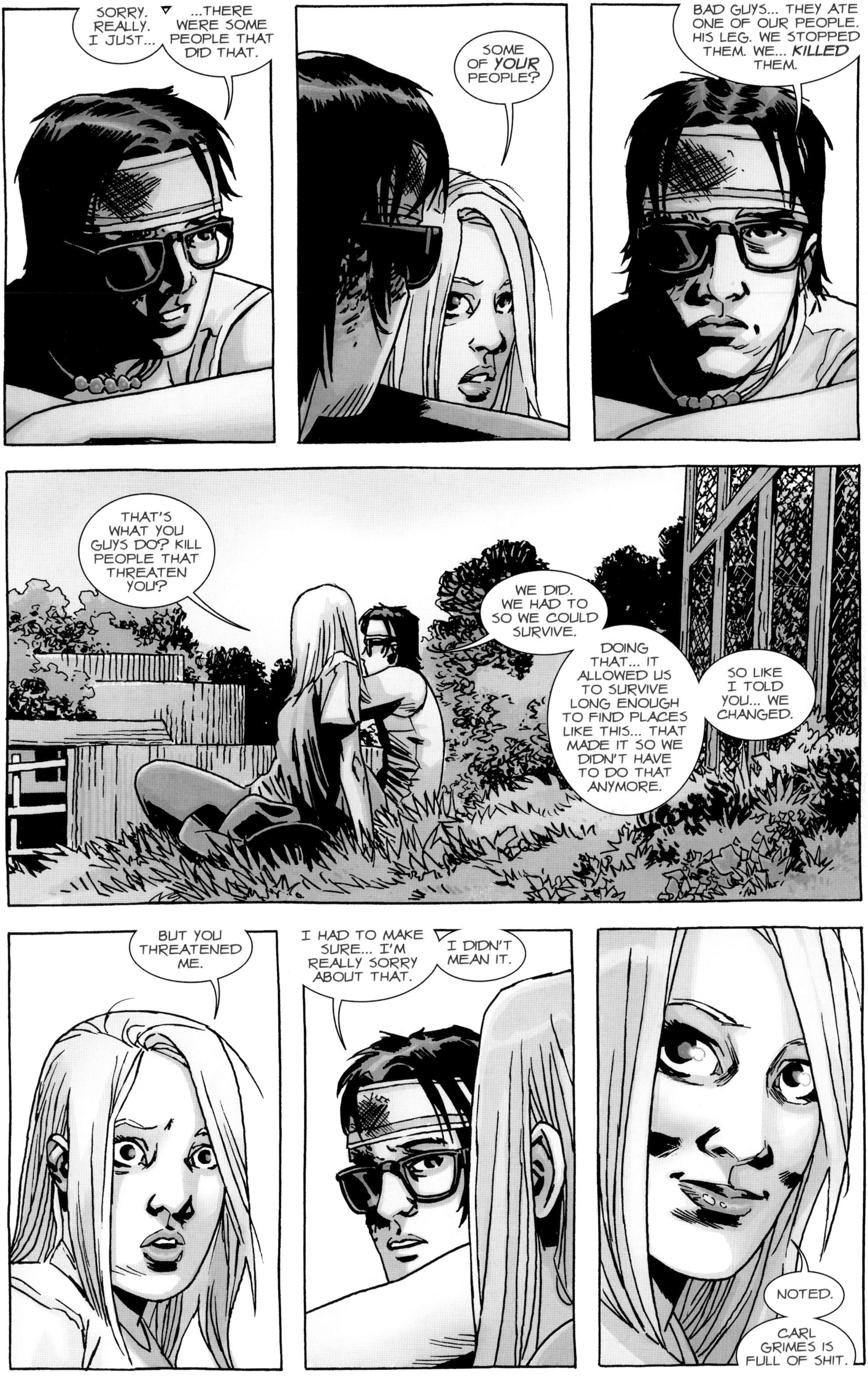
SORRY. REALLY. I JUST...
...THERE WERE SOME PEOPLE THAT DID THAT.
SOME OF YOUR PEOPLE?
BAD GUYS... THEY ATE ONE OF OUR PEOPLE. HIS LEG. WE STOPPED THEM. WE... KILLED THEM.
THAT'S WHAT YOU GUYS DO? KILL PEOPLE THAT THREATEN YOU?
WE DID. WE HAD TO SO WE COULD SURVIVE.
DOING THAT... IT ALLOWED US TO SURVIVE LONG ENOUGH TO FIND PLACES LIKE THIS... THAT MADE IT SO WE DIDN'T HAVE TO DO THAT ANYMORE.
SO LIKE I TOLD YOU... WE CHANGED.
BUT YOU THREATENED ME.
I HAD TO MAKE SURE... I'M REALLY SORRY ABOUT THAT.
I DIDN'T MEAN IT.
NOTED.
CARL GRIMES IS FULL OF SHIT.

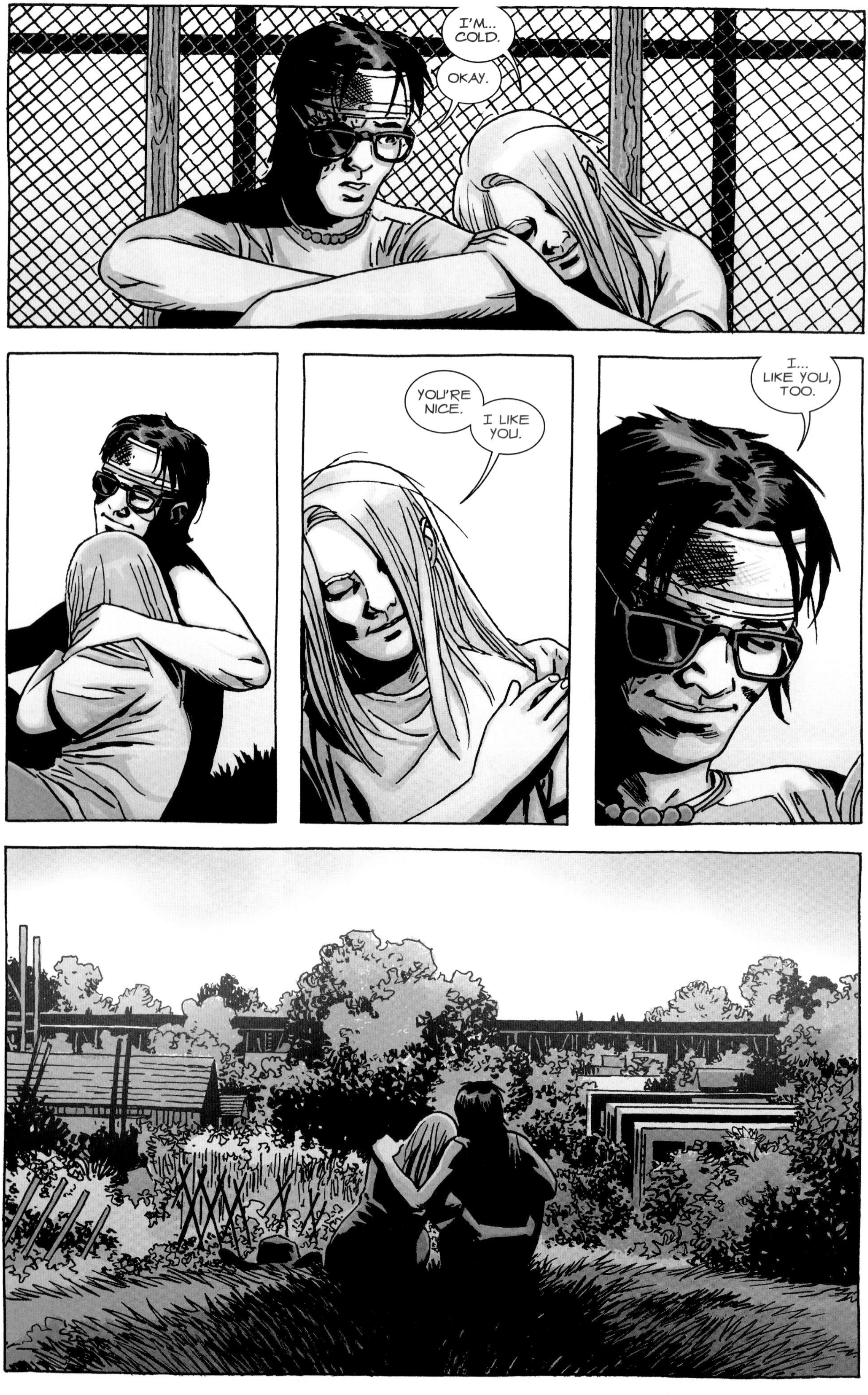
I'M... COLD.
OKAY.
YOU'RE NICE.
I LIKE YOU.
I... LIKE YOU, TOO.

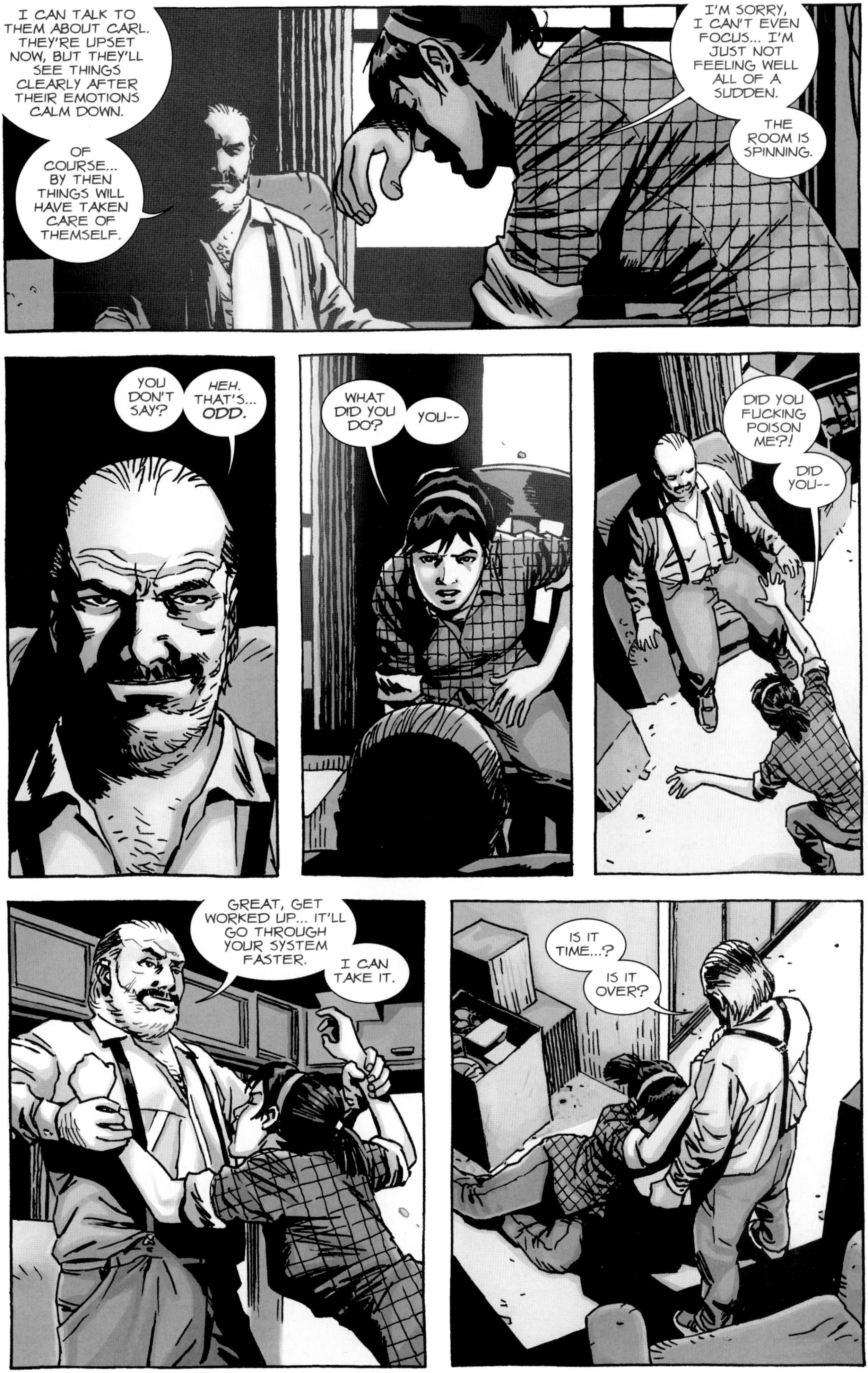
I CAN TALK TO THEM ABOUT CARL. THEY'RE UPSET NOW, BUT THEY'LL SEE THINGS CLEARLY AFTER THEIR EMOTIONS CALM DOWN.
OF COURSE... BY THEN THINGS WILL HAVE TAKEN CARE OF THEMSELF.
I'M SORRY, I CAN'T EVEN FOCUS... I'M JUST NOT FEELING WELL ALL OF A SUDDEN.
THE ROOM IS SPINNING.
YOU DON'T SAY?
HEH. THAT'S... ODD.
WHAT DID YOU DO?
YOU--
DID YOU FUCKING POISON ME?!
DID YOU--
GREAT, GET WORKED UP... IT'LL GO THROUGH YOUR SYSTEM FASTER.
I CAN TAKE IT.
IS IT TIME...?
IS IT OVER?

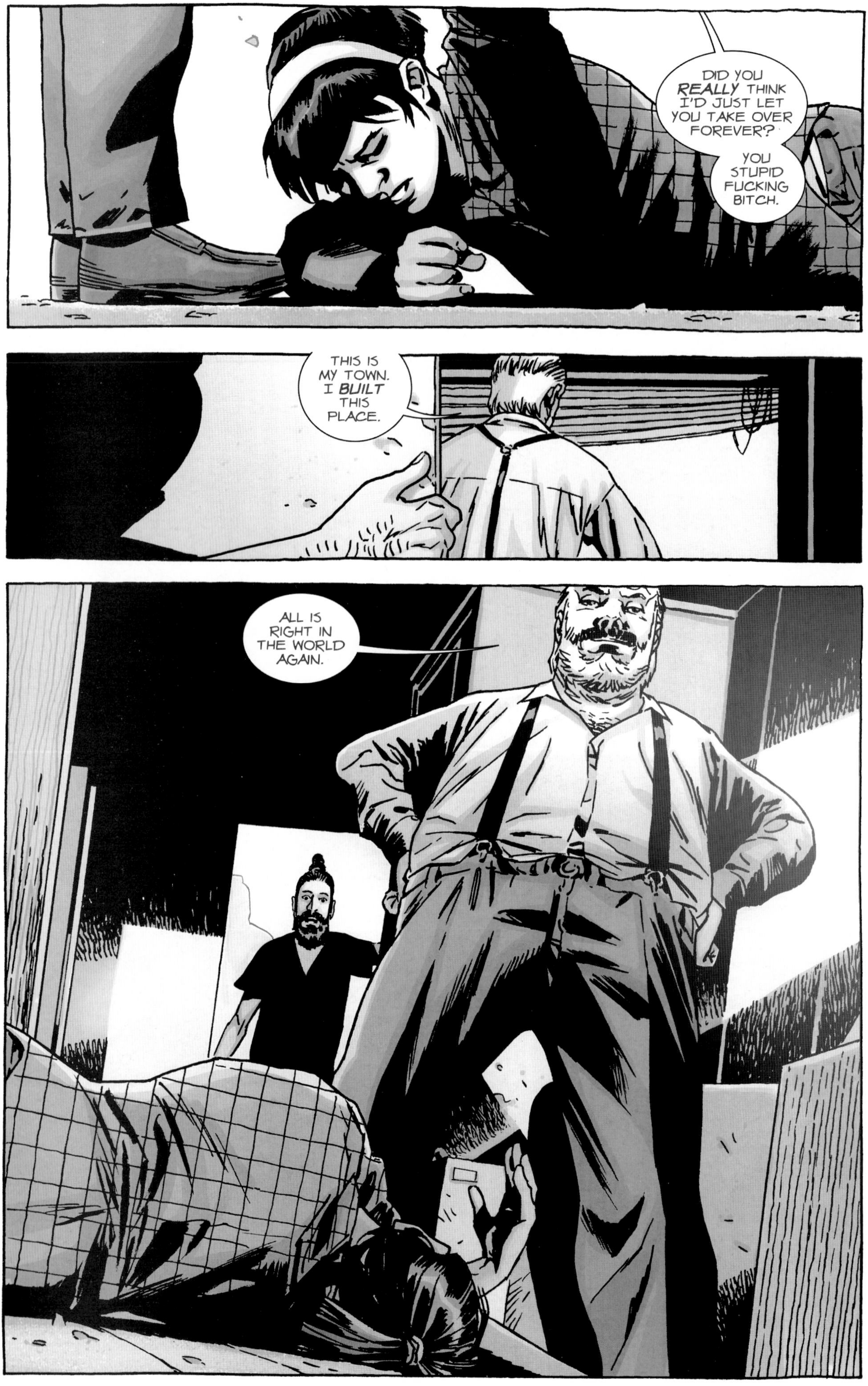
DID YOU REALLY THINK I'D JUST LET YOU TAKE OVER FOREVER?
YOU STUPID FUCKING BITCH.
THIS IS MY TOWN. I BUILT THIS PLACE.
ALL IS RIGHT IN THE WORLD AGAIN.

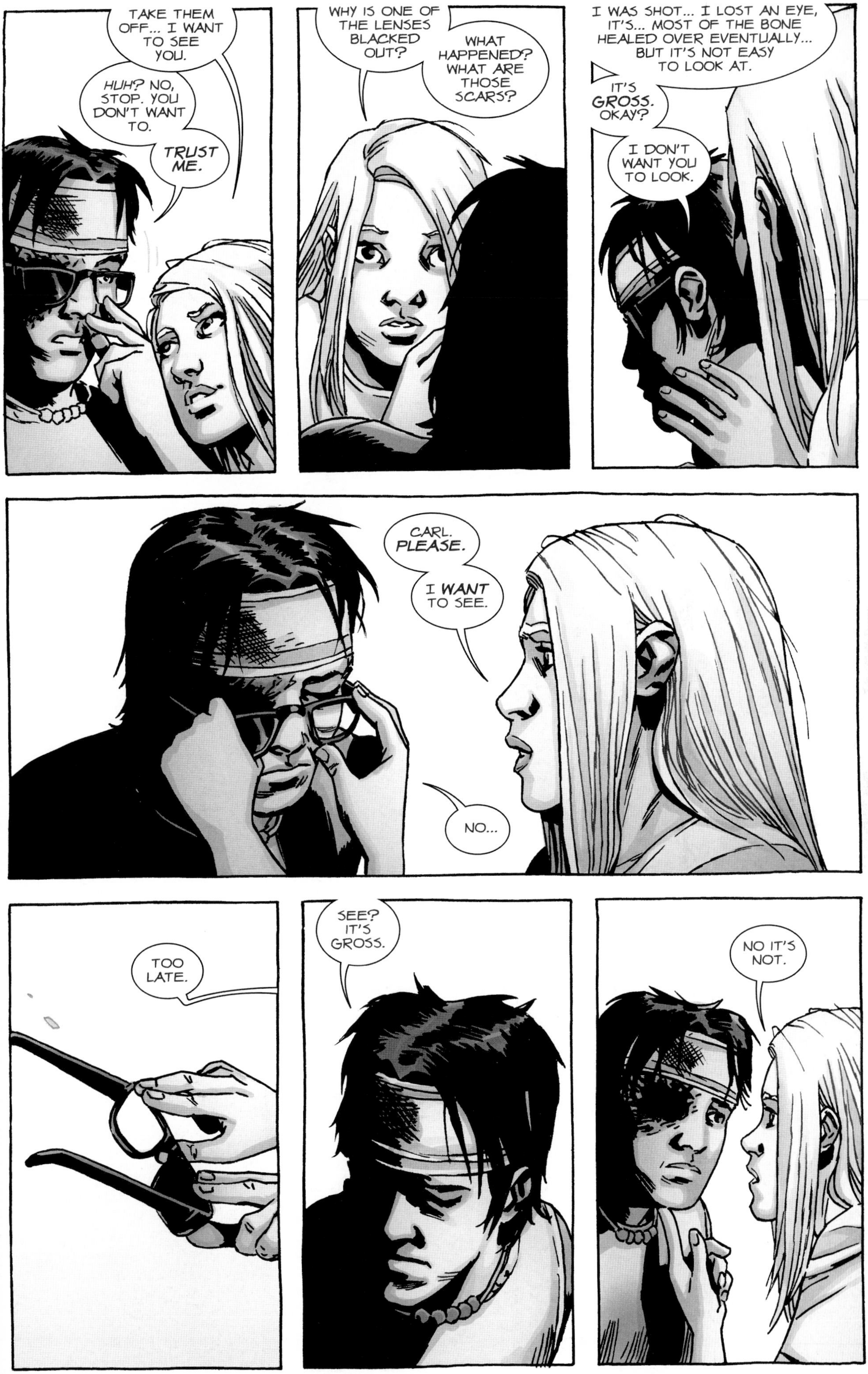
TAKE THEM OFF... I WANT TO SEE YOU.
HUH? NO, STOP. YOU DON'T WANT TO.
TRUST ME.
WHY IS ONE OF THE LENSES BLACKED OUT?
WHAT HAPPENED? WHAT ARE THOSE SCARS?
I WAS SHOT... I LOST AN EYE, IT'S... MOST OF THE BONE HEALED OVER EVENTUALLY... BUT IT'S NOT EASY TO LOOK AT.
IT'S GROSS. OKAY?
I DON'T WANT YOU TO LOOK.
CARL. PLEASE.
I WANT TO SEE.
NO...
TOO LATE.
SEE? IT'S GROSS.
NO IT'S NOT.

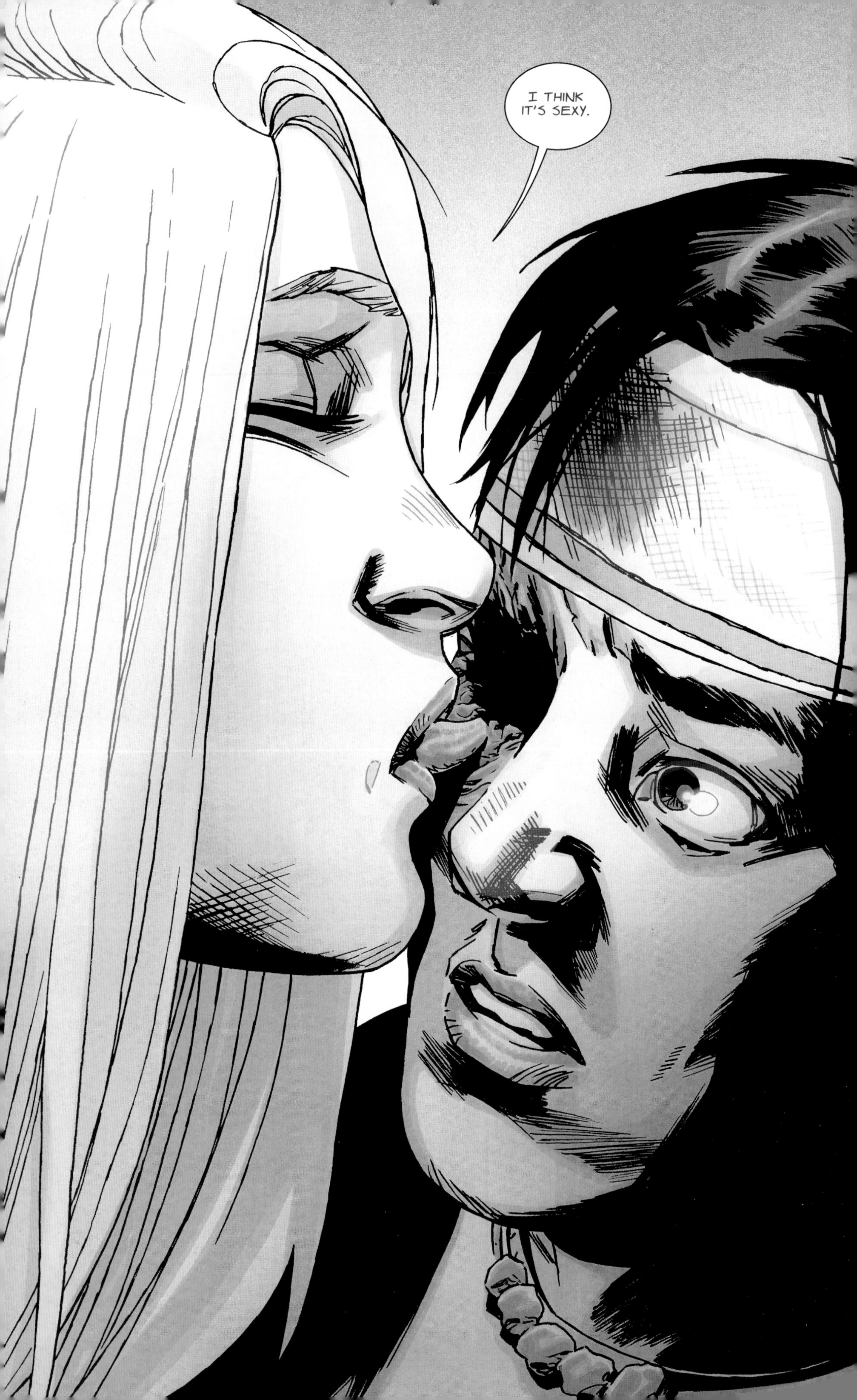
I THINK IT'S SEXY.

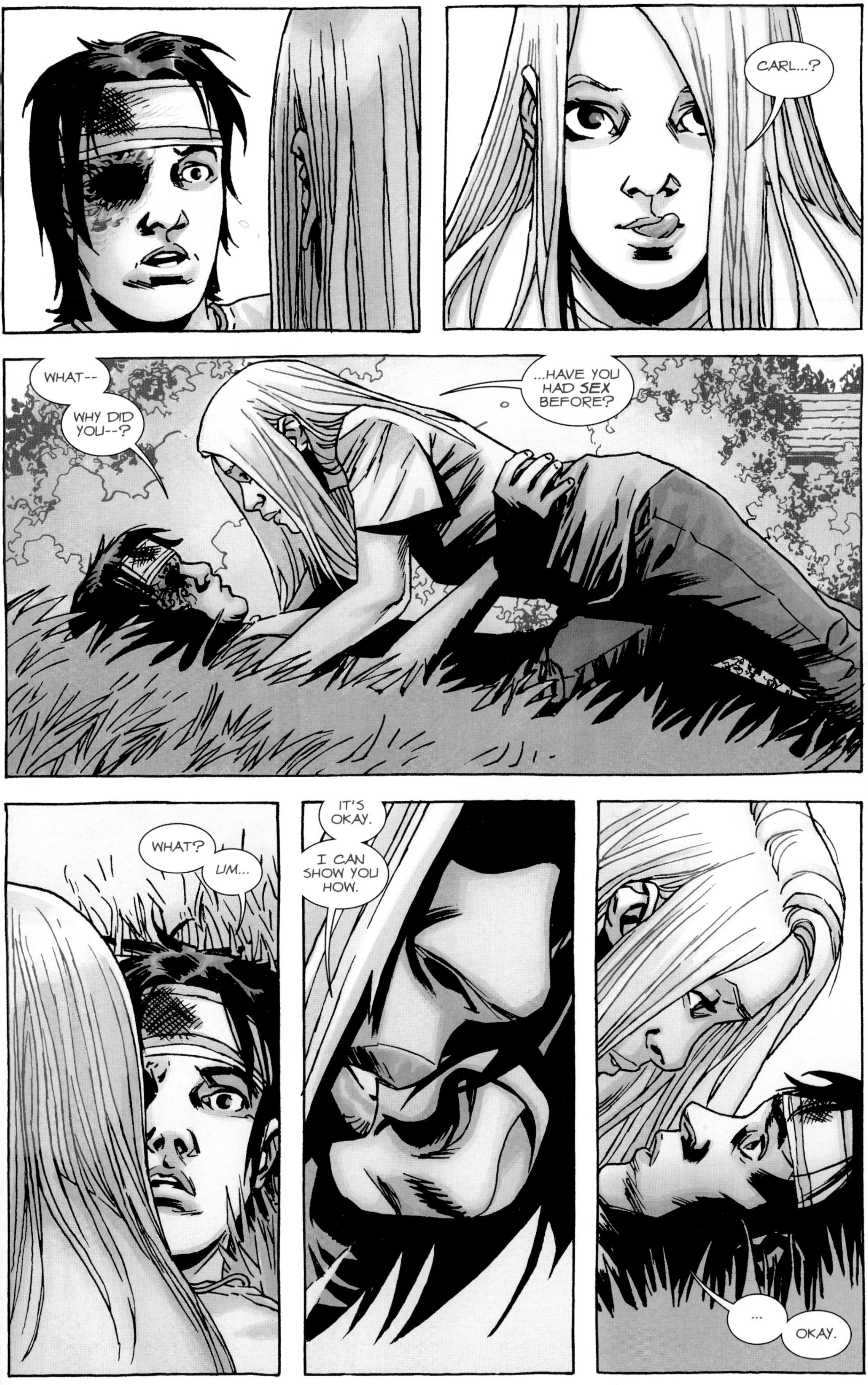
CARL...?
WHAT--
WHY DID YOU--?
...HAVE YOU HAD SEX BEFORE?
WHAT?
UM...
IT'S OKAY.
I CAN SHOW YOU HOW.
...
OKAY.

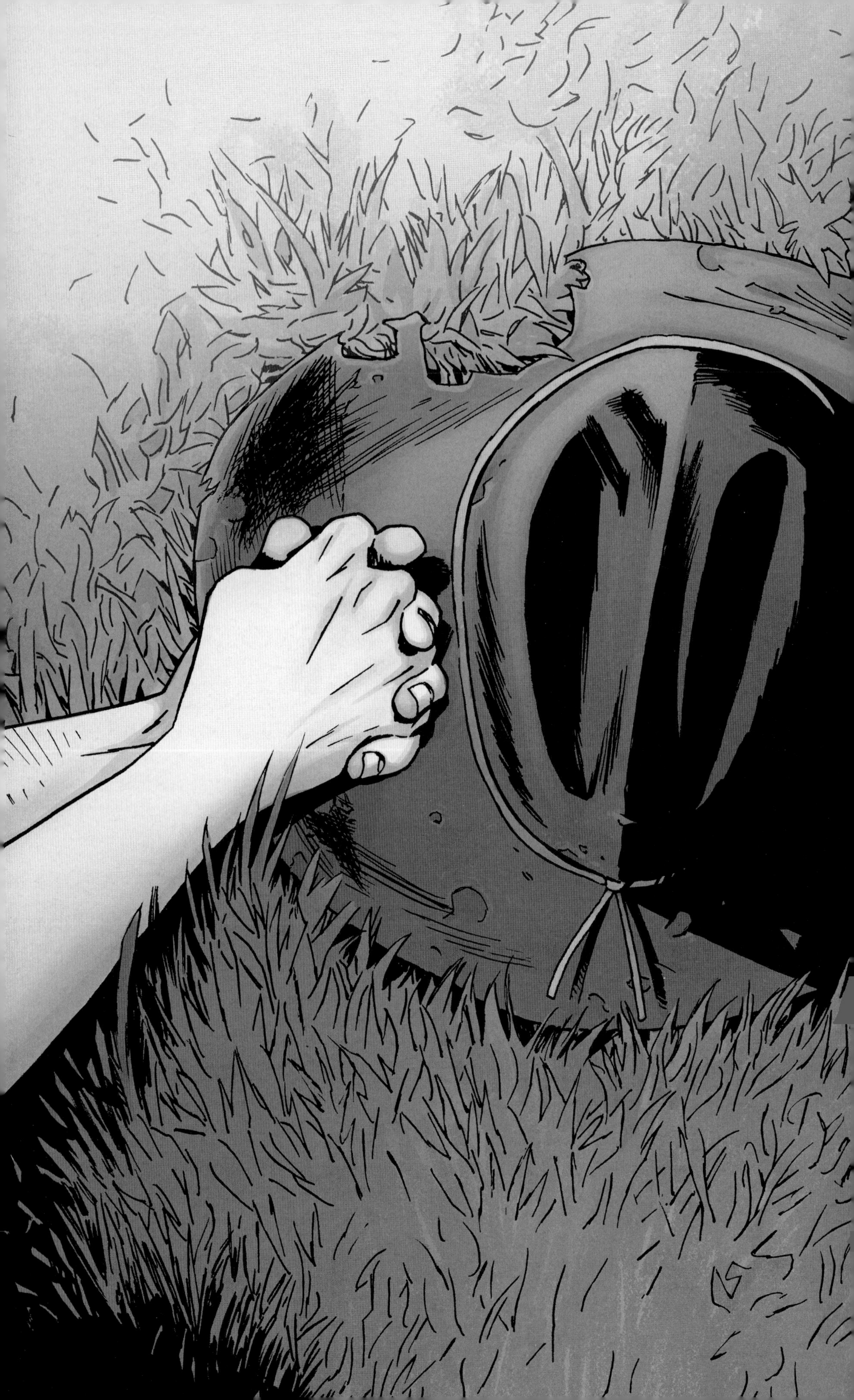

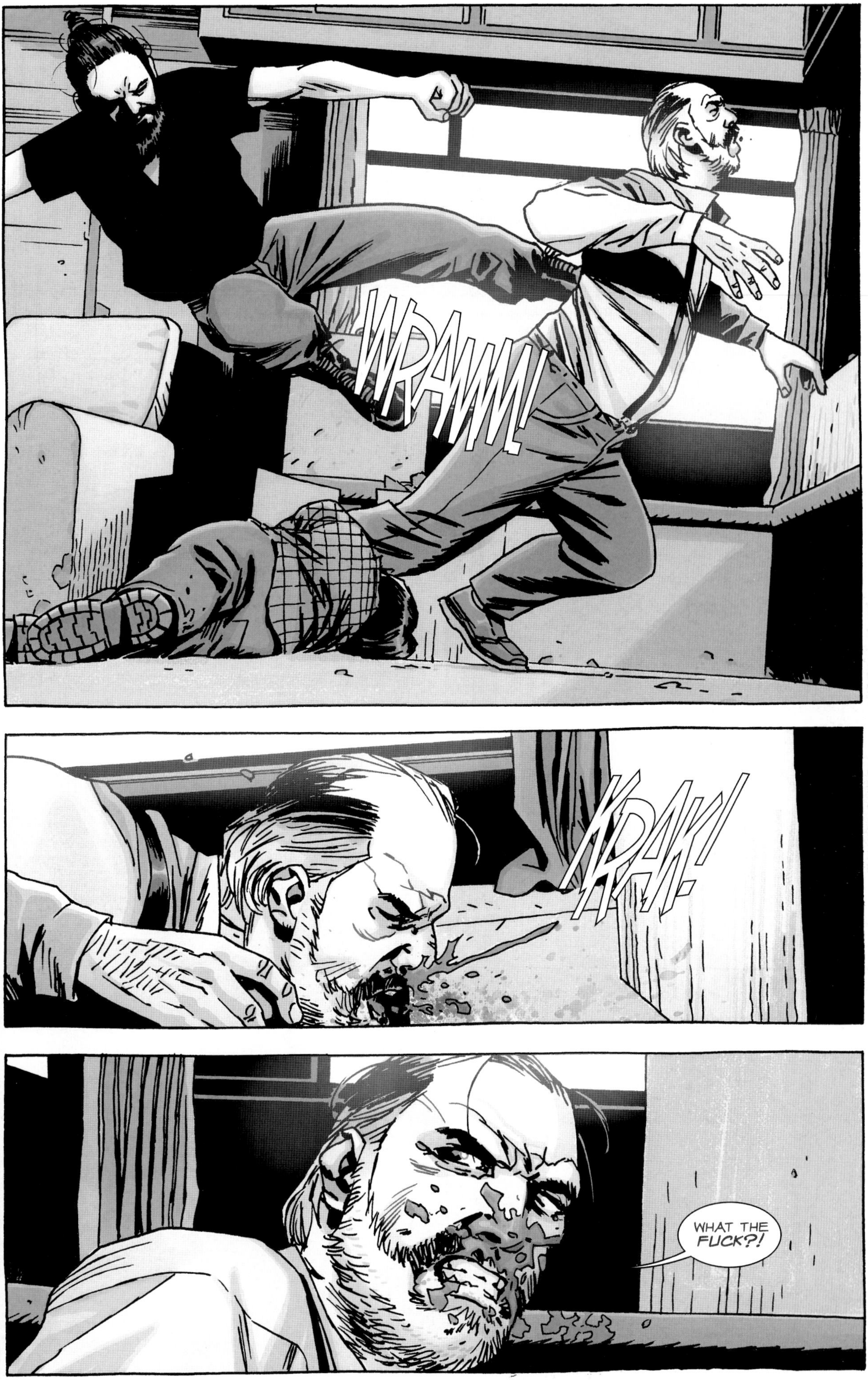
WRAMM!
KRAK!
WHAT THE FUCK?!

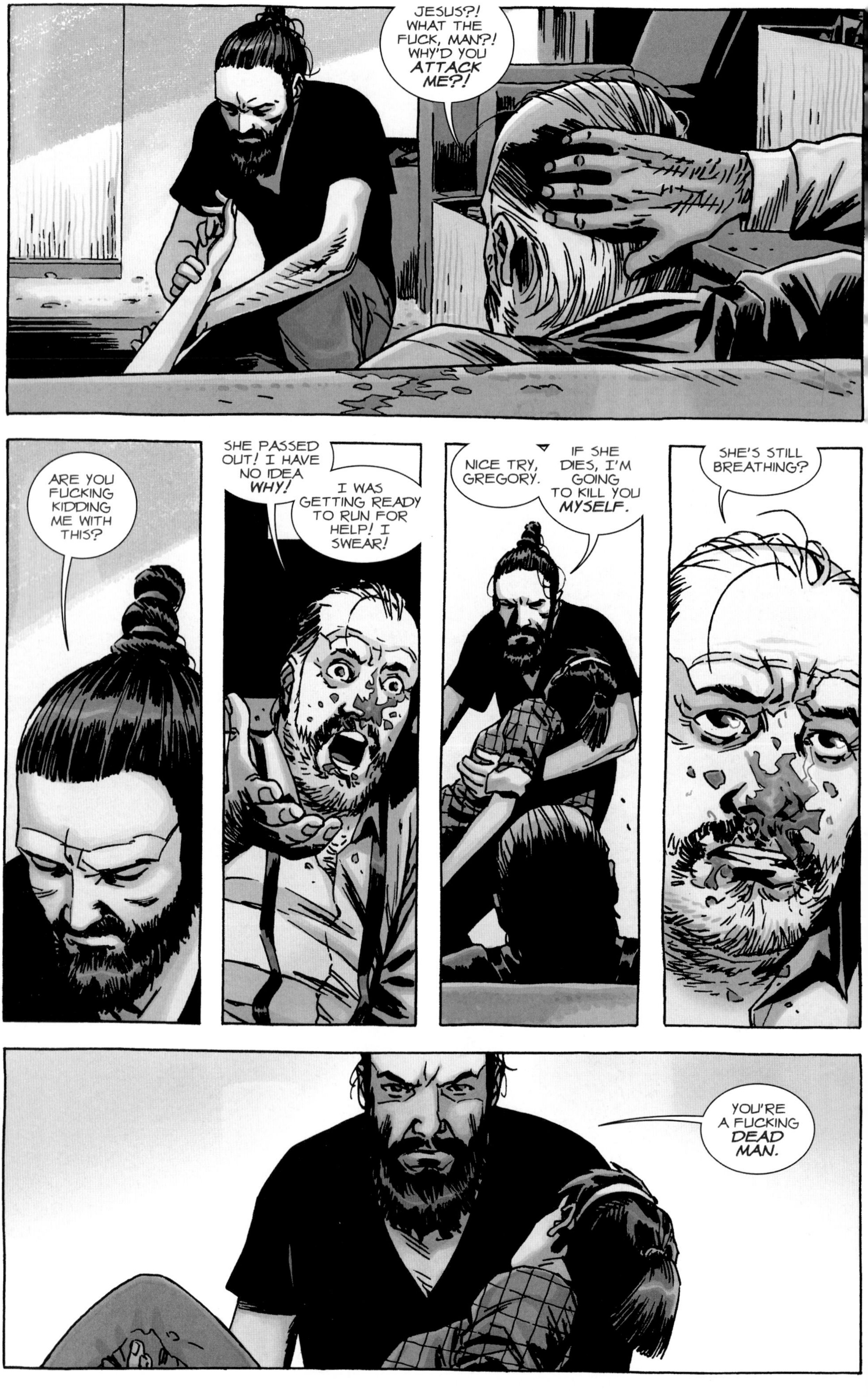

JESUS?! WHAT THE FUCK, MAN?! WHY'D YOU ATTACK ME?!
ARE YOU FUCKING KIDDING ME WITH THIS?
SHE PASSED OUT! I HAVE NO IDEA WHY!
I WAS GETTING READY TO RUN FOR HELP! I SWEAR!
NICE TRY, GREGORY.
IF SHE DIES, I'M GOING TO KILL YOU MYSELF.
SHE'S STILL BREATHING?
YOU'RE A FUCKING DEAD MAN.

NO. NOBODY IS KILLING...

ANYONE...

PUT ME DOWN, JESUS... I'M... I'M OKAY... I THINK.

I'M NOT--

I'M OKAY.

DON'T LEAVE HIM ALONE HERE. TAKE *HIM*, SEND DOC CARSON ON YOUR WAY... LOCK...

LOCK HIM UP... AND THEN COME BACK AND SEARCH THIS PLACE... FIND OUT WHAT HE GAVE ME.

MAGGIE, YOU HAVE *NO REASON* TO SUSPECT ME OF--

SHUT THE FUCK UP, GREGORY.

YOU WANT TO BE THE LEADER OF THIS COMMUNITY?

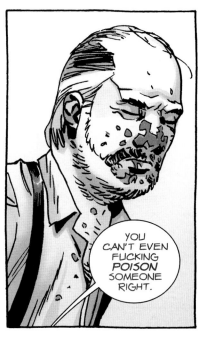

YOU CAN'T EVEN FUCKING *POISON* SOMEONE RIGHT.

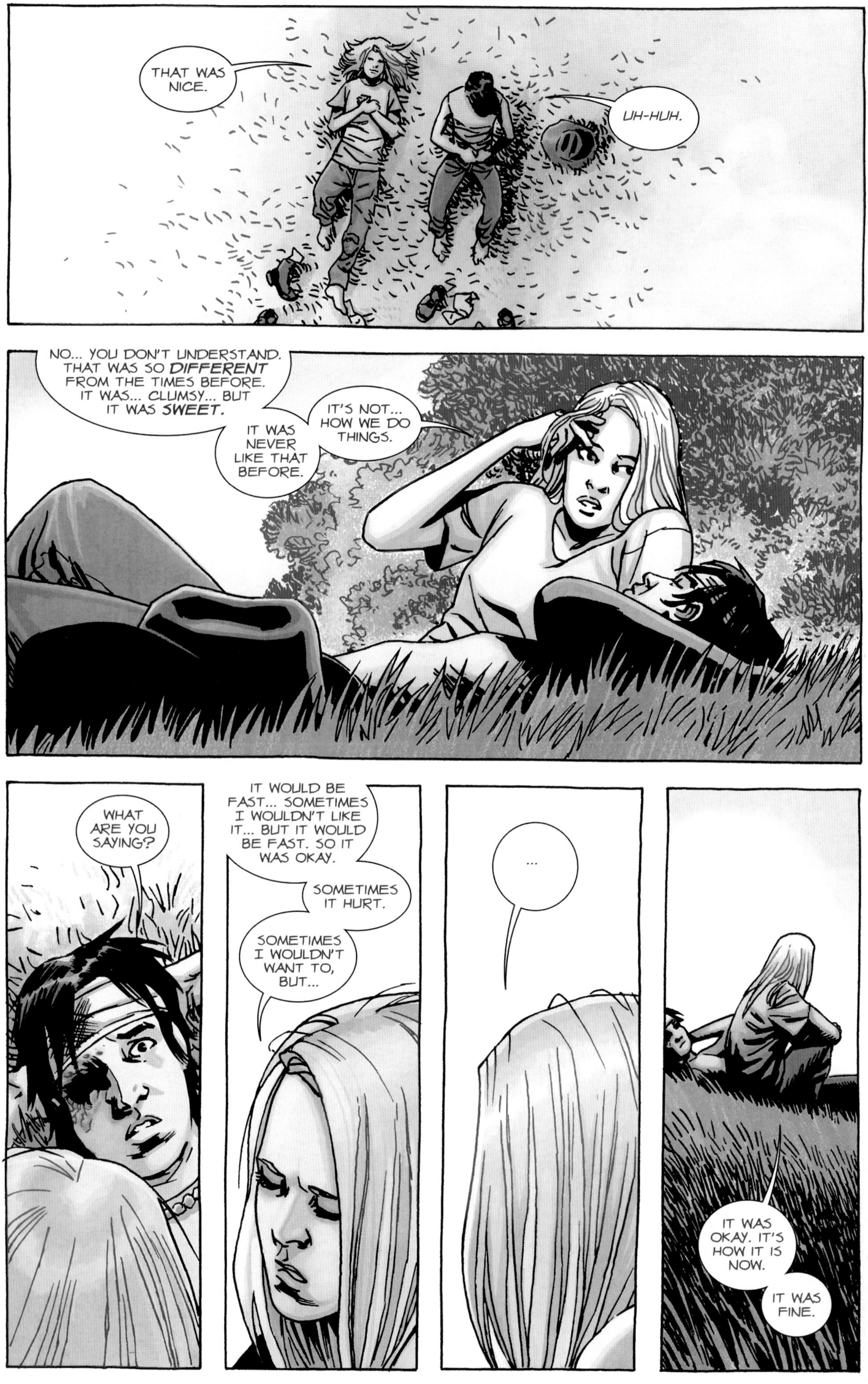
THAT WAS NICE.
UH-HUH.
NO... YOU DON'T UNDERSTAND. THAT WAS SO DIFFERENT FROM THE TIMES BEFORE. IT WAS... CLUMSY... BUT IT WAS SWEET.
IT WAS NEVER LIKE THAT BEFORE.
IT'S NOT... HOW WE DO THINGS.
WHAT ARE YOU SAYING?
IT WOULD BE FAST... SOMETIMES I WOULDN'T LIKE IT... BUT IT WOULD BE FAST. SO IT WAS OKAY.
SOMETIMES IT HURT.
SOMETIMES I WOULDN'T WANT TO, BUT...
...
IT WAS OKAY. IT'S HOW IT IS NOW.
IT WAS FINE.

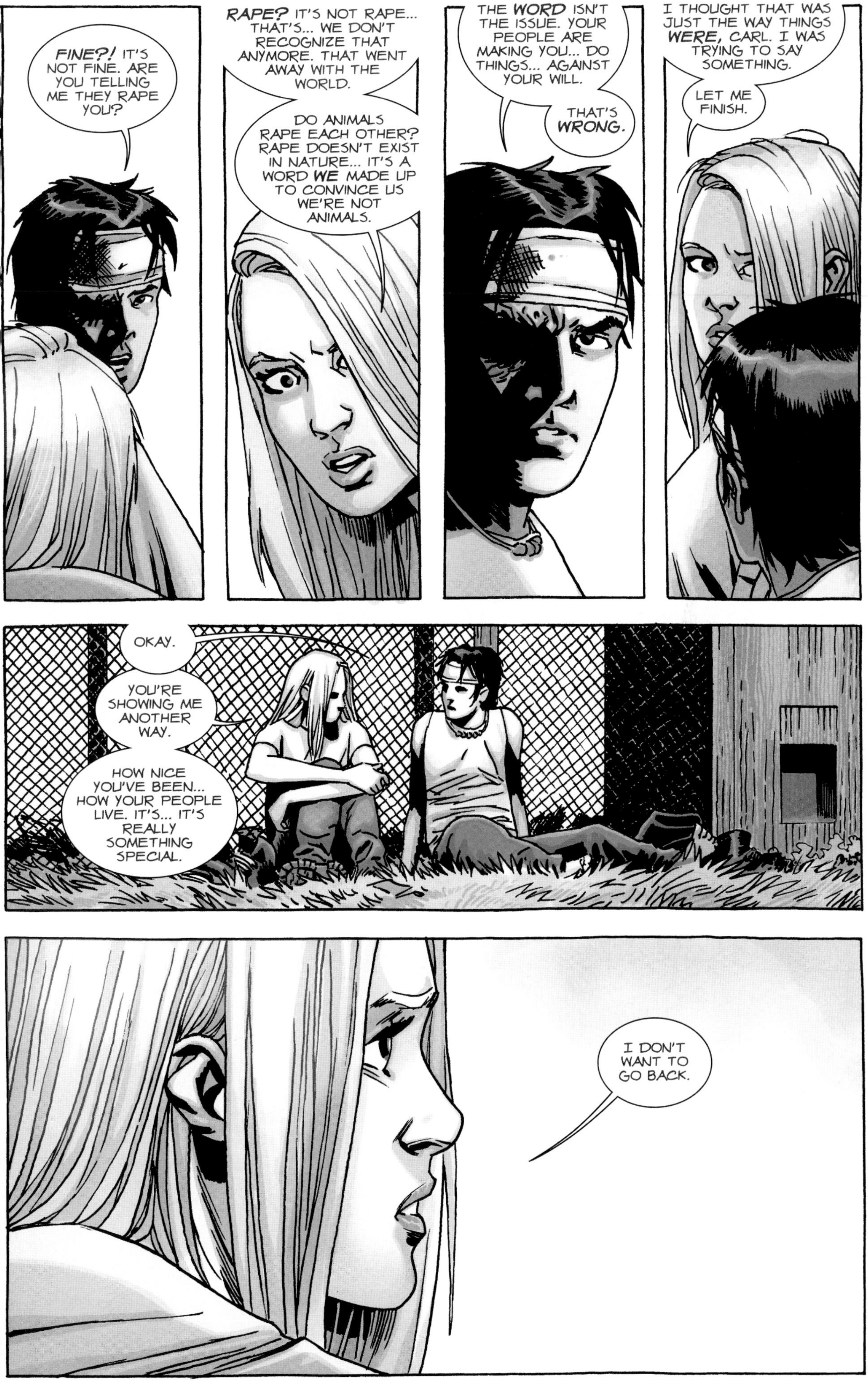
FINE?! IT'S NOT FINE. ARE YOU TELLING ME THEY RAPE YOU?
RAPE? IT'S NOT RAPE... THAT'S... WE DON'T RECOGNIZE THAT ANYMORE. THAT WENT AWAY WITH THE WORLD.
DO ANIMALS RAPE EACH OTHER? RAPE DOESN'T EXIST IN NATURE... IT'S A WORD WE MADE UP TO CONVINCE US WE'RE NOT ANIMALS.
THE WORD ISN'T THE ISSUE. YOUR PEOPLE ARE MAKING YOU... DO THINGS... AGAINST YOUR WILL.
THAT'S WRONG.
I THOUGHT THAT WAS JUST THE WAY THINGS WERE, CARL. I WAS TRYING TO SAY SOMETHING.
LET ME FINISH.
OKAY.
YOU'RE SHOWING ME ANOTHER WAY.
HOW NICE YOU'VE BEEN... HOW YOUR PEOPLE LIVE. IT'S... IT'S REALLY SOMETHING SPECIAL.
I DON'T WANT TO GO BACK.

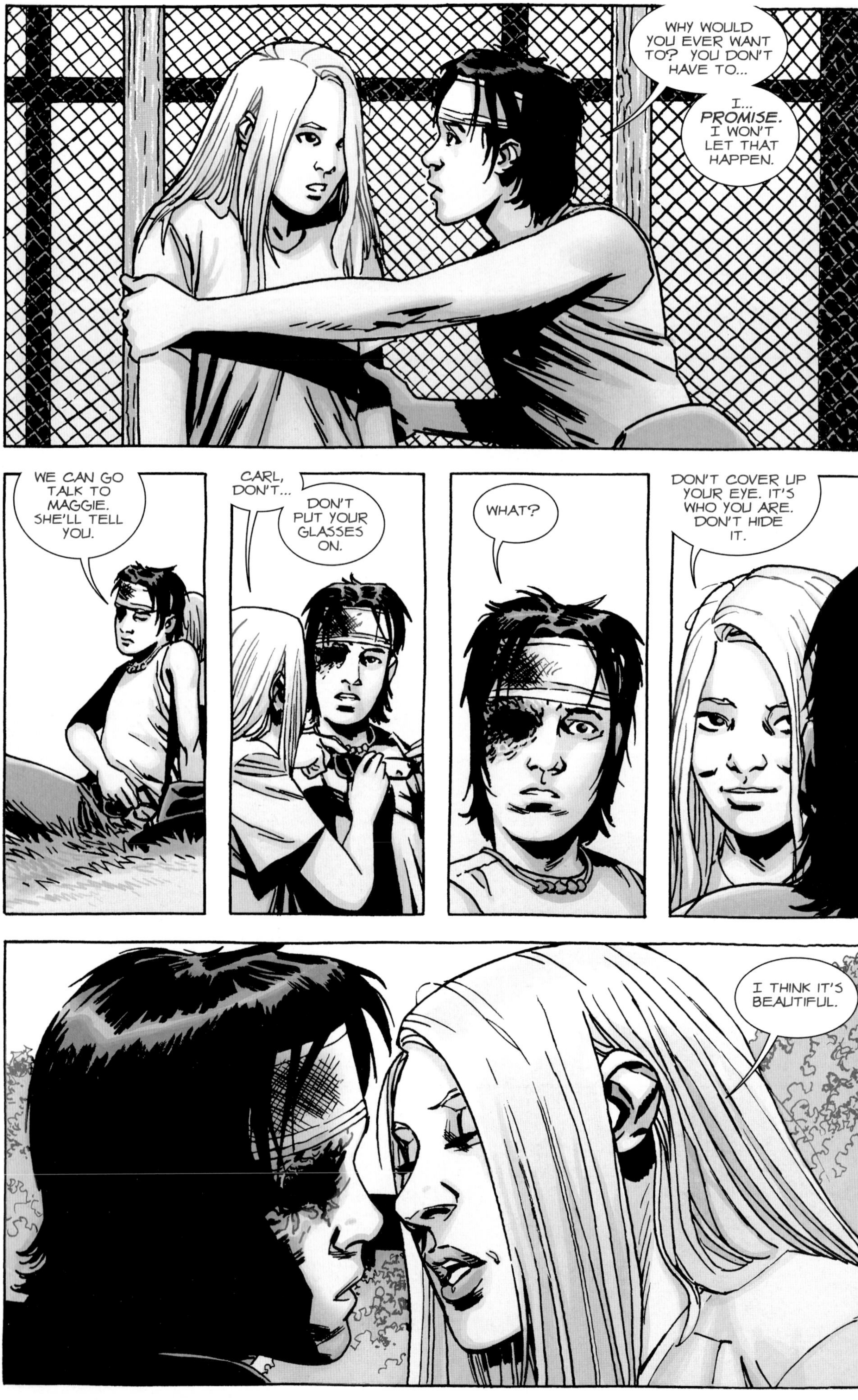
WHY WOULD YOU EVER WANT TO? YOU DON'T HAVE TO...
I... *PROMISE.* I WON'T LET THAT HAPPEN.
WE CAN GO TALK TO MAGGIE. SHE'LL TELL YOU.
CARL, DON'T...
DON'T PUT YOUR GLASSES ON.
WHAT?
DON'T COVER UP YOUR EYE. IT'S WHO YOU ARE. DON'T HIDE IT.
I THINK IT'S BEAUTIFUL.

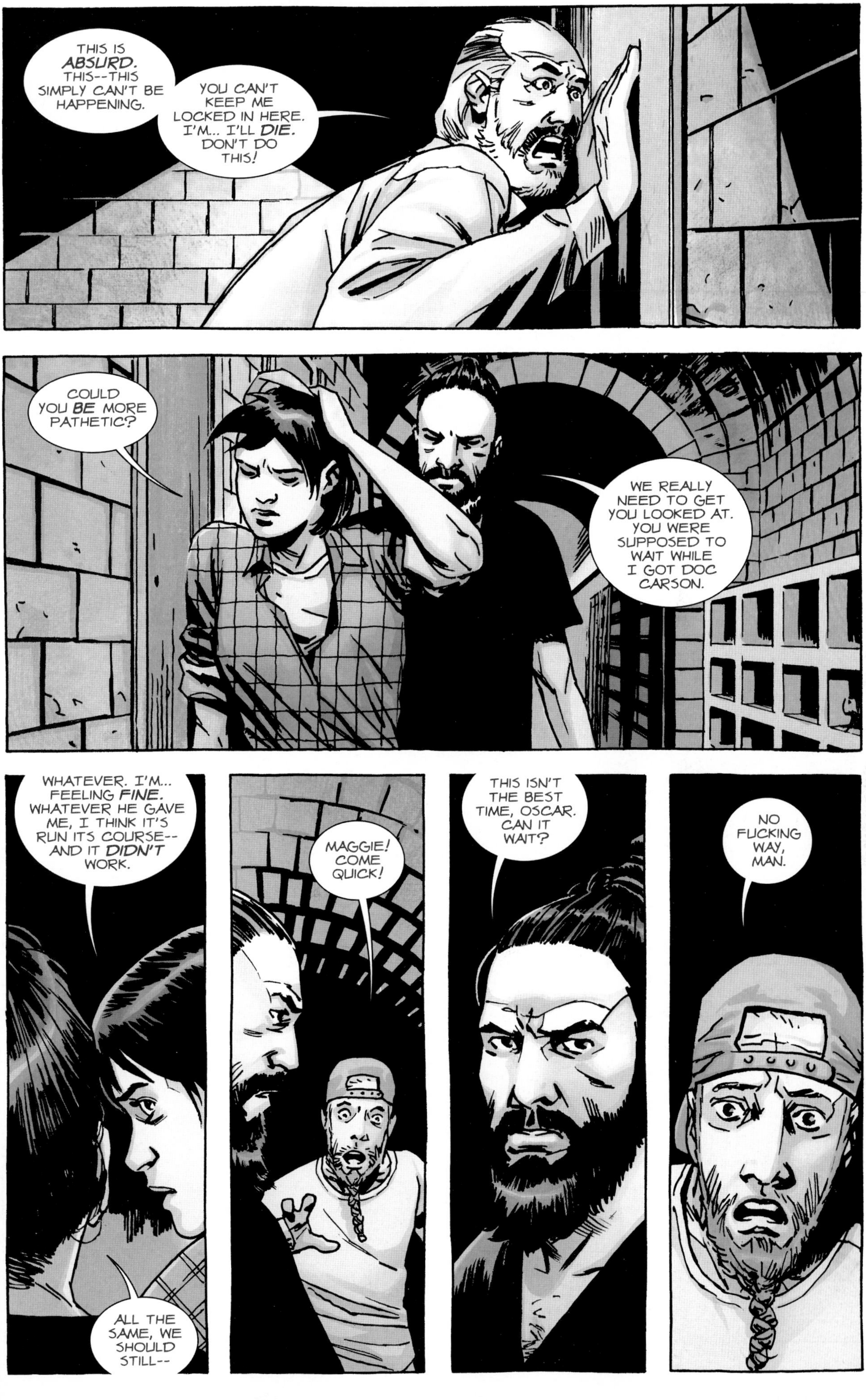

THIS IS ABSURD. THIS--THIS SIMPLY CAN'T BE HAPPENING.
YOU CAN'T KEEP ME LOCKED IN HERE. I'M... I'LL DIE. DON'T DO THIS!
COULD YOU BE MORE PATHETIC?
WE REALLY NEED TO GET YOU LOOKED AT. YOU WERE SUPPOSED TO WAIT WHILE I GOT DOC CARSON.
WHATEVER. I'M... FEELING FINE. WHATEVER HE GAVE ME, I THINK IT'S RUN ITS COURSE-- AND IT DIDN'T WORK.
ALL THE SAME, WE SHOULD STILL--
MAGGIE! COME QUICK!
THIS ISN'T THE BEST TIME, OSCAR. CAN IT WAIT?
NO FUCKING WAY, MAN.

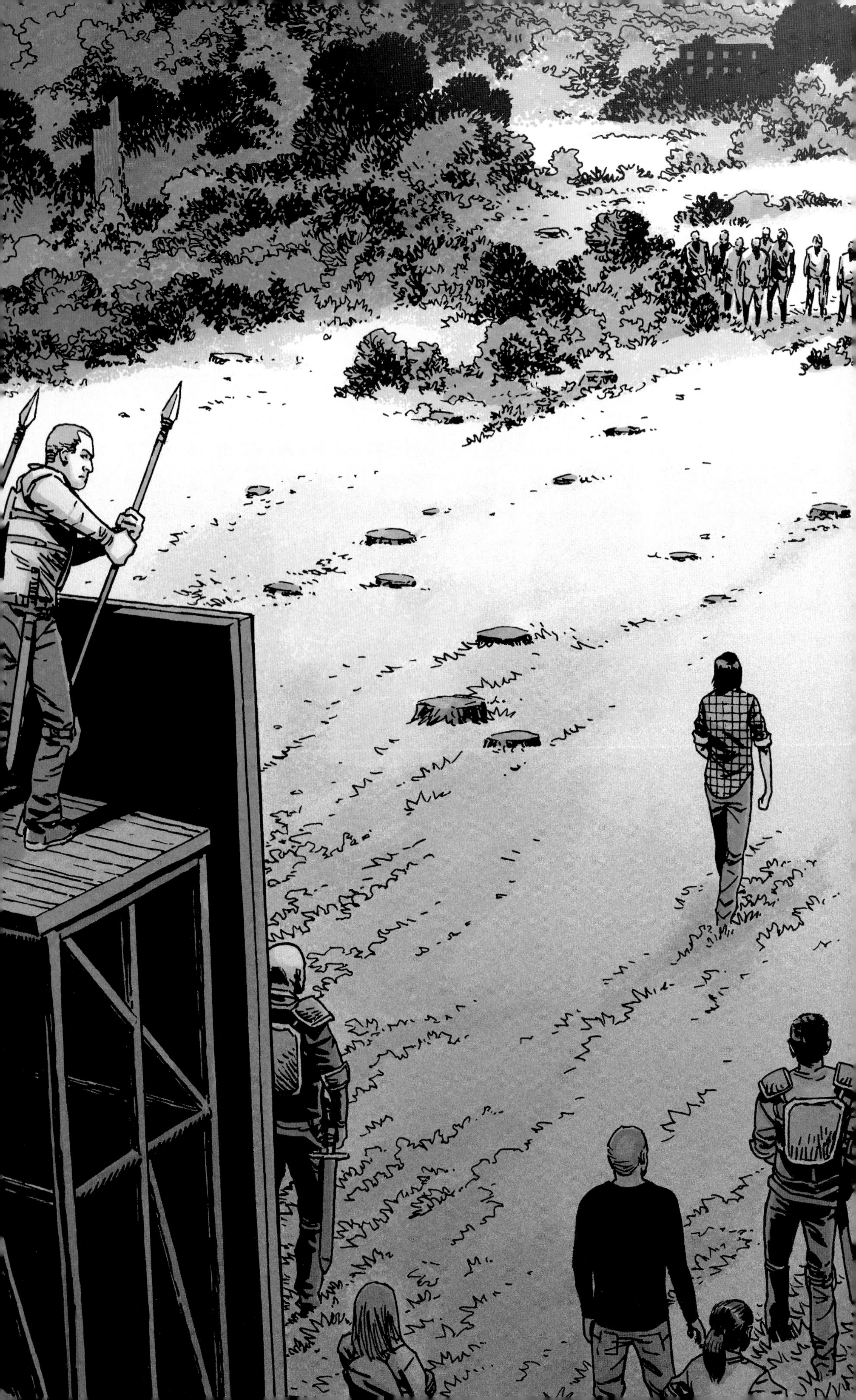

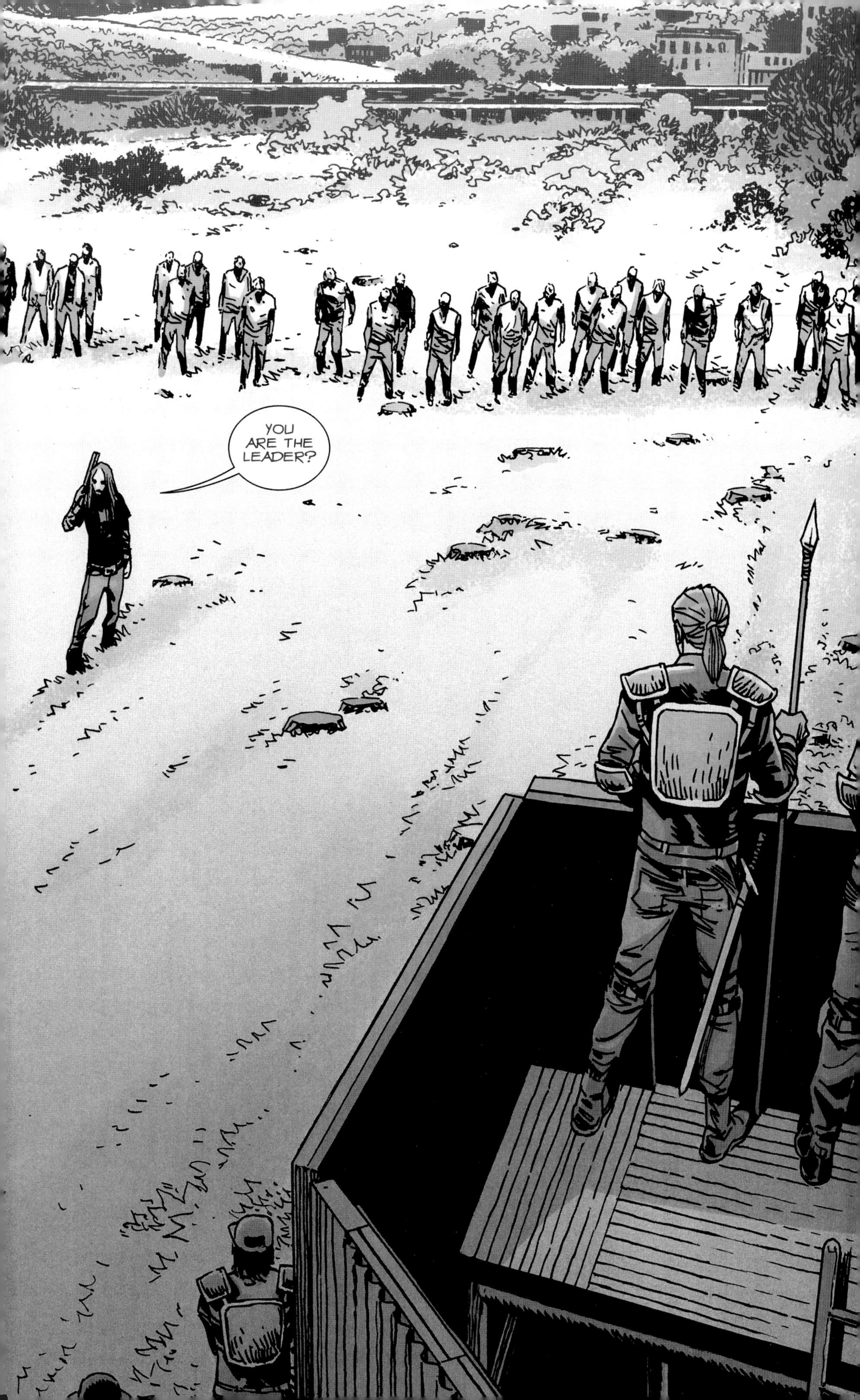
YOU ARE THE LEADER?

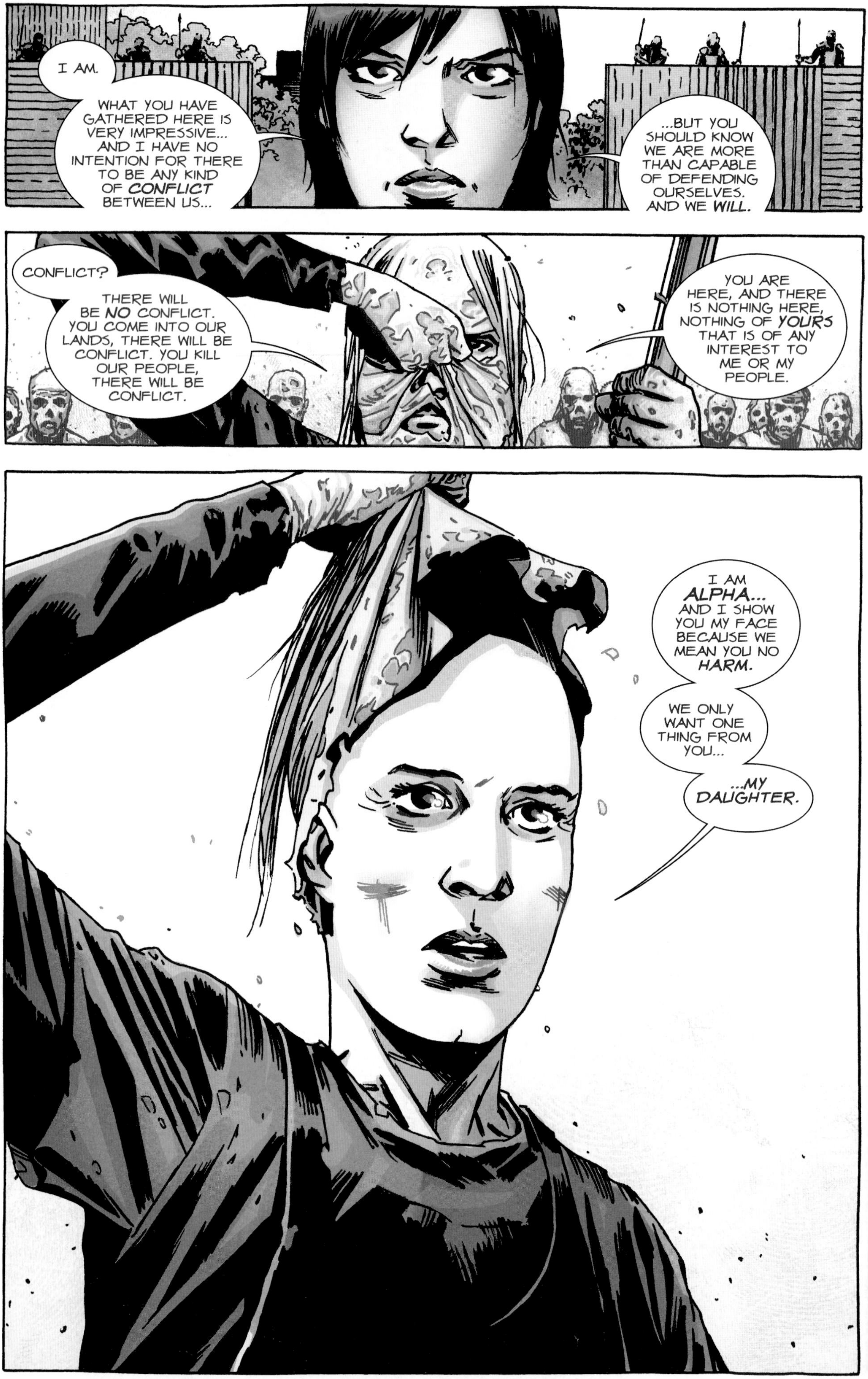
I AM.
WHAT YOU HAVE GATHERED HERE IS VERY IMPRESSIVE... AND I HAVE NO INTENTION FOR THERE TO BE ANY KIND OF CONFLICT BETWEEN US...
...BUT YOU SHOULD KNOW WE ARE MORE THAN CAPABLE OF DEFENDING OURSELVES. AND WE WILL.
CONFLICT?
THERE WILL BE NO CONFLICT. YOU COME INTO OUR LANDS, THERE WILL BE CONFLICT. YOU KILL OUR PEOPLE, THERE WILL BE CONFLICT.
YOU ARE HERE, AND THERE IS NOTHING HERE, NOTHING OF YOURS THAT IS OF ANY INTEREST TO ME OR MY PEOPLE.
I AM ALPHA... AND I SHOW YOU MY FACE BECAUSE WE MEAN YOU NO HARM.
WE ONLY WANT ONE THING FROM YOU...
...MY DAUGHTER.

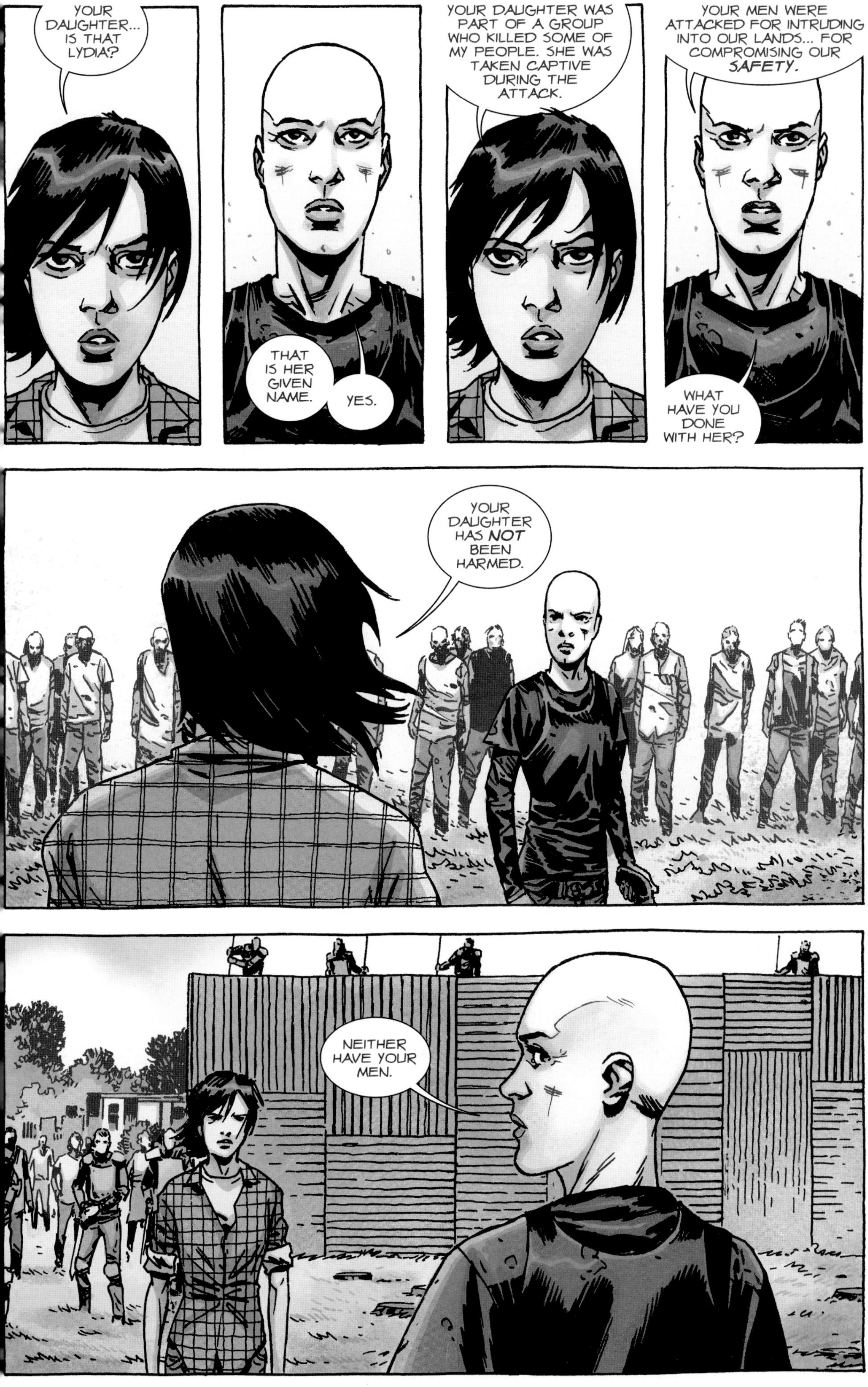
YOUR DAUGHTER... IS THAT LYDIA?
THAT IS HER GIVEN NAME.
YES.
YOUR DAUGHTER WAS PART OF A GROUP WHO KILLED SOME OF MY PEOPLE. SHE WAS TAKEN CAPTIVE DURING THE ATTACK.
YOUR MEN WERE ATTACKED FOR INTRUDING INTO OUR LANDS... FOR COMPROMISING OUR SAFETY.
WHAT HAVE YOU DONE WITH HER?
YOUR DAUGHTER HAS NOT BEEN HARMED.
NEITHER HAVE YOUR MEN.

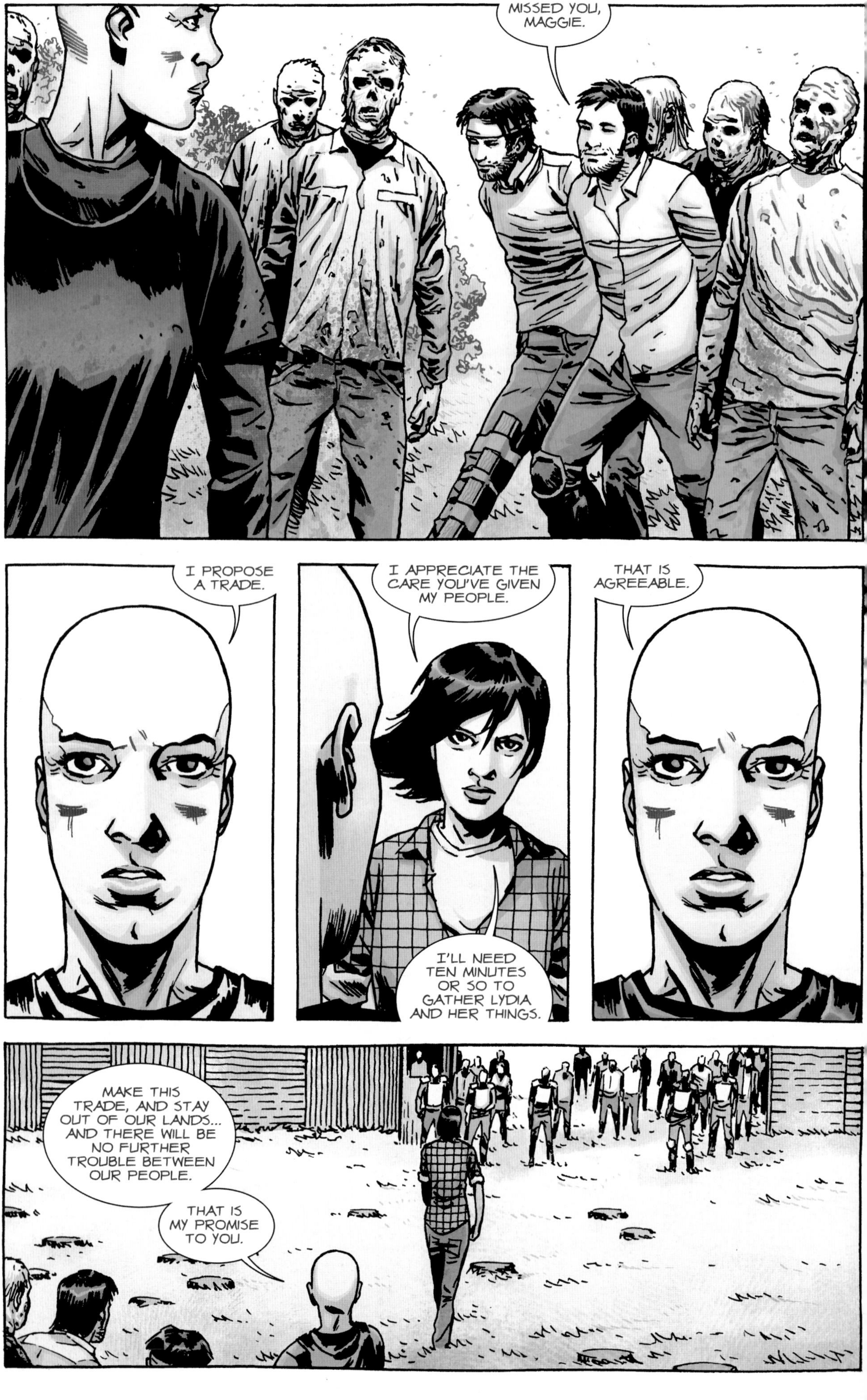
MISSED YOU, MAGGIE.
I PROPOSE A TRADE.
I APPRECIATE THE CARE YOU'VE GIVEN MY PEOPLE.
I'LL NEED TEN MINUTES OR SO TO GATHER LYDIA AND HER THINGS.
THAT IS AGREEABLE.
MAKE THIS TRADE, AND STAY OUT OF OUR LANDS... AND THERE WILL BE NO FURTHER TROUBLE BETWEEN OUR PEOPLE.
THAT IS MY PROMISE TO YOU.

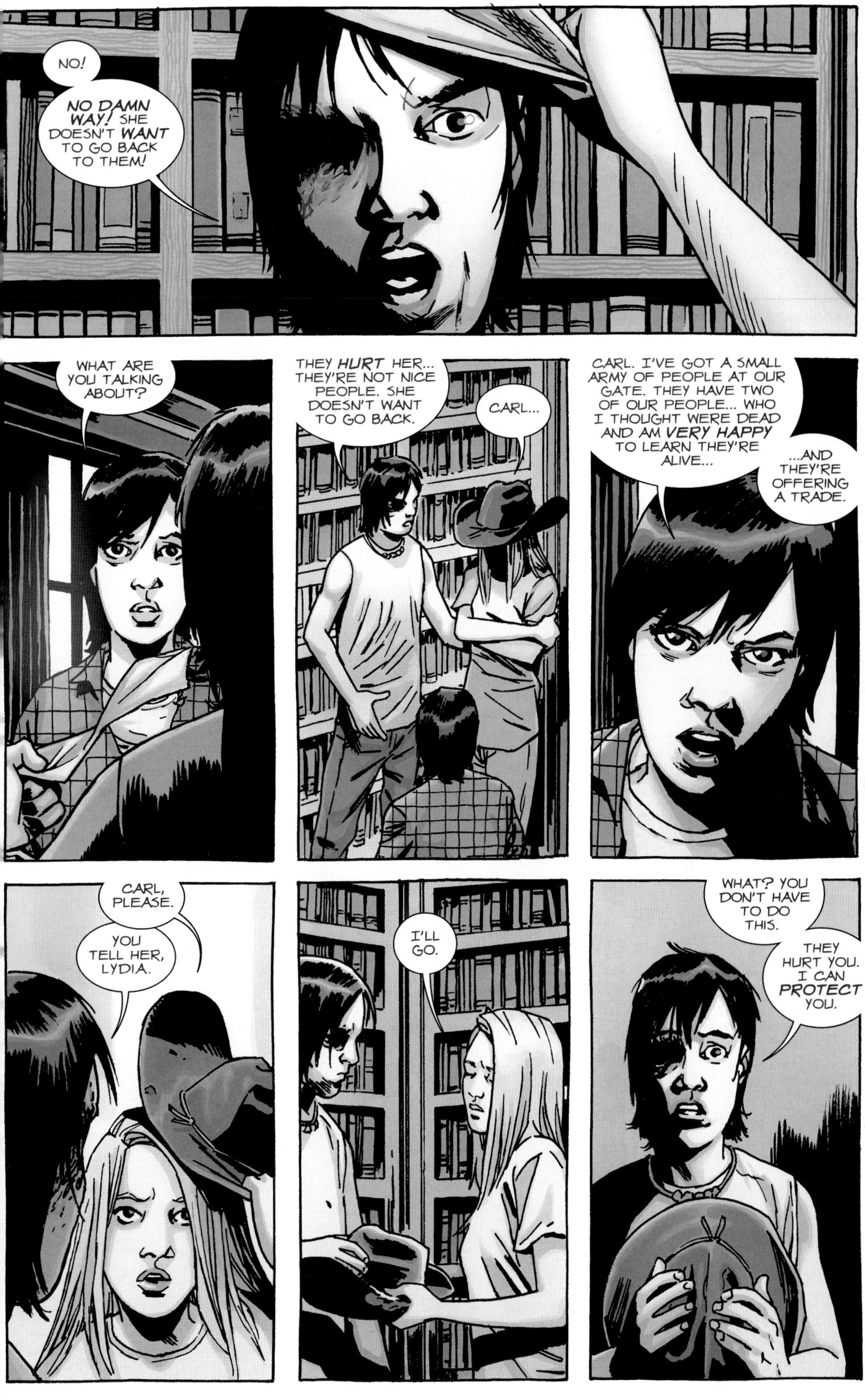
NO!
NO DAMN WAY! SHE DOESN'T WANT TO GO BACK TO THEM!
WHAT ARE YOU TALKING ABOUT?
THEY HURT HER... THEY'RE NOT NICE PEOPLE. SHE DOESN'T WANT TO GO BACK.
CARL...
CARL. I'VE GOT A SMALL ARMY OF PEOPLE AT OUR GATE. THEY HAVE TWO OF OUR PEOPLE... WHO I THOUGHT WERE DEAD AND AM VERY HAPPY TO LEARN THEY'RE ALIVE...
...AND THEY'RE OFFERING A TRADE.
CARL, PLEASE.
YOU TELL HER, LYDIA.
I'LL GO.
WHAT? YOU DON'T HAVE TO DO THIS.
THEY HURT YOU. I CAN PROTECT YOU.

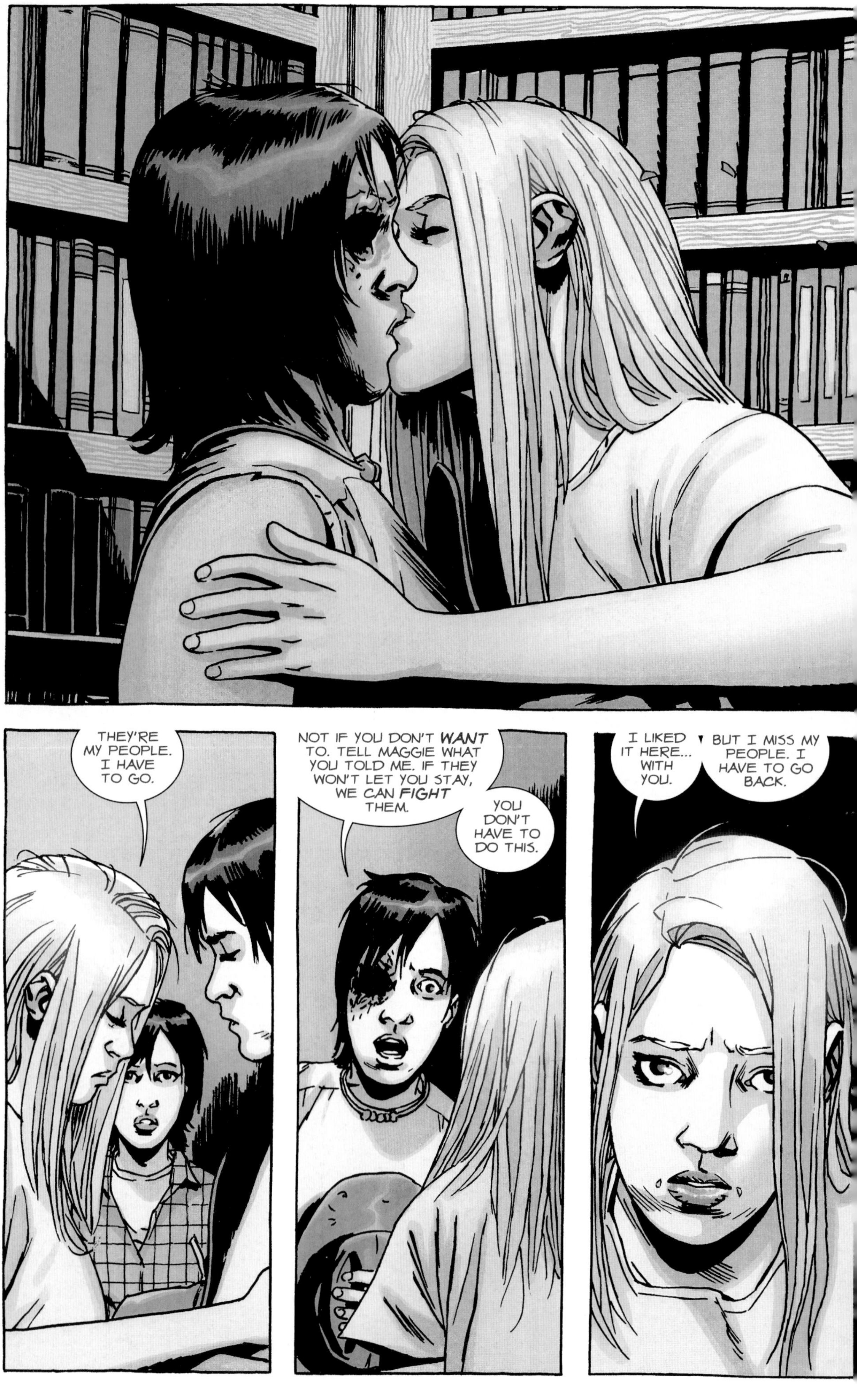
THEY'RE MY PEOPLE. I HAVE TO GO.
NOT IF YOU DON'T WANT TO. TELL MAGGIE WHAT YOU TOLD ME. IF THEY WON'T LET YOU STAY, WE CAN FIGHT THEM.
YOU DON'T HAVE TO DO THIS.
I LIKED IT HERE... WITH YOU.
BUT I MISS MY PEOPLE. I HAVE TO GO BACK.

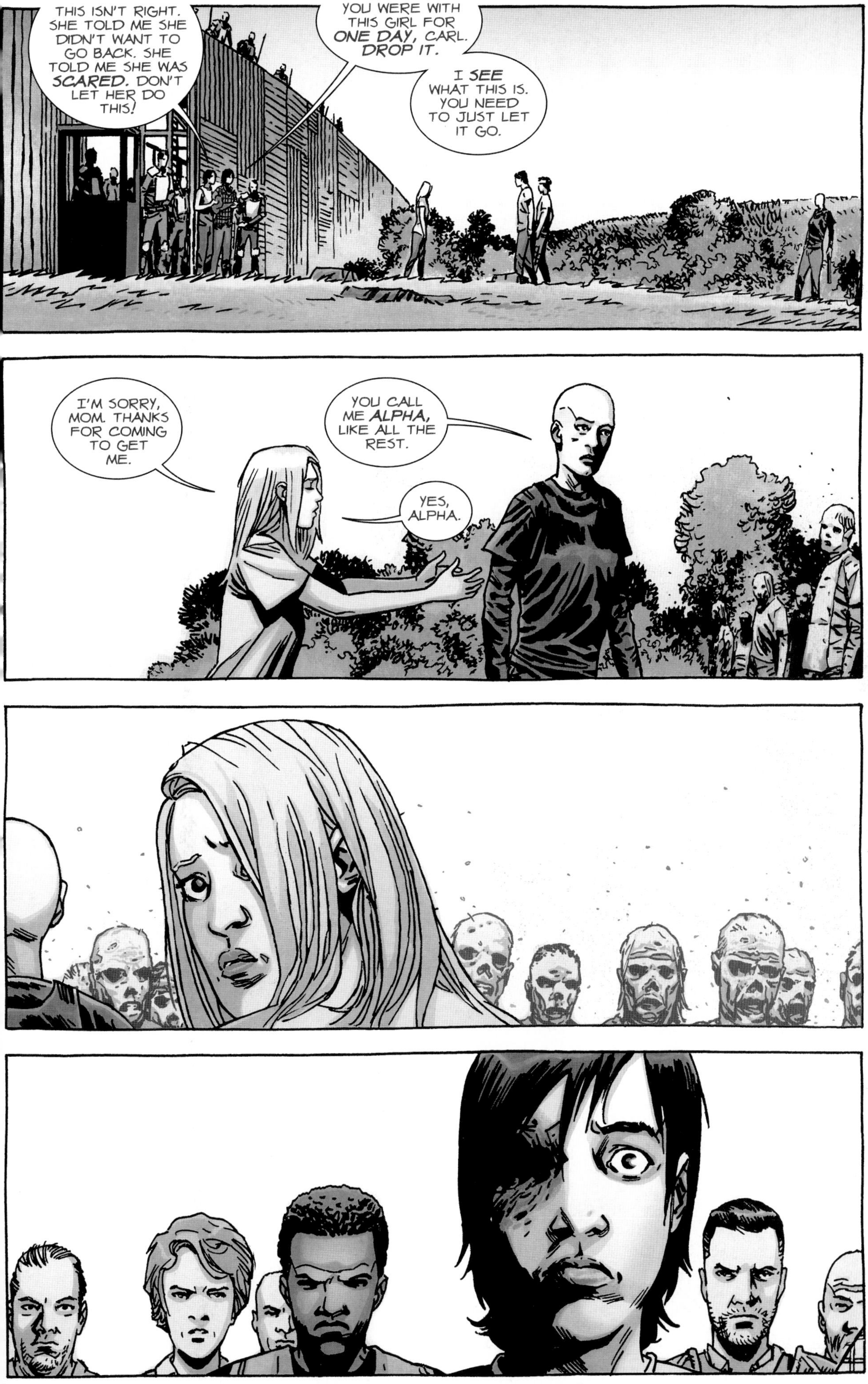
THIS ISN'T RIGHT. SHE TOLD ME SHE DIDN'T WANT TO GO BACK. SHE TOLD ME SHE WAS SCARED. DON'T LET HER DO THIS!
YOU WERE WITH THIS GIRL FOR ONE DAY, CARL. DROP IT.
I SEE WHAT THIS IS. YOU NEED TO JUST LET IT GO.
I'M SORRY, MOM. THANKS FOR COMING TO GET ME.
YOU CALL ME ALPHA, LIKE ALL THE REST.
YES, ALPHA.

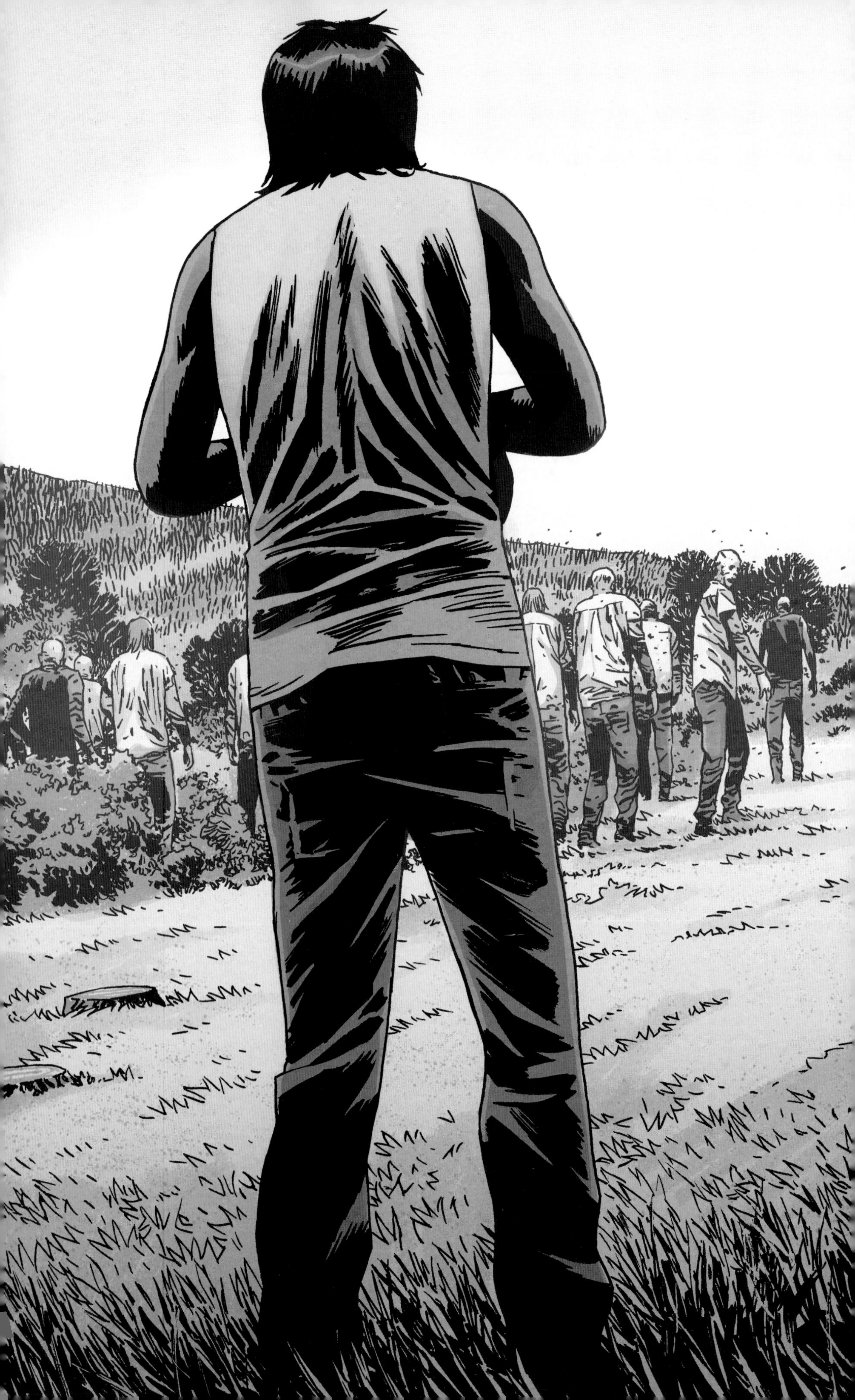

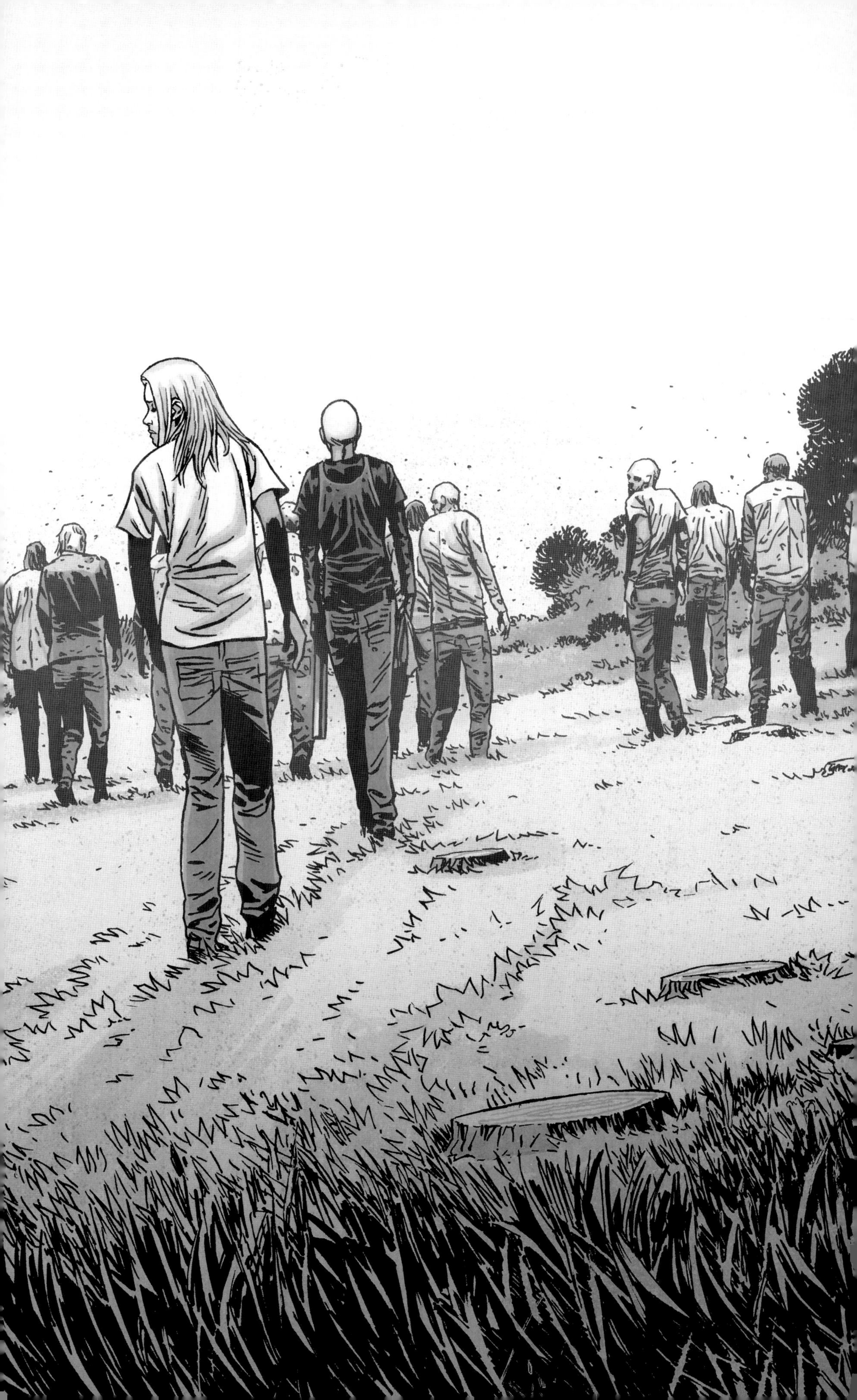

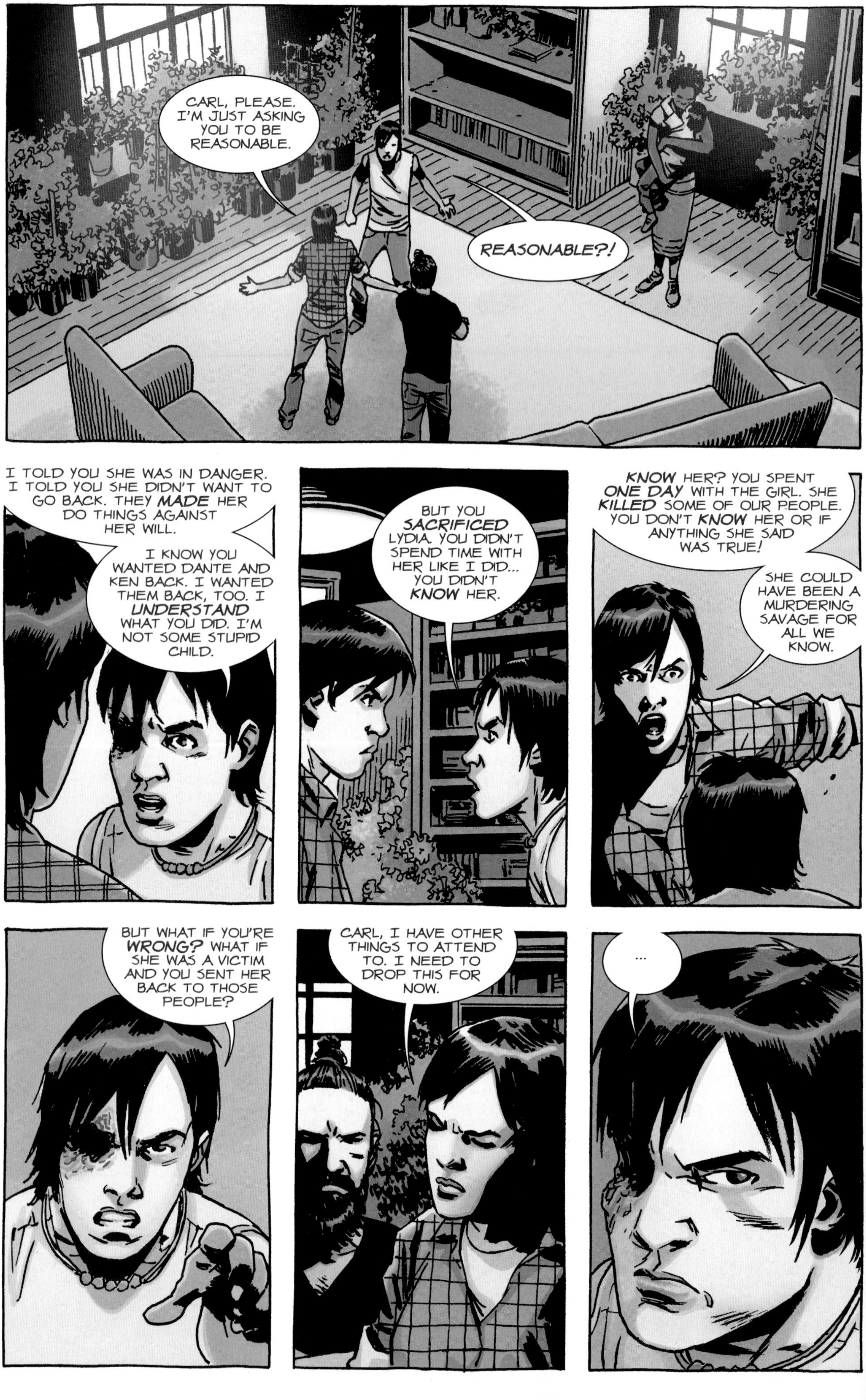
CARL, PLEASE. I'M JUST ASKING YOU TO BE REASONABLE.
REASONABLE?!
I TOLD YOU SHE WAS IN DANGER. I TOLD YOU SHE DIDN'T WANT TO GO BACK. THEY MADE HER DO THINGS AGAINST HER WILL.
I KNOW YOU WANTED DANTE AND KEN BACK. I WANTED THEM BACK, TOO. I UNDERSTAND WHAT YOU DID. I'M NOT SOME STUPID CHILD.
BUT YOU SACRIFICED LYDIA. YOU DIDN'T SPEND TIME WITH HER LIKE I DID... YOU DIDN'T KNOW HER.
KNOW HER? YOU SPENT ONE DAY WITH THE GIRL. SHE KILLED SOME OF OUR PEOPLE. YOU DON'T KNOW HER OR IF ANYTHING SHE SAID WAS TRUE!
SHE COULD HAVE BEEN A MURDERING SAVAGE FOR ALL WE KNOW.
BUT WHAT IF YOU'RE WRONG? WHAT IF SHE WAS A VICTIM AND YOU SENT HER BACK TO THOSE PEOPLE?
CARL, I HAVE OTHER THINGS TO ATTEND TO. I NEED TO DROP THIS FOR NOW.
...

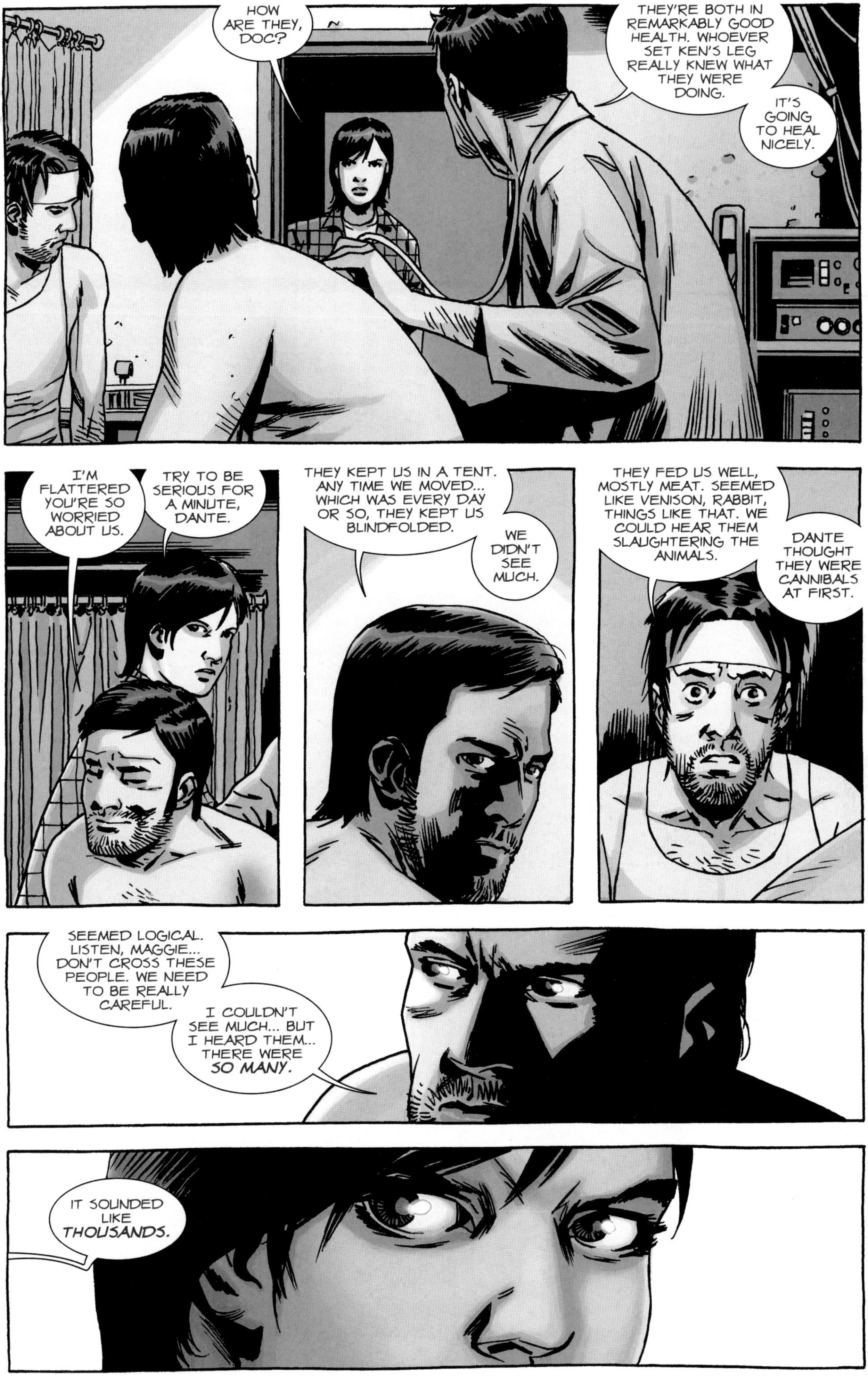
HOW ARE THEY, DOC?
THEY'RE BOTH IN REMARKABLY GOOD HEALTH. WHOEVER SET KEN'S LEG REALLY KNEW WHAT THEY WERE DOING.
IT'S GOING TO HEAL NICELY.
I'M FLATTERED YOU'RE SO WORRIED ABOUT US.
TRY TO BE SERIOUS FOR A MINUTE, DANTE.
THEY KEPT US IN A TENT. ANY TIME WE MOVED... WHICH WAS EVERY DAY OR SO, THEY KEPT US BLINDFOLDED.
WE DIDN'T SEE MUCH.
THEY FED US WELL, MOSTLY MEAT. SEEMED LIKE VENISON, RABBIT, THINGS LIKE THAT. WE COULD HEAR THEM SLAUGHTERING THE ANIMALS.
DANTE THOUGHT THEY WERE CANNIBALS AT FIRST.
SEEMED LOGICAL. LISTEN, MAGGIE... DON'T CROSS THESE PEOPLE. WE NEED TO BE REALLY CAREFUL.
I COULDN'T SEE MUCH... BUT I HEARD THEM... THERE WERE *SO MANY.*
IT SOUNDED LIKE *THOUSANDS.*

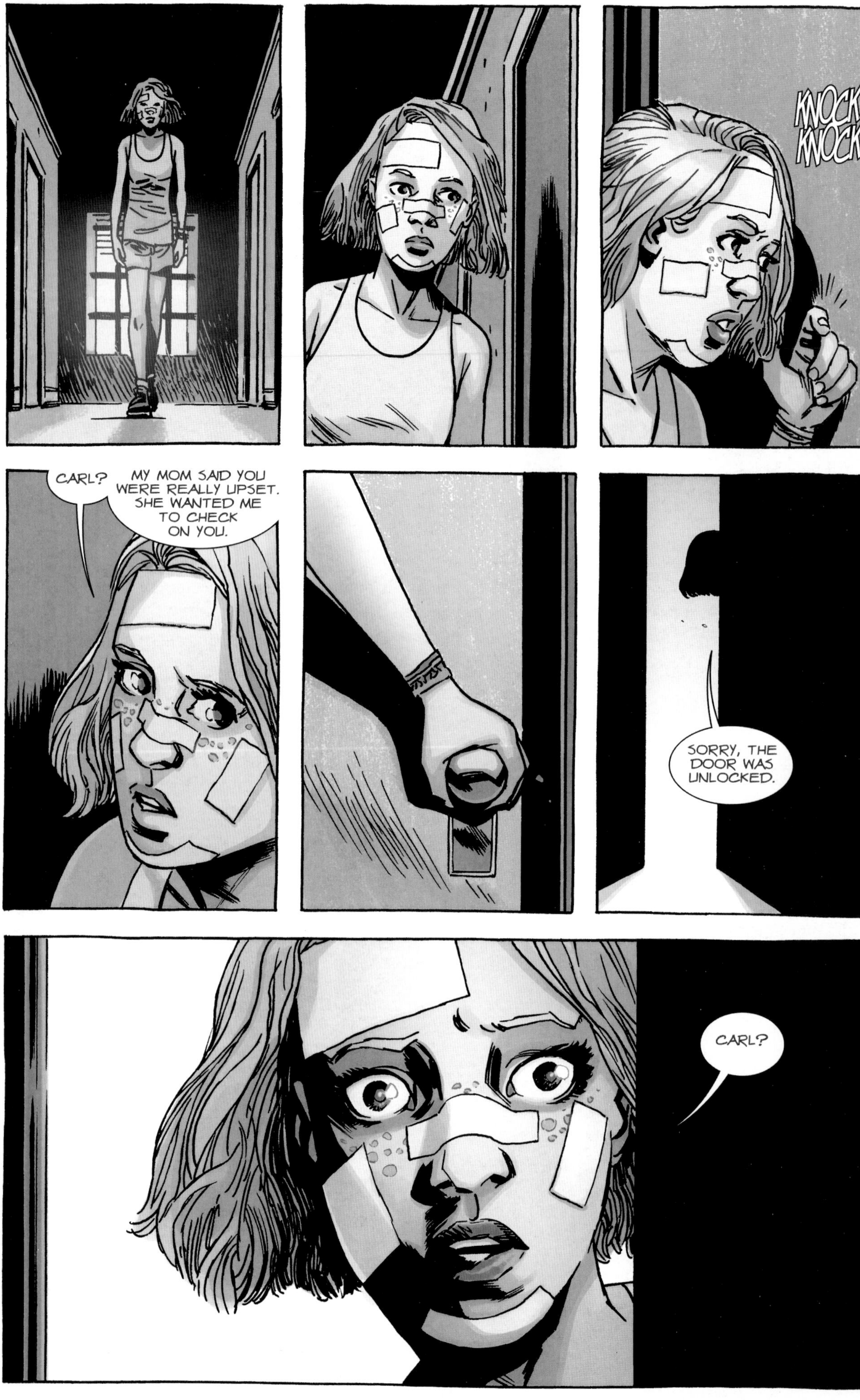
KNOCK KNOCK
CARL?
MY MOM SAID YOU WERE REALLY UPSET. SHE WANTED ME TO CHECK ON YOU.
SORRY, THE DOOR WAS UNLOCKED.
CARL?

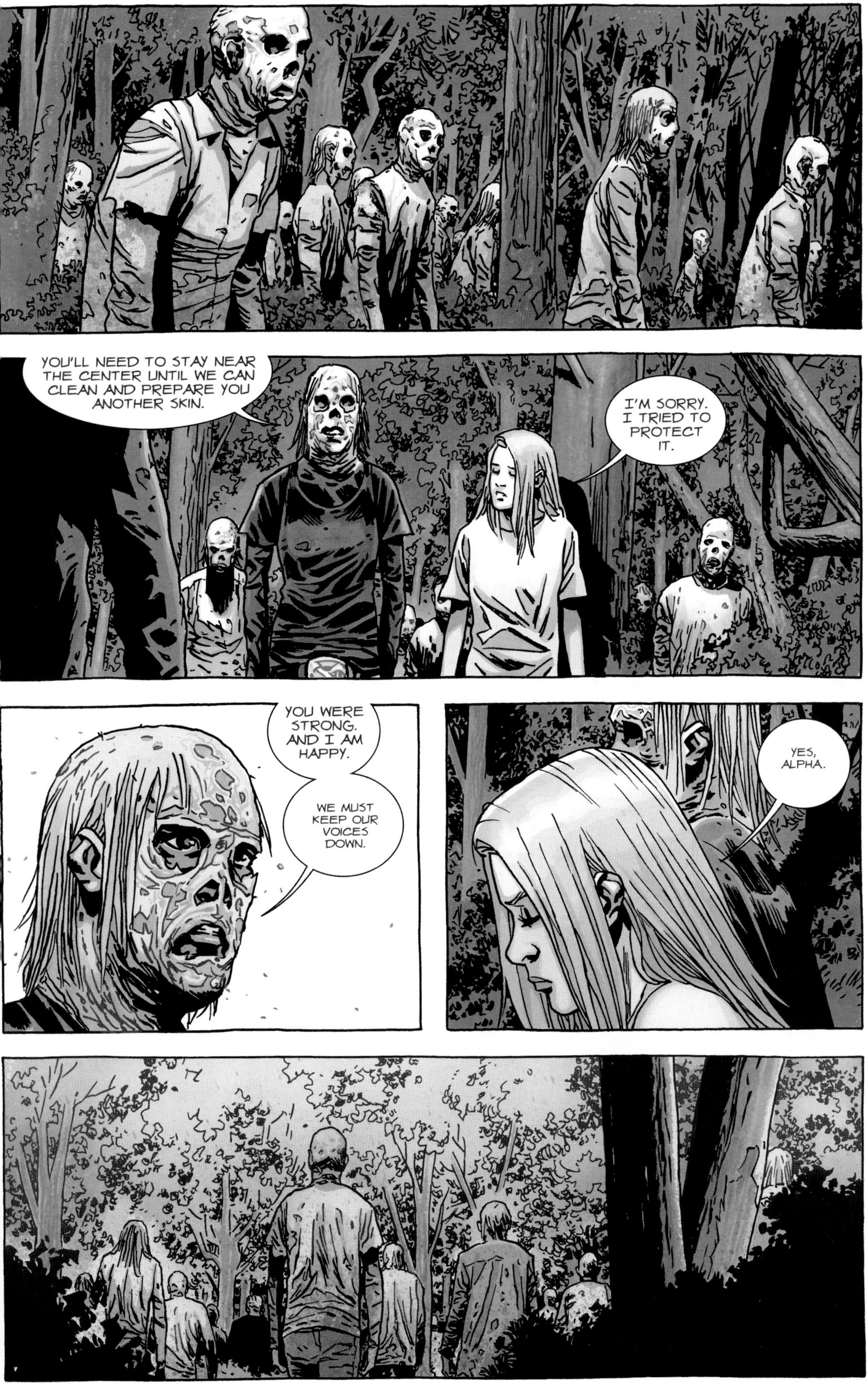
YOU'LL NEED TO STAY NEAR THE CENTER UNTIL WE CAN CLEAN AND PREPARE YOU ANOTHER SKIN.
I'M SORRY. I TRIED TO PROTECT IT.
YOU WERE STRONG. AND I AM HAPPY.
WE MUST KEEP OUR VOICES DOWN.
YES, ALPHA.

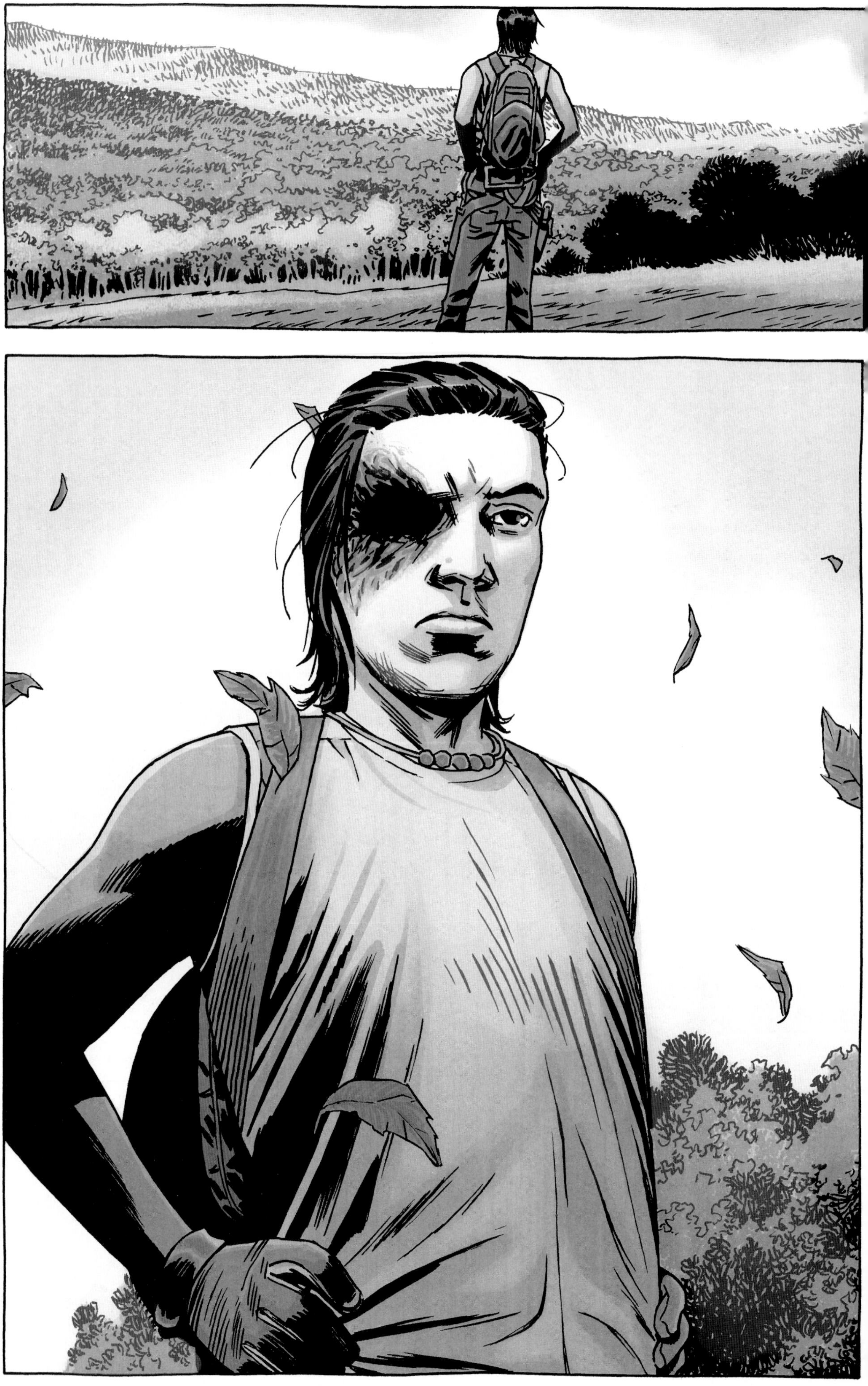

Chapter Twenty-Four:
Life and Death

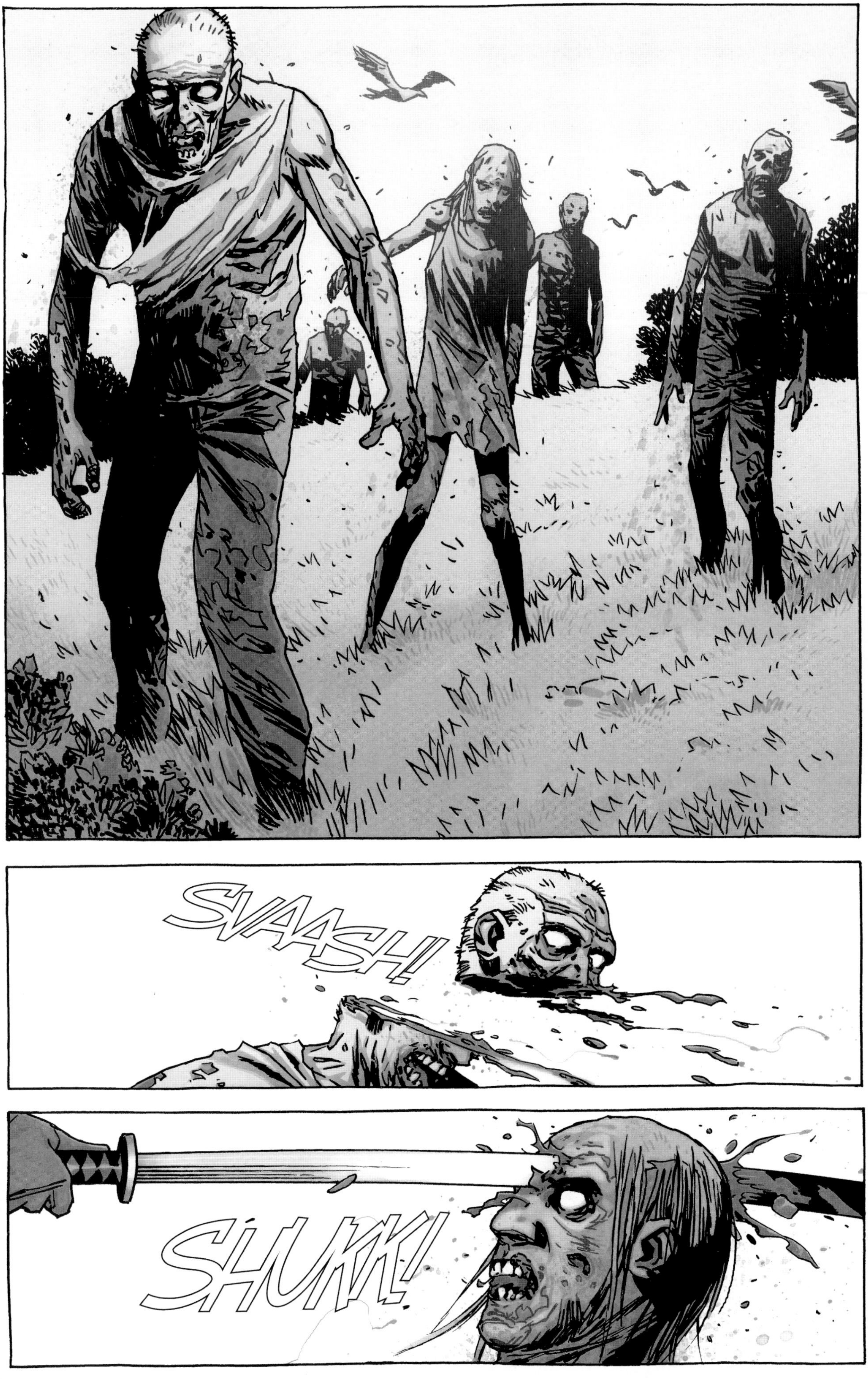
SVAASH!
SHUKK!

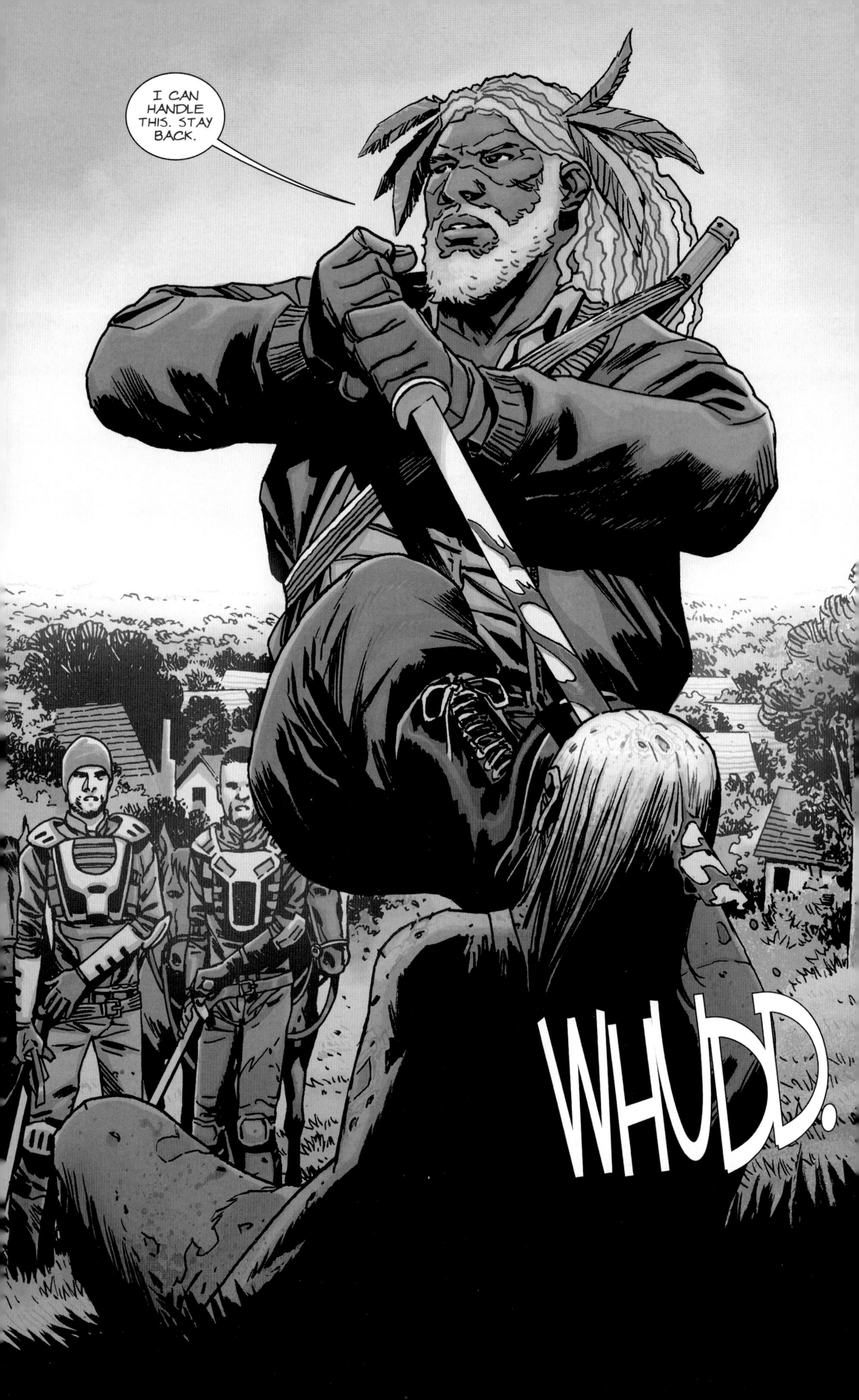
I CAN HANDLE THIS. STAY BACK.
WHUDD.

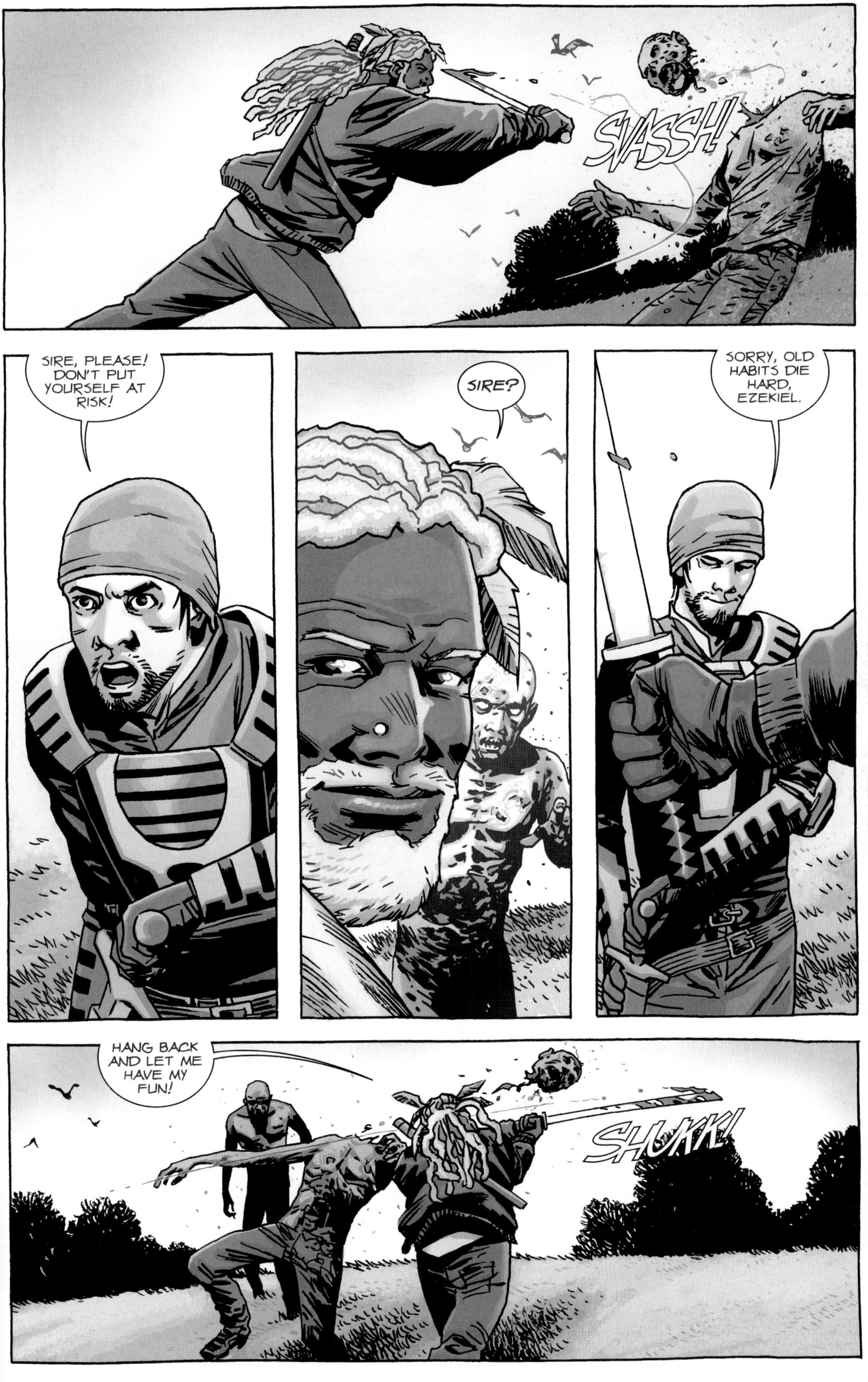
SVASSH!
SIRE, PLEASE! DON'T PUT YOURSELF AT RISK!
SIRE?
SORRY, OLD HABITS DIE HARD, EZEKIEL.
HANG BACK AND LET ME HAVE MY FUN!
SHUKK!

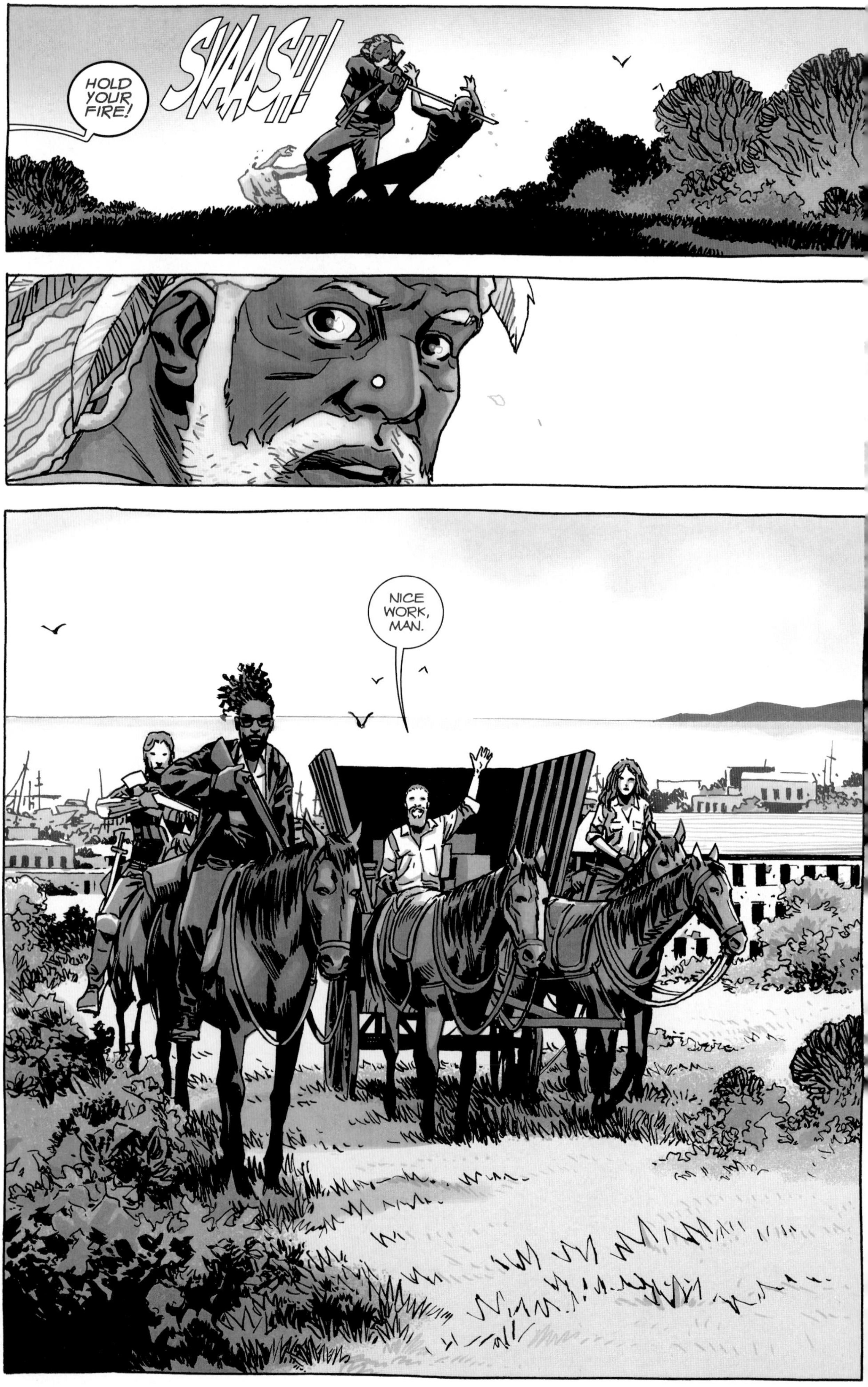
HOLD YOUR FIRE!
SVAASH!!
NICE WORK, MAN.

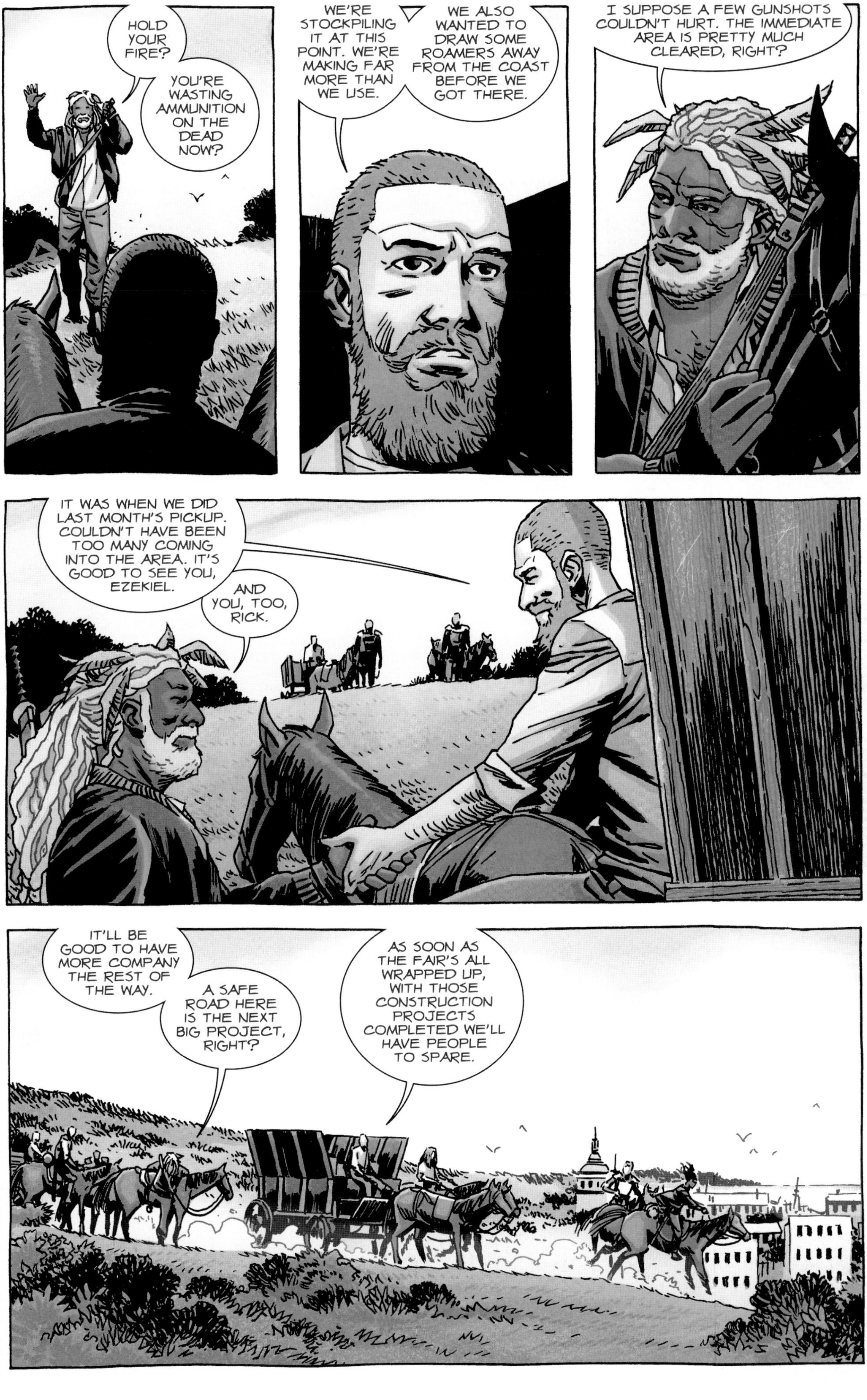
HOLD YOUR FIRE?
YOU'RE WASTING AMMUNITION ON THE DEAD NOW?
WE'RE STOCKPILING IT AT THIS POINT. WE'RE MAKING FAR MORE THAN WE USE.
WE ALSO WANTED TO DRAW SOME ROAMERS AWAY FROM THE COAST BEFORE WE GOT THERE.
I SUPPOSE A FEW GUNSHOTS COULDN'T HURT. THE IMMEDIATE AREA IS PRETTY MUCH CLEARED, RIGHT?
IT WAS WHEN WE DID LAST MONTH'S PICKUP. COULDN'T HAVE BEEN TOO MANY COMING INTO THE AREA. IT'S GOOD TO SEE YOU, EZEKIEL.
AND YOU, TOO, RICK.
IT'LL BE GOOD TO HAVE MORE COMPANY THE REST OF THE WAY.
A SAFE ROAD HERE IS THE NEXT BIG PROJECT, RIGHT?
AS SOON AS THE FAIR'S ALL WRAPPED UP, WITH THOSE CONSTRUCTION PROJECTS COMPLETED WE'LL HAVE PEOPLE TO SPARE.

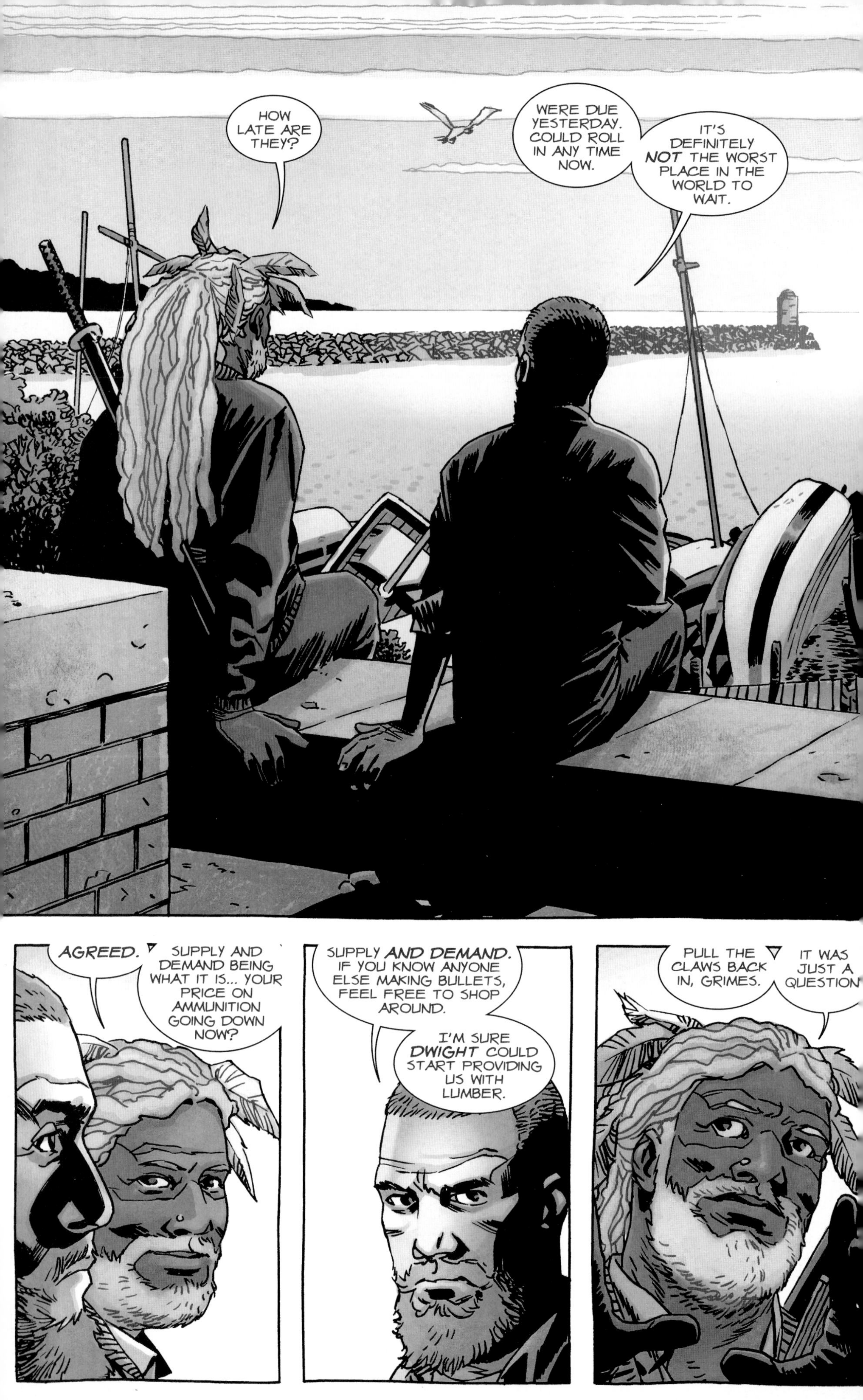
HOW LATE ARE THEY?
WERE DUE YESTERDAY. COULD ROLL IN ANY TIME NOW.
IT'S DEFINITELY **NOT** THE WORST PLACE IN THE WORLD TO WAIT.
AGREED.
SUPPLY AND DEMAND BEING WHAT IT IS... YOUR PRICE ON AMMUNITION GOING DOWN NOW?
SUPPLY **AND DEMAND.** IF YOU KNOW ANYONE ELSE MAKING BULLETS, FEEL FREE TO SHOP AROUND.
I'M SURE **DWIGHT** COULD START PROVIDING US WITH LUMBER.
PULL THE CLAWS BACK IN, GRIMES.
IT WAS JUST A QUESTION

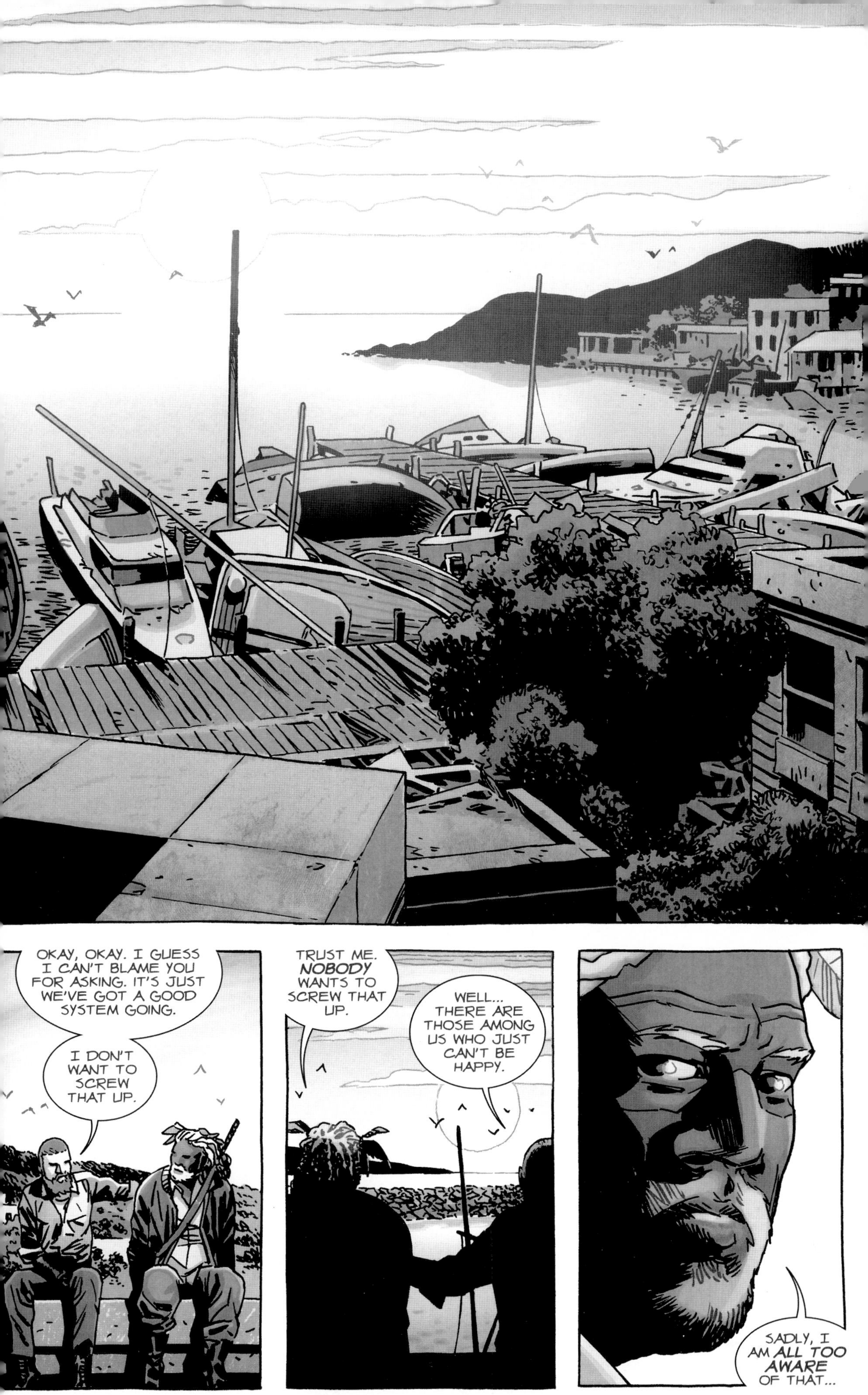
OKAY, OKAY. I GUESS I CAN'T BLAME YOU FOR ASKING. IT'S JUST WE'VE GOT A GOOD SYSTEM GOING.
I DON'T WANT TO SCREW THAT UP.
TRUST ME. NOBODY WANTS TO SCREW THAT UP.
WELL... THERE ARE THOSE AMONG US WHO JUST CAN'T BE HAPPY.
SADLY, I AM ALL TOO AWARE OF THAT...

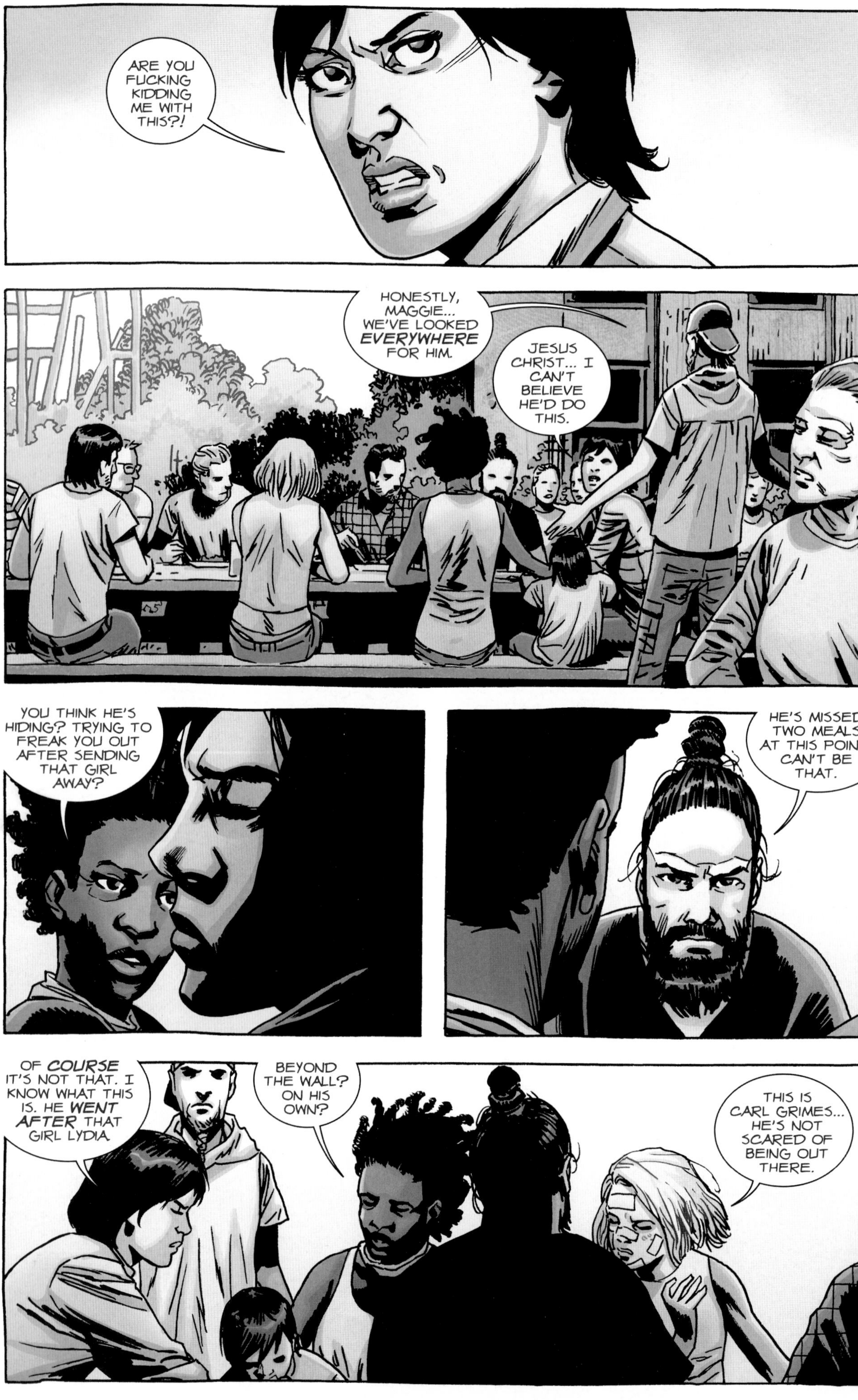
ARE YOU FUCKING KIDDING ME WITH THIS?!
HONESTLY, MAGGIE... WE'VE LOOKED EVERYWHERE FOR HIM.
JESUS CHRIST... I CAN'T BELIEVE HE'D DO THIS.
YOU THINK HE'S HIDING? TRYING TO FREAK YOU OUT AFTER SENDING THAT GIRL AWAY?
HE'S MISSED TWO MEALS AT THIS POINT. CAN'T BE THAT.
OF COURSE IT'S NOT THAT. I KNOW WHAT THIS IS. HE WENT AFTER THAT GIRL LYDIA.
BEYOND THE WALL? ON HIS OWN?
THIS IS CARL GRIMES... HE'S NOT SCARED OF BEING OUT THERE.

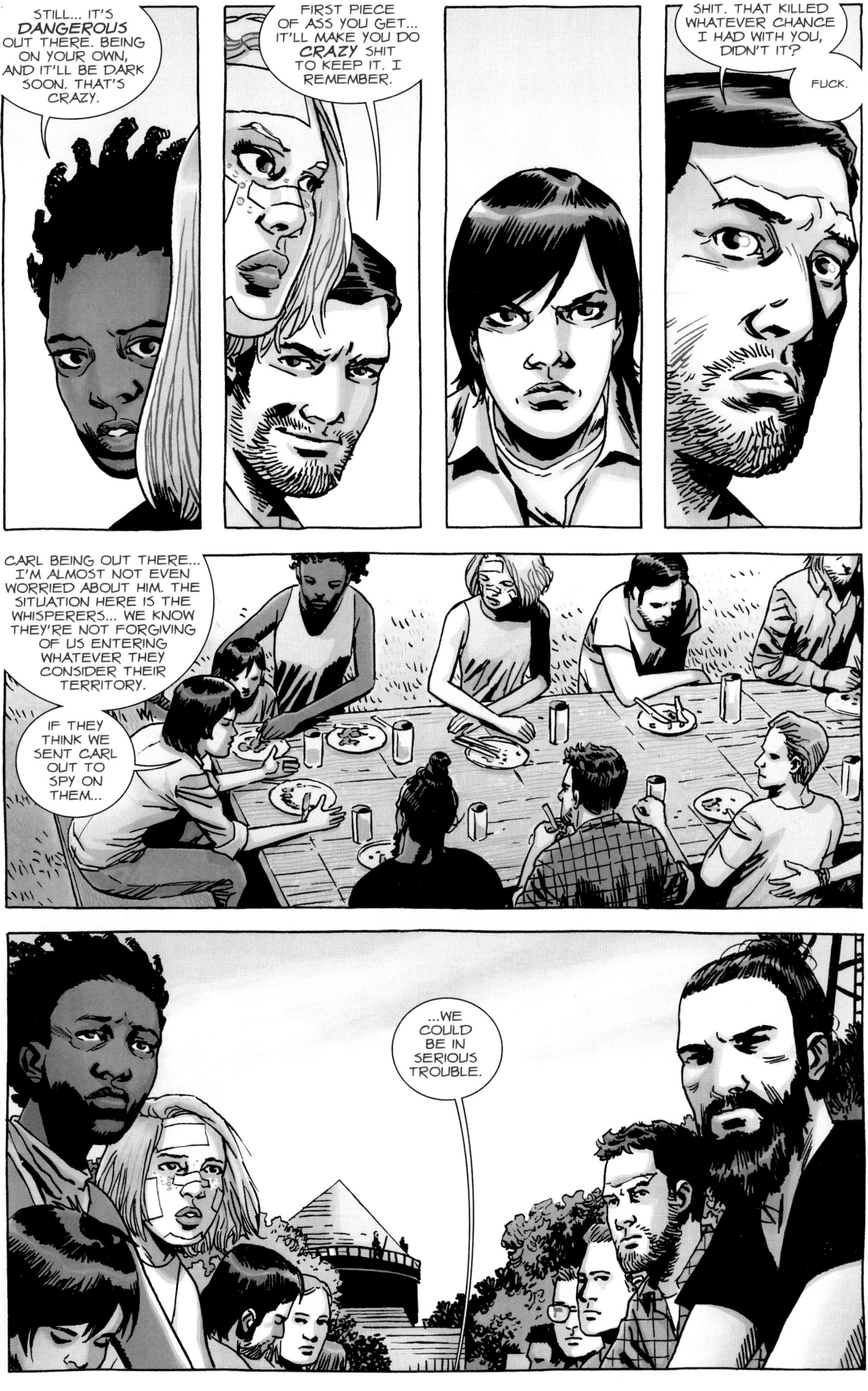
STILL... IT'S DANGEROUS OUT THERE. BEING ON YOUR OWN, AND IT'LL BE DARK SOON. THAT'S CRAZY.
FIRST PIECE OF ASS YOU GET... IT'LL MAKE YOU DO CRAZY SHIT TO KEEP IT. I REMEMBER.
SHIT. THAT KILLED WHATEVER CHANCE I HAD WITH YOU, DIDN'T IT?
FUCK.
CARL BEING OUT THERE... I'M ALMOST NOT EVEN WORRIED ABOUT HIM. THE SITUATION HERE IS THE WHISPERERS... WE KNOW THEY'RE NOT FORGIVING OF US ENTERING WHATEVER THEY CONSIDER THEIR TERRITORY.
IF THEY THINK WE SENT CARL OUT TO SPY ON THEM...
...WE COULD BE IN SERIOUS TROUBLE.

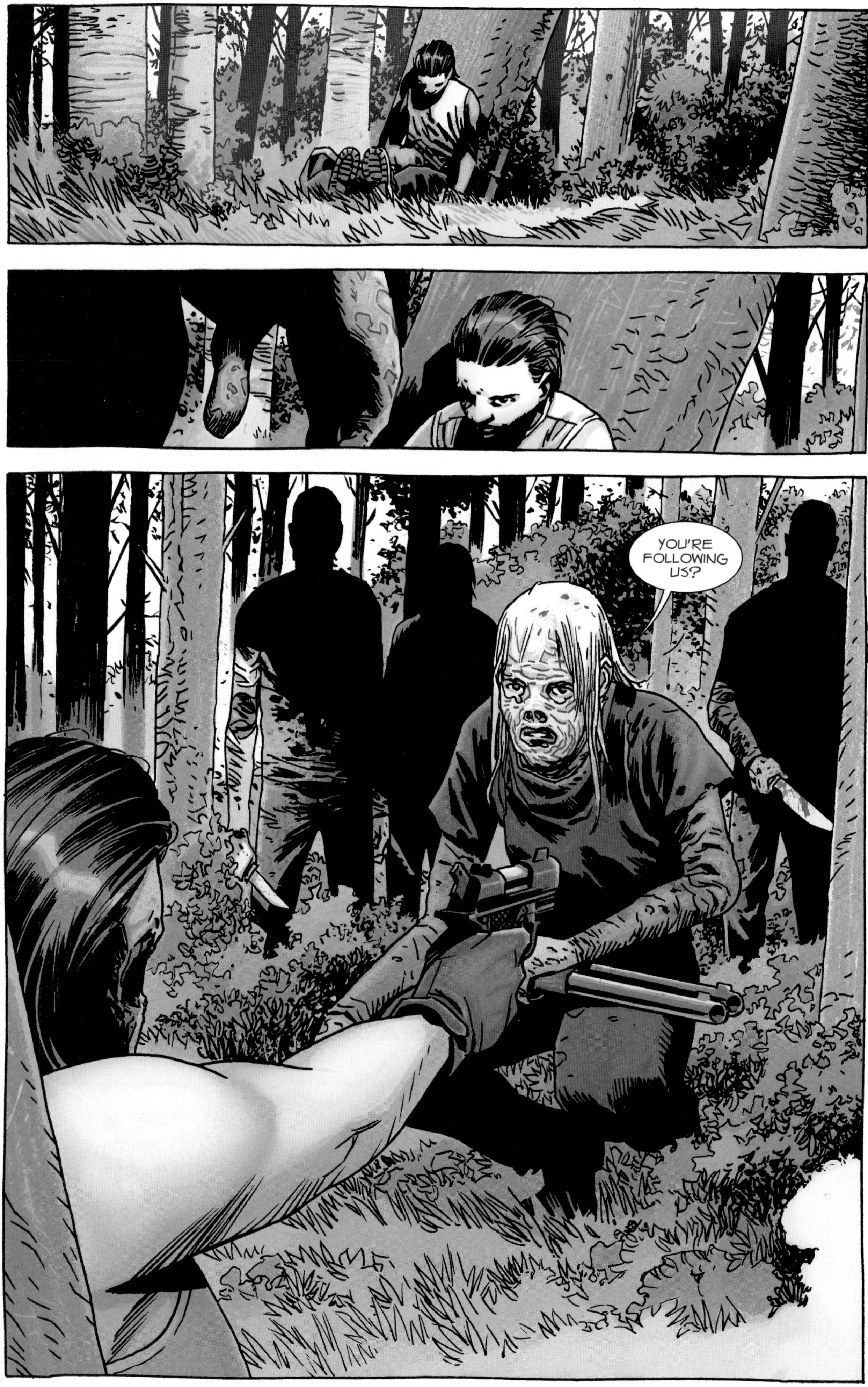
YOU'RE FOLLOWING US?

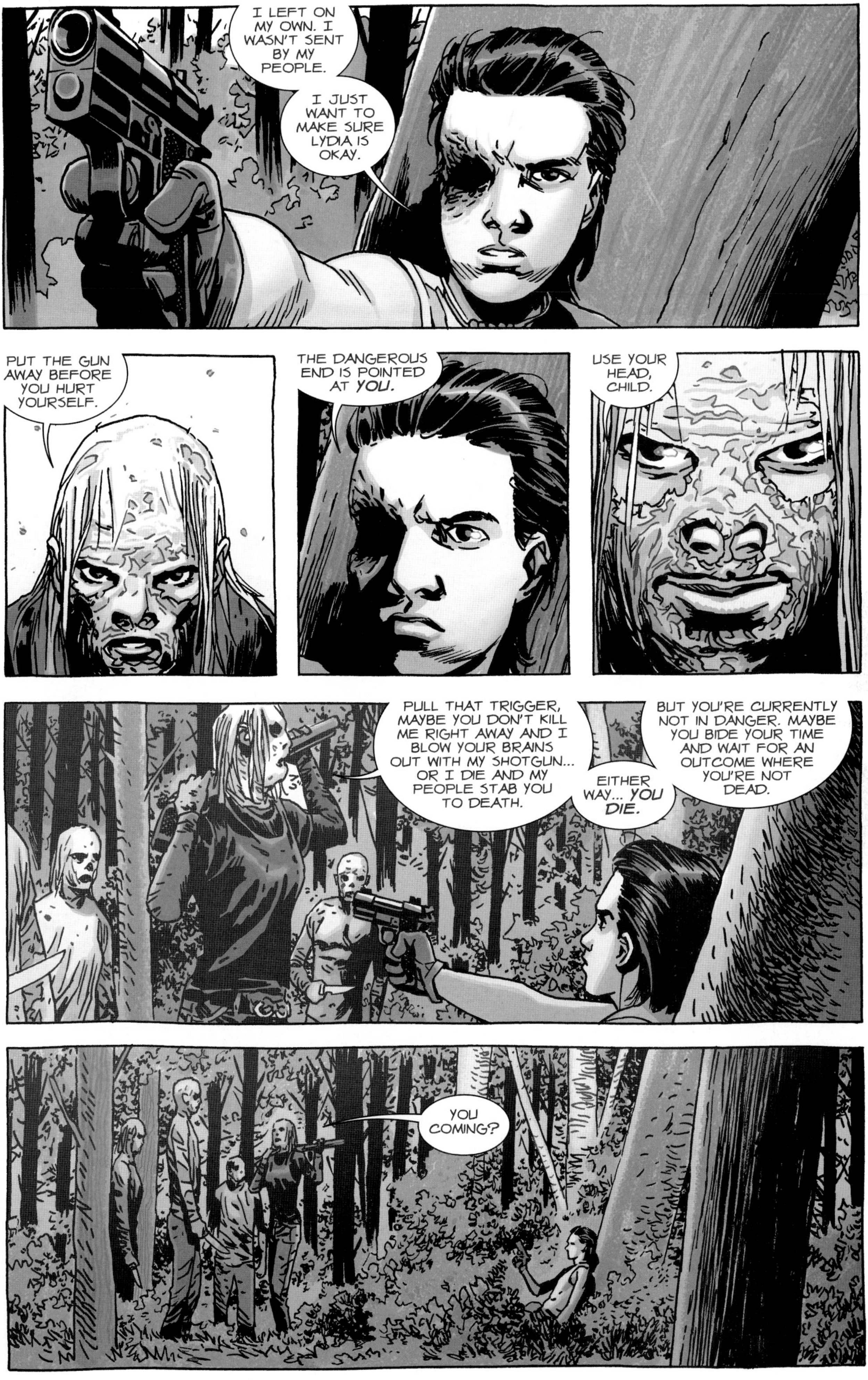
I LEFT ON MY OWN. I WASN'T SENT BY MY PEOPLE.
I JUST WANT TO MAKE SURE LYDIA IS OKAY.
PUT THE GUN AWAY BEFORE YOU HURT YOURSELF.
THE DANGEROUS END IS POINTED AT *YOU.*
USE YOUR HEAD, CHILD.
PULL THAT TRIGGER, MAYBE YOU DON'T KILL ME RIGHT AWAY AND I BLOW YOUR BRAINS OUT WITH MY SHOTGUN... OR I DIE AND MY PEOPLE STAB YOU TO DEATH.
EITHER WAY... *YOU DIE.*
BUT YOU'RE CURRENTLY NOT IN DANGER. MAYBE YOU BIDE YOUR TIME AND WAIT FOR AN OUTCOME WHERE YOU'RE NOT DEAD.
YOU COMING?

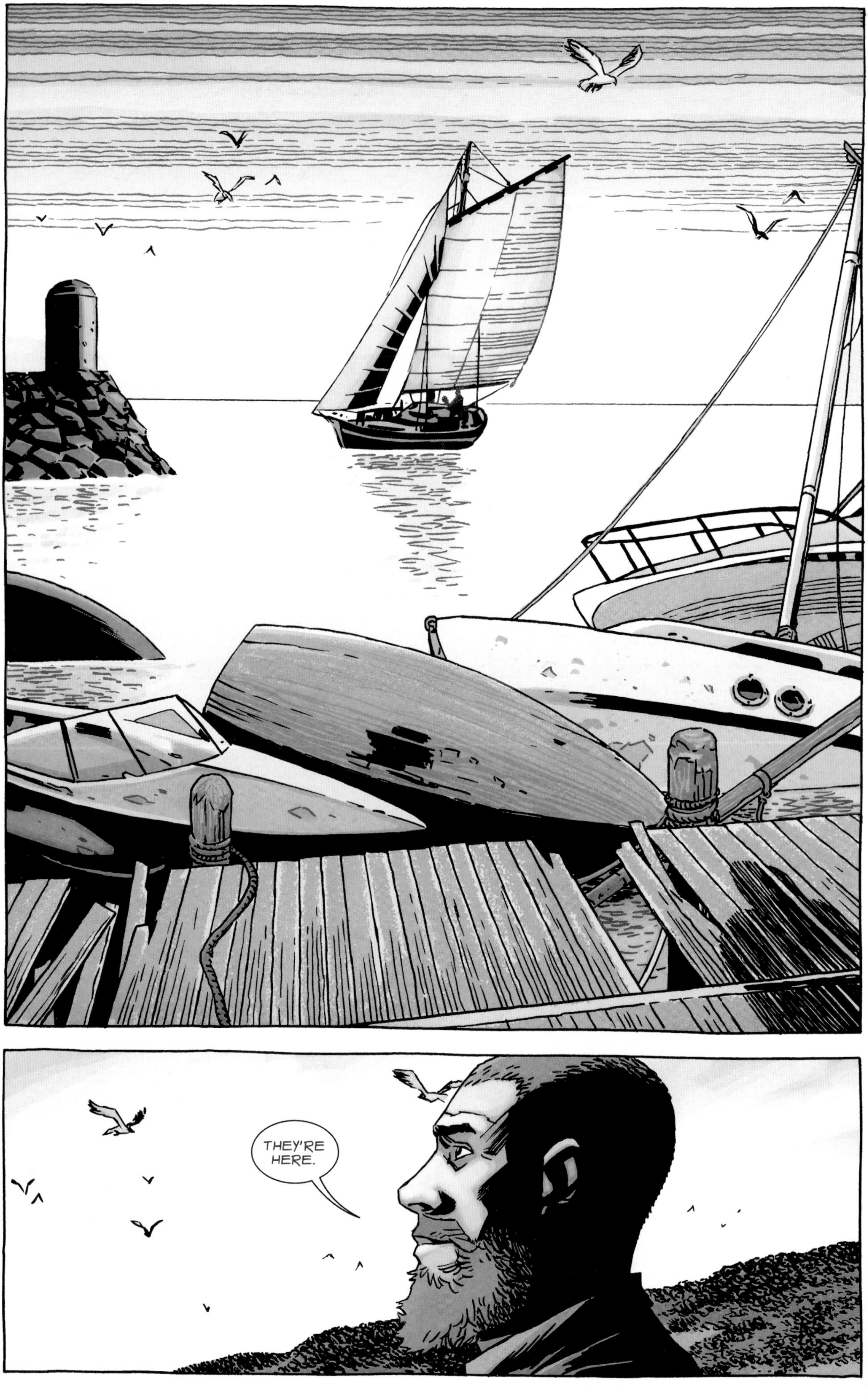
THEY'RE HERE.

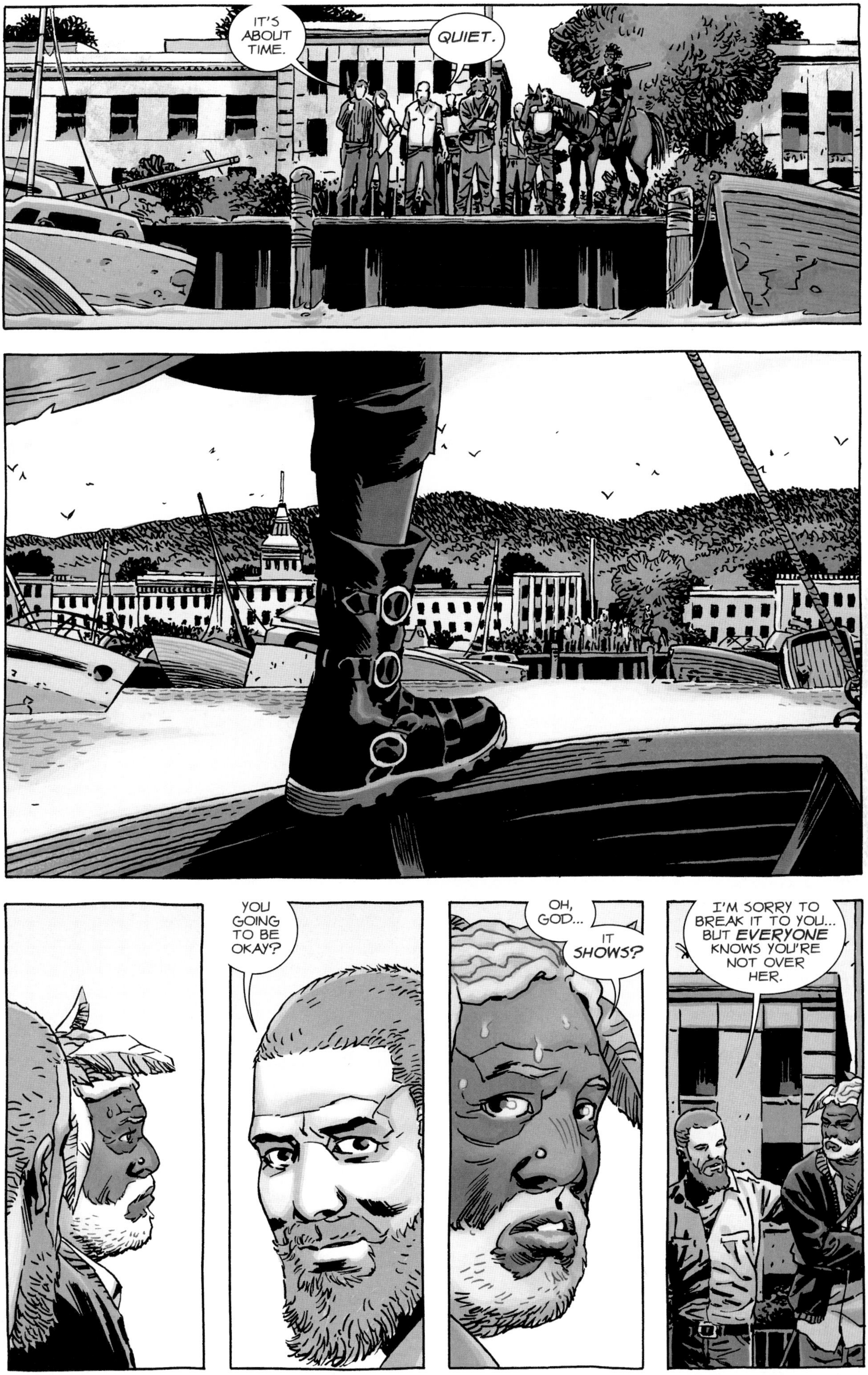

IT'S ABOUT TIME.
QUIET.
YOU GOING TO BE OKAY?
OH, GOD...
IT SHOWS?
I'M SORRY TO BREAK IT TO YOU... BUT EVERYONE KNOWS YOU'RE NOT OVER HER.

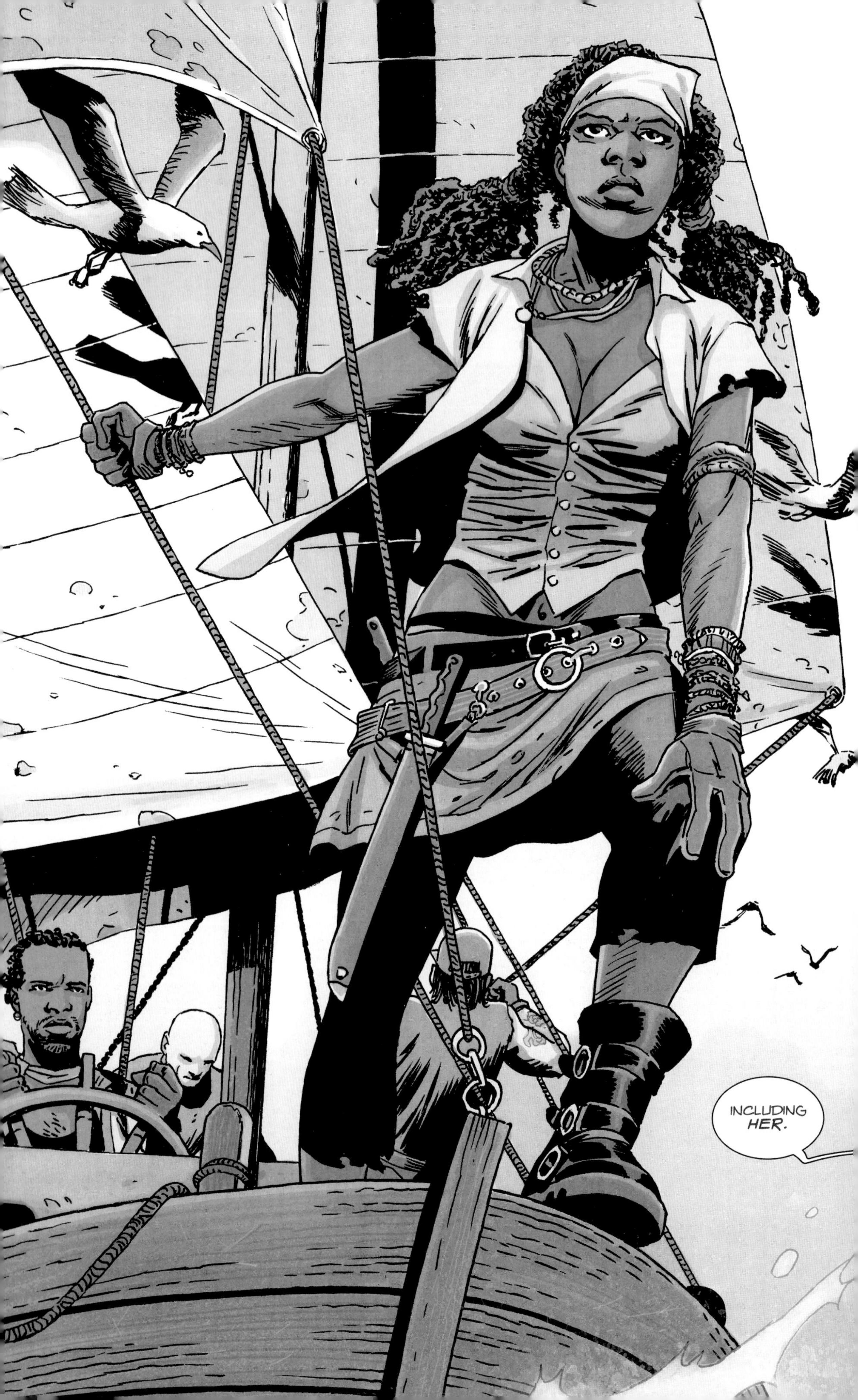
INCLUDING HER.

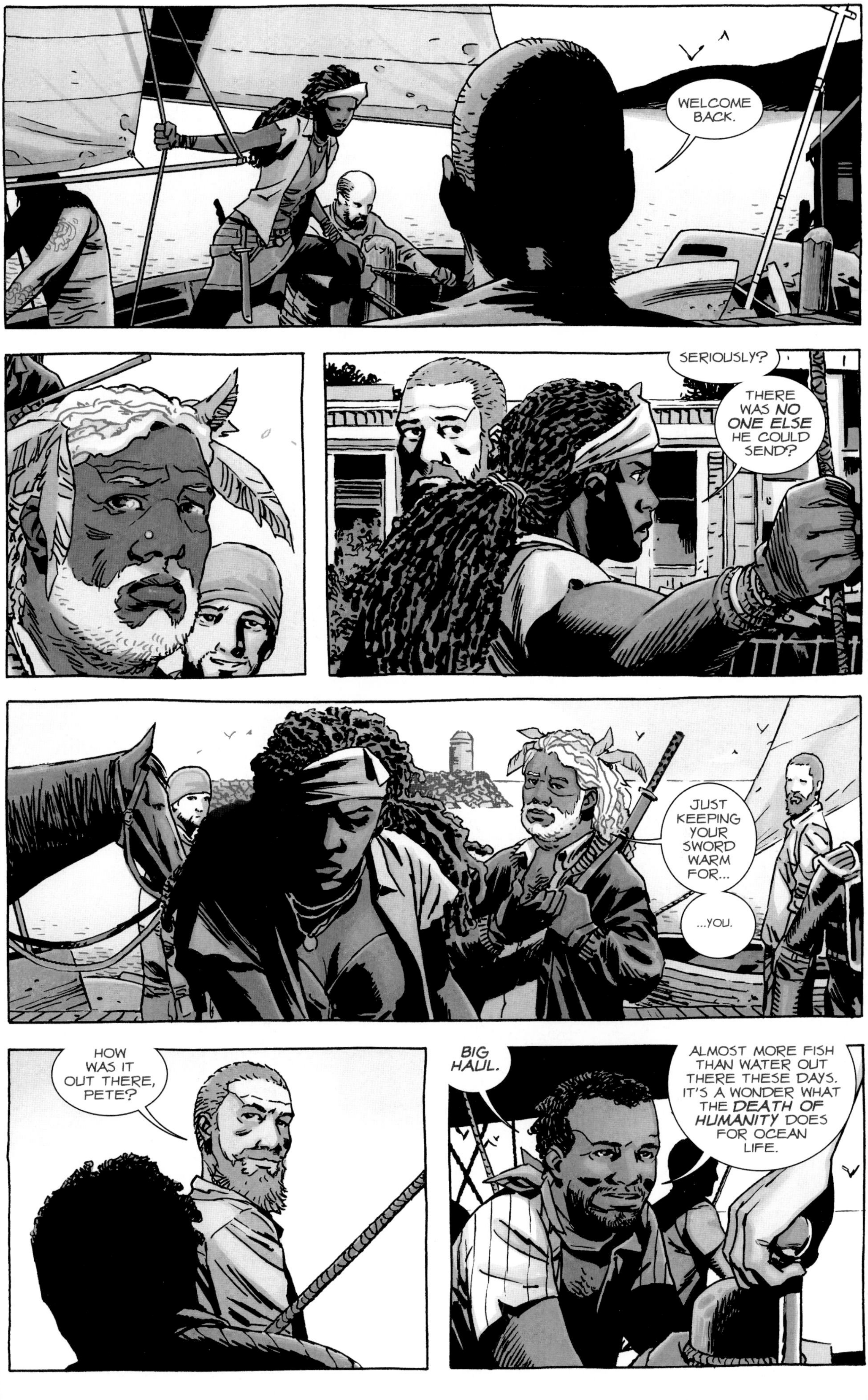
WELCOME BACK.
SERIOUSLY?
THERE WAS NO ONE ELSE HE COULD SEND?
JUST KEEPING YOUR SWORD WARM FOR...
...YOU.
HOW WAS IT OUT THERE, PETE?
BIG HAUL.
ALMOST MORE FISH THAN WATER OUT THERE THESE DAYS. IT'S A WONDER WHAT THE DEATH OF HUMANITY DOES FOR OCEAN LIFE.

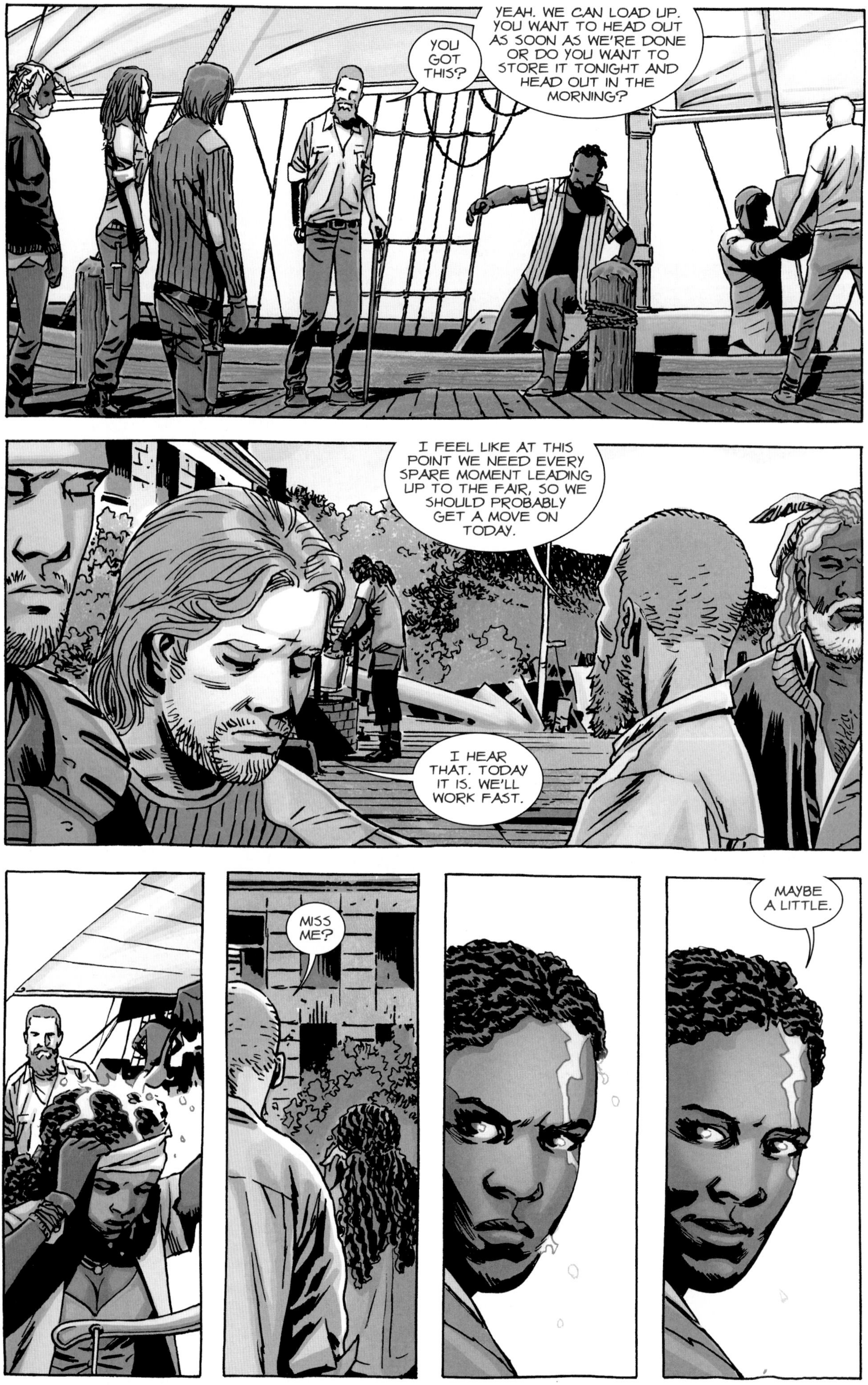
YOU GOT THIS?
YEAH. WE CAN LOAD UP. YOU WANT TO HEAD OUT AS SOON AS WE'RE DONE OR DO YOU WANT TO STORE IT TONIGHT AND HEAD OUT IN THE MORNING?
I FEEL LIKE AT THIS POINT WE NEED EVERY SPARE MOMENT LEADING UP TO THE FAIR, SO WE SHOULD PROBABLY GET A MOVE ON TODAY.
I HEAR THAT. TODAY IT IS. WE'LL WORK FAST.
MISS ME?
MAYBE A LITTLE.

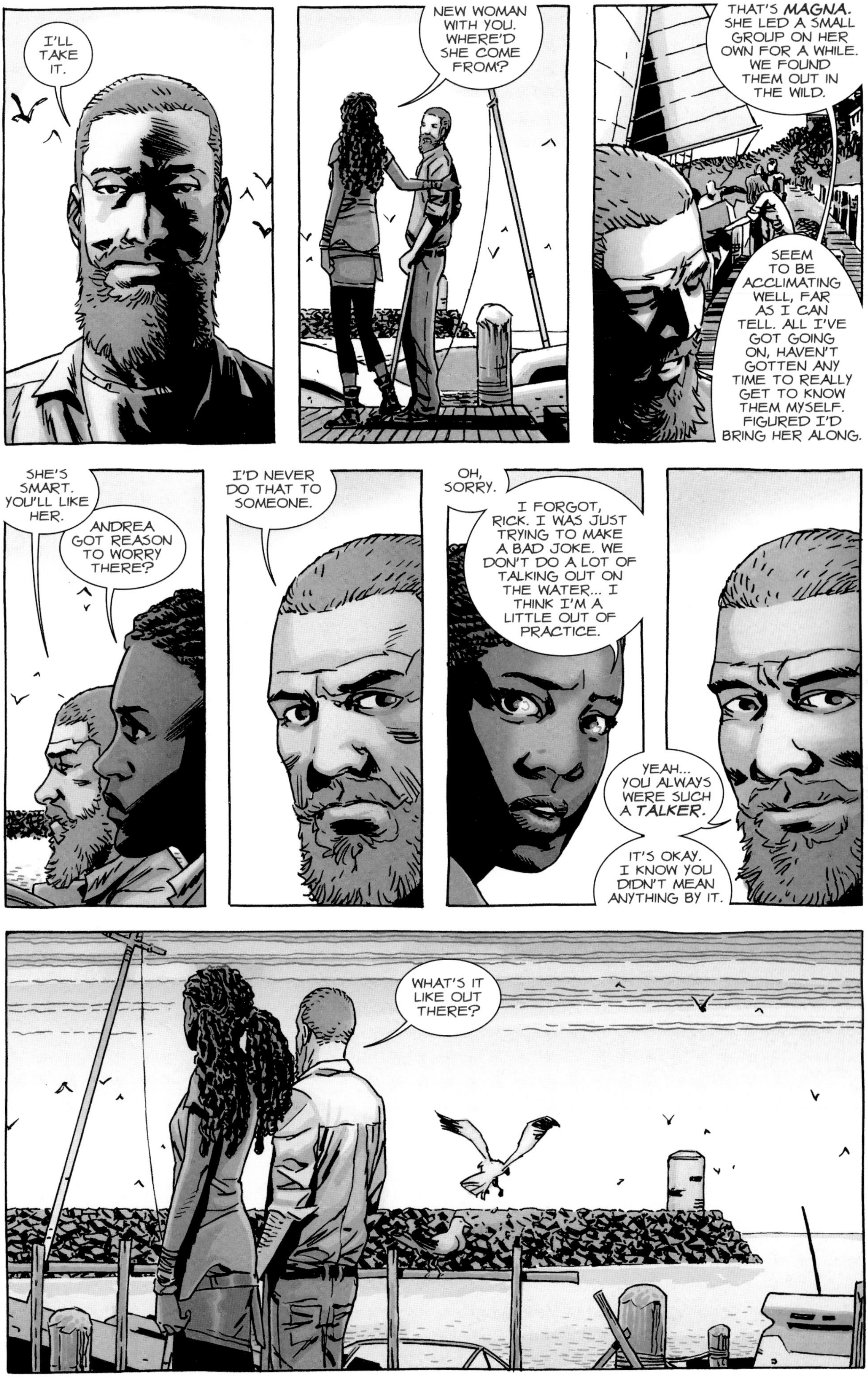

I'LL TAKE IT.
NEW WOMAN WITH YOU. WHERE'D SHE COME FROM?
THAT'S MAGNA. SHE LED A SMALL GROUP ON HER OWN FOR A WHILE. WE FOUND THEM OUT IN THE WILD.
SEEM TO BE ACCLIMATING WELL, FAR AS I CAN TELL. ALL I'VE GOT GOING ON, HAVEN'T GOTTEN ANY TIME TO REALLY GET TO KNOW THEM MYSELF. FIGURED I'D BRING HER ALONG.
SHE'S SMART. YOU'LL LIKE HER.
ANDREA GOT REASON TO WORRY THERE?
I'D NEVER DO THAT TO SOMEONE.
OH, SORRY.
I FORGOT, RICK. I WAS JUST TRYING TO MAKE A BAD JOKE. WE DON'T DO A LOT OF TALKING OUT ON THE WATER... I THINK I'M A LITTLE OUT OF PRACTICE.
YEAH... YOU ALWAYS WERE SUCH A TALKER.
IT'S OKAY. I KNOW YOU DIDN'T MEAN ANYTHING BY IT.
WHAT'S IT LIKE OUT THERE?

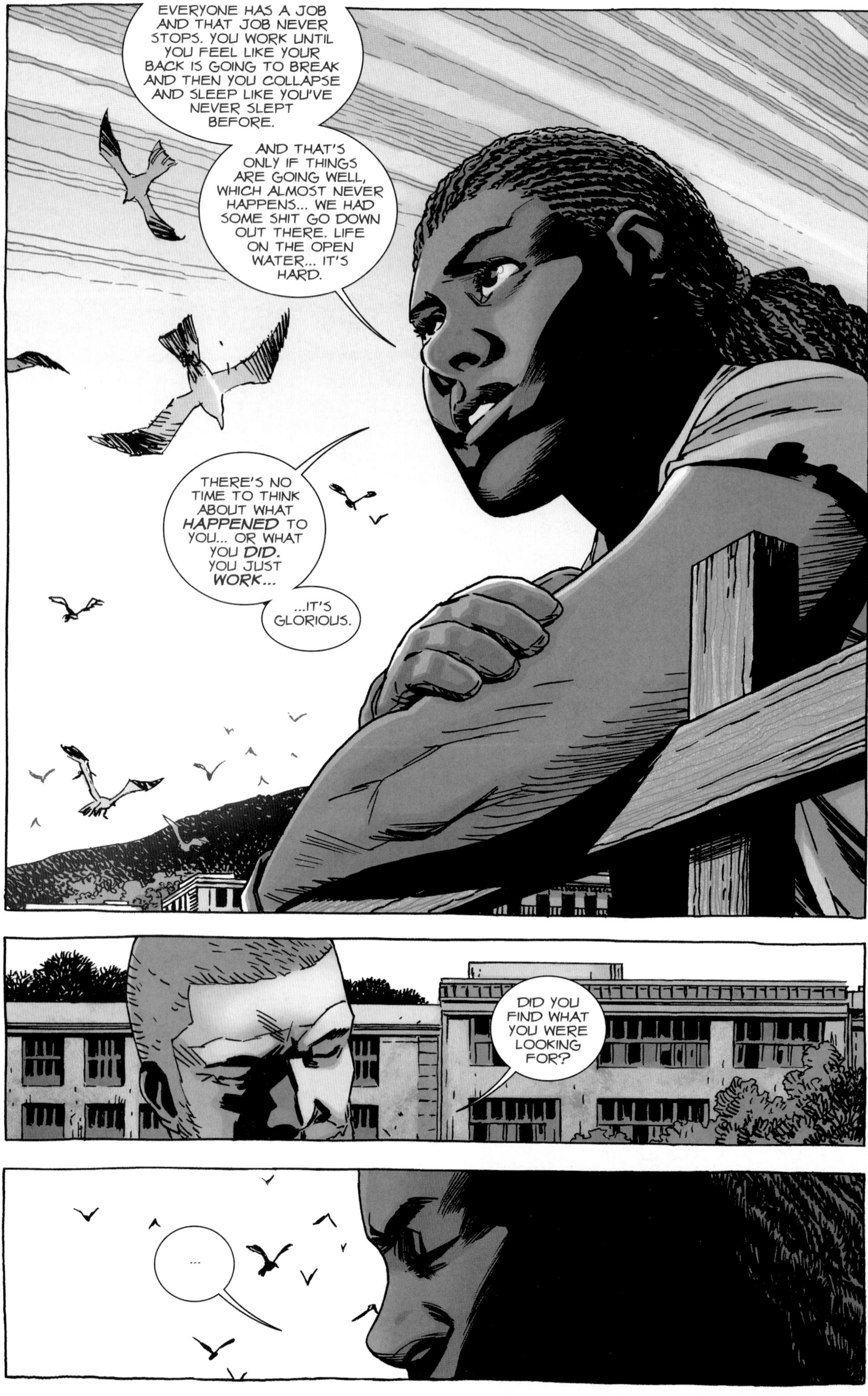
EVERYONE HAS A JOB AND THAT JOB NEVER STOPS. YOU WORK UNTIL YOU FEEL LIKE YOUR BACK IS GOING TO BREAK AND THEN YOU COLLAPSE AND SLEEP LIKE YOU'VE NEVER SLEPT BEFORE.
AND THAT'S ONLY IF THINGS ARE GOING WELL, WHICH ALMOST NEVER HAPPENS... WE HAD SOME SHIT GO DOWN OUT THERE. LIFE ON THE OPEN WATER... IT'S HARD.
THERE'S NO TIME TO THINK ABOUT WHAT HAPPENED TO YOU... OR WHAT YOU DID. YOU JUST WORK...
...IT'S GLORIOUS.
DID YOU FIND WHAT YOU WERE LOOKING FOR?
...

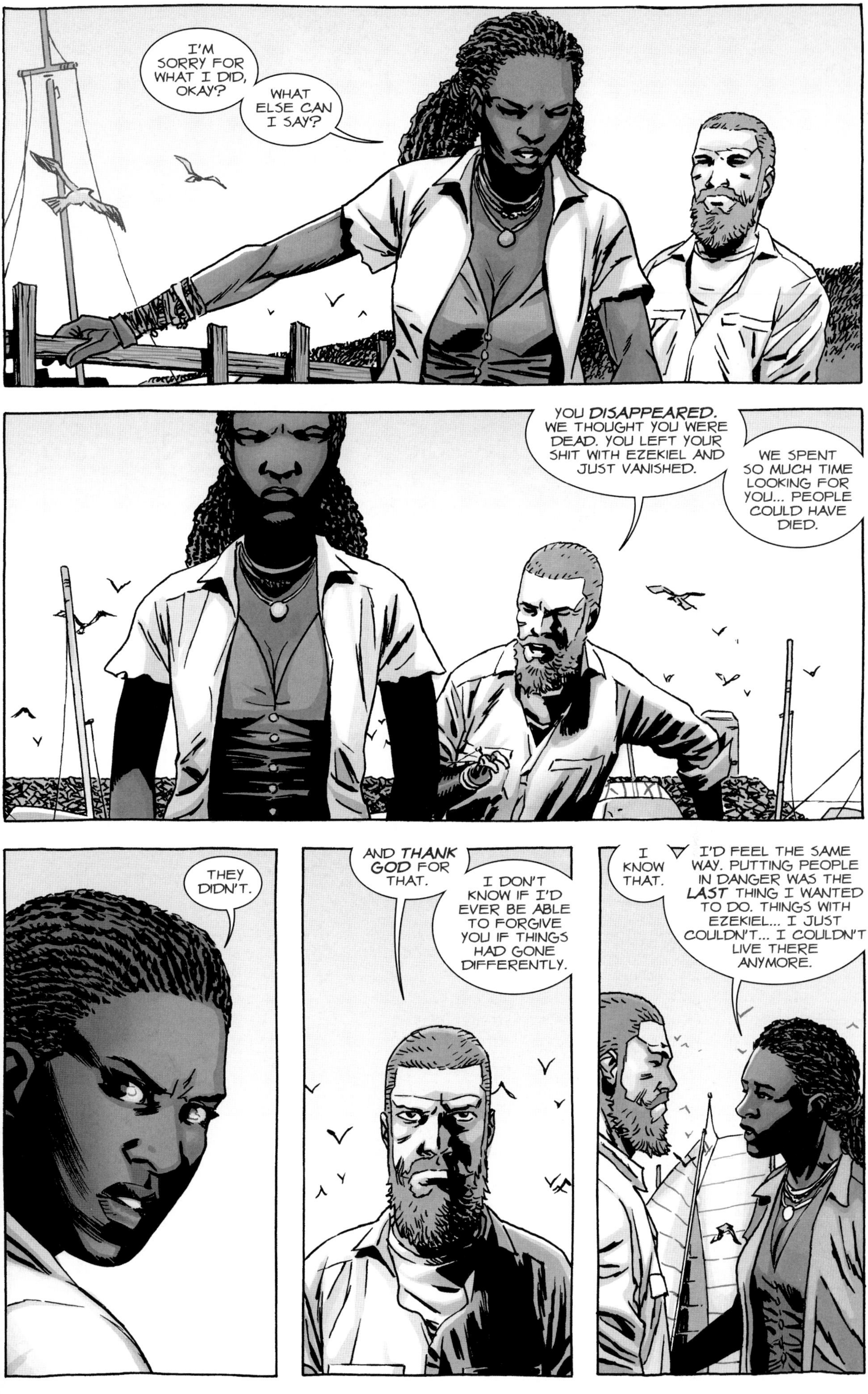
I'M SORRY FOR WHAT I DID, OKAY?
WHAT ELSE CAN I SAY?
YOU DISAPPEARED. WE THOUGHT YOU WERE DEAD. YOU LEFT YOUR SHIT WITH EZEKIEL AND JUST VANISHED.
WE SPENT SO MUCH TIME LOOKING FOR YOU... PEOPLE COULD HAVE DIED.
THEY DIDN'T.
AND THANK GOD FOR THAT.
I DON'T KNOW IF I'D EVER BE ABLE TO FORGIVE YOU IF THINGS HAD GONE DIFFERENTLY.
I KNOW THAT.
I'D FEEL THE SAME WAY. PUTTING PEOPLE IN DANGER WAS THE LAST THING I WANTED TO DO. THINGS WITH EZEKIEL... I JUST COULDN'T... I COULDN'T LIVE THERE ANYMORE.

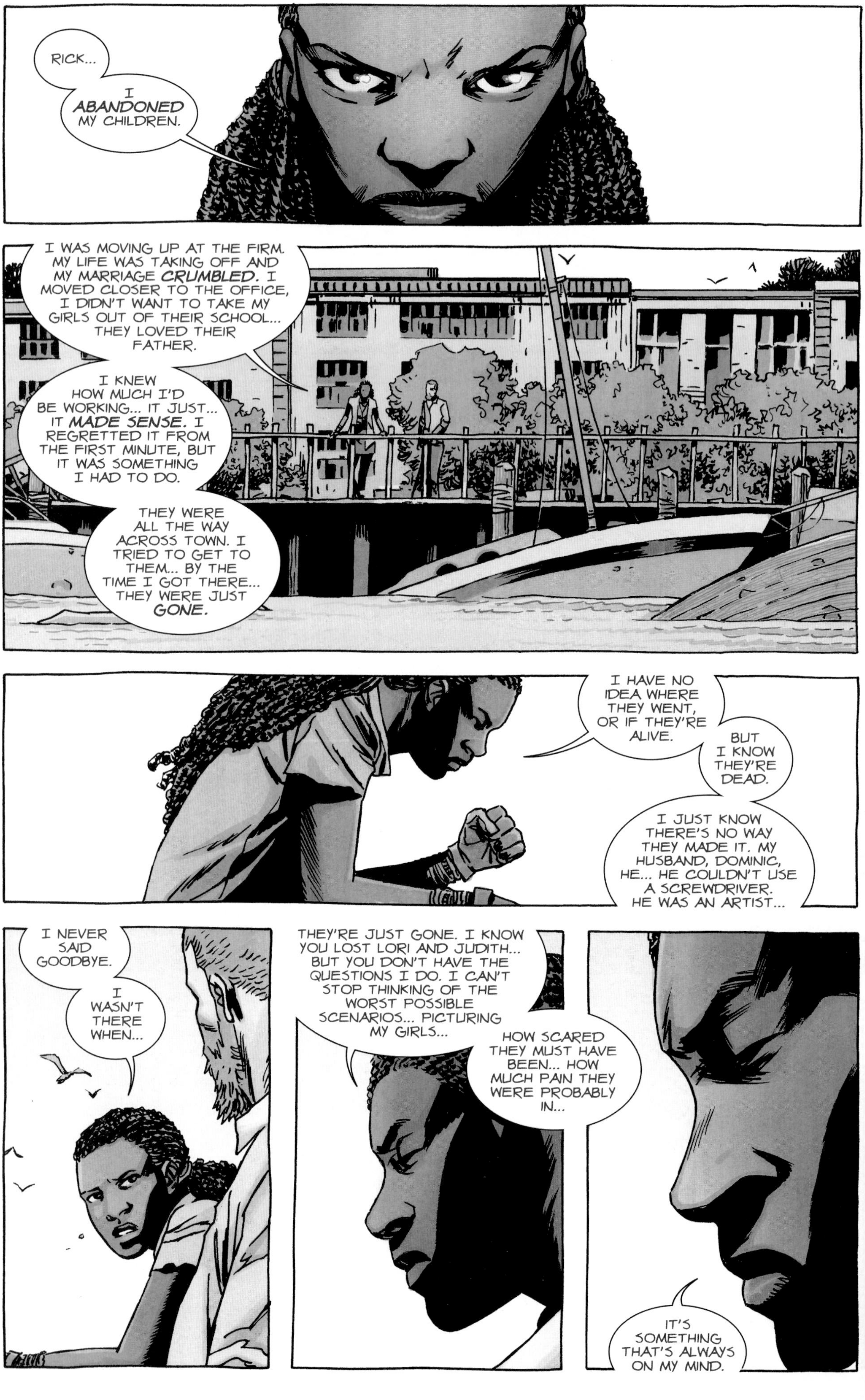
RICK...
I ABANDONED MY CHILDREN.
I WAS MOVING UP AT THE FIRM. MY LIFE WAS TAKING OFF AND MY MARRIAGE CRUMBLED. I MOVED CLOSER TO THE OFFICE, I DIDN'T WANT TO TAKE MY GIRLS OUT OF THEIR SCHOOL... THEY LOVED THEIR FATHER.
I KNEW HOW MUCH I'D BE WORKING... IT JUST... IT MADE SENSE. I REGRETTED IT FROM THE FIRST MINUTE, BUT IT WAS SOMETHING I HAD TO DO.
THEY WERE ALL THE WAY ACROSS TOWN. I TRIED TO GET TO THEM... BY THE TIME I GOT THERE... THEY WERE JUST GONE.
I HAVE NO IDEA WHERE THEY WENT, OR IF THEY'RE ALIVE.
BUT I KNOW THEY'RE DEAD.
I JUST KNOW THERE'S NO WAY THEY MADE IT. MY HUSBAND, DOMINIC, HE... HE COULDN'T USE A SCREWDRIVER. HE WAS AN ARTIST...
I NEVER SAID GOODBYE.
I WASN'T THERE WHEN...
THEY'RE JUST GONE. I KNOW YOU LOST LORI AND JUDITH... BUT YOU DON'T HAVE THE QUESTIONS I DO. I CAN'T STOP THINKING OF THE WORST POSSIBLE SCENARIOS... PICTURING MY GIRLS...
HOW SCARED THEY MUST HAVE BEEN... HOW MUCH PAIN THEY WERE PROBABLY IN...
IT'S SOMETHING THAT'S ALWAYS ON MY MIND.

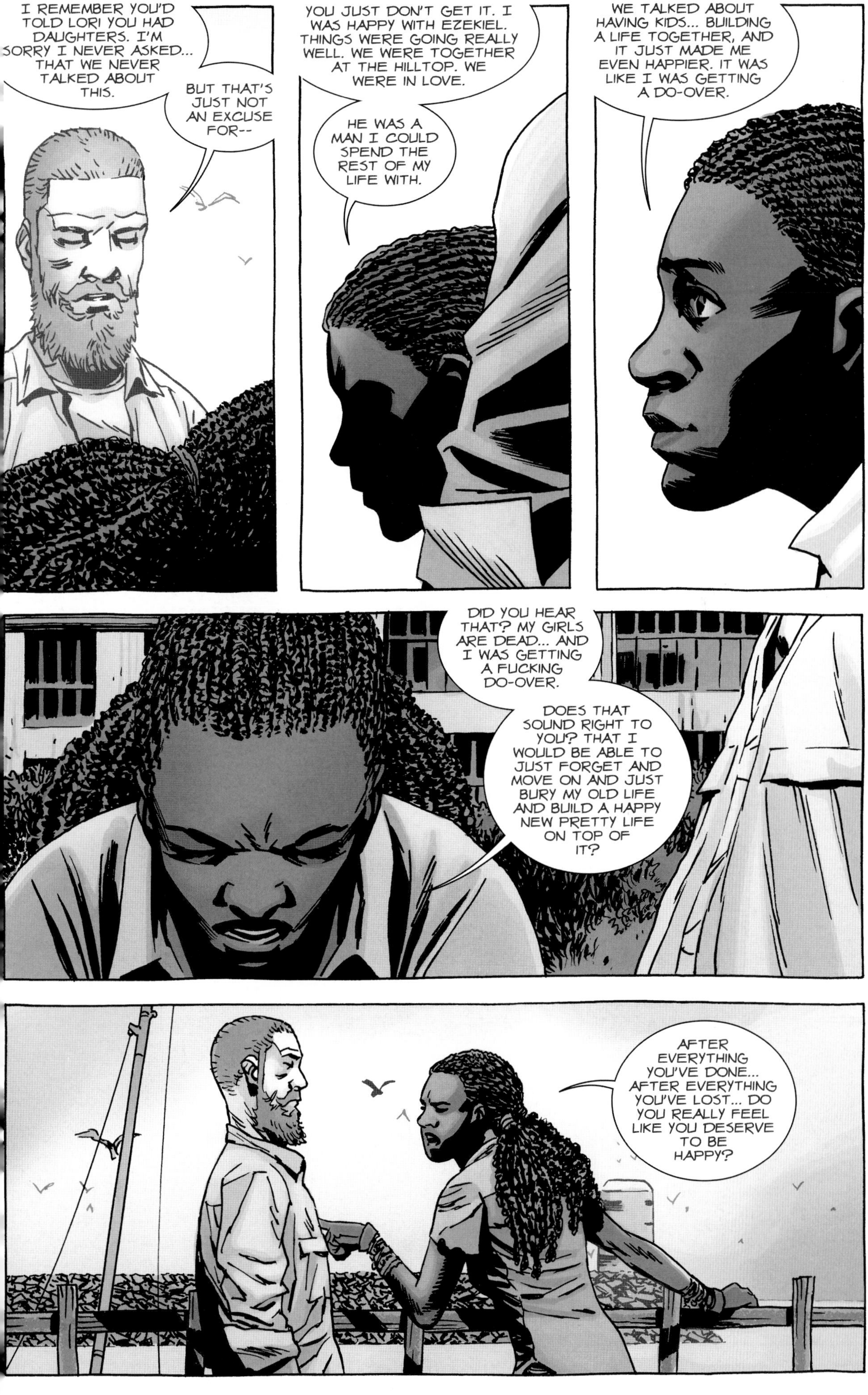
I REMEMBER YOU'D TOLD LORI YOU HAD DAUGHTERS. I'M SORRY I NEVER ASKED... THAT WE NEVER TALKED ABOUT THIS.
BUT THAT'S JUST NOT AN EXCUSE FOR--
YOU JUST DON'T GET IT. I WAS HAPPY WITH EZEKIEL. THINGS WERE GOING REALLY WELL. WE WERE TOGETHER AT THE HILLTOP. WE WERE IN LOVE.
HE WAS A MAN I COULD SPEND THE REST OF MY LIFE WITH.
WE TALKED ABOUT HAVING KIDS... BUILDING A LIFE TOGETHER, AND IT JUST MADE ME EVEN HAPPIER. IT WAS LIKE I WAS GETTING A DO-OVER.
DID YOU HEAR THAT? MY GIRLS ARE DEAD... AND I WAS GETTING A FUCKING DO-OVER.
DOES THAT SOUND RIGHT TO YOU? THAT I WOULD BE ABLE TO JUST FORGET AND MOVE ON AND JUST BURY MY OLD LIFE AND BUILD A HAPPY NEW PRETTY LIFE ON TOP OF IT?
AFTER EVERYTHING YOU'VE DONE... AFTER EVERYTHING YOU'VE LOST... DO YOU REALLY FEEL LIKE YOU DESERVE TO BE HAPPY?

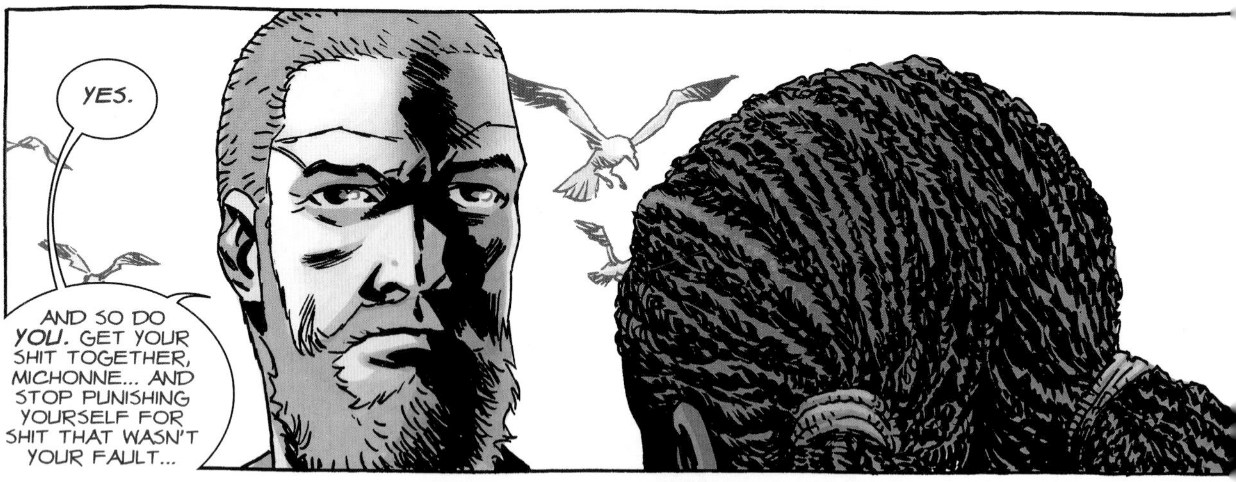
YES.
AND SO DO YOU. GET YOUR SHIT TOGETHER, MICHONNE... AND STOP PUNISHING YOURSELF FOR SHIT THAT WASN'T YOUR FAULT...

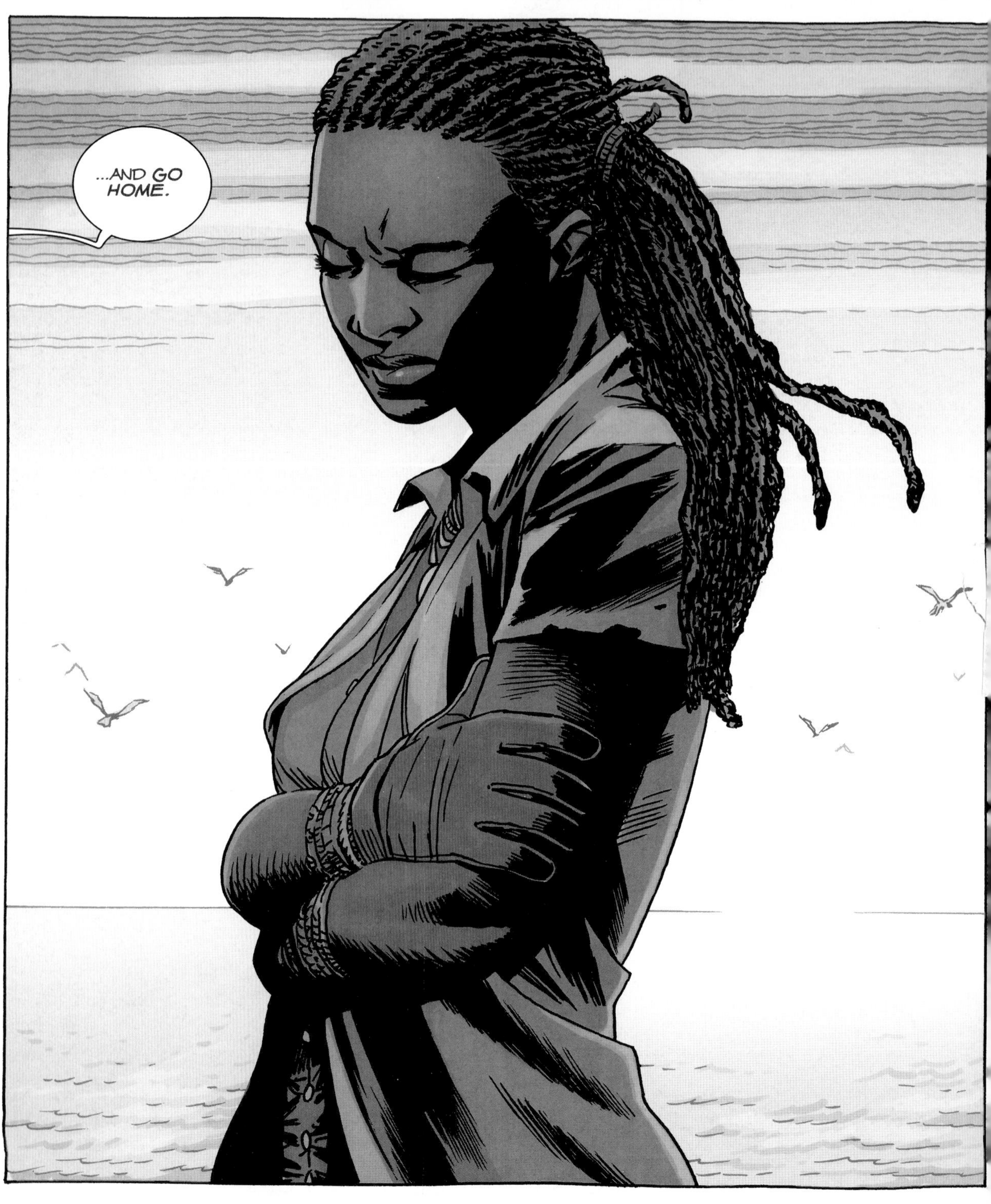
...AND GO HOME.

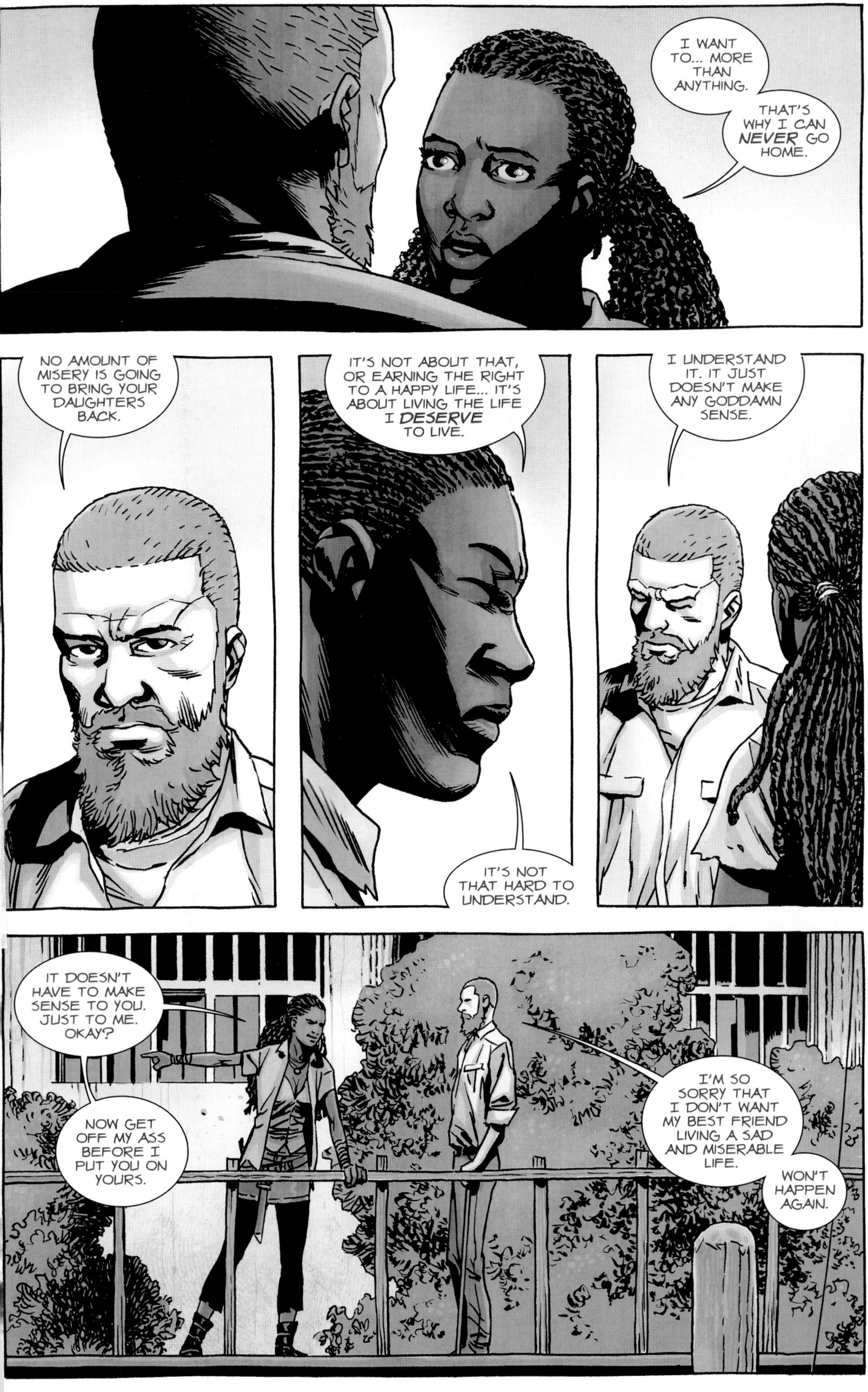

I WANT TO... MORE THAN ANYTHING.
THAT'S WHY I CAN NEVER GO HOME.
NO AMOUNT OF MISERY IS GOING TO BRING YOUR DAUGHTERS BACK.
IT'S NOT ABOUT THAT, OR EARNING THE RIGHT TO A HAPPY LIFE... IT'S ABOUT LIVING THE LIFE I DESERVE TO LIVE.
IT'S NOT THAT HARD TO UNDERSTAND.
I UNDERSTAND IT. IT JUST DOESN'T MAKE ANY GODDAMN SENSE.
IT DOESN'T HAVE TO MAKE SENSE TO YOU. JUST TO ME. OKAY?
NOW GET OFF MY ASS BEFORE I PUT YOU ON YOURS.
I'M SO SORRY THAT I DON'T WANT MY BEST FRIEND LIVING A SAD AND MISERABLE LIFE.
WON'T HAPPEN AGAIN.

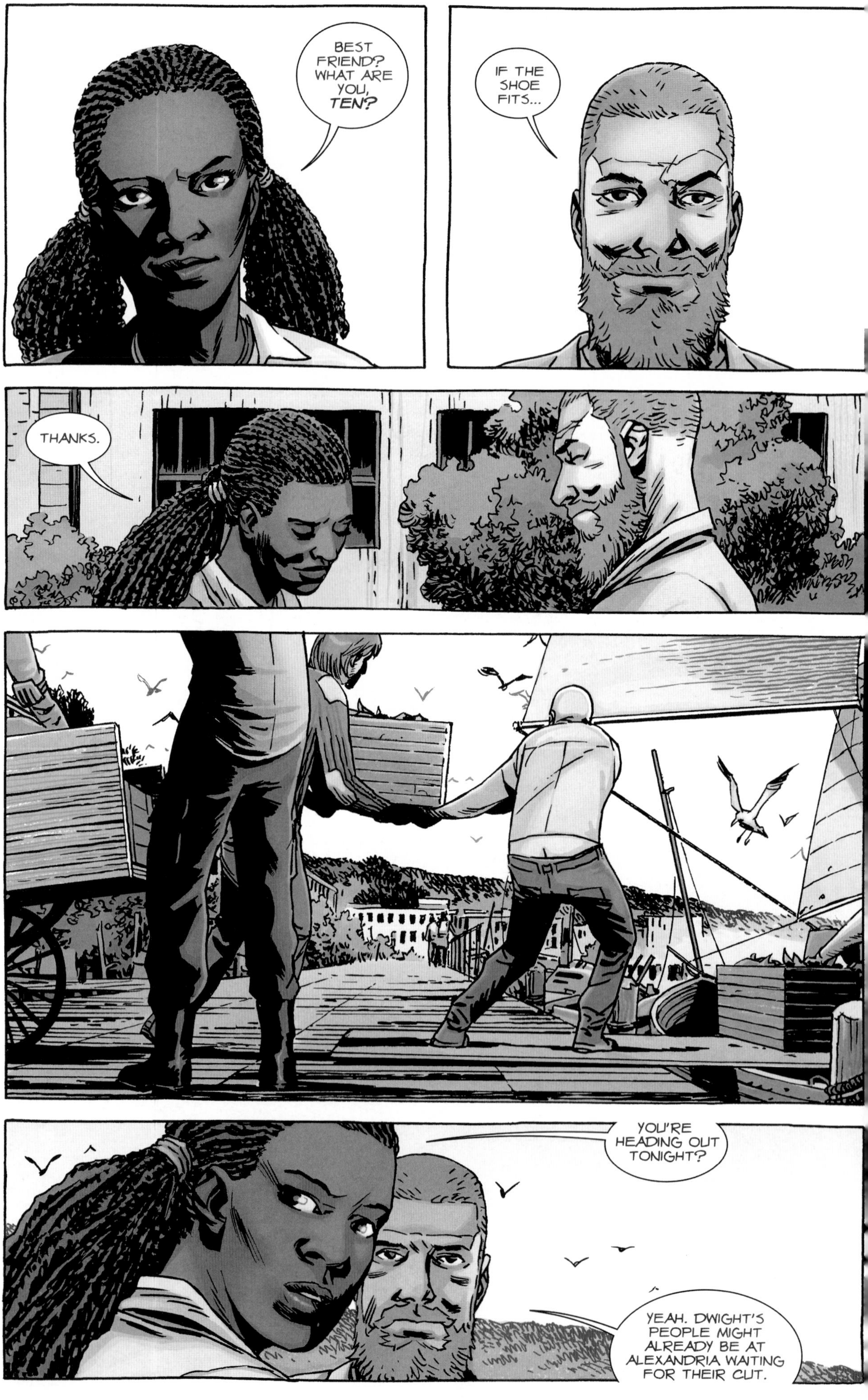
BEST FRIEND? WHAT ARE YOU, TEN?
IF THE SHOE FITS...
THANKS.
YOU'RE HEADING OUT TONIGHT?
YEAH. DWIGHT'S PEOPLE MIGHT ALREADY BE AT ALEXANDRIA WAITING FOR THEIR CUT.

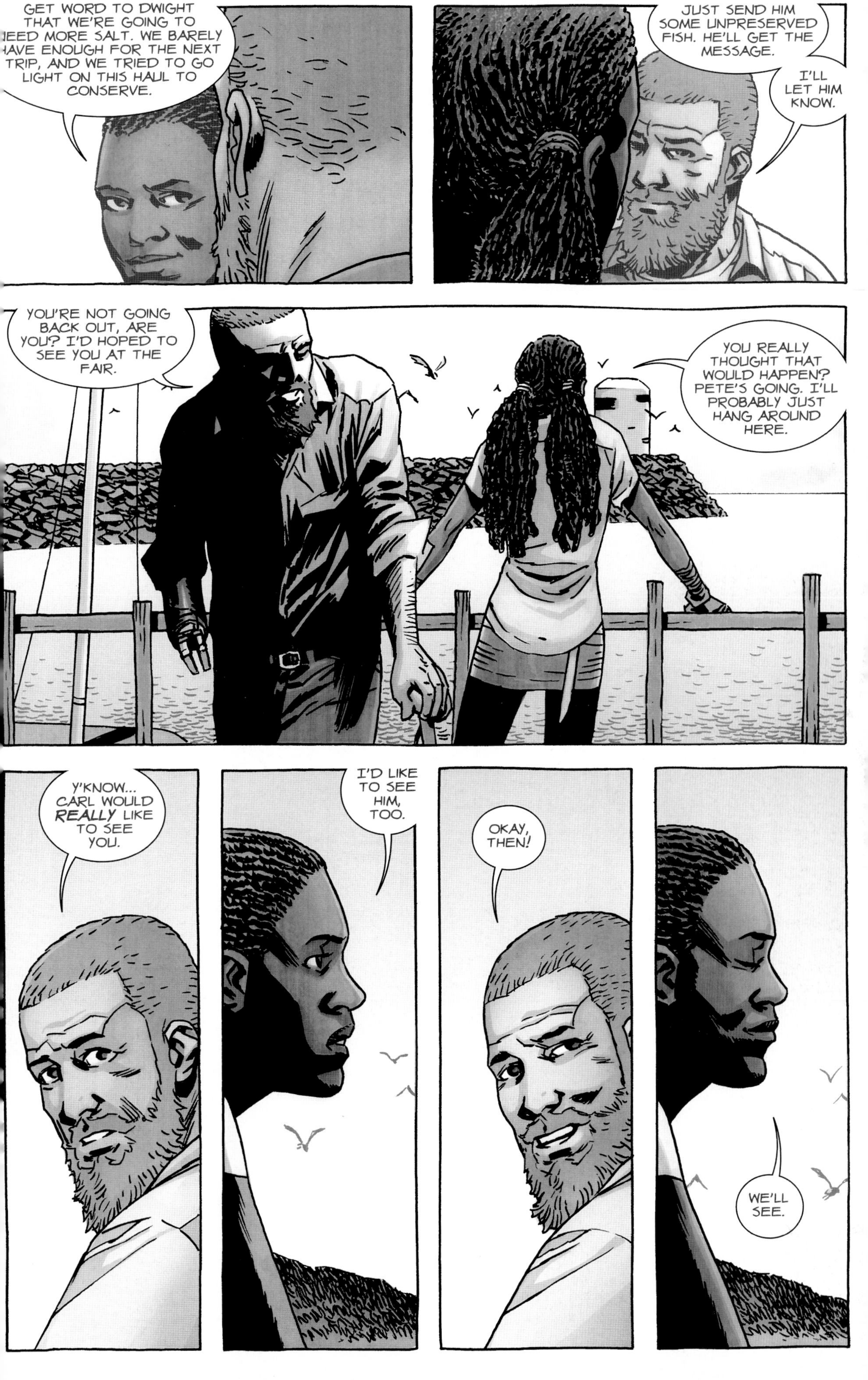
GET WORD TO DWIGHT THAT WE'RE GOING TO NEED MORE SALT. WE BARELY HAVE ENOUGH FOR THE NEXT TRIP, AND WE TRIED TO GO LIGHT ON THIS HAUL TO CONSERVE.
JUST SEND HIM SOME UNPRESERVED FISH. HE'LL GET THE MESSAGE.
I'LL LET HIM KNOW.
YOU'RE NOT GOING BACK OUT, ARE YOU? I'D HOPED TO SEE YOU AT THE FAIR.
YOU REALLY THOUGHT THAT WOULD HAPPEN? PETE'S GOING. I'LL PROBABLY JUST HANG AROUND HERE.
Y'KNOW... CARL WOULD REALLY LIKE TO SEE YOU.
I'D LIKE TO SEE HIM, TOO.
OKAY, THEN!
WE'LL SEE.

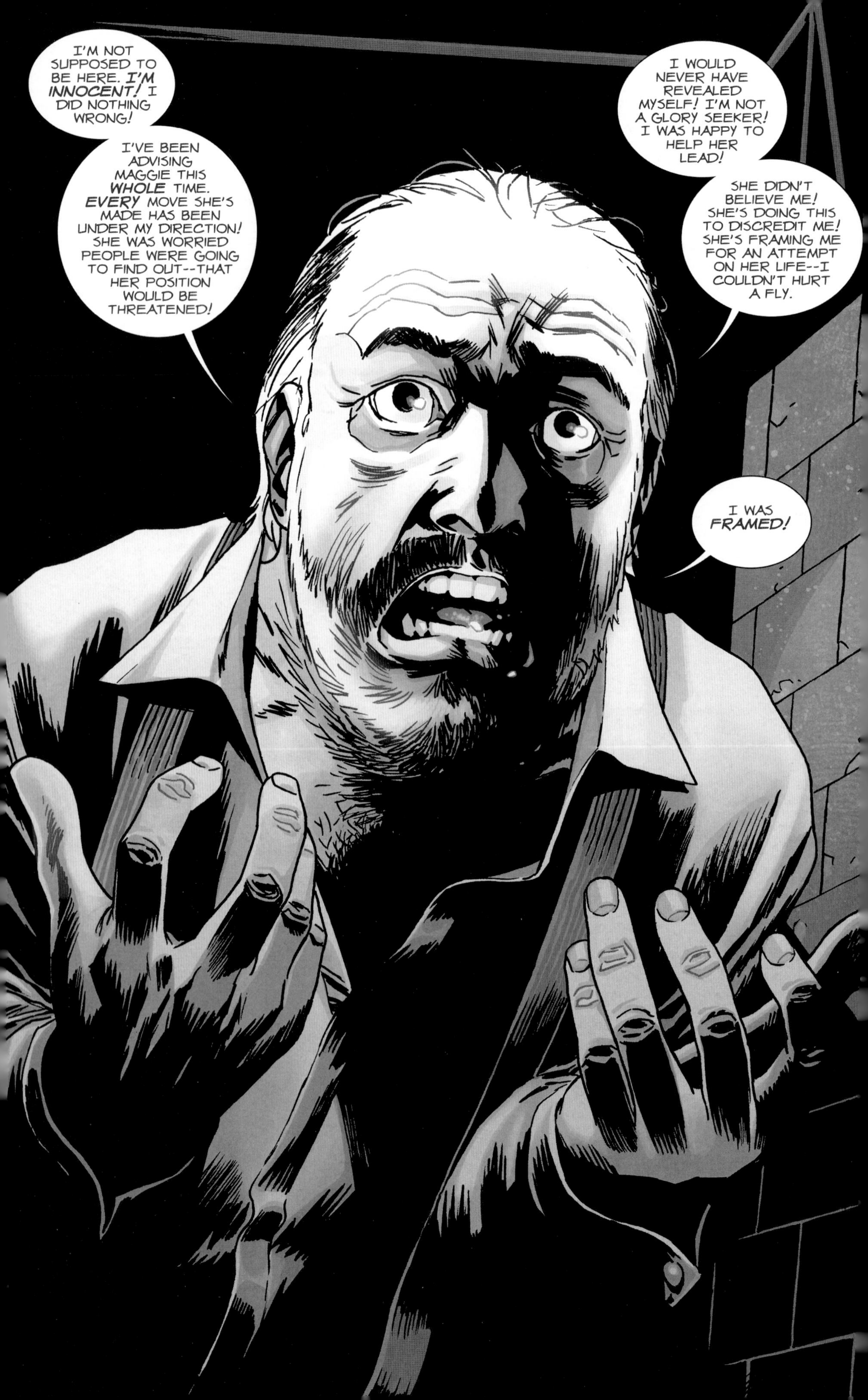
I'M NOT SUPPOSED TO BE HERE. *I'M INNOCENT!* I DID NOTHING WRONG!
I'VE BEEN ADVISING MAGGIE THIS *WHOLE* TIME. *EVERY* MOVE SHE'S MADE HAS BEEN UNDER MY DIRECTION! SHE WAS WORRIED PEOPLE WERE GOING TO FIND OUT--THAT HER POSITION WOULD BE THREATENED!
I WOULD NEVER HAVE REVEALED MYSELF! I'M NOT A GLORY SEEKER! I WAS HAPPY TO HELP HER LEAD!
SHE DIDN'T BELIEVE ME! SHE'S DOING THIS TO DISCREDIT ME! SHE'S FRAMING ME FOR AN ATTEMPT ON HER LIFE--I COULDN'T HURT A FLY.
I WAS *FRAMED!*

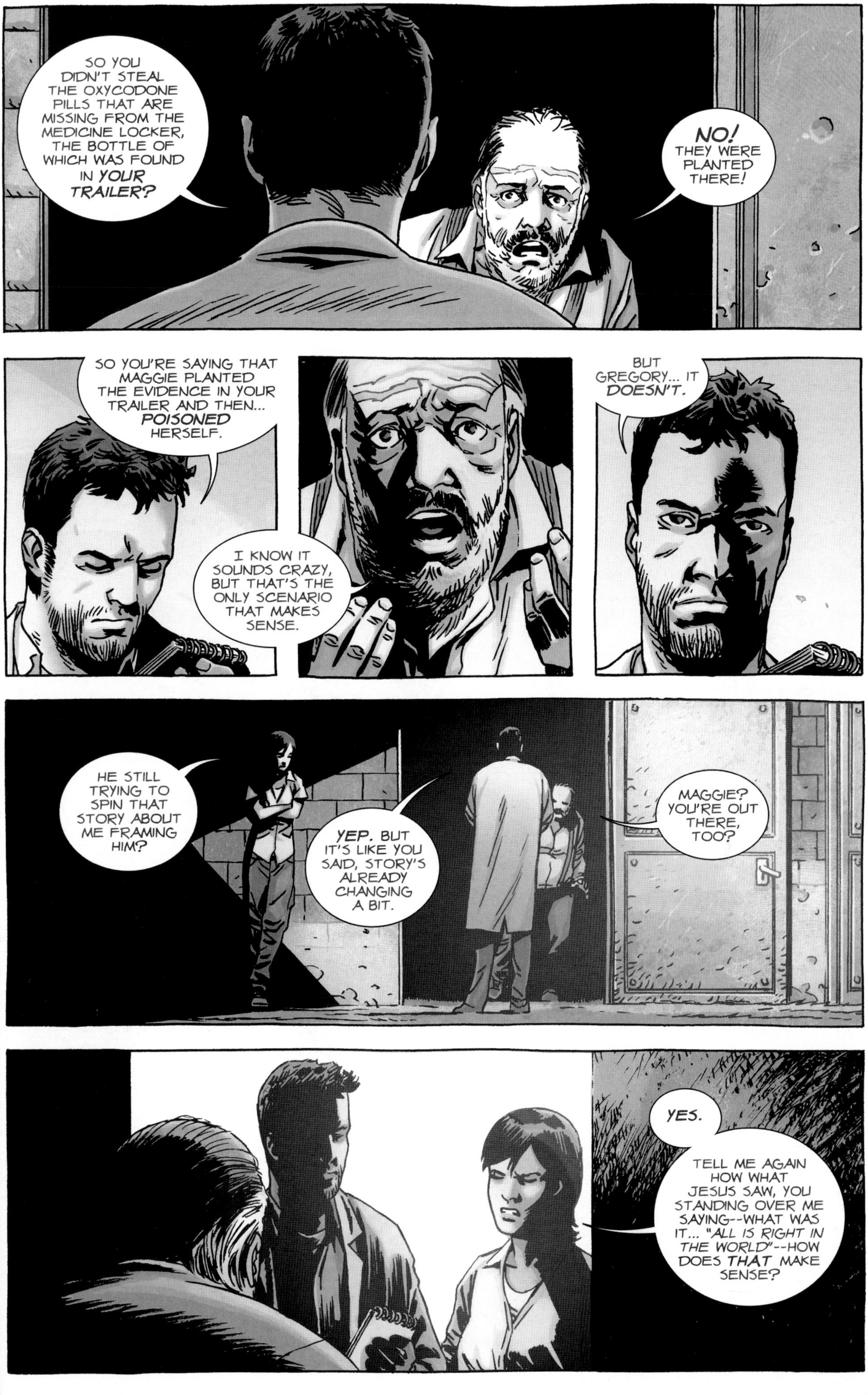
SO YOU DIDN'T STEAL THE OXYCODONE PILLS THAT ARE MISSING FROM THE MEDICINE LOCKER, THE BOTTLE OF WHICH WAS FOUND IN YOUR TRAILER?
NO! THEY WERE PLANTED THERE!
SO YOU'RE SAYING THAT MAGGIE PLANTED THE EVIDENCE IN YOUR TRAILER AND THEN... POISONED HERSELF.
I KNOW IT SOUNDS CRAZY, BUT THAT'S THE ONLY SCENARIO THAT MAKES SENSE.
BUT GREGORY... IT DOESN'T.
HE STILL TRYING TO SPIN THAT STORY ABOUT ME FRAMING HIM?
YEP. BUT IT'S LIKE YOU SAID, STORY'S ALREADY CHANGING A BIT.
MAGGIE? YOU'RE OUT THERE, TOO?
YES.
TELL ME AGAIN HOW WHAT JESUS SAW, YOU STANDING OVER ME SAYING--WHAT WAS IT... "ALL IS RIGHT IN THE WORLD"--HOW DOES THAT MAKE SENSE?

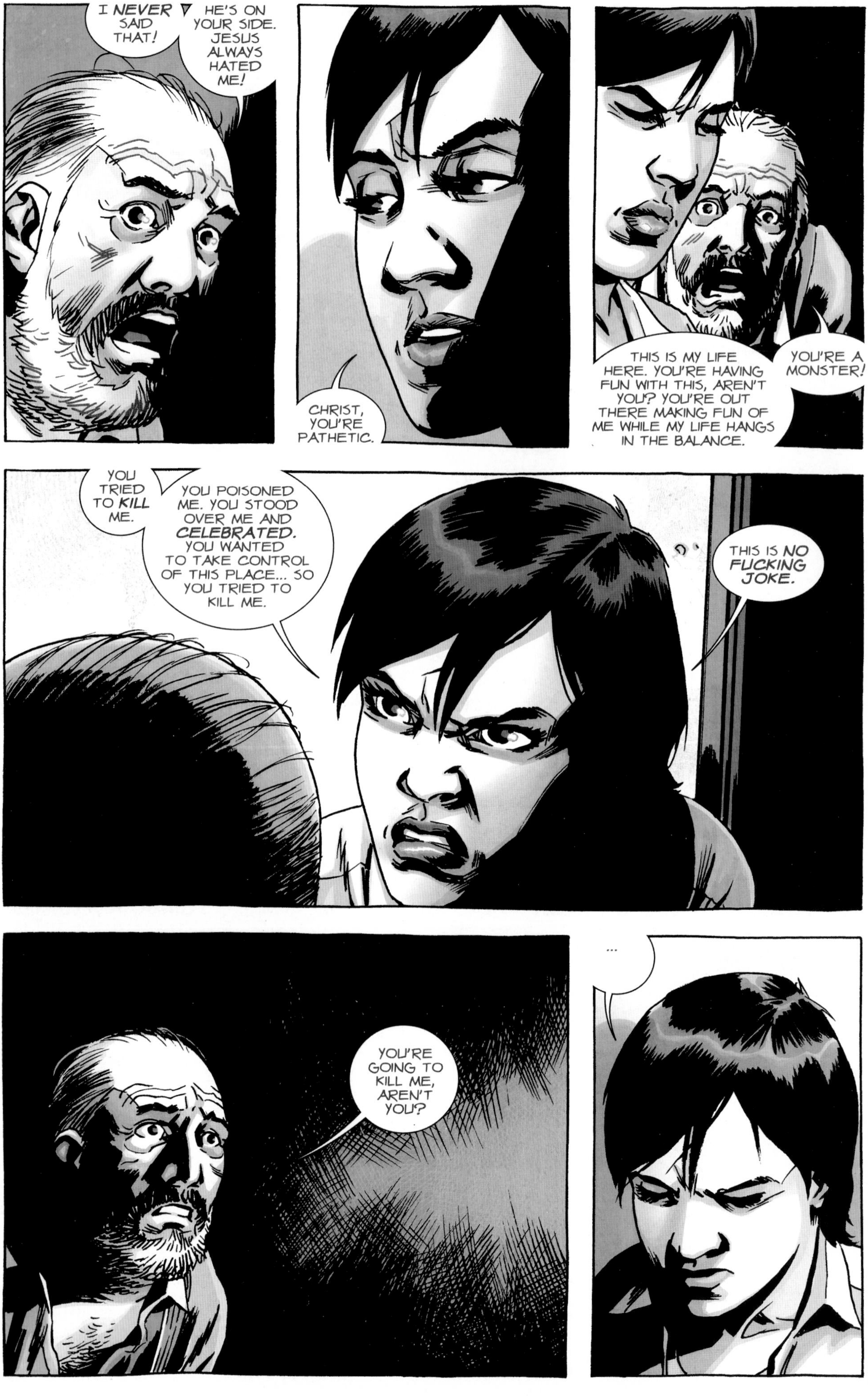
I NEVER SAID THAT!
HE'S ON YOUR SIDE. JESUS ALWAYS HATED ME!
CHRIST, YOU'RE PATHETIC.
THIS IS MY LIFE HERE. YOU'RE HAVING FUN WITH THIS, AREN'T YOU? YOU'RE OUT THERE MAKING FUN OF ME WHILE MY LIFE HANGS IN THE BALANCE.
YOU'RE A MONSTER!
YOU TRIED TO KILL ME.
YOU POISONED ME. YOU STOOD OVER ME AND CELEBRATED. YOU WANTED TO TAKE CONTROL OF THIS PLACE... SO YOU TRIED TO KILL ME.
THIS IS NO FUCKING JOKE.
YOU'RE GOING TO KILL ME, AREN'T YOU?
...

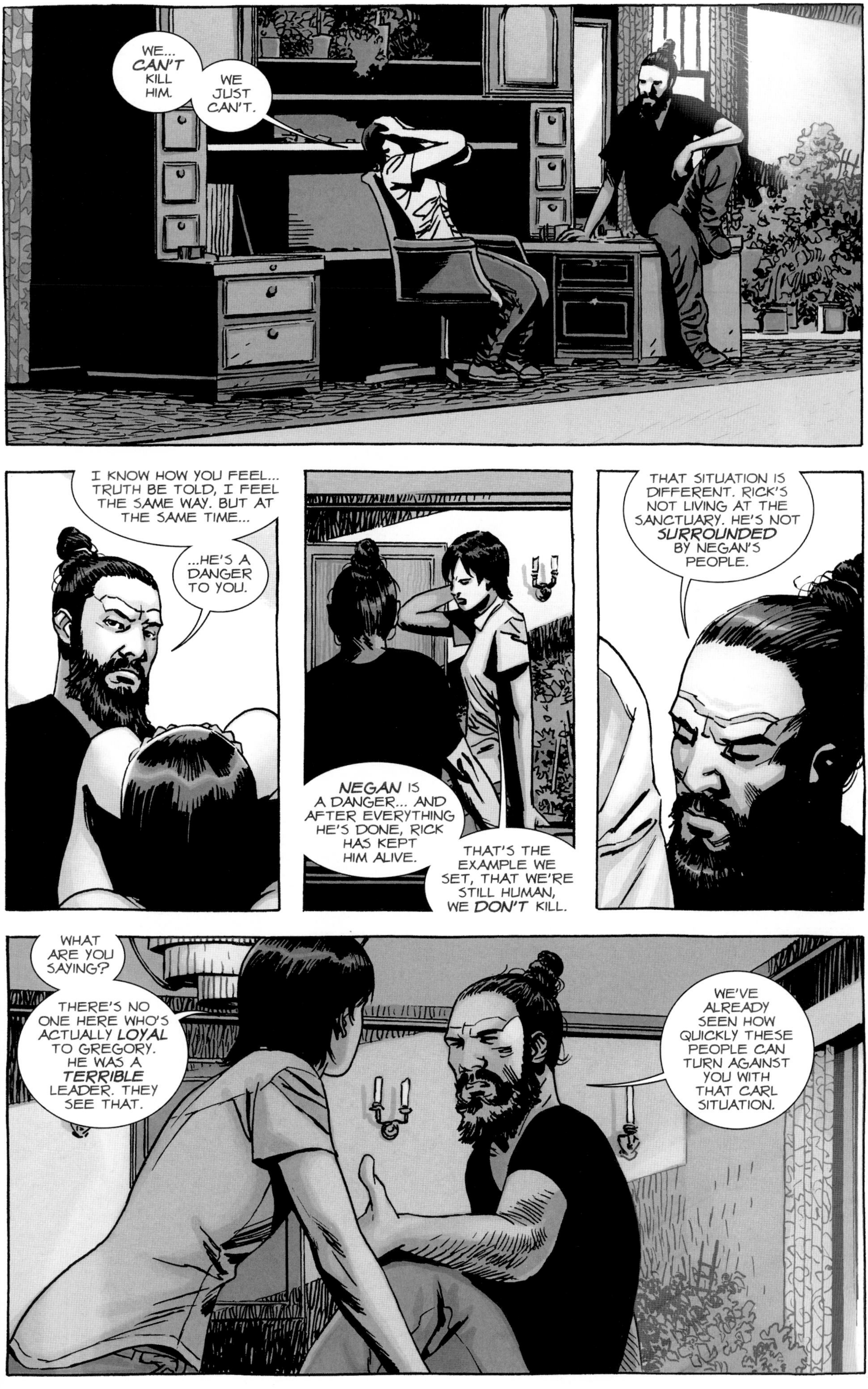

WE... CAN'T KILL HIM.
WE JUST CAN'T.
I KNOW HOW YOU FEEL... TRUTH BE TOLD, I FEEL THE SAME WAY. BUT AT THE SAME TIME...
...HE'S A DANGER TO YOU.
NEGAN IS A DANGER... AND AFTER EVERYTHING HE'S DONE, RICK HAS KEPT HIM ALIVE.
THAT'S THE EXAMPLE WE SET, THAT WE'RE STILL HUMAN, WE DON'T KILL.
THAT SITUATION IS DIFFERENT. RICK'S NOT LIVING AT THE SANCTUARY. HE'S NOT SURROUNDED BY NEGAN'S PEOPLE.
WHAT ARE YOU SAYING?
THERE'S NO ONE HERE WHO'S ACTUALLY LOYAL TO GREGORY. HE WAS A TERRIBLE LEADER. THEY SEE THAT.
WE'VE ALREADY SEEN HOW QUICKLY THESE PEOPLE CAN TURN AGAINST YOU WITH THAT CARL SITUATION.

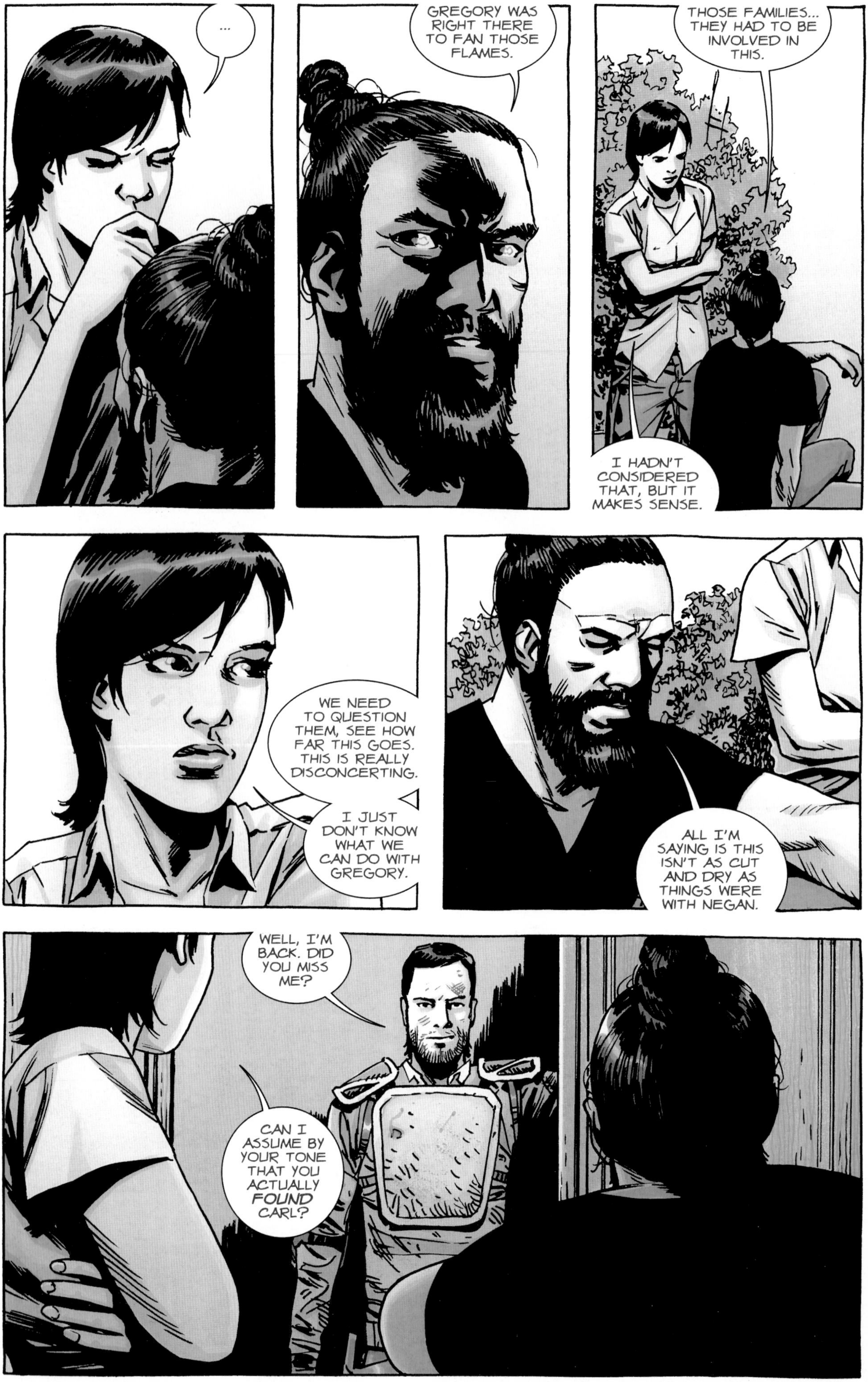
...
GREGORY WAS RIGHT THERE TO FAN THOSE FLAMES.
THOSE FAMILIES... THEY HAD TO BE INVOLVED IN THIS.
I HADN'T CONSIDERED THAT, BUT IT MAKES SENSE.
WE NEED TO QUESTION THEM, SEE HOW FAR THIS GOES. THIS IS REALLY DISCONCERTING.
I JUST DON'T KNOW WHAT WE CAN DO WITH GREGORY.
ALL I'M SAYING IS THIS ISN'T AS CUT AND DRY AS THINGS WERE WITH NEGAN.
WELL, I'M BACK. DID YOU MISS ME?
CAN I ASSUME BY YOUR TONE THAT YOU ACTUALLY FOUND CARL?

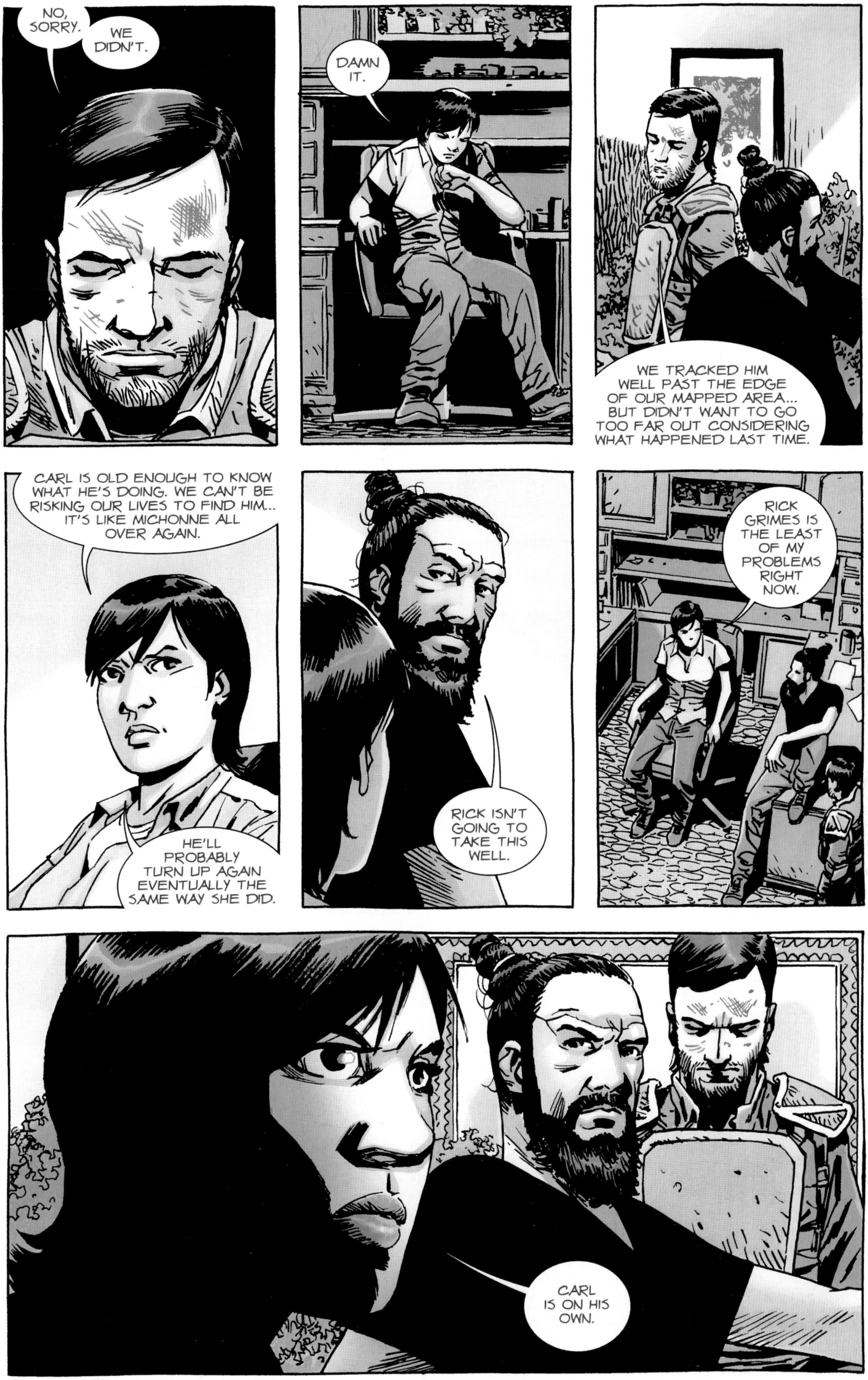
NO, SORRY.
WE DIDN'T.
DAMN IT.
WE TRACKED HIM WELL PAST THE EDGE OF OUR MAPPED AREA... BUT DIDN'T WANT TO GO TOO FAR OUT CONSIDERING WHAT HAPPENED LAST TIME.
CARL IS OLD ENOUGH TO KNOW WHAT HE'S DOING. WE CAN'T BE RISKING OUR LIVES TO FIND HIM... IT'S LIKE MICHONNE ALL OVER AGAIN.
HE'LL PROBABLY TURN UP AGAIN EVENTUALLY THE SAME WAY SHE DID.
RICK ISN'T GOING TO TAKE THIS WELL.
RICK GRIMES IS THE LEAST OF MY PROBLEMS RIGHT NOW.
CARL IS ON HIS OWN.

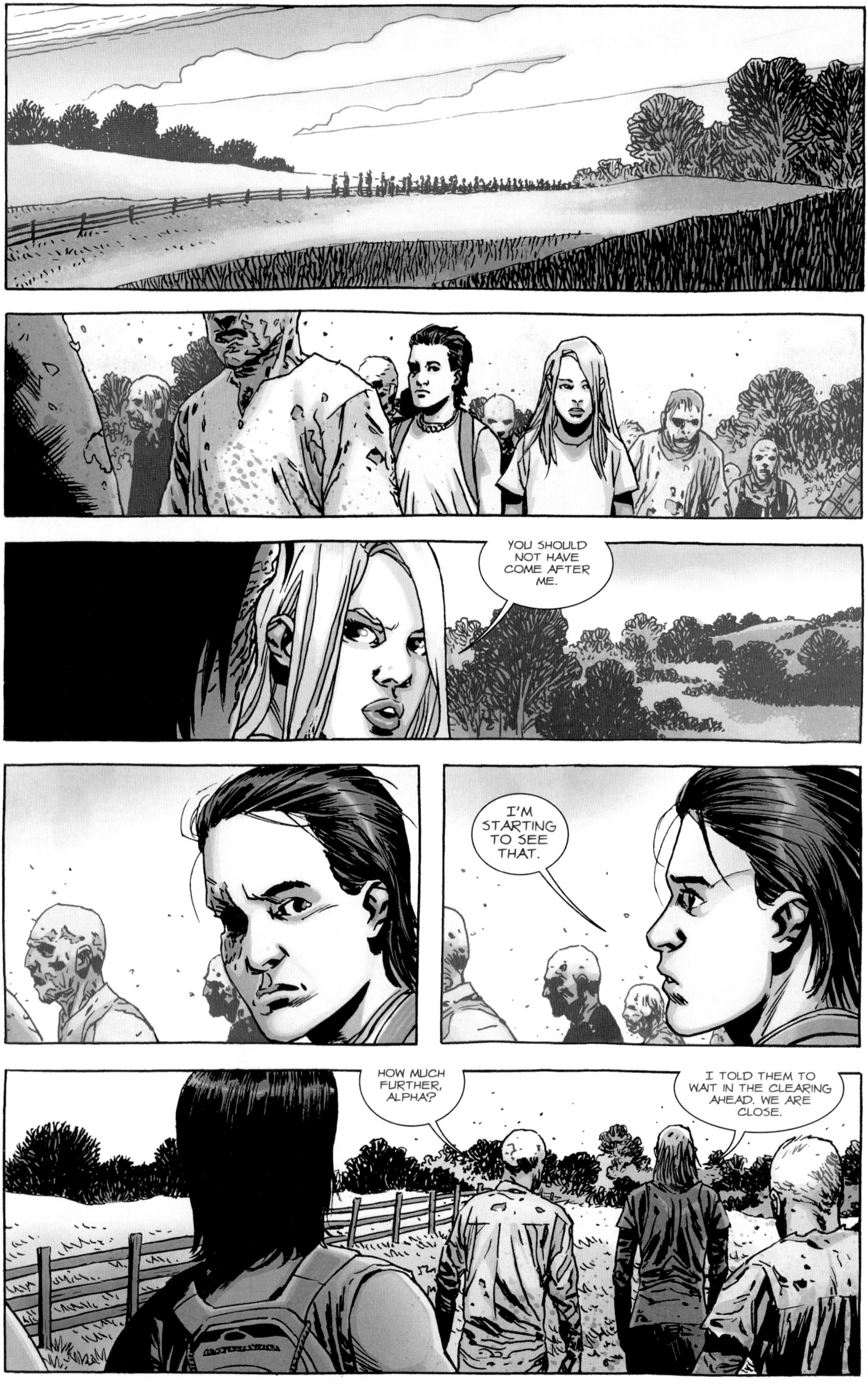
YOU SHOULD NOT HAVE COME AFTER ME.
I'M STARTING TO SEE THAT.
HOW MUCH FURTHER, ALPHA?
I TOLD THEM TO WAIT IN THE CLEARING AHEAD. WE ARE CLOSE.

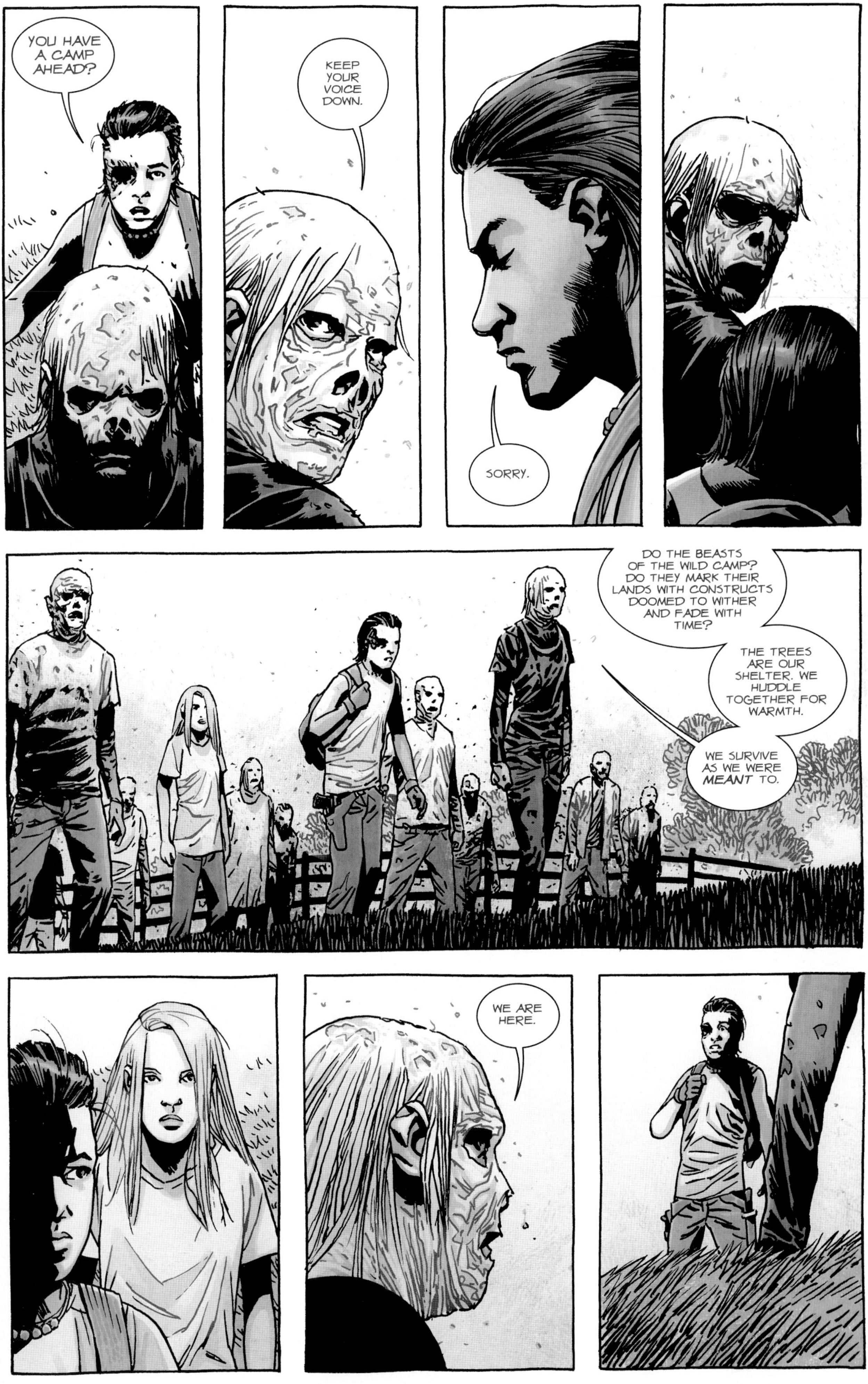
YOU HAVE A CAMP AHEAD?
KEEP YOUR VOICE DOWN.
SORRY.
DO THE BEASTS OF THE WILD CAMP? DO THEY MARK THEIR LANDS WITH CONSTRUCTS DOOMED TO WITHER AND FADE WITH TIME?
THE TREES ARE OUR SHELTER. WE HUDDLE TOGETHER FOR WARMTH.
WE SURVIVE AS WE WERE MEANT TO.
WE ARE HERE.

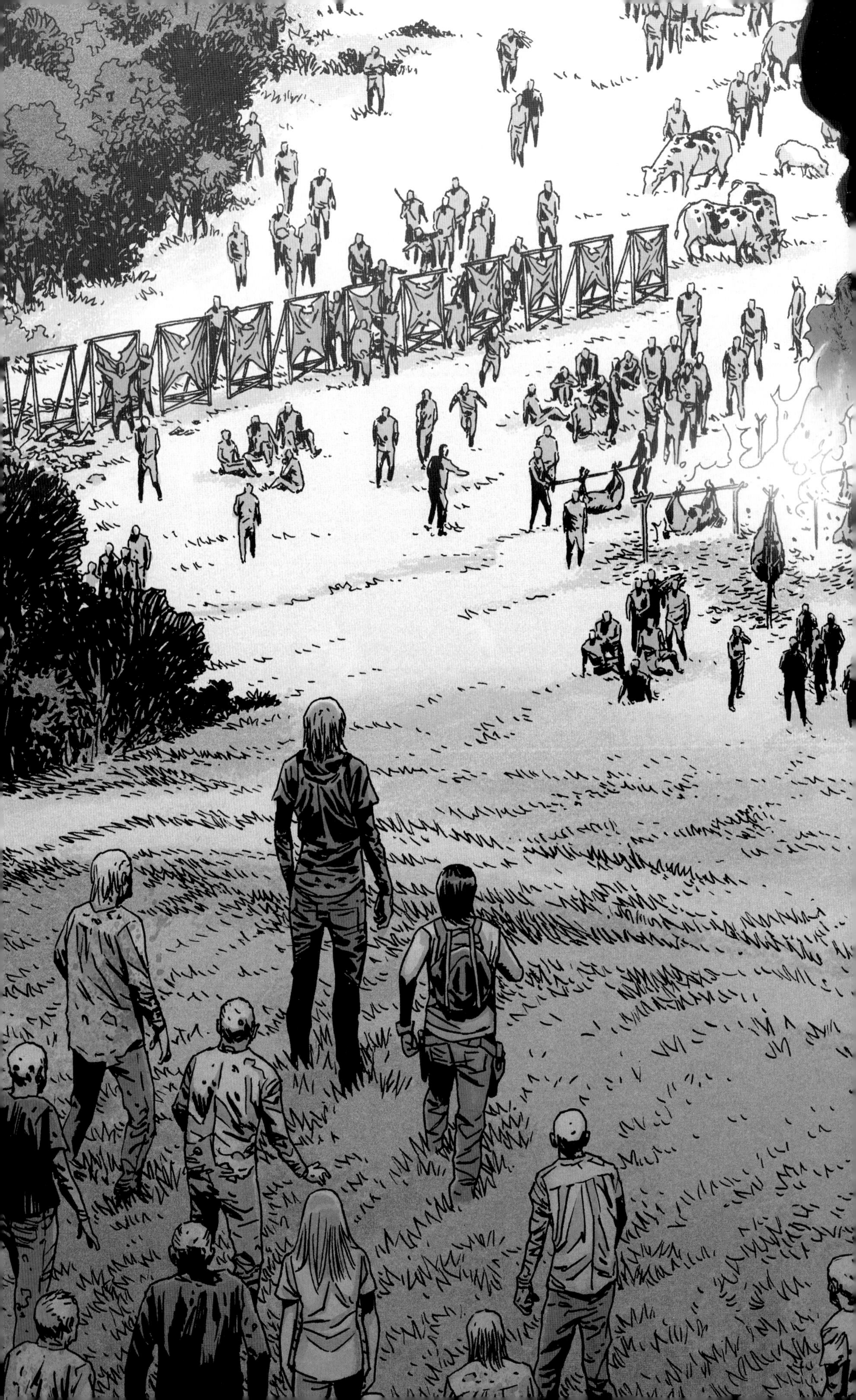

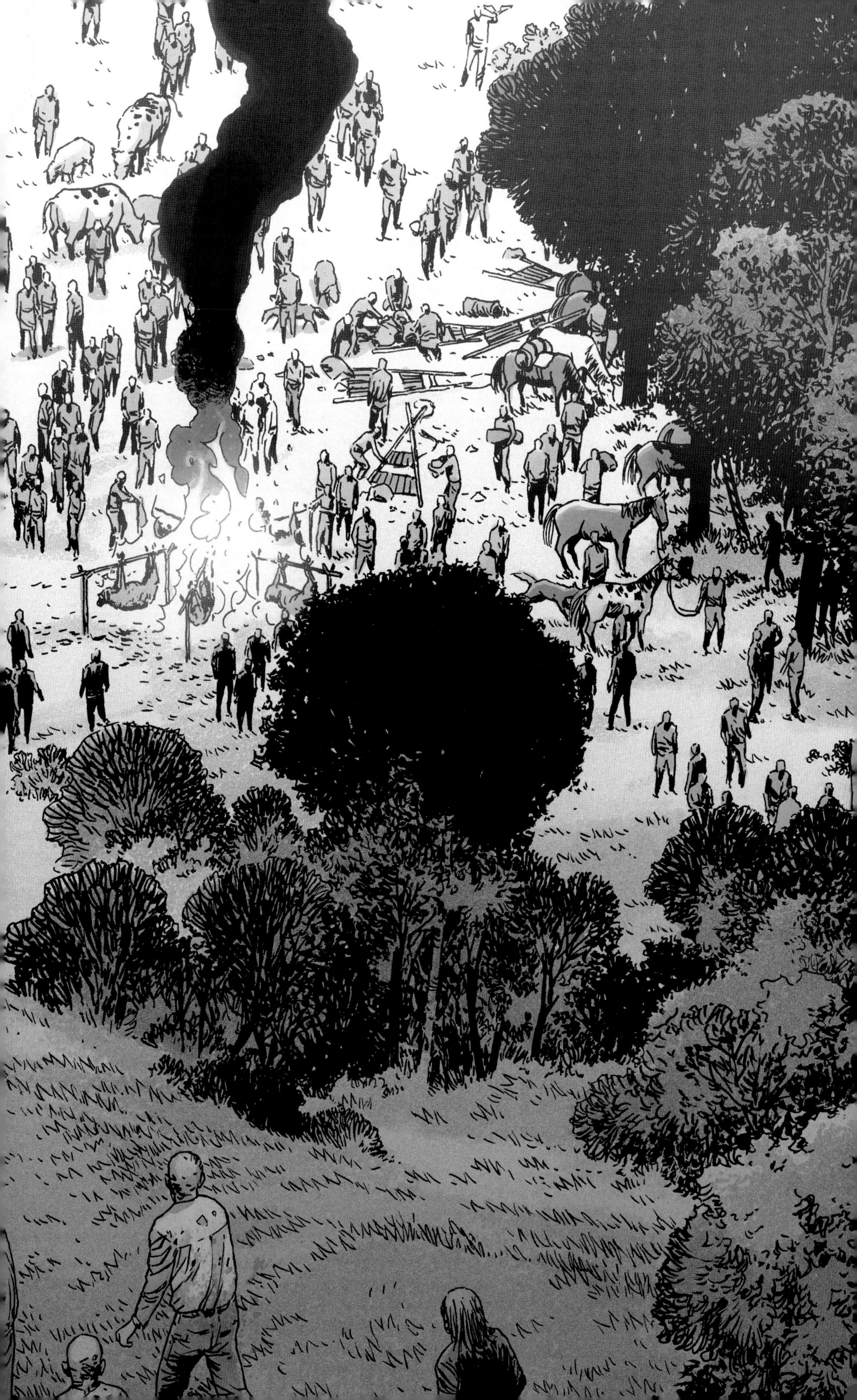

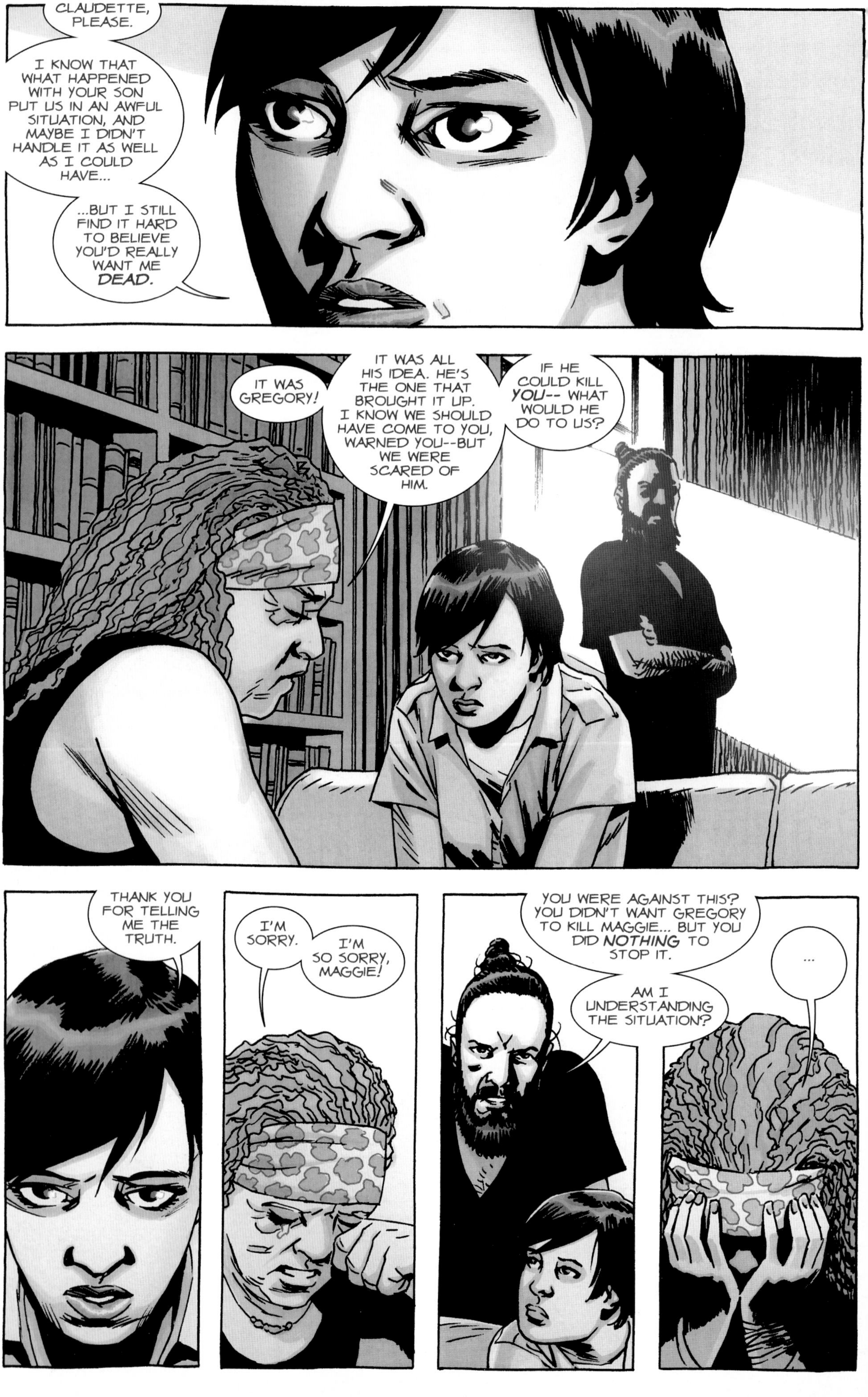
CLAUDETTE, PLEASE.
I KNOW THAT WHAT HAPPENED WITH YOUR SON PUT US IN AN AWFUL SITUATION, AND MAYBE I DIDN'T HANDLE IT AS WELL AS I COULD HAVE...
...BUT I STILL FIND IT HARD TO BELIEVE YOU'D REALLY WANT ME DEAD.
IT WAS GREGORY!
IT WAS ALL HIS IDEA. HE'S THE ONE THAT BROUGHT IT UP. I KNOW WE SHOULD HAVE COME TO YOU, WARNED YOU--BUT WE WERE SCARED OF HIM.
IF HE COULD KILL YOU-- WHAT WOULD HE DO TO US?
THANK YOU FOR TELLING ME THE TRUTH.
I'M SORRY.
I'M SO SORRY, MAGGIE!
YOU WERE AGAINST THIS? YOU DIDN'T WANT GREGORY TO KILL MAGGIE... BUT YOU DID NOTHING TO STOP IT.
AM I UNDERSTANDING THE SITUATION?
...

I WAS *ANGRY*.

MY SON WAS HURT, YOU WERE ACTING LIKE IT WAS HIS FAULT. I THOUGHT I WAS GOING TO *LOSE* HIM.

SO... I WOULDN'T HAVE BEEN UPSET IF YOU'D DIED.

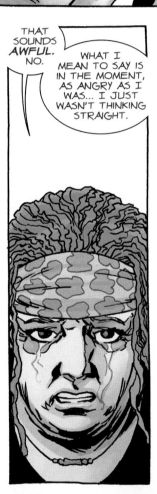

THAT SOUNDS *AWFUL*. NO.

WHAT I MEAN TO SAY IS IN THE MOMENT, AS ANGRY AS I WAS... I JUST WASN'T THINKING STRAIGHT.

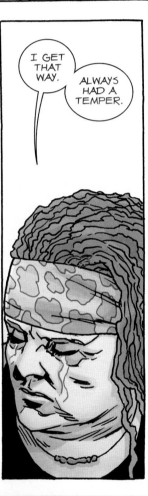

I GET THAT WAY.

ALWAYS HAD A TEMPER.

AND YOUR HUSBAND, MORTON? AND THE HARLAN FAMILY?

THEY HAVE THE SAME TEMPER?

WELL...

GREGORY CAN BE REALLY PERSUASIVE.

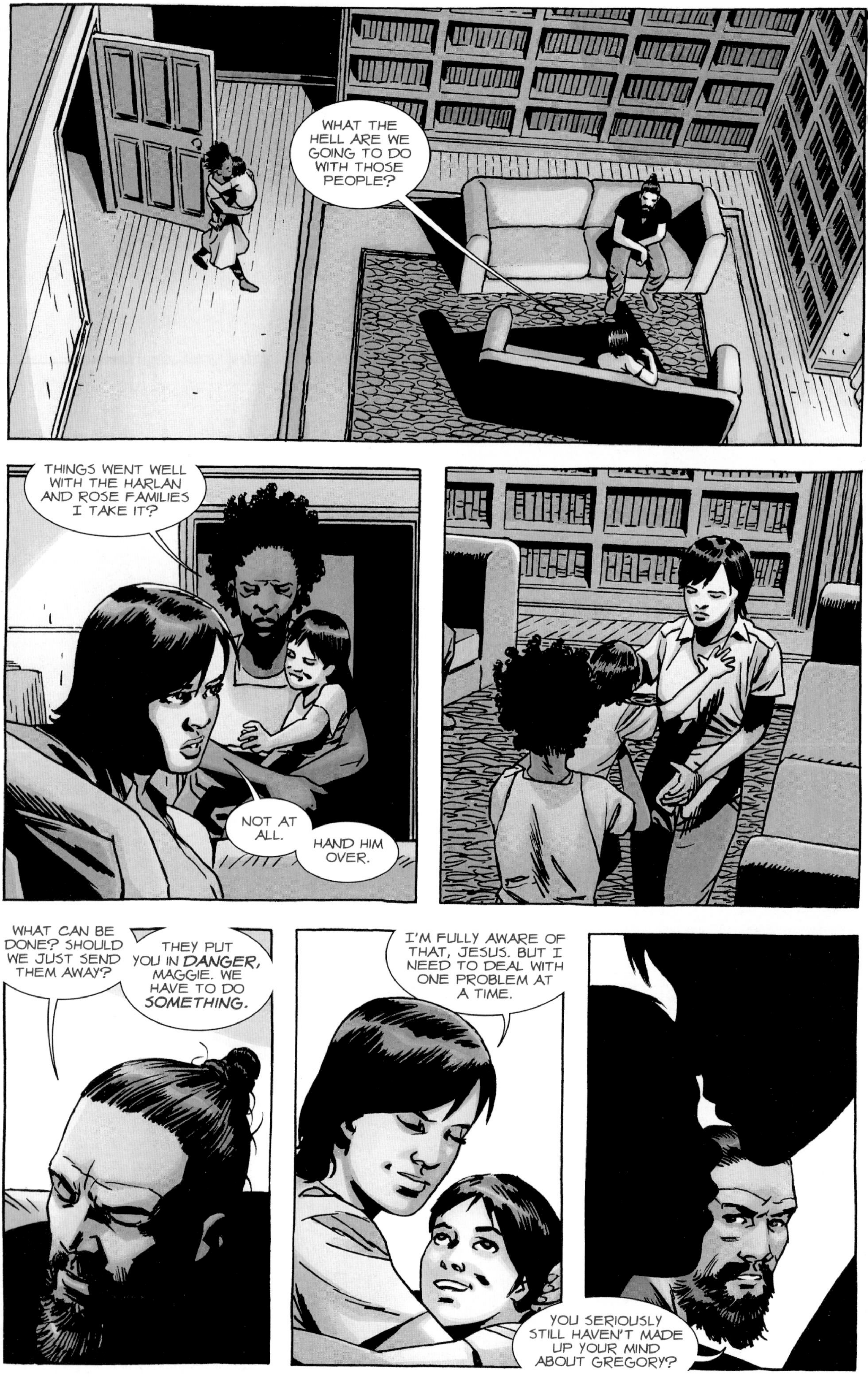
WHAT THE HELL ARE WE GOING TO DO WITH THOSE PEOPLE?
THINGS WENT WELL WITH THE HARLAN AND ROSE FAMILIES I TAKE IT?
NOT AT ALL.
HAND HIM OVER.
WHAT CAN BE DONE? SHOULD WE JUST SEND THEM AWAY?
THEY PUT YOU IN DANGER, MAGGIE. WE HAVE TO DO SOMETHING.
I'M FULLY AWARE OF THAT, JESUS. BUT I NEED TO DEAL WITH ONE PROBLEM AT A TIME.
YOU SERIOUSLY STILL HAVEN'T MADE UP YOUR MIND ABOUT GREGORY?

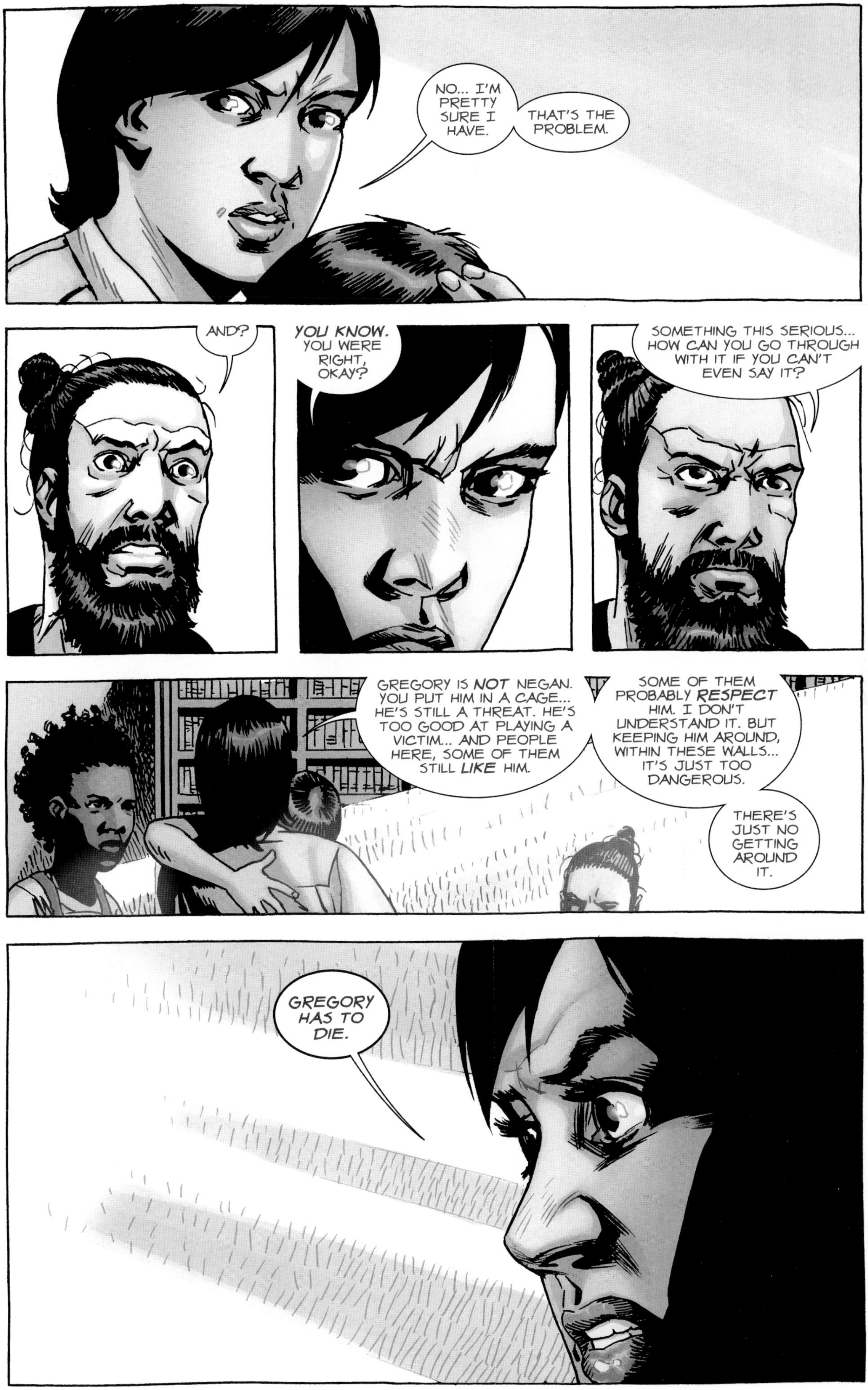
NO... I'M PRETTY SURE I HAVE.
THAT'S THE PROBLEM.
AND?
YOU KNOW. YOU WERE RIGHT, OKAY?
SOMETHING THIS SERIOUS... HOW CAN YOU GO THROUGH WITH IT IF YOU CAN'T EVEN SAY IT?
GREGORY IS NOT NEGAN. YOU PUT HIM IN A CAGE... HE'S STILL A THREAT. HE'S TOO GOOD AT PLAYING A VICTIM... AND PEOPLE HERE, SOME OF THEM STILL LIKE HIM.
SOME OF THEM PROBABLY RESPECT HIM. I DON'T UNDERSTAND IT. BUT KEEPING HIM AROUND, WITHIN THESE WALLS... IT'S JUST TOO DANGEROUS.
THERE'S JUST NO GETTING AROUND IT.
GREGORY HAS TO DIE.

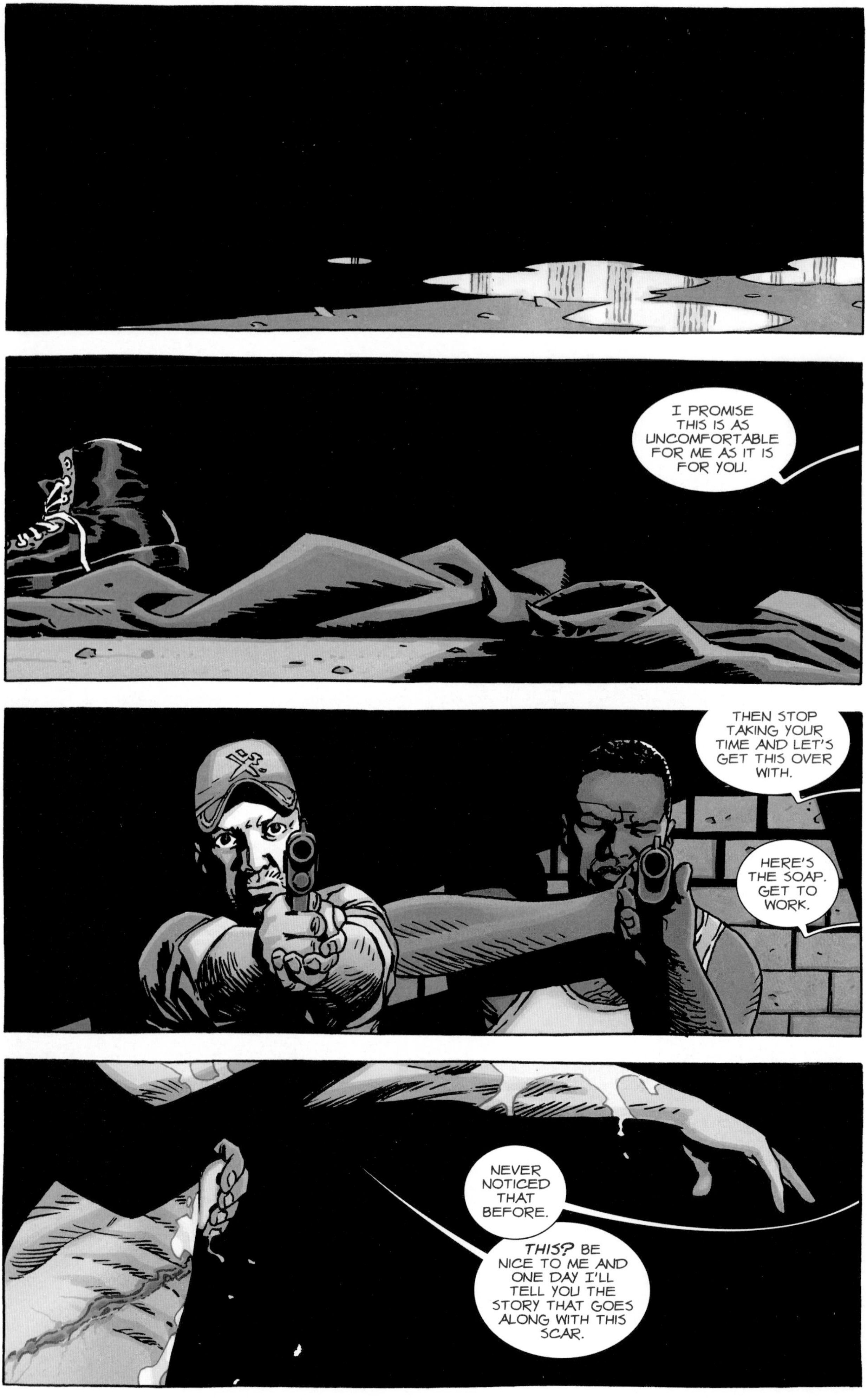
I PROMISE THIS IS AS UNCOMFORTABLE FOR ME AS IT IS FOR YOU.
THEN STOP TAKING YOUR TIME AND LET'S GET THIS OVER WITH.
HERE'S THE SOAP. GET TO WORK.
NEVER NOTICED THAT BEFORE.
THIS? BE NICE TO ME AND ONE DAY I'LL TELL YOU THE STORY THAT GOES ALONG WITH THIS SCAR.

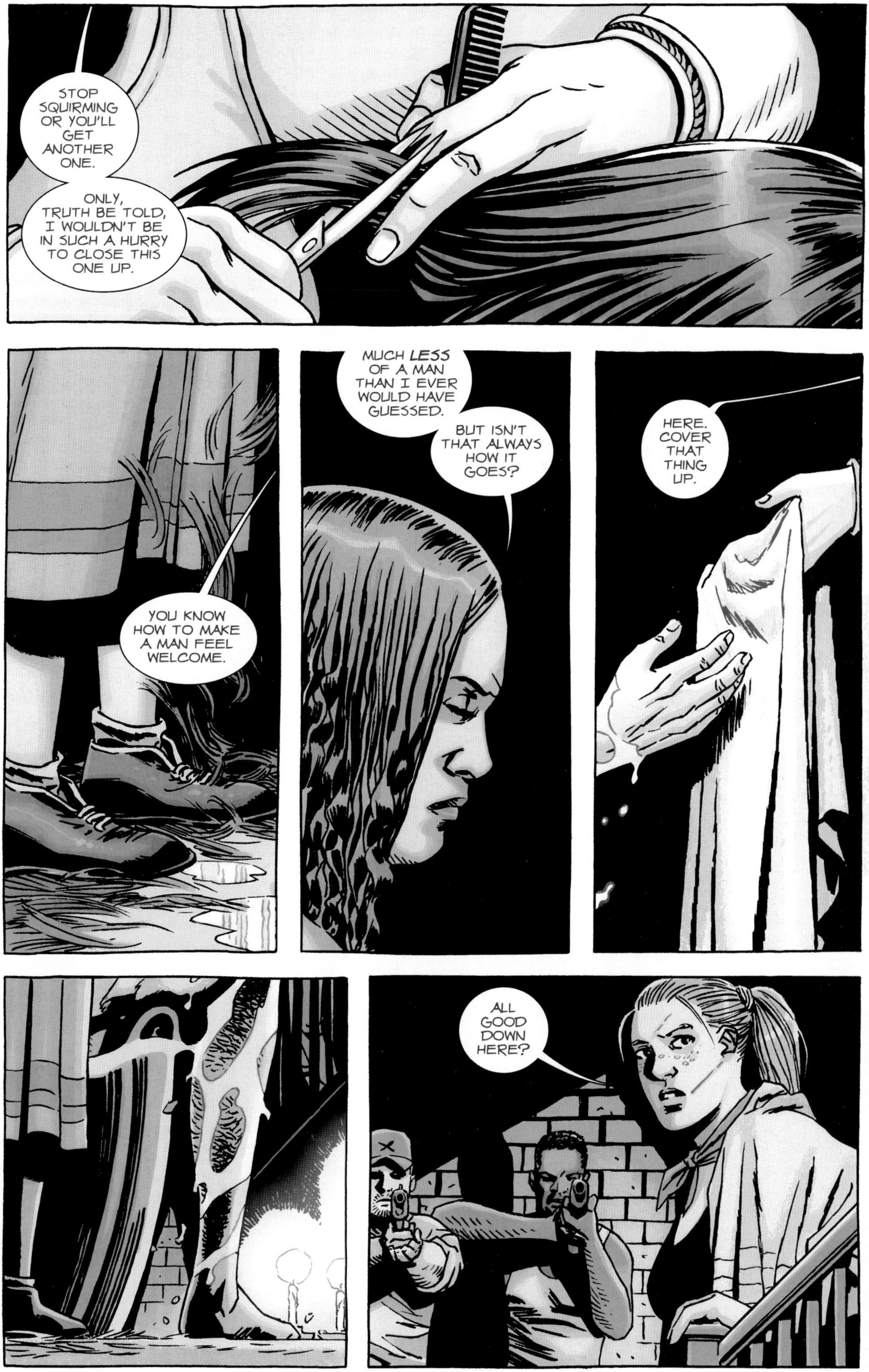
STOP SQUIRMING OR YOU'LL GET ANOTHER ONE.
ONLY, TRUTH BE TOLD, I WOULDN'T BE IN SUCH A HURRY TO CLOSE THIS ONE UP.
YOU KNOW HOW TO MAKE A MAN FEEL WELCOME.
MUCH LESS OF A MAN THAN I EVER WOULD HAVE GUESSED.
BUT ISN'T THAT ALWAYS HOW IT GOES?
HERE. COVER THAT THING UP.
ALL GOOD DOWN HERE?

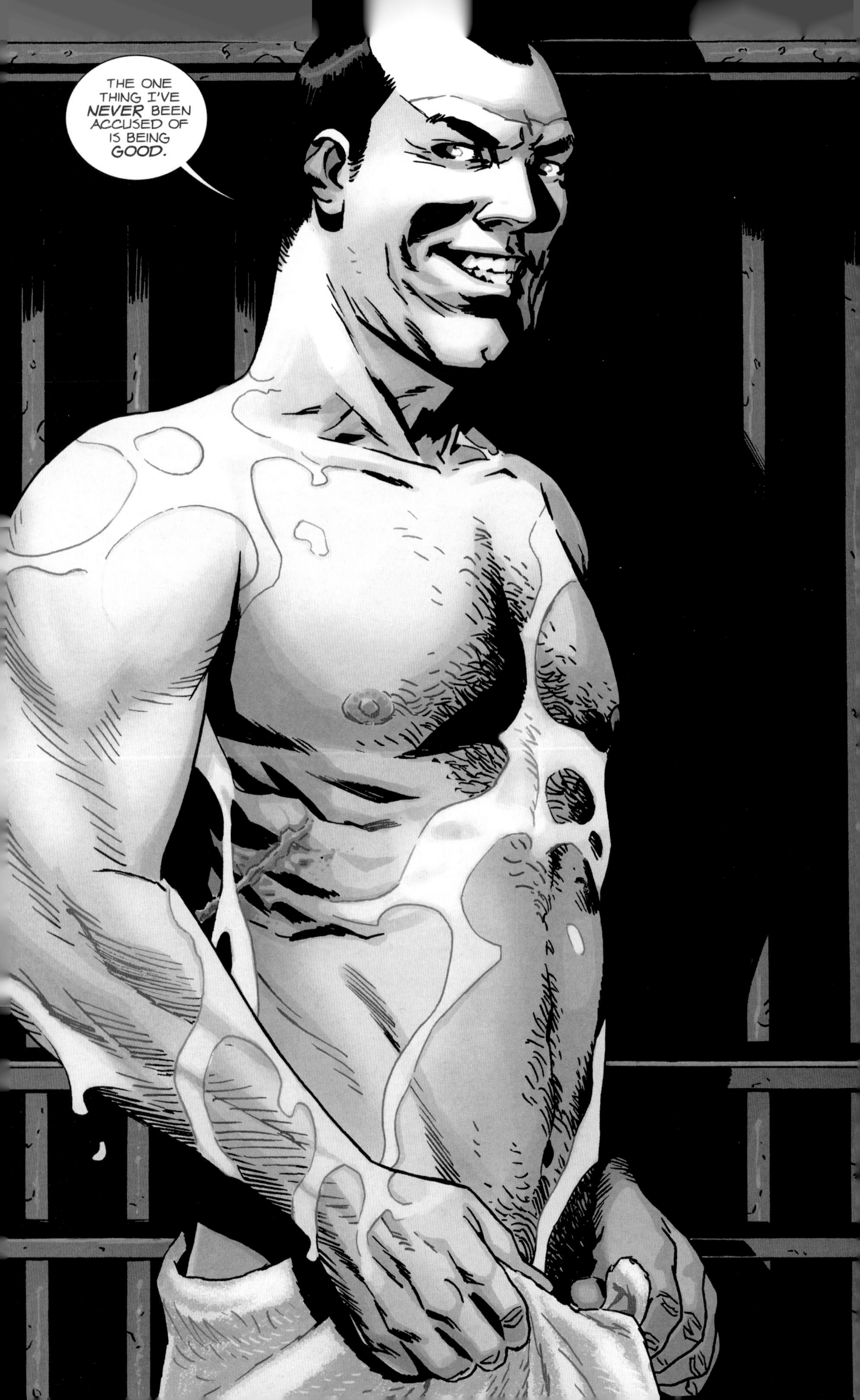
THE ONE THING I'VE NEVER BEEN ACCUSED OF IS BEING GOOD.

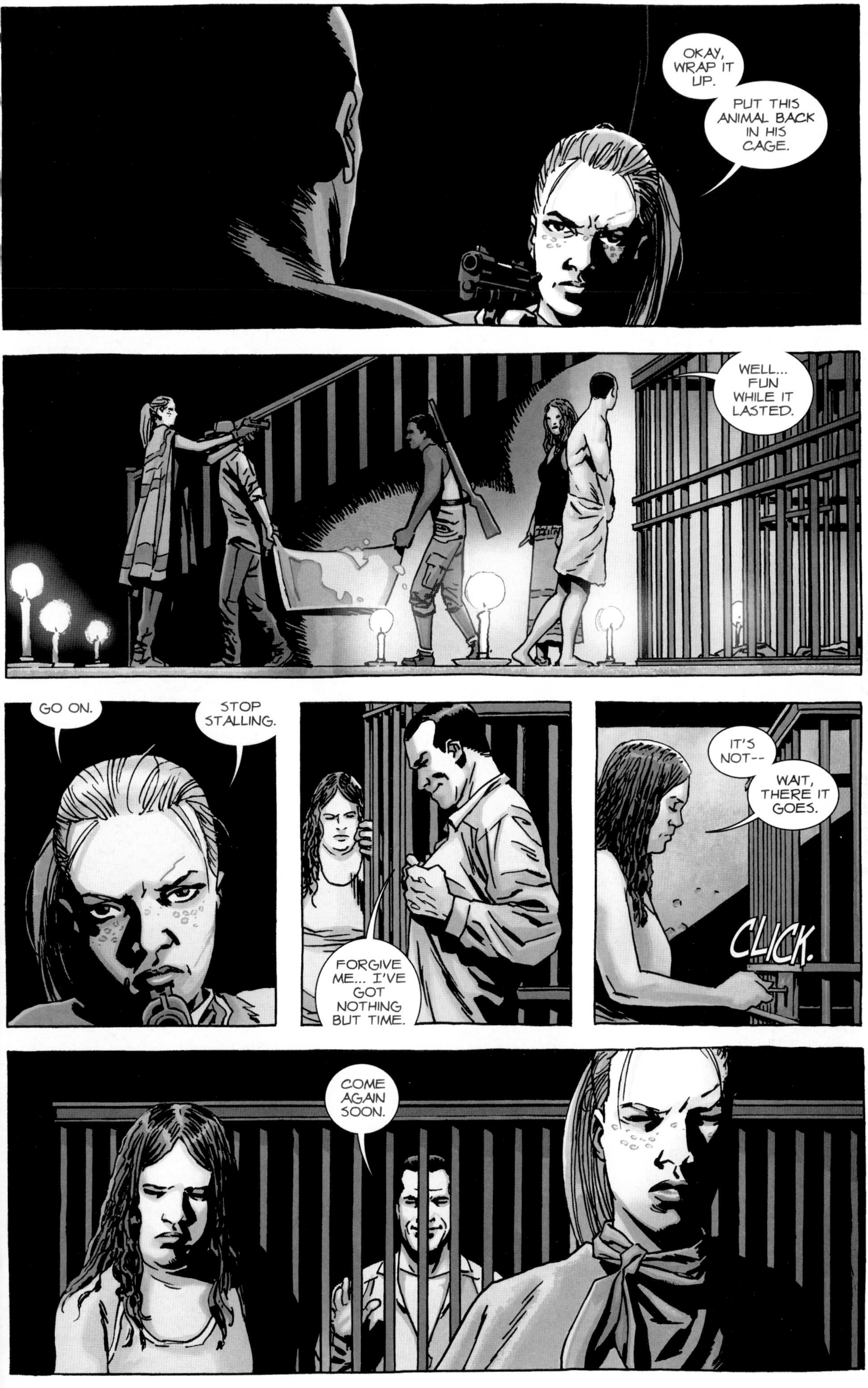
OKAY, WRAP IT UP.
PUT THIS ANIMAL BACK IN HIS CAGE.
WELL... FUN WHILE IT LASTED.
GO ON.
STOP STALLING.
FORGIVE ME... I'VE GOT NOTHING BUT TIME.
IT'S NOT--
WAIT, THERE IT GOES.
CLICK.
COME AGAIN SOON.

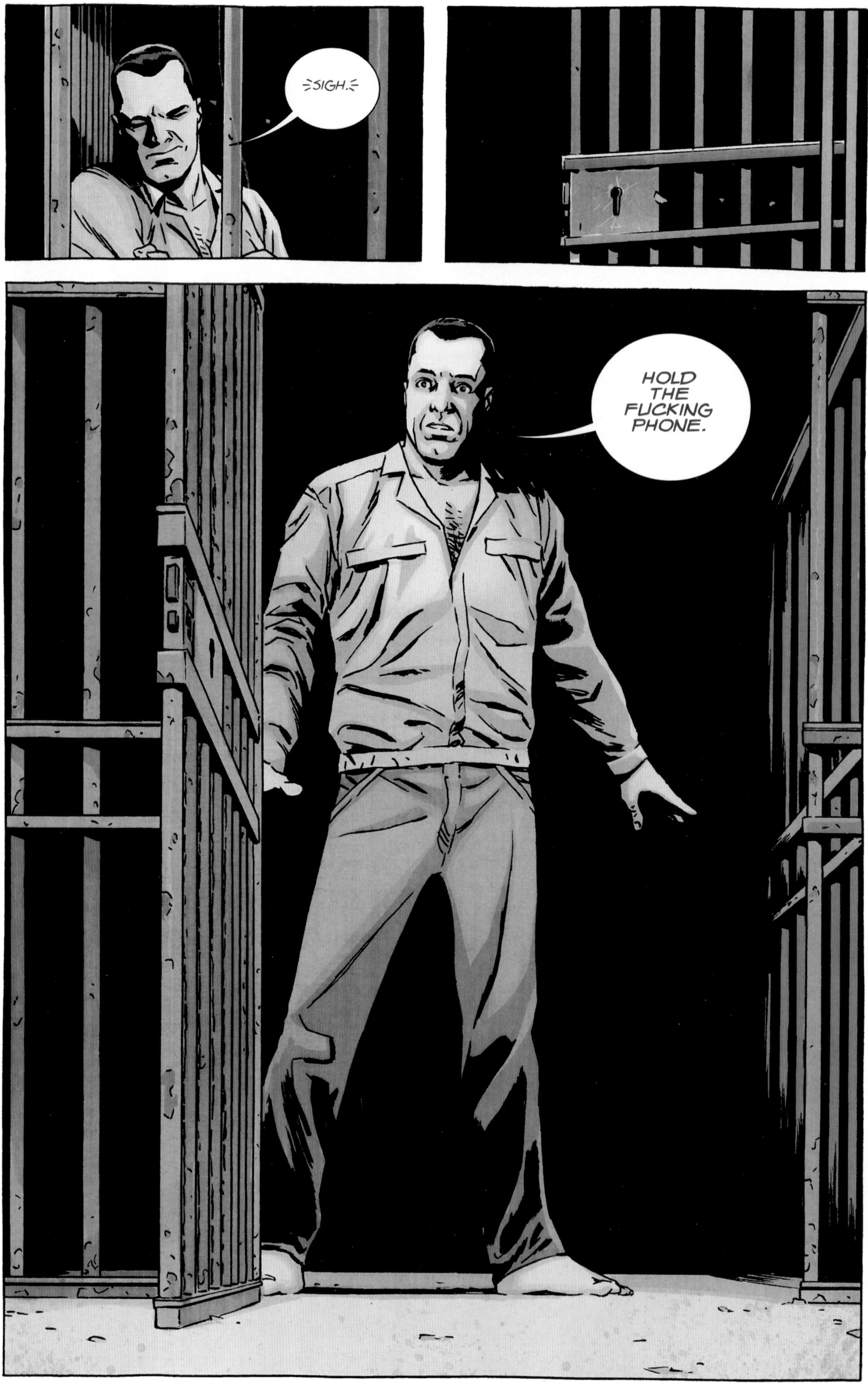

SIGH.
HOLD THE FUCKING PHONE.

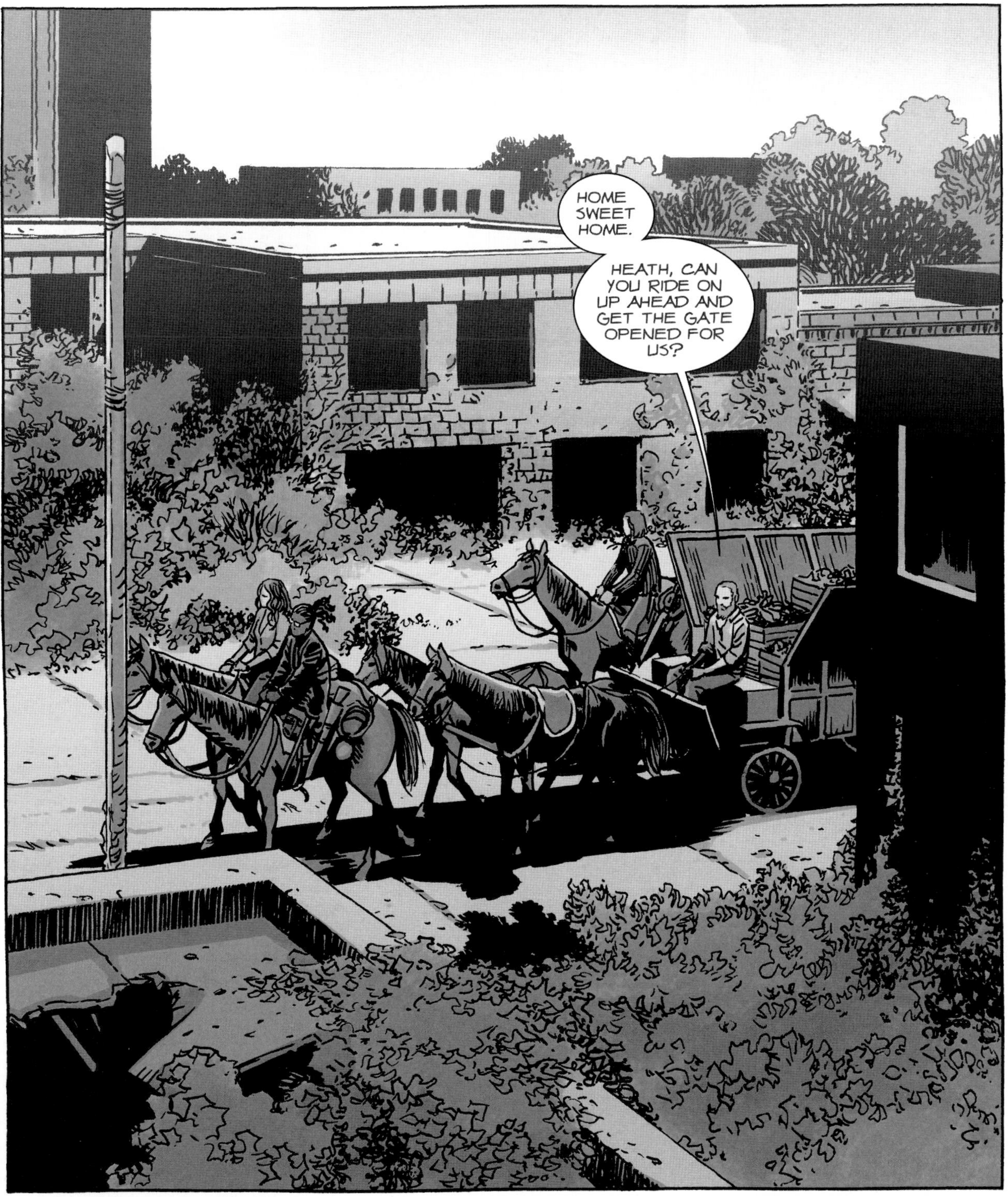
HOME SWEET HOME.
HEATH, CAN YOU RIDE ON UP AHEAD AND GET THE GATE OPENED FOR US?

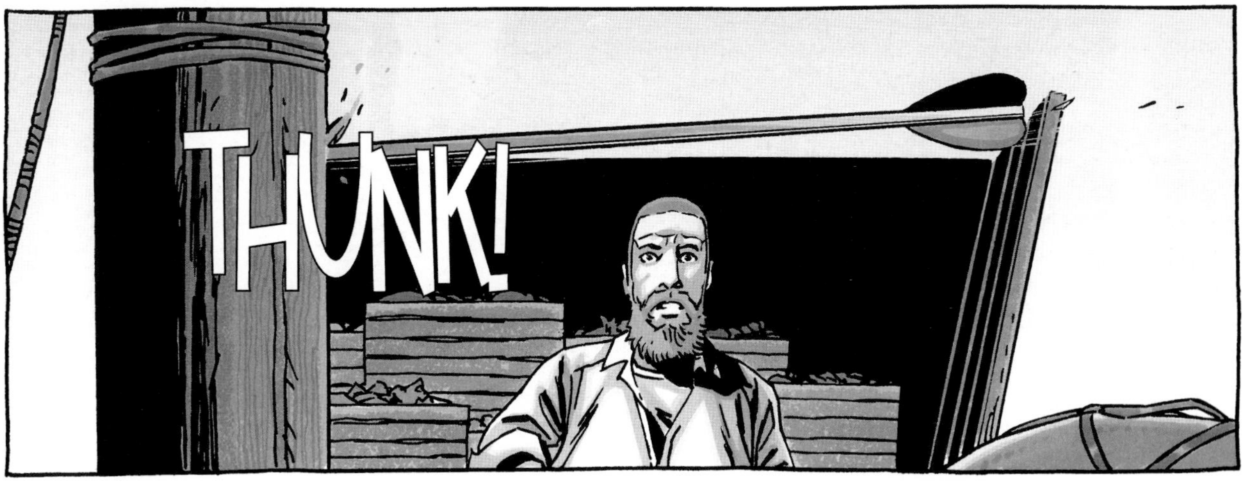
THUNK!

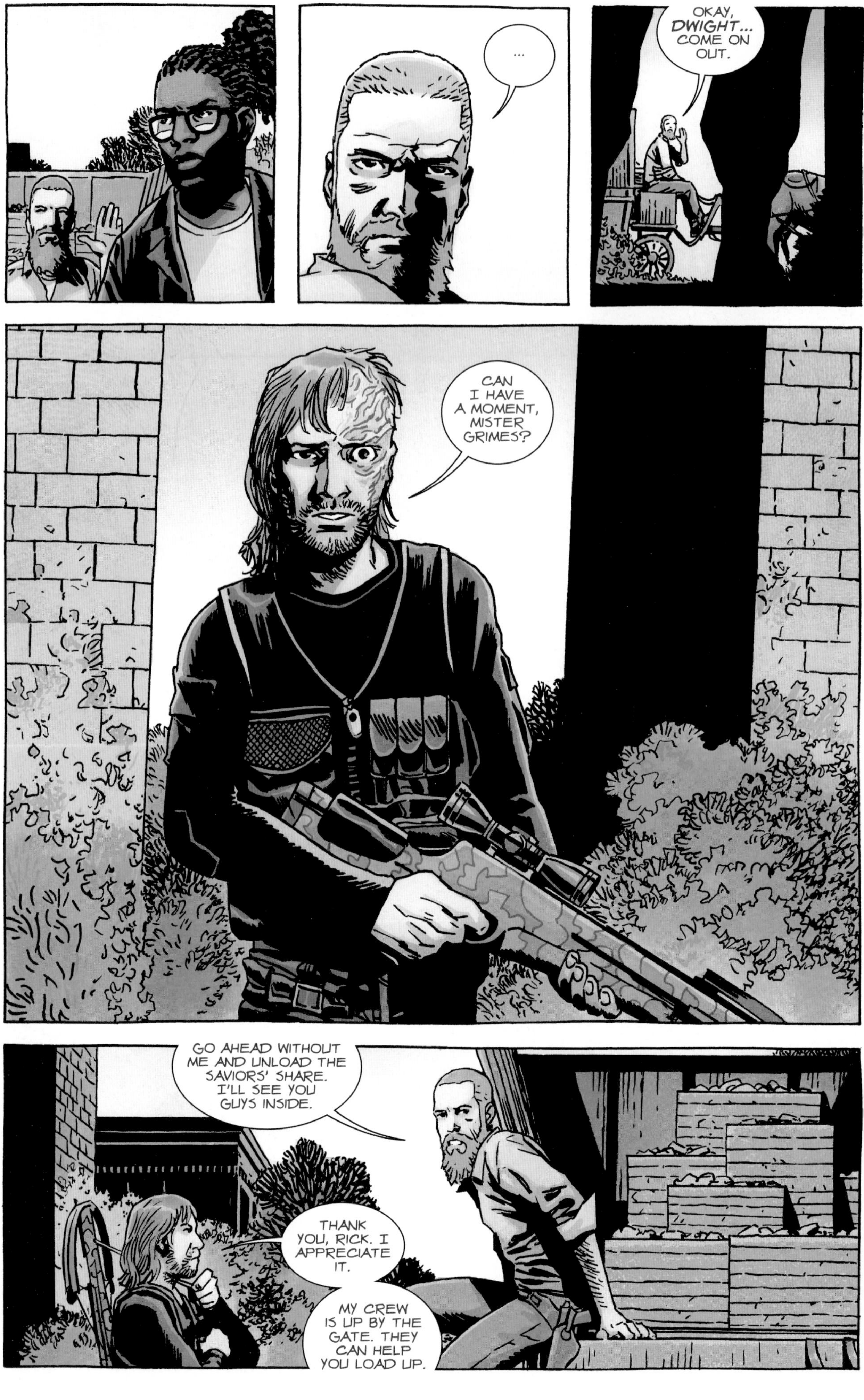
...
OKAY, DWIGHT... COME ON OUT.
CAN I HAVE A MOMENT, MISTER GRIMES?
GO AHEAD WITHOUT ME AND UNLOAD THE SAVIORS' SHARE. I'LL SEE YOU GUYS INSIDE.
THANK YOU, RICK. I APPRECIATE IT.
MY CREW IS UP BY THE GATE. THEY CAN HELP YOU LOAD UP.

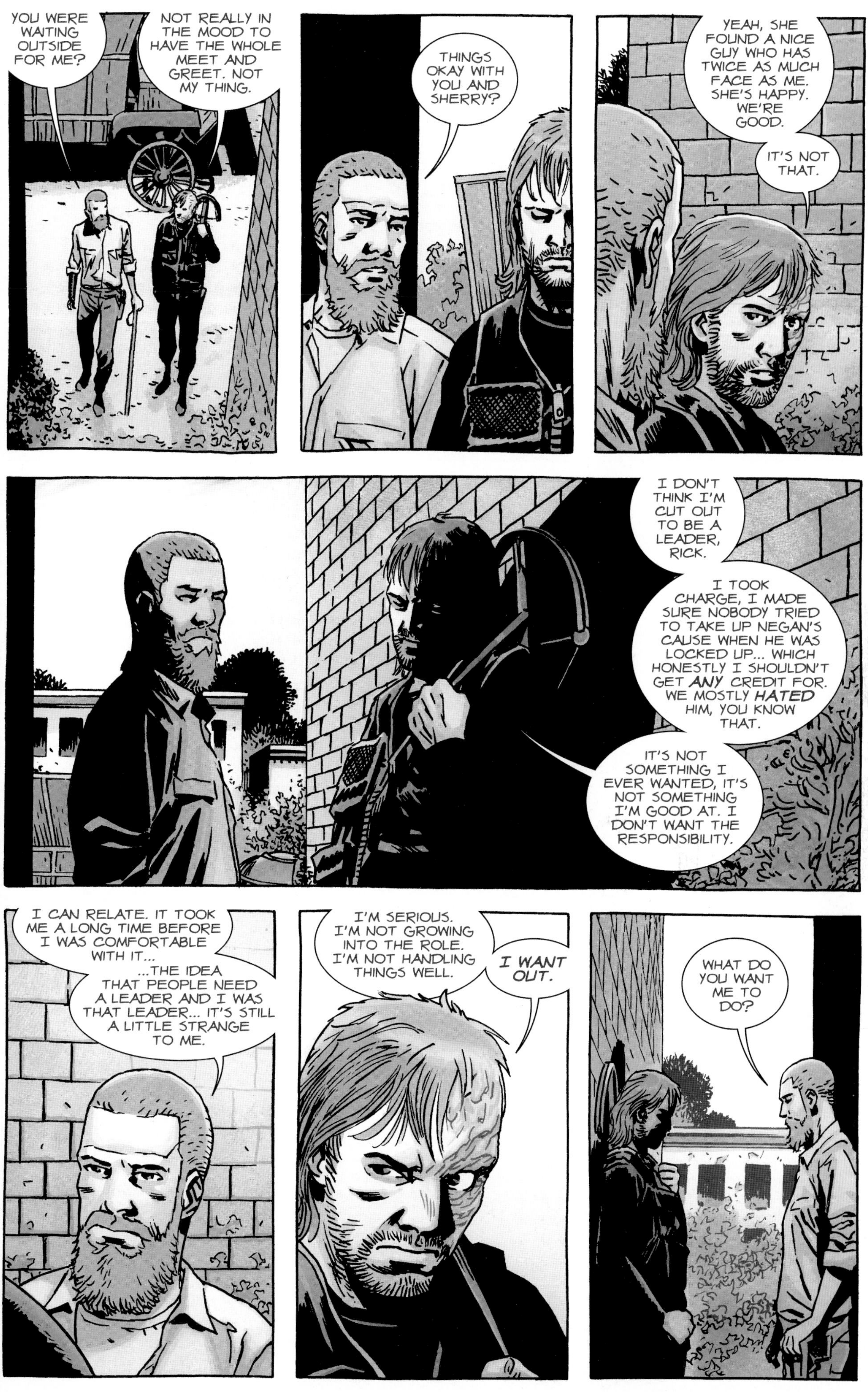

YOU WERE WAITING OUTSIDE FOR ME?
NOT REALLY IN THE MOOD TO HAVE THE WHOLE MEET AND GREET. NOT MY THING.
THINGS OKAY WITH YOU AND SHERRY?
YEAH, SHE FOUND A NICE GUY WHO HAS TWICE AS MUCH FACE AS ME. SHE'S HAPPY. WE'RE GOOD.
IT'S NOT THAT.
I DON'T THINK I'M CUT OUT TO BE A LEADER, RICK.
I TOOK CHARGE, I MADE SURE NOBODY TRIED TO TAKE UP NEGAN'S CAUSE WHEN HE WAS LOCKED UP... WHICH HONESTLY I SHOULDN'T GET ANY CREDIT FOR. WE MOSTLY HATED HIM, YOU KNOW THAT.
IT'S NOT SOMETHING I EVER WANTED, IT'S NOT SOMETHING I'M GOOD AT. I DON'T WANT THE RESPONSIBILITY.
I CAN RELATE. IT TOOK ME A LONG TIME BEFORE I WAS COMFORTABLE WITH IT...
...THE IDEA THAT PEOPLE NEED A LEADER AND I WAS THAT LEADER... IT'S STILL A LITTLE STRANGE TO ME.
I'M SERIOUS. I'M NOT GROWING INTO THE ROLE. I'M NOT HANDLING THINGS WELL.
I WANT OUT.
WHAT DO YOU WANT ME TO DO?

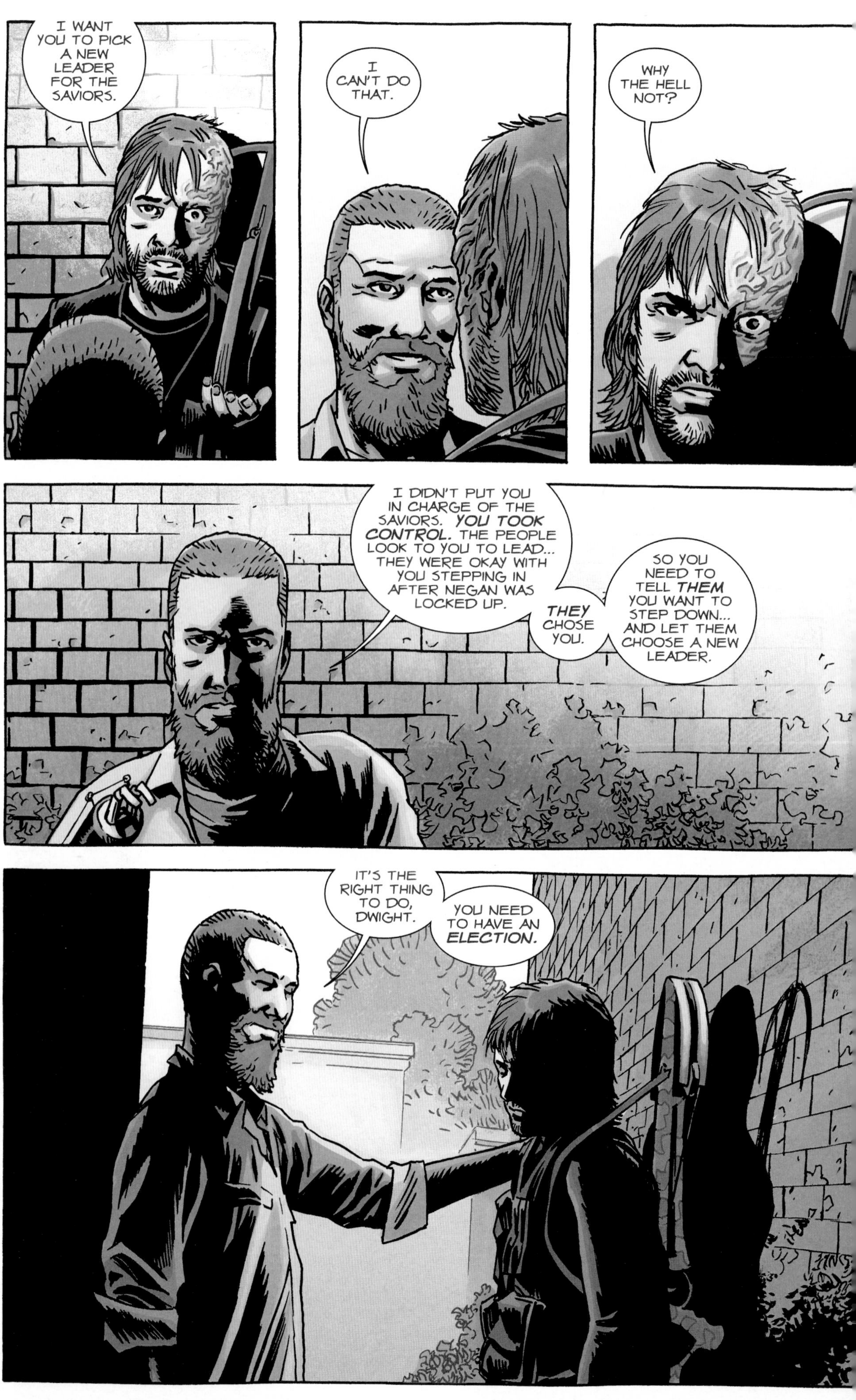
I WANT YOU TO PICK A NEW LEADER FOR THE SAVIORS.
I CAN'T DO THAT.
WHY THE HELL NOT?
I DIDN'T PUT YOU IN CHARGE OF THE SAVIORS. YOU TOOK CONTROL. THE PEOPLE LOOK TO YOU TO LEAD... THEY WERE OKAY WITH YOU STEPPING IN AFTER NEGAN WAS LOCKED UP.
THEY CHOSE YOU.
SO YOU NEED TO TELL THEM YOU WANT TO STEP DOWN... AND LET THEM CHOOSE A NEW LEADER.
IT'S THE RIGHT THING TO DO, DWIGHT.
YOU NEED TO HAVE AN ELECTION.

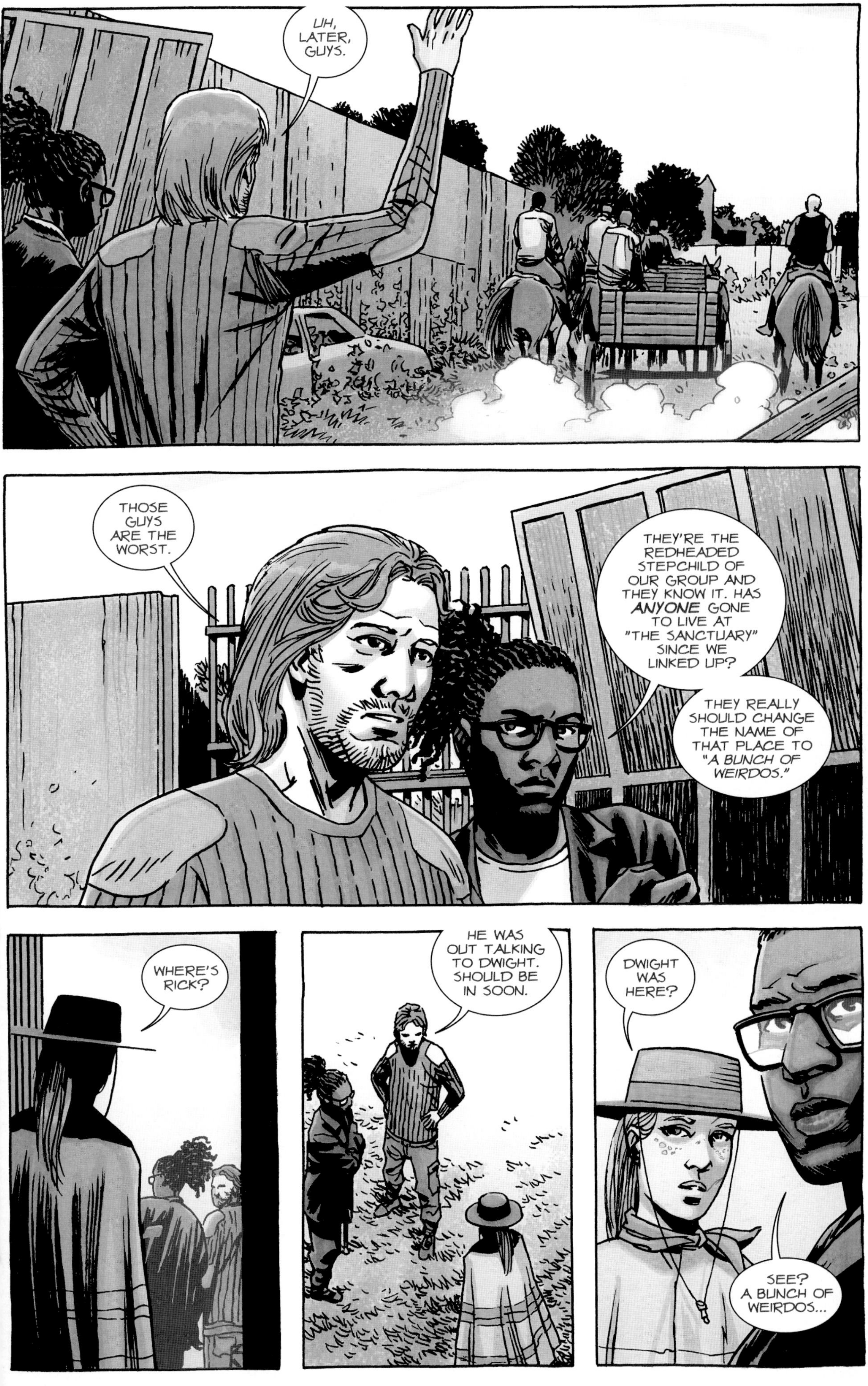
UH, LATER, GUYS.
THOSE GUYS ARE THE WORST.
THEY'RE THE REDHEADED STEPCHILD OF OUR GROUP AND THEY KNOW IT. HAS ANYONE GONE TO LIVE AT "THE SANCTUARY" SINCE WE LINKED UP?
THEY REALLY SHOULD CHANGE THE NAME OF THAT PLACE TO "A BUNCH OF WEIRDOS."
WHERE'S RICK?
HE WAS OUT TALKING TO DWIGHT. SHOULD BE IN SOON.
DWIGHT WAS HERE?
SEE? A BUNCH OF WEIRDOS...

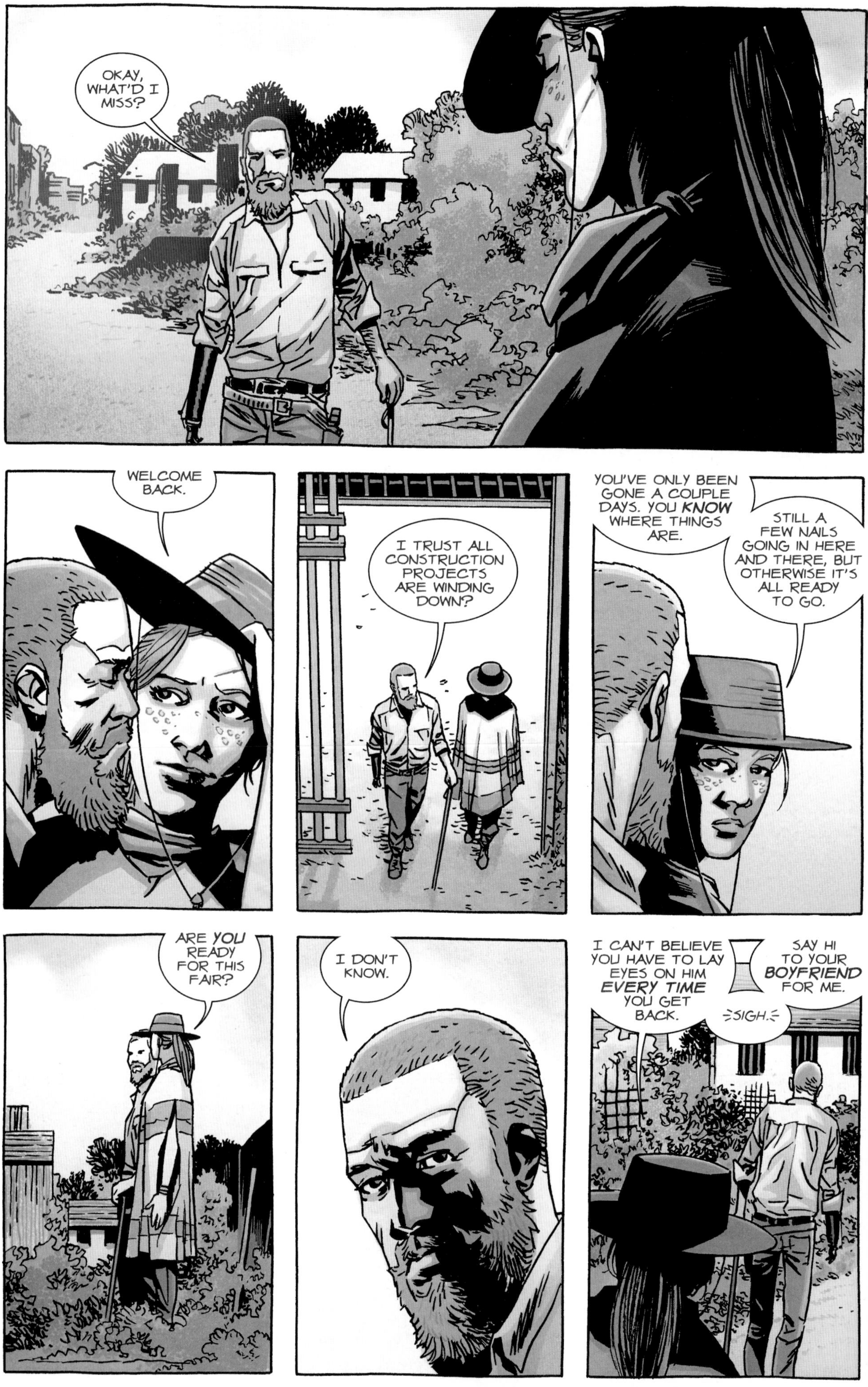
OKAY, WHAT'D I MISS?
WELCOME BACK.
I TRUST ALL CONSTRUCTION PROJECTS ARE WINDING DOWN?
YOU'VE ONLY BEEN GONE A COUPLE DAYS. YOU **KNOW** WHERE THINGS ARE.
STILL A FEW NAILS GOING IN HERE AND THERE, BUT OTHERWISE IT'S ALL READY TO GO.
ARE **YOU** READY FOR THIS FAIR?
I DON'T KNOW.
I CAN'T BELIEVE YOU HAVE TO LAY EYES ON HIM **EVERY TIME** YOU GET BACK.
SAY HI TO YOUR **BOYFRIEND** FOR ME.
SIGH.

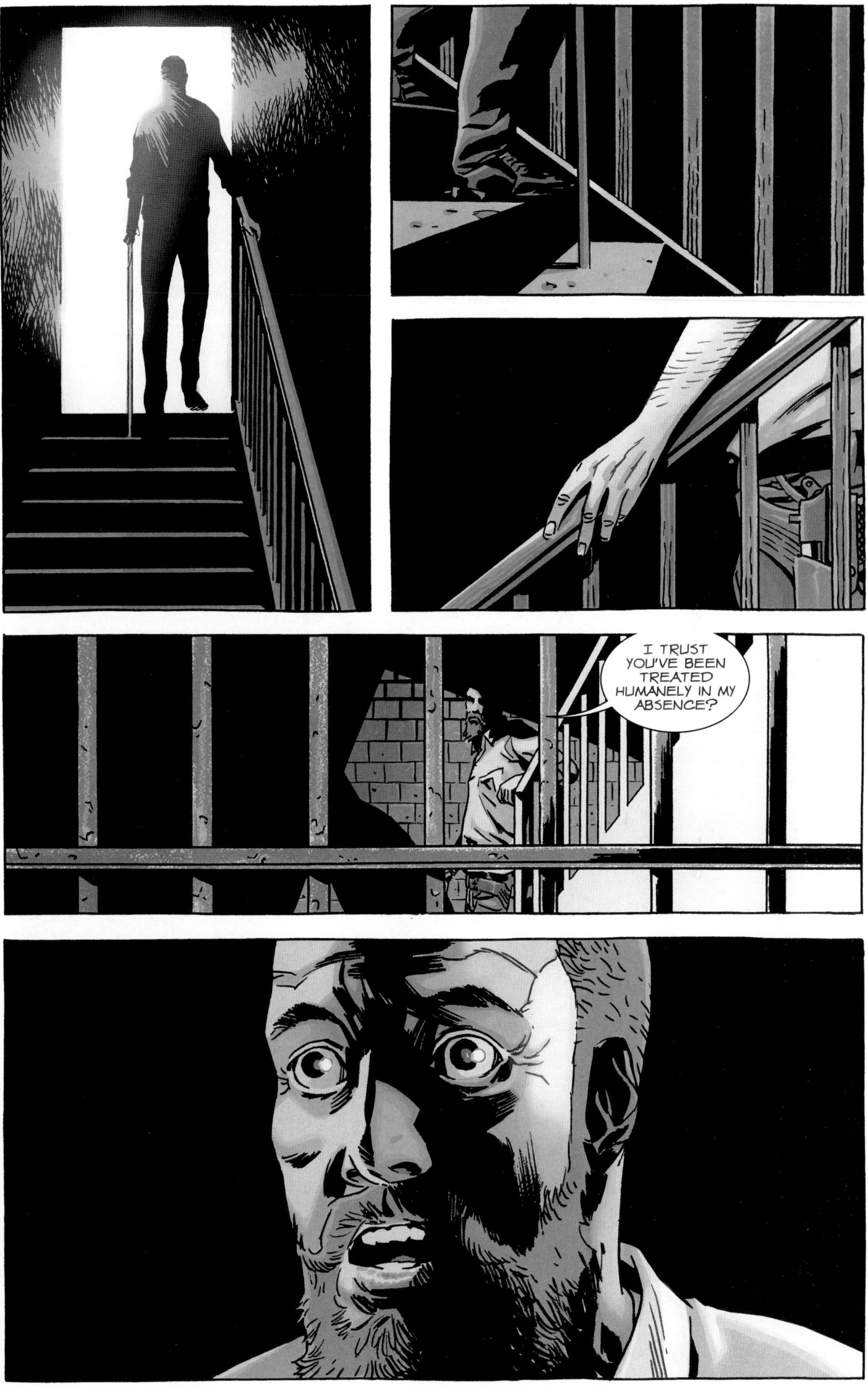
I TRUST YOU'VE BEEN TREATED HUMANELY IN MY ABSENCE?

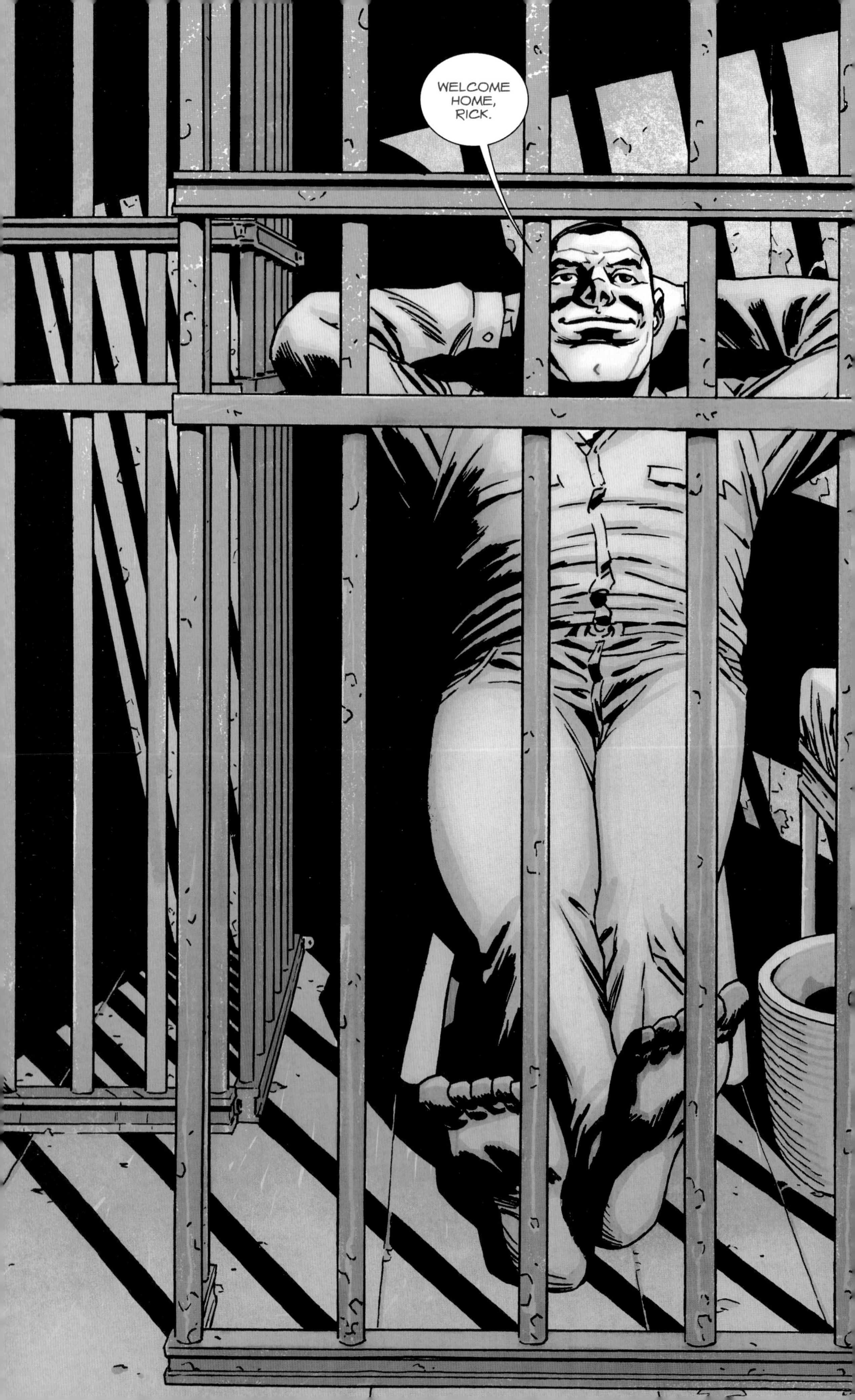
WELCOME HOME, RICK.

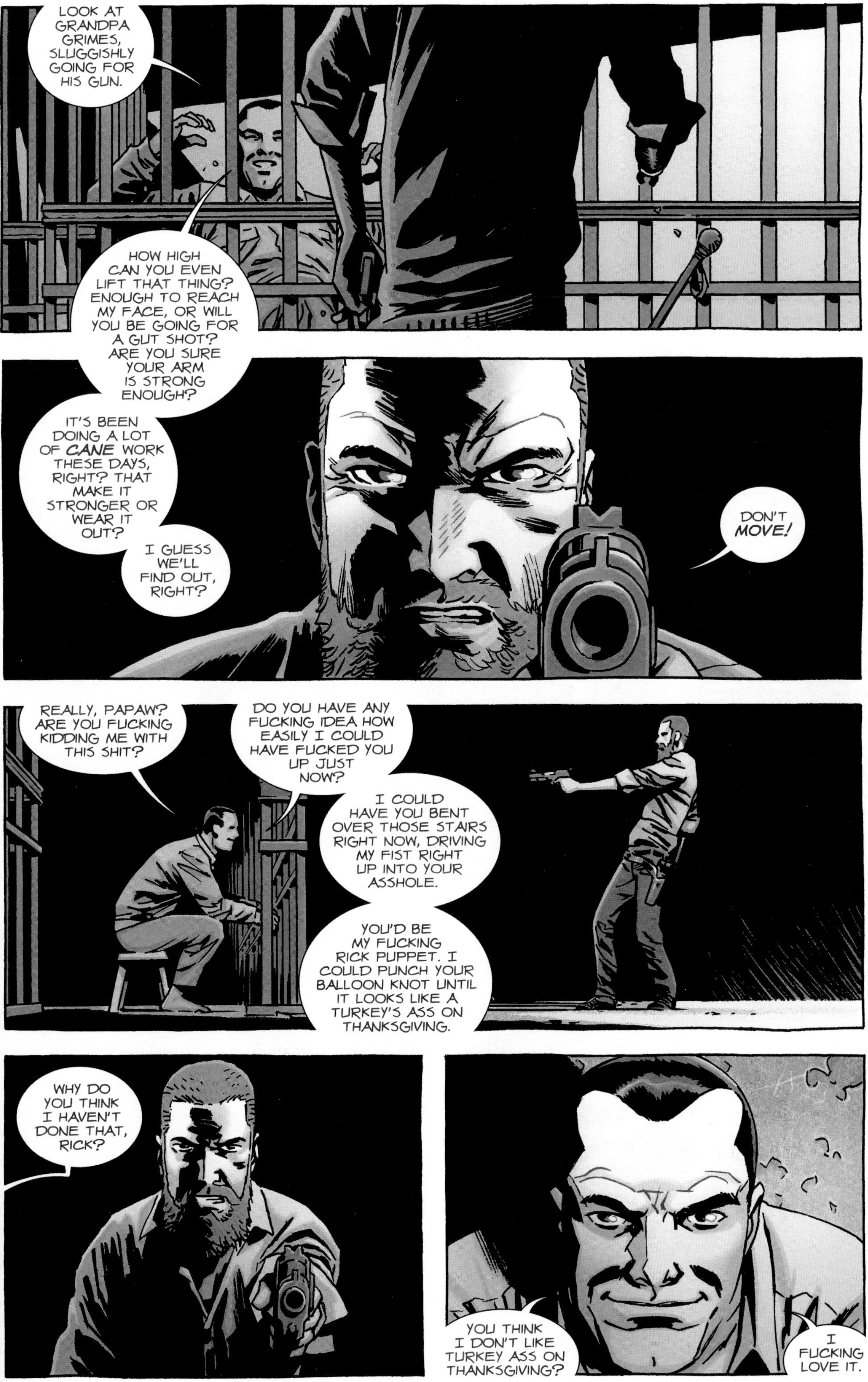
LOOK AT GRANDPA GRIMES, SLUGGISHLY GOING FOR HIS GUN.
HOW HIGH CAN YOU EVEN LIFT THAT THING? ENOUGH TO REACH MY FACE, OR WILL YOU BE GOING FOR A GUT SHOT? ARE YOU SURE YOUR ARM IS STRONG ENOUGH?
IT'S BEEN DOING A LOT OF *CANE* WORK THESE DAYS, RIGHT? THAT MAKE IT STRONGER OR WEAR IT OUT?
I GUESS WE'LL FIND OUT, RIGHT?
DON'T *MOVE!*
REALLY, PAPAW? ARE YOU FUCKING KIDDING ME WITH THIS SHIT?
DO YOU HAVE ANY FUCKING IDEA HOW EASILY I COULD HAVE FUCKED YOU UP JUST NOW?
I COULD HAVE YOU BENT OVER THOSE STAIRS RIGHT NOW, DRIVING MY FIST RIGHT UP INTO YOUR ASSHOLE.
YOU'D BE MY FUCKING RICK PUPPET. I COULD PUNCH YOUR BALLOON KNOT UNTIL IT LOOKS LIKE A TURKEY'S ASS ON THANKSGIVING.
WHY DO YOU THINK I HAVEN'T DONE THAT, RICK?
YOU THINK I DON'T LIKE TURKEY ASS ON THANKSGIVING?
I FUCKING LOVE IT.

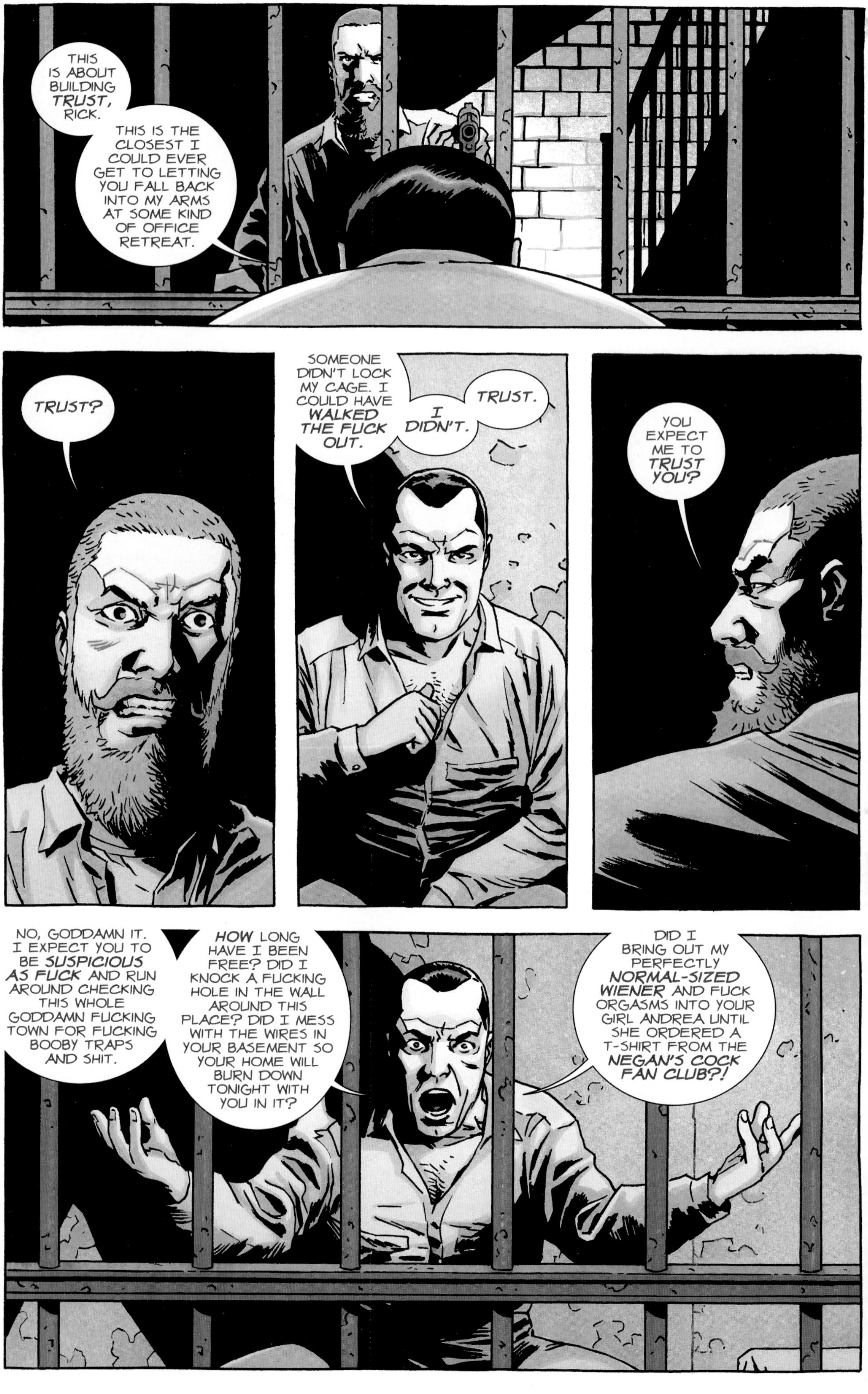
THIS IS ABOUT BUILDING TRUST, RICK.
THIS IS THE CLOSEST I COULD EVER GET TO LETTING YOU FALL BACK INTO MY ARMS AT SOME KIND OF OFFICE RETREAT.
TRUST?
SOMEONE DIDN'T LOCK MY CAGE. I COULD HAVE WALKED THE FUCK OUT.
I DIDN'T.
TRUST.
YOU EXPECT ME TO TRUST YOU?
NO, GODDAMN IT. I EXPECT YOU TO BE SUSPICIOUS AS FUCK AND RUN AROUND CHECKING THIS WHOLE GODDAMN FUCKING TOWN FOR FUCKING BOOBY TRAPS AND SHIT.
HOW LONG HAVE I BEEN FREE? DID I KNOCK A FUCKING HOLE IN THE WALL AROUND THIS PLACE? DID I MESS WITH THE WIRES IN YOUR BASEMENT SO YOUR HOME WILL BURN DOWN TONIGHT WITH YOU IN IT?
DID I BRING OUT MY PERFECTLY NORMAL-SIZED WIENER AND FUCK ORGASMS INTO YOUR GIRL ANDREA UNTIL SHE ORDERED A T-SHIRT FROM THE NEGAN'S COCK FAN CLUB?!

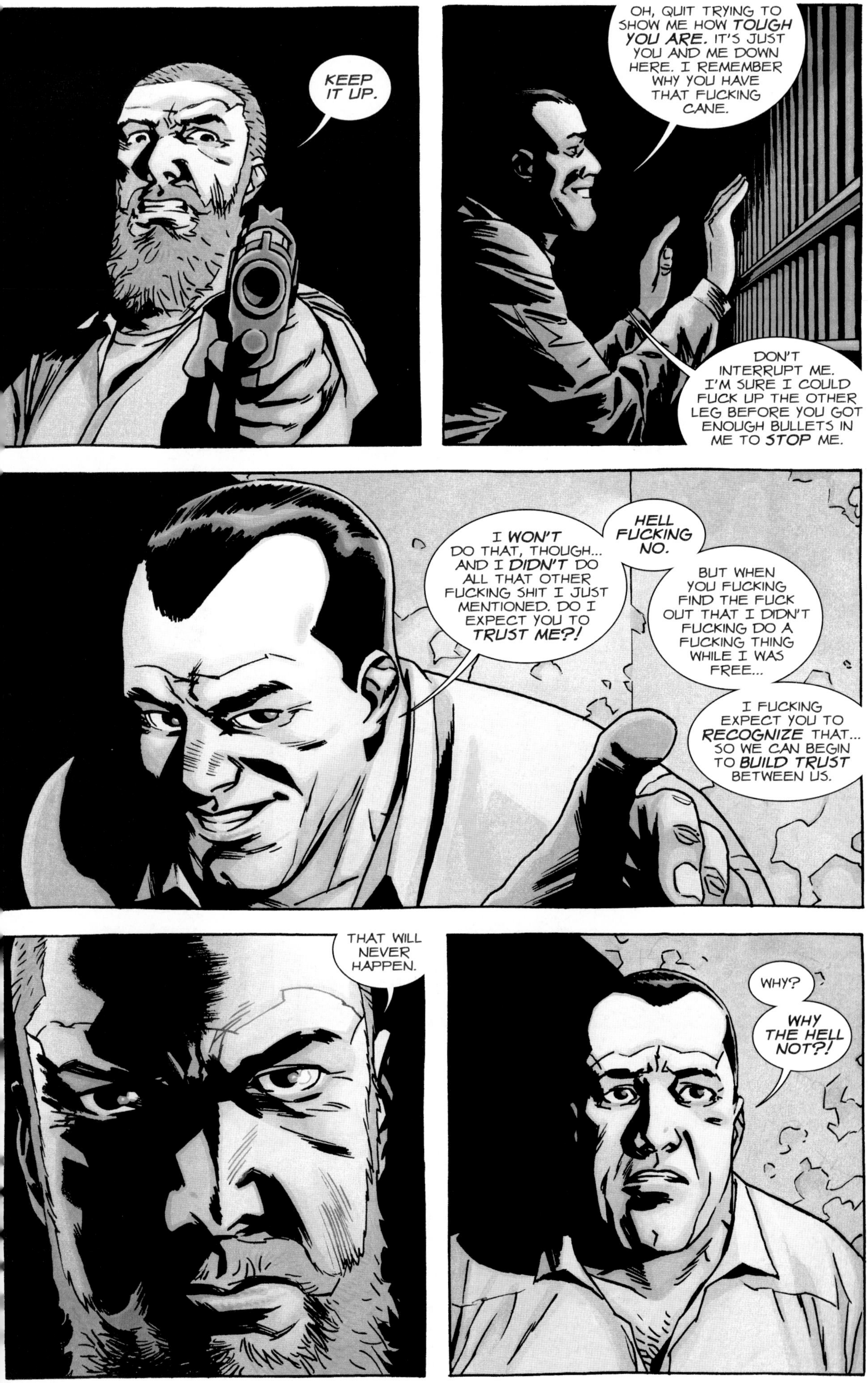
KEEP IT UP.
OH, QUIT TRYING TO SHOW ME HOW TOUGH YOU ARE. IT'S JUST YOU AND ME DOWN HERE. I REMEMBER WHY YOU HAVE THAT FUCKING CANE.
DON'T INTERRUPT ME. I'M SURE I COULD FUCK UP THE OTHER LEG BEFORE YOU GOT ENOUGH BULLETS IN ME TO STOP ME.
I WON'T DO THAT, THOUGH... AND I DIDN'T DO ALL THAT OTHER FUCKING SHIT I JUST MENTIONED. DO I EXPECT YOU TO TRUST ME?!
HELL FUCKING NO.
BUT WHEN YOU FUCKING FIND THE FUCK OUT THAT I DIDN'T FUCKING DO A FUCKING THING WHILE I WAS FREE...
I FUCKING EXPECT YOU TO RECOGNIZE THAT... SO WE CAN BEGIN TO BUILD TRUST BETWEEN US.
THAT WILL NEVER HAPPEN.
WHY?
WHY THE HELL NOT?!

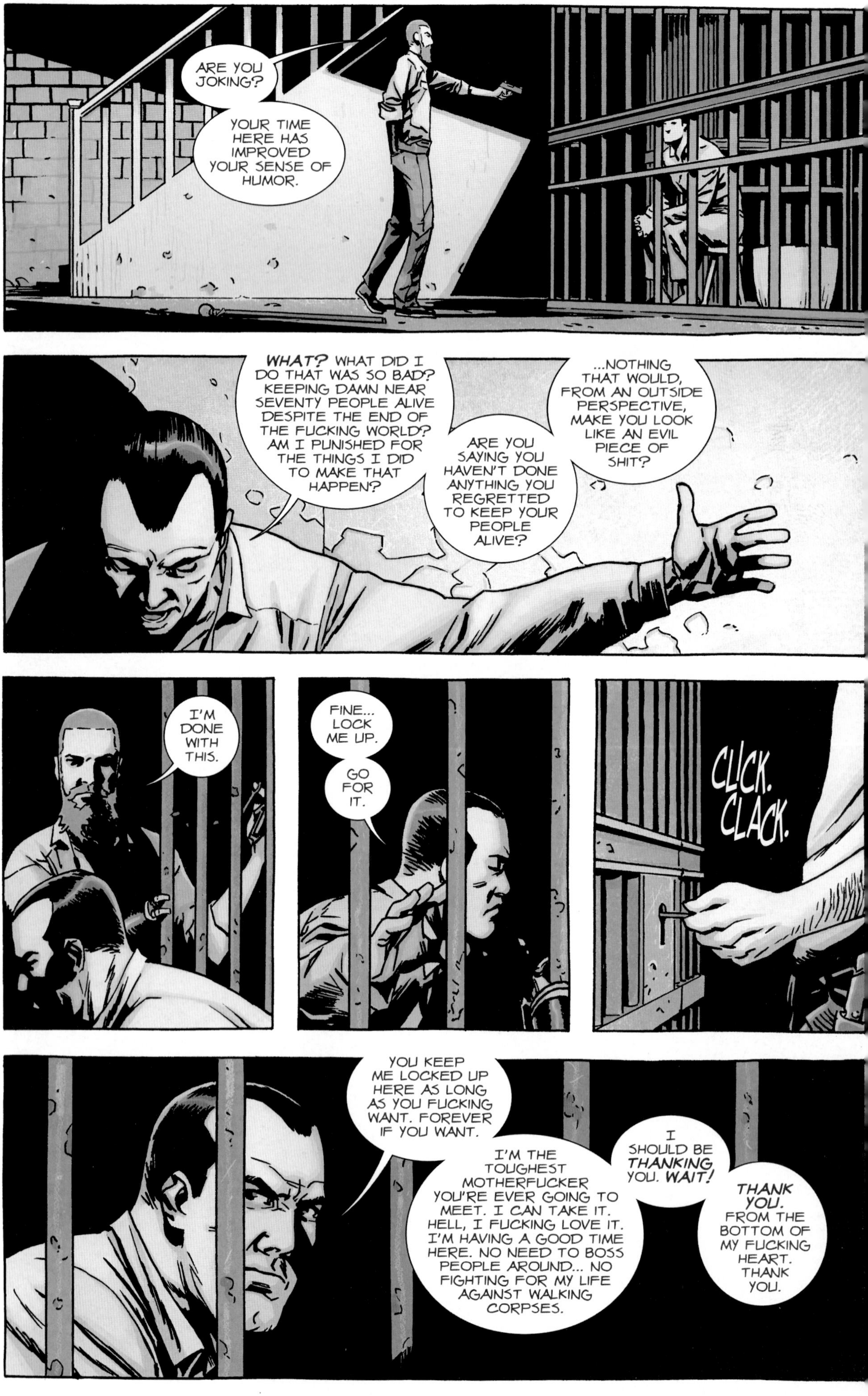
ARE YOU JOKING?
YOUR TIME HERE HAS IMPROVED YOUR SENSE OF HUMOR.
WHAT? WHAT DID I DO THAT WAS SO BAD? KEEPING DAMN NEAR SEVENTY PEOPLE ALIVE DESPITE THE END OF THE FUCKING WORLD? AM I PUNISHED FOR THE THINGS I DID TO MAKE THAT HAPPEN?
ARE YOU SAYING YOU HAVEN'T DONE ANYTHING YOU REGRETTED TO KEEP YOUR PEOPLE ALIVE?
...NOTHING THAT WOULD, FROM AN OUTSIDE PERSPECTIVE, MAKE YOU LOOK LIKE AN EVIL PIECE OF SHIT?
I'M DONE WITH THIS.
FINE... LOCK ME UP.
GO FOR IT.
CLICK. CLACK.
YOU KEEP ME LOCKED UP HERE AS LONG AS YOU FUCKING WANT. FOREVER IF YOU WANT.
I'M THE TOUGHEST MOTHERFUCKER YOU'RE EVER GOING TO MEET. I CAN TAKE IT. HELL, I FUCKING LOVE IT. I'M HAVING A GOOD TIME HERE. NO NEED TO BOSS PEOPLE AROUND... NO FIGHTING FOR MY LIFE AGAINST WALKING CORPSES.
I SHOULD BE THANKING YOU. WAIT!
THANK YOU. FROM THE BOTTOM OF MY FUCKING HEART. THANK YOU.

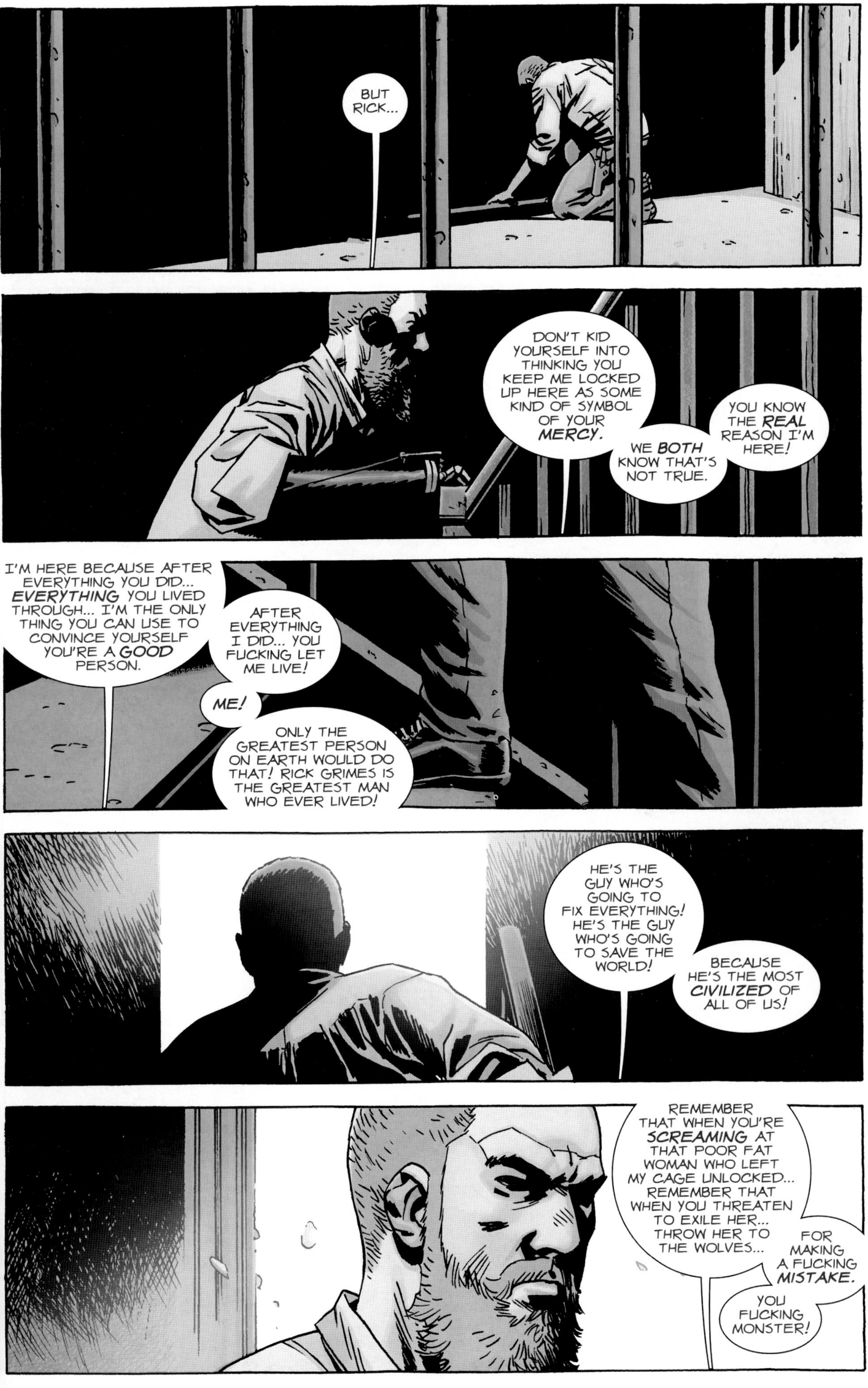
BUT RICK...
DON'T KID YOURSELF INTO THINKING YOU KEEP ME LOCKED UP HERE AS SOME KIND OF SYMBOL OF YOUR MERCY.
WE BOTH KNOW THAT'S NOT TRUE.
YOU KNOW THE REAL REASON I'M HERE!
I'M HERE BECAUSE AFTER EVERYTHING YOU DID... EVERYTHING YOU LIVED THROUGH... I'M THE ONLY THING YOU CAN USE TO CONVINCE YOURSELF YOU'RE A GOOD PERSON.
AFTER EVERYTHING I DID... YOU FUCKING LET ME LIVE!
ME!
ONLY THE GREATEST PERSON ON EARTH WOULD DO THAT! RICK GRIMES IS THE GREATEST MAN WHO EVER LIVED!
HE'S THE GUY WHO'S GOING TO FIX EVERYTHING! HE'S THE GUY WHO'S GOING TO SAVE THE WORLD!
BECAUSE HE'S THE MOST CIVILIZED OF ALL OF US!
REMEMBER THAT WHEN YOU'RE SCREAMING AT THAT POOR FAT WOMAN WHO LEFT MY CAGE UNLOCKED... REMEMBER THAT WHEN YOU THREATEN TO EXILE HER... THROW HER TO THE WOLVES...
FOR MAKING A FUCKING MISTAKE.
YOU FUCKING MONSTER!

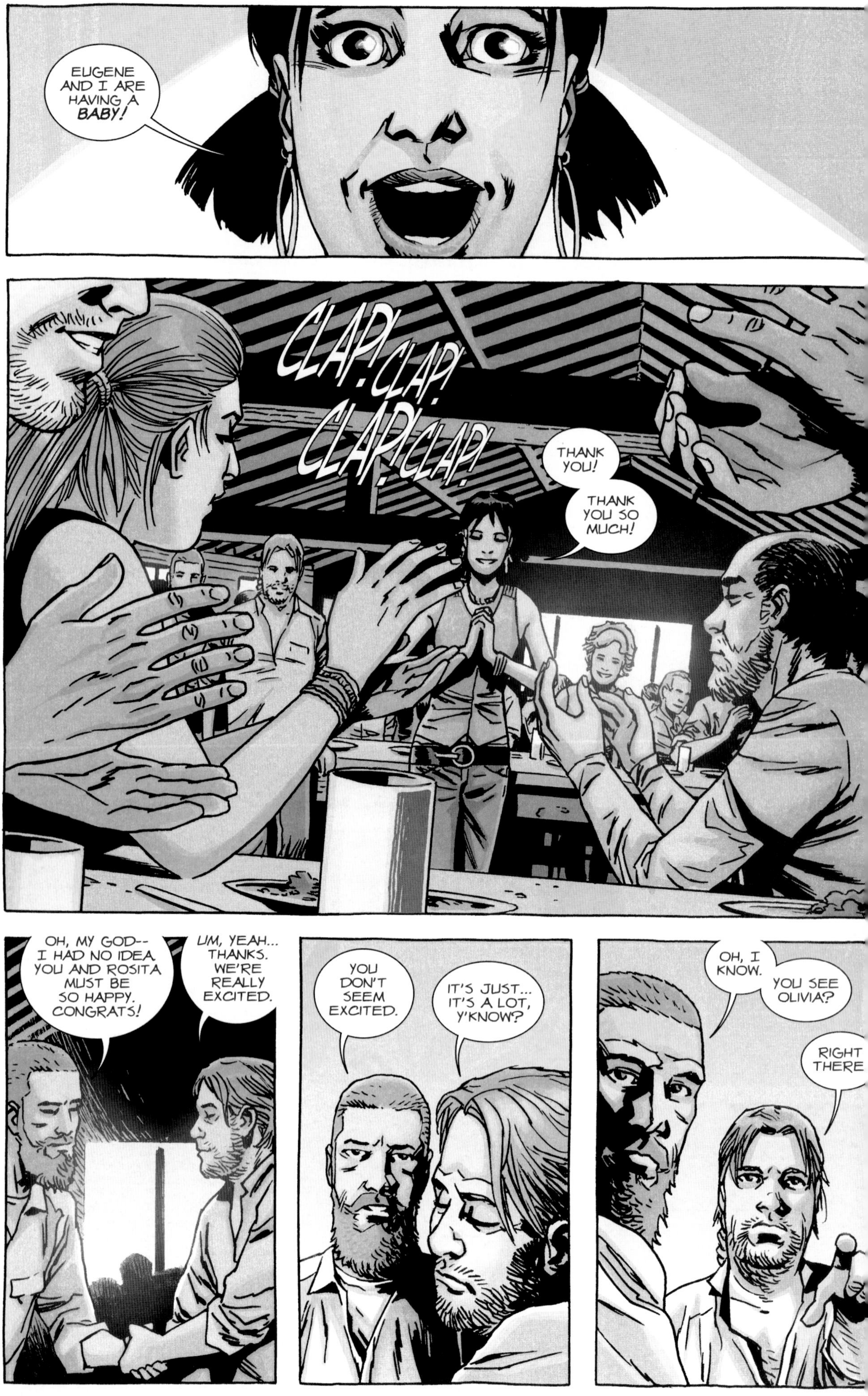
EUGENE AND I ARE HAVING A BABY!
CLAP! CLAP! CLAP! CLAP!
THANK YOU!
THANK YOU SO MUCH!
OH, MY GOD-- I HAD NO IDEA. YOU AND ROSITA MUST BE SO HAPPY. CONGRATS!
UM, YEAH... THANKS. WE'RE REALLY EXCITED.
YOU DON'T SEEM EXCITED.
IT'S JUST... IT'S A LOT, Y'KNOW?
OH, I KNOW.
YOU SEE OLIVIA?
RIGHT THERE

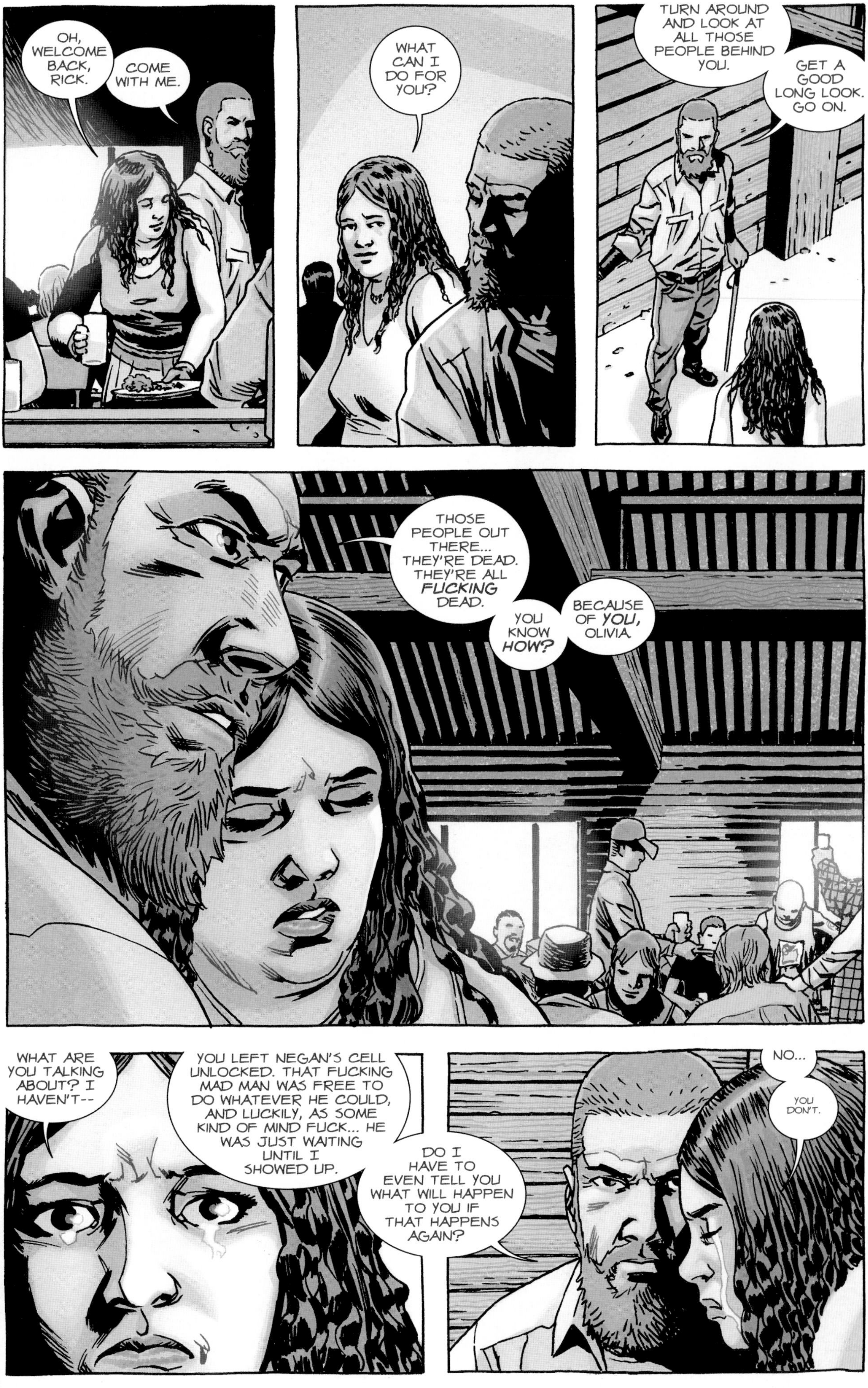
OH, WELCOME BACK, RICK.
COME WITH ME.
WHAT CAN I DO FOR YOU?
TURN AROUND AND LOOK AT ALL THOSE PEOPLE BEHIND YOU.
GET A GOOD LONG LOOK. GO ON.
THOSE PEOPLE OUT THERE... THEY'RE DEAD. THEY'RE ALL FUCKING DEAD.
YOU KNOW HOW?
BECAUSE OF YOU, OLIVIA.
WHAT ARE YOU TALKING ABOUT? I HAVEN'T--
YOU LEFT NEGAN'S CELL UNLOCKED. THAT FUCKING MAD MAN WAS FREE TO DO WHATEVER HE COULD, AND LUCKILY, AS SOME KIND OF MIND FUCK... HE WAS JUST WAITING UNTIL I SHOWED UP.
DO I HAVE TO EVEN TELL YOU WHAT WILL HAPPEN TO YOU IF THAT HAPPENS AGAIN?
NO...
YOU DON'T.

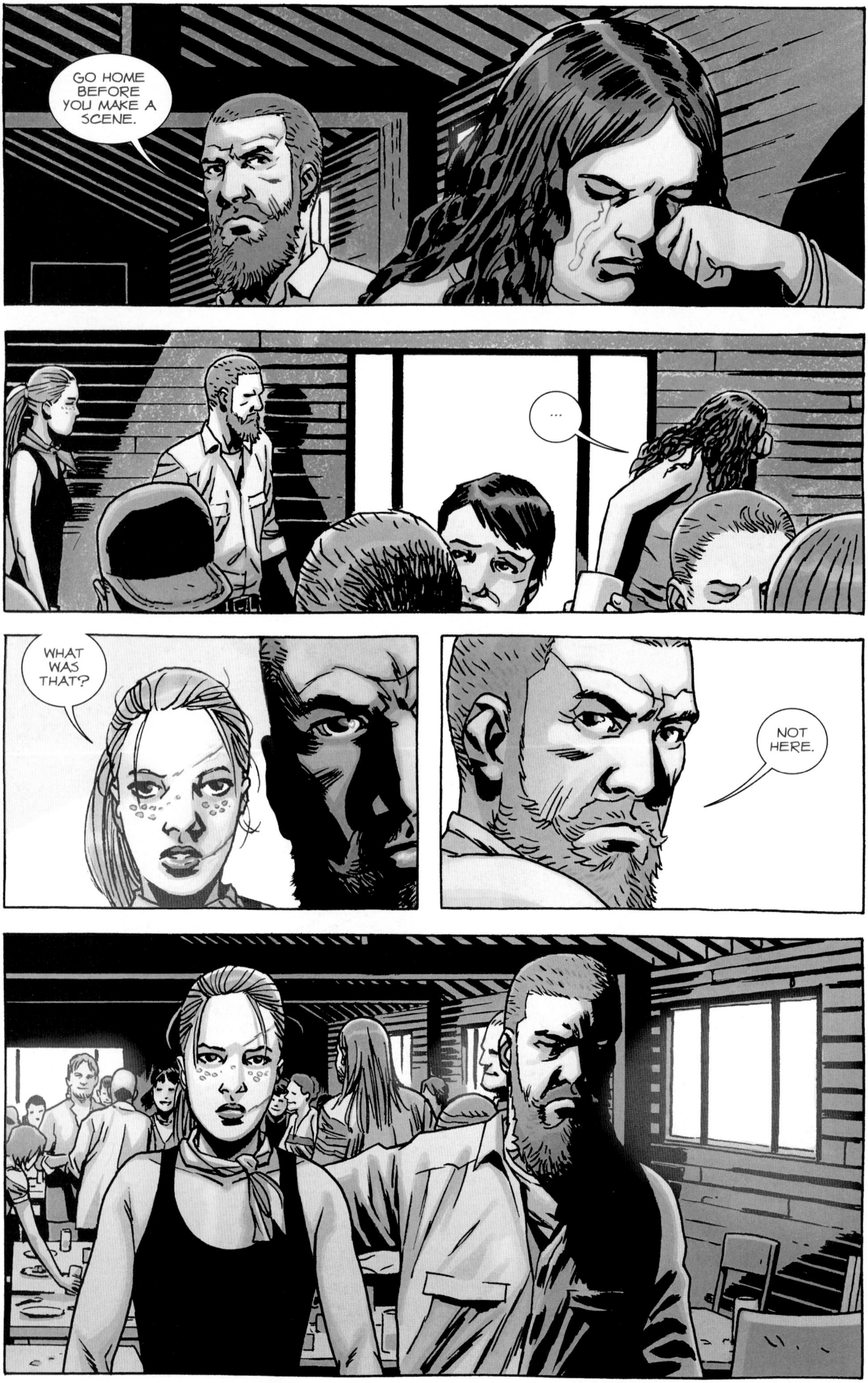
GO HOME BEFORE YOU MAKE A SCENE.
...
WHAT WAS THAT?
NOT HERE.

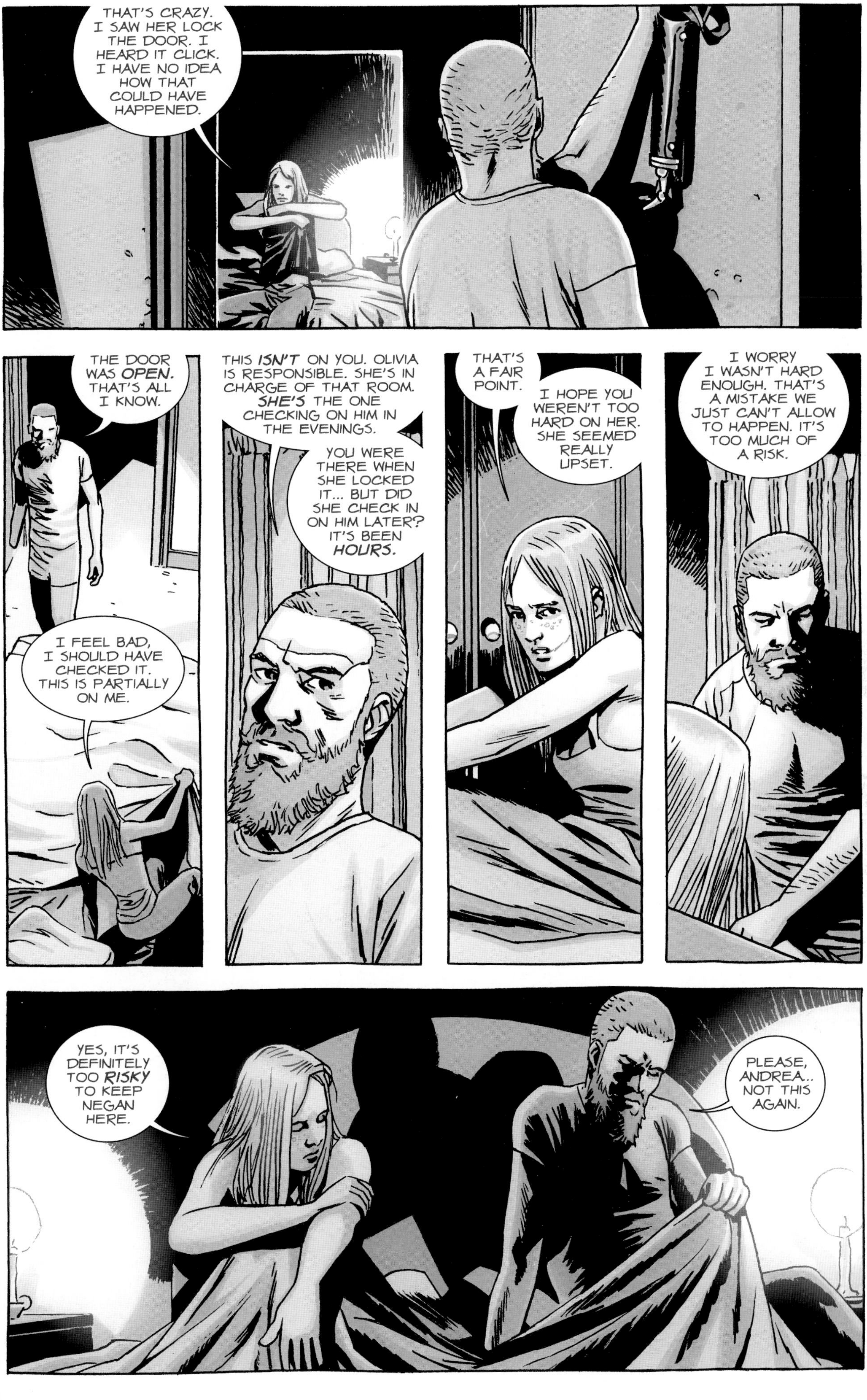
THAT'S CRAZY. I SAW HER LOCK THE DOOR. I HEARD IT CLICK. I HAVE NO IDEA HOW THAT COULD HAVE HAPPENED.
THE DOOR WAS OPEN. THAT'S ALL I KNOW.
I FEEL BAD, I SHOULD HAVE CHECKED IT. THIS IS PARTIALLY ON ME.
THIS ISN'T ON YOU. OLIVIA IS RESPONSIBLE. SHE'S IN CHARGE OF THAT ROOM. SHE'S THE ONE CHECKING ON HIM IN THE EVENINGS.
YOU WERE THERE WHEN SHE LOCKED IT... BUT DID SHE CHECK IN ON HIM LATER? IT'S BEEN HOURS.
THAT'S A FAIR POINT.
I HOPE YOU WEREN'T TOO HARD ON HER. SHE SEEMED REALLY UPSET.
I WORRY I WASN'T HARD ENOUGH. THAT'S A MISTAKE WE JUST CAN'T ALLOW TO HAPPEN. IT'S TOO MUCH OF A RISK.
YES, IT'S DEFINITELY TOO RISKY TO KEEP NEGAN HERE.
PLEASE, ANDREA.. NOT THIS AGAIN.

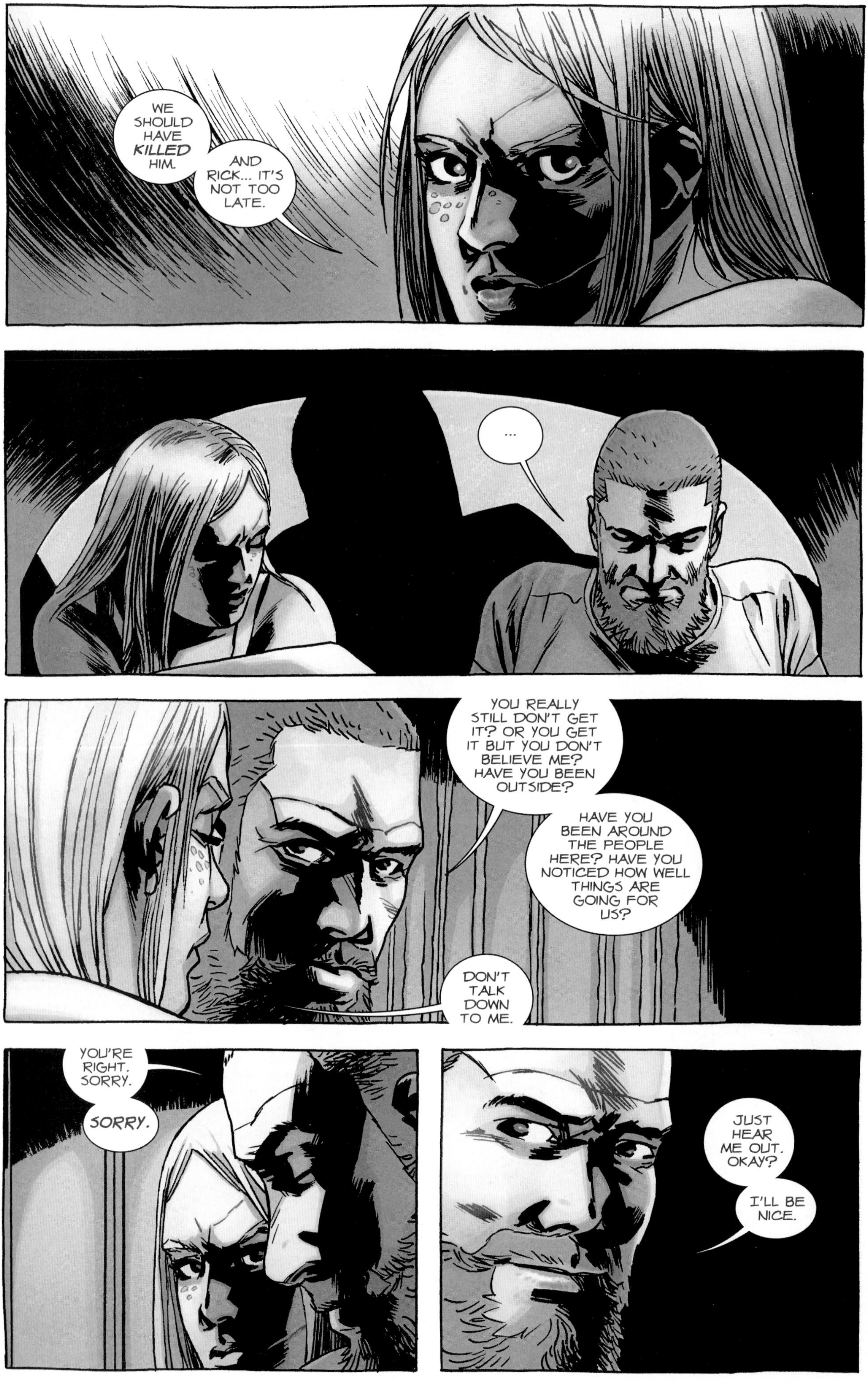
WE SHOULD HAVE KILLED HIM.
AND RICK... IT'S NOT TOO LATE.
...
YOU REALLY STILL DON'T GET IT? OR YOU GET IT BUT YOU DON'T BELIEVE ME? HAVE YOU BEEN OUTSIDE?
HAVE YOU BEEN AROUND THE PEOPLE HERE? HAVE YOU NOTICED HOW WELL THINGS ARE GOING FOR US?
DON'T TALK DOWN TO ME.
YOU'RE RIGHT. SORRY.
SORRY.
JUST HEAR ME OUT. OKAY?
I'LL BE NICE.

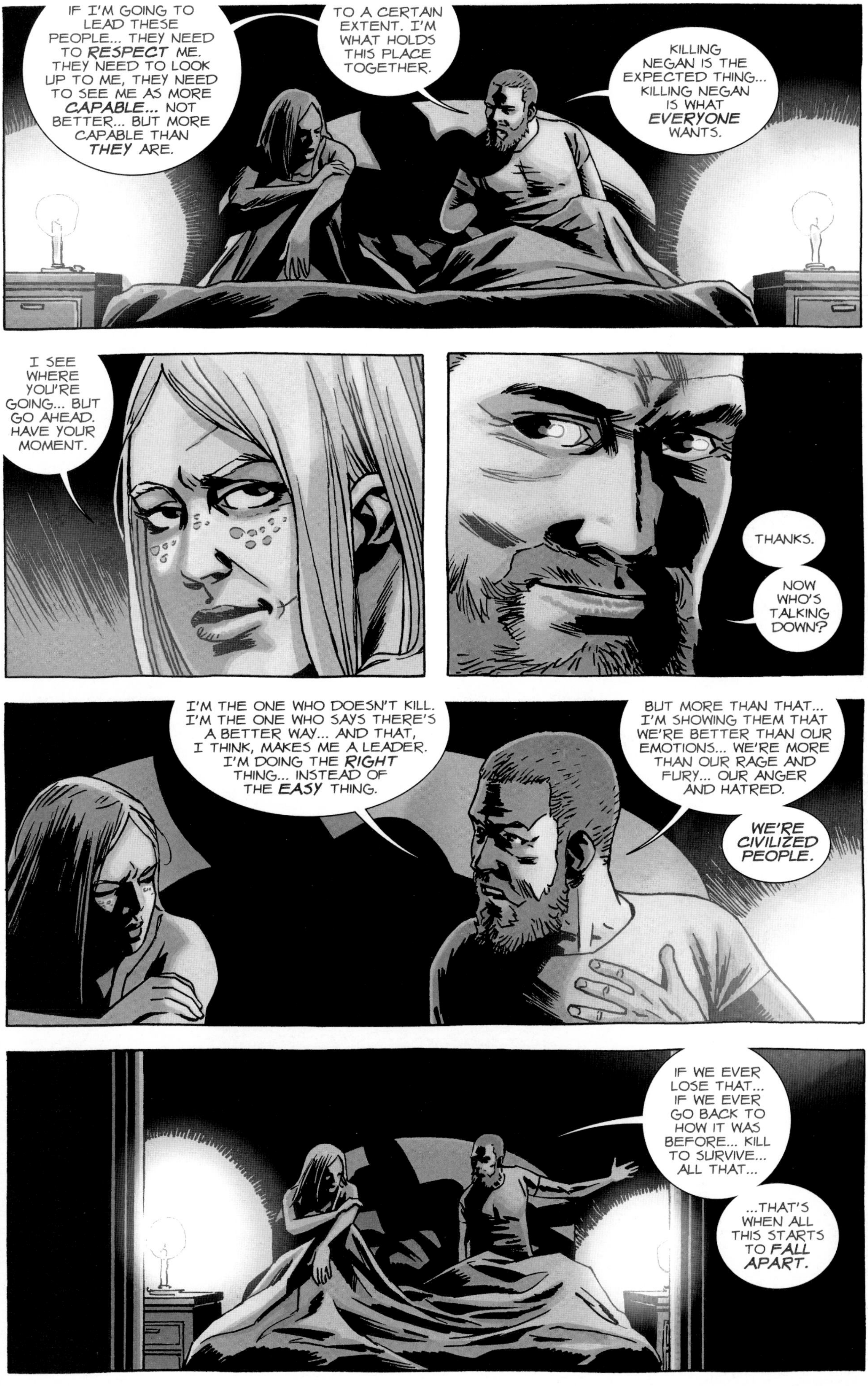
IF I'M GOING TO LEAD THESE PEOPLE... THEY NEED TO RESPECT ME. THEY NEED TO LOOK UP TO ME, THEY NEED TO SEE ME AS MORE CAPABLE... NOT BETTER... BUT MORE CAPABLE THAN THEY ARE.
TO A CERTAIN EXTENT. I'M WHAT HOLDS THIS PLACE TOGETHER.
KILLING NEGAN IS THE EXPECTED THING... KILLING NEGAN IS WHAT EVERYONE WANTS.
I SEE WHERE YOU'RE GOING... BUT GO AHEAD. HAVE YOUR MOMENT.
THANKS.
NOW WHO'S TALKING DOWN?
I'M THE ONE WHO DOESN'T KILL. I'M THE ONE WHO SAYS THERE'S A BETTER WAY... AND THAT, I THINK, MAKES ME A LEADER. I'M DOING THE RIGHT THING... INSTEAD OF THE EASY THING.
BUT MORE THAN THAT... I'M SHOWING THEM THAT WE'RE BETTER THAN OUR EMOTIONS... WE'RE MORE THAN OUR RAGE AND FURY... OUR ANGER AND HATRED.
WE'RE CIVILIZED PEOPLE.
IF WE EVER LOSE THAT... IF WE EVER GO BACK TO HOW IT WAS BEFORE... KILL TO SURVIVE... ALL THAT...
...THAT'S WHEN ALL THIS STARTS TO FALL APART.

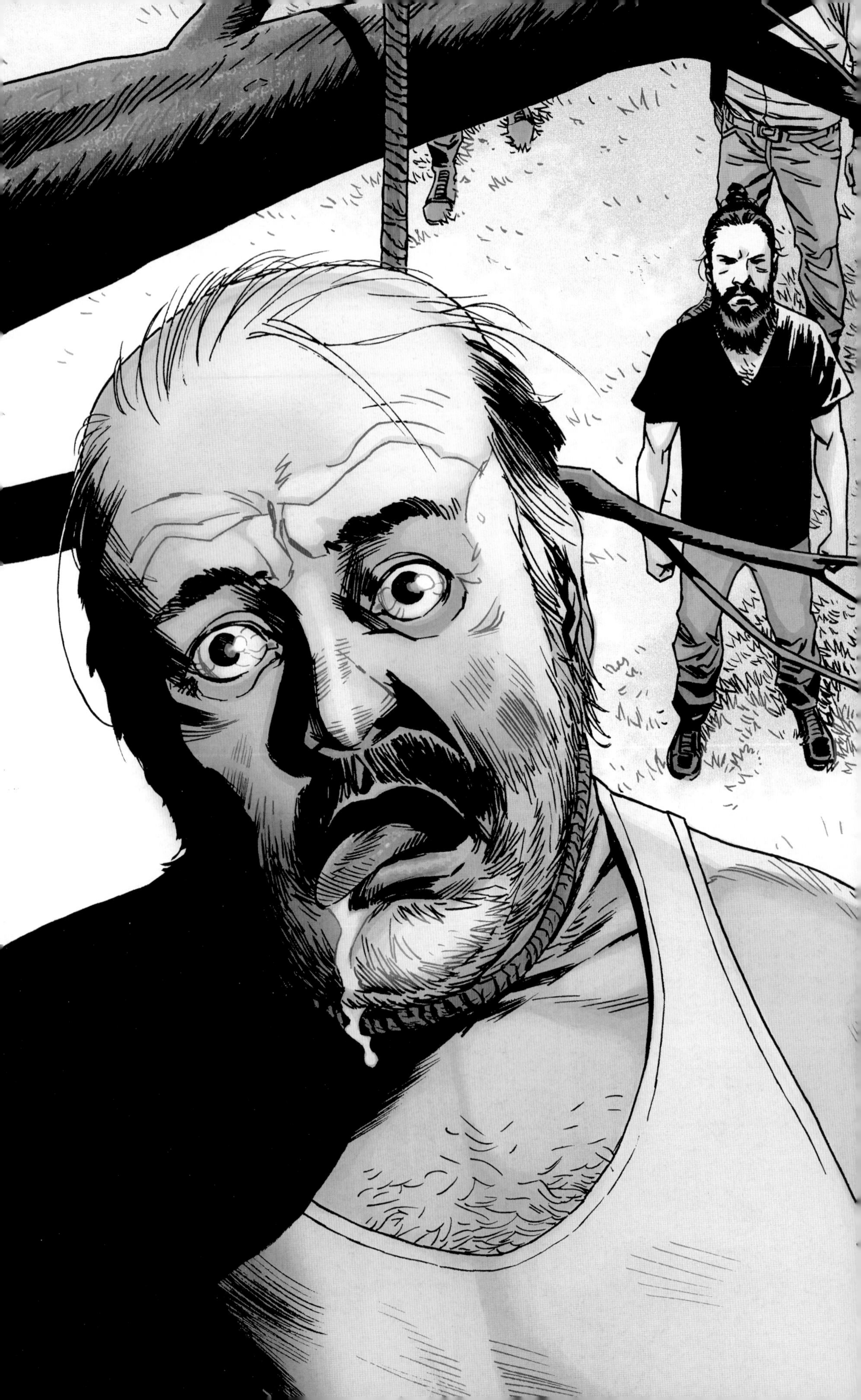

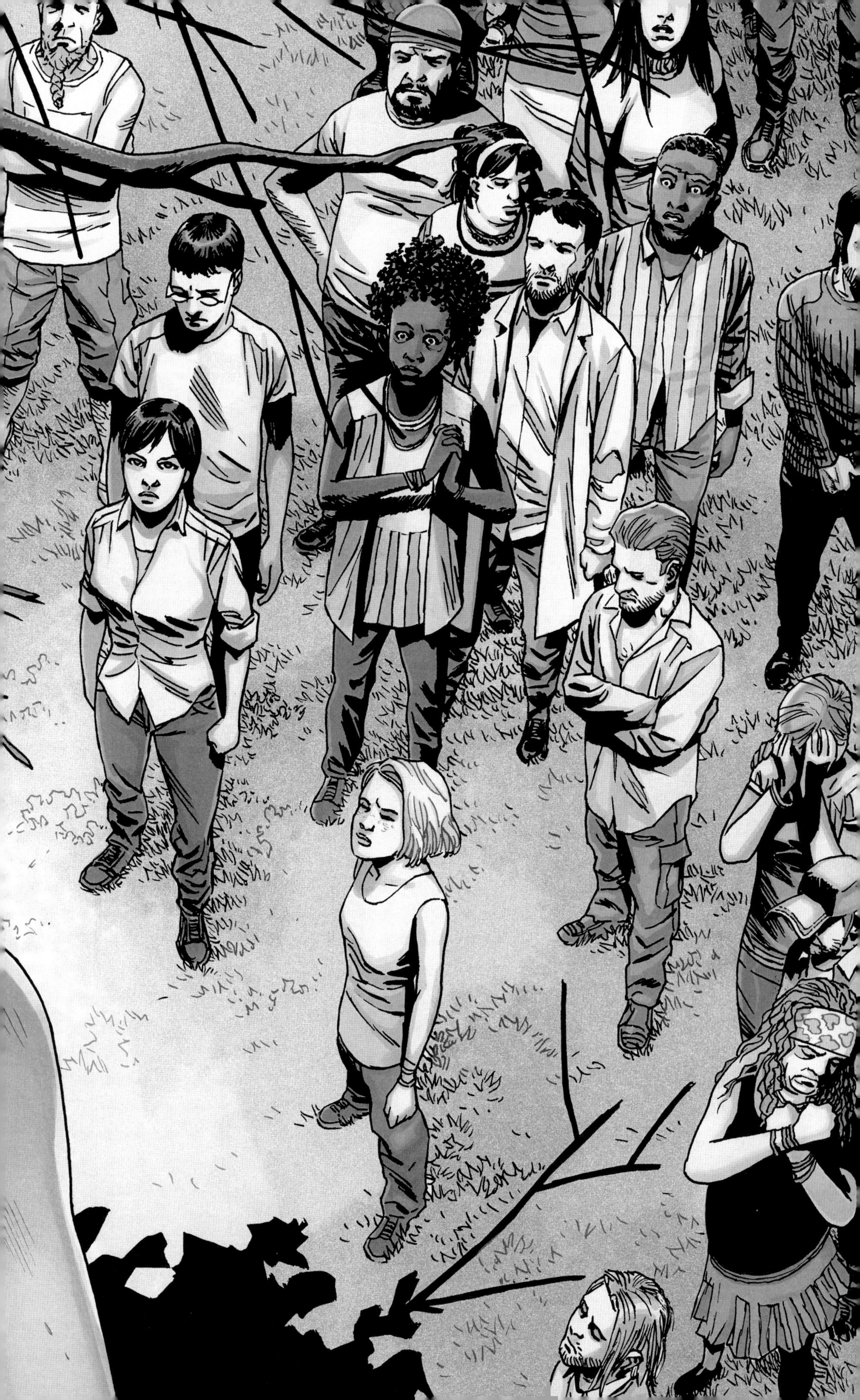

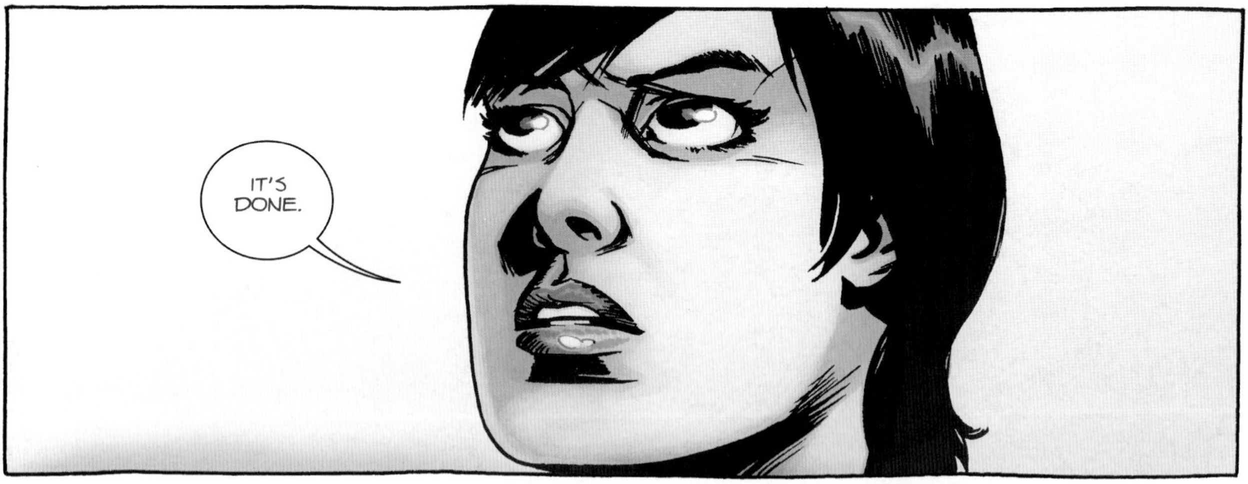
IT'S DONE.
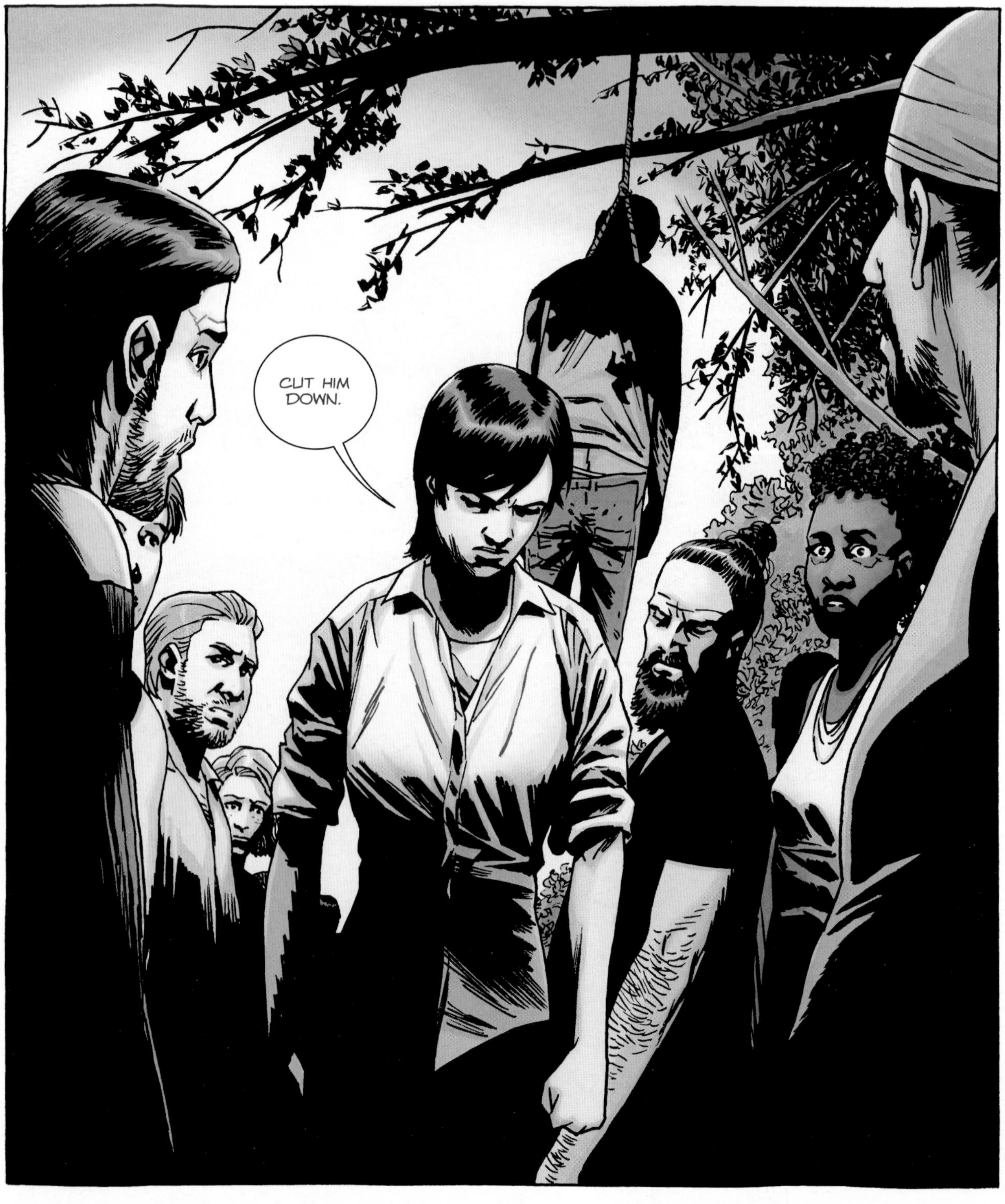
CUT HIM DOWN.

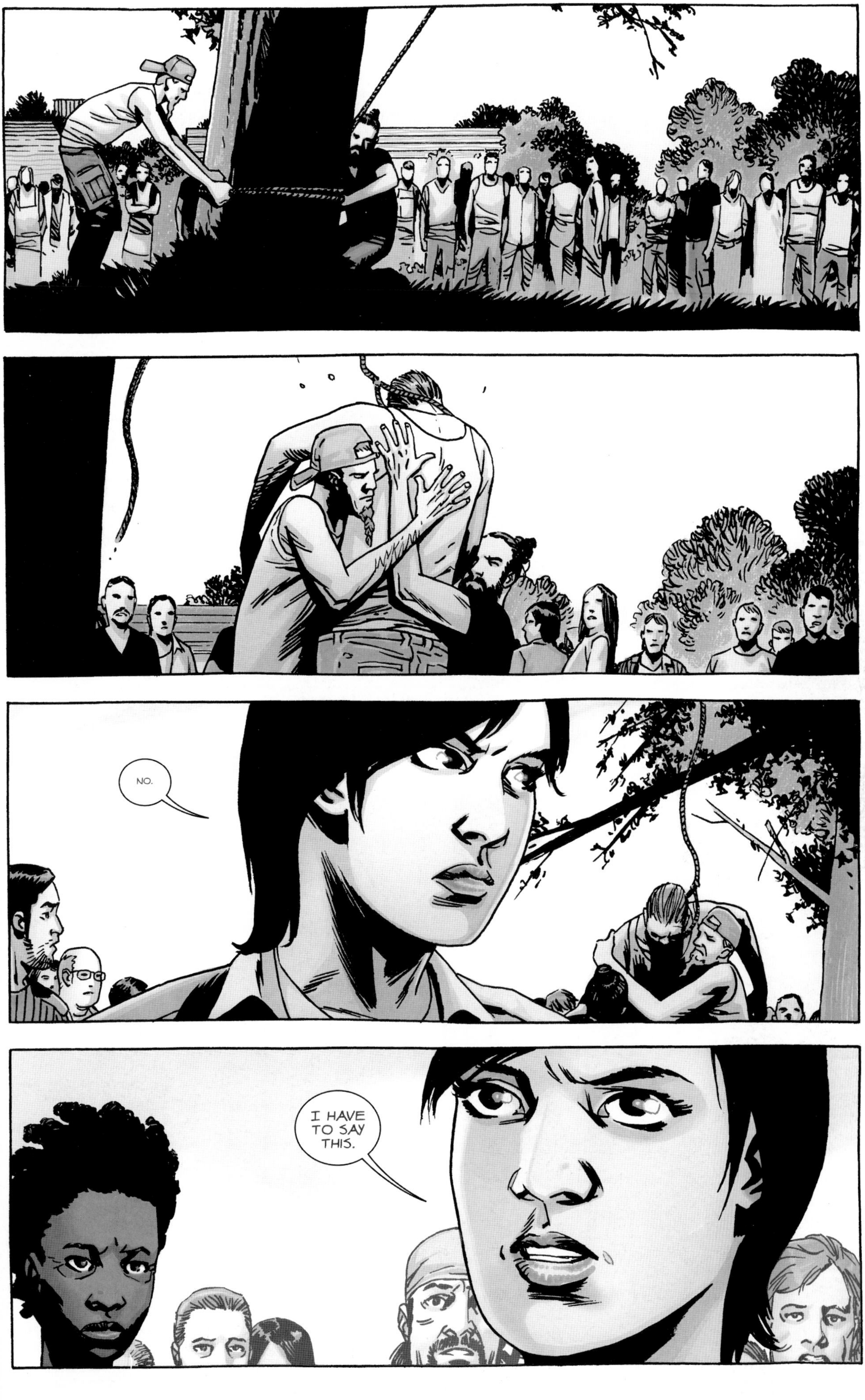
NO.
I HAVE TO SAY THIS.

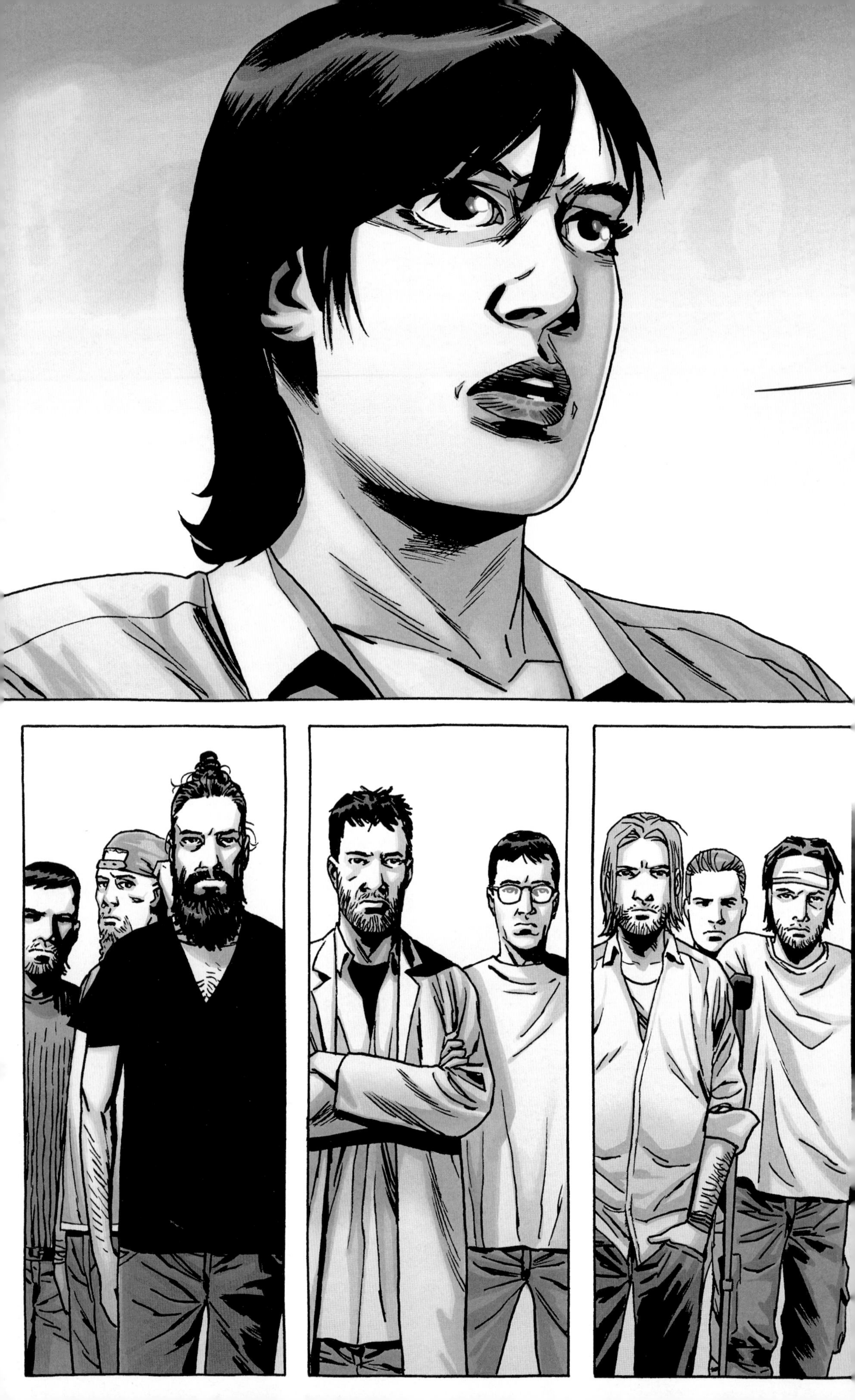

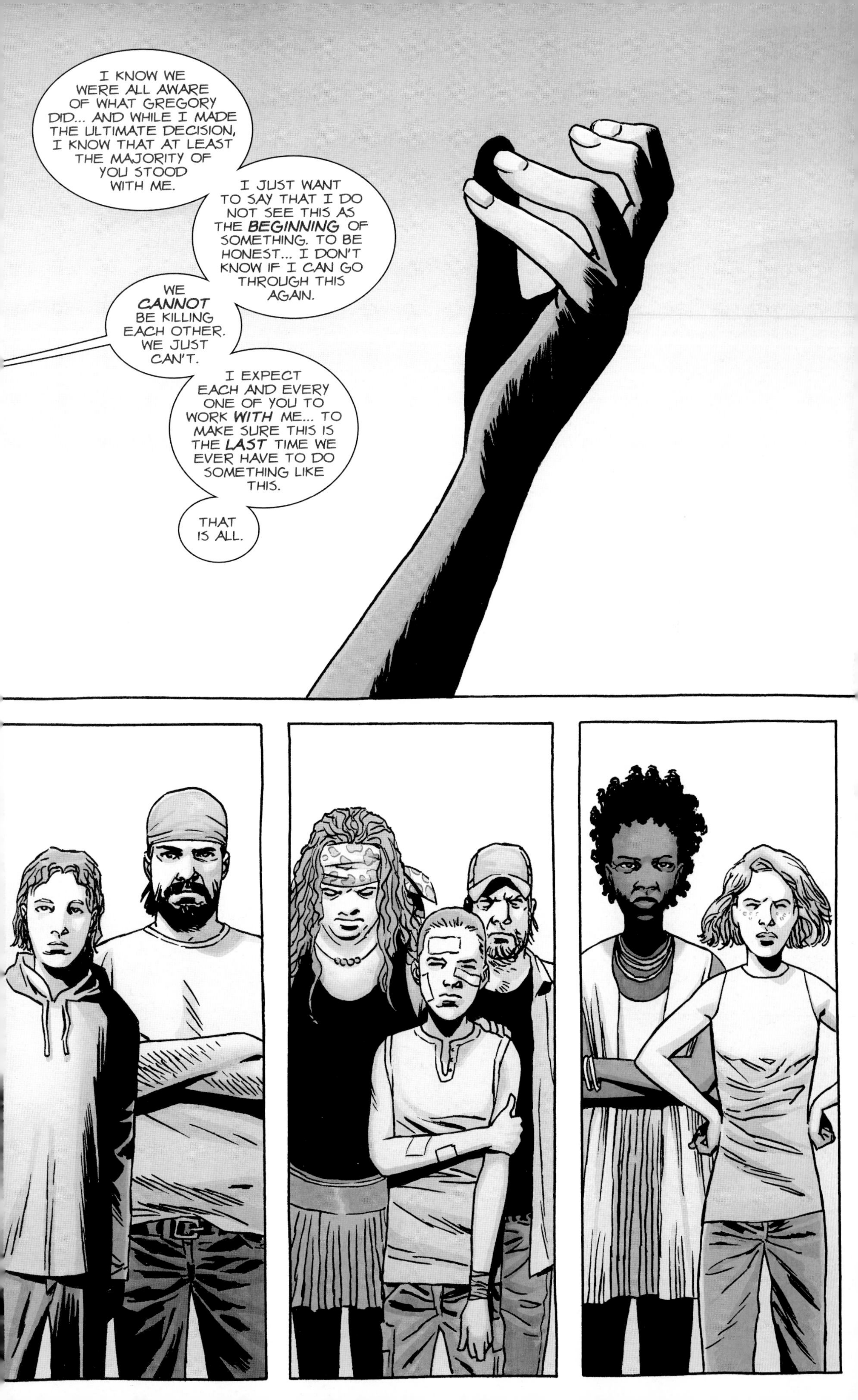
I KNOW WE WERE ALL AWARE OF WHAT GREGORY DID... AND WHILE I MADE THE ULTIMATE DECISION, I KNOW THAT AT LEAST THE MAJORITY OF YOU STOOD WITH ME.
I JUST WANT TO SAY THAT I DO NOT SEE THIS AS THE BEGINNING OF SOMETHING. TO BE HONEST... I DON'T KNOW IF I CAN GO THROUGH THIS AGAIN.
WE CANNOT BE KILLING EACH OTHER. WE JUST CAN'T.
I EXPECT EACH AND EVERY ONE OF YOU TO WORK WITH ME... TO MAKE SURE THIS IS THE LAST TIME WE EVER HAVE TO DO SOMETHING LIKE THIS.
THAT IS ALL.

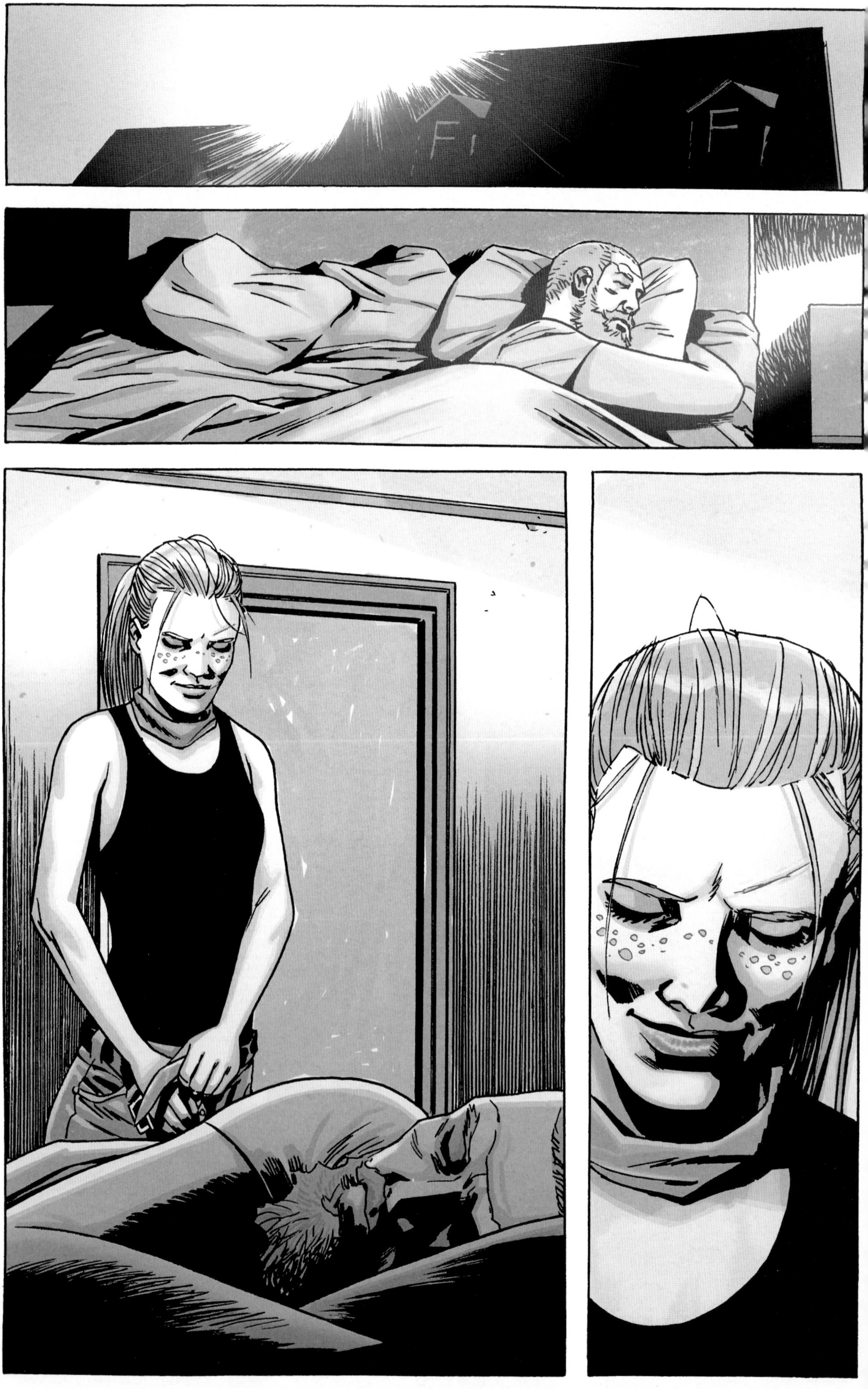

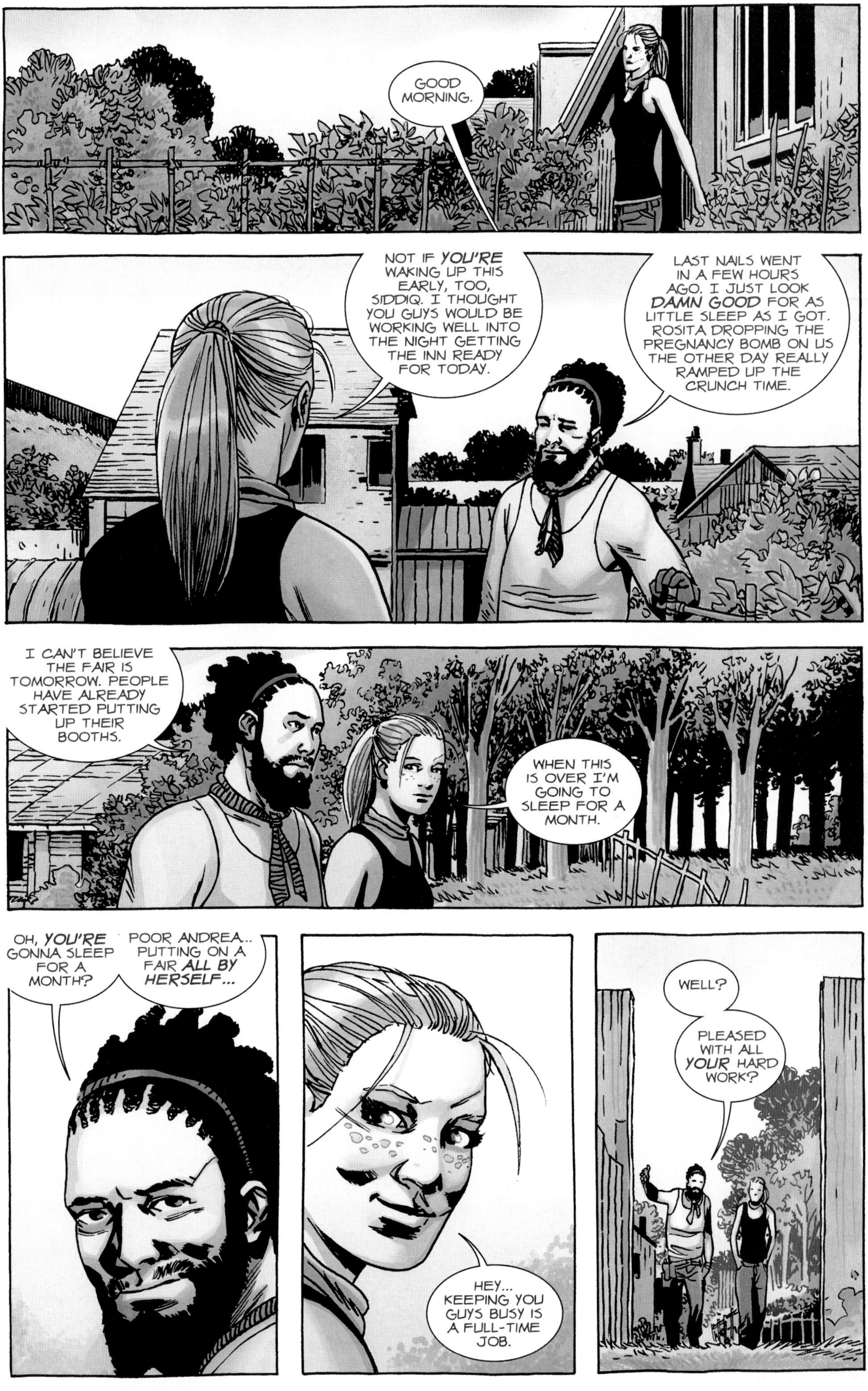
GOOD MORNING.
NOT IF YOU'RE WAKING UP THIS EARLY, TOO, SIDDIQ. I THOUGHT YOU GUYS WOULD BE WORKING WELL INTO THE NIGHT GETTING THE INN READY FOR TODAY.
LAST NAILS WENT IN A FEW HOURS AGO. I JUST LOOK DAMN GOOD FOR AS LITTLE SLEEP AS I GOT. ROSITA DROPPING THE PREGNANCY BOMB ON US THE OTHER DAY REALLY RAMPED UP THE CRUNCH TIME.
I CAN'T BELIEVE THE FAIR IS TOMORROW. PEOPLE HAVE ALREADY STARTED PUTTING UP THEIR BOOTHS.
WHEN THIS IS OVER I'M GOING TO SLEEP FOR A MONTH.
OH, YOU'RE GONNA SLEEP FOR A MONTH?
POOR ANDREA.. PUTTING ON A FAIR ALL BY HERSELF...
HEY... KEEPING YOU GUYS BUSY IS A FULL-TIME JOB.
WELL?
PLEASED WITH ALL YOUR HARD WORK?

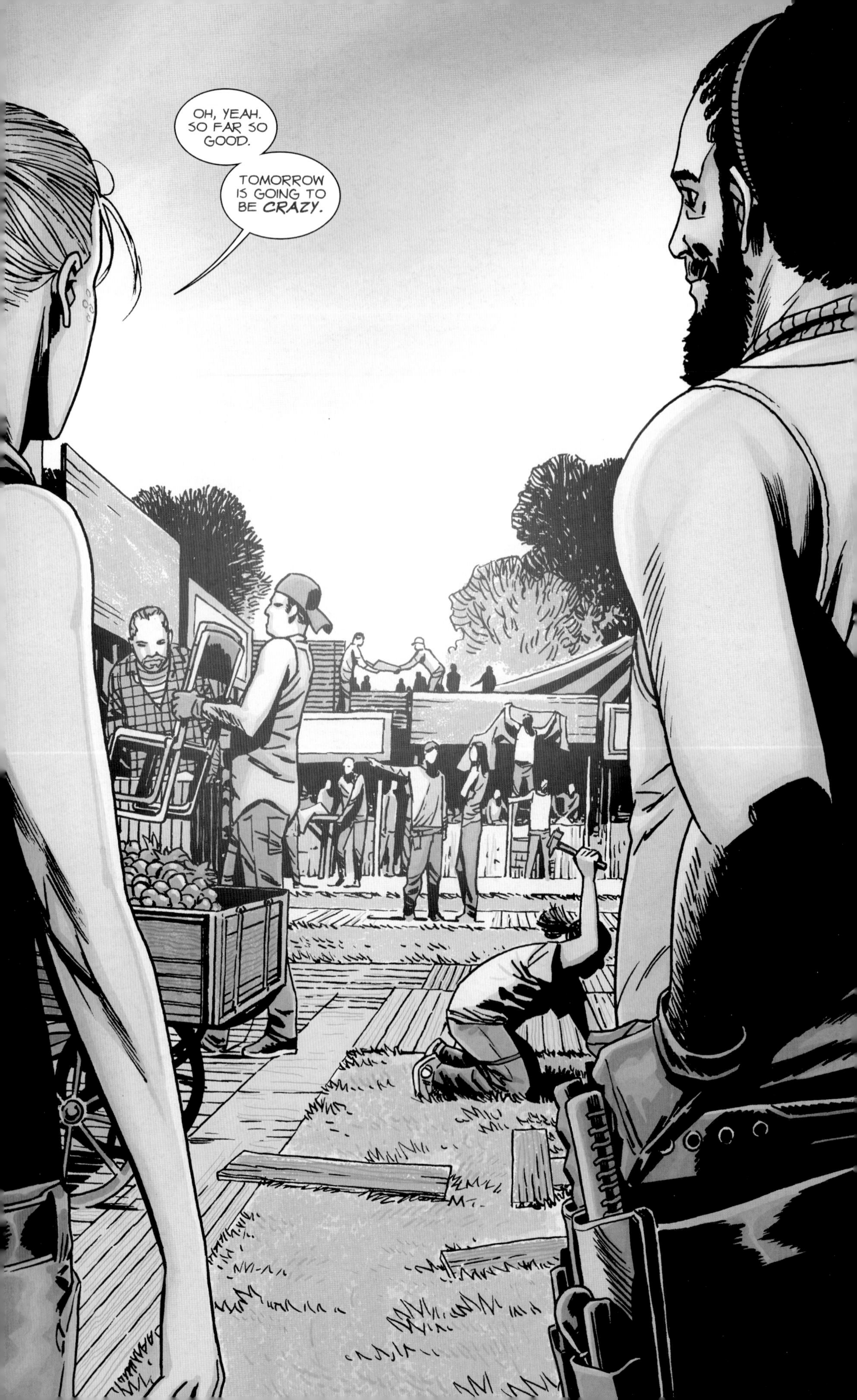
OH, YEAH. SO FAR SO GOOD.
TOMORROW IS GOING TO BE *CRAZY*.

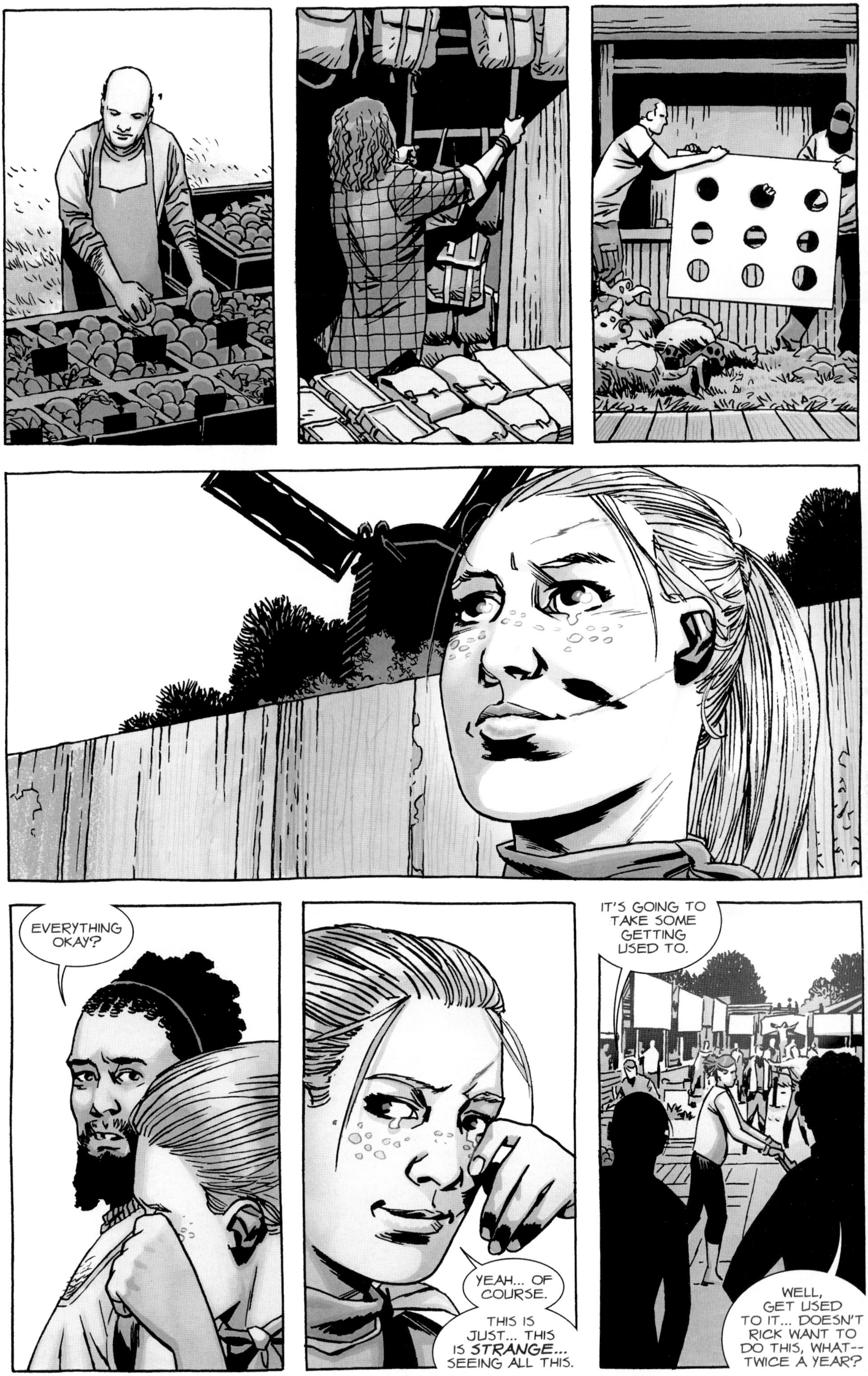
EVERYTHING OKAY?
YEAH... OF COURSE.
THIS IS JUST... THIS IS STRANGE... SEEING ALL THIS.
IT'S GOING TO TAKE SOME GETTING USED TO.
WELL, GET USED TO IT... DOESN'T RICK WANT TO DO THIS, WHAT-- TWICE A YEAR?

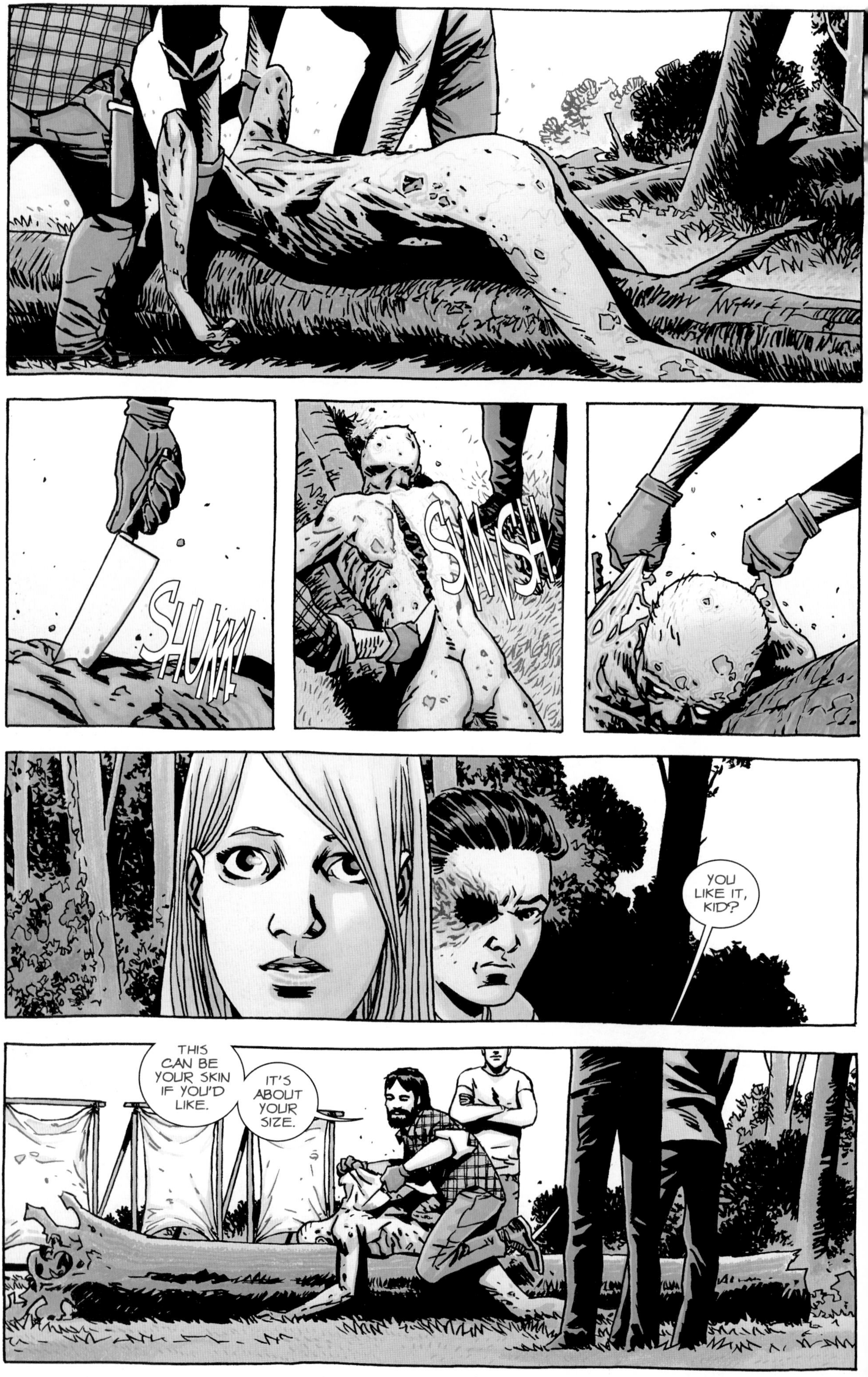
SHUKK!
SWISH!
YOU LIKE IT, KID?
THIS CAN BE YOUR SKIN IF YOU'D LIKE.
IT'S ABOUT YOUR SIZE.

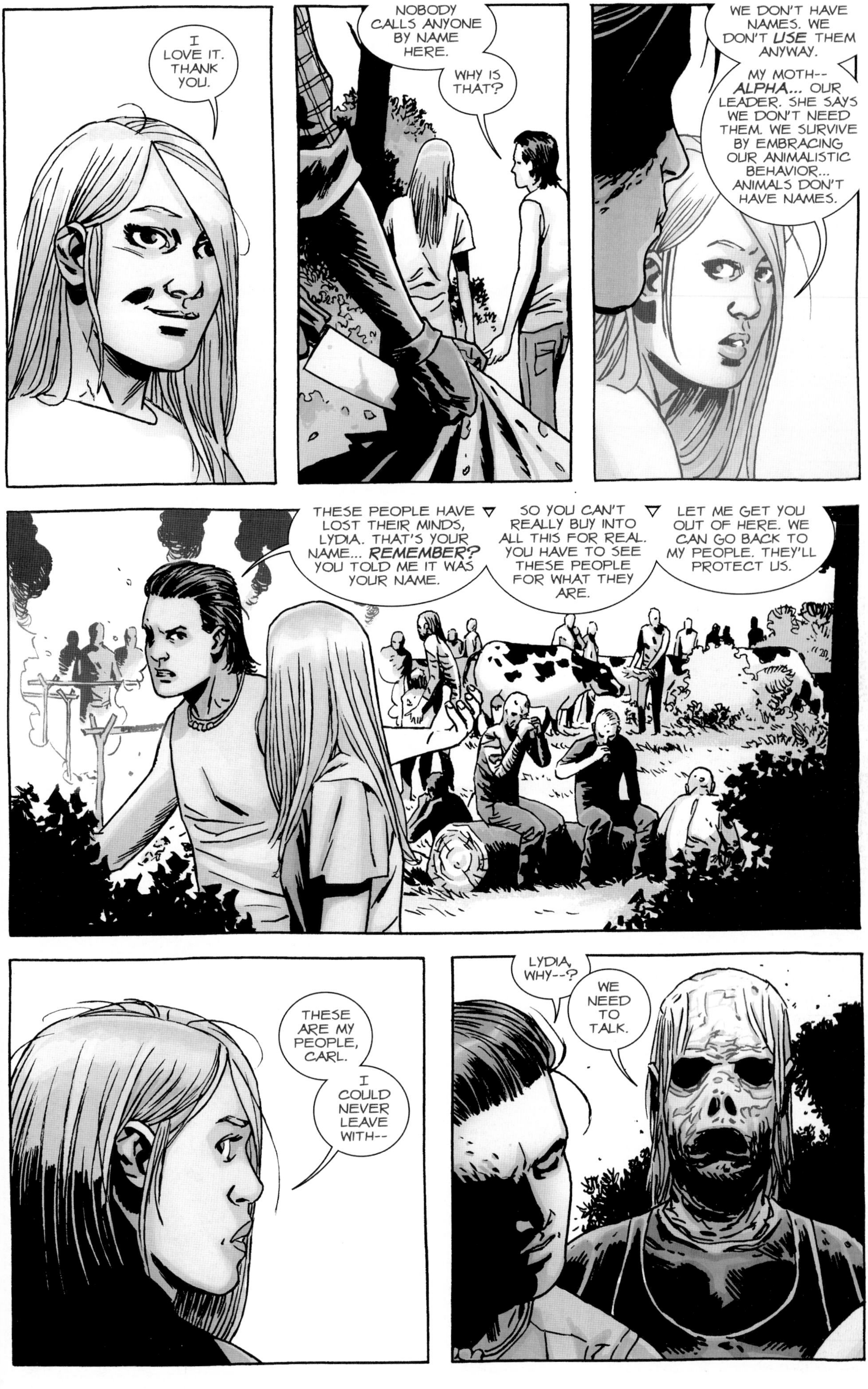
I LOVE IT. THANK YOU.
NOBODY CALLS ANYONE BY NAME HERE.
WHY IS THAT?
WE DON'T HAVE NAMES. WE DON'T *USE* THEM ANYWAY.
MY MOTH-- ***ALPHA...*** OUR LEADER. SHE SAYS WE DON'T NEED THEM. WE SURVIVE BY EMBRACING OUR ANIMALISTIC BEHAVIOR... ANIMALS DON'T HAVE NAMES.
THESE PEOPLE HAVE LOST THEIR MINDS, LYDIA. THAT'S YOUR NAME... ***REMEMBER?*** YOU TOLD ME IT WAS YOUR NAME.
SO YOU CAN'T REALLY BUY INTO ALL THIS FOR REAL. YOU HAVE TO SEE THESE PEOPLE FOR WHAT THEY ARE.
LET ME GET YOU OUT OF HERE. WE CAN GO BACK TO MY PEOPLE. THEY'LL PROTECT US.
THESE ARE MY PEOPLE, CARL.
I COULD NEVER LEAVE WITH--
LYDIA, WHY--?
WE NEED TO TALK.

YOU ARE VERY SMART, I CAN SEE THAT.

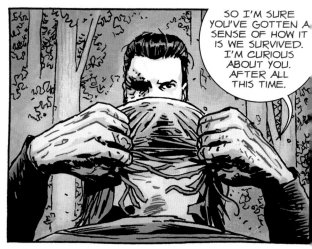

SO I'M SURE YOU'VE GOTTEN A SENSE OF HOW IT IS WE SURVIVED. I'M CURIOUS ABOUT YOU. AFTER ALL THIS TIME.

HOW DID *YOU* SURVIVE?

MY DAD KEPT US ALIVE.

HE DID IT WITH NAMES AND PEOPLE ACTING LIKE HUMANS AND WITHOUT HALLOWEEN MASKS MADE OUT OF HUMAN SKIN.

YOU'D DO WELL TO REMEMBER YOU ARE MY CAPTIVE.

IS THAT WHAT THIS IS? AM I A HOSTAGE?

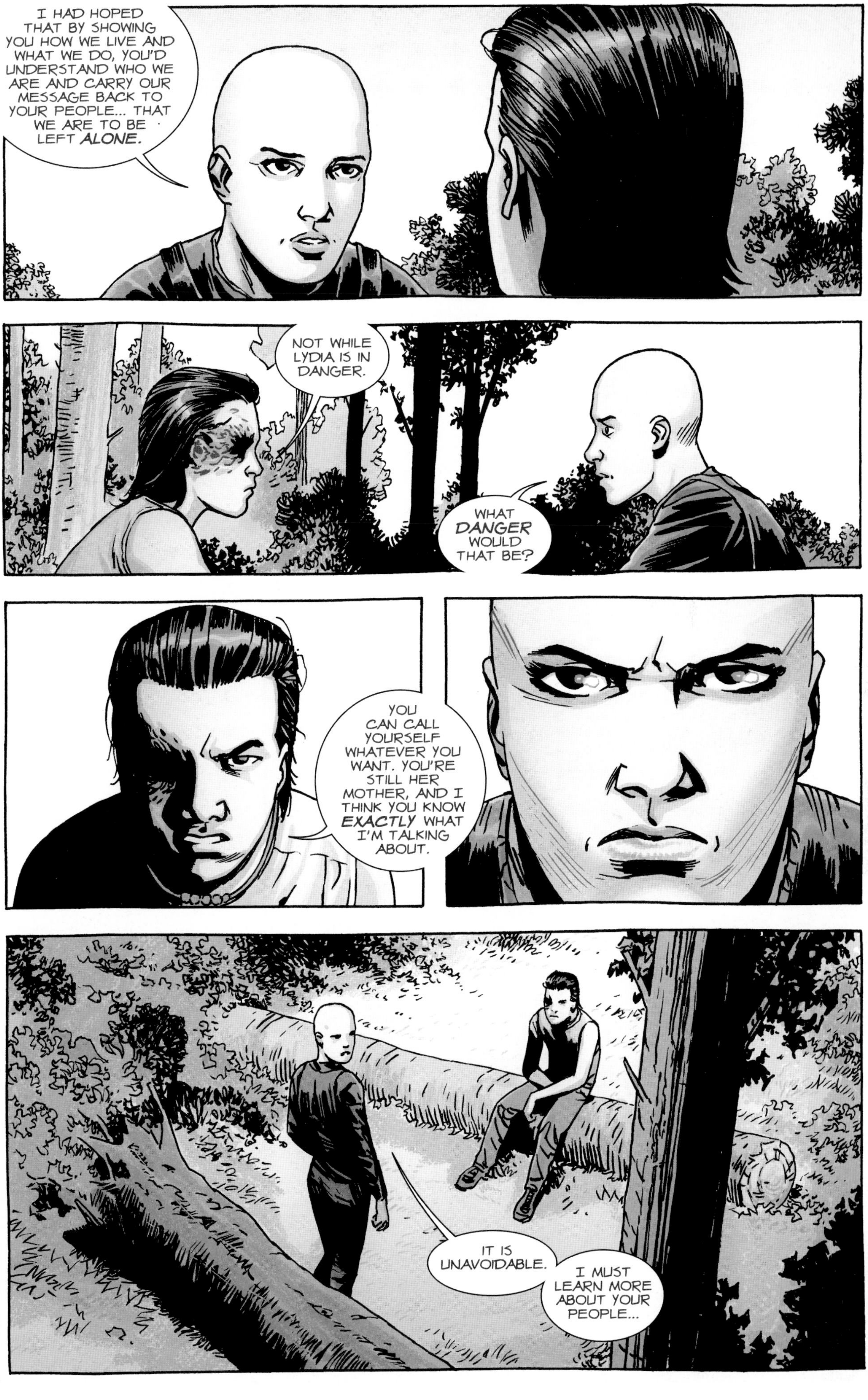
I HAD HOPED THAT BY SHOWING YOU HOW WE LIVE AND WHAT WE DO, YOU'D UNDERSTAND WHO WE ARE AND CARRY OUR MESSAGE BACK TO YOUR PEOPLE... THAT WE ARE TO BE LEFT ALONE.
NOT WHILE LYDIA IS IN DANGER.
WHAT DANGER WOULD THAT BE?
YOU CAN CALL YOURSELF WHATEVER YOU WANT. YOU'RE STILL HER MOTHER, AND I THINK YOU KNOW EXACTLY WHAT I'M TALKING ABOUT.
IT IS UNAVOIDABLE.
I MUST LEARN MORE ABOUT YOUR PEOPLE...

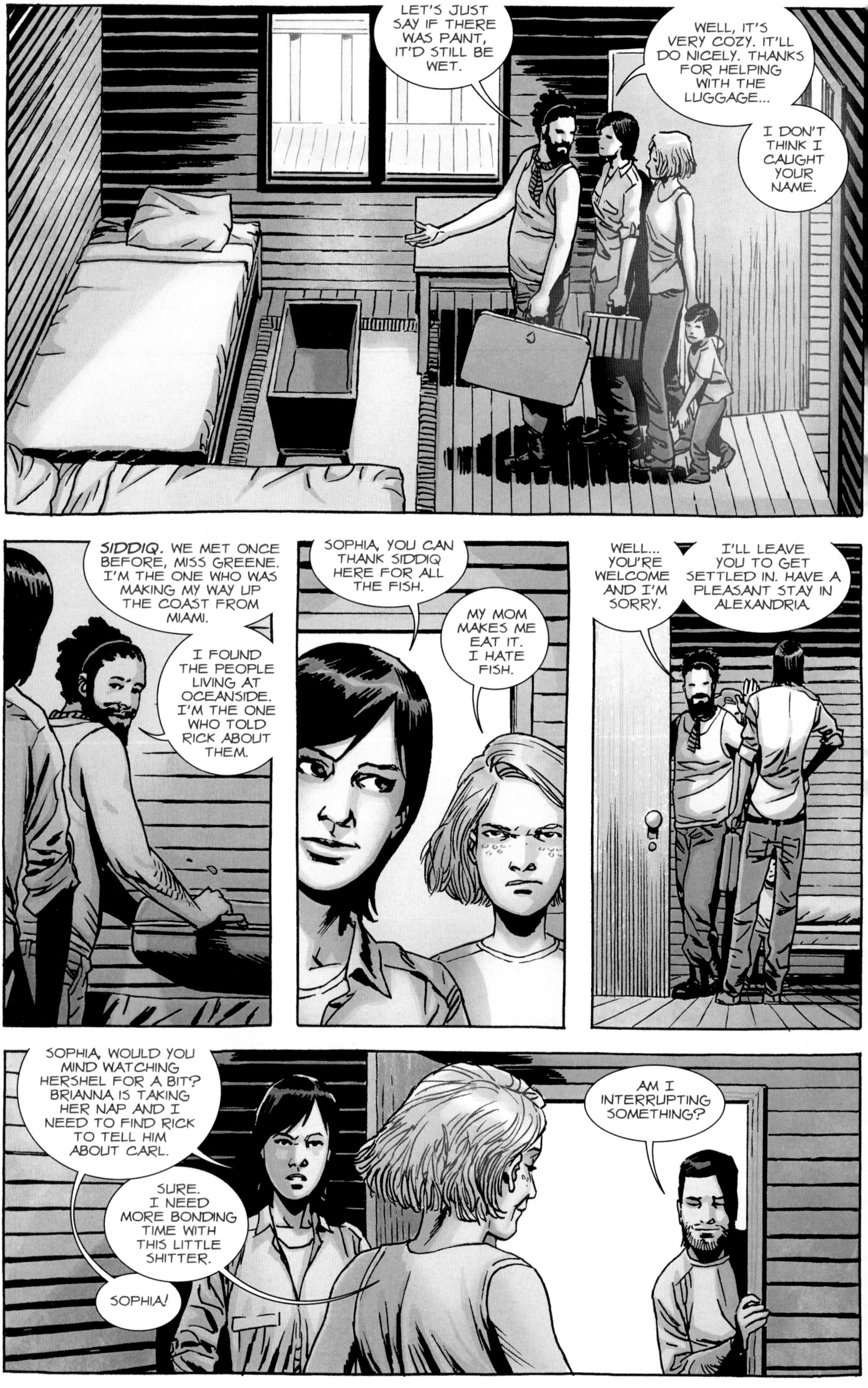
LET'S JUST SAY IF THERE WAS PAINT, IT'D STILL BE WET.
WELL, IT'S VERY COZY. IT'LL DO NICELY. THANKS FOR HELPING WITH THE LUGGAGE...
I DON'T THINK I CAUGHT YOUR NAME.
SIDDIQ. WE MET ONCE BEFORE, MISS GREENE. I'M THE ONE WHO WAS MAKING MY WAY UP THE COAST FROM MIAMI.
I FOUND THE PEOPLE LIVING AT OCEANSIDE. I'M THE ONE WHO TOLD RICK ABOUT THEM.
SOPHIA, YOU CAN THANK SIDDIQ HERE FOR ALL THE FISH.
MY MOM MAKES ME EAT IT. I HATE FISH.
WELL... YOU'RE WELCOME AND I'M SORRY.
I'LL LEAVE YOU TO GET SETTLED IN. HAVE A PLEASANT STAY IN ALEXANDRIA.
SOPHIA, WOULD YOU MIND WATCHING HERSHEL FOR A BIT? BRIANNA IS TAKING HER NAP AND I NEED TO FIND RICK TO TELL HIM ABOUT CARL.
SURE. I NEED MORE BONDING TIME WITH THIS LITTLE SHITTER.
SOPHIA!
AM I INTERRUPTING SOMETHING?

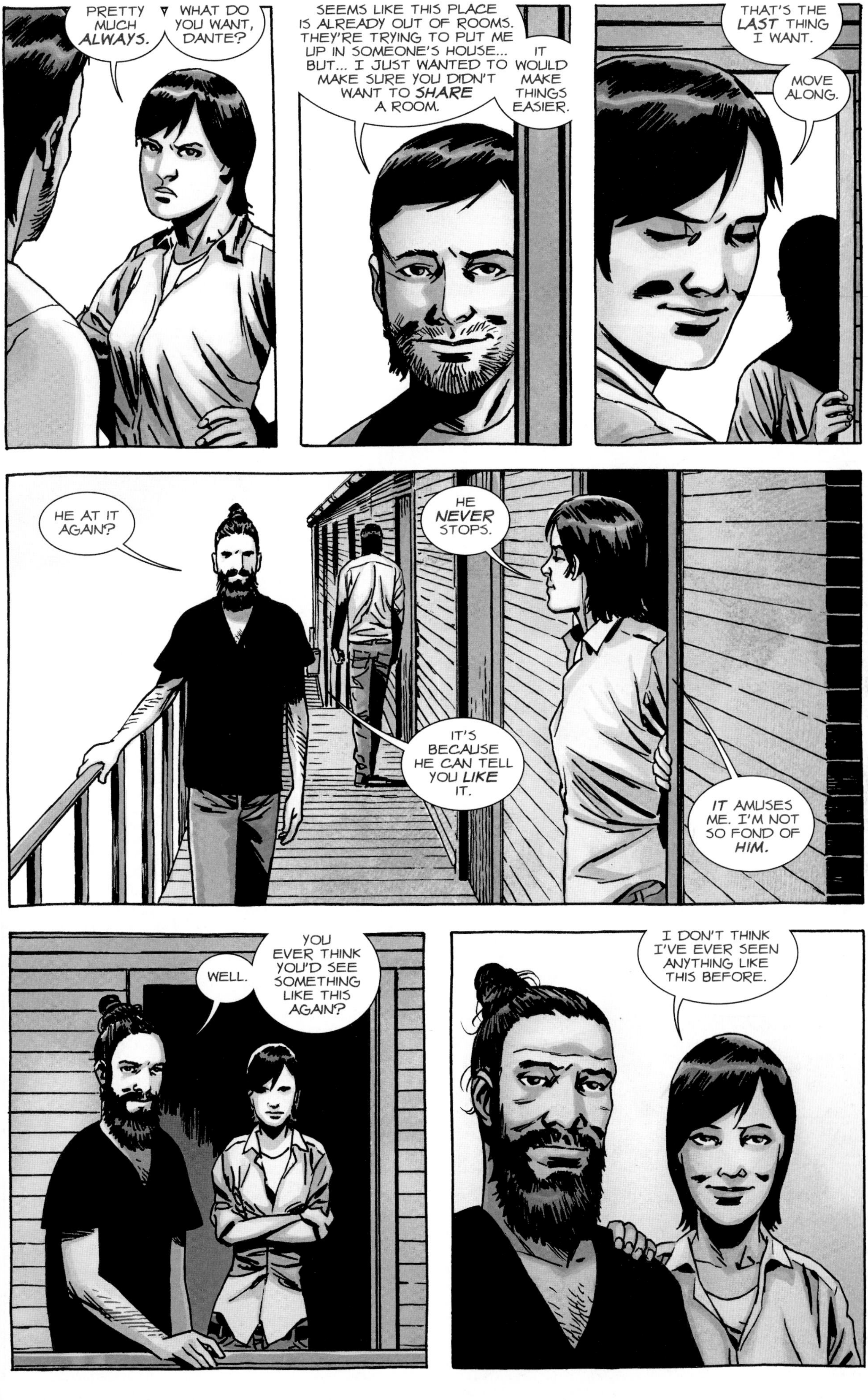
PRETTY MUCH ALWAYS.
WHAT DO YOU WANT, DANTE?
SEEMS LIKE THIS PLACE IS ALREADY OUT OF ROOMS. THEY'RE TRYING TO PUT ME UP IN SOMEONE'S HOUSE... BUT... I JUST WANTED TO MAKE SURE YOU DIDN'T WANT TO SHARE A ROOM.
IT WOULD MAKE THINGS EASIER.
THAT'S THE LAST THING I WANT.
MOVE ALONG.
HE AT IT AGAIN?
HE NEVER STOPS.
IT'S BECAUSE HE CAN TELL YOU LIKE IT.
IT AMUSES ME. I'M NOT SO FOND OF HIM.
WELL.
YOU EVER THINK YOU'D SEE SOMETHING LIKE THIS AGAIN?
I DON'T THINK I'VE EVER SEEN ANYTHING LIKE THIS BEFORE.

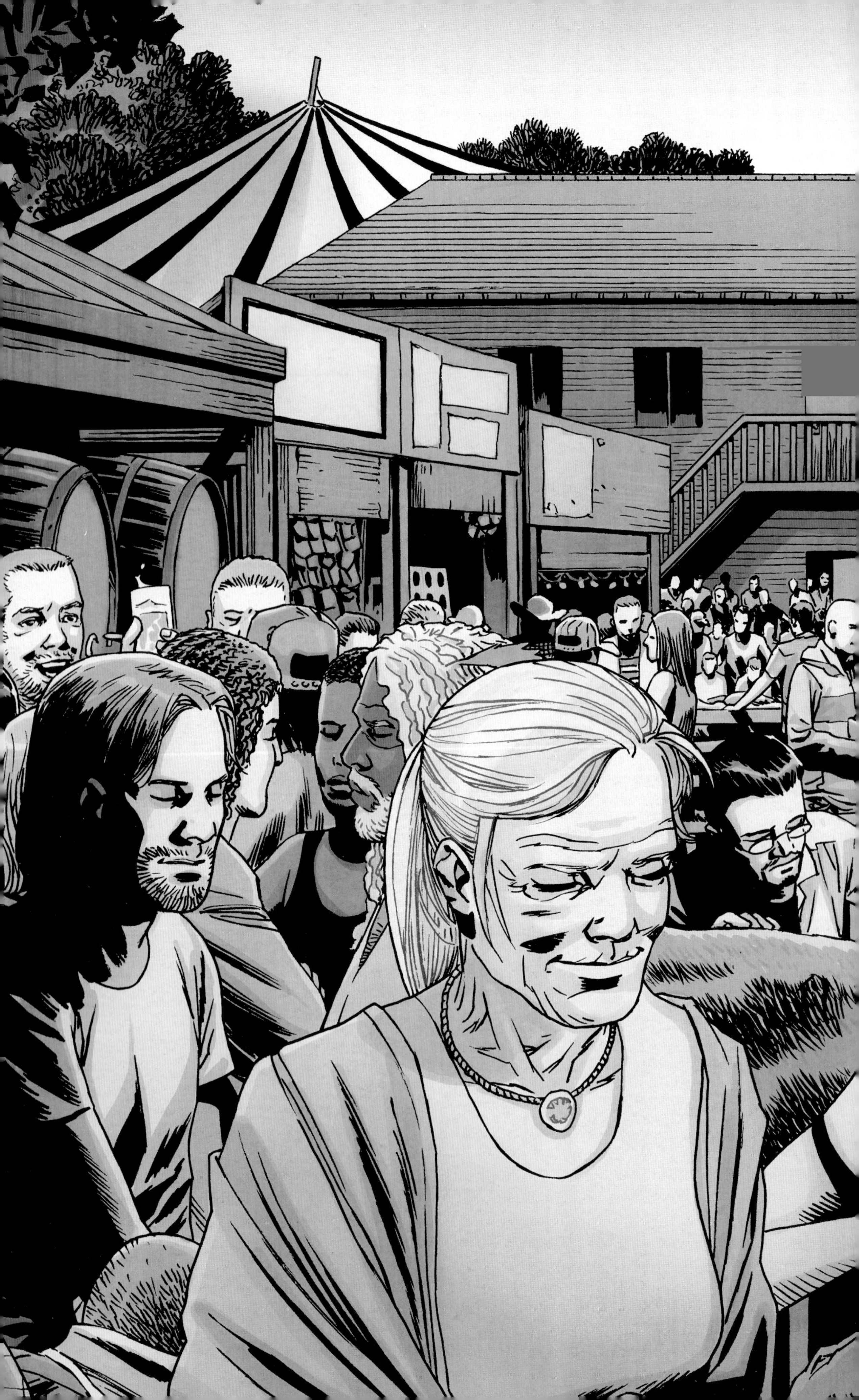

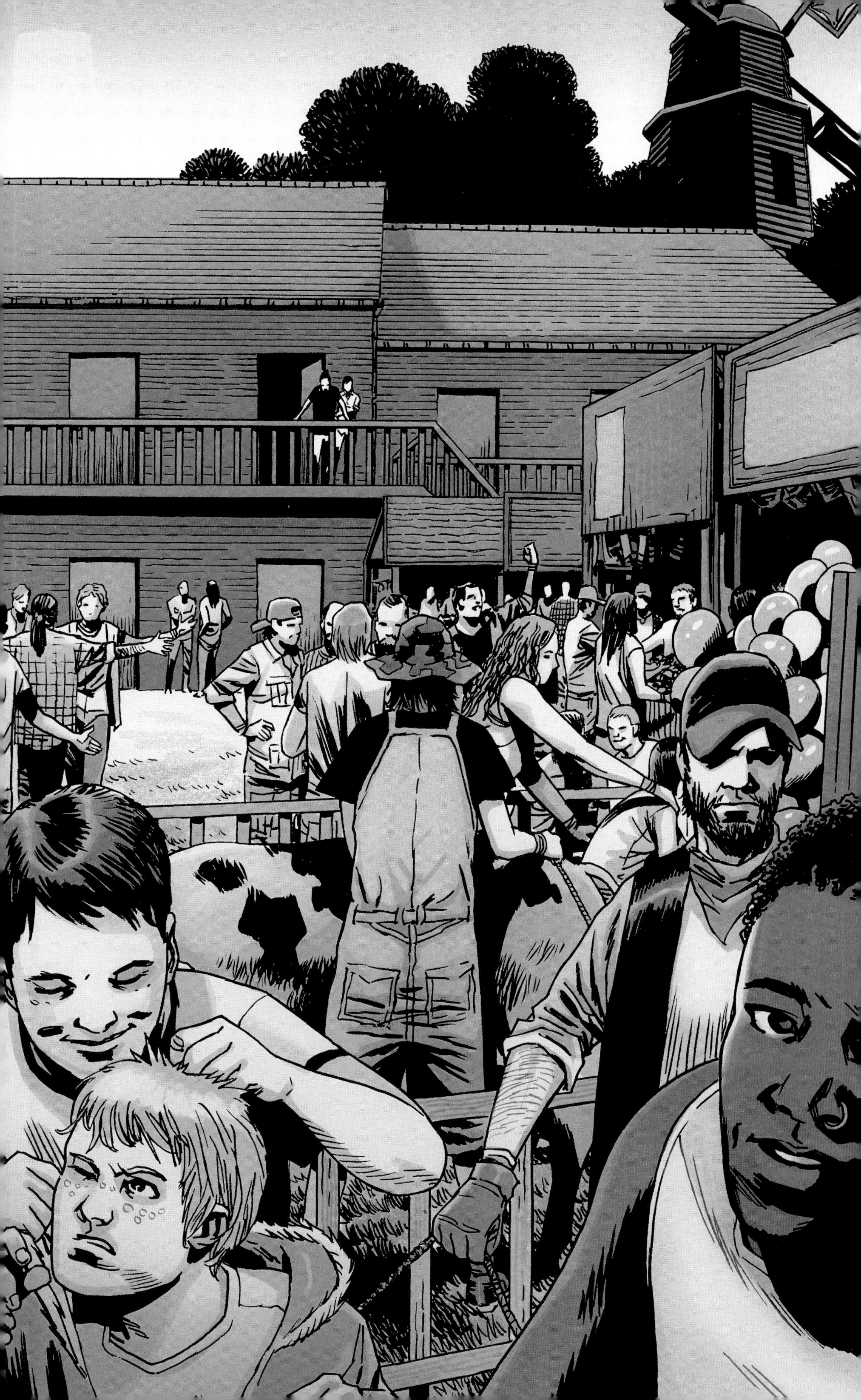

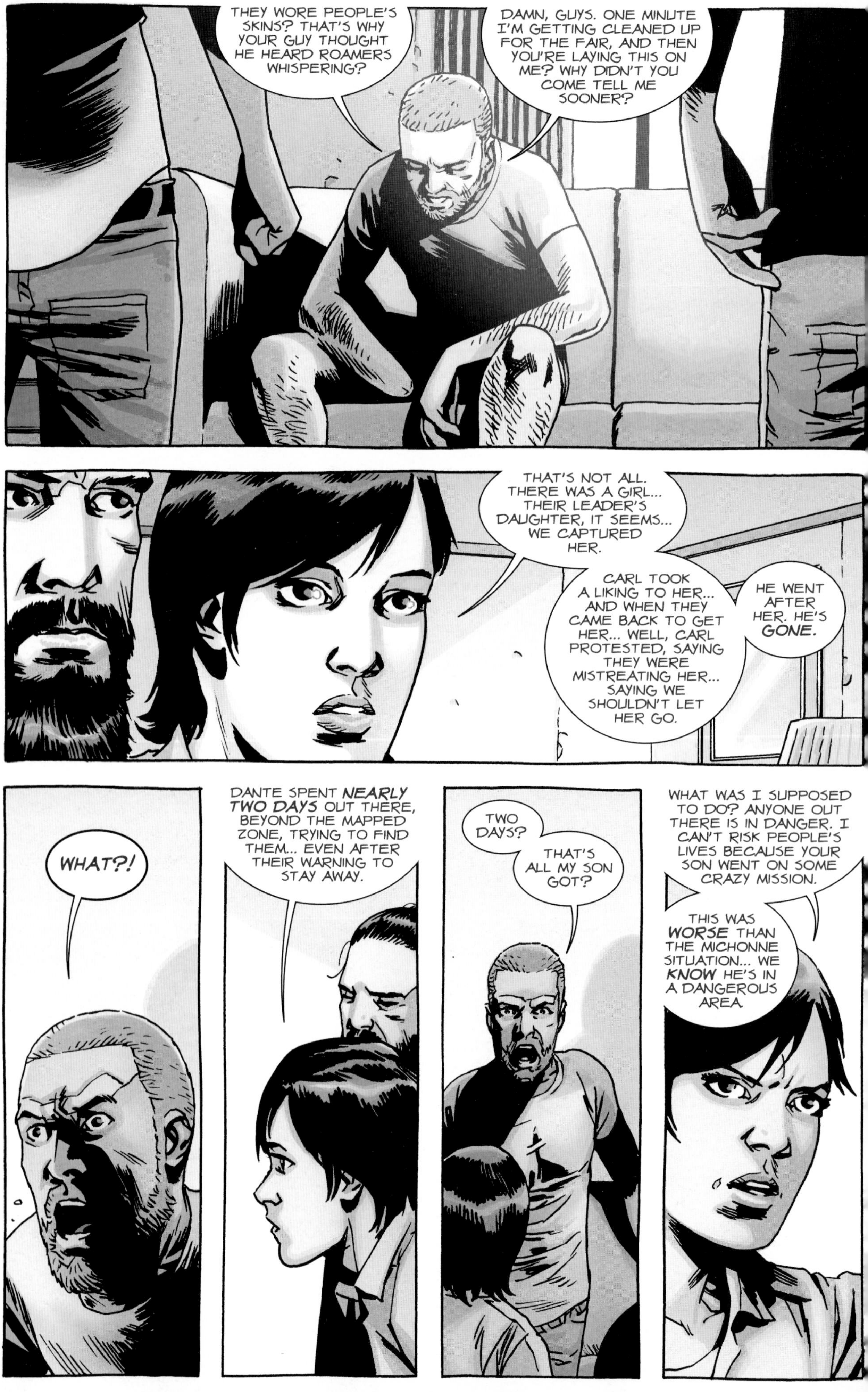
THEY WORE PEOPLE'S SKINS? THAT'S WHY YOUR GUY THOUGHT HE HEARD ROAMERS WHISPERING?
DAMN, GUYS. ONE MINUTE I'M GETTING CLEANED UP FOR THE FAIR, AND THEN YOU'RE LAYING THIS ON ME? WHY DIDN'T YOU COME TELL ME SOONER?
THAT'S NOT ALL. THERE WAS A GIRL... THEIR LEADER'S DAUGHTER, IT SEEMS... WE CAPTURED HER.
CARL TOOK A LIKING TO HER... AND WHEN THEY CAME BACK TO GET HER... WELL, CARL PROTESTED, SAYING THEY WERE MISTREATING HER... SAYING WE SHOULDN'T LET HER GO.
HE WENT AFTER HER. HE'S GONE.
WHAT?!
DANTE SPENT NEARLY TWO DAYS OUT THERE, BEYOND THE MAPPED ZONE, TRYING TO FIND THEM... EVEN AFTER THEIR WARNING TO STAY AWAY.
TWO DAYS?
THAT'S ALL MY SON GOT?
WHAT WAS I SUPPOSED TO DO? ANYONE OUT THERE IS IN DANGER. I CAN'T RISK PEOPLE'S LIVES BECAUSE YOUR SON WENT ON SOME CRAZY MISSION.
THIS WAS WORSE THAN THE MICHONNE SITUATION... WE KNOW HE'S IN A DANGEROUS AREA.

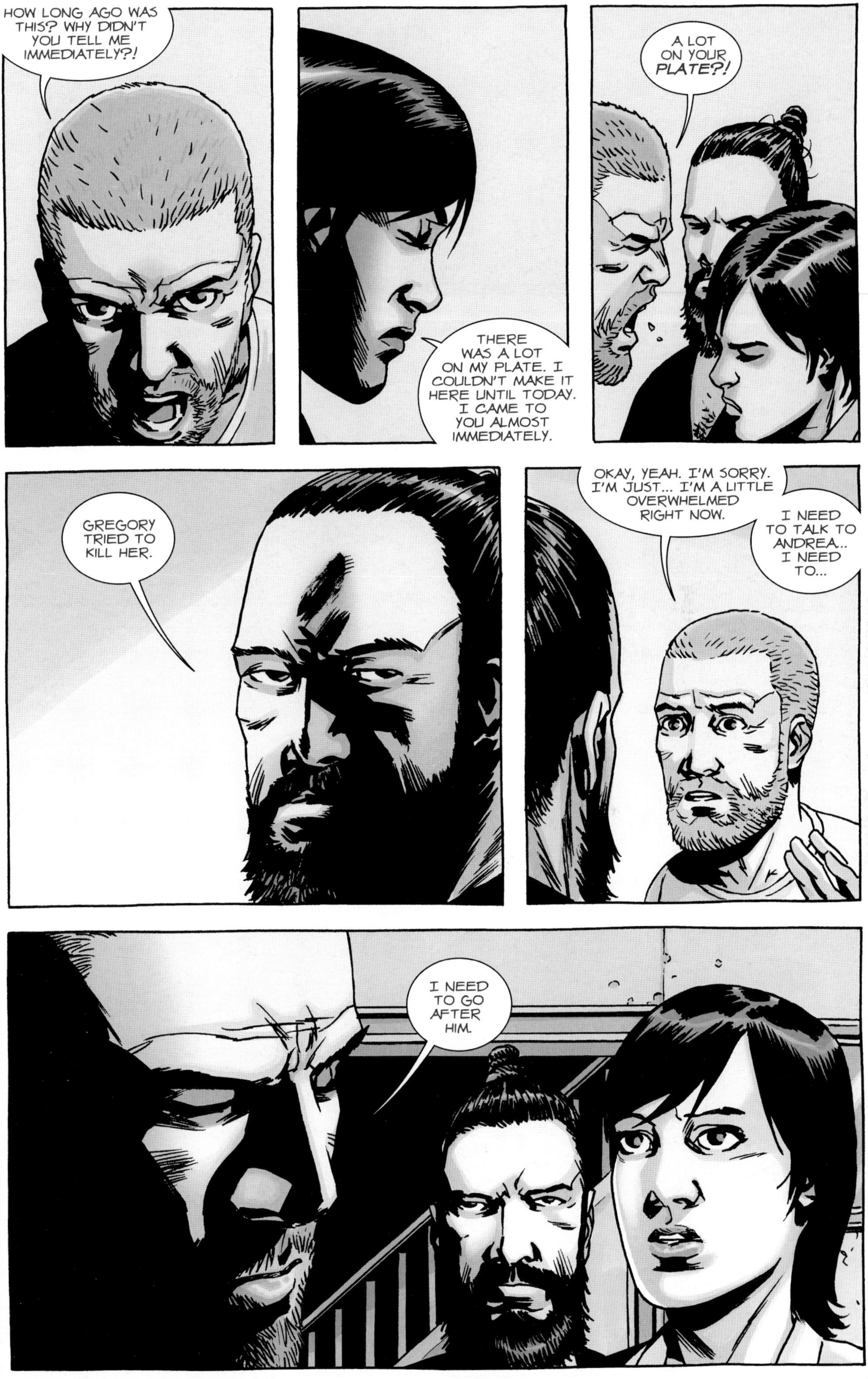
HOW LONG AGO WAS THIS? WHY DIDN'T YOU TELL ME IMMEDIATELY?!
THERE WAS A LOT ON MY PLATE. I COULDN'T MAKE IT HERE UNTIL TODAY. I CAME TO YOU ALMOST IMMEDIATELY.
A LOT ON YOUR PLATE?!
GREGORY TRIED TO KILL HER.
OKAY, YEAH. I'M SORRY. I'M JUST... I'M A LITTLE OVERWHELMED RIGHT NOW.
I NEED TO TALK TO ANDREA... I NEED TO...
I NEED TO GO AFTER HIM.

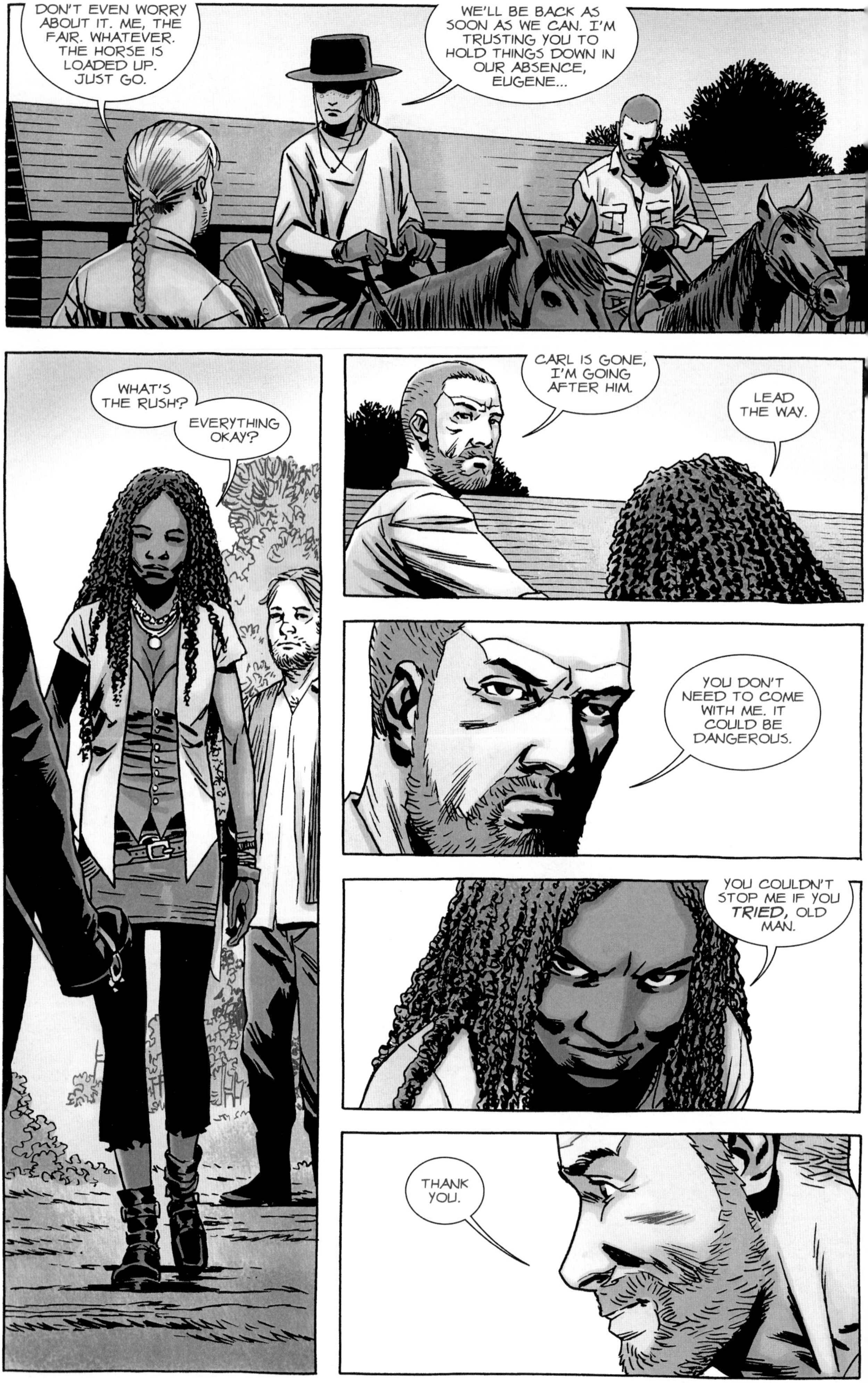
DON'T EVEN WORRY ABOUT IT. ME, THE FAIR. WHATEVER. THE HORSE IS LOADED UP. JUST GO.
WE'LL BE BACK AS SOON AS WE CAN. I'M TRUSTING YOU TO HOLD THINGS DOWN IN OUR ABSENCE, EUGENE...
WHAT'S THE RUSH?
EVERYTHING OKAY?
CARL IS GONE, I'M GOING AFTER HIM.
LEAD THE WAY.
YOU DON'T NEED TO COME WITH ME. IT COULD BE DANGEROUS.
YOU COULDN'T STOP ME IF YOU *TRIED*, OLD MAN.
THANK YOU.

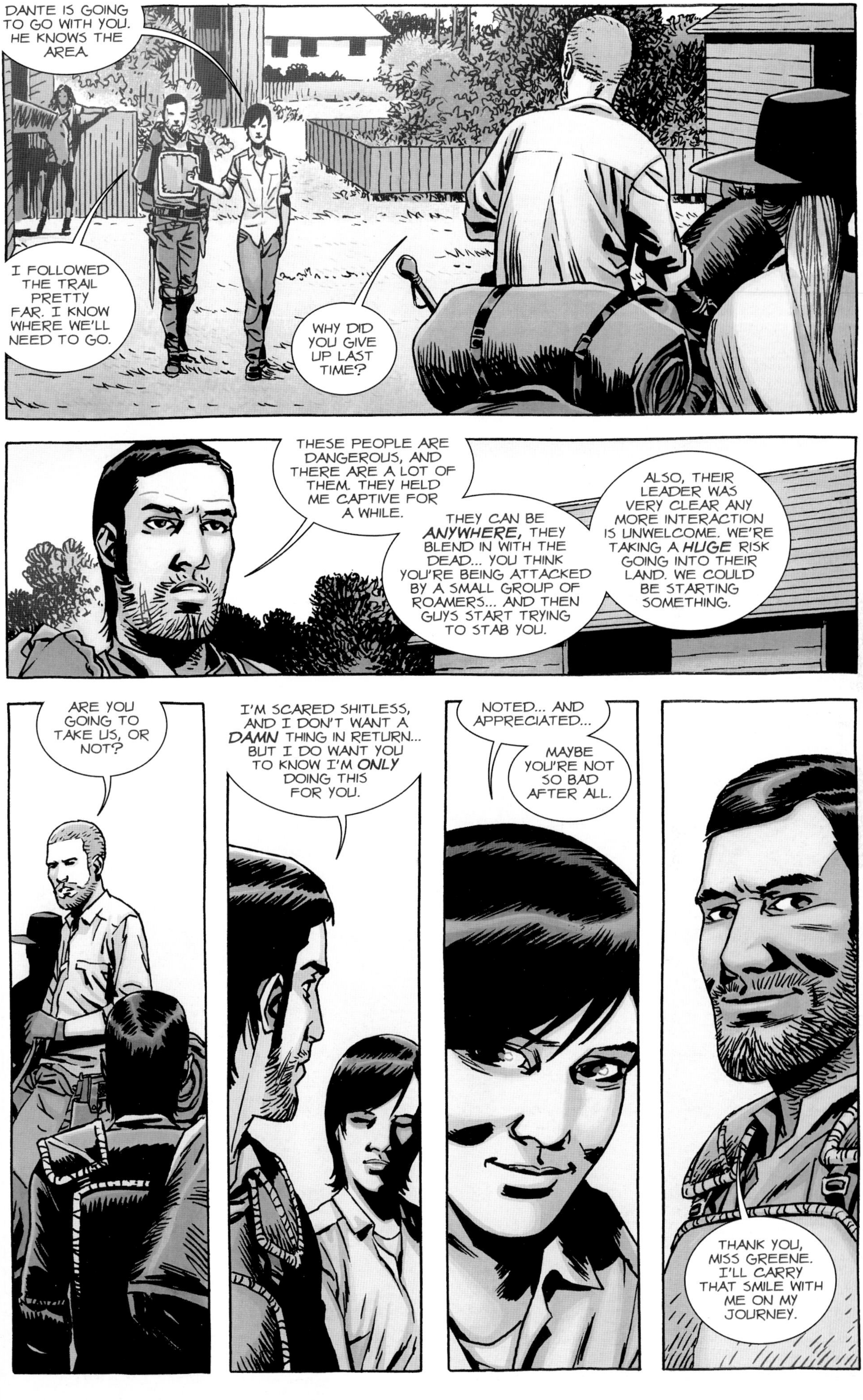
DANTE IS GOING TO GO WITH YOU. HE KNOWS THE AREA.
I FOLLOWED THE TRAIL PRETTY FAR. I KNOW WHERE WE'LL NEED TO GO.
WHY DID YOU GIVE UP LAST TIME?
THESE PEOPLE ARE DANGEROUS, AND THERE ARE A LOT OF THEM. THEY HELD ME CAPTIVE FOR A WHILE.
THEY CAN BE ANYWHERE, THEY BLEND IN WITH THE DEAD... YOU THINK YOU'RE BEING ATTACKED BY A SMALL GROUP OF ROAMERS... AND THEN GUYS START TRYING TO STAB YOU.
ALSO, THEIR LEADER WAS VERY CLEAR ANY MORE INTERACTION IS UNWELCOME. WE'RE TAKING A HUGE RISK GOING INTO THEIR LAND. WE COULD BE STARTING SOMETHING.
ARE YOU GOING TO TAKE US, OR NOT?
I'M SCARED SHITLESS, AND I DON'T WANT A DAMN THING IN RETURN... BUT I DO WANT YOU TO KNOW I'M ONLY DOING THIS FOR YOU.
NOTED... AND APPRECIATED...
MAYBE YOU'RE NOT SO BAD AFTER ALL.
THANK YOU, MISS GREENE. I'LL CARRY THAT SMILE WITH ME ON MY JOURNEY.

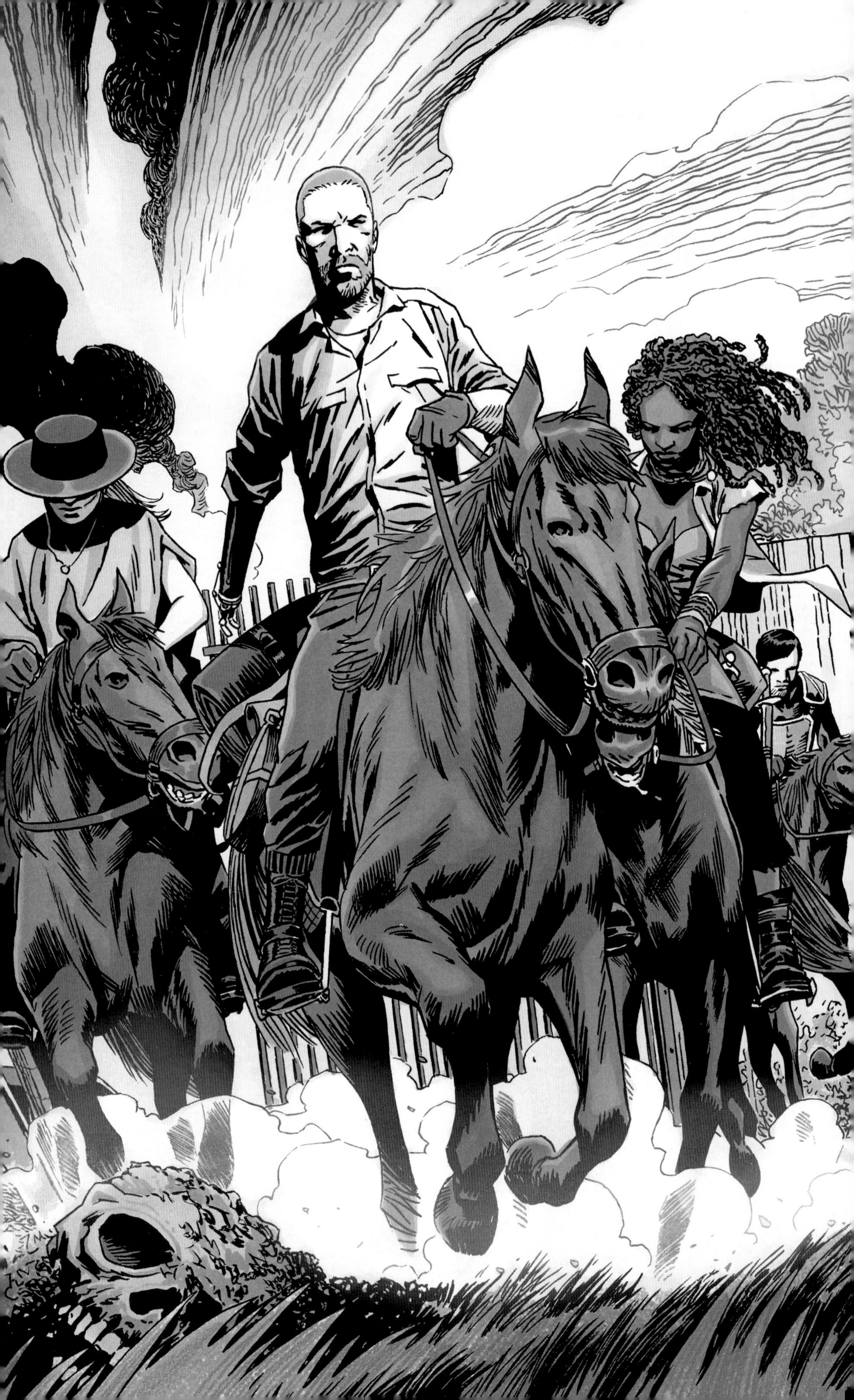

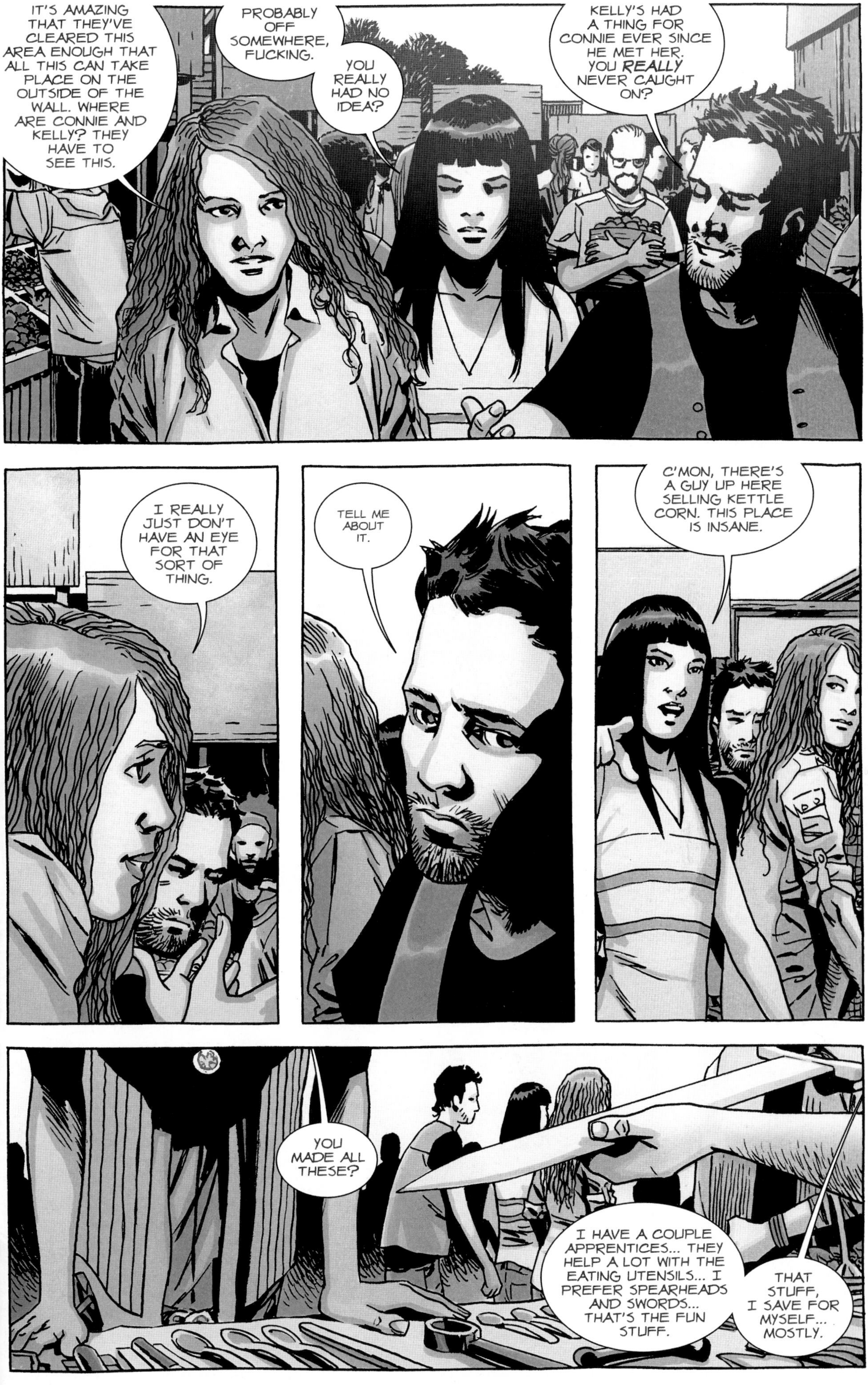
IT'S AMAZING THAT THEY'VE CLEARED THIS AREA ENOUGH THAT ALL THIS CAN TAKE PLACE ON THE OUTSIDE OF THE WALL. WHERE ARE CONNIE AND KELLY? THEY HAVE TO SEE THIS.
PROBABLY OFF SOMEWHERE, FUCKING.
YOU REALLY HAD NO IDEA?
KELLY'S HAD A THING FOR CONNIE EVER SINCE HE MET HER. YOU REALLY NEVER CAUGHT ON?
I REALLY JUST DON'T HAVE AN EYE FOR THAT SORT OF THING.
TELL ME ABOUT IT.
C'MON, THERE'S A GUY UP HERE SELLING KETTLE CORN. THIS PLACE IS INSANE.
YOU MADE ALL THESE?
I HAVE A COUPLE APPRENTICES... THEY HELP A LOT WITH THE EATING UTENSILS... I PREFER SPEARHEADS AND SWORDS... THAT'S THE FUN STUFF.
THAT STUFF, I SAVE FOR MYSELF... MOSTLY.

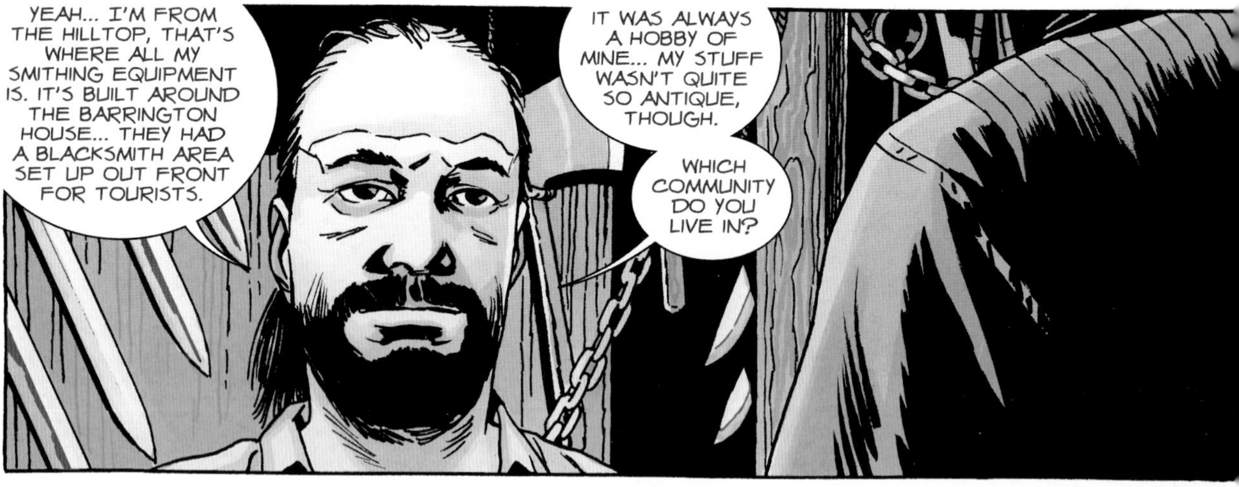
YEAH... I'M FROM THE HILLTOP, THAT'S WHERE ALL MY SMITHING EQUIPMENT IS. IT'S BUILT AROUND THE BARRINGTON HOUSE... THEY HAD A BLACKSMITH AREA SET UP OUT FRONT FOR TOURISTS.
IT WAS ALWAYS A HOBBY OF MINE... MY STUFF WASN'T QUITE SO ANTIQUE, THOUGH.
WHICH COMMUNITY DO YOU LIVE IN?
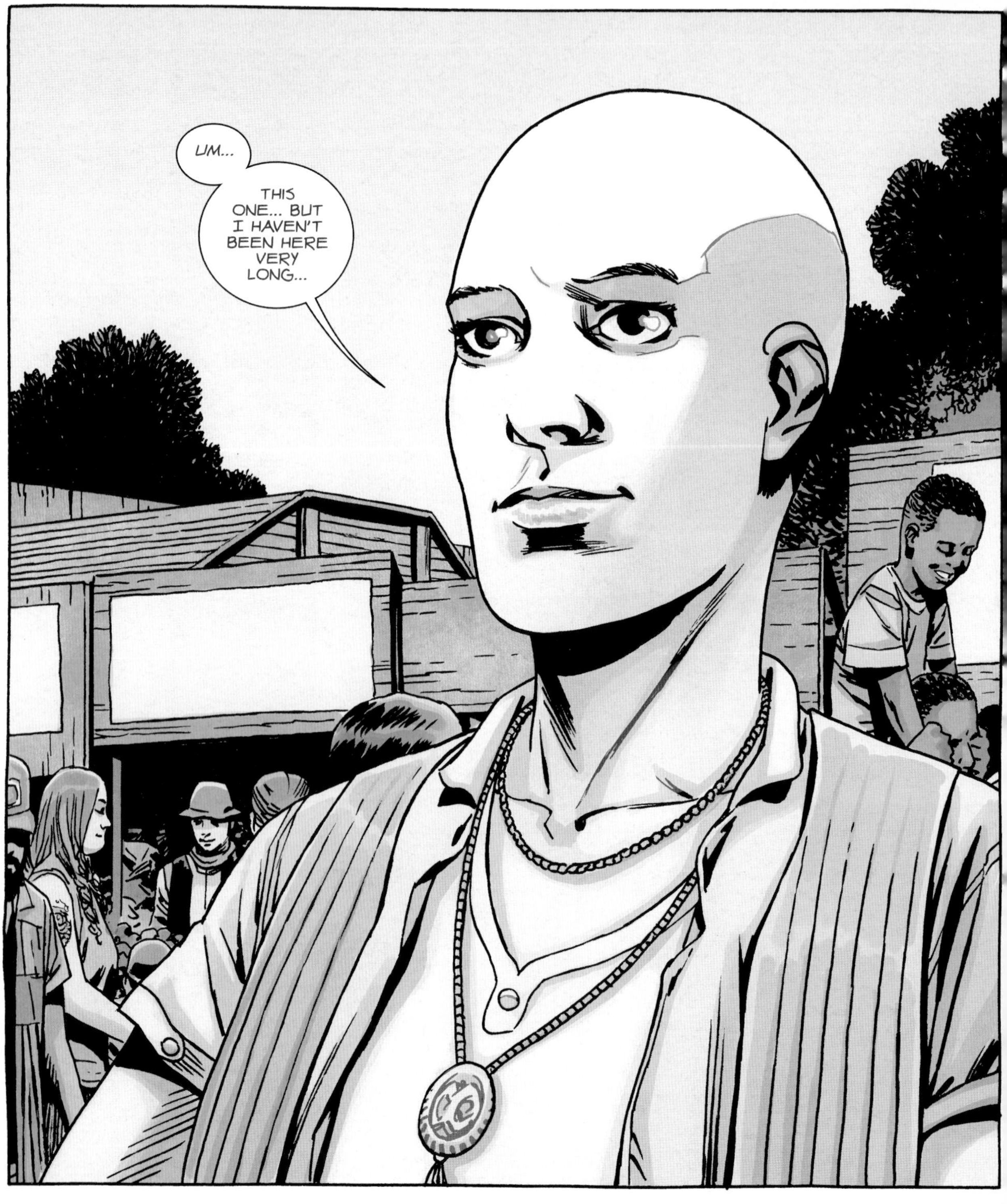
UM...
THIS ONE... BUT I HAVEN'T BEEN HERE VERY LONG...

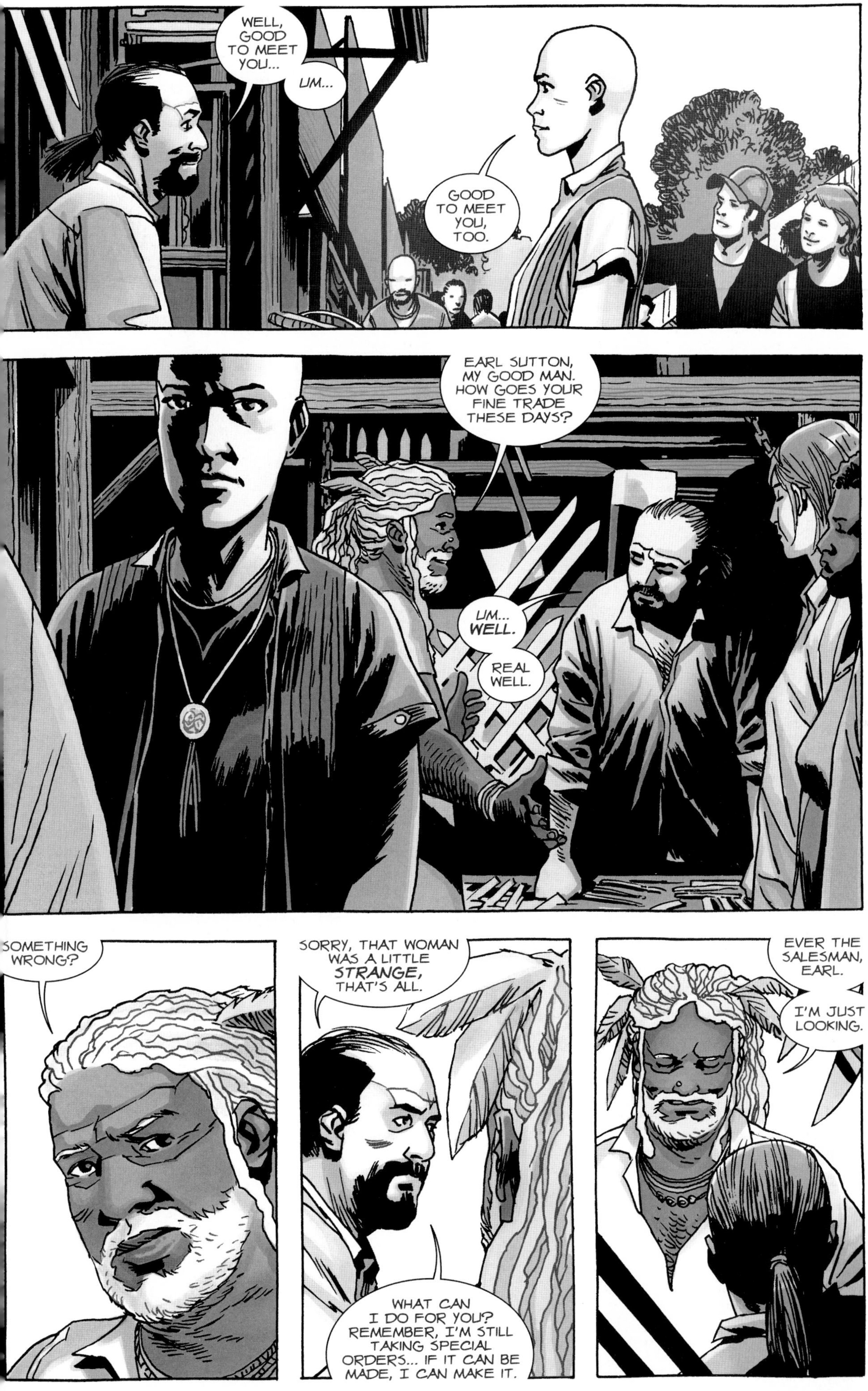
WELL, GOOD TO MEET YOU...
UM...
GOOD TO MEET YOU, TOO.
EARL SUTTON, MY GOOD MAN. HOW GOES YOUR FINE TRADE THESE DAYS?
UM... WELL.
REAL WELL.
SOMETHING WRONG?
SORRY, THAT WOMAN WAS A LITTLE STRANGE, THAT'S ALL.
WHAT CAN I DO FOR YOU? REMEMBER, I'M STILL TAKING SPECIAL ORDERS... IF IT CAN BE MADE, I CAN MAKE IT.
EVER THE SALESMAN, EARL.
I'M JUST LOOKING.

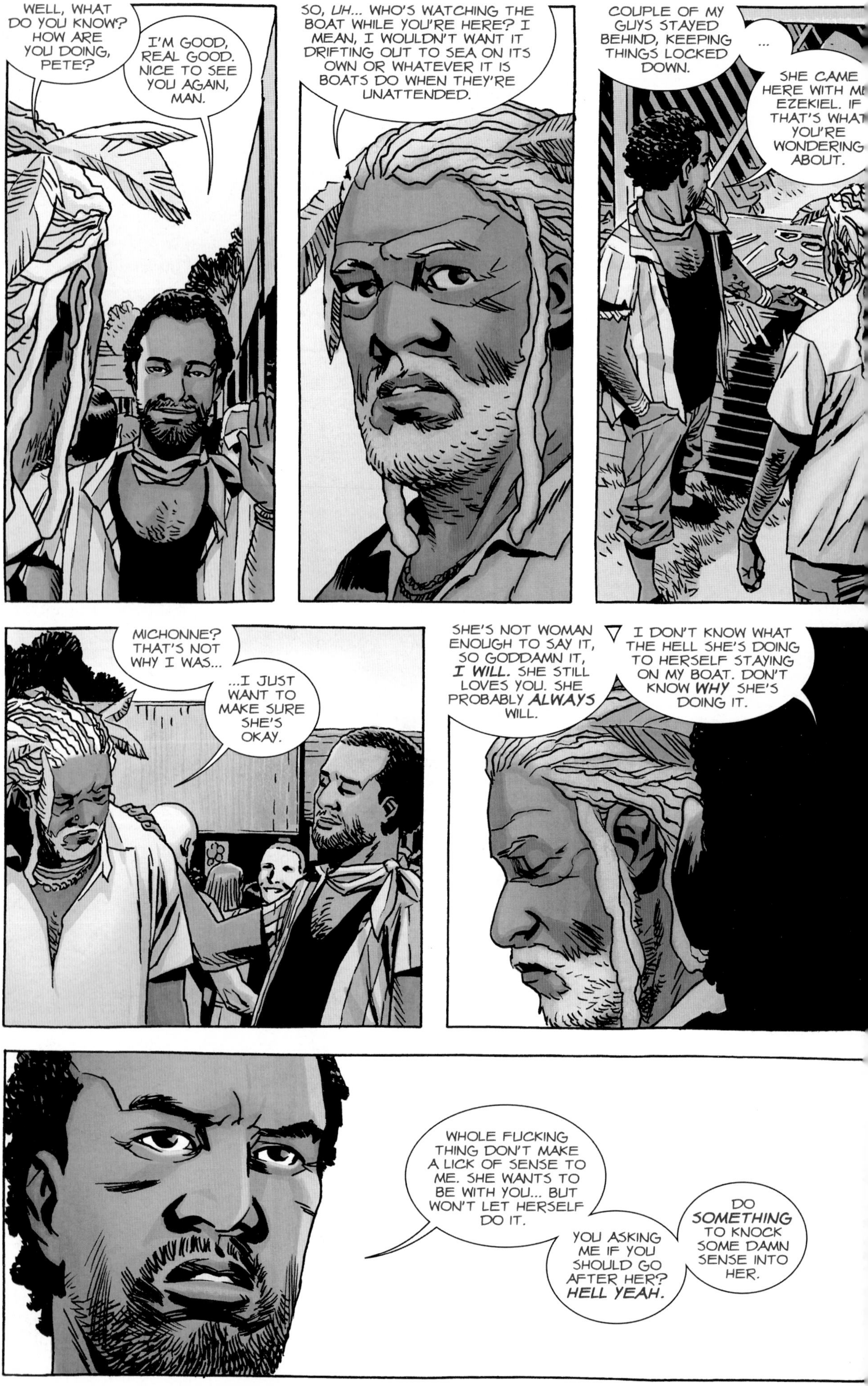
WELL, WHAT DO YOU KNOW? HOW ARE YOU DOING, PETE?
I'M GOOD, REAL GOOD. NICE TO SEE YOU AGAIN, MAN.
SO, UH... WHO'S WATCHING THE BOAT WHILE YOU'RE HERE? I MEAN, I WOULDN'T WANT IT DRIFTING OUT TO SEA ON ITS OWN OR WHATEVER IT IS BOATS DO WHEN THEY'RE UNATTENDED.
COUPLE OF MY GUYS STAYED BEHIND, KEEPING THINGS LOCKED DOWN.
...
SHE CAME HERE WITH ME, EZEKIEL. IF THAT'S WHAT YOU'RE WONDERING ABOUT.
MICHONNE? THAT'S NOT WHY I WAS...
...I JUST WANT TO MAKE SURE SHE'S OKAY.
I DON'T KNOW WHAT THE HELL SHE'S DOING TO HERSELF STAYING ON MY BOAT. DON'T KNOW WHY SHE'S DOING IT.
SHE'S NOT WOMAN ENOUGH TO SAY IT, SO GODDAMN IT, I WILL. SHE STILL LOVES YOU. SHE PROBABLY ALWAYS WILL.
WHOLE FUCKING THING DON'T MAKE A LICK OF SENSE TO ME. SHE WANTS TO BE WITH YOU... BUT WON'T LET HERSELF DO IT.
YOU ASKING ME IF YOU SHOULD GO AFTER HER? HELL YEAH.
DO SOMETHING TO KNOCK SOME DAMN SENSE INTO HER.

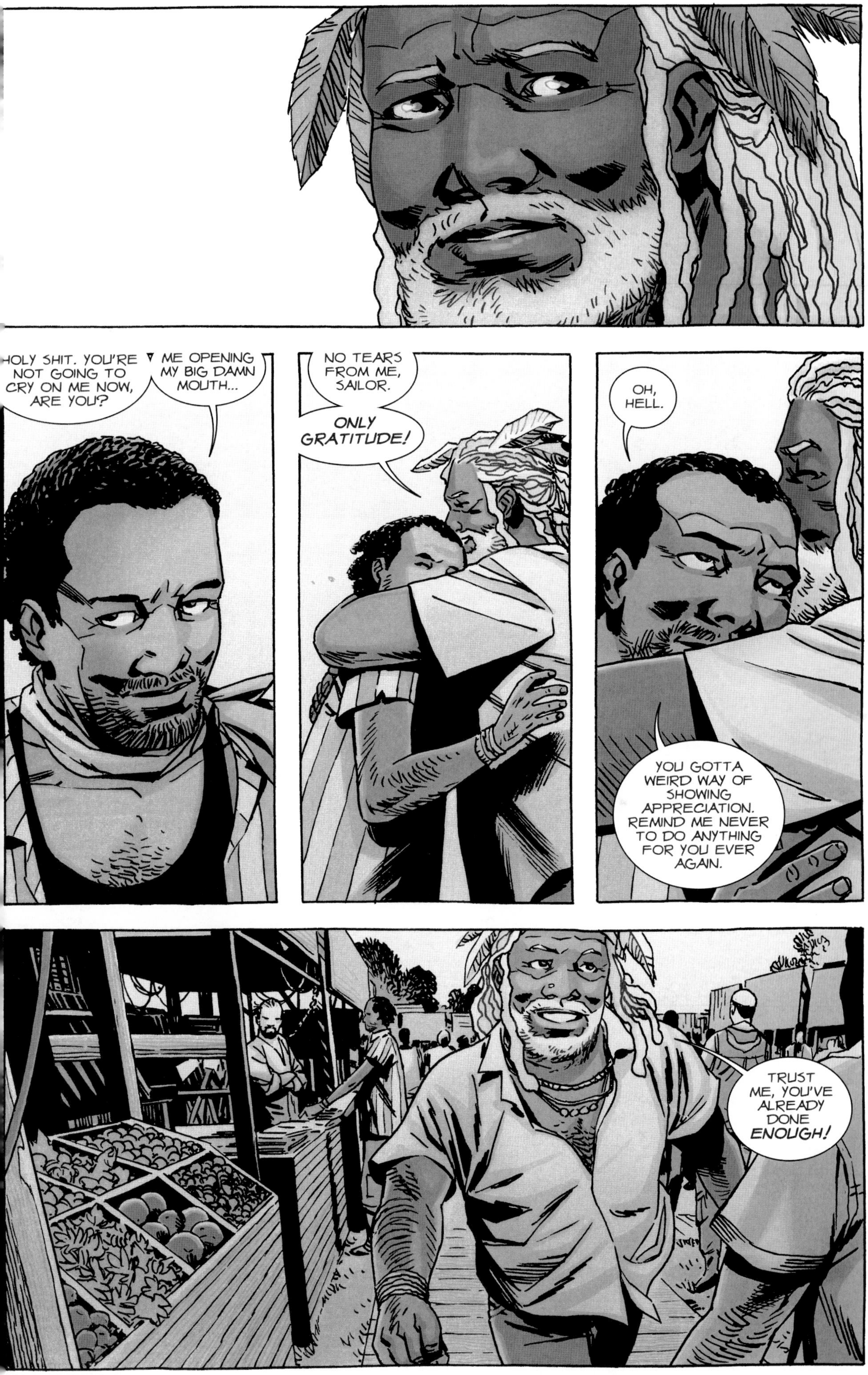
HOLY SHIT. YOU'RE NOT GOING TO CRY ON ME NOW, ARE YOU?
ME OPENING MY BIG DAMN MOUTH...
NO TEARS FROM ME, SAILOR.
ONLY GRATITUDE!
OH, HELL.
YOU GOTTA WEIRD WAY OF SHOWING APPRECIATION. REMIND ME NEVER TO DO ANYTHING FOR YOU EVER AGAIN.
TRUST ME, YOU'VE ALREADY DONE ENOUGH!

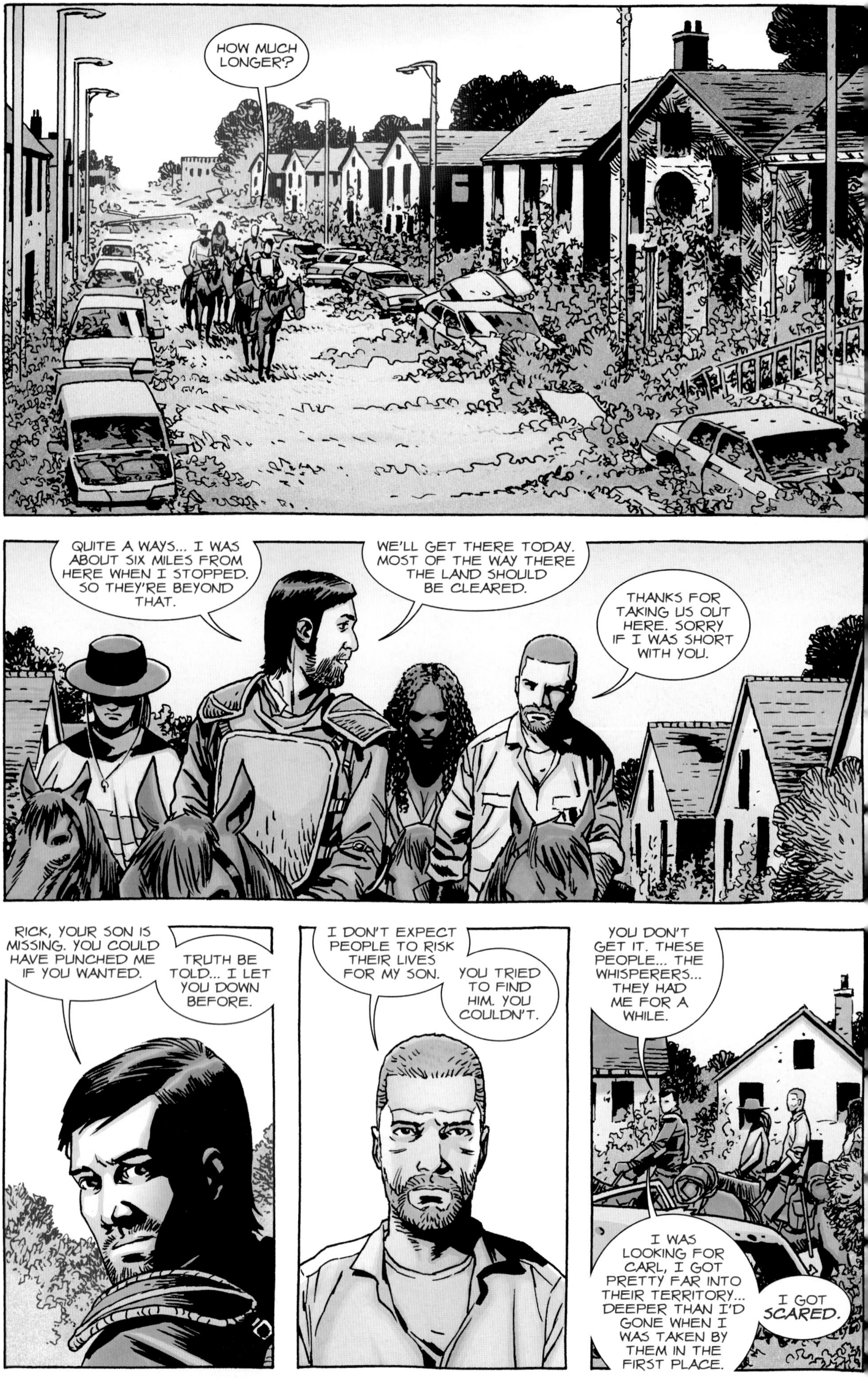
HOW MUCH LONGER?
QUITE A WAYS... I WAS ABOUT SIX MILES FROM HERE WHEN I STOPPED. SO THEY'RE BEYOND THAT.
WE'LL GET THERE TODAY. MOST OF THE WAY THERE THE LAND SHOULD BE CLEARED.
THANKS FOR TAKING US OUT HERE. SORRY IF I WAS SHORT WITH YOU.
RICK, YOUR SON IS MISSING. YOU COULD HAVE PUNCHED ME IF YOU WANTED.
TRUTH BE TOLD... I LET YOU DOWN BEFORE.
I DON'T EXPECT PEOPLE TO RISK THEIR LIVES FOR MY SON.
YOU TRIED TO FIND HIM. YOU COULDN'T.
YOU DON'T GET IT. THESE PEOPLE... THE WHISPERERS... THEY HAD ME FOR A WHILE.
I WAS LOOKING FOR CARL, I GOT PRETTY FAR INTO THEIR TERRITORY... DEEPER THAN I'D GONE WHEN I WAS TAKEN BY THEM IN THE FIRST PLACE.
I GOT SCARED.

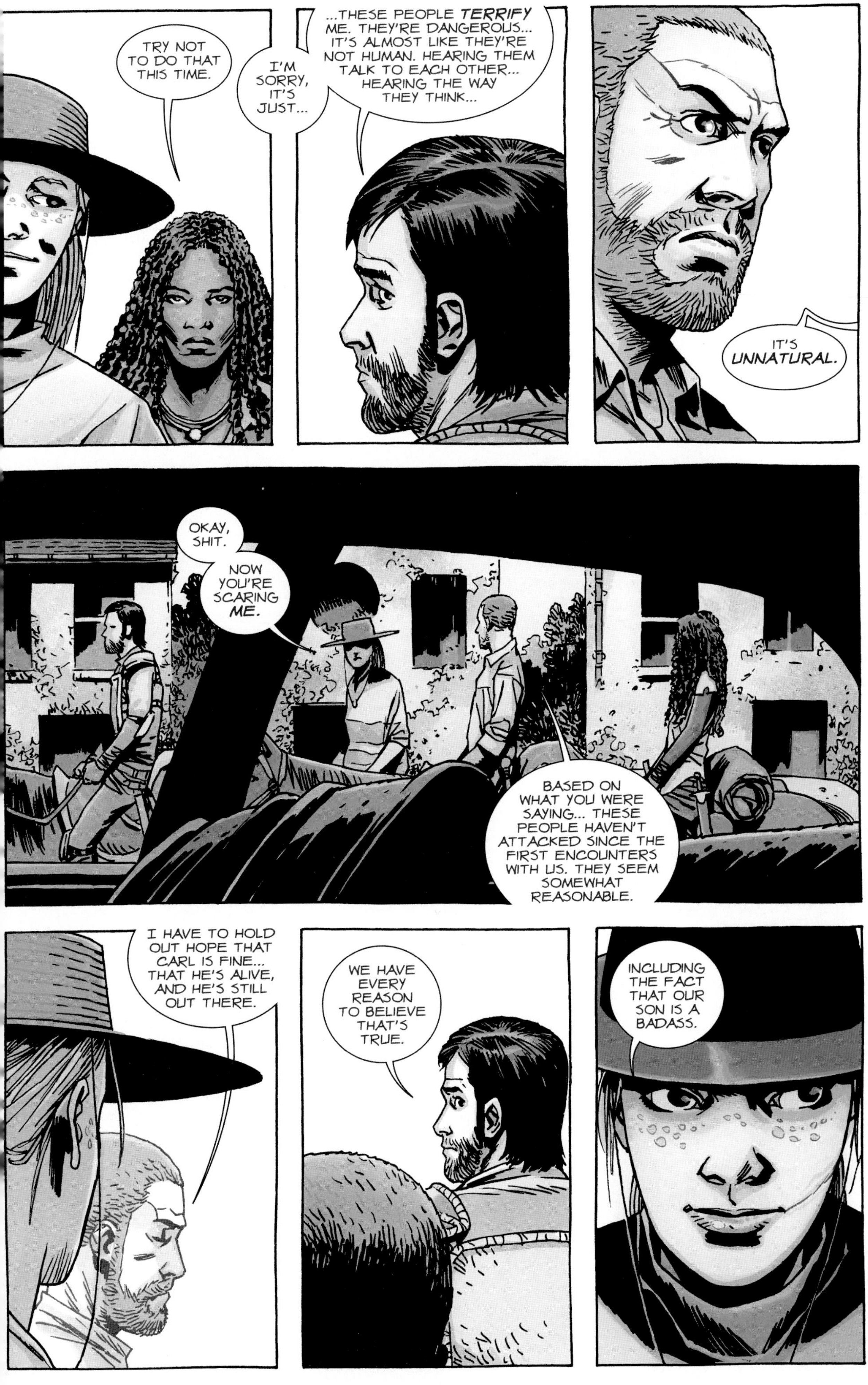
TRY NOT TO DO THAT THIS TIME.
I'M SORRY, IT'S JUST...
...THESE PEOPLE TERRIFY ME. THEY'RE DANGEROUS... IT'S ALMOST LIKE THEY'RE NOT HUMAN. HEARING THEM TALK TO EACH OTHER... HEARING THE WAY THEY THINK...
IT'S UNNATURAL.
OKAY, SHIT.
NOW YOU'RE SCARING ME.
BASED ON WHAT YOU WERE SAYING... THESE PEOPLE HAVEN'T ATTACKED SINCE THE FIRST ENCOUNTERS WITH US. THEY SEEM SOMEWHAT REASONABLE.
I HAVE TO HOLD OUT HOPE THAT CARL IS FINE... THAT HE'S ALIVE, AND HE'S STILL OUT THERE.
WE HAVE EVERY REASON TO BELIEVE THAT'S TRUE.
INCLUDING THE FACT THAT OUR SON IS A BADASS.

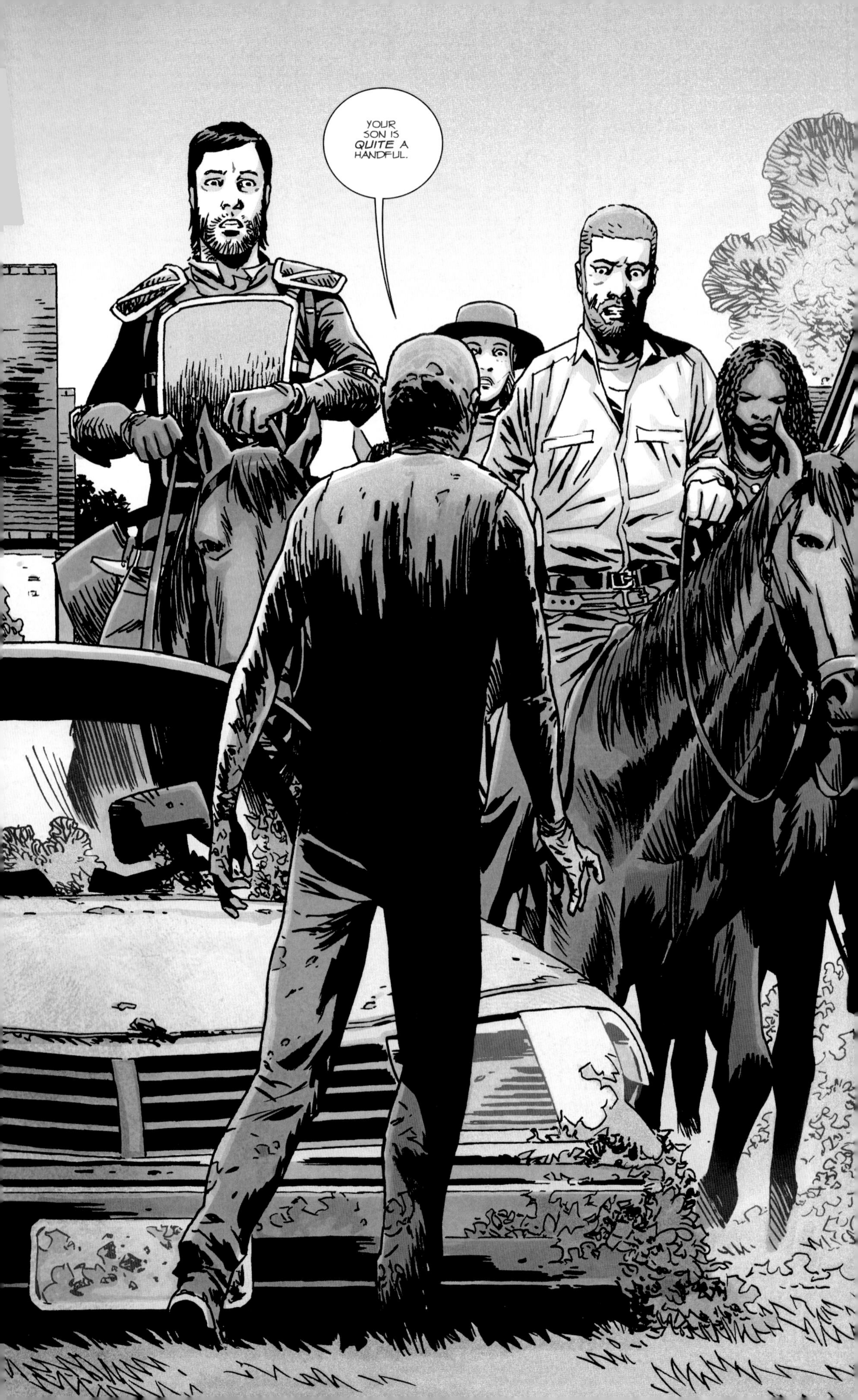
YOUR SON IS QUITE A HANDFUL.

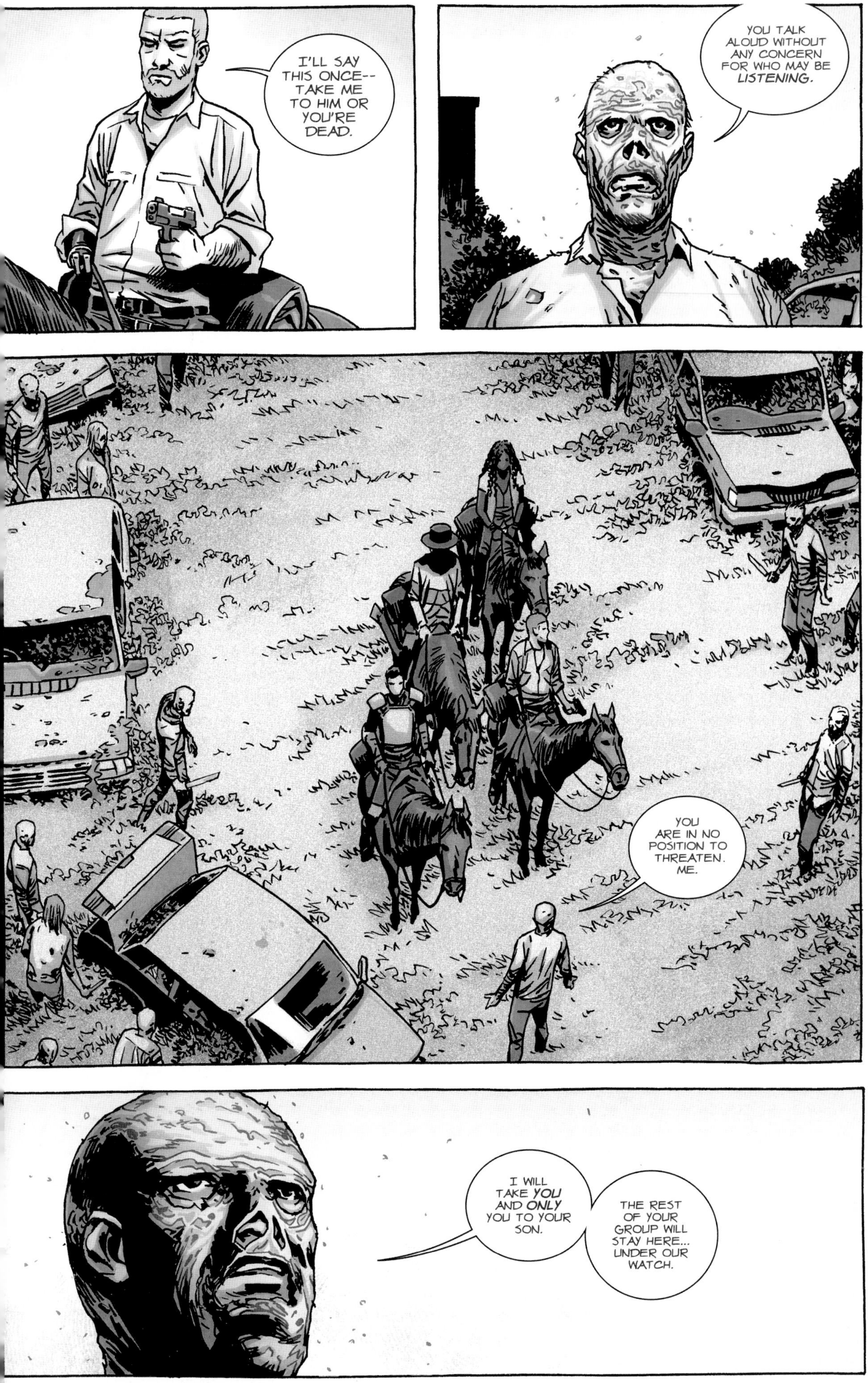
I'LL SAY THIS ONCE-- TAKE ME TO HIM OR YOU'RE DEAD.
YOU TALK ALOUD WITHOUT ANY CONCERN FOR WHO MAY BE *LISTENING.*
YOU ARE IN NO POSITION TO THREATEN. ME.
I WILL TAKE *YOU* AND *ONLY* YOU TO YOUR SON.
THE REST OF YOUR GROUP WILL STAY HERE... UNDER OUR WATCH.

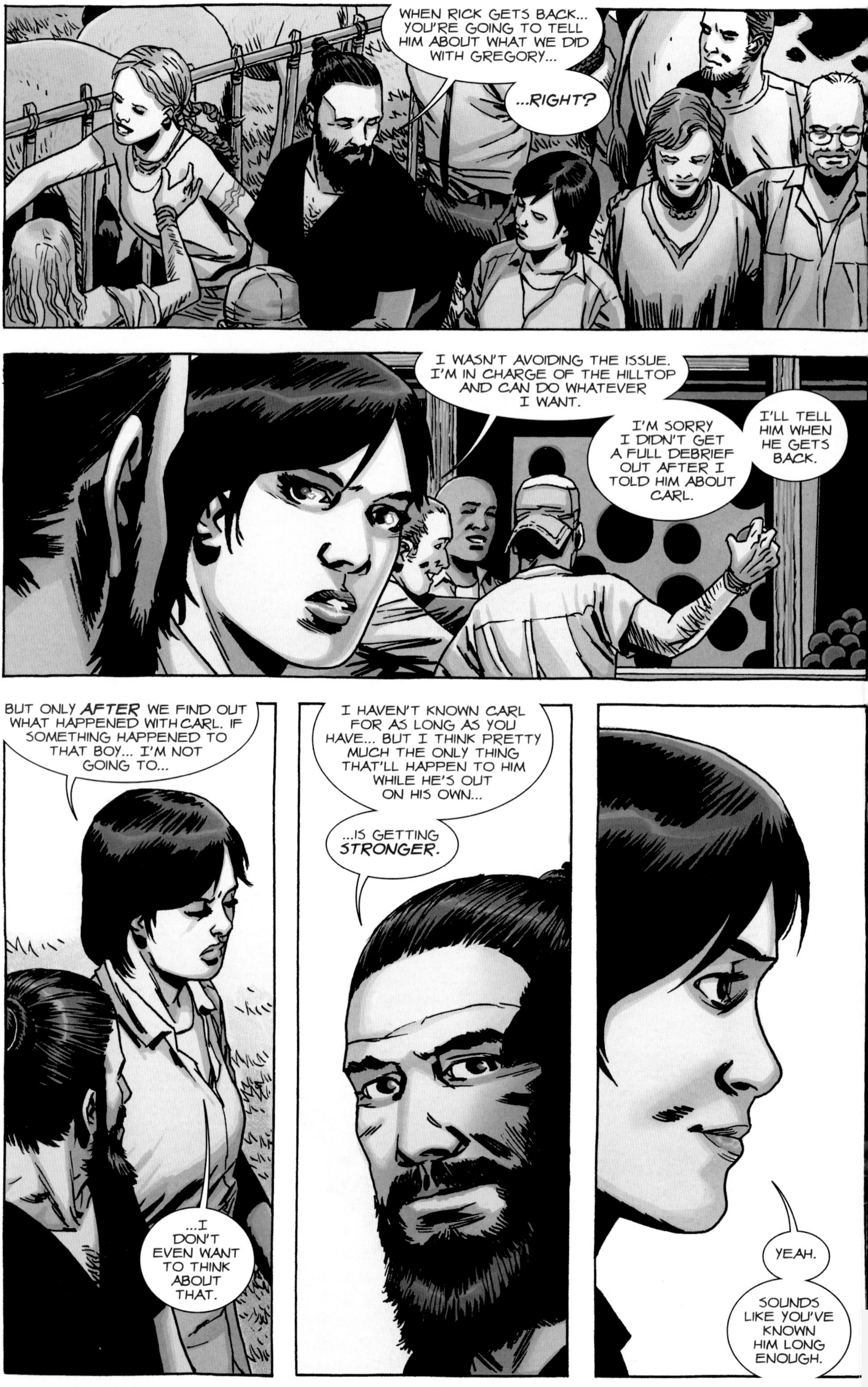
WHEN RICK GETS BACK... YOU'RE GOING TO TELL HIM ABOUT WHAT WE DID WITH GREGORY...
...RIGHT?
I WASN'T AVOIDING THE ISSUE. I'M IN CHARGE OF THE HILLTOP AND CAN DO WHATEVER I WANT.
I'M SORRY I DIDN'T GET A FULL DEBRIEF OUT AFTER I TOLD HIM ABOUT CARL.
I'LL TELL HIM WHEN HE GETS BACK.
BUT ONLY AFTER WE FIND OUT WHAT HAPPENED WITH CARL. IF SOMETHING HAPPENED TO THAT BOY... I'M NOT GOING TO...
...I DON'T EVEN WANT TO THINK ABOUT THAT.
I HAVEN'T KNOWN CARL FOR AS LONG AS YOU HAVE... BUT I THINK PRETTY MUCH THE ONLY THING THAT'LL HAPPEN TO HIM WHILE HE'S OUT ON HIS OWN...
...IS GETTING STRONGER.
YEAH.
SOUNDS LIKE YOU'VE KNOWN HIM LONG ENOUGH.

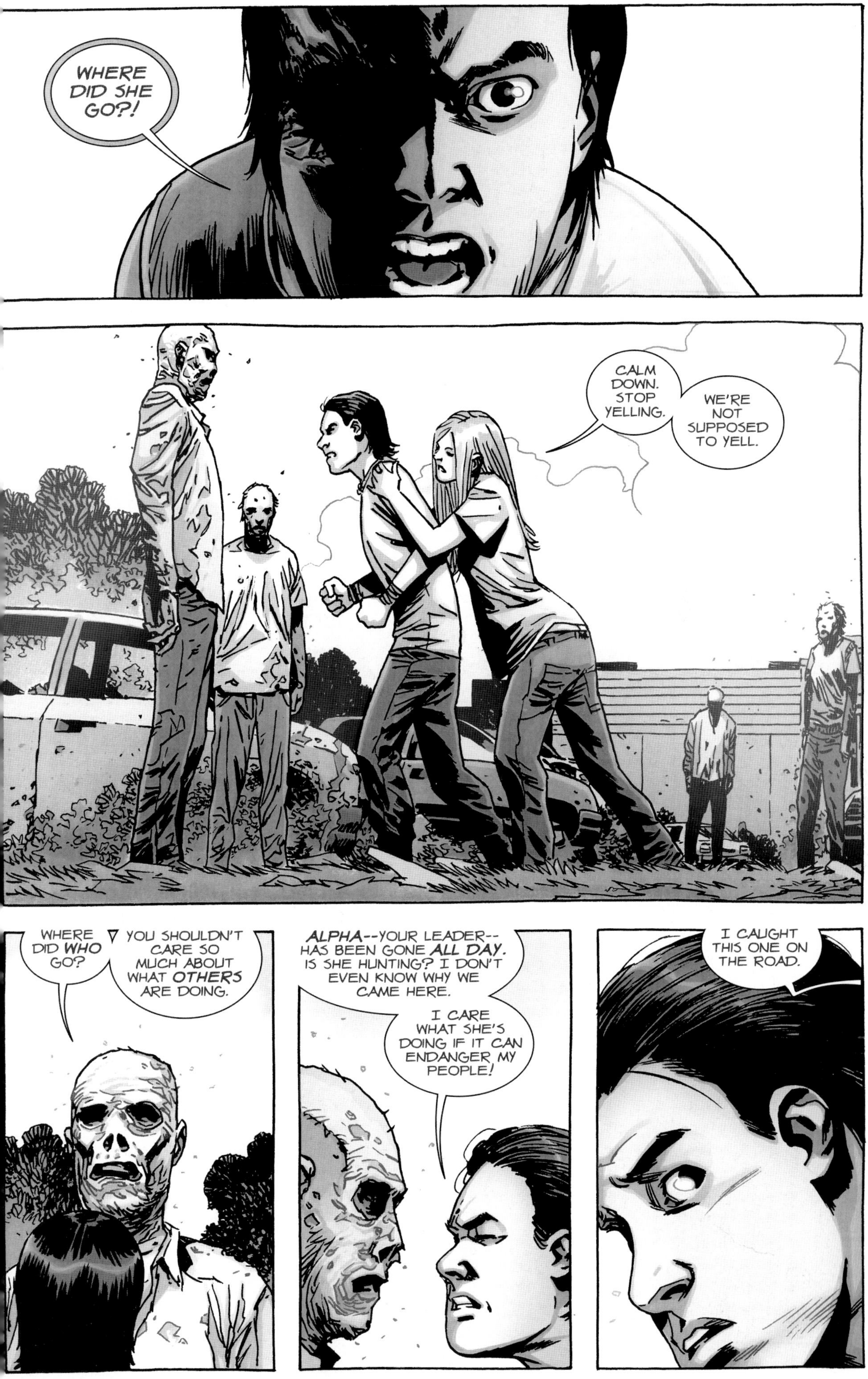
WHERE DID SHE GO?!
CALM DOWN. STOP YELLING.
WE'RE NOT SUPPOSED TO YELL.
WHERE DID WHO GO?
YOU SHOULDN'T CARE SO MUCH ABOUT WHAT OTHERS ARE DOING.
ALPHA--YOUR LEADER--HAS BEEN GONE ALL DAY. IS SHE HUNTING? I DON'T EVEN KNOW WHY WE CAME HERE.
I CARE WHAT SHE'S DOING IF IT CAN ENDANGER MY PEOPLE!
I CAUGHT THIS ONE ON THE ROAD.

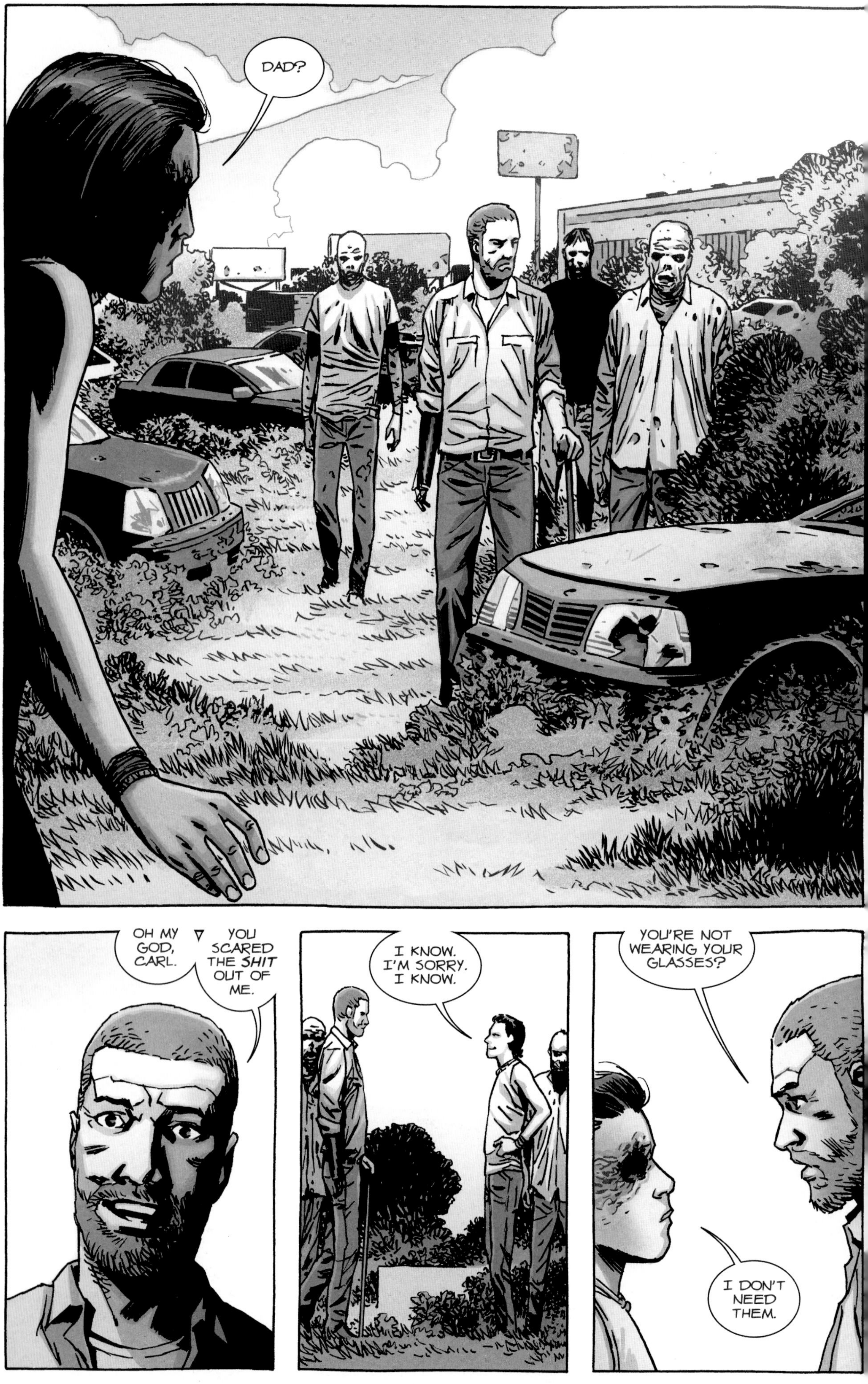
DAD?
OH MY GOD, CARL.
YOU SCARED THE SHIT OUT OF ME.
I KNOW. I'M SORRY. I KNOW.
YOU'RE NOT WEARING YOUR GLASSES?
I DON'T NEED THEM.

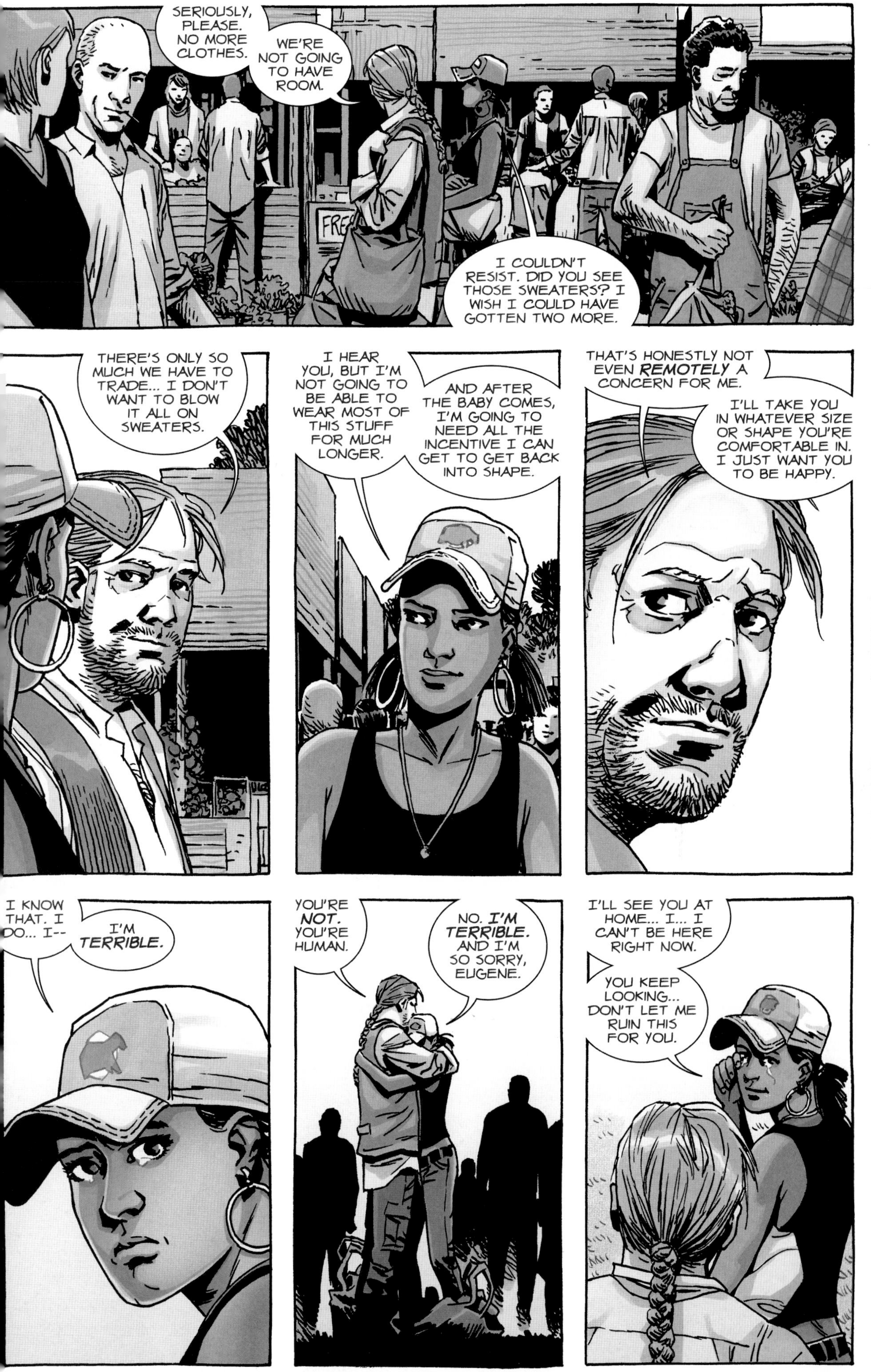
SERIOUSLY, PLEASE. NO MORE CLOTHES.
WE'RE NOT GOING TO HAVE ROOM.
I COULDN'T RESIST. DID YOU SEE THOSE SWEATERS? I WISH I COULD HAVE GOTTEN TWO MORE.
FRE
THERE'S ONLY SO MUCH WE HAVE TO TRADE... I DON'T WANT TO BLOW IT ALL ON SWEATERS.
I HEAR YOU, BUT I'M NOT GOING TO BE ABLE TO WEAR MOST OF THIS STUFF FOR MUCH LONGER.
AND AFTER THE BABY COMES, I'M GOING TO NEED ALL THE INCENTIVE I CAN GET TO GET BACK INTO SHAPE.
THAT'S HONESTLY NOT EVEN REMOTELY A CONCERN FOR ME.
I'LL TAKE YOU IN WHATEVER SIZE OR SHAPE YOU'RE COMFORTABLE IN. I JUST WANT YOU TO BE HAPPY.
I KNOW THAT. I DO... I--
I'M TERRIBLE.
YOU'RE NOT. YOU'RE HUMAN.
NO. I'M TERRIBLE. AND I'M SO SORRY, EUGENE.
I'LL SEE YOU AT HOME... I... I CAN'T BE HERE RIGHT NOW.
YOU KEEP LOOKING... DON'T LET ME RUIN THIS FOR YOU.

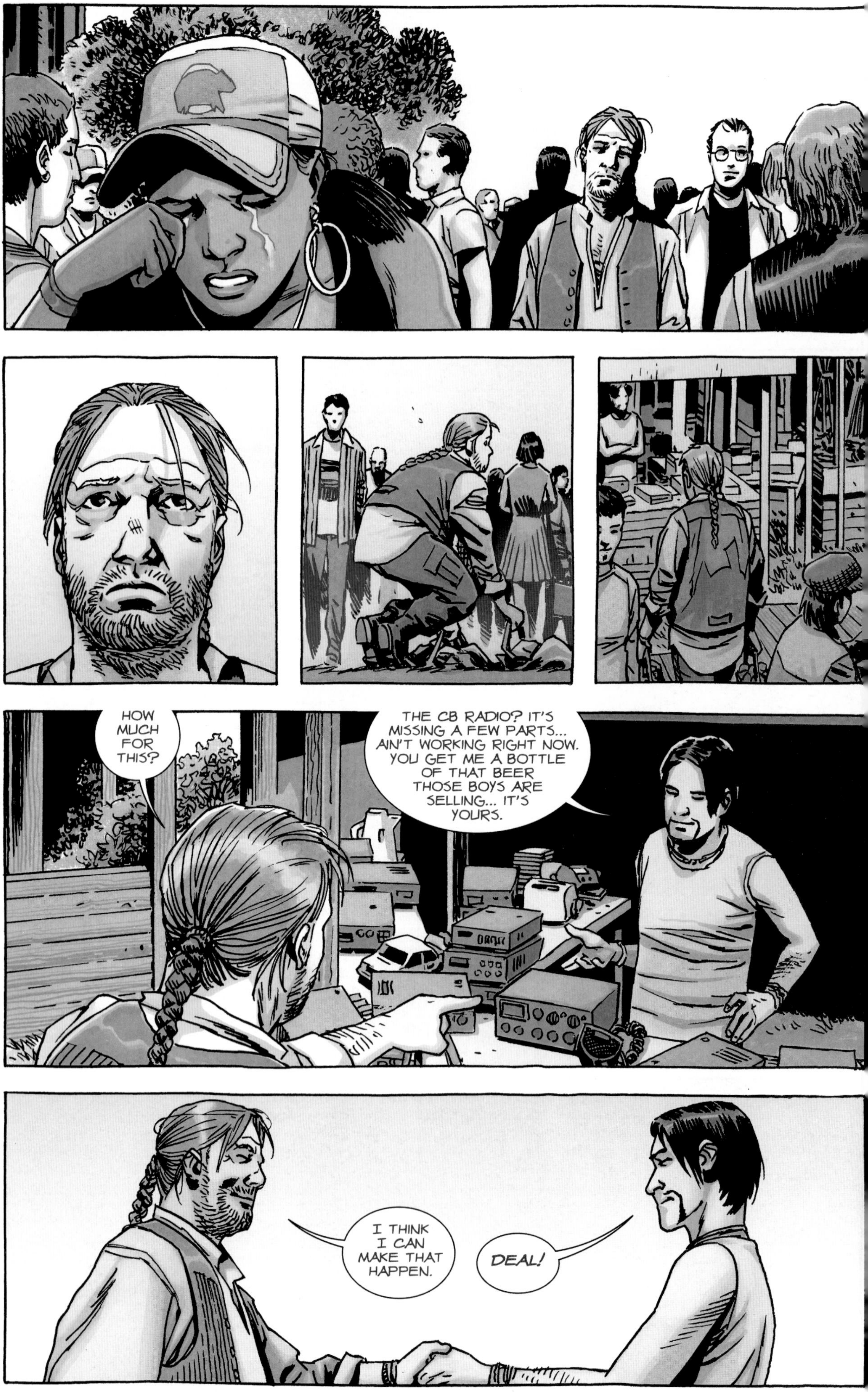
HOW MUCH FOR THIS?
THE CB RADIO? IT'S MISSING A FEW PARTS... AIN'T WORKING RIGHT NOW. YOU GET ME A BOTTLE OF THAT BEER THOSE BOYS ARE SELLING... IT'S YOURS.
I THINK I CAN MAKE THAT HAPPEN.
DEAL!

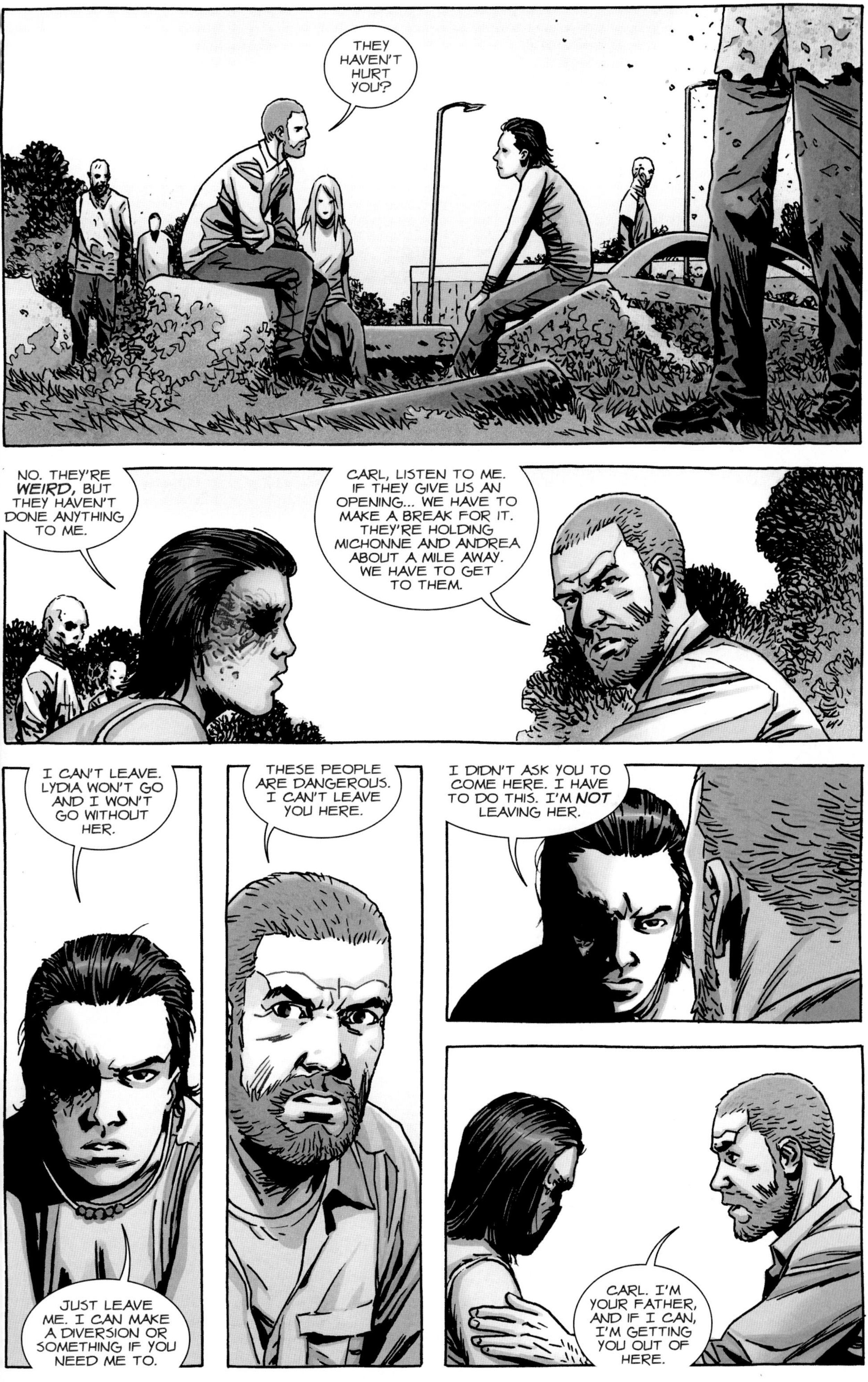
THEY HAVEN'T HURT YOU?
NO. THEY'RE *WEIRD,* BUT THEY HAVEN'T DONE ANYTHING TO ME.
CARL, LISTEN TO ME. IF THEY GIVE US AN OPENING... WE HAVE TO MAKE A BREAK FOR IT. THEY'RE HOLDING MICHONNE AND ANDREA ABOUT A MILE AWAY. WE HAVE TO GET TO THEM.
I CAN'T LEAVE. LYDIA WON'T GO AND I WON'T GO WITHOUT HER.
JUST LEAVE ME. I CAN MAKE A DIVERSION OR SOMETHING IF YOU NEED ME TO.
THESE PEOPLE ARE DANGEROUS. I CAN'T LEAVE YOU HERE.
I DIDN'T ASK YOU TO COME HERE. I HAVE TO DO THIS. I'M *NOT* LEAVING HER.
CARL. I'M YOUR FATHER, AND IF I CAN, I'M GETTING YOU OUT OF HERE.

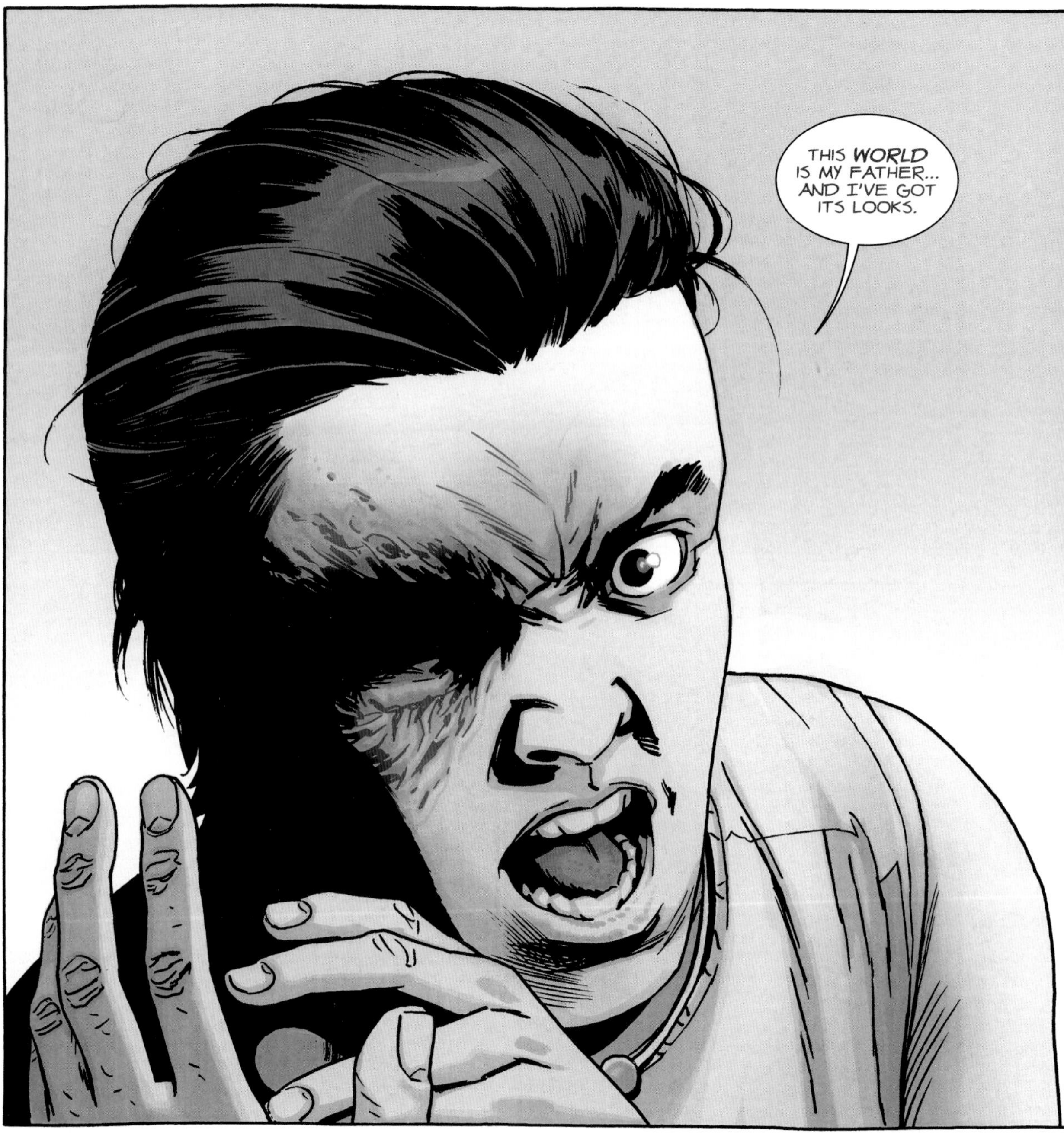
THIS *WORLD* IS MY FATHER... AND I'VE GOT ITS LOOKS.

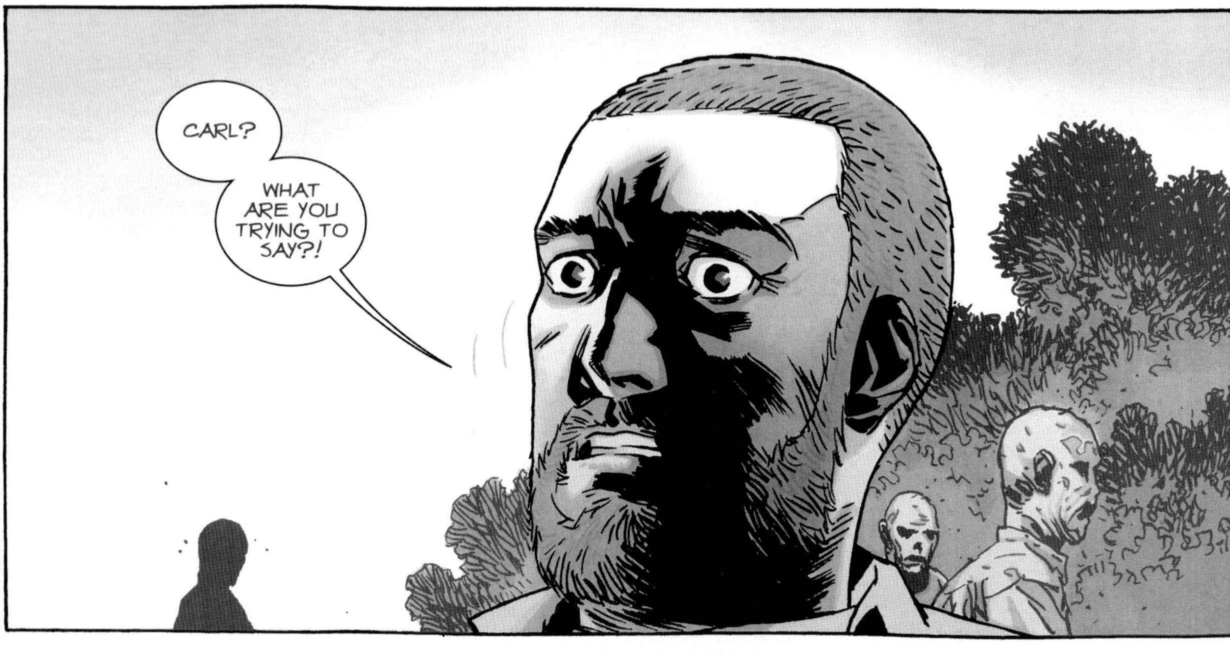
CARL?
WHAT ARE YOU TRYING TO SAY?!

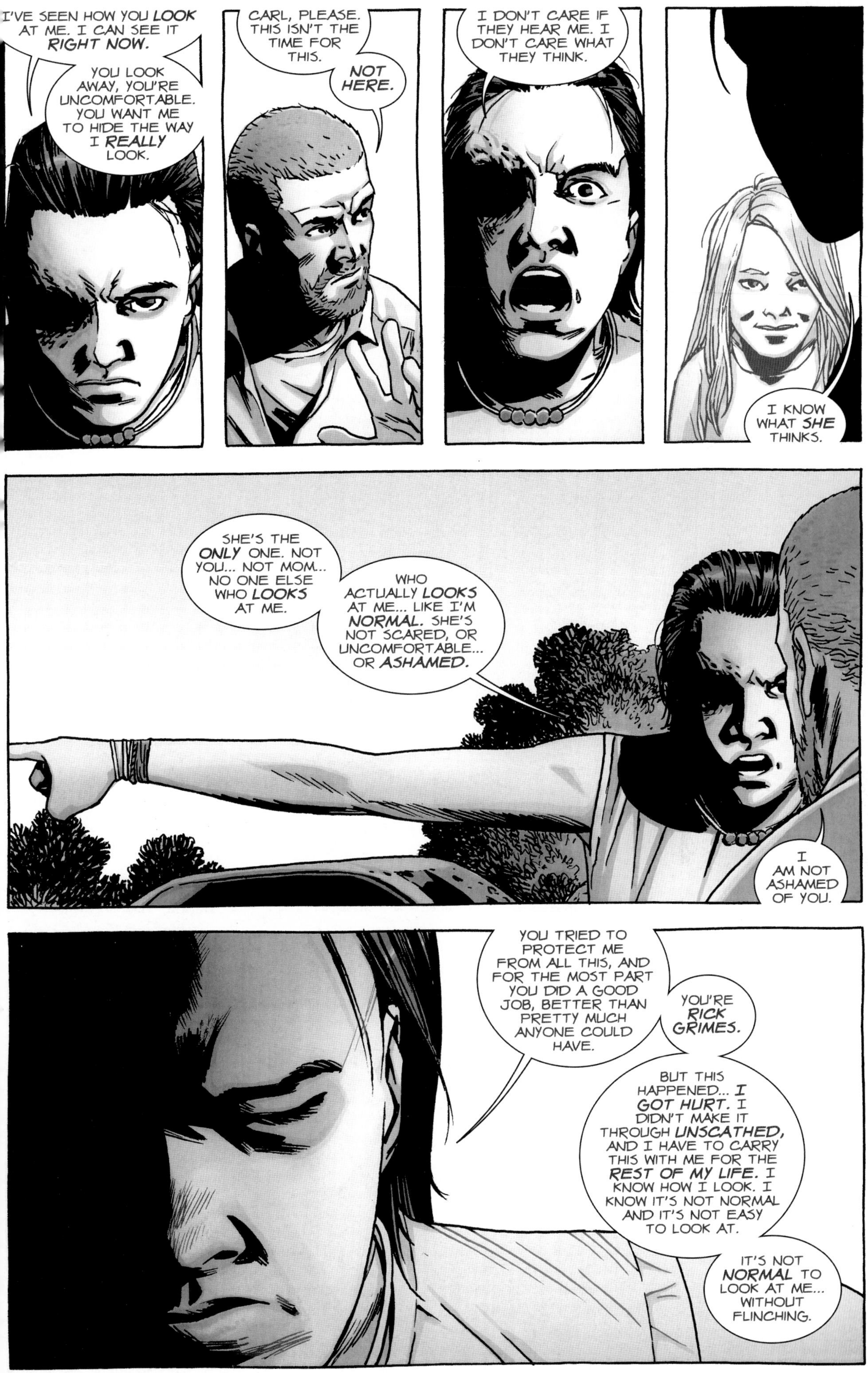
I'VE SEEN HOW YOU LOOK AT ME. I CAN SEE IT RIGHT NOW.
YOU LOOK AWAY, YOU'RE UNCOMFORTABLE. YOU WANT ME TO HIDE THE WAY I REALLY LOOK.
CARL, PLEASE. THIS ISN'T THE TIME FOR THIS.
NOT HERE.
I DON'T CARE IF THEY HEAR ME. I DON'T CARE WHAT THEY THINK.
I KNOW WHAT SHE THINKS.
SHE'S THE ONLY ONE. NOT YOU... NOT MOM... NO ONE ELSE WHO LOOKS AT ME.
WHO ACTUALLY LOOKS AT ME... LIKE I'M NORMAL. SHE'S NOT SCARED, OR UNCOMFORTABLE... OR ASHAMED.
I AM NOT ASHAMED OF YOU.
YOU TRIED TO PROTECT ME FROM ALL THIS, AND FOR THE MOST PART YOU DID A GOOD JOB, BETTER THAN PRETTY MUCH ANYONE COULD HAVE.
YOU'RE RICK GRIMES.
BUT THIS HAPPENED... I GOT HURT. I DIDN'T MAKE IT THROUGH UNSCATHED, AND I HAVE TO CARRY THIS WITH ME FOR THE REST OF MY LIFE. I KNOW HOW I LOOK. I KNOW IT'S NOT NORMAL AND IT'S NOT EASY TO LOOK AT.
IT'S NOT NORMAL TO LOOK AT ME... WITHOUT FLINCHING.

BUT SOMEHOW... *SHE* DOES IT.

▽ SHE'S SPECIAL TO ME. I *CARE* ABOUT HER.

SO I'M NOT GOING TO LEAVE HER. I'VE FINALLY FOUND SOMEONE WHO CAN TRULY ACCEPT ME FOR *WHO I AM*, INSTEAD OF WHO I WAS, OR WHO MY FATHER IS...

...SO I'M GOING TO HOLD ONTO THAT.

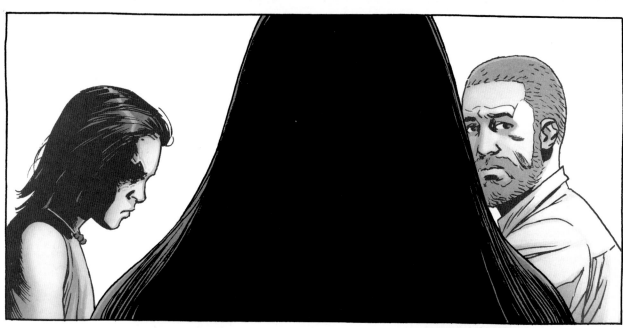

...

OKAY. I UNDERSTAND.

I'M SORRY.

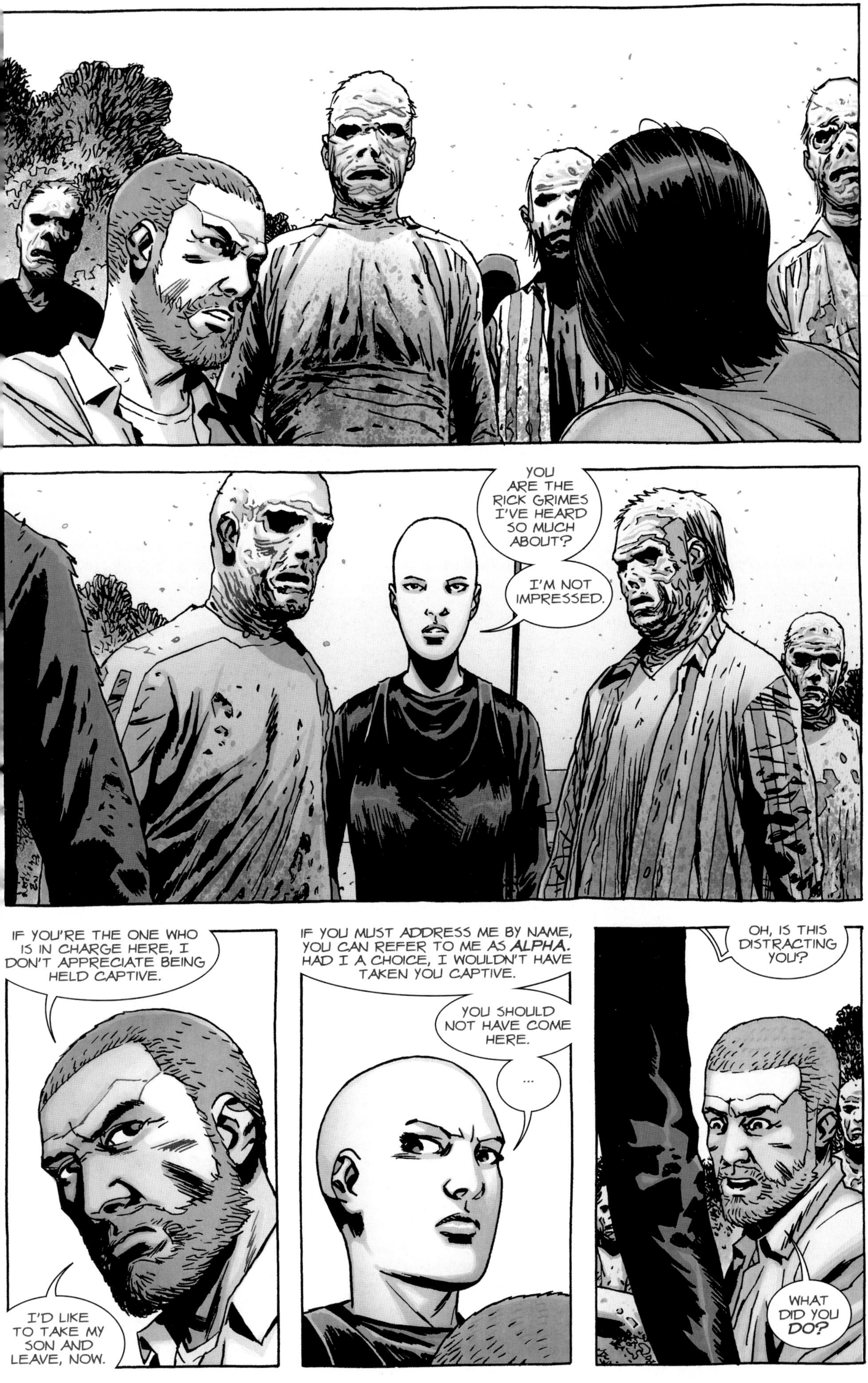
YOU ARE THE RICK GRIMES I'VE HEARD SO MUCH ABOUT?
I'M NOT IMPRESSED.
IF YOU'RE THE ONE WHO IS IN CHARGE HERE, I DON'T APPRECIATE BEING HELD CAPTIVE.
I'D LIKE TO TAKE MY SON AND LEAVE, NOW.
IF YOU MUST ADDRESS ME BY NAME, YOU CAN REFER TO ME AS ALPHA. HAD I A CHOICE, I WOULDN'T HAVE TAKEN YOU CAPTIVE.
YOU SHOULD NOT HAVE COME HERE.
...
OH, IS THIS DISTRACTING YOU?
WHAT DID YOU DO?

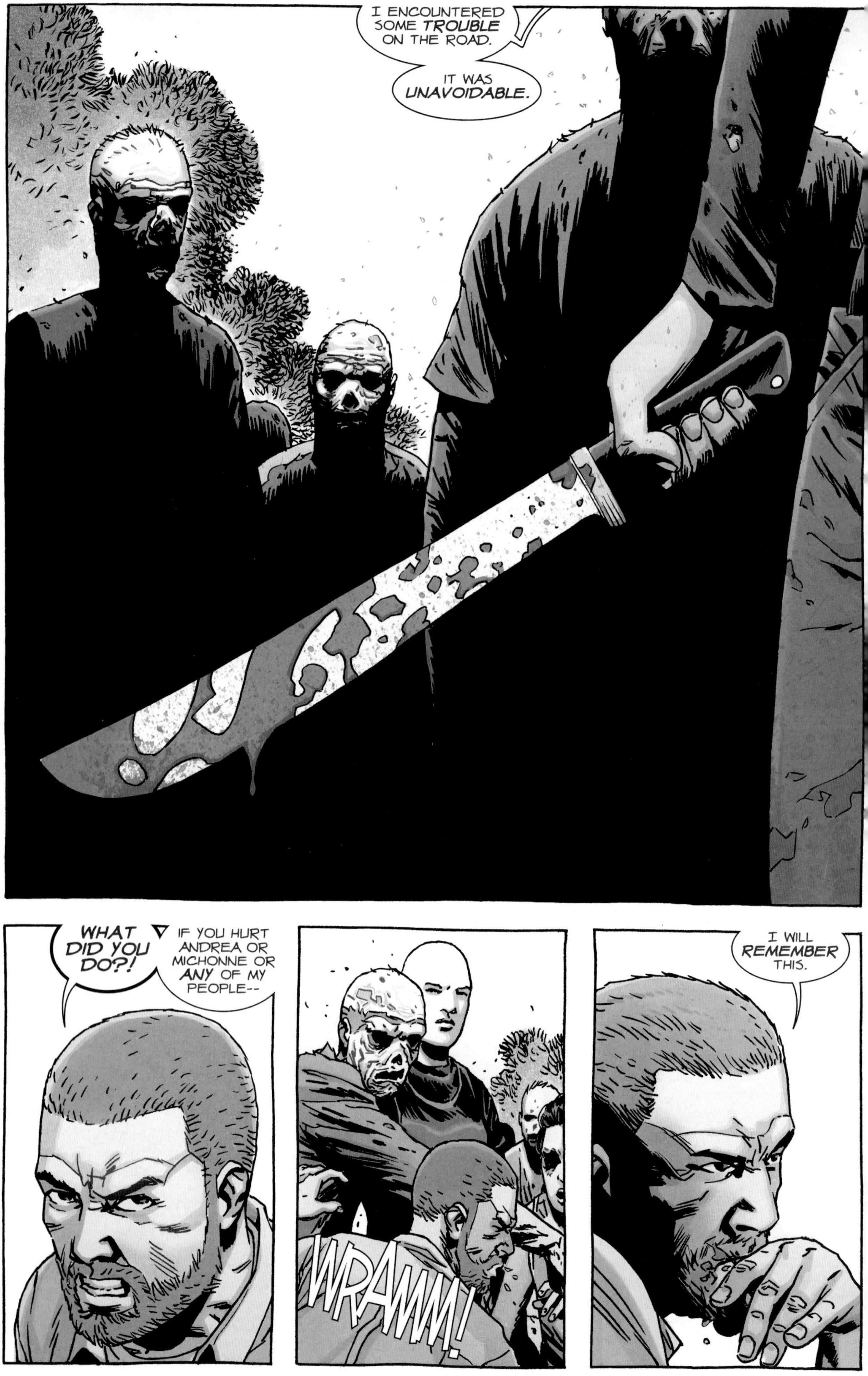
I ENCOUNTERED SOME TROUBLE ON THE ROAD.
IT WAS UNAVOIDABLE.
WHAT DID YOU DO?!
IF YOU HURT ANDREA OR MICHONNE OR ANY OF MY PEOPLE--
WRAMM!
I WILL REMEMBER THIS.

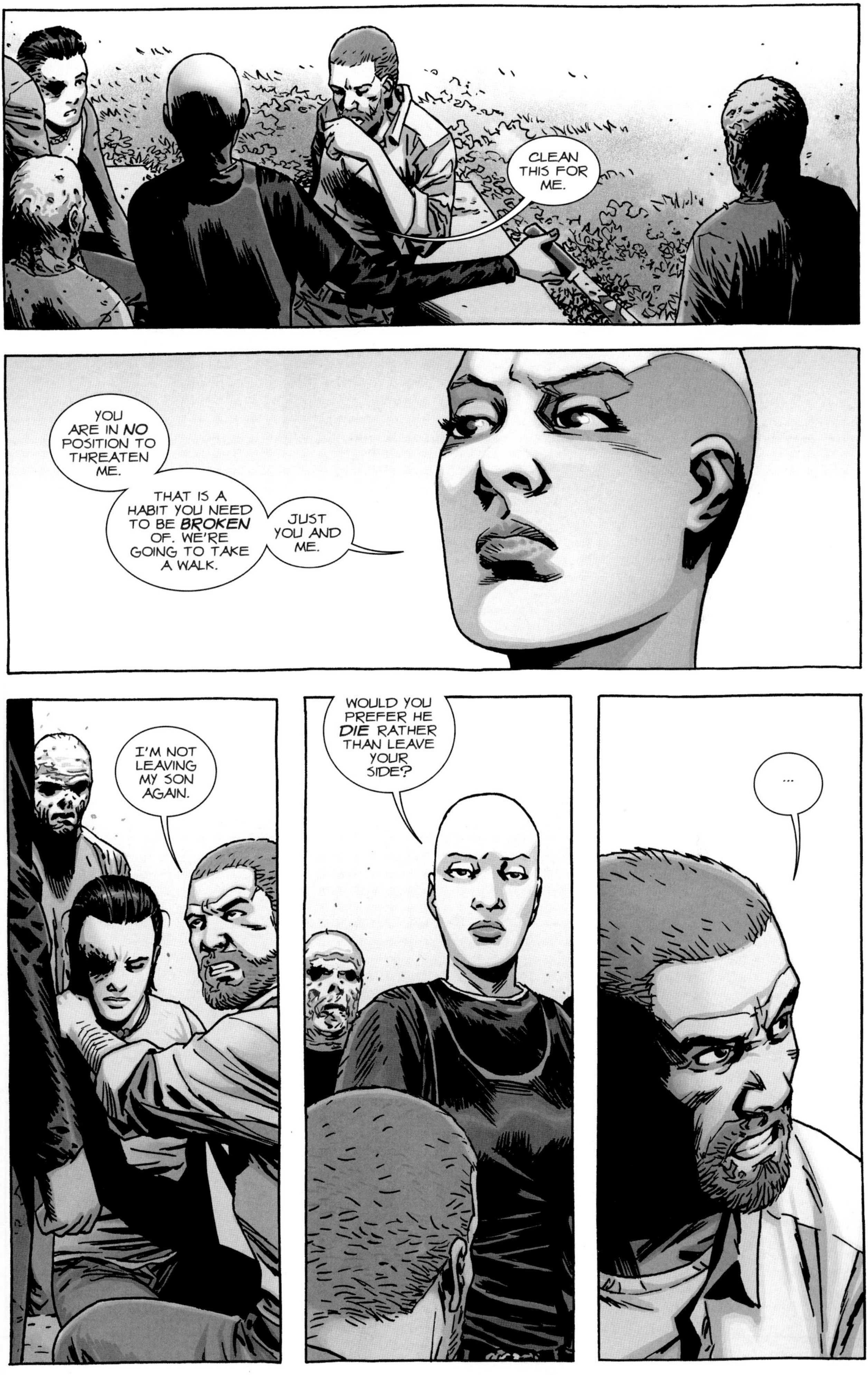
CLEAN THIS FOR ME.
YOU ARE IN NO POSITION TO THREATEN ME.
THAT IS A HABIT YOU NEED TO BE BROKEN OF. WE'RE GOING TO TAKE A WALK.
JUST YOU AND ME.
I'M NOT LEAVING MY SON AGAIN.
WOULD YOU PREFER HE DIE RATHER THAN LEAVE YOUR SIDE?
...

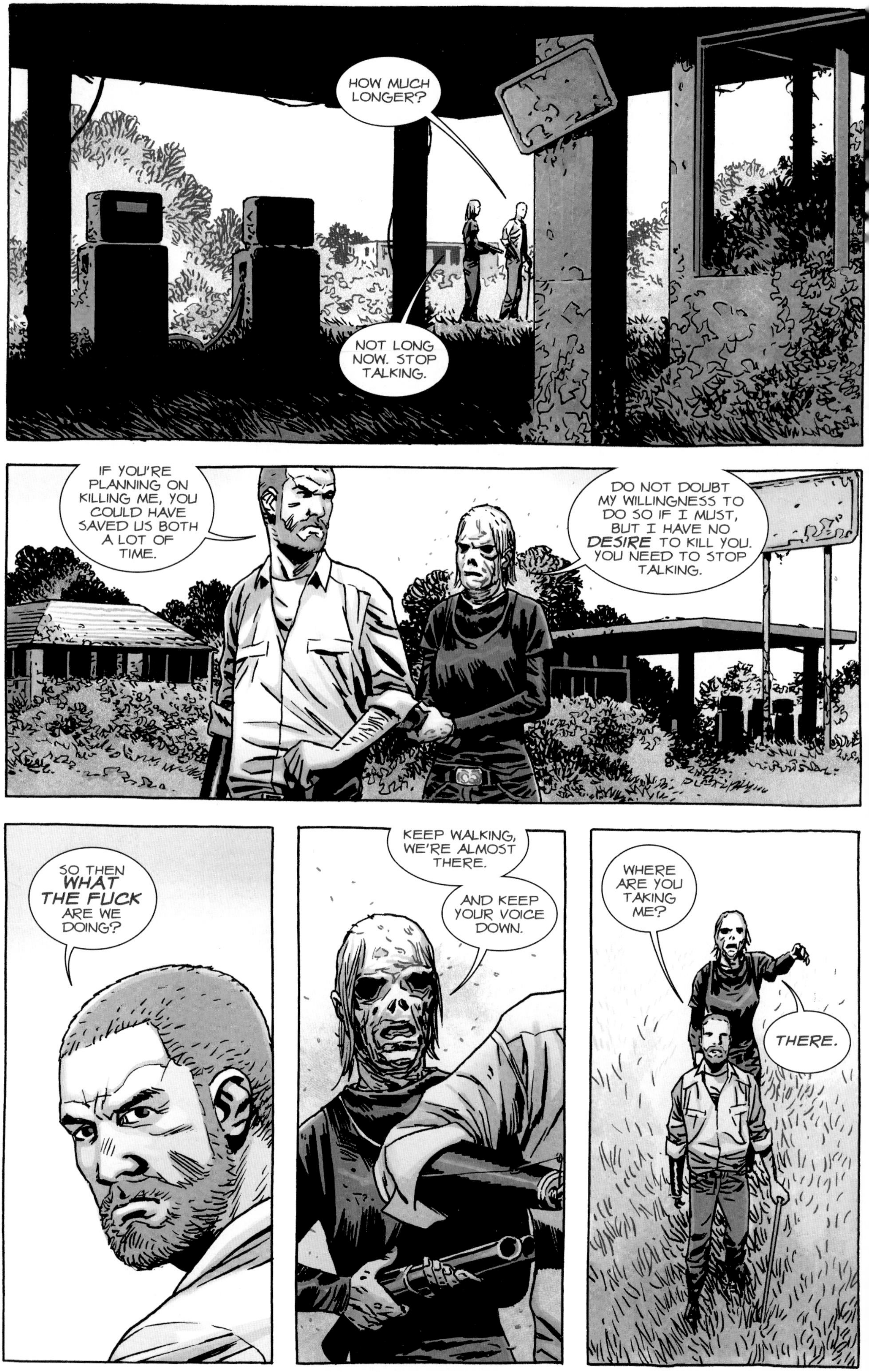
HOW MUCH LONGER?
NOT LONG NOW. STOP TALKING.
IF YOU'RE PLANNING ON KILLING ME, YOU COULD HAVE SAVED US BOTH A LOT OF TIME.
DO NOT DOUBT MY WILLINGNESS TO DO SO IF I MUST, BUT I HAVE NO DESIRE TO KILL YOU. YOU NEED TO STOP TALKING.
SO THEN WHAT THE FUCK ARE WE DOING?
KEEP WALKING, WE'RE ALMOST THERE.
AND KEEP YOUR VOICE DOWN.
WHERE ARE YOU TAKING ME?
THERE.

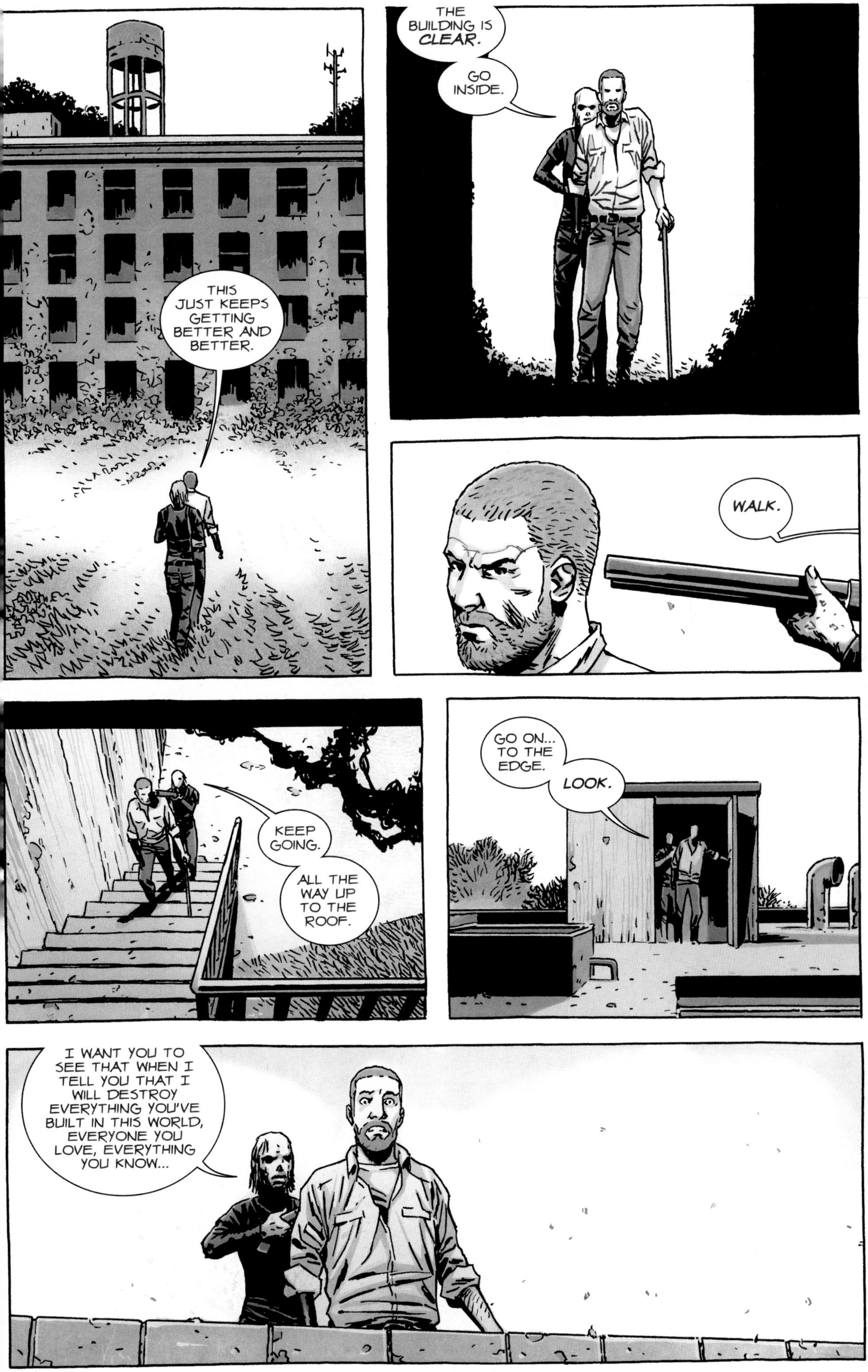
THIS JUST KEEPS GETTING BETTER AND BETTER.
THE BUILDING IS CLEAR.
GO INSIDE.
WALK.
KEEP GOING.
ALL THE WAY UP TO THE ROOF.
GO ON... TO THE EDGE.
LOOK.
I WANT YOU TO SEE THAT WHEN I TELL YOU THAT I WILL DESTROY EVERYTHING YOU'VE BUILT IN THIS WORLD, EVERYONE YOU LOVE, EVERYTHING YOU KNOW...

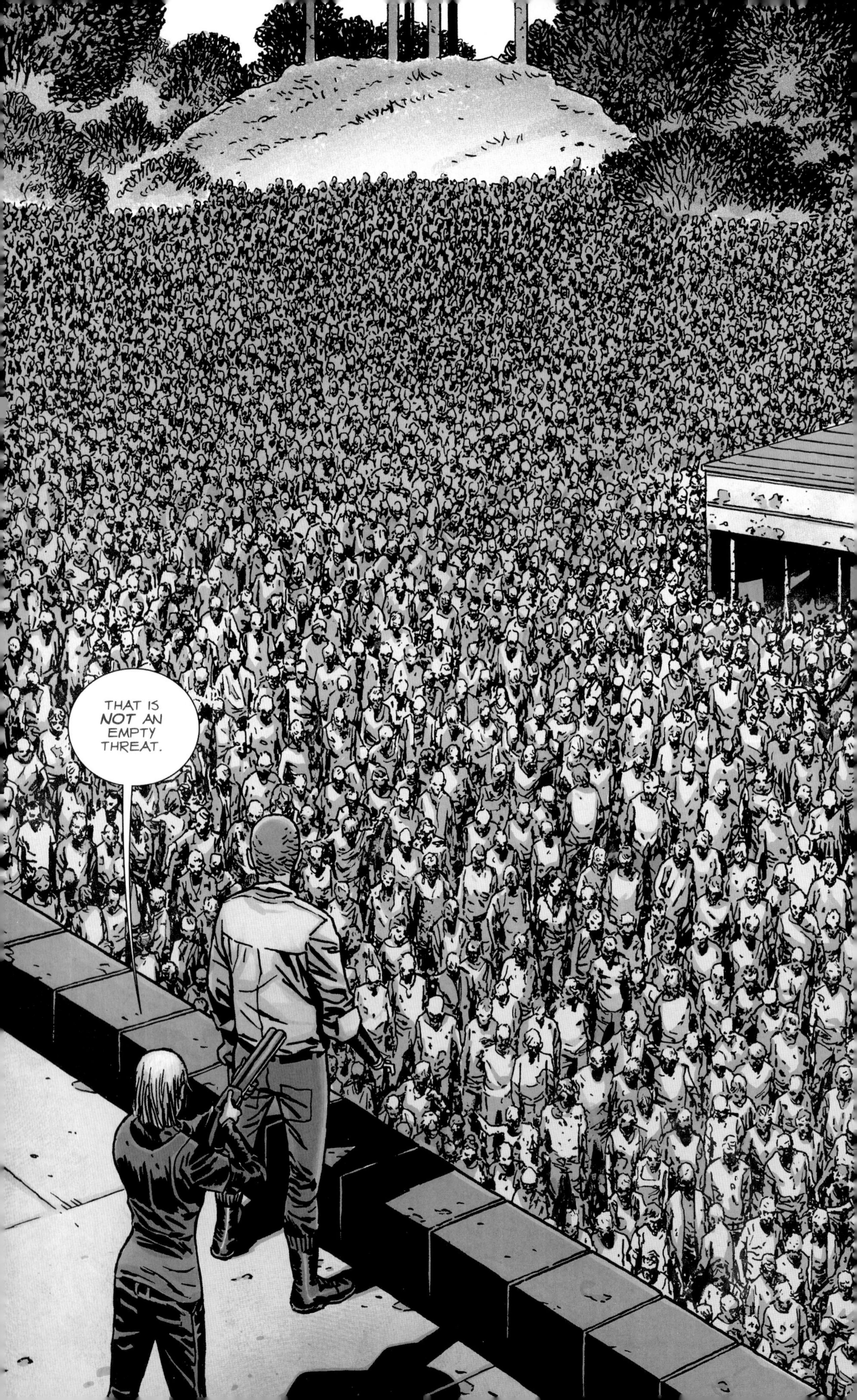
THAT IS *NOT* AN EMPTY THREAT.

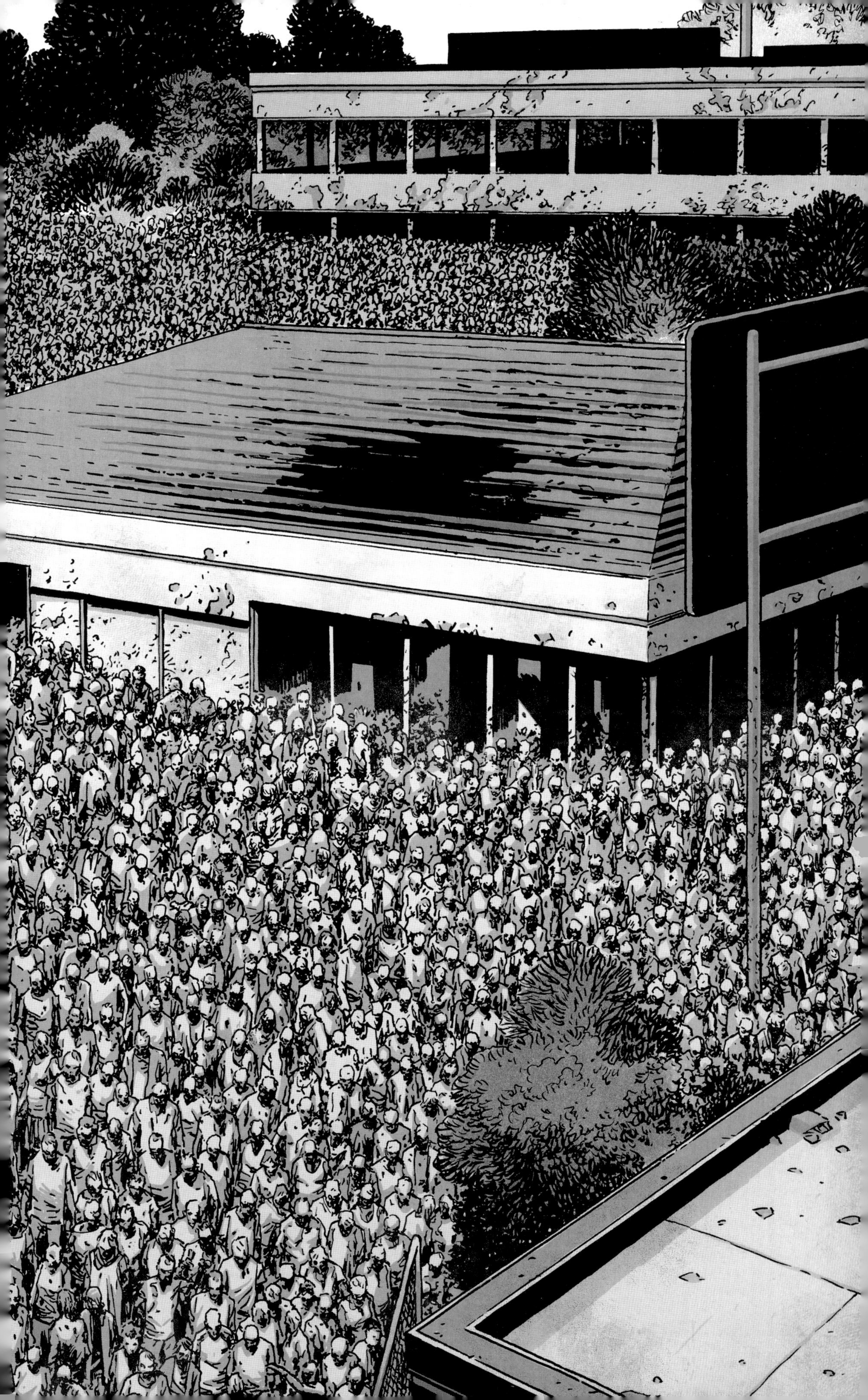

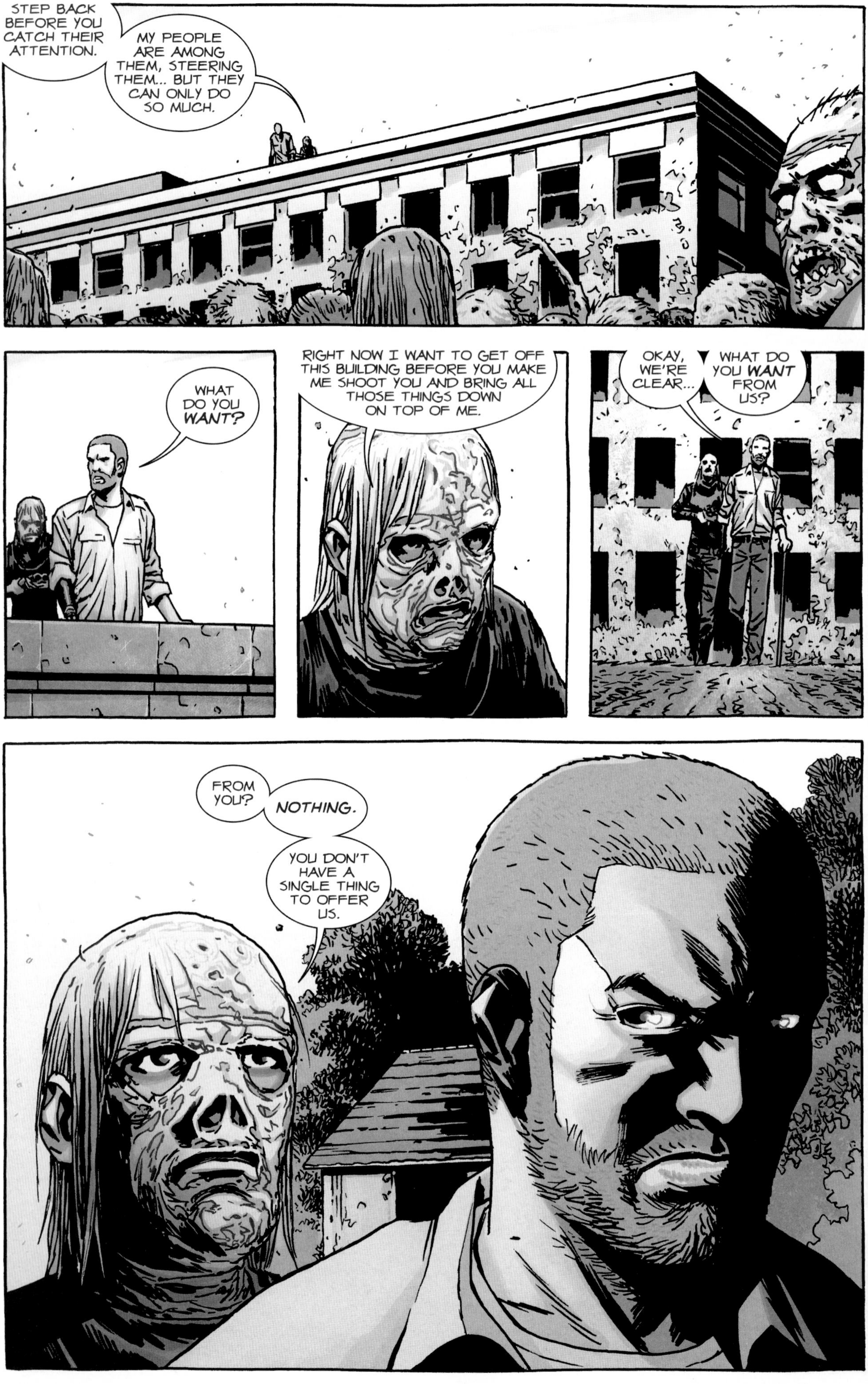
STEP BACK BEFORE YOU CATCH THEIR ATTENTION.
MY PEOPLE ARE AMONG THEM, STEERING THEM... BUT THEY CAN ONLY DO SO MUCH.
WHAT DO YOU WANT?
RIGHT NOW I WANT TO GET OFF THIS BUILDING BEFORE YOU MAKE ME SHOOT YOU AND BRING ALL THOSE THINGS DOWN ON TOP OF ME.
OKAY, WE'RE CLEAR...
WHAT DO YOU WANT FROM US?
FROM YOU?
NOTHING.
YOU DON'T HAVE A SINGLE THING TO OFFER US.

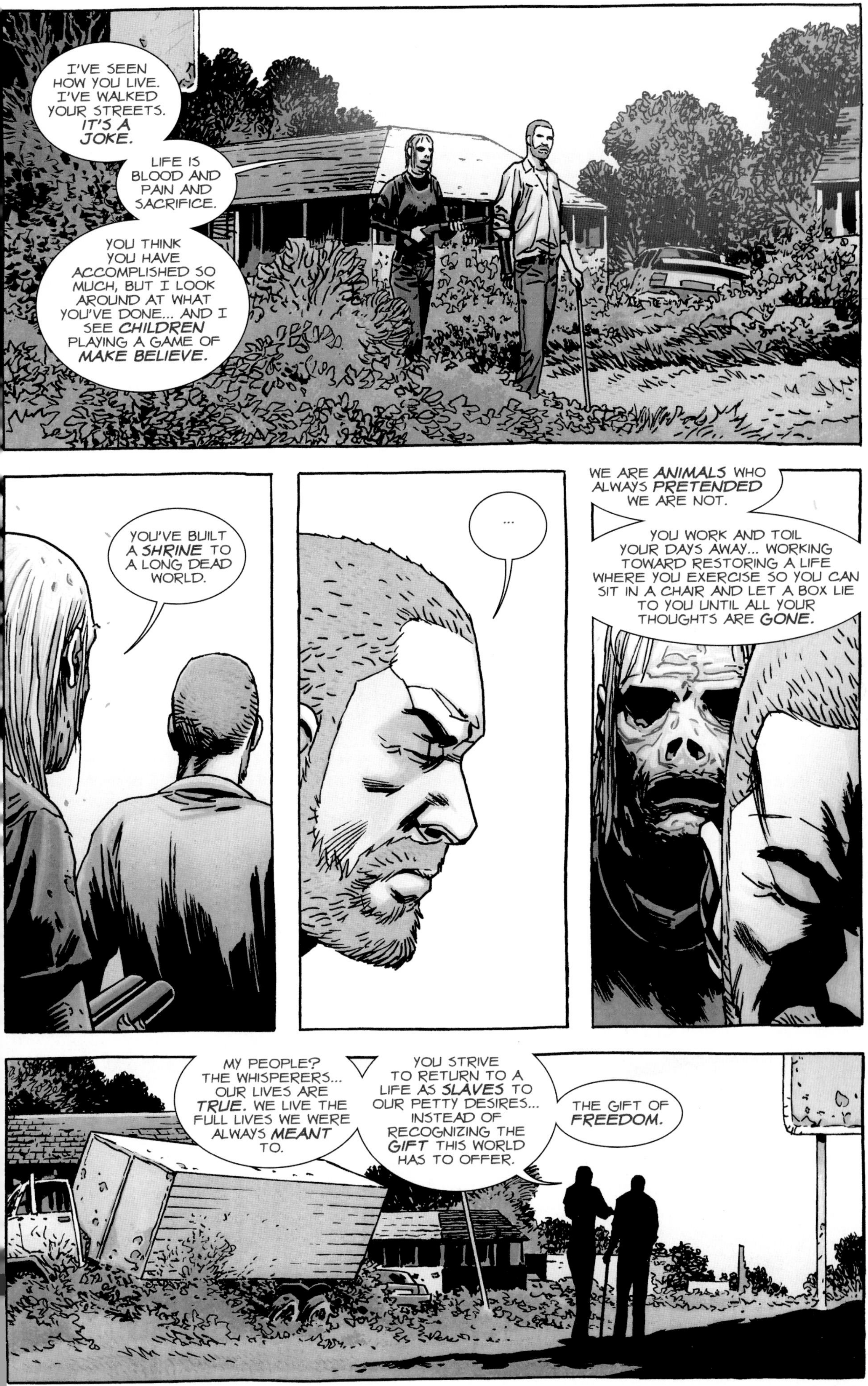
I'VE SEEN HOW YOU LIVE. I'VE WALKED YOUR STREETS. IT'S A JOKE.
LIFE IS BLOOD AND PAIN AND SACRIFICE.
YOU THINK YOU HAVE ACCOMPLISHED SO MUCH, BUT I LOOK AROUND AT WHAT YOU'VE DONE... AND I SEE CHILDREN PLAYING A GAME OF MAKE BELIEVE.
YOU'VE BUILT A SHRINE TO A LONG DEAD WORLD.
...
WE ARE ANIMALS WHO ALWAYS PRETENDED WE ARE NOT.
YOU WORK AND TOIL YOUR DAYS AWAY... WORKING TOWARD RESTORING A LIFE WHERE YOU EXERCISE SO YOU CAN SIT IN A CHAIR AND LET A BOX LIE TO YOU UNTIL ALL YOUR THOUGHTS ARE GONE.
MY PEOPLE? THE WHISPERERS... OUR LIVES ARE TRUE. WE LIVE THE FULL LIVES WE WERE ALWAYS MEANT TO.
YOU STRIVE TO RETURN TO A LIFE AS SLAVES TO OUR PETTY DESIRES... INSTEAD OF RECOGNIZING THE GIFT THIS WORLD HAS TO OFFER.
THE GIFT OF FREEDOM.

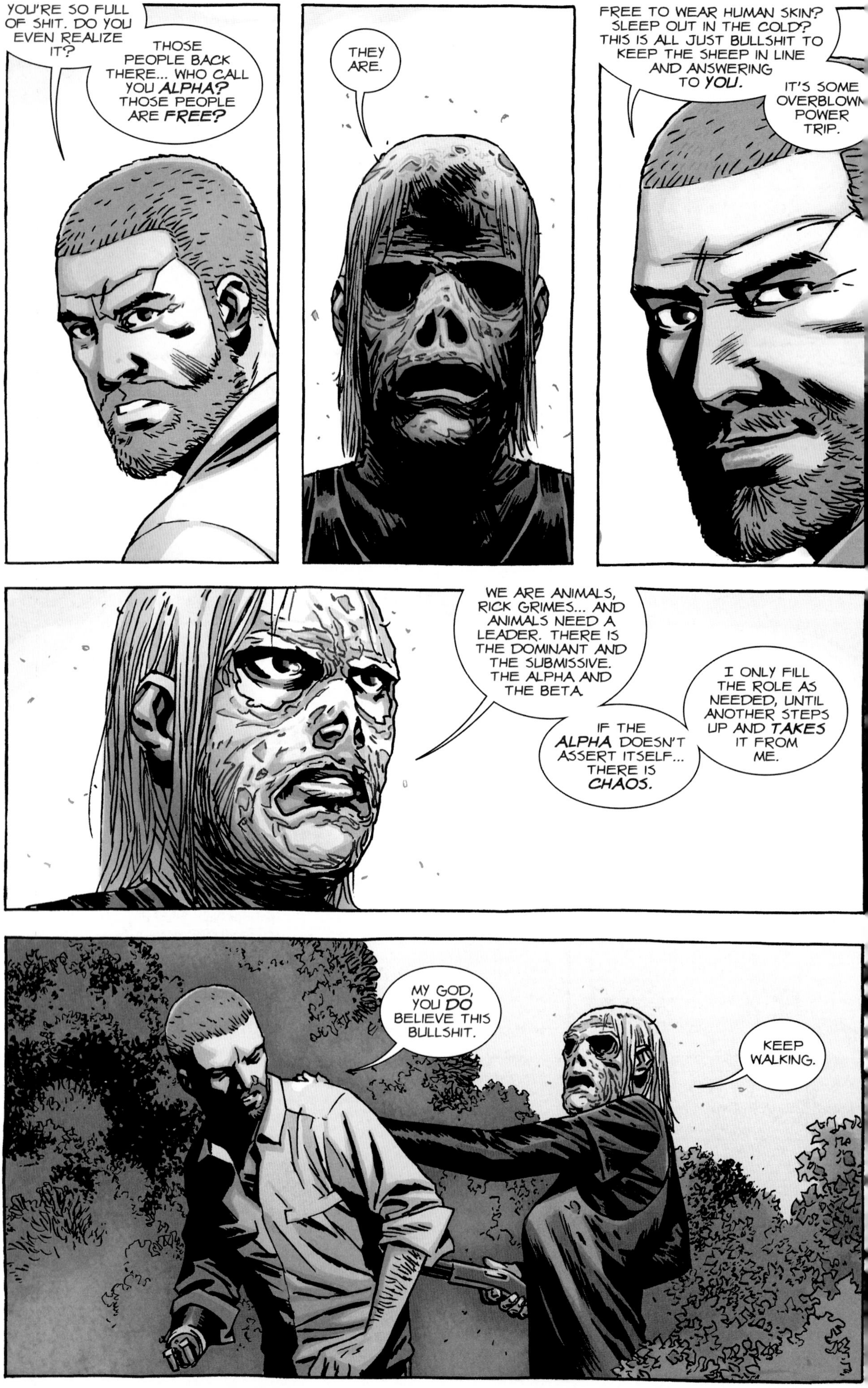
YOU'RE SO FULL OF SHIT. DO YOU EVEN REALIZE IT?
THOSE PEOPLE BACK THERE... WHO CALL YOU ALPHA? THOSE PEOPLE ARE FREE?
THEY ARE.
FREE TO WEAR HUMAN SKIN? SLEEP OUT IN THE COLD? THIS IS ALL JUST BULLSHIT TO KEEP THE SHEEP IN LINE AND ANSWERING TO YOU.
IT'S SOME OVERBLOWN POWER TRIP.
WE ARE ANIMALS, RICK GRIMES... AND ANIMALS NEED A LEADER. THERE IS THE DOMINANT AND THE SUBMISSIVE. THE ALPHA AND THE BETA.
IF THE ALPHA DOESN'T ASSERT ITSELF... THERE IS CHAOS.
I ONLY FILL THE ROLE AS NEEDED, UNTIL ANOTHER STEPS UP AND TAKES IT FROM ME.
MY GOD, YOU DO BELIEVE THIS BULLSHIT.
KEEP WALKING.

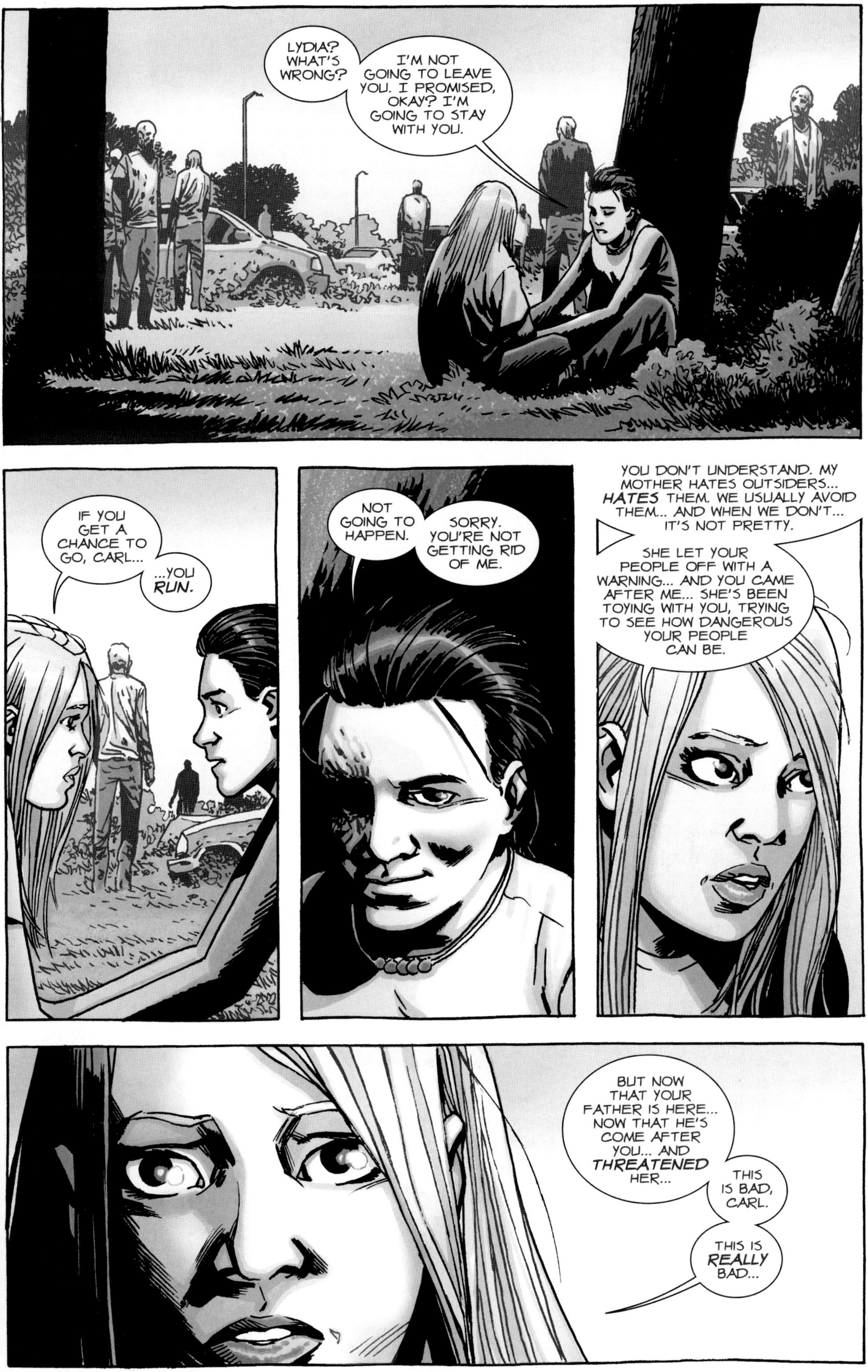
LYDIA? WHAT'S WRONG?
I'M NOT GOING TO LEAVE YOU. I PROMISED, OKAY? I'M GOING TO STAY WITH YOU.
IF YOU GET A CHANCE TO GO, CARL...
...YOU *RUN.*
NOT GOING TO HAPPEN.
SORRY. YOU'RE NOT GETTING RID OF ME.
YOU DON'T UNDERSTAND. MY MOTHER HATES OUTSIDERS... *HATES* THEM. WE USUALLY AVOID THEM... AND WHEN WE DON'T... IT'S NOT PRETTY.
SHE LET YOUR PEOPLE OFF WITH A WARNING... AND YOU CAME AFTER ME... SHE'S BEEN TOYING WITH YOU, TRYING TO SEE HOW DANGEROUS YOUR PEOPLE CAN BE.
BUT NOW THAT YOUR FATHER IS HERE... NOW THAT HE'S COME AFTER YOU... AND *THREATENED* HER...
THIS IS BAD, CARL.
THIS IS *REALLY* BAD...

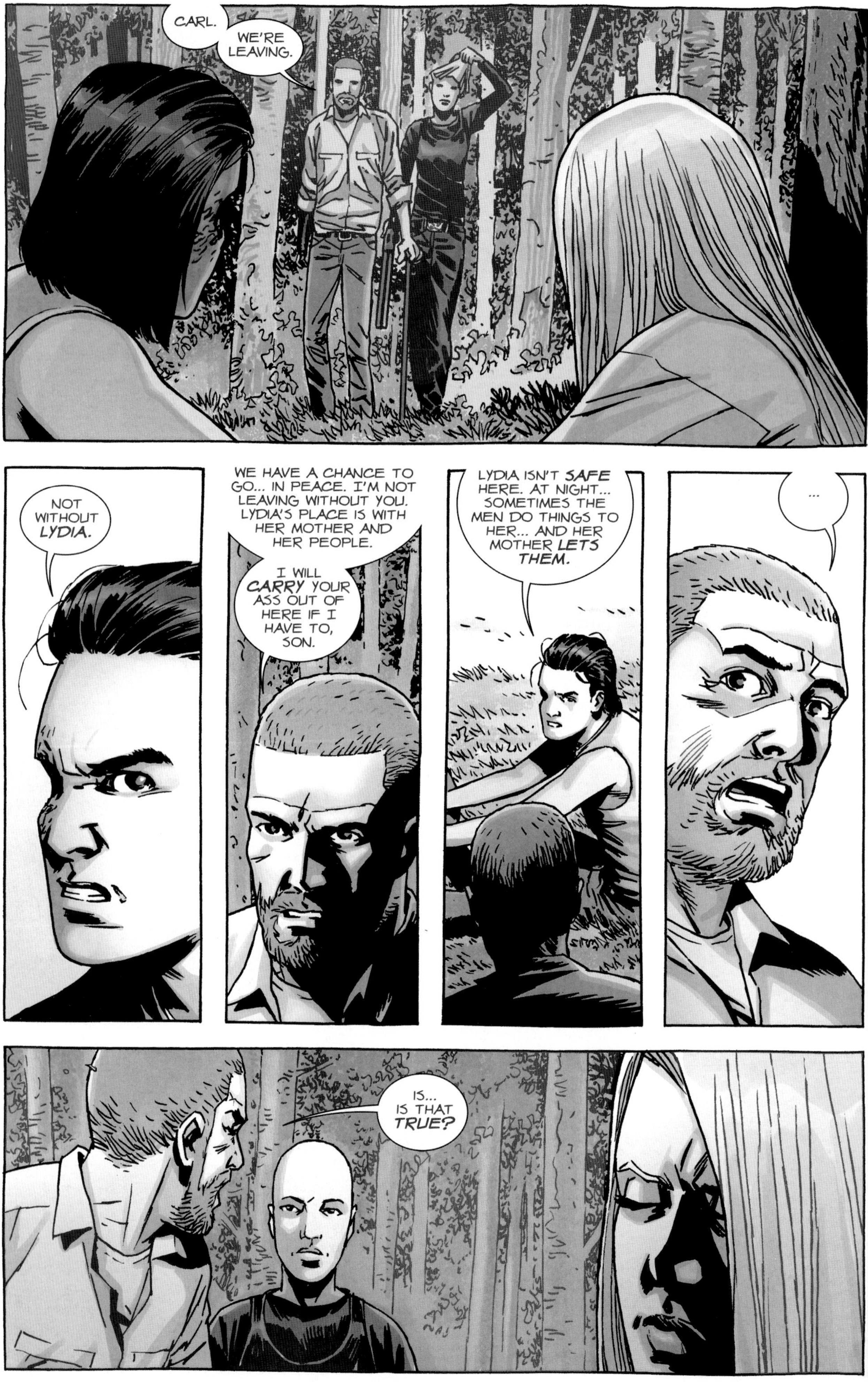
CARL.
WE'RE LEAVING.
NOT WITHOUT LYDIA.
WE HAVE A CHANCE TO GO... IN PEACE. I'M NOT LEAVING WITHOUT YOU. LYDIA'S PLACE IS WITH HER MOTHER AND HER PEOPLE.
I WILL CARRY YOUR ASS OUT OF HERE IF I HAVE TO, SON.
LYDIA ISN'T SAFE HERE. AT NIGHT... SOMETIMES THE MEN DO THINGS TO HER... AND HER MOTHER LETS THEM.
...
IS... IS THAT TRUE?

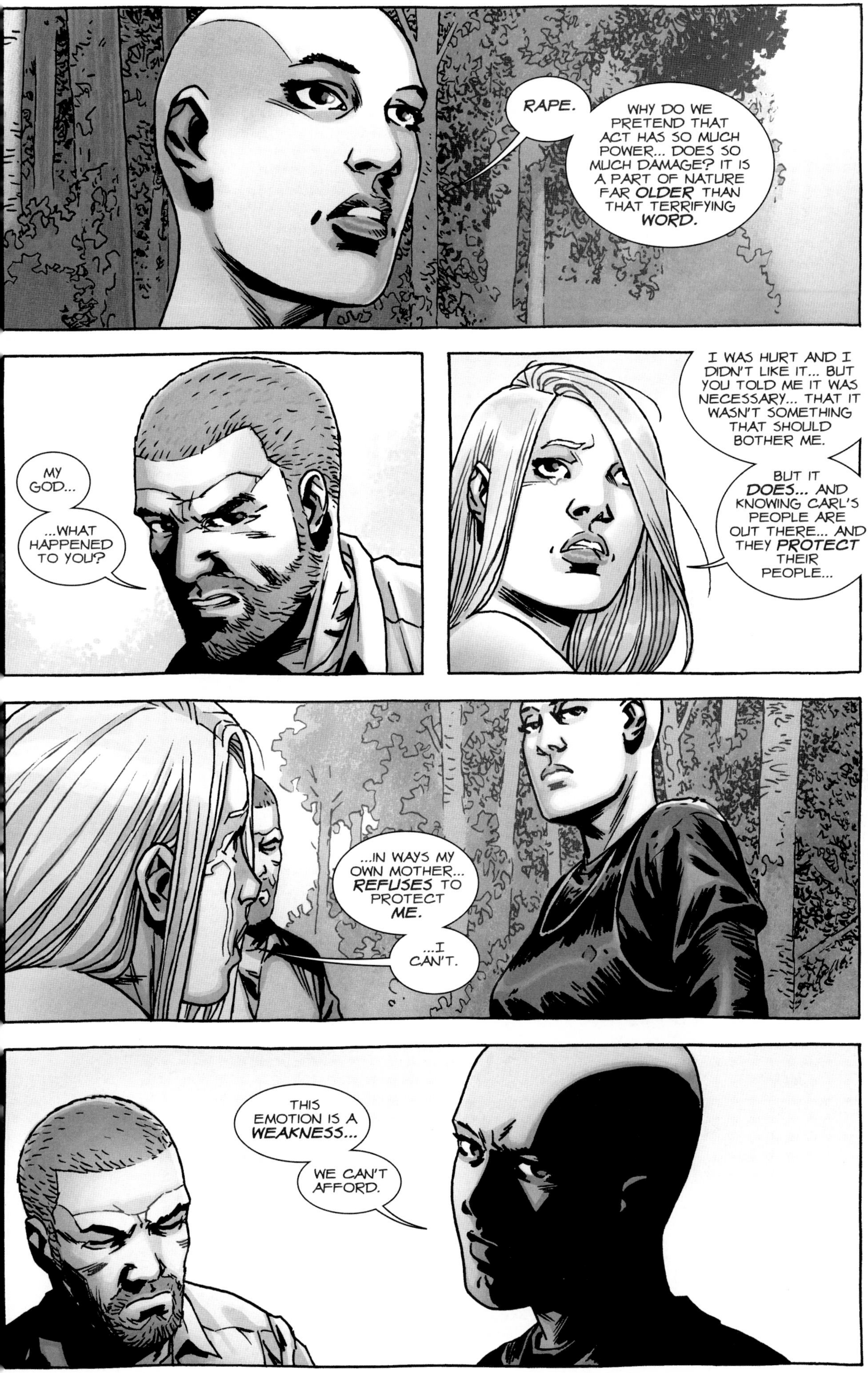
RAPE.
WHY DO WE PRETEND THAT ACT HAS SO MUCH POWER... DOES SO MUCH DAMAGE? IT IS A PART OF NATURE FAR OLDER THAN THAT TERRIFYING WORD.
MY GOD...
...WHAT HAPPENED TO YOU?
I WAS HURT AND I DIDN'T LIKE IT... BUT YOU TOLD ME IT WAS NECESSARY... THAT IT WASN'T SOMETHING THAT SHOULD BOTHER ME.
BUT IT DOES... AND KNOWING CARL'S PEOPLE ARE OUT THERE... AND THEY PROTECT THEIR PEOPLE...
...IN WAYS MY OWN MOTHER... REFUSES TO PROTECT ME.
...I CAN'T.
THIS EMOTION IS A WEAKNESS...
WE CAN'T AFFORD.

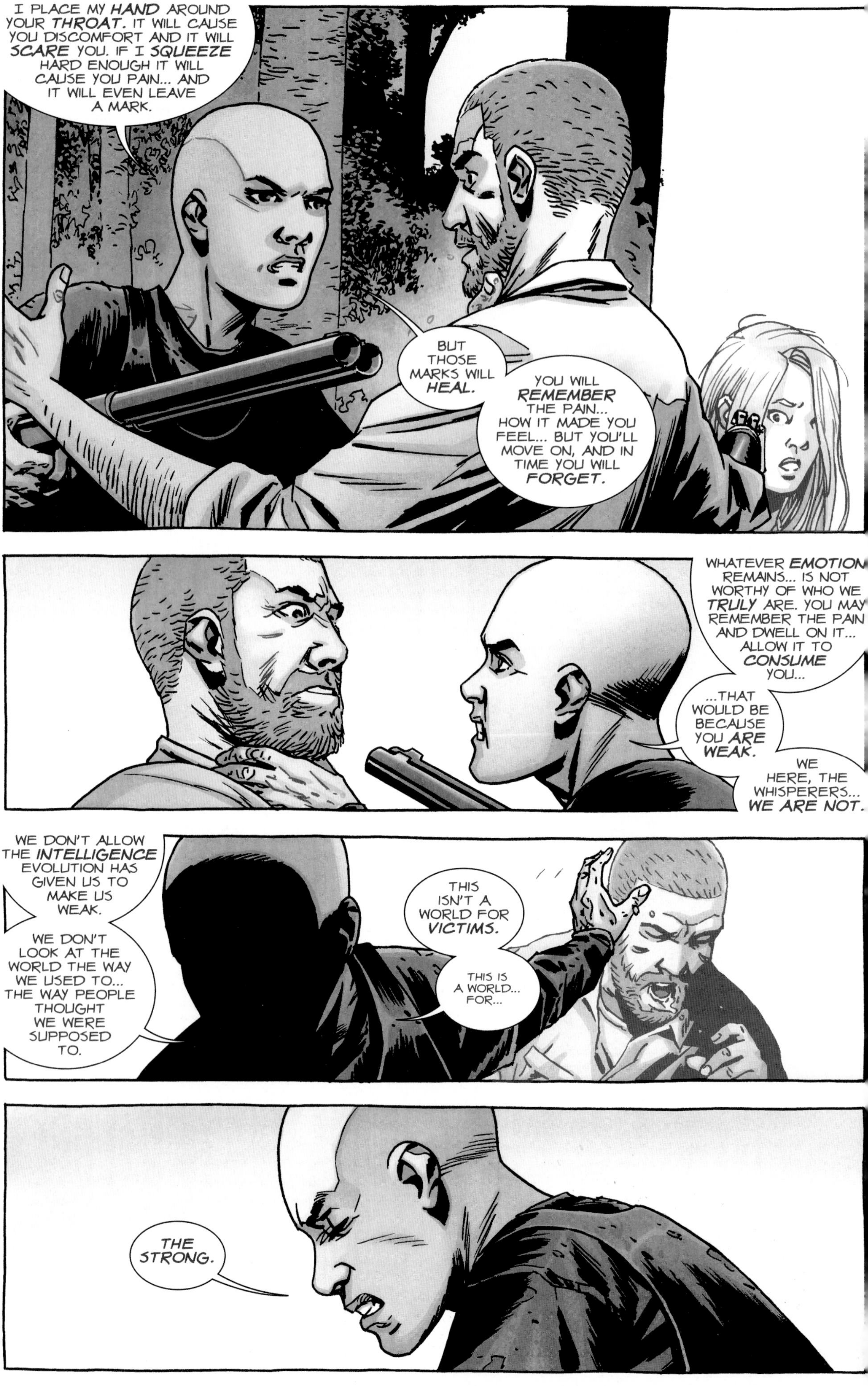
I PLACE MY HAND AROUND YOUR THROAT. IT WILL CAUSE YOU DISCOMFORT AND IT WILL SCARE YOU. IF I SQUEEZE HARD ENOUGH IT WILL CAUSE YOU PAIN... AND IT WILL EVEN LEAVE A MARK.
BUT THOSE MARKS WILL HEAL.
YOU WILL REMEMBER THE PAIN... HOW IT MADE YOU FEEL... BUT YOU'LL MOVE ON, AND IN TIME YOU WILL FORGET.
WHATEVER EMOTION REMAINS... IS NOT WORTHY OF WHO WE TRULY ARE. YOU MAY REMEMBER THE PAIN AND DWELL ON IT... ALLOW IT TO CONSUME YOU...
...THAT WOULD BE BECAUSE YOU ARE WEAK.
WE HERE, THE WHISPERERS... WE ARE NOT.
WE DON'T ALLOW THE INTELLIGENCE EVOLUTION HAS GIVEN US TO MAKE US WEAK.
WE DON'T LOOK AT THE WORLD THE WAY WE USED TO... THE WAY PEOPLE THOUGHT WE WERE SUPPOSED TO.
THIS ISN'T A WORLD FOR VICTIMS.
THIS IS A WORLD... FOR...
THE STRONG.

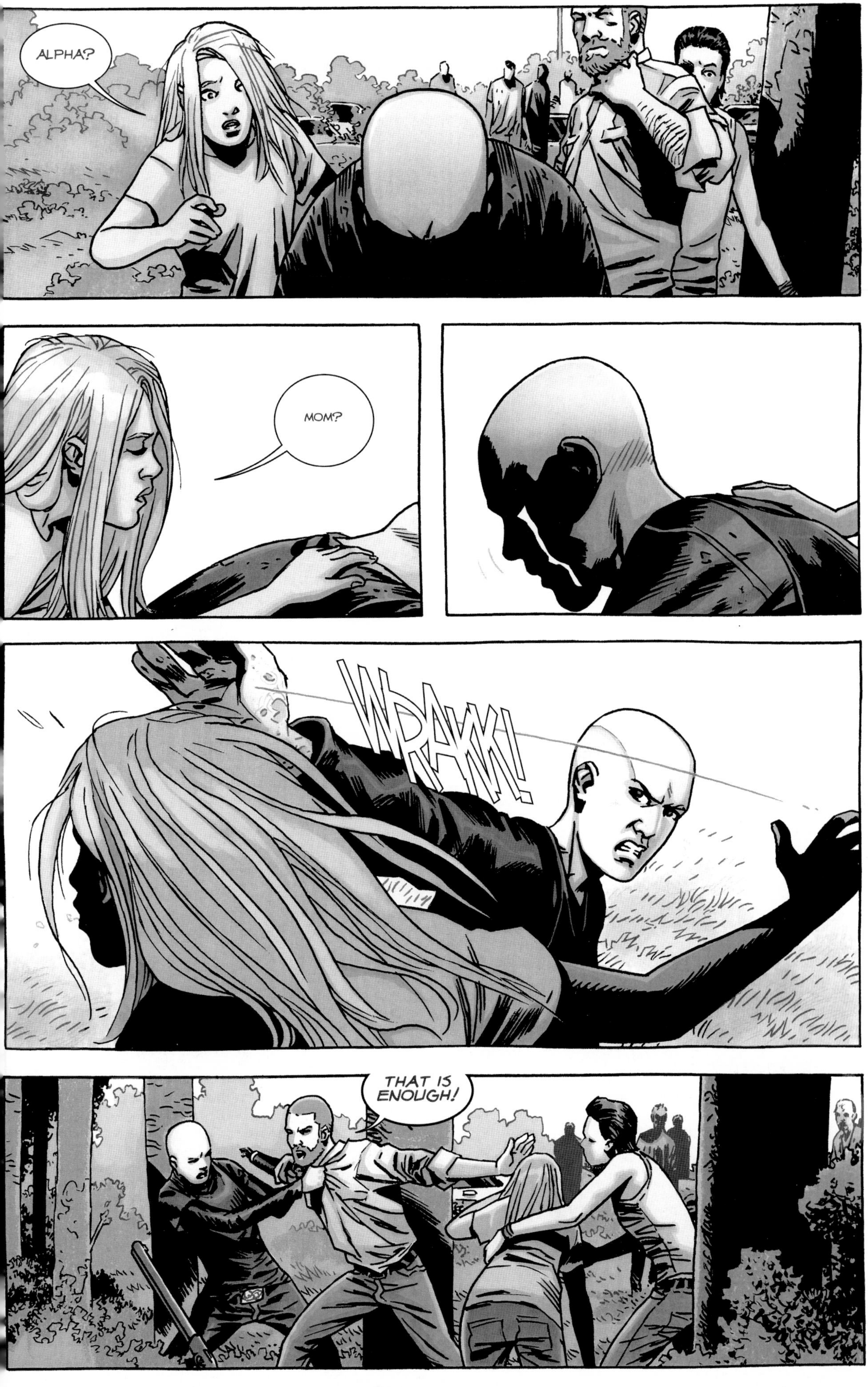
ALPHA?
MOM?
WRAKK!
THAT IS ENOUGH!

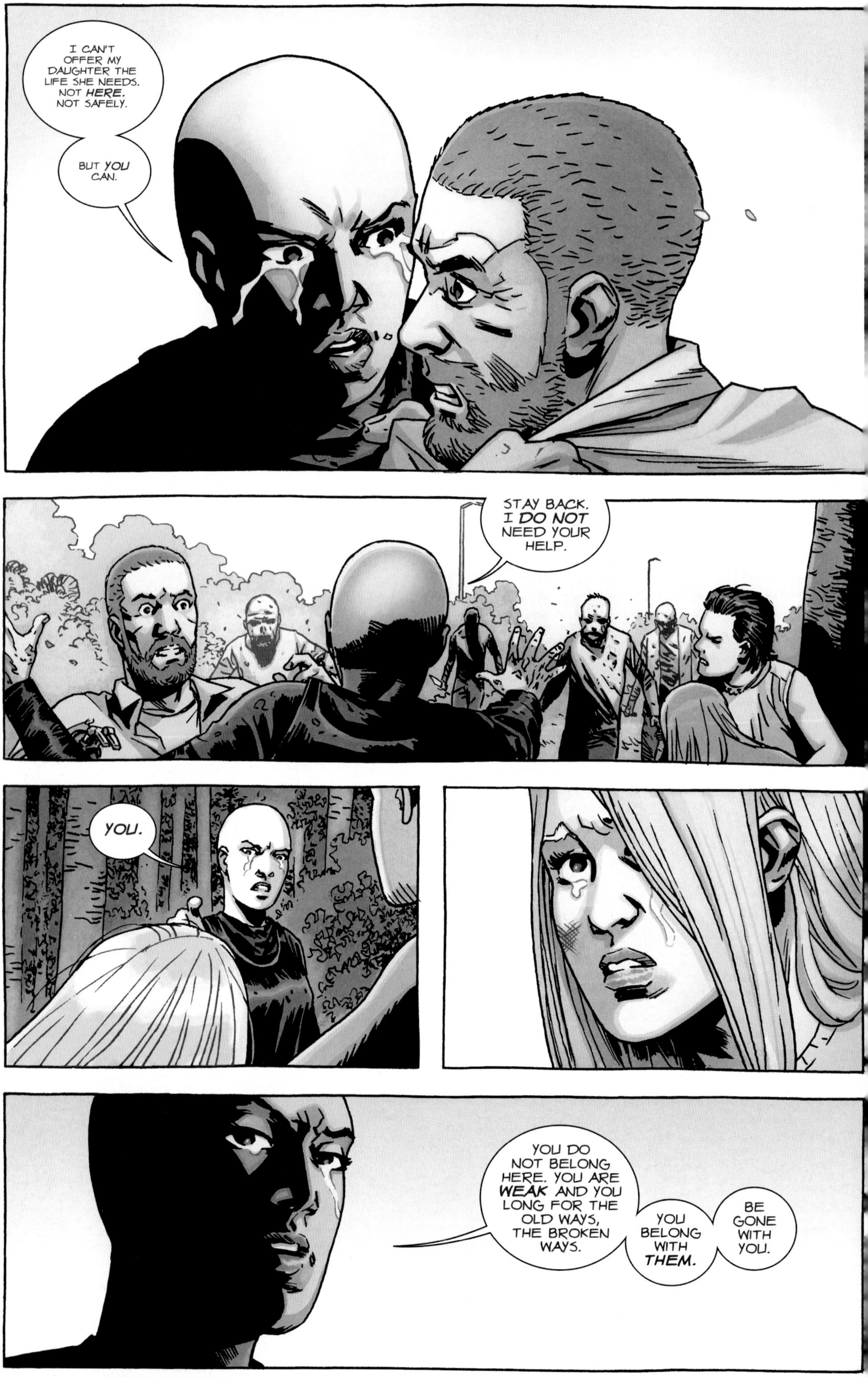
I CAN'T OFFER MY DAUGHTER THE LIFE SHE NEEDS. NOT *HERE.* NOT SAFELY.
BUT *YOU* CAN.
STAY BACK. I *DO NOT* NEED YOUR HELP.
YOU.
YOU DO NOT BELONG HERE. YOU ARE *WEAK* AND YOU LONG FOR THE OLD WAYS, THE BROKEN WAYS.
YOU BELONG WITH *THEM.*
BE GONE WITH YOU.

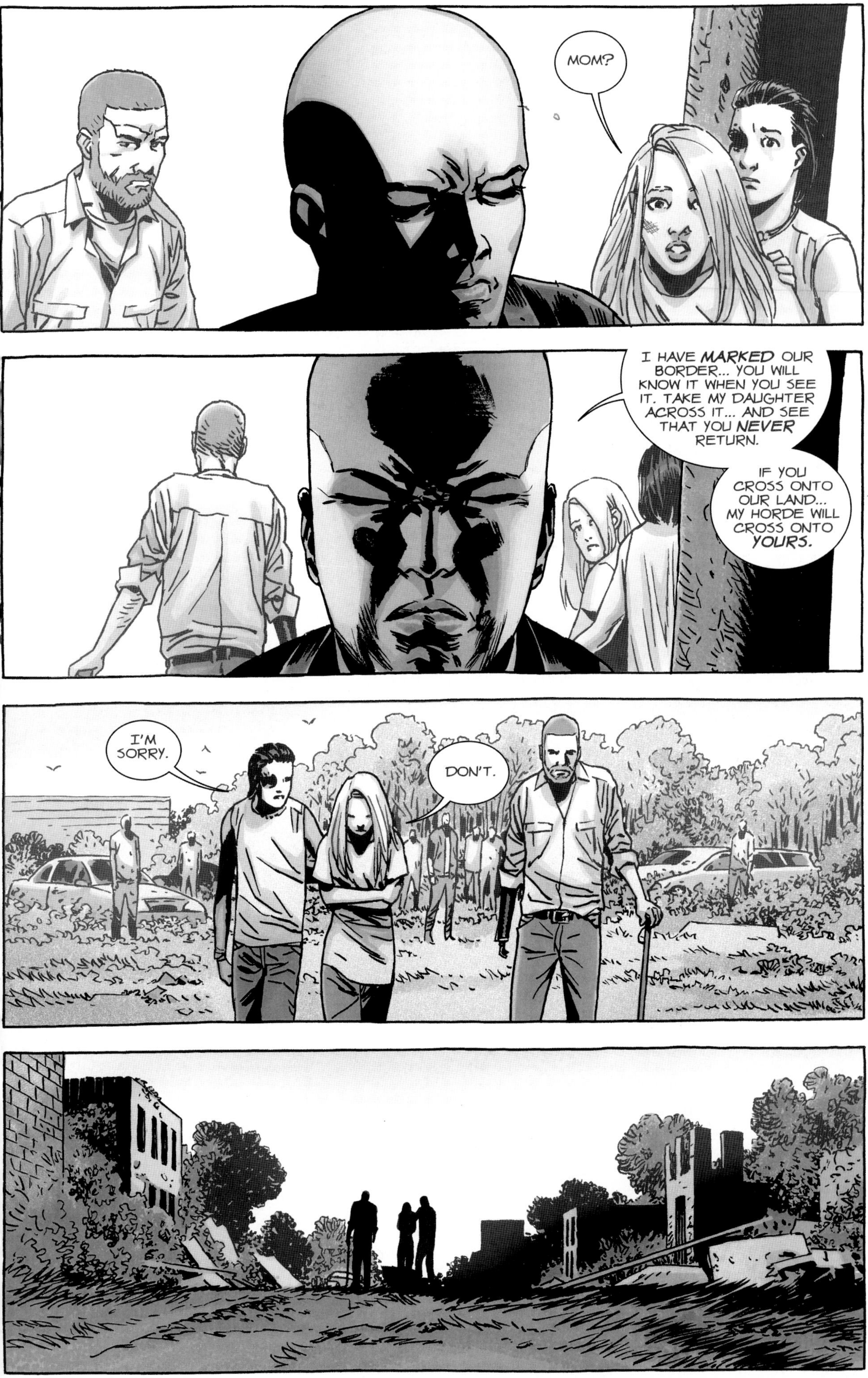
MOM?
I HAVE MARKED OUR BORDER... YOU WILL KNOW IT WHEN YOU SEE IT. TAKE MY DAUGHTER ACROSS IT... AND SEE THAT YOU NEVER RETURN.
IF YOU CROSS ONTO OUR LAND... MY HORDE WILL CROSS ONTO YOURS.
I'M SORRY.
DON'T.

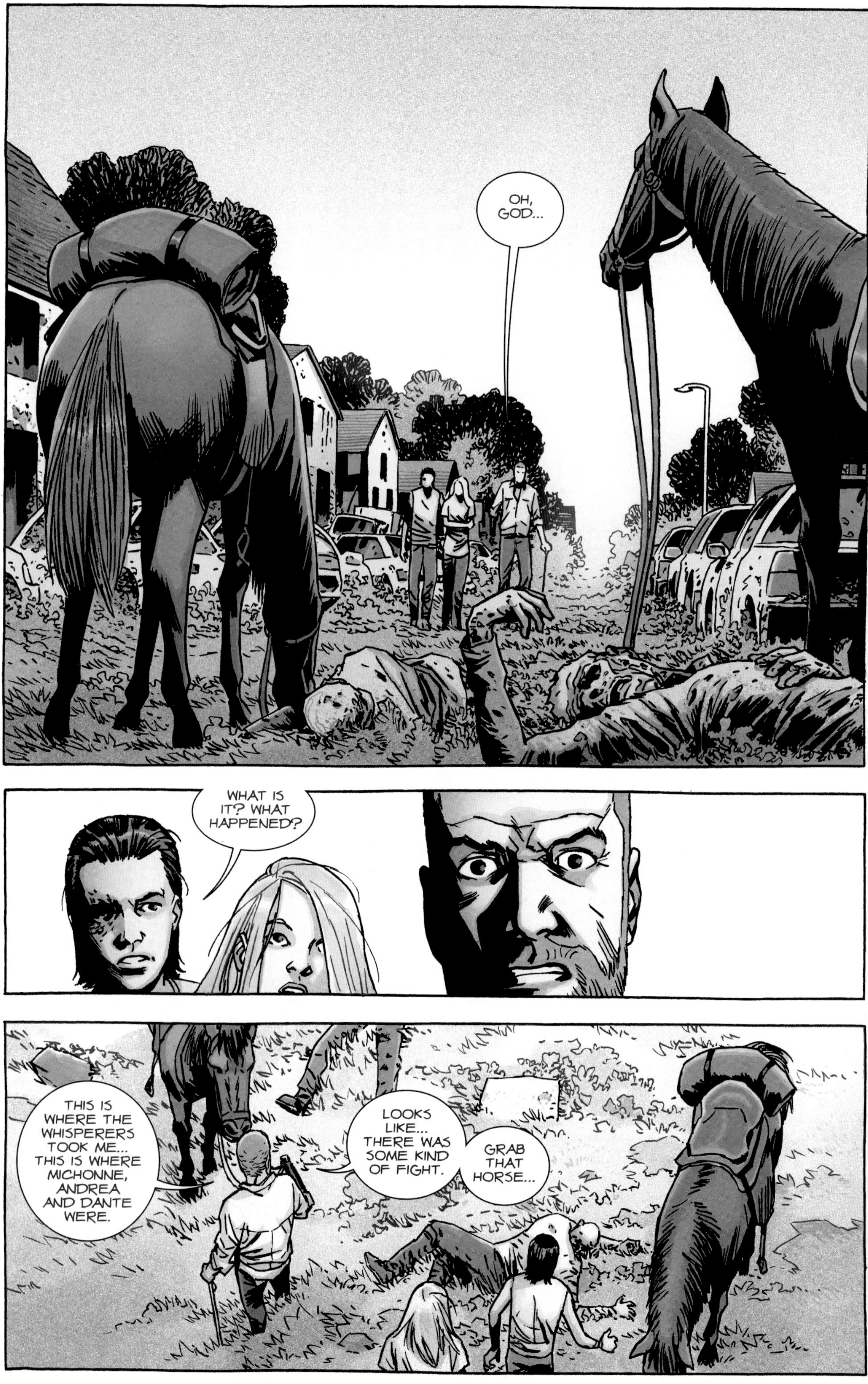
OH, GOD...
WHAT IS IT? WHAT HAPPENED?
THIS IS WHERE THE WHISPERERS TOOK ME... THIS IS WHERE MICHONNE, ANDREA AND DANTE WERE.
LOOKS LIKE... THERE WAS SOME KIND OF FIGHT.
GRAB THAT HORSE...

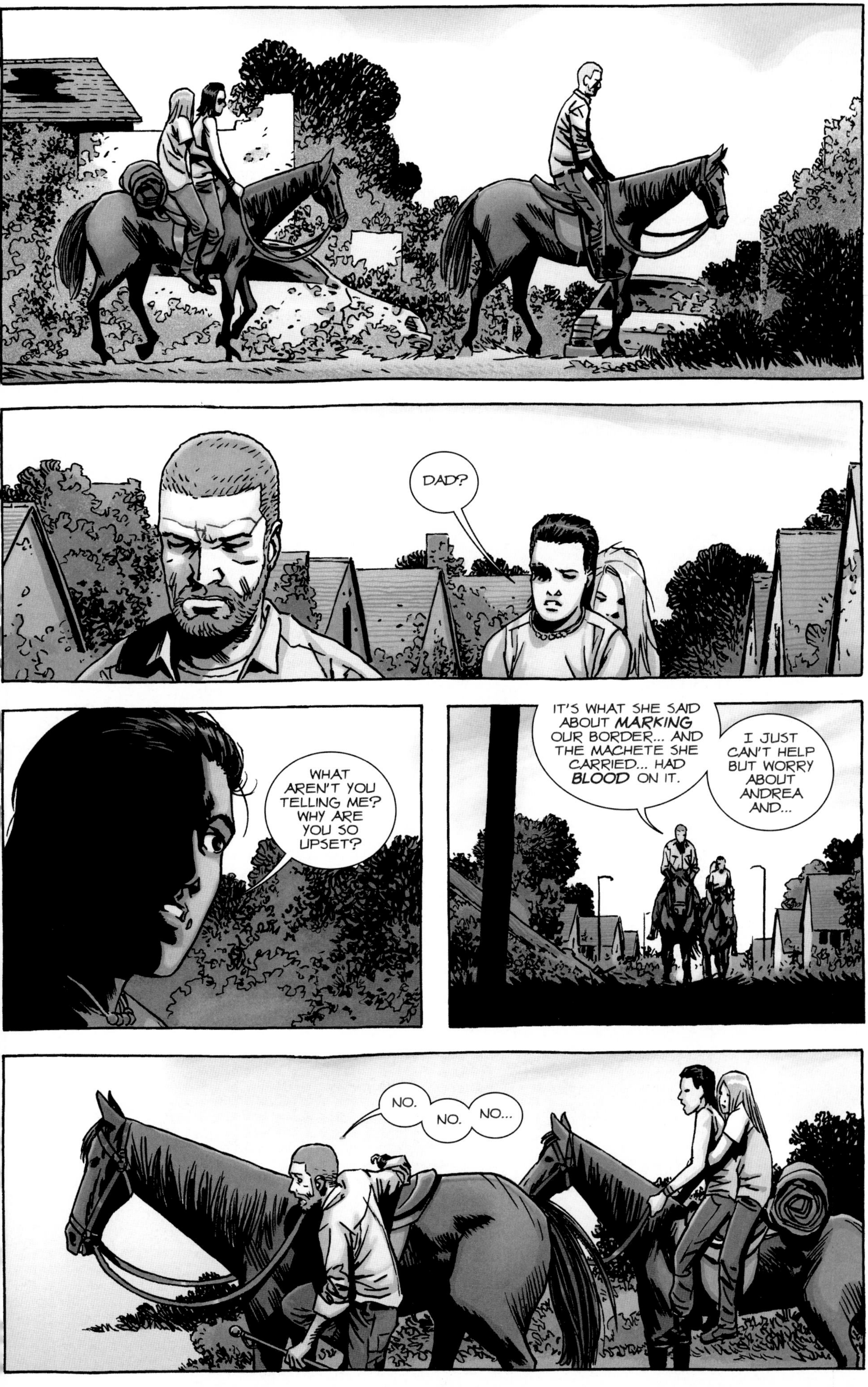
DAD?
WHAT AREN'T YOU TELLING ME? WHY ARE YOU SO UPSET?
IT'S WHAT SHE SAID ABOUT MARKING OUR BORDER... AND THE MACHETE SHE CARRIED... HAD BLOOD ON IT.
I JUST CAN'T HELP BUT WORRY ABOUT ANDREA AND...
NO.
NO.
NO...

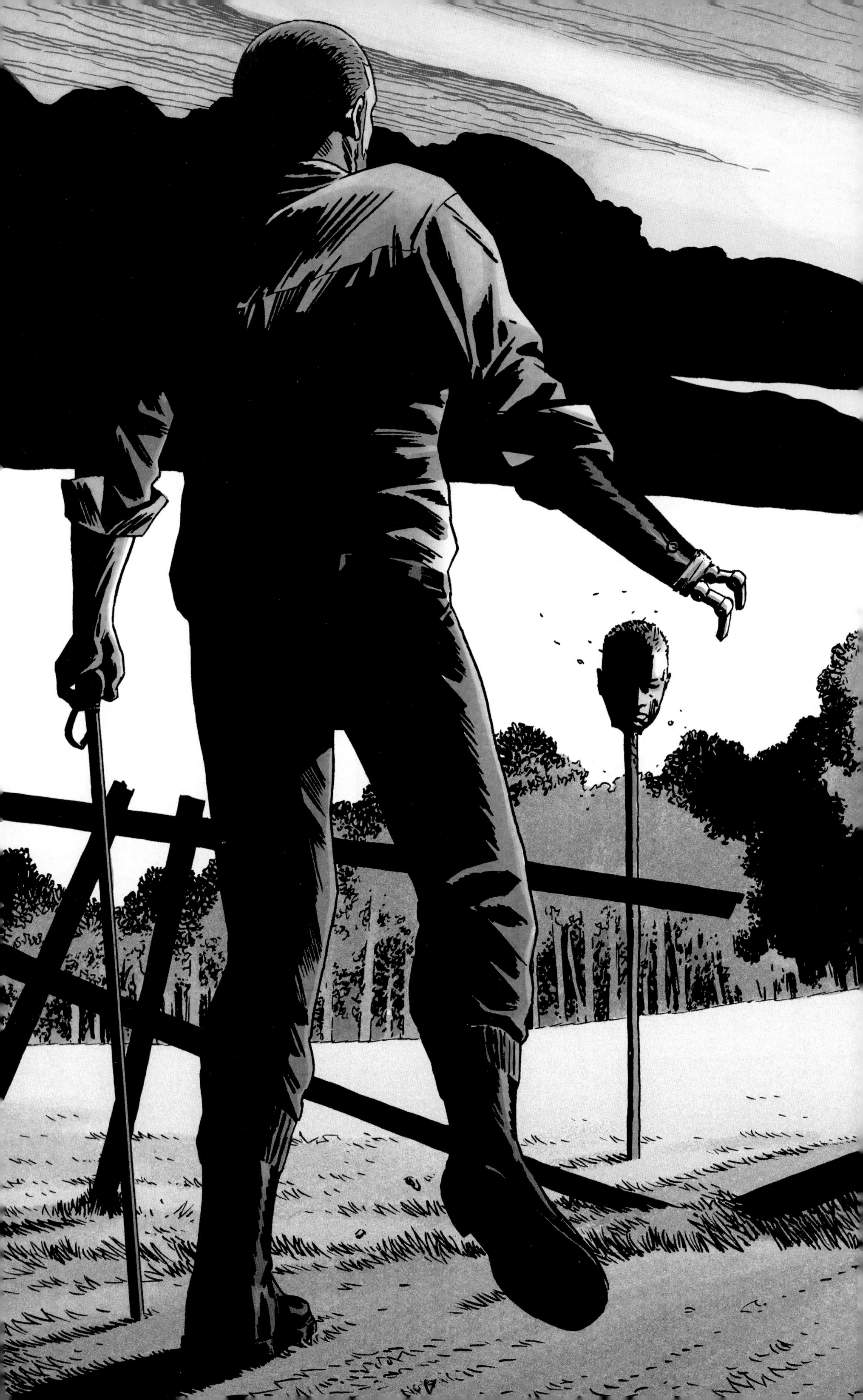

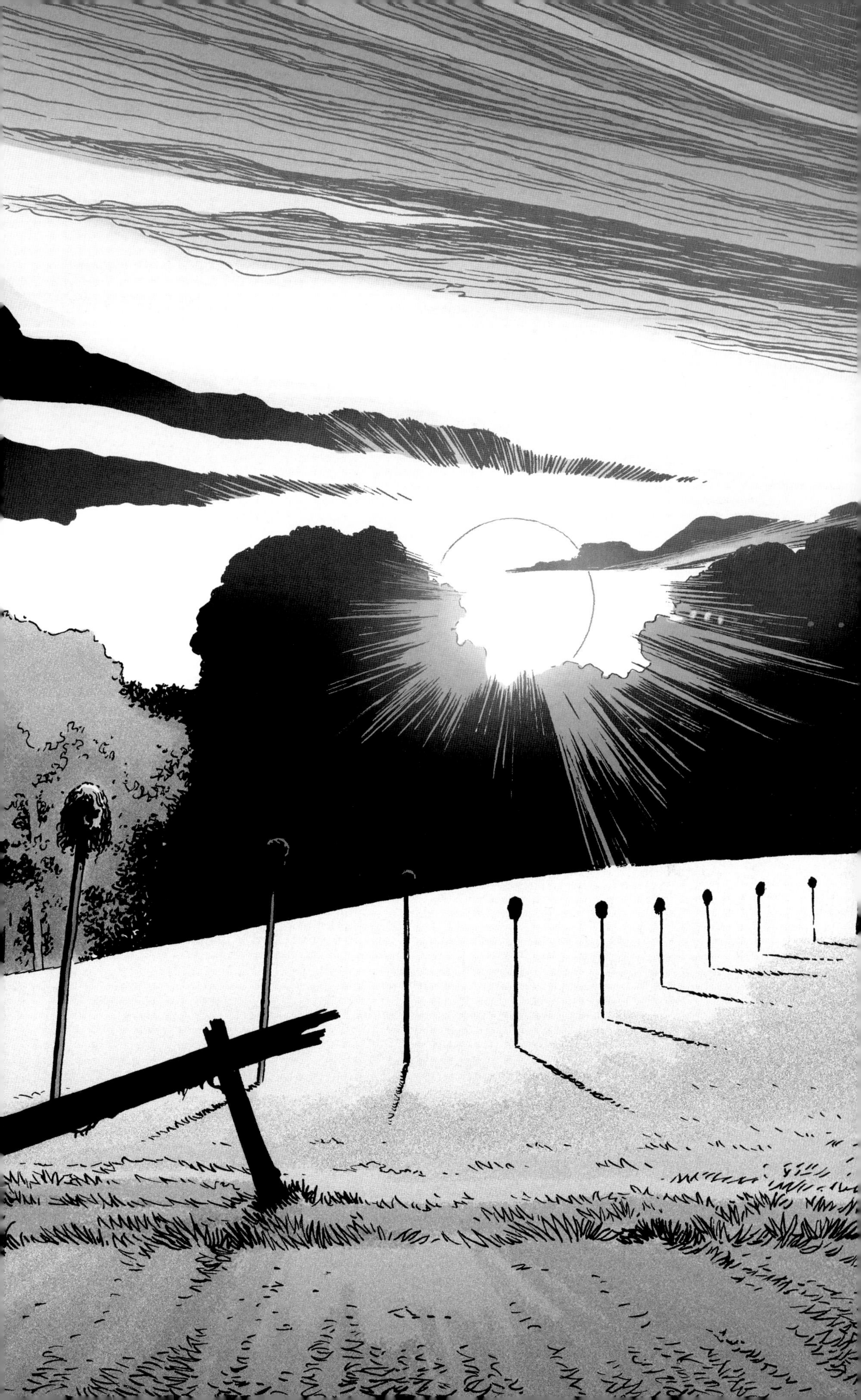

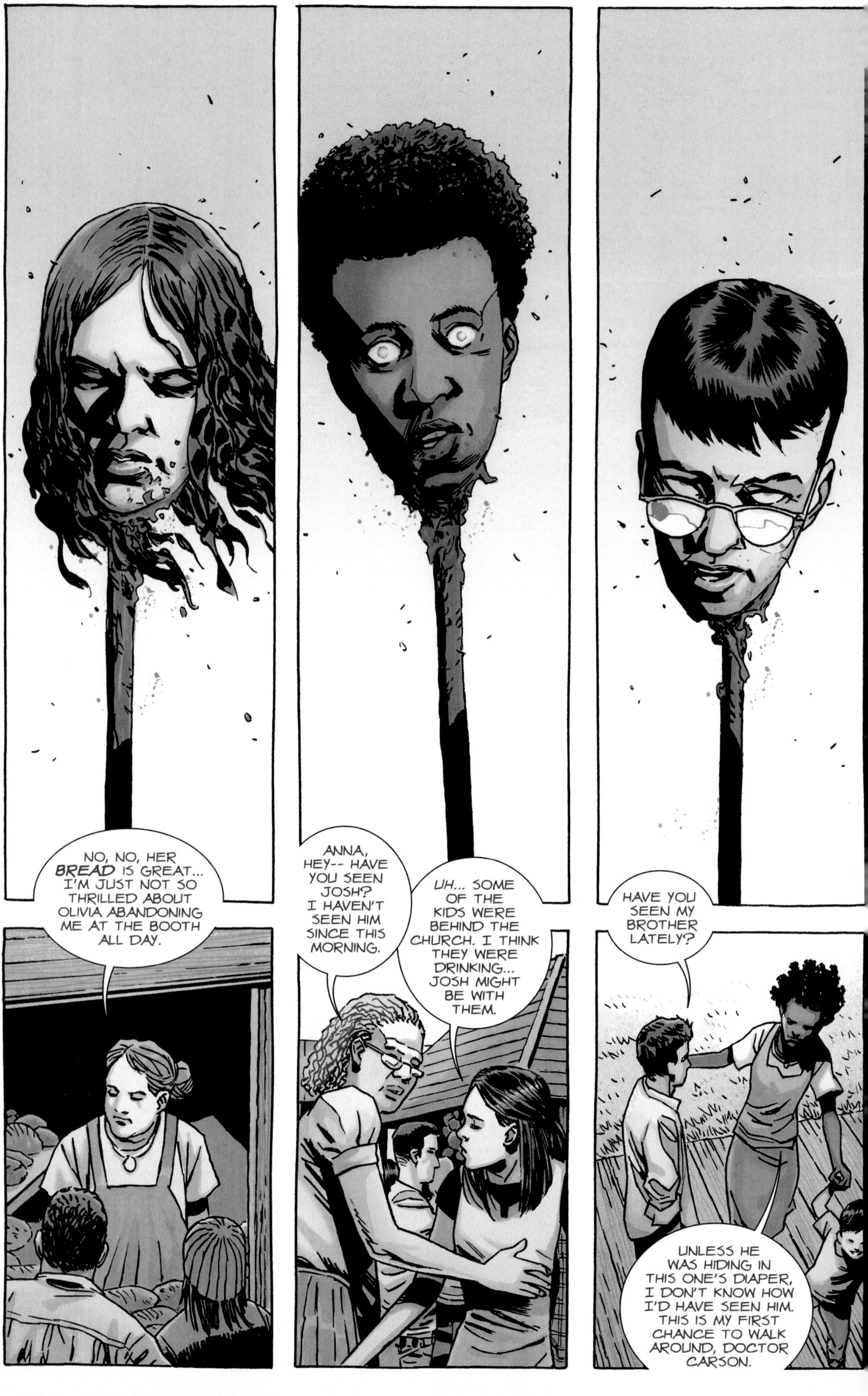
NO, NO, HER BREAD IS GREAT... I'M JUST NOT SO THRILLED ABOUT OLIVIA ABANDONING ME AT THE BOOTH ALL DAY.
ANNA, HEY-- HAVE YOU SEEN JOSH? I HAVEN'T SEEN HIM SINCE THIS MORNING.
UH... SOME OF THE KIDS WERE BEHIND THE CHURCH. I THINK THEY WERE DRINKING... JOSH MIGHT BE WITH THEM.
HAVE YOU SEEN MY BROTHER LATELY?
UNLESS HE WAS HIDING IN THIS ONE'S DIAPER, I DON'T KNOW HOW I'D HAVE SEEN HIM. THIS IS MY FIRST CHANCE TO WALK AROUND, DOCTOR CARSON.

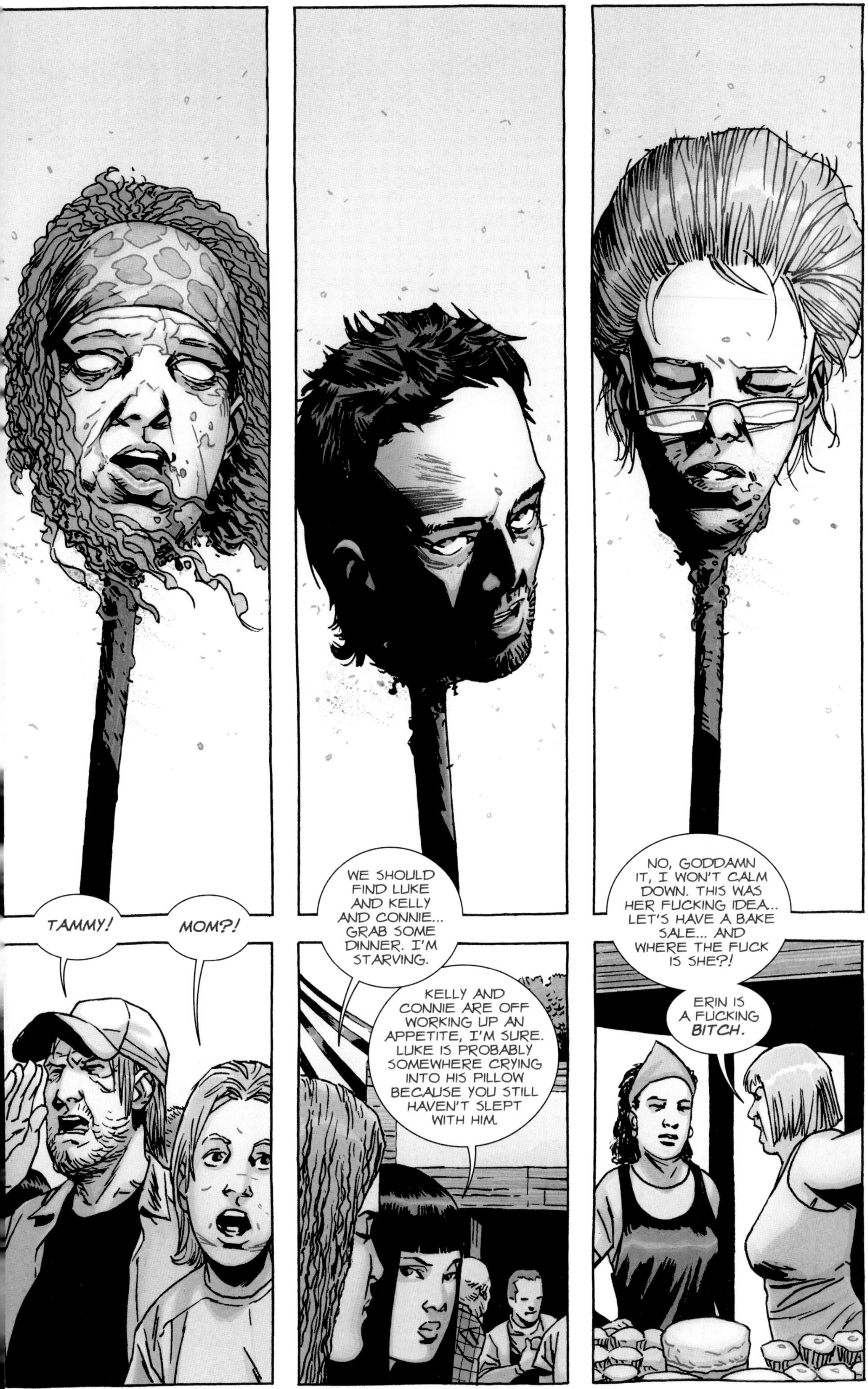
TAMMY!
MOM?!
WE SHOULD FIND LUKE AND KELLY AND CONNIE... GRAB SOME DINNER. I'M STARVING.
KELLY AND CONNIE ARE OFF WORKING UP AN APPETITE, I'M SURE. LUKE IS PROBABLY SOMEWHERE CRYING INTO HIS PILLOW BECAUSE YOU STILL HAVEN'T SLEPT WITH HIM.
NO, GODDAMN IT, I WON'T CALM DOWN. THIS WAS HER FUCKING IDEA.. LET'S HAVE A BAKE SALE... AND WHERE THE FUCK IS SHE?!
ERIN IS A FUCKING *BITCH*.

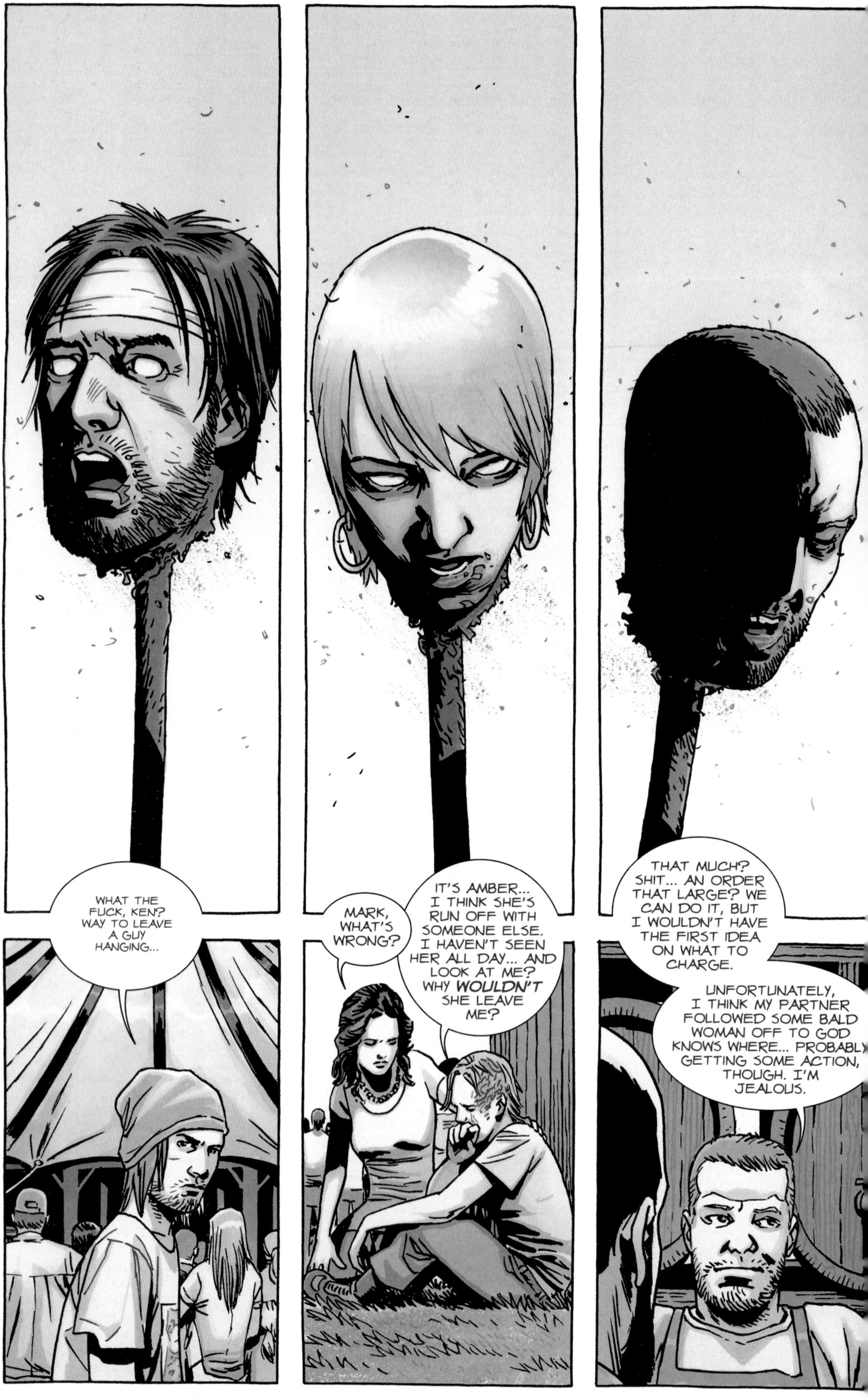
WHAT THE FUCK, KEN? WAY TO LEAVE A GUY HANGING...
MARK, WHAT'S WRONG?
IT'S AMBER... I THINK SHE'S RUN OFF WITH SOMEONE ELSE. I HAVEN'T SEEN HER ALL DAY... AND LOOK AT ME? WHY WOULDN'T SHE LEAVE ME?
THAT MUCH? SHIT... AN ORDER THAT LARGE? WE CAN DO IT, BUT I WOULDN'T HAVE THE FIRST IDEA ON WHAT TO CHARGE.
UNFORTUNATELY, I THINK MY PARTNER FOLLOWED SOME BALD WOMAN OFF TO GOD KNOWS WHERE... PROBABLY GETTING SOME ACTION, THOUGH. I'M JEALOUS.

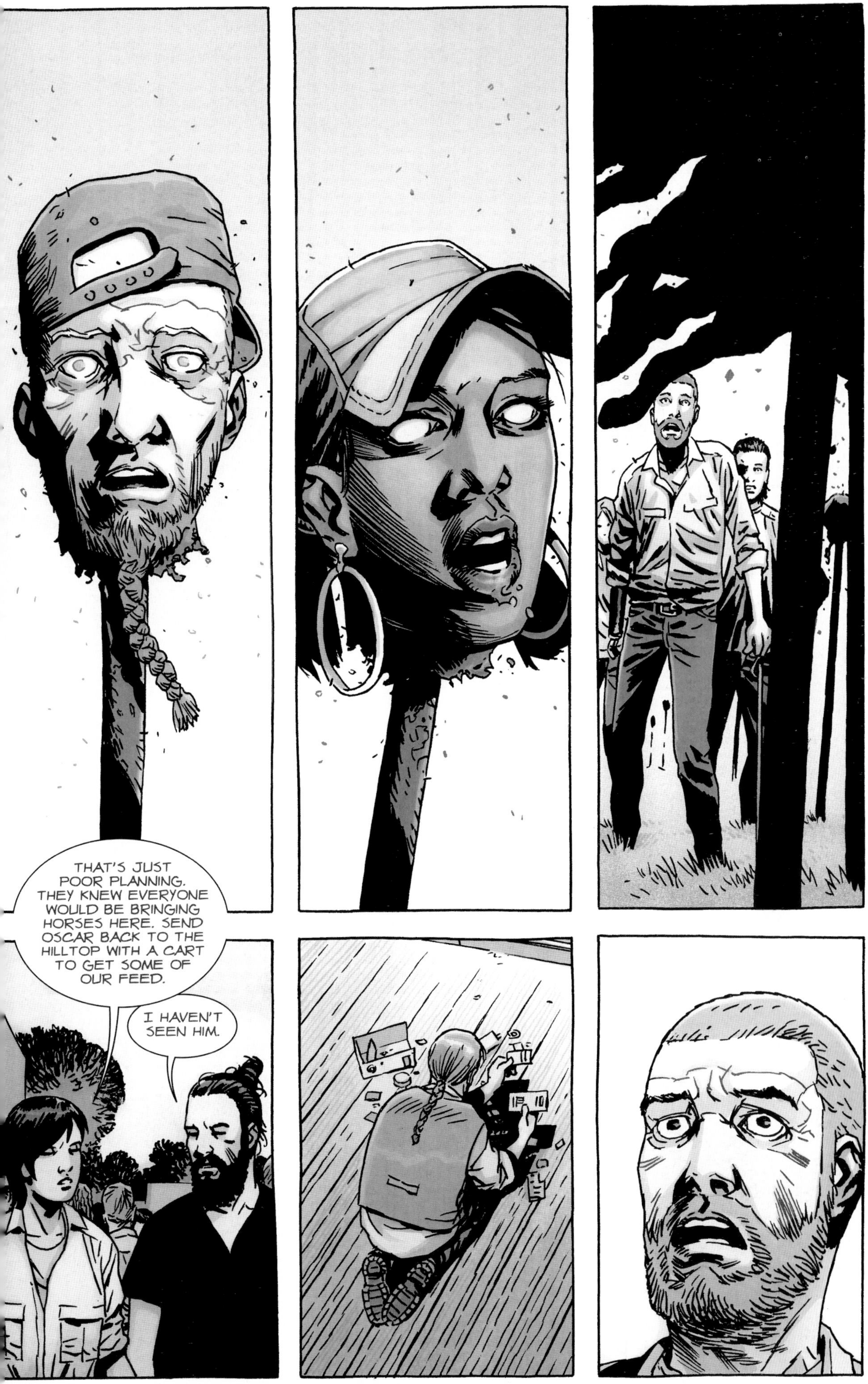
THAT'S JUST POOR PLANNING. THEY KNEW EVERYONE WOULD BE BRINGING HORSES HERE. SEND OSCAR BACK TO THE HILLTOP WITH A CART TO GET SOME OF OUR FEED.
I HAVEN'T SEEN HIM.

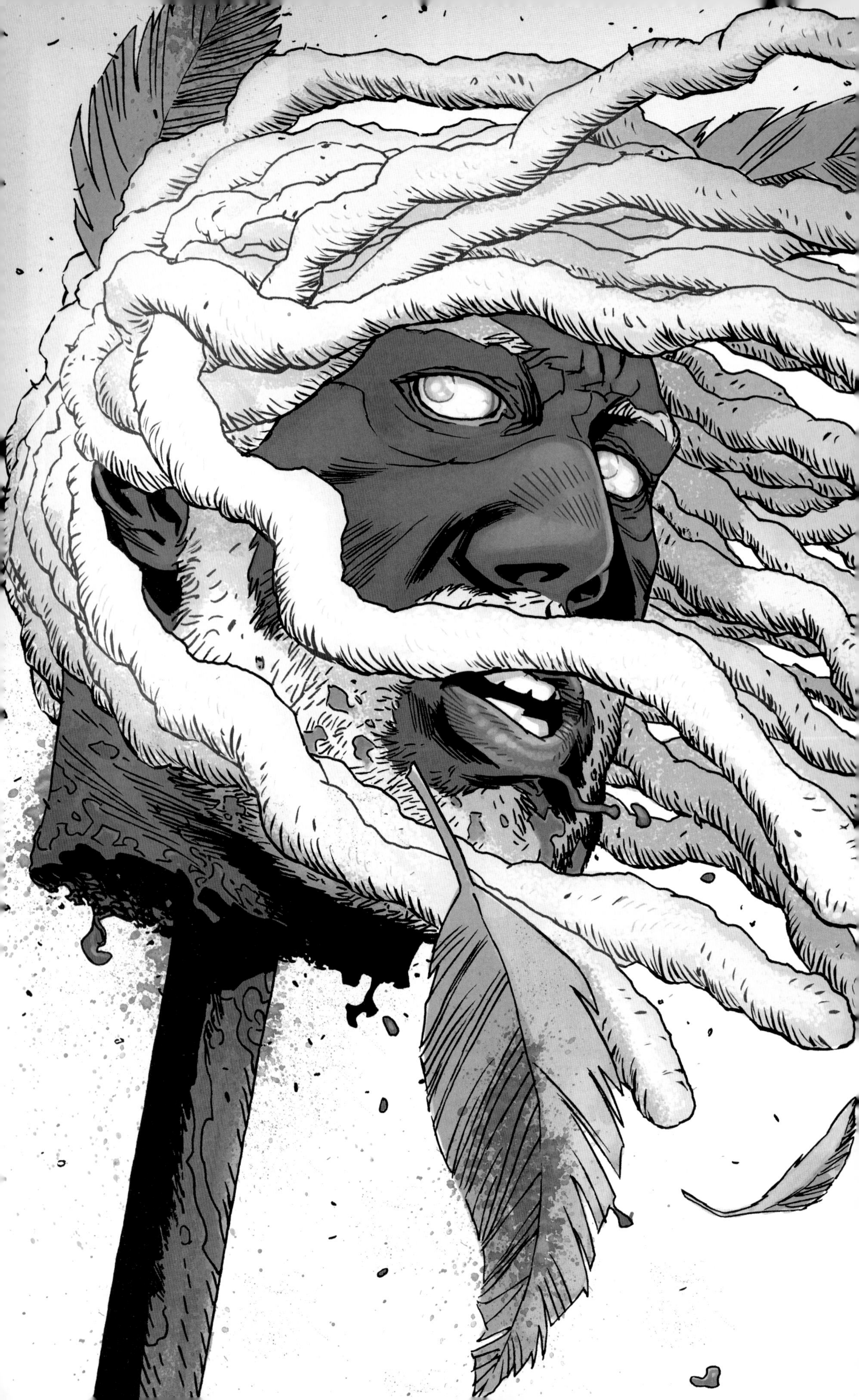

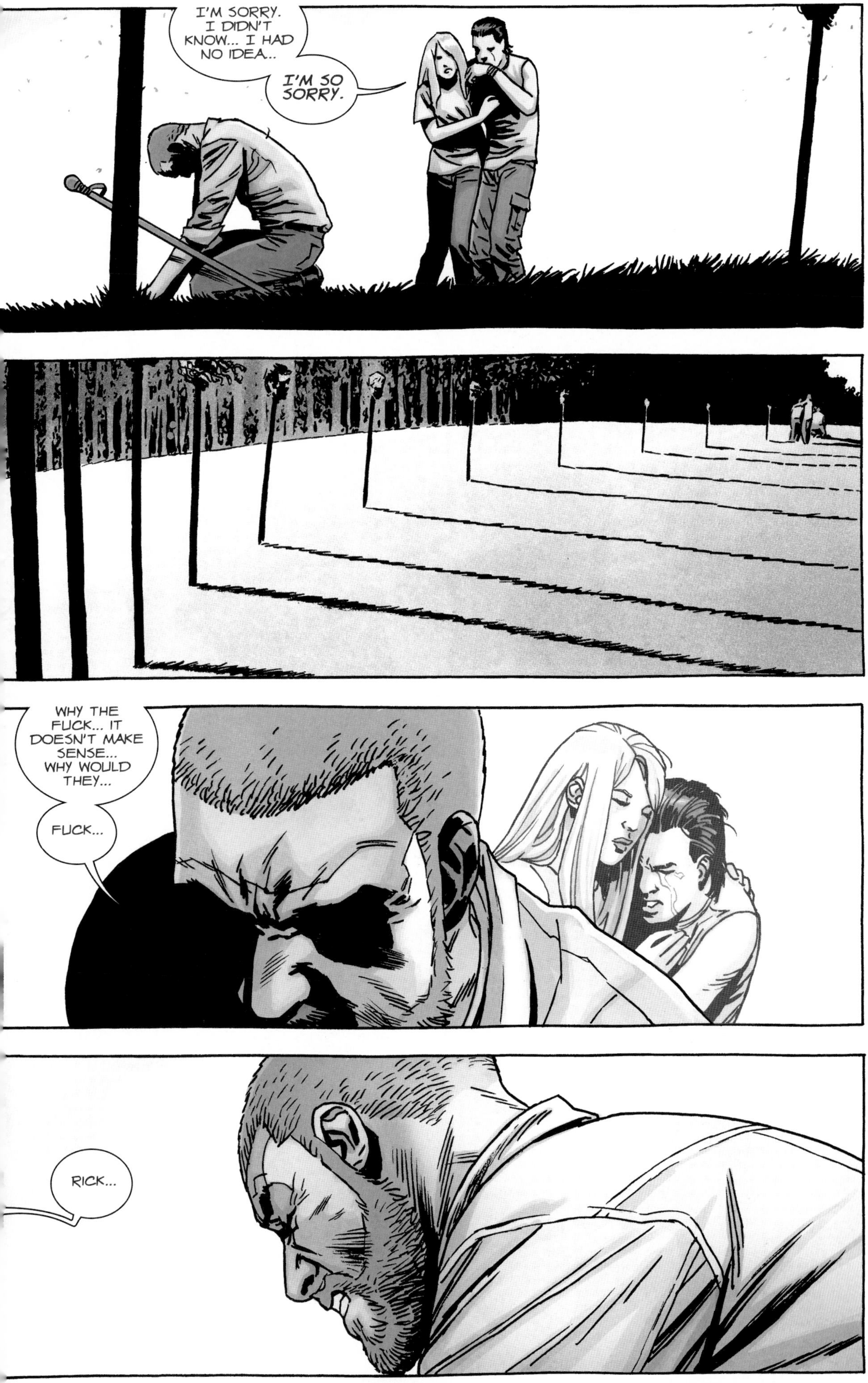
I'M SORRY. I DIDN'T KNOW... I HAD NO IDEA...
I'M SO SORRY.
WHY THE FUCK... IT DOESN'T MAKE SENSE... WHY WOULD THEY...
FUCK...
RICK...

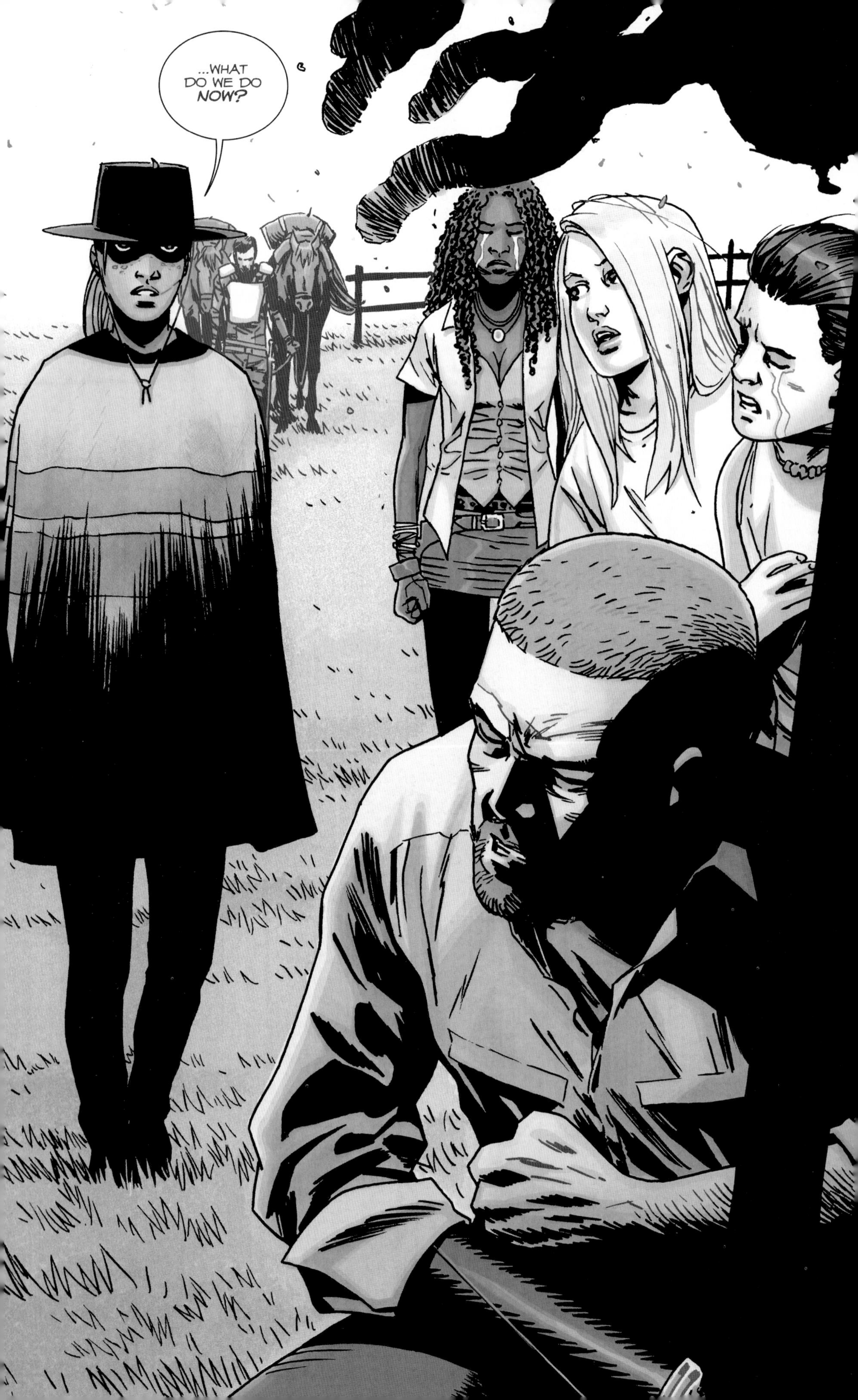
...WHAT DO WE DO NOW?

to be continued...

Sketchbook

Hello and welcome to this glorious sketchbook section where we give you a peek into what goes on behind the scenes on THE WALKING DEAD. On this page you'll see Charlie's pencils for page 14 of issue 139 where we reintroduced Michonne after over a year of her not being in the book. After so much time away, I really wanted a cool iconic shot to debut "pirate Michonne" and Charlie delivered! As he always does.

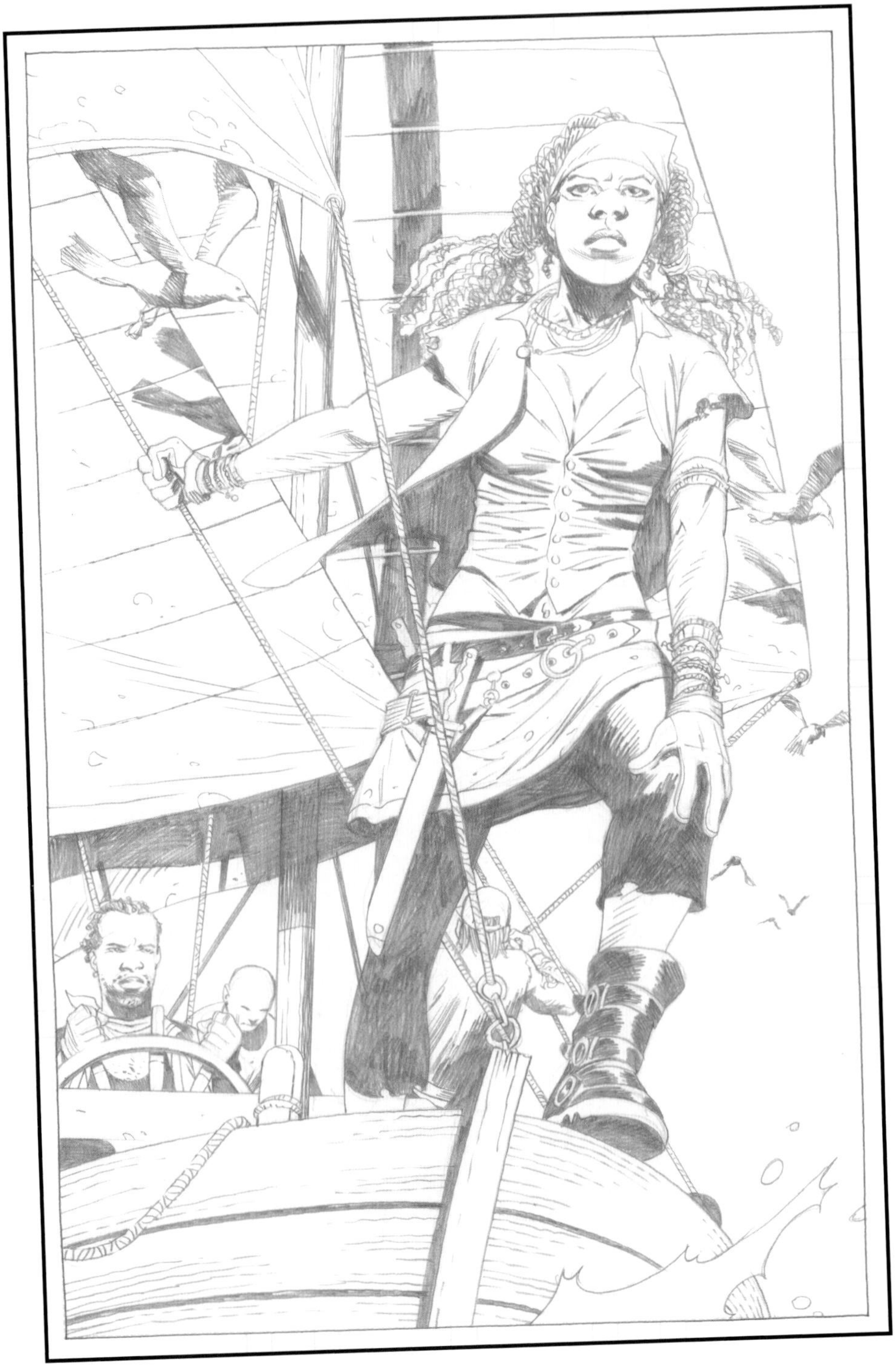

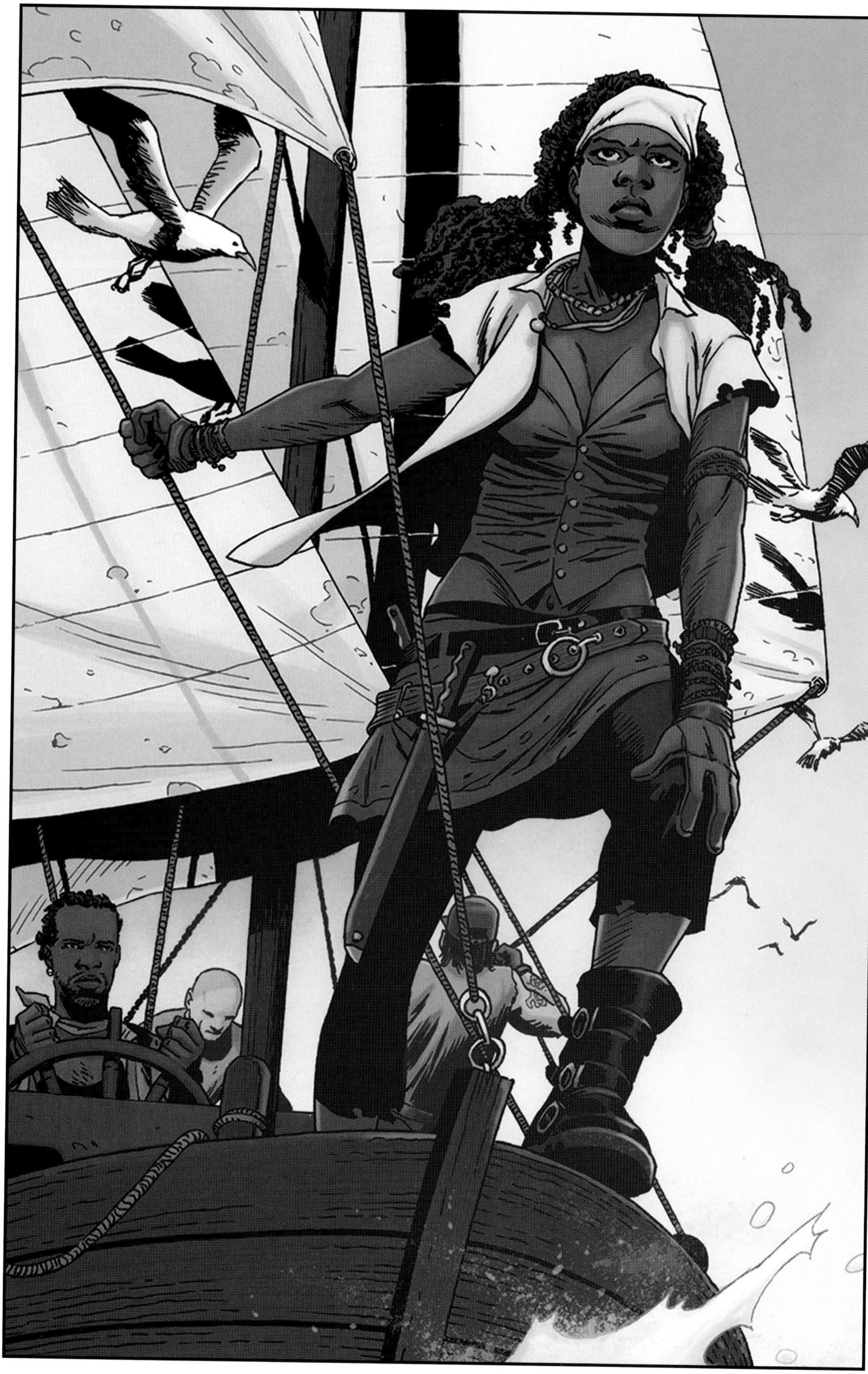

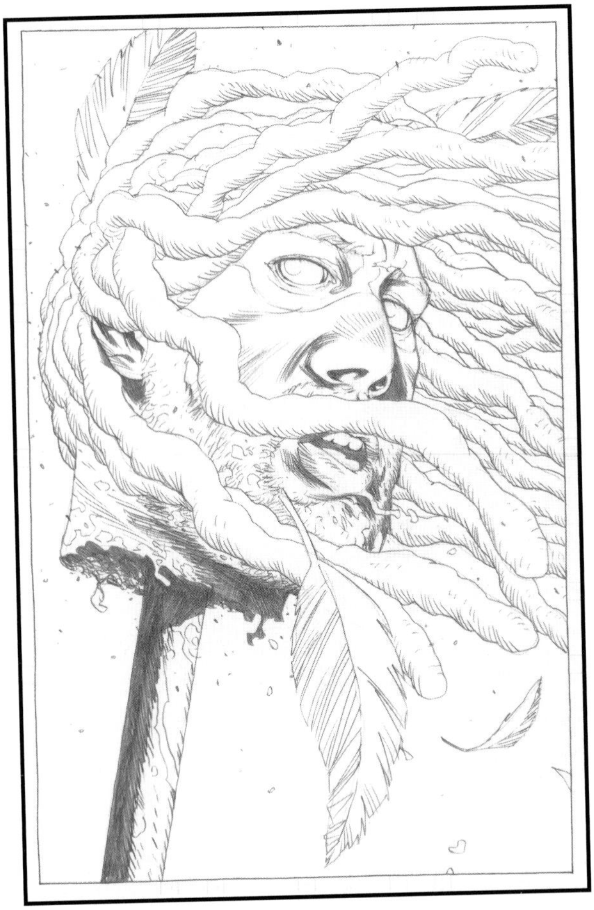

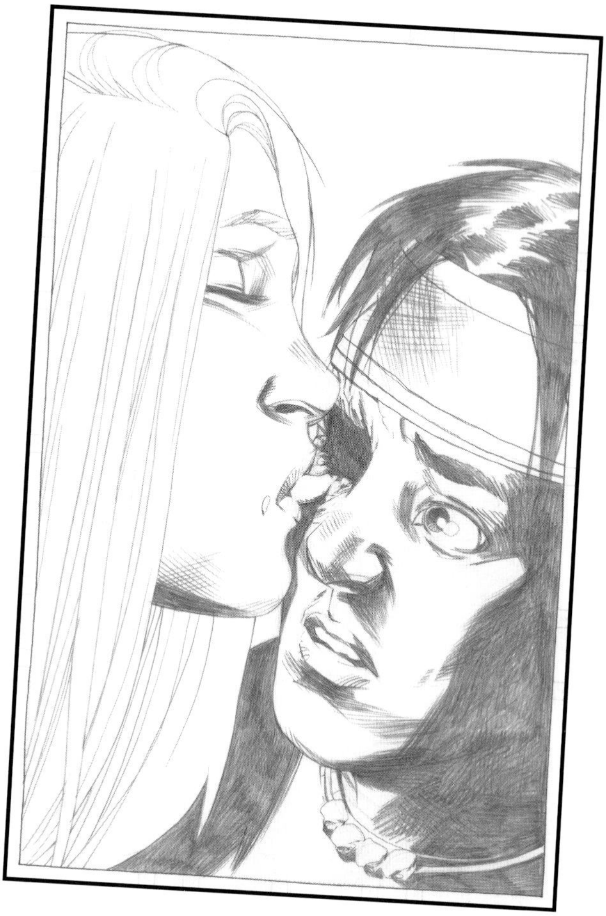

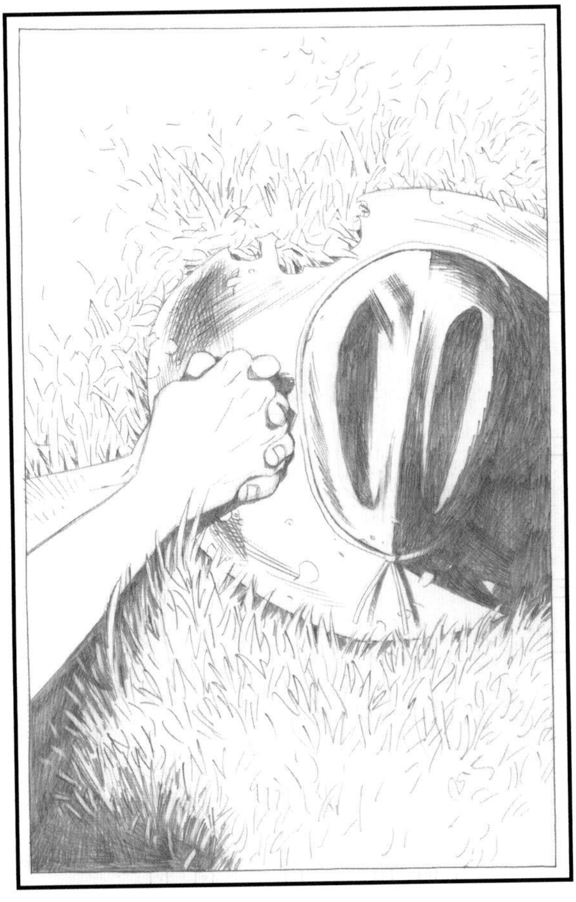

MORE of Charlie's lovely pencils so you can see his awesome work before Stefano comes in and works his magic.

This image was a print Charlie did for
a signing he did at Gosh Comics in
London.

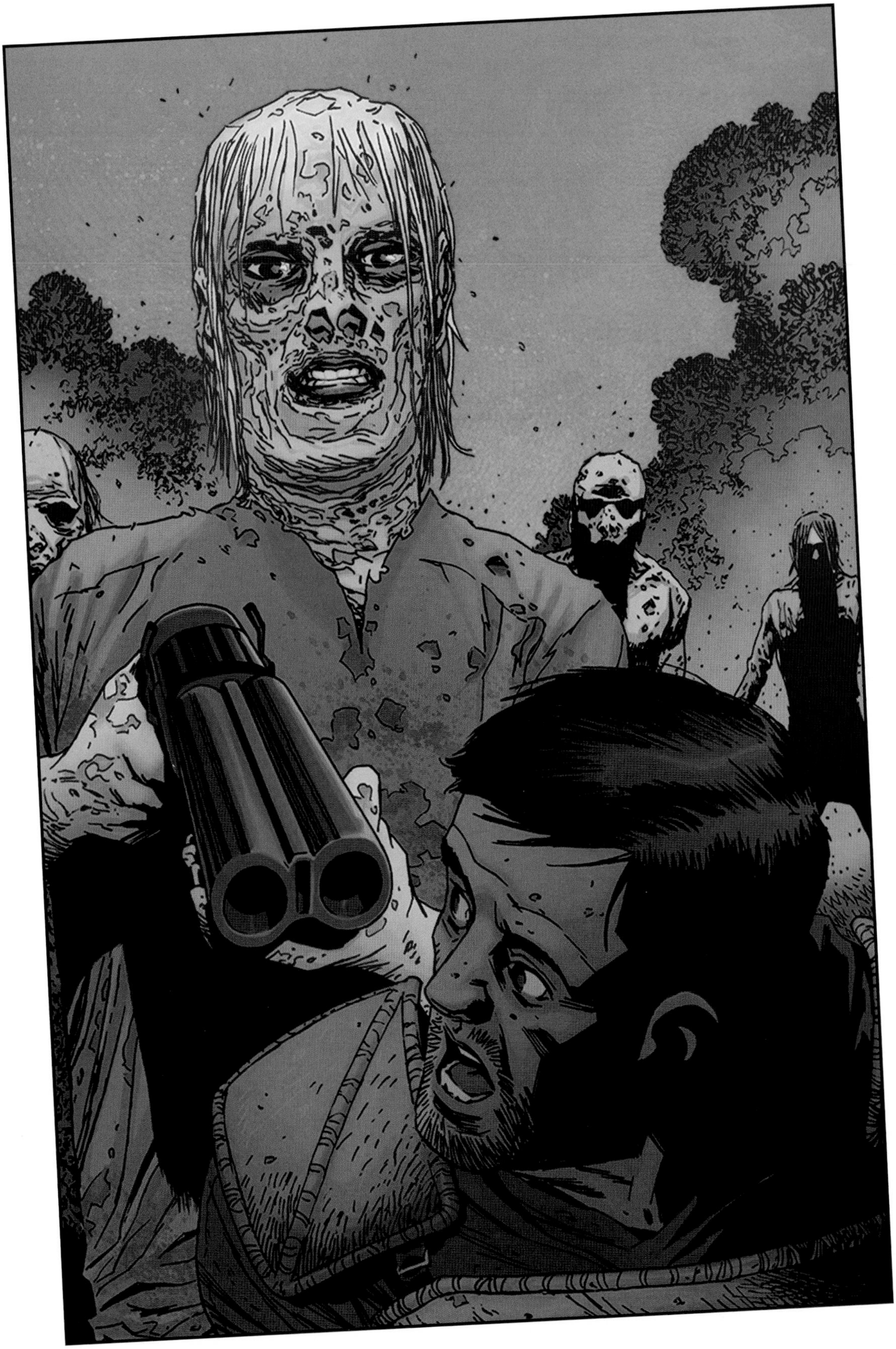

Another color image from Charlie, Stefano, and Cliff for *The Walking Dead Magazine* featuring the first appearance of ALPHA.

This image was used as a Comic-Con exclusive variant cover of issue 144, and it was also half of our big 20 foot tall banner at the Skybound booth in 2015. It's always awesome to see this stuff bigger than a billboard. The other half was an Outcast image by Paul Azaceta that connected to this image to promote both series together. But I'm far too classy to plug my other work here. (Buy OUTCAST BY KIRKMAN & AZACETA, it's a great series! Coming to television on Cinemax in 2016!)

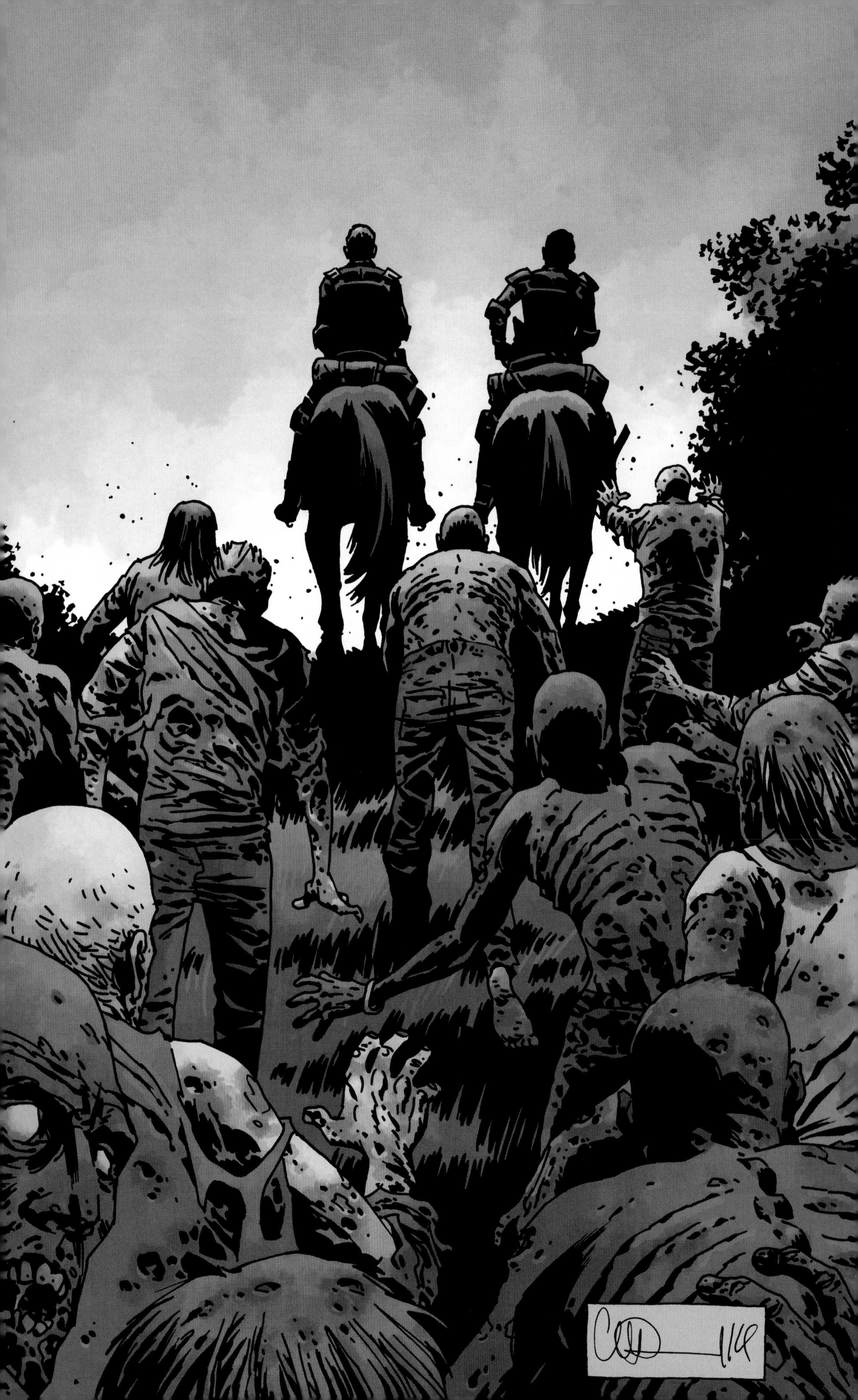

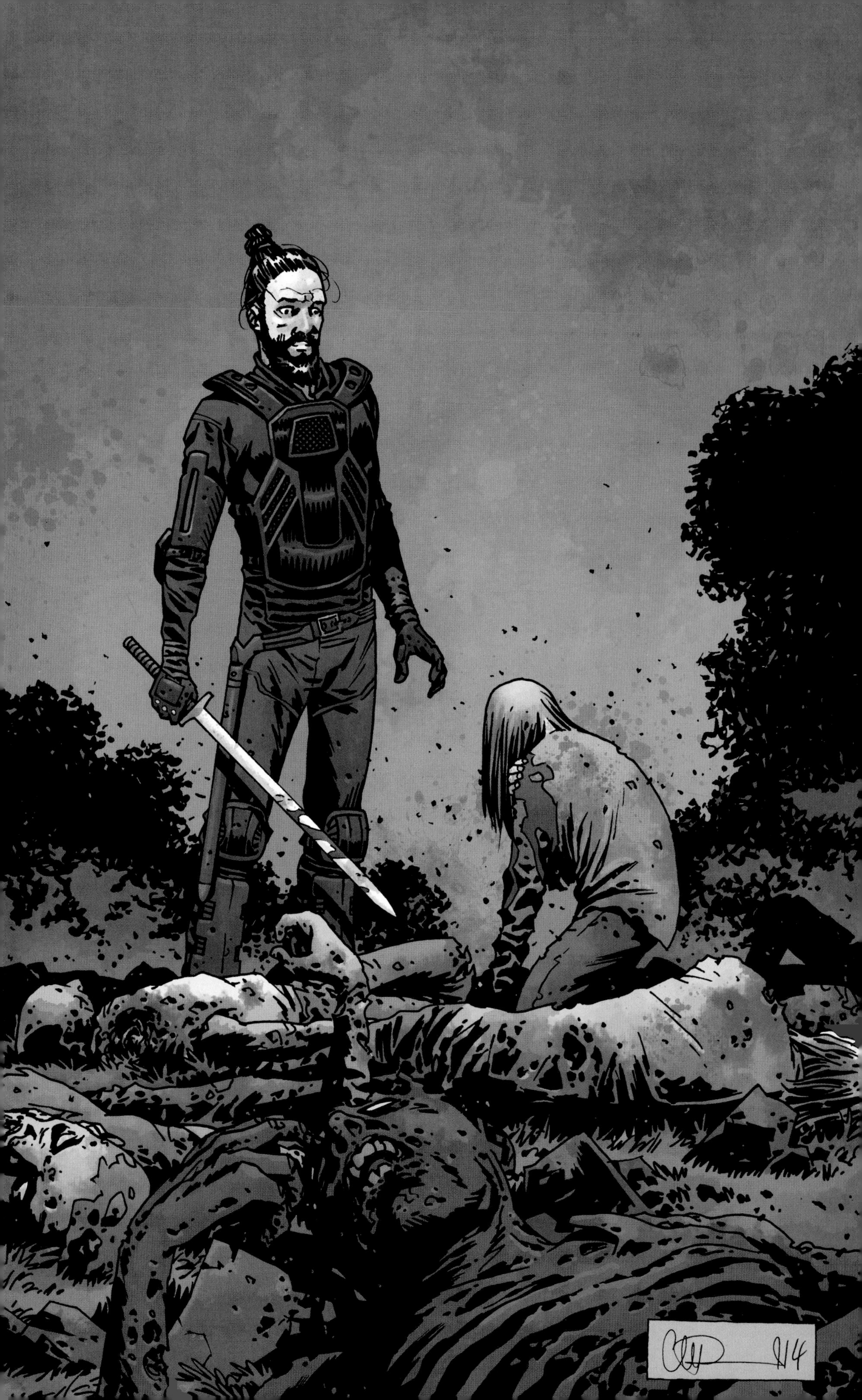

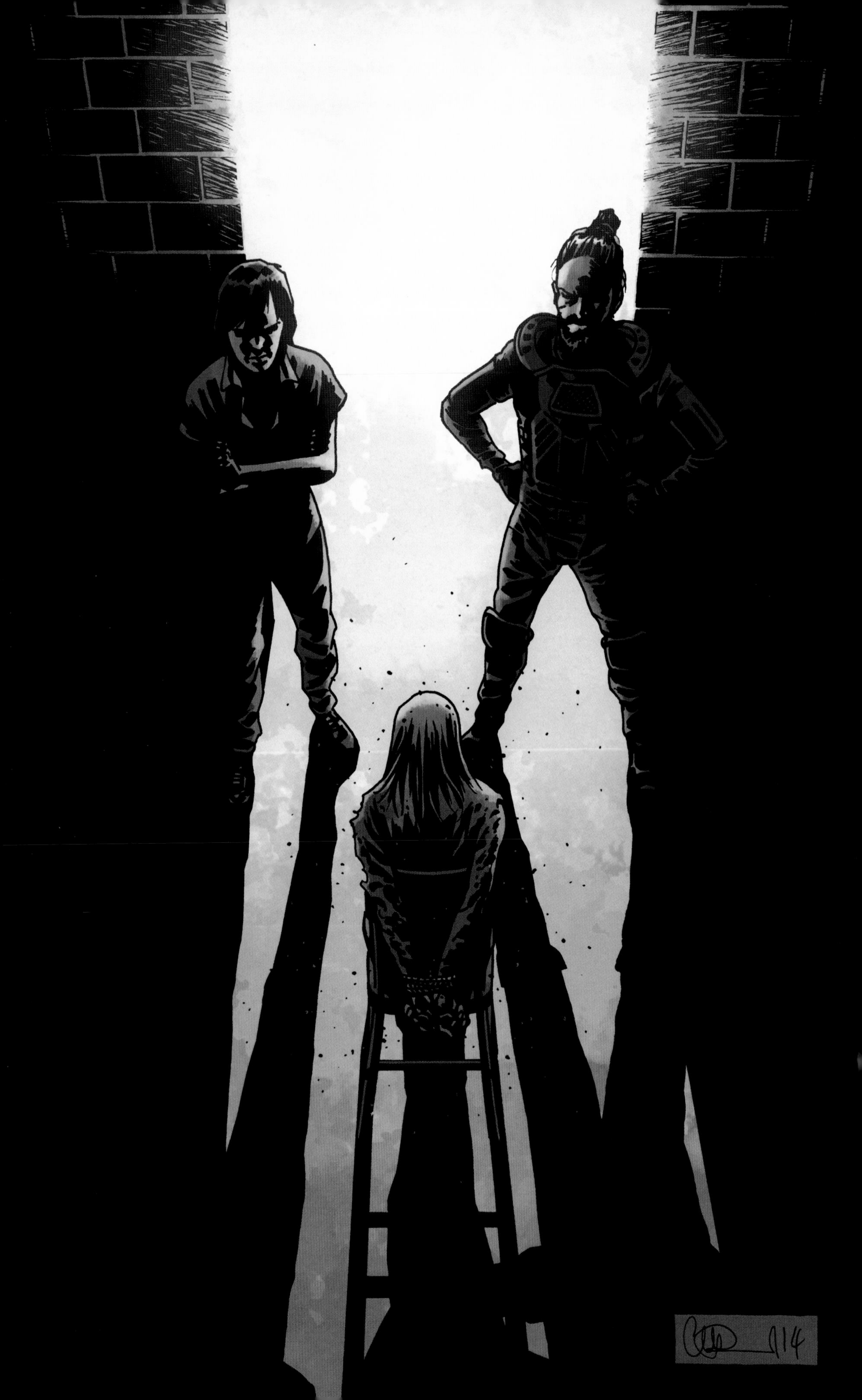

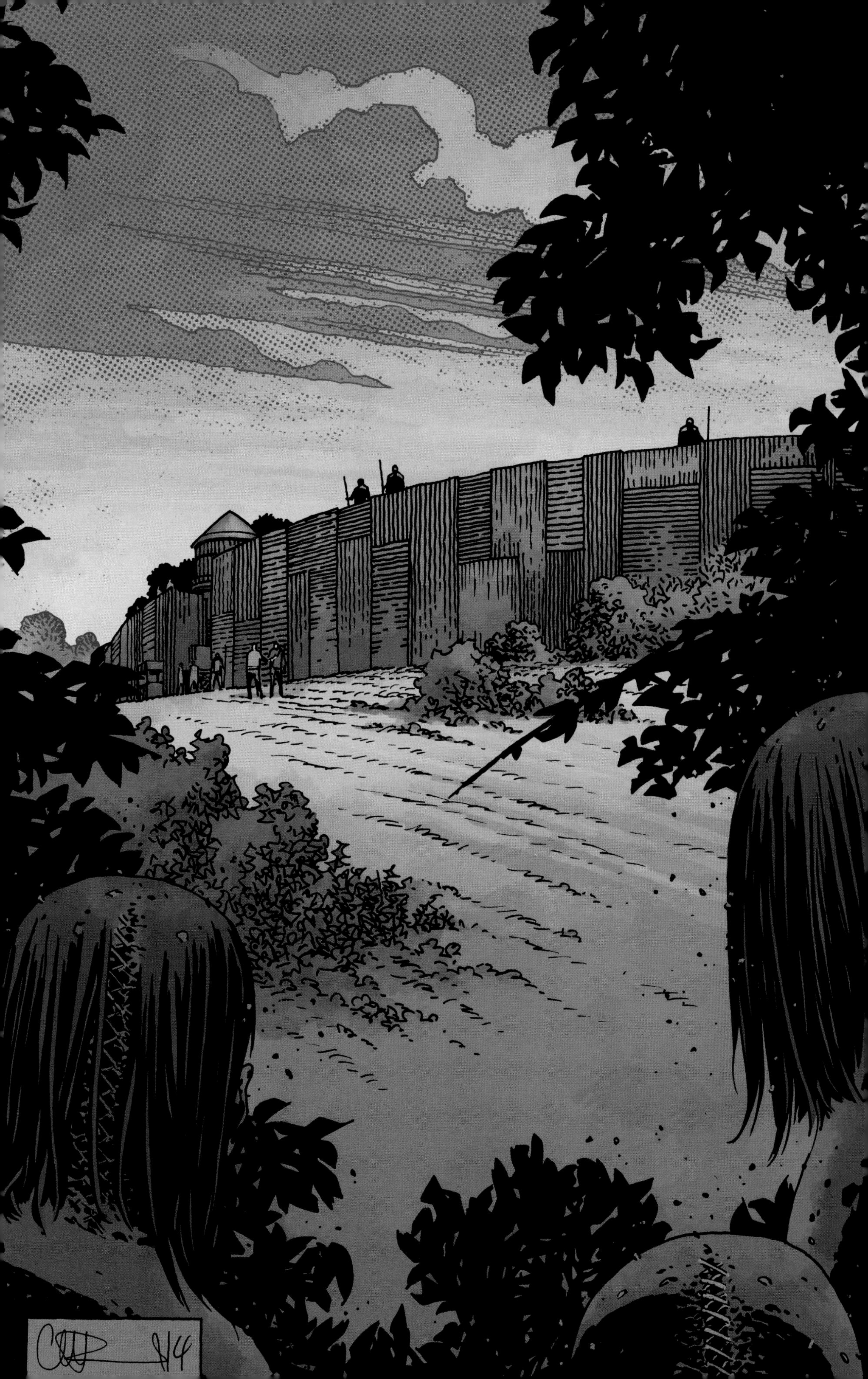

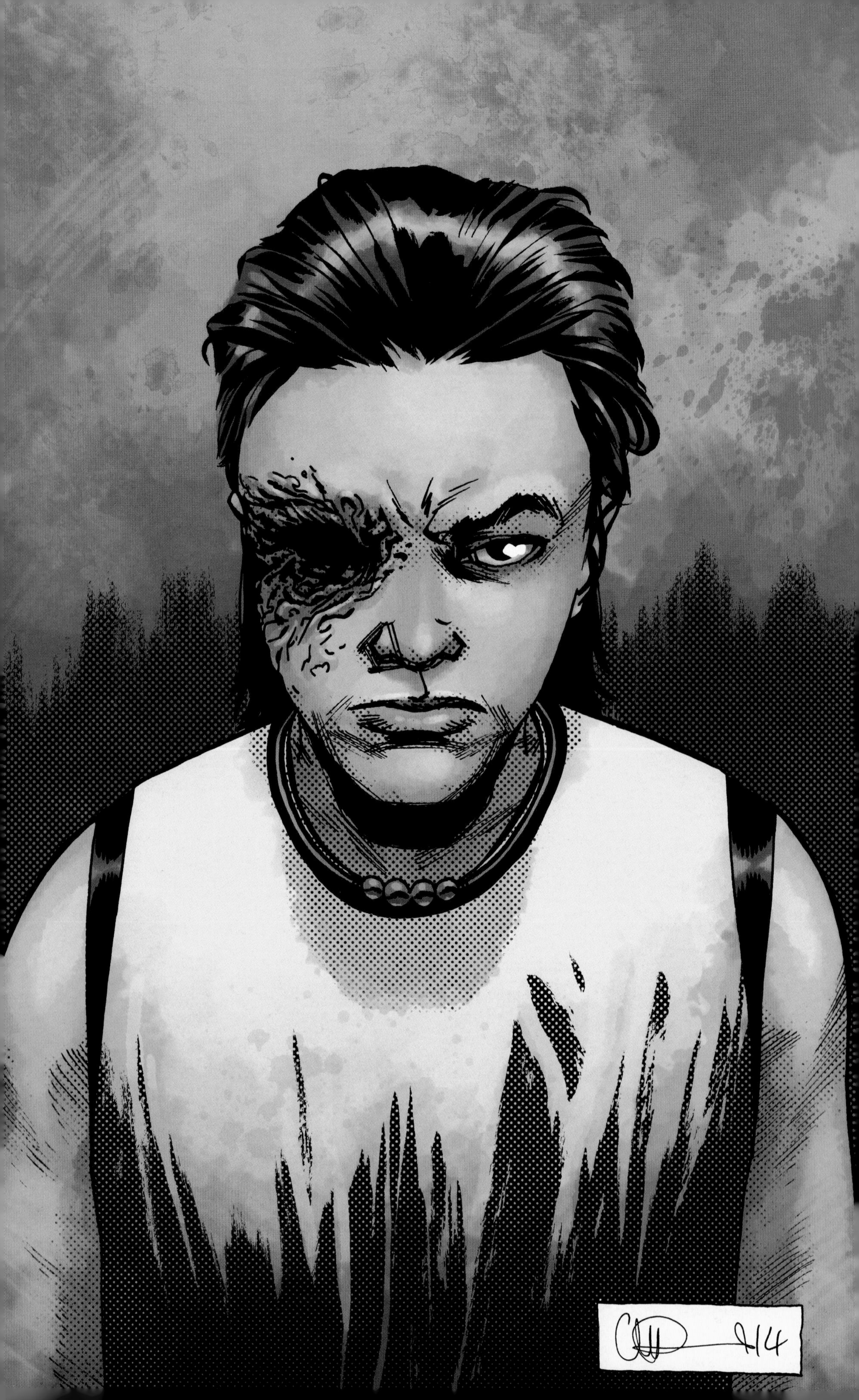

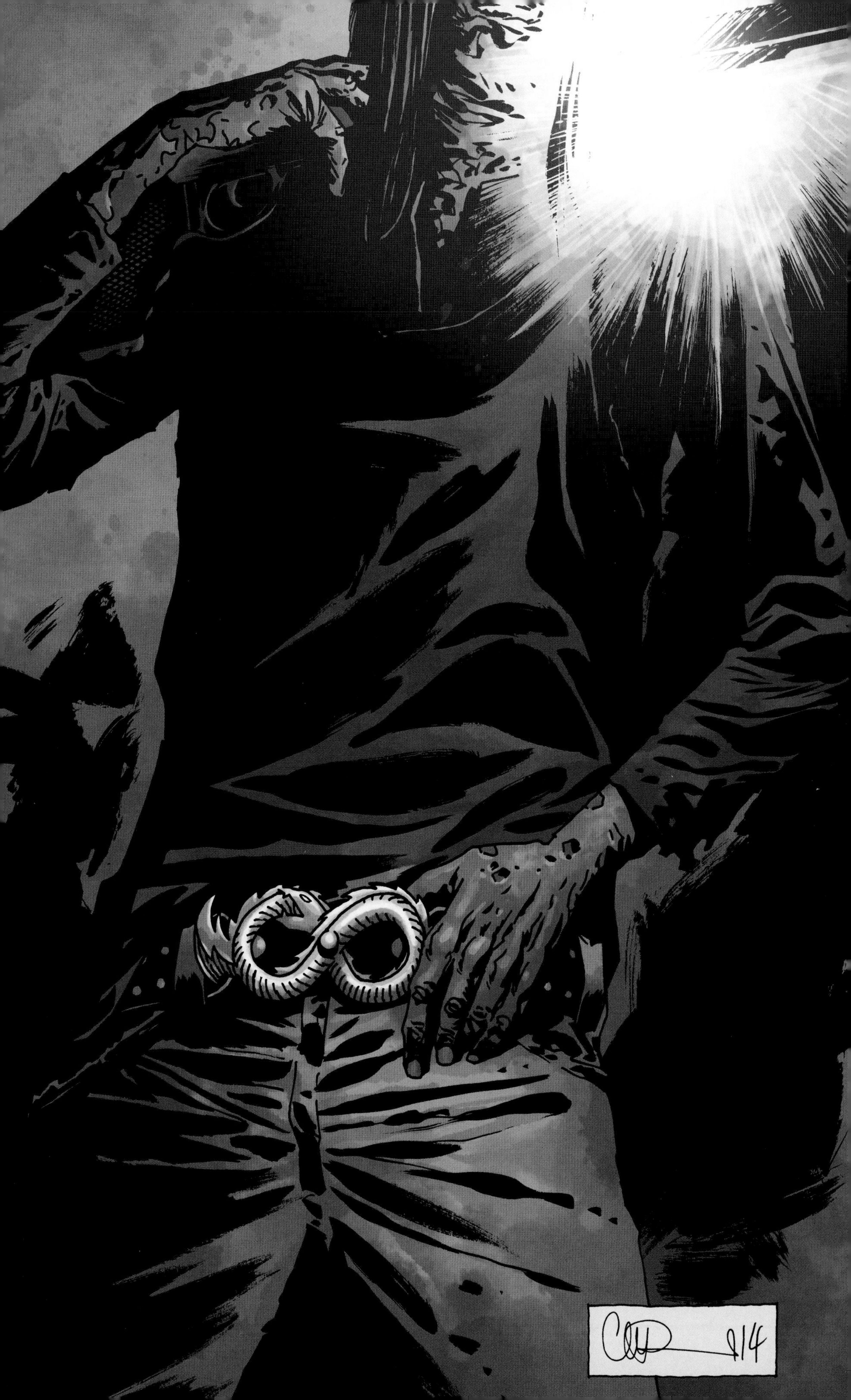

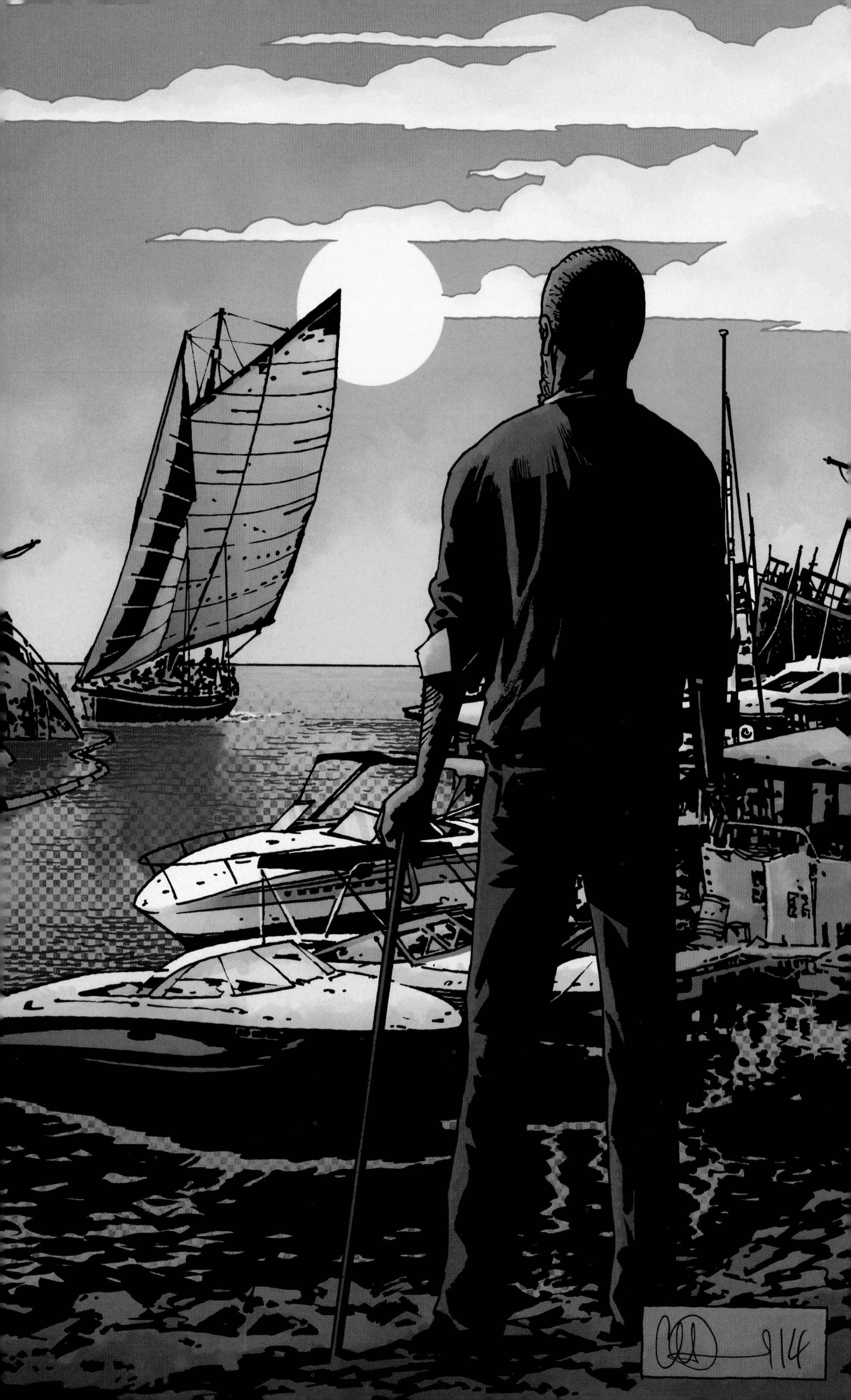

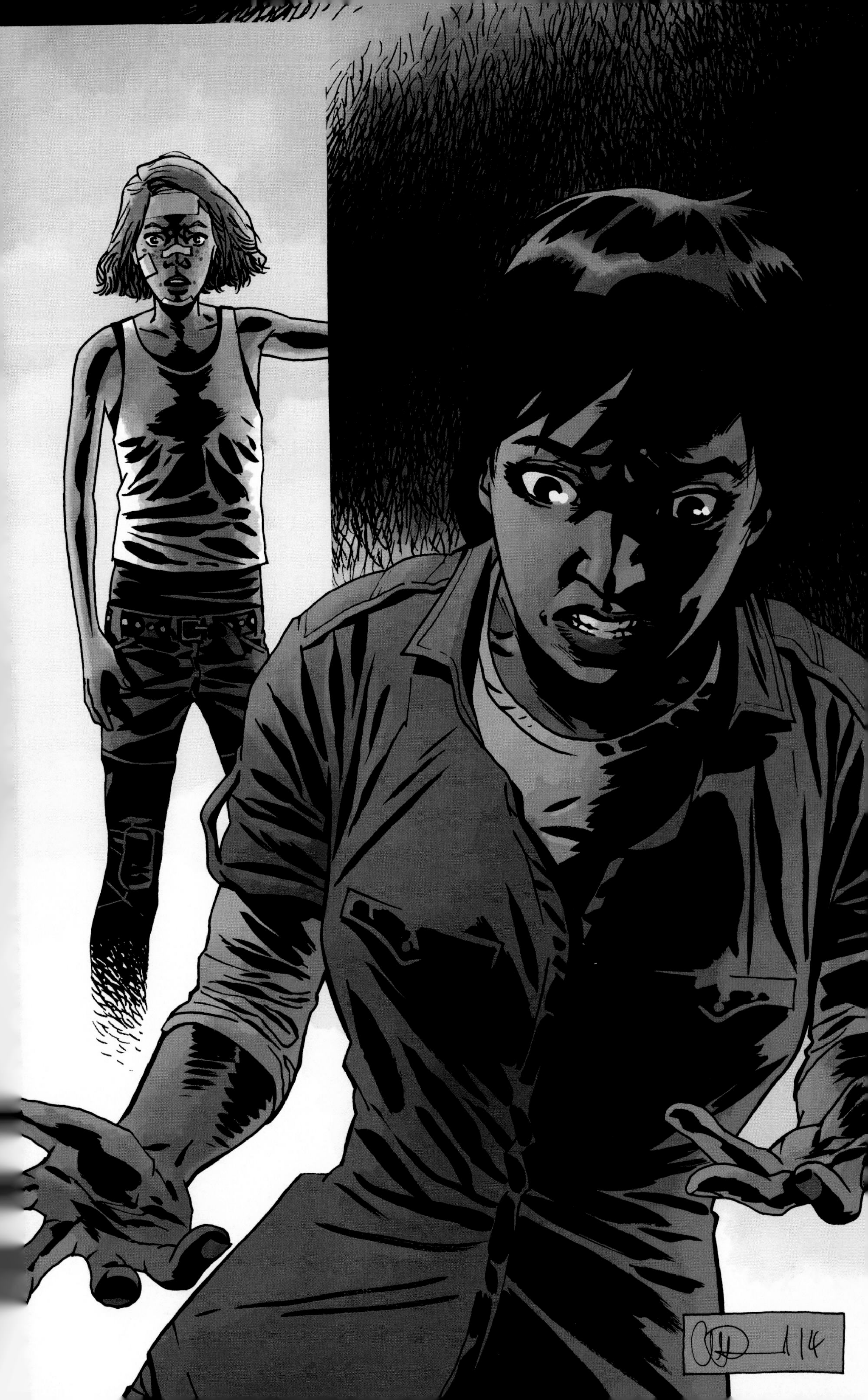

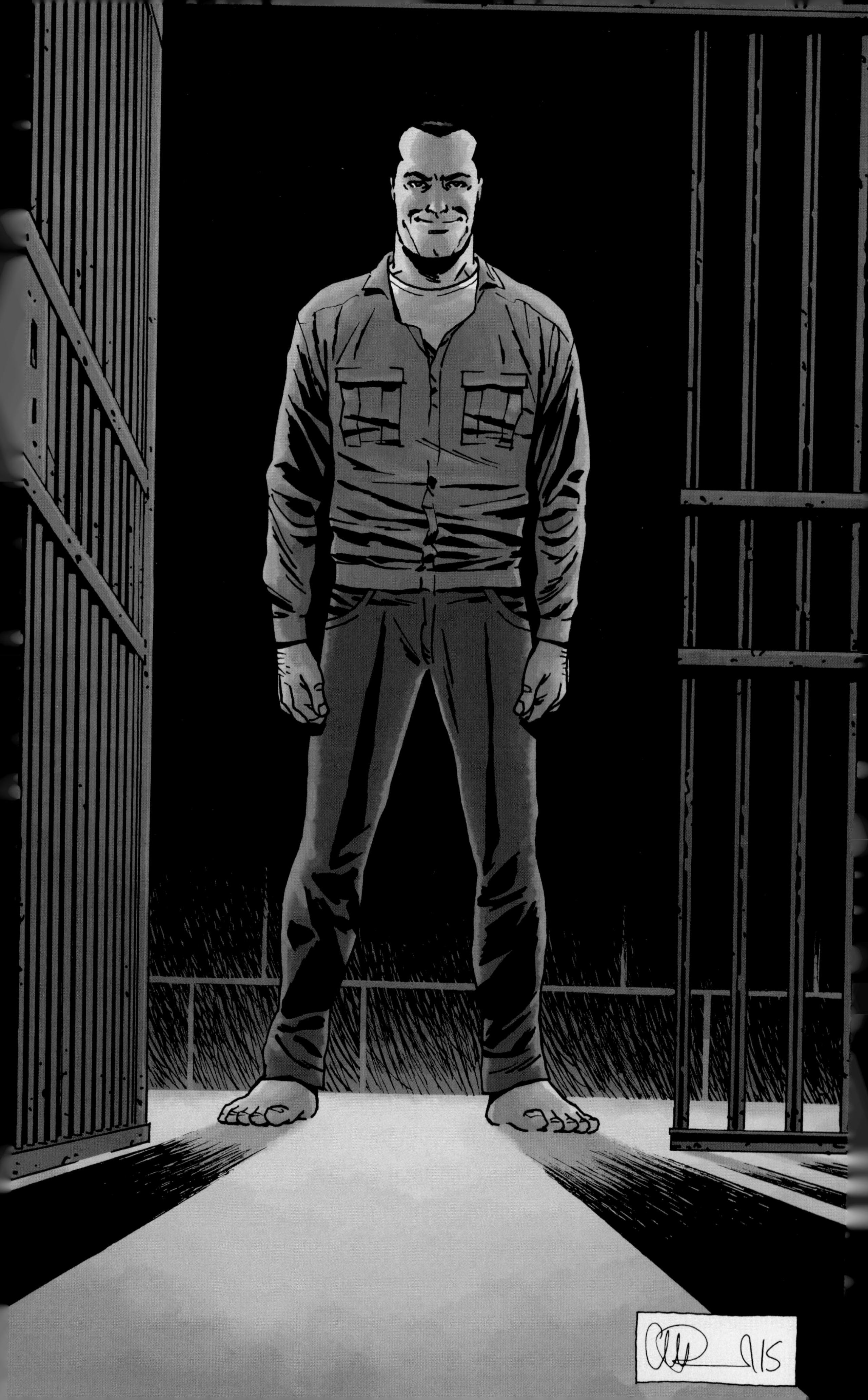

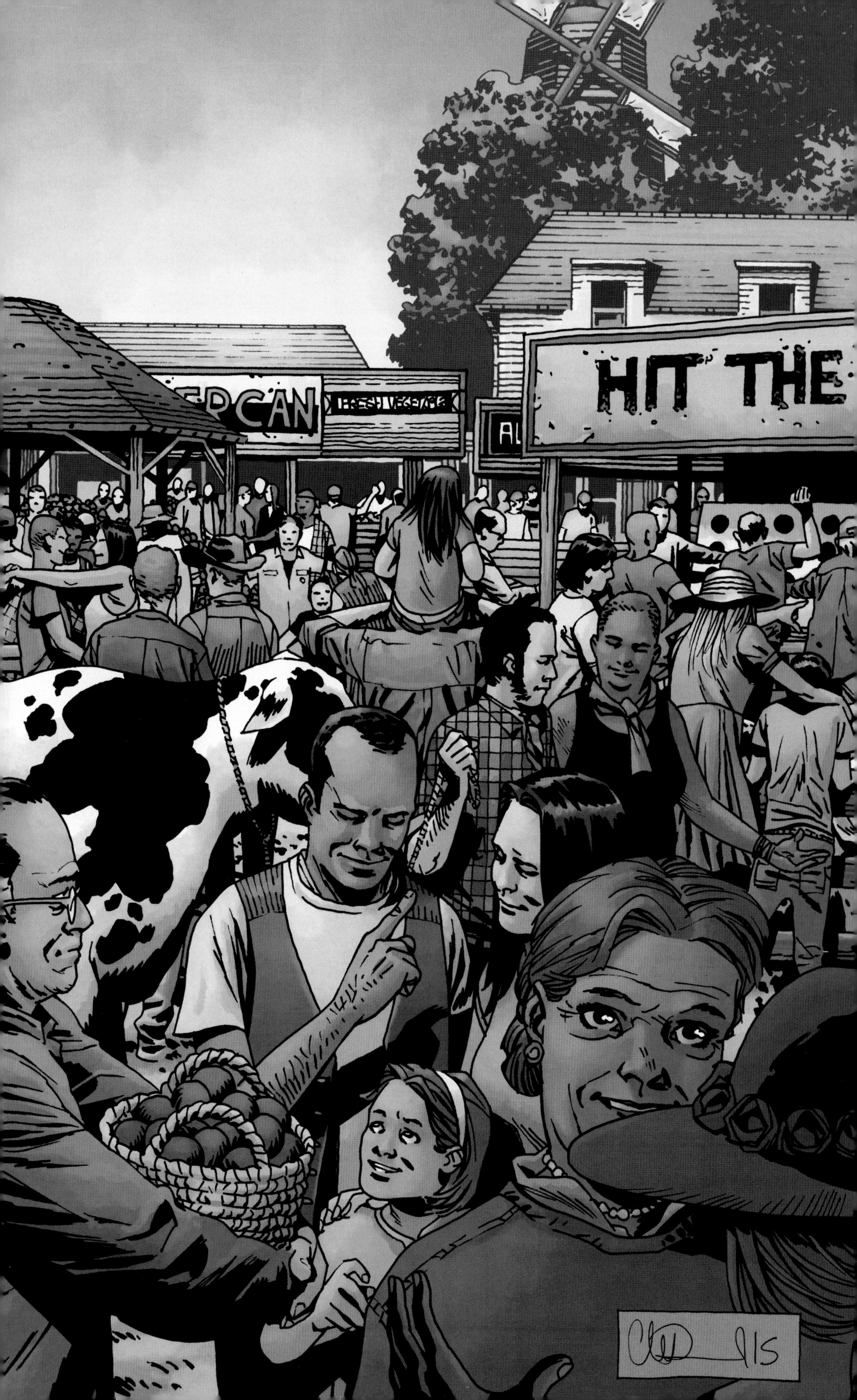
ERCAN
HIT THE

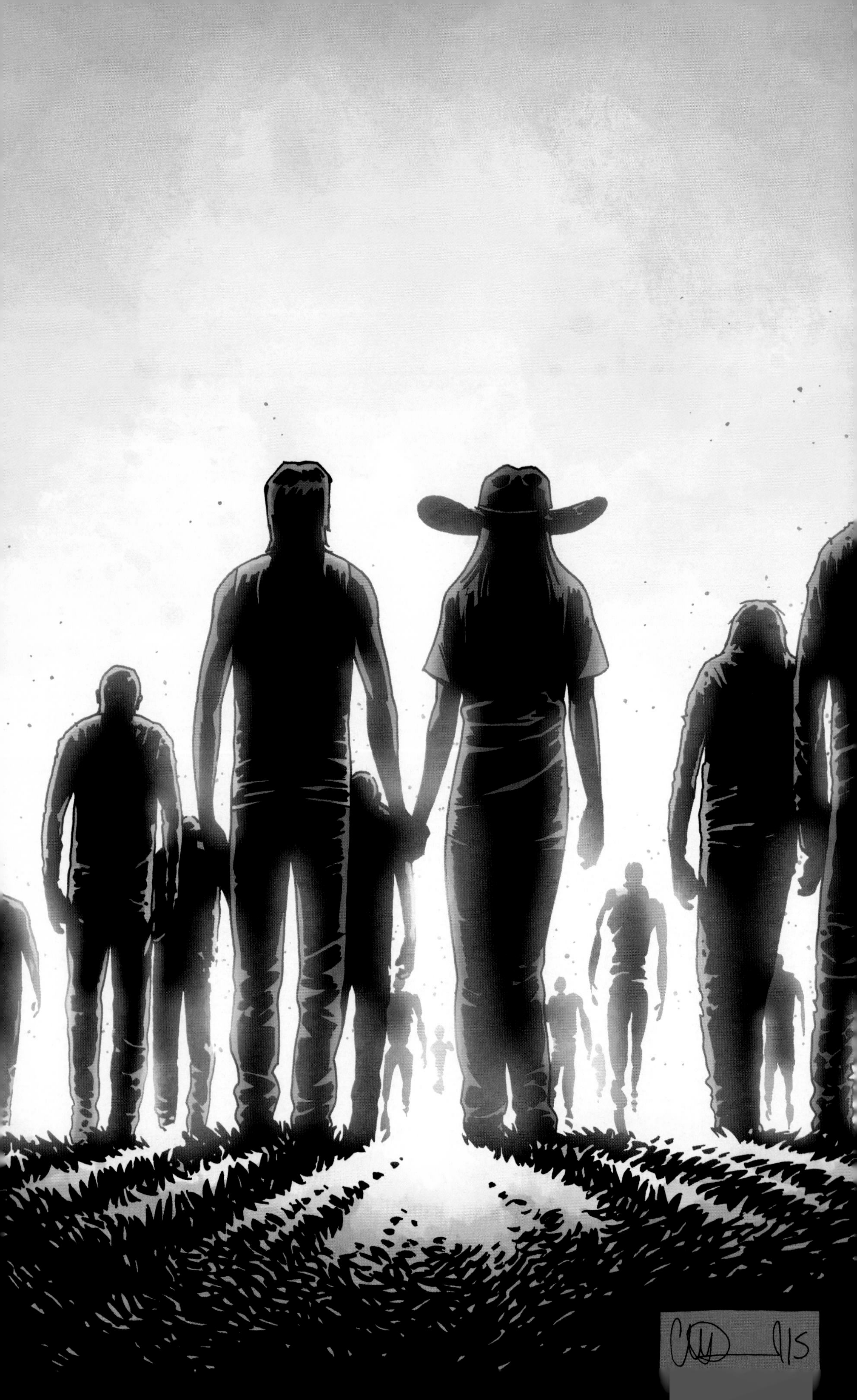

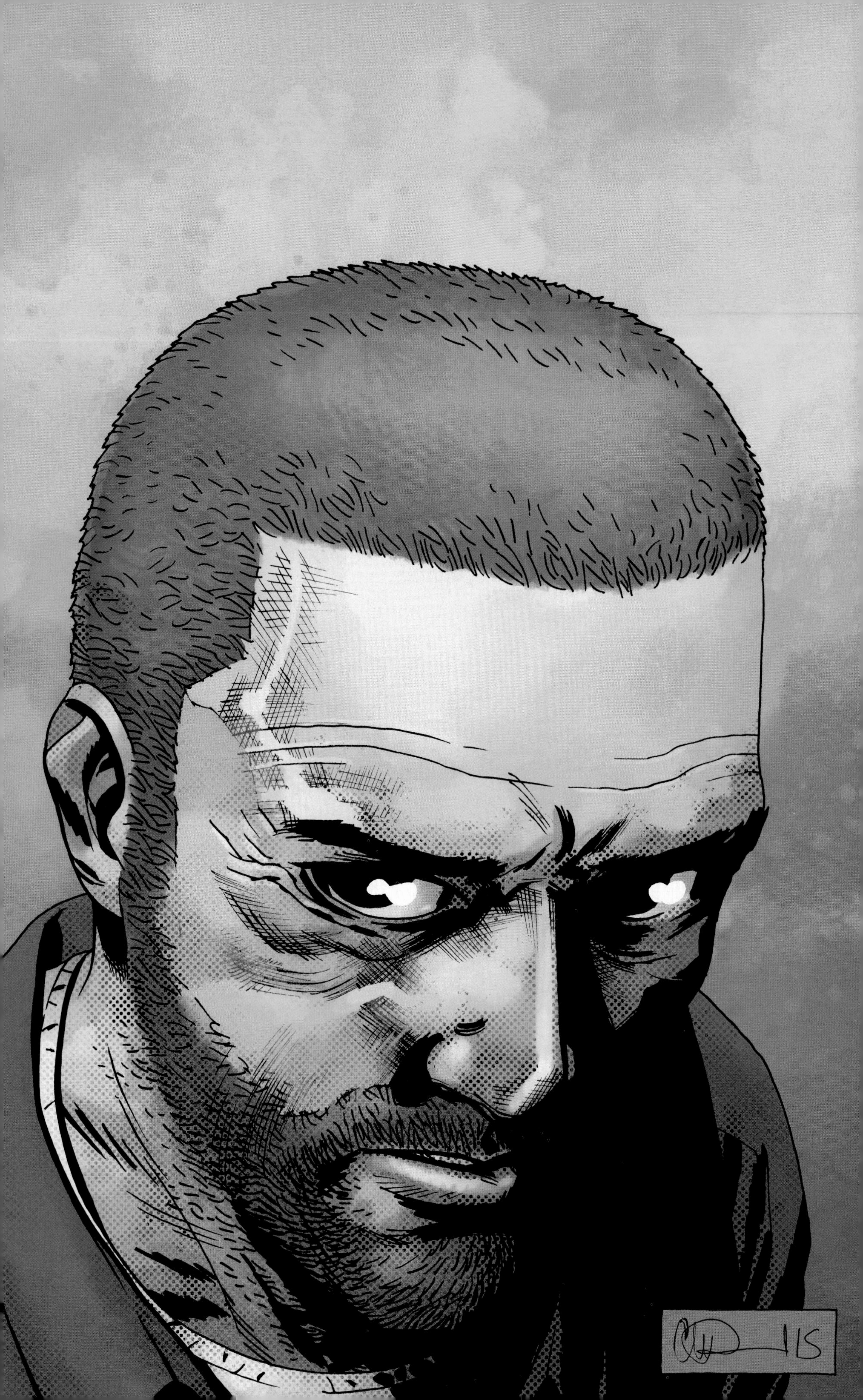

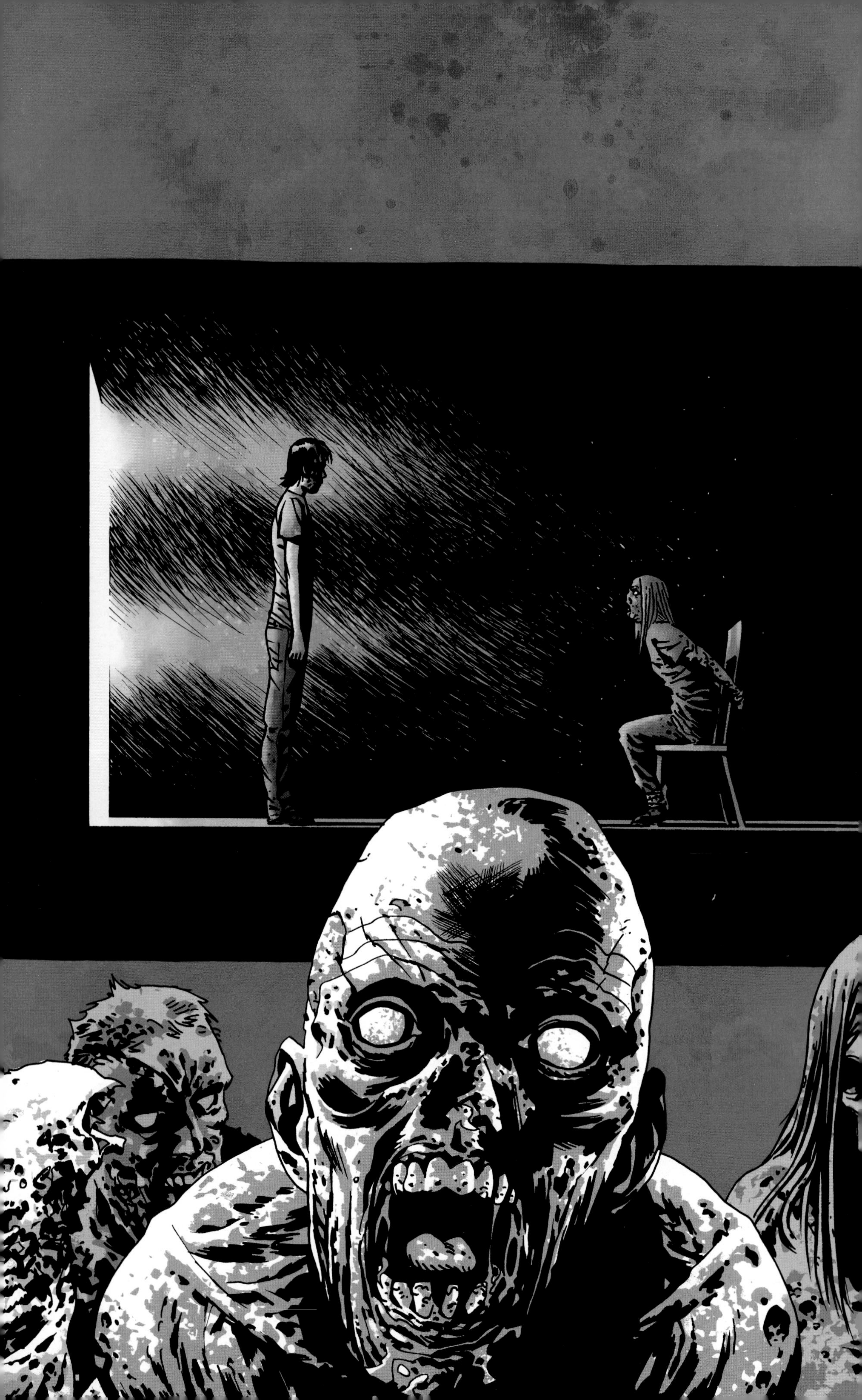

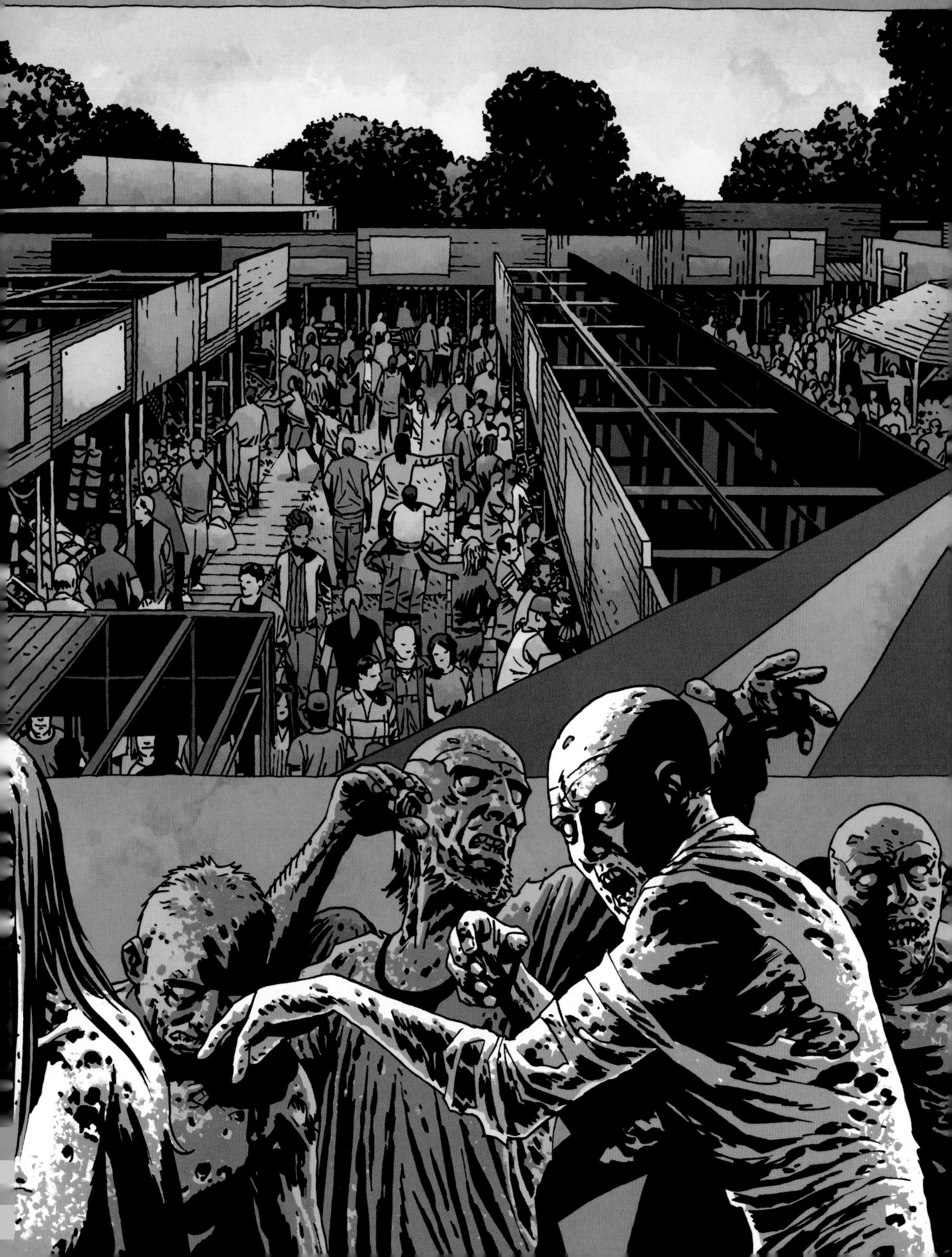

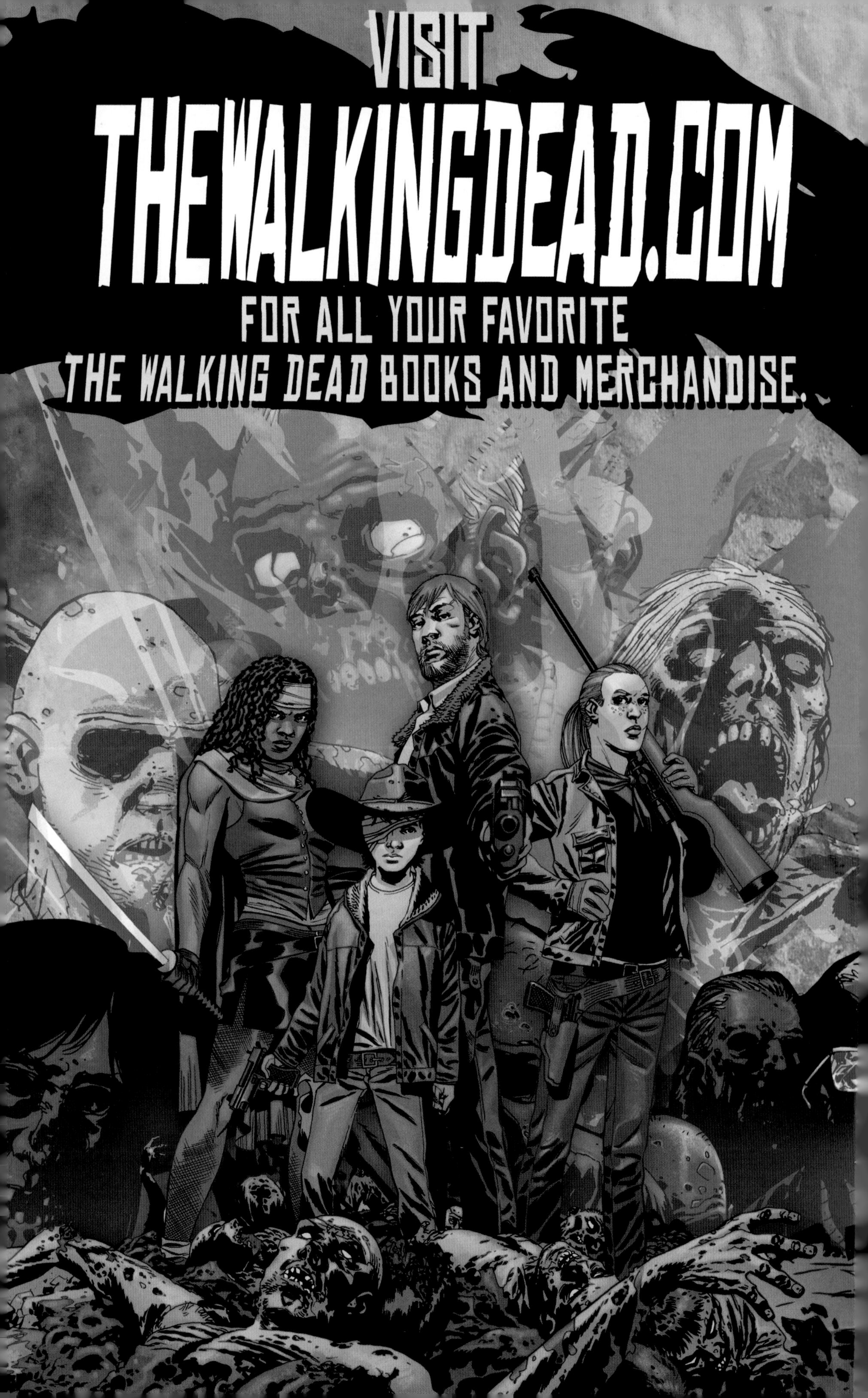
VISIT
THEWALKINGDEAD.COM
FOR ALL YOUR FAVORITE
THE WALKING DEAD BOOKS AND MERCHANDISE.

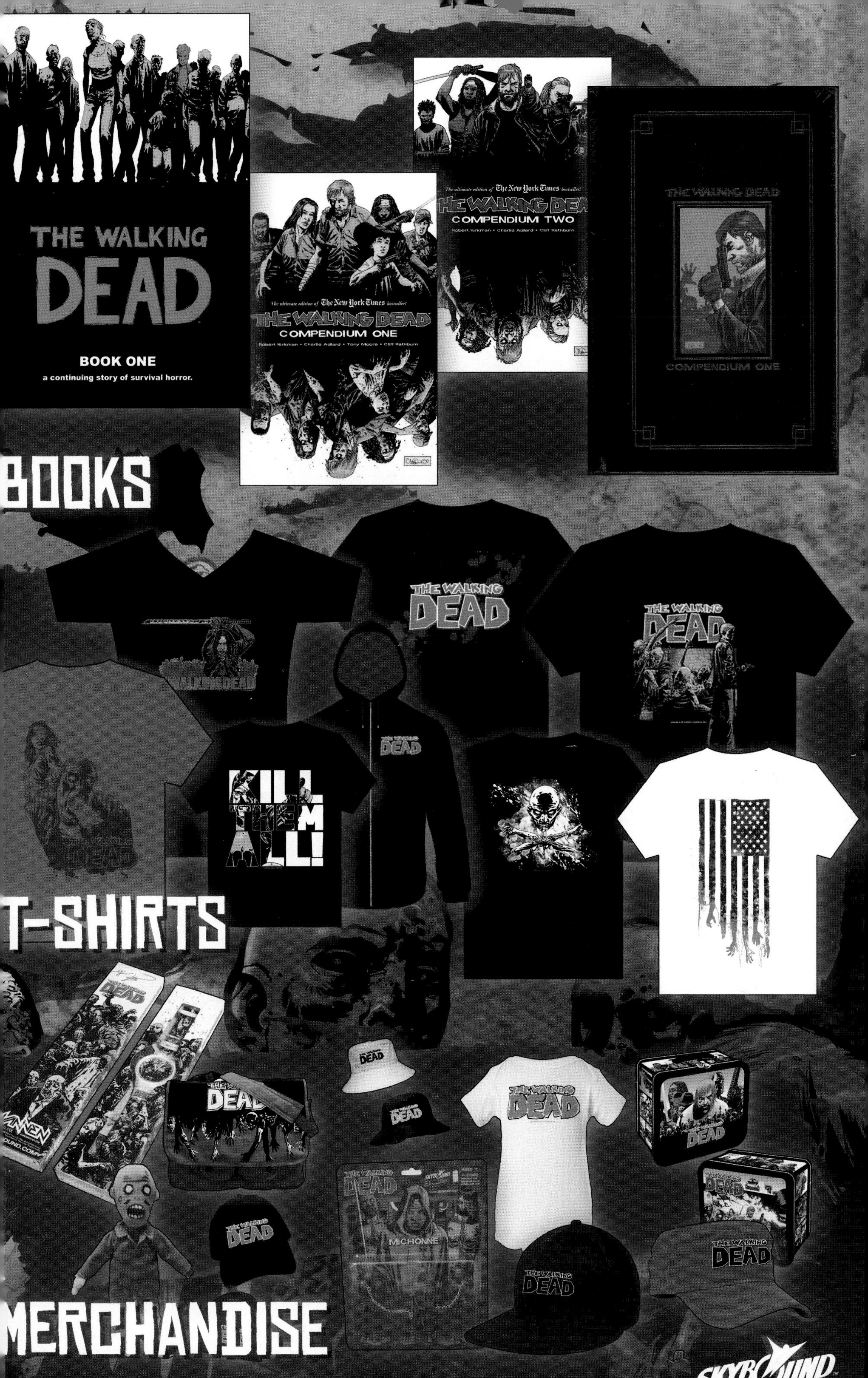
THE WALKING DEAD
BOOK ONE
a continuing story of survival horror.
The ultimate edition of The New York Times bestseller!
THE WALKING DEAD
COMPENDIUM ONE
Robert Kirkman • Charlie Adlard • Tony Moore • Cliff Rathburn
The ultimate edition of The New York Times bestseller!
THE WALKING DEAD
COMPENDIUM TWO
Robert Kirkman • Charlie Adlard • Cliff Rathburn
THE WALKING DEAD
COMPENDIUM ONE
BOOKS
THE WALKING DEAD
KILL THEM ALL!
T-SHIRTS
MICHONNE
MERCHANDISE
SKYBOUND

for more tales from ROBERT KIRKMAN and SKYBOUND

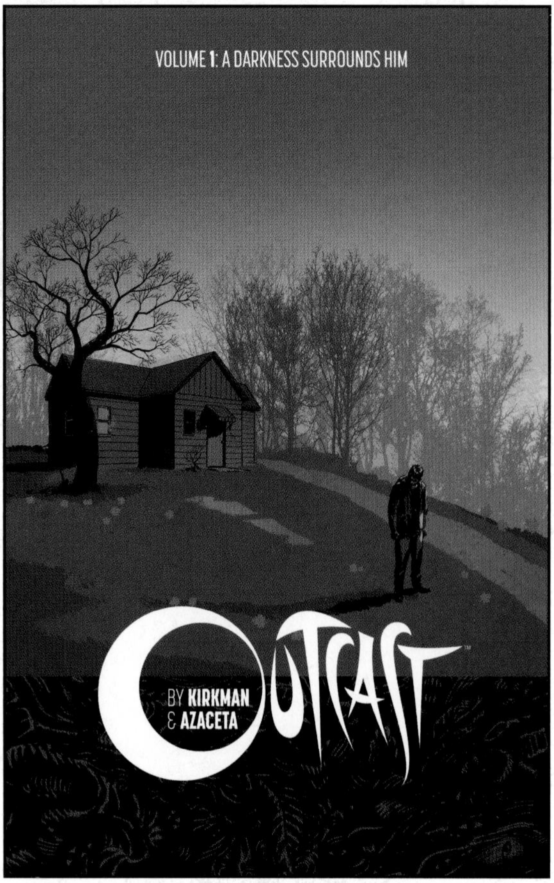
VOLUME 1: A DARKNESS SURROUNDS HIM
OUTCAST
BY KIRKMAN & AZACETA

VOL. 1: A DARKNESS SURROUNDS HIM TP
ISBN: 978-1-63215-053-0
$9.99

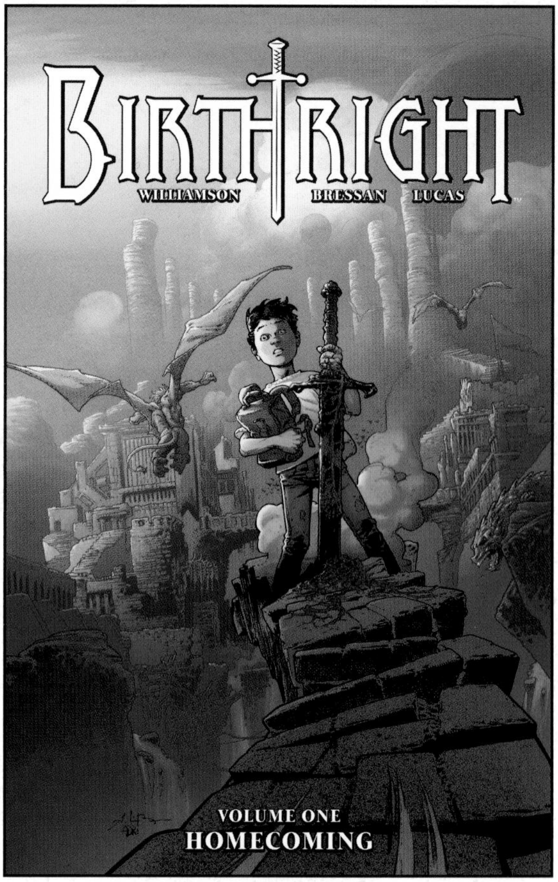
BIRTHRIGHT
WILLIAMSON BRESSAN LUCAS
VOLUME ONE
HOMECOMING

VOL. 1: HOMECOMING TP
ISBN: 978-1-63215-231-2
$9.99

VOL. 2: CALL TO ADVENTURE TP
ISBN: 978-1-63215-446-0
$12.99

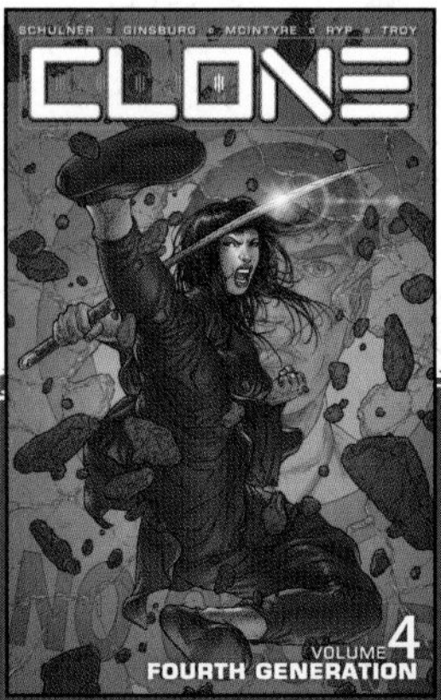
SCHULNER • GINSBURG • MCINTYRE • RYP • TROY
CLONE
VOLUME 4
FOURTH GENERATION

VOL. 1: FIRST GENERATION TP
ISBN: 978-1-60706-683-5
$12.99

VOL. 2: SECOND GENERATION TP
ISBN: 978-1-60706-830-3
$12.99

VOL. 3: THIRD GENERATION TP
ISBN: 978-1-60706-939-3
$12.99

VOL. 4: FOURTH GENERATION TP
ISBN: 978-1-63215-036-3
$12.99

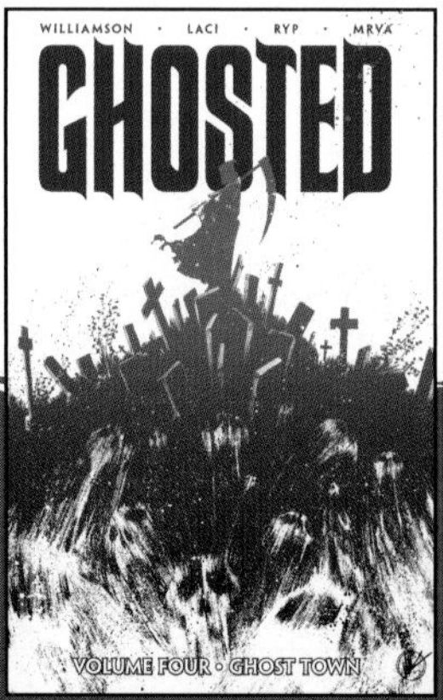
WILLIAMSON • LACI • RYP • MRVA
GHOSTED
VOLUME FOUR • GHOST TOWN

VOL. 1: HAUNTED HEIST TP
ISBN: 978-1-60706-836-5
$9.99

VOL. 2: BOOKS OF THE DEAD TP
ISBN: 978-1-63215-046-2
$12.99

VOL. 3: DEATH WISH TP
ISBN: 978-1-63215-051-6
$12.99

VOL. 4: GHOST TOWN TP
ISBN: 978-1-63215-317-3
$12.99

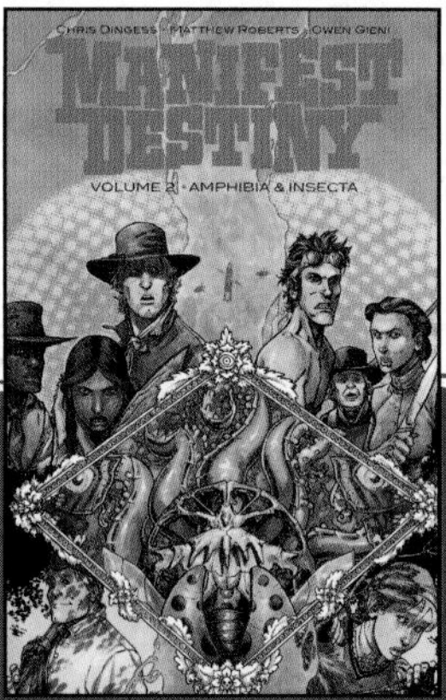
CHRIS DINGESS • MATTHEW ROBERTS • OWEN GIENI
MANIFEST DESTINY
VOLUME 2 • AMPHIBIA & INSECTA

VOL. 1: FLORA & FAUNA TP
ISBN: 978-1-60706-982-9
$9.99

VOL. 2: AMPHIBIA & INSECTA TP
ISBN: 978-1-63215-052-3
$14.99

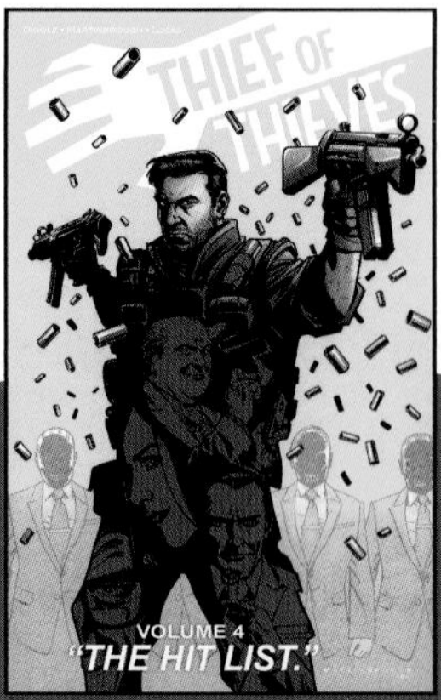
THIEF OF THIEVES
VOLUME 4
"THE HIT LIST."

VOL. 1: "I QUIT."
ISBN: 978-1-60706-592-0
$14.99

VOL. 2: "HELP ME."
ISBN: 978-1-60706-676-7
$14.99

VOL. 3: "VENICE."
ISBN: 978-1-60706-844-0
$14.99

VOL. 4: "THE HIT LIST."
ISBN: 978-1-63215-037-0
$14.99